A Stone's Throw Away

Also by Linda M. Mutty

Cadences

How Far Do You Want to Go?

A Stone's Throw Away

Linda M. Mutty

For Geoffrey and Jason who kept me safely anchored by their love and trust in me as their mother.

And for John, my husband, who will always be my true north.

≈

As far as the locals could collectively recall, a couple had last occupied it. And long before that, a family. However, what they thought they knew about the family and what had occurred there was little more than hearsay due to the passage of time. Although the structure was unoccupied, it was evident to the curious who ignored the posted "Do Not Trespass" signs that it was not neglected. Enough upkeep was evident to give trespassers pause and cause them to turn back, thinking twice about confronting the resident. It sat deep within the coastal redwood groves and the drive leading to it was enticing, an easy turn off the highway. The dampness saturated its exterior throughout the winter months as the inevitable blanket of fog wrapped its walls, clung to its roof, and dripped from the ancient boughs only to give way to the coastal storms that, once passed, were replaced by brief, temporary warmth, although never enough to dry out waterlogged surfaces. And then the inevitable shroud of gray would reappear. Only in the golden autumn months could it expect rescue from the damp and even then, nothing was certain. And so it sat, what had once been a small cabin in the woods, someone's makeshift shelter long ago, its metamorphosis the result of the needs of its occupants as the years passed so that, at first glimpse, the description of "cabin" would not come to mind.

Part I

Intersections

Chapter 1

He told her that he owned three outright, all on the East Coast, as he had always wanted to experience living in New England. Anything south did not interest him. He loved the history of the region, the coastline's ruggedness as well as its broad beaches and the change of seasons. His first job promotion at twenty-four solidified his career path in investing and further promotions soon followed until he found himself comfortably ensconced in three different East Coast homes during a period of twenty-one years.

The guesthouse, as he liked to refer to it, was nestled on the southern beachfront in Maine. To spend time here was an escape from the pressures of his job, a job that he fell into by knowing the right people at the right time and leaving the rest up to fate. He always seemed to land upright from the highest drop, never experiencing the bruising that some of his colleagues had suffered and from which they had never recovered. He considered himself fortunate or maybe blessed. He wasn't really sure what kept him out of harm's way.

The main house was on the Cape. He managed to procure it from one of his unfortunate supervisors who had fallen flat on his face. Stephen felt badly about the man's fate; loss of house and consequently, the eventual loss of wife and children, only to be left with visitation rights that sounded reasonable at the time but proved to be even less than a "Sunday father", as Sting, one of his favorite music artists, lamented in a heartfelt lyric about divorce. This husband, father, homeowner, and successful businessman had sung these lyrics along with Sting so many times on his way to and from the office, never imagining that what was then fiction would soon become his reality.

After the purchase of the home, Stephen dropped any connection with the man, for no reason. He did enjoy entertaining in this house and stayed there as often as he could.

It was large and lent itself to occupation rather than seclusion. There were very few weekends that Stephen did not open his home to his friends and acquaintances. His circle of friends was not lacking membership, but it did lack staying power. People seemed to drift in and out of his life, when present always supplying a great intensity of friendship but once separated from the circle for any reason, never pursued by Stephen. He knew in his private thoughts that he was a lousy friend, really. However, there was always someone new to replace what had seemed irreplaceable at the time. And, strangely, no one seemed to mind.

It was one of these friends who led him to his final investment while living in New England, which, in turn, led him to Eliza. Intrigued by the historic nature of the region, he had always wanted to own a home with a bronze plaque secured near the entrance with the date, perhaps going as far back as the early eighteenth century, and possibly the names of the original owners, neatly engraved into the worn metal. Though not a true history buff, Stephen had felt a connection to the past and the desire to vicariously experience it.

The information about the Hanover House came to him during one of the dinner-party conversations he was having with work colleagues who were also interested in New England history. Most of them were imports from west of the Mississippi, as he was, and who had come east for the experience. Of this group, Damian, who had worked side by side with Stephen at the investment firm for the past year, owned a historic house and was going on about the pros and cons of this kind of home ownership. Stephen became completely absorbed in Damian's words and pulled him aside during a convenient lag in the conversation, while the rest of the group sought out refills at the bar and a more stimulating conversation with others. Most of them had listened to Damian's viewpoint numerous times and were over it. Stephen, on the other hand, could not get enough. Did Damian know of any such homes available? Were there any specific requirements for a potential buyer when dealing with a historical building? Was it costly? However, that really didn't matter, as he was in a financial position to comfortably procure whatever he desired. But he was still curious. It was as if they had both found a long-lost brother as well as an eager audience, and by the end of the evening, Stephen had all his questions answered, a brain full of new information, and a burning desire to make his dream come true.

There were two houses that Damian knew about that had just gone on the market; one was in Boston and the other in Gettysburg. Gettysburg, being smaller than Boston, might not be the best choice, Damian offered, if Stephen was looking for some seclusion from the curious. However, Boston held what he was hoping for. Set off from the main thoroughfares and certainly off the historic paths visited by thousands each year, the Hanover House was in a quiet residential district of similar homes that had not yet been given any historical designation. In fact, this house had been designated just two months earlier. The seller, retired and recently widowed, was a born-in-the-cradle Easterner whose children in Oregon had convinced him to come live with them to escape the harshness of cold winters and the horribly hot summers. In a moment of exhaustion brought on by his numerous explanations as to why he wouldn't move from all that he had known, the widower gave in just to have peace and quiet. He put the house on the market with hopes that there would be little interest in purchasing what could become a rather public place.

Unfortunately for the seller, the stars were aligned so that he and Stephen would find their way to one another and complete the sale of the home, with Stephen settling quite comfortably into his dream house while the seller, exhausted, heartbroken, and left lonely by his wife's death, boarded a plane headed west.

Chapter 2

Eliza was not a tourist. She'd come to Boston from California a little less than a year ago with the intention of developing a new career, while privately hoping that the dormant writer within her would come along. An acquaintance had mentioned that perhaps new sights, a new living situation, and new people in her life would inspire her to get beyond whatever was preventing her from letting her words flow on paper. Her frustration with her inability to think creatively after a prolonged and successful writing career, the kind of career that allowed her to get by, if barely, beginning at the age of nineteen, was a strong enough reason to find a new path. She loved reading about Boston's historic sites, their rich and intriguing pasts. Most importantly, Boston was a place she had never explored. All this had captivated her. She left San Jose, her birthplace, in which she had spent the first forty years of her life. She left behind no living parents and had never had siblings, husbands, or children; she left behind the known for the unknown.

Not able to immediately afford the purchase of her own place, she was fortunate enough, through her new small group of like-minded writer acquaintances, to find a shared space in the heart of Boston in which to live and to write. Granted, peace and quiet were not always the day's fare, but between her two roommates and herself, time was allotted for each of them to have a few hours alone in the loft each day. Eliza cherished this time and found that just breathing the city's air inspired her to write. Her notion of beginning a new career was the farthest thing from her mind now as the blank pages on her laptop rapidly filled with her ideas. Her publisher, uniquely understanding, knew, perhaps more than Eliza did, that her efforts would eventually produce her next success.

She lost herself in her work each day, never concerned that she was still essentially alone in the world. After all, she had many friends; they might be fictional, but to her they were as real as Stephen's friends were to him. The difference was that she could return to her friends whenever she felt the need and then leave them by simply closing the book and placing it on her bookshelf. They were always there and were enough for her.

The fall of her second year in Boston was of the sort that hurt the eyes and stimulated the mind. The air, with a biting clarity, was clean and crisp. The ever-changing golden light from a sun that had worked long and hard throughout a sweltering Boston summer aided in illuminating the dying leaves' colors. Nature's transitions inspired her creative process, and she was beginning to glimpse the resolution of her current story. A satisfying sense of completion blanketed her from the loft's many drafts as she devoured each day's allotted time for her writing. She became a regular at the local coffeehouse, spending many hours pounding out a steady stream of words as she consumed too much caffeine.

Eliza's decision to go east had not become a regret. She sensed that fate had led her here, opened the doors for her, and still had more in store. She did not want to look around the corners of the unknown, however, and she did not want to suppose or desire beyond the moment at hand. The familiar was best and safe.

Chapter 3

Traveling from house to house proved to be more of a chore than an adventure as the months passed. Now thirty-six, Stephen frequently toyed with the idea of settling down. He had his favorite place, of course, and found himself spending as much time as possible in Boston. Because of its historic designation, he could do very little to his home to enhance it, which was perfectly all right with him. He realized one evening that he did not even own a toolbox and depended upon an old screwdriver and hammer that he found in what was now a one-car garage attached to the house. The idea of having tools at hand for specific jobs caused him to grin, as he would not know what to do with them even if he did own them. It was one of those gaps in his upbringing. No dad role model to teach him the ways of a man and his domain. He'd never taken shop in school, even though his advisor thought it would round out his education. And, quite frankly, in looking back, he still had no use for manual labor of that sort. Someone was always there to take on the work for him, and he was never disappointed in the outcome.

The home was built in 1765, one of the earliest dwellings that was not in the center of the city. It had been owned and occupied by the Hanover family consistently until 1955, when the last of this generation of Hanovers passed away at the age of ninety-eight. The younger generations had no interest in keeping the home in the family. They were living in many different parts of the country and absorbed in their own lives and families. The house was on the market for over a year before it sold. The neighbors were relieved when the FOR SALE sign was taken down, for the home whose appearance had been barely kept up by the realty company was truly appearing neglected to those who knew it well. The sadness of an empty building weighs heavily on those familiar with it—even more so when it is an empty home.

Born and bred in New England, the new owners, the

Pollepecks, were a young couple with no children yet. They moved into the home with the intention of raising their children there, having their children bring the grandchildren to visit, and retiring peacefully together to enjoy the final years of their lives. Nothing remarkable about this plan. However, intentions, as good as they may be, are no match for fate.

The family grew at a rapid clip, with the addition of five children within the first eight years. Each one of the offspring grew a family of his or her own and, as planned by the senior Pollepecks, returned to the family home whenever they could. The years were full of noise and laughter, little ones learning how to climb up and down the staircase, tearful evenings when the parents left the children with the grandparents for a night out, holiday celebrations that never went as planned just because of the numbers of characters involved, until the house grew quiet again. The families began to explore their options. They moved to other towns and out of state, but no one stayed in Boston. The senior Pollepecks found themselves saying tearful goodbyes over and over again until the visits dwindled to infrequent ones, if any. Too old to travel, they had not enjoyed the final years of their lives as they had expected. The wife fell ill and never recovered completely, only to die on a bitterly cold February morning in her own bed and in her husband's arms. The house was full again, but only for a few short days as the family buried its matriarch. Her husband, left completely alone, had reassured his grown children that he was perfectly capable of managing without help. His stubbornness was self-defense against the forces that he knew could change his life at this late date, and he was not going to tolerate anyone's interference.

He managed to get through the winter and when a late spring came, he breathed a sigh of relief along with all of Mother Nature, knowing that warmth and light had returned. He forced himself to open the dresser drawers and cupboards that held his wife's clothing and belongings. He gathered the garments, the jewelry, and the knickknacks and boxed them for storage so that if any of the children came back, they could search through their mother's belongings, taking what was meaningful to them. He did not want to be present when this occurred, however. He rearranged the furniture to suit his needs and spent some of the insurance money on purchases that he had not made when his wife was alive. Then, they either couldn't afford it, or his wife saw no need for it. Now, he decided if it was needed and, inevitably, it was.

The following spring found him not at all healthy. He had difficulty moving about the home, and climbing stairs was so painful that he forced himself to try only on the few good days that he experienced. Soon, those good days did not exist. His life became confined to the first floor.

To go into detail is not necessary, but one can imagine the state of affairs found by the second oldest son when he surprised his father while on a business trip to Boston. It was from that visit that the senior Pollepeck's life changed. This son, who lived in Oregon, insisted that his father come to live with his family. And that was the end. The senior Pollepeck did not agree to sell his home, did not agree to leave the only place that he really knew and loved, did not agree to be transplanted three thousand miles west of Boston. However, the forces that he knew were waiting for him to buckle under in a weakened state had won. All else was lost. Except the house. Stephen had rescued the house to make it a home as only he knew how to do.

Chapter 4

Daily, people intersect with one another while on separate life journeys. From these exchanges, brief or extended, friendships may evolve. Eliza had found this to be a comforting thought as her frequent visits to the coffeehouse to work on her draft placed her at many intersections, if she paid attention to her surroundings. She didn't do this at first. Once settled at a corner table away from the general commotion of customers rattling off their coffee orders, she grasped her warm cup of soy chai tea with both hands. A ritual, seemingly, as she did this each time before touching fingertips to her keyboard. It helped her to calm down and focus before rereading the draft so that she could find her way through the next section yet to materialize on the screen. When the ideas came, the confusion of thought intensified in her so that she physically sagged under its weight. But to write fed her soul, propelling her to places of pure joy. The anticipation of experiencing this euphoria got her out of bed each day, disciplined her to use every moment of her assigned time in the loft and then to wend her way to the coffee shop, consciously forcing herself not to mind waiting in line with others whose only anticipation, it seemed to her, was the first sip of their morning jolt.

Observation was a strong quality in Eliza. She prided herself on always noticing the details and remembering them. When she was very young, sitting in the backseat of her father's car, she would watch from her window as the world flew by, focusing her attention on the ever-changing scenery. Missing a moment of fleeting life beyond the confines of the car seemed unbearable, much like the urge to turn the pages of a good story to finish the chapter because closing the book before doing so was unthinkable. Her father had understood. His sensitivity to her need to be alone while being with others was familiar to him. As he observed her from his rearview mirror, he wondered about his child. Would she be like him, caught up in the tides of life and never finding the high ground upon which to hear himself think? To be himself? To be alone, just for a while? He loved his family with all his being, but the longing to discover more of himself always lay beneath the surface of his existence. Eliza was young enough then not to have gotten caught in the tides. Not yet.

Her voice broke through her parents' chatter to say, "I wonder what it would have been like to have lived here when people first came to this land." She wasn't asking anyone in particular; it was just an observation that had escaped her lips as the miles of farmland and old family homes sped by. Her father had paid attention to it, though. Looking at her through the rearview mirror, he commented, "What an interesting observation, Eliza." She had remembered her father's words, his kindness, and his connection with her during that moment before he returned his eyes to the road ahead and she to the world outside. No more was ever said between them about that exchange, but she held onto it as the special gift that her father had given her so long ago.

Much of her composing depended on her mental files. Those memories that had not been visited for so long surprised her with their unannounced appearances as she wrote. Not so much that they boggled her brain with unnecessary details, but enough for her to consider using them, somehow slipping one or two into her creation. A quick note to herself on a possible idea did not take that much time, and so at the end of a writing period, she had an abbreviated list of memories scribbled in her notebook. This exercise comforted her. Somewhere in her subconscious, she held onto the fear that neglecting these memories was the ticket to losing them forever. Whether or not they found their way into her composing was not as critical to her as recording them. She had recognized them and had welcomed them back. That was enough.

Chapter 5

Stephen had always harbored an aversion to chain-brand coffeehouses. His lament was that each one of them looked exactly the same, smelled the same, offered the same "chalkboard" menu, and served the same kind of clientele. It was distressing to him that variety seemed to be of less and less importance in this world.

Living in this Boston neighborhood had treated him to some wonderful family-run businesses, the kind that had weathered the ups and downs of the economic woes; the kind that made you feel like you were opening the door to a good home full of good neighbors, the kind where "everyone knows your name and they're glad you came." He was not that frequent of a customer, but when he craved that good cup of coffee, he always found himself at Gregario's Java Hut. The name itself seemed to be steeped in the fifties or sixties, historic enough to have outlasted the winds of change. The coffee shop had been lovingly preserved by three generations of Gregarios. It was a place where you could sit quietly and be alone among the customers or join the old hipsters who reminisced about their youth for hours on end, many of them sitting at the same tables that they had occupied since their late teens. The place, upon entering, reeked of life, present and long past. Stephen found great comfort here.

So it was to his great consternation one morning in early fall when Stephen found his way to Gregario's only to find a CLOSED sign on the door. Not convinced that the sign spoke the truth, he tried the door and found it locked. He peered through the window. The place was dark and empty.

"Do you know why they're not open?"

He turned to the stranger seeking the same solace as he and heard in her voice the surprise and disappointment that he was feeling all in her one simple question.

"Haven't a clue, but this doesn't start my morning well."

Stephen's voice communicated to Eliza disappointment with a tinge of sour humor thrown in. Not the end-of-the-world-type comment, she thought. She felt the same way. Her routine had been interrupted, and she felt strangely uncomfortable as to what her next move should be. She couldn't go back to the flat; it wasn't her allotted time. The library was within walking distance. Not a problem but finding a good hot soy chai made the Gregario way would be her challenge for the morning.

"Do you know anyplace close?" Stephen started to move from the door and back out to the sidewalk, throwing the question over his shoulder as he did so.

"Not really. There's a coffee shop two blocks south, but it's part of a chain and I swore I wouldn't patronize it. I want to see Gregario's stay in business for the next three generations." Eliza was a bit surprised to hear her words spoken aloud, especially to a stranger. She considered herself conservatively shy, having plenty of opinions but never comfortable sharing them out loud for fear of having to defend herself. She did not like conflict.

"I agree. This place is a great find. I hope that this closing isn't an indication of things to come. They really seemed to be doing well."

Eliza had joined him in the middle of the sidewalk, keeping a safe distance. "Are you new to the neighborhood?"

"No. Been here for eight years. You?" This was the first time Stephen had focused on the woman in front of him. A personal question to a stranger almost demands some eye contact. However, he couldn't release his gaze from her eyes. Nor could she his.

Eliza felt such ease with this man who could be any one of several nefarious characters for all she knew. But something about him produced comfort and security in his presence. His smile unlocked her hesitation in proceeding with the conversation. She had been ready to walk in any direction, just not the same one he was headed. That fleeting plan no longer existed. Instead, she moved a bit closer, and Stephen stood his ground.

"I moved from California about two years ago. You know, the itch to see and be somewhere new. Boston seemed a good choice, so different from what I was used to." She stopped short and shifted her bag to her other shoulder, afraid that she was saying too much, revealing too much. After all, he had come for a cup of coffee, not to hear her life story. "Well, I need to get going. Hope you find your morning coffee. I won't think any less of you if you decide to head south." Her forced laugh was embarrassing to her. How could she be so flippant with this stranger? But his reaction calmed her nerves immediately.

"I think that I can pass up on it today. Our limited conversation has been enough to get me going. I'm Stephen, by the way. Stephen Bingham. And you?"

"Eliza. Eliza Whick." She offered her hand and he did the same. Very businesslike, she thought. The fabric of his suit sleeve brushed against the top of her hand. At that moment, she allowed herself to take him all in. A beautifully tailored suit, European cut, to be sure, emphasized his physique, slim yet muscular and well maintained. He was taller, but he did not tower over all five-foot-six inches of her. His thick ebony hair had been styled to look casually windblown. And his eyes, that moments ago would not release her, were dark, the irises seemingly jet black against the whites of his eyes. They were pools of mystery, so dense and striking. Long, rich dark lashes framed them. Swarthy. Yes, swarthy, she thought, was the right word to describe his facial features.

"Well, Eliza Whick." He released his hand from hers. "Perhaps fortune will shine down on us once again and tomorrow morning we'll find ourselves reading an 'open' sign and life will be good again. What do you think?" He just couldn't let her walk off; he couldn't break his contact with her eyes. She was holding onto him without physically doing so. He felt drawn to her somehow. Beyond a sexual attraction, although the potential could not be denied.

"There's always tomorrow." Did she really say that? Could she be more cliché?

"Well, I'm planning on it. There's still so much coffee to

drink before I end up at the heavenly coffee bar. Okay then. Perhaps tomorrow we can pick up where we left off today?"

Once again, he had gracefully made her feel comfortable after her verbal blunder. Now all she had to do was respond intelligently. "I bring my work here for a few hours each morning. If you are here around eight thirty and the sign on the door is in our favor, I'd enjoy a few moments of conversation with you, but I do need to work. I hope you understand." Intelligent and somewhat professional sounding, as well as conservative and limiting in the invitation, she thought.

"I'll be here and do understand. Not a problem. However, if it's better for you that we just dump this whole idea right now, no harm done." Stephen watched her face for any indication of rejection; after all, he had just given her the perfect out and wouldn't be surprised if she took it. He wondered what she really thought of him breaching the borders of familiarity. He was conscious of the beads of sweat forming on his upper lip and hoped that she had not detected it. This woman was dragging him into her space, or was it he who was pushing his way closer?

Eliza's smile was enough. He knew immediately that he would see her again. He shifted his weight realizing that he had been in an uncomfortable stance the whole time, tense muscles and sweating glands all taking over so that this minor adjustment brought relief to a physical body that he had mentally left behind in his struggle not to lose this woman from his sight. He even managed to artfully guide his index finger along his wet upper lip as one might do to quell an itch and thus blot away the telltale sign that his body had recently betrayed him.

She had not noticed. After struggling to maintain her part of the conversation, she felt relieved. He was a gentle man and, in the few moments that they had been together for the very first time, she sensed that he was much more. "I can make time. Good to have met you, Stephen. See you, then, tomorrow?"

"Absolutely. Pray to the coffee gods for an open door." He watched her cross the street as she headed north.

Chapter 6

In the following weeks, their early-morning meetings at Gregario's were becoming a part of both of their morning rituals. The one-day closing, they found out, was due to a family member's death. Although sympathetic to the family, they secretly rejoiced that that was all it was. The time spent over a warm cup of coffee and tea nourished them so that the conversations extended into the later morning hours. No one pressured them to give up their table for other customers, neither one of their own internal clocks checked in with them to alert them of time's passage, and the necessity to get their individual days under way was the farthest thought from their minds. Stephen had a future planned for them. He did not divulge this to Eliza. Frightening her off was the last thing he wanted to do, and he really wasn't sure of her feelings for him. True, these morning get-togethers were a good sign. The relationship was strengthening as both found ever-increasing familiarity with each other.

They seemed to have so much in common yet were so different. This one observation on Eliza's part provided the flame that kept some internal fire burning. He was four years older, but he did not seem forty-six. Never mind how in shape and ruggedly handsome he was. More importantly, he had accomplished so much, was so successful, while she still shared an apartment. She was not sure that Stephen found her all that interesting but thought something must be present for him to meet her each day. She longed for the confidence to accept who she was; it would allow her to understand Stephen's acceptance of her. Was she confusing the issue? Why not sit back and enjoy this wonderful ride? After all, the other choice for any companionship was her ongoing relationship with her laptop. She wondered, more frequently than she was comfortable doing, which relationship was more real to her. In her composing, she lost herself in the tide of emotions that only her words could bring forth. Finding herself adrift in sorrow or in happiness as the words appeared before her was not only comforting but also allowed her to escape momentarily from the loft, from the city's constant commotion, from her worries, and from the nagging thought that she needed to get to know who she really was and what she truly wanted from life. Always postponing the latter because there was still time was beginning to prey heavily on her as each birthday came and went without any significant revelations. Moving from one coast to the other was a subconscious decision on her part, after all, to start the process. As the mornings passed with Stephen, it became evident that he was to be a part of the process.

And because of this, Eliza said yes to Stephen's proposal of marriage. The path was quite clear for her as the months of being with Stephen passed. She allowed him in. He sat with her for hours at a time in the comfort of his home, listening to her read her most recent work to him. He never interrupted, never critiqued while she read. Once she'd finished, he allowed her to voice her criticism, to ask him his opinion, and to practice the stance of self-preservation by self-deprecation. She hated herself every time she did this and recalled vividly a T-shirt given to her as she completed a summer writing workshop in graduate school. The kelly-green print, dead center on the front, was enclosed in a circle of the same color with a diagonal slash mark across it. The intended message stood out from the deep mustard-yellow background and stated clearly, "Don't apologize. Just read the crap!" It always made her smile to remember the moment when she received it along with her fellow graduate students in Creative Writing. They had been commanded to put the shirts on, right there and then. No exceptions. And they had laughed to see the professor's constant reprimand now glaring at them from someone else's chest. And in their delight, they each recalled their moments of insecurity and unwillingness to share their creations as the patient professor waited them out until there was no escape, nothing to do but "read the crap!"

On a golden afternoon in the early fall, exactly one year since their first encounter at Gregarios, Eliza and Stephen married. The whole affair was very low key, as Stephen had wanted. Only Eliza's roommates and three of Stephen's current associates from work attended. Eliza had asked Stephen if their honeymoon could be in Europe, somewhere romantic and rich in history. She had always wanted to see the Mediterranean area, especially Greece. He hadn't refused but had wanted her to at least consider other places. She had said that she would, but knowing that he would eventually agree, she began to anticipate this new journey and the wealth of information that she would gather, the memories that she would make with Stephen at her side.

Stephen approached the subject of a honeymoon again during a late-night dinner a few weeks after their wedding. The restaurant was one of their favorites, small and quiet, a place where a conversation could develop and be enjoyed. He told her that there was no rush to take a honeymoon. Why be like everyone else? He said that he felt comfortable with the idea of letting Eliza settle into his home, her new home, before they began any travels. They had the rest of their lives to travel the world. Eliza listened to Stephen's empty words trying desperately to conceal her disappointment, her surprise, and her anger. How many hours had they spent planning their future together, including the talk of a honeymoon destination? He had been so enthusiastic about this first journey together and so open to suggestions from her. What had happened? Why had he turned everything upside down in a matter of moments? How could she feel such deep contempt for her new husband? This last thought stayed with her as hot tears began to form while he droned on.

Fortunately, there were many more happy moments than disturbing ones for Eliza as she shared her days with Stephen. She found comfort in the quiet times in the house when Stephen went to work each morning. Her writing continued to be a place of solace and of challenge. Not the challenge that she had faced when juggling her work between the flat and the coffee shop, but one that forced her to move even more deeply into herself to find fodder for composing. Finding herself in these deeper places was at once satisfying and frightening to her if she let herself examine these places too closely. They seemed to lie in wait, undisturbed, having slumbered within since birth. If she let herself explore them, she did so timidly and with caution, ready to retreat at the first sign of discomfort. However, the satisfaction of having made the attempt washed over her, and a longing to return lingered with her as she composed. She wondered how she had stumbled upon them after all these years, and then realized that she had been unaware that they existed until she married Stephen.

The early days of her marriage were filled with varied attempts to transform Stephen's home into "their home." She was careful never to remove or change anything in the house without asking him first, which was not difficult because Stephen had been more than generous and sensitive to her needs to feel at home. Never having had a home to call her own and to do with as her imagination directed, Eliza found happiness as she rearranged furniture, added a knickknack here and there, dug into her few boxes of belongings, and began to give the light of day to long forgotten items from childhood and her teen years that, although mere trinkets to the stranger's eyes, were invaluable to her, carrying with them some of her strongest memories of a time before. Each found a special place on the shelves of bookcases that lined so many walls in the house. The shelves of books were one of the reasons that Eliza was so attracted to Stephen. He read the books and loved to discuss them with her. How many people had she met who had collections of literature but had never cracked open the books, and if they had read them, did so only because they had been forced down their throats in a required Lit course in college?

As she came to one of the last boxes, she knew the contents by heart. It held those books that she considered her dearest friends and mentors. She pored over each one as she drew them from the box. Specific moments in time were vibrantly alive for very brief moments as she flipped through the pages, catching glimpses of sentences, phrases, a word that drew her into the blurring print on the page. There was no need for her to read on, as her imagination formed the scene immediately.

Then she would move to the next book, only to experience the same familiarity. It was as though she dissolved into the pages of each book. She was the black ink; she was a thread woven into the texture of the paper; she was the fragrance of stored paper and cardboard; she was lost in what was so intimately familiar and loved. She remembered, as she emptied the box of the last book, how many books she had parted with when she left California. She had given away so many, had sold a few to help fund her venture east, and had recycled the dime-store paperbacks that she had procured along the way because everyone was reading them at the time. The few books that she had kept with her she would always keep with her.

Stephen never failed to mention something about her creative endeavors with the house. He would come home each night, lovingly embrace her while asking how her day had gone, and then move through each room on his way to the bedroom, noting any changes or additions. Eliza found herself eager for him to compliment her. She was proud of her newfound creative flair when it came to enhancing their living space. And Stephen never failed to do so. This alone was enough for Eliza, for she wanted to please her husband as well as herself. And so, over the years, they comfortably nested in "their home" as their love grew.

Neither was interested in sharing their home with dependents. They decided that they were too far along in life to fairly bring a child into this world and then be interested enough to nurture it for eighteen years or so. That decision left them, then, to focus on themselves and each other. Stephen was closing in on another promotion with the investment firm that would not only be a bigger feather in his cap, which he loved to wear on any occasion, but also place them in an income bracket that neither of them had dreamed they would reach. A second book of Eliza's poetry was published about the same time, and she found that the royalty checks were a welcome bit of income that Stephen had insisted she keep for herself. The meager checks from her first attempt at writing poetry for publication when she was in her twenties continued to arrive and had served as incentive to attempt a second volume. The additional twenty years of life experiences under her belt had produced richly textured thoughts that poured from her without the struggle to create that she had dealt with when younger. The subject matter varied, but she had known that underlying each poem's foundation was her insecurity, and even now she could not identify its source.

It was in the ninth year of their marriage that they revisited the honeymoon conversation. There had been no further thoughts about a honeymoon after that one night, but there had been a few small trips that seemed to make up for Stephen's unsettling behavior then. Eliza had considered the subject closed until Stephen asked her over dinner one evening if she would like to go to Greece.

"Why not go now while we can? I can finagle it so that it's a business trip of sorts. Save us some cash doing that. Remember, you wanted to go to the Mediterranean?" Stephen was leaning in to her from across the dining room table.

She saw in his eyes that he meant what he said, and his enthusiasm caught her by surprise. Eliza felt that she was dissolving into her own confused memories. Wounds do not always heal completely, she thought. Would he even mention anything about their conversation so long ago? It felt like yesterday to her and as she began to feel the sting of salty tears forming, she drew herself back to the present with every ounce of her being, smiling and hearing her own excited voice. She knew that she had pleased Stephen with her response as he leaned all the way across the table and planted a kiss on her lips.

"Well, I'll go online and see what I can find. How does a cruise sound, or would you rather we just hoof it and see the sights on our own time and wherewithal?"

"A cruise, Stephen, I think. I've never been on one. Have you?"

"One or two. Good choice. That's what we'll do, then. Any time not work for you with your writing? I'm pretty much my own boss when it comes to my time, so tell me what works best for you, sweetheart."

As he spoke, his love for her came over her as suddenly as the tears of hurt just moments ago threatened to reveal her feelings to Stephen. Was this the way it was supposed to be? The ups and downs, the emotional roller coaster of which she was the only passenger?

Chapter 7

The cruise was more than Eliza expected. Even though the stops in the various ports never were long enough for her, Eliza made sure that they saw and experienced as much as possible. She filled her notebooks with details that were all so new to her: the language and its beauty, the colors of the natural and unnatural, the people and the heritage of which they seemed so proud, the ancient ruins as well as the bustling modern cities, and the music and dance that she was somewhat familiar with because of a Greek friend in college who insisted on exposing her to everything Greek, namely food and dance. In a way, she felt at home here, nurtured by the vibrancy of life that she encountered wherever she and Stephen ventured.

"I hate to even bring this up, but I am missing being home." Stephen had interjected this remark rather loudly during an excited exchange between Eliza and a shopkeeper who recognized Eliza's last name and wondered if she was related to an American who had stayed in the village for the summer maybe twenty-five or so years ago. His name was Michael Bingham from Los Angeles, California. Did they know him? The shopkeeper smiled as he recalled how well-liked Michael was by the people of the area and that if he should ever return, he would always have a place to stay.

Eliza turned to Stephen, ignoring for the moment his last remark. "Are we related to Michael Bingham, Stephen? Wouldn't that be something, to come all this way to find one of your relatives blazing the path before us? I wonder what the odds are of this happening—I mean, meeting this gentleman in a small shop in a small village in Greece who has met one of your own?" Eliza was a bit breathless in her excitement for Stephen.

Stephen blanched at the mention of Michael but regained his composure while consciously making the effort to remove himself from this conversation. "No, I don't think so. I haven't heard of a Michael in the family. Bingham is a very common name in America. I think it comes from Britain originally," he said without looking at either Eliza or the shopkeeper. He seemed to be focused on something above them, as his eyes remained directed toward the very low ceiling.

That was rude, Eliza thought. Not like Stephen to avoid eye contact, much less respond in such a curt manner. She tried to engage him once again. "It would be fun to do a little research and find out if he is related, don't you think?"

The smiling shopkeeper nodded his head in agreement with Eliza. "Oh yes. That would be something. You could come back here together, perhaps. Spend time here with us. Michael's relatives are always welcomed here. If you don't mind me saying so, there is a reason that you have found your way to us and that you have come to my shop to spend time. I think this is a sign." He heartily laughed, extending his arms to Eliza and Stephen in a gesture of embrace. Stephen stepped back abruptly, almost knocking over a display table but catching himself just in time. Eliza had already moved in for the embrace but was taken aback by Stephen's behavior. "No problem, no problem," the shopkeeper reassured Stephen, pointing to the table. "I am sorry if I may have offended you. I can get a bit excited. Please accept my apology, Mr. Bingham."

Stephen looked the shopkeeper in the eye, suddenly engaged. "No apology needed. My fault entirely. Very sorry." Abruptly turning to Eliza, he asked, "Are we done here?" There remained a note of disdain in his voice. She wasn't sure for whom.

Perhaps the mention of Los Angeles or the American "relation" compelled Stephen to voice his desire to return home, but no matter what the reason, Eliza was dismayed by his timing. More so, that he wanted to leave this beautiful place. Their days were growing shorter, of course, as the cruise was coming to an end within a few days. She didn't like counting down time, never had. However, time was rudely brought to her attention by Stephen's remark, and what had felt like such a magical experience for her was now no more than three more days on a ship with her husband and then home.

The shopkeeper, sensing that further conversation with these people was not wise, smiled gently at Eliza, who felt his discomfort now as an interloper. Averting his eyes from the couple so that they could finish what had just begun, he excused himself and moved to the other side of the shop.

Straining to keep her voice only between them, she turned to Stephen. "I am not sure how you would like me to respond, Stephen. If the truth be told, I am loving it here and wish we had a whole summer to spend here. I am sorry that you are missing Boston and I guess we'll be there soon enough. Can't you just enjoy these last few days?"

Stephen's face held an expression that Eliza had never seen before. It was one of hurt, but his eyes concealed darkness, an anger that weirdly disagreed with the rest of his face. He looked beyond her toward the shopkeeper, who had begun a conversation with another couple. Their voices seemed to fill the room with a cacophony of verbiage and very loud laughter. It was difficult for Stephen to think clearly. He saw Eliza standing in front of him, waiting for his reassuring response that of course he would enjoy himself, that he was just a bit travel weary.

"Stephen, perhaps we should just go back to the ship. Maybe spend the rest of the day lounging by the pool? Naps are good, and I could sure use one. Stephen? What do you think?" He seemed so far away from her. She couldn't begin to read him, to bring him back to her.

After an awkward passage of time and without a response from him, she decided not to waste her precious afternoon waiting for him to come around. There was so much still to see. Besides, he could do his own thing, and he knew his way back to the ship as well as she did. Miffed with him, she left the shop without looking back and moved down the cobbled street to find another interesting shop and perhaps a human being who would enjoy an exchange of words.

Returning to the ship that afternoon was difficult for Eliza. Unfinished business nagged at her. Her abrupt departure from the shop and from her husband both demanded her attention. Because of this, she decided to return to the first shop to apologize for their behavior. She would deal with Stephen later.

Unperturbed and happy to see her again, the shopkeeper picked up their initial conversation as if nothing untoward had occurred between them. He captivated Eliza with his stories and explanations about the history of his shop, of his family, of the village, and of the island's birth mother, whose caldera the inhabitants had settled upon. Not comfortable with pulling out her notebook and recording his words as he spoke, his eye contact penetrating and deliberate, an unspoken demand that she be present, she focused on his every word, trying to commit to memory all that he shared with her. Once outside the shop she would find a quiet place to record his words before she could not.

She asked so many questions the more he went on. Trying not to appear completely ignorant, she gauged her questions to him by watching his facial expression. His wrinkled parchment face remained placid when he spoke of family, the shop, and the village. Not because these were not important topics to him, she knew, but because this information must be somewhat mundane from his point of view, as he probably shared these topics on a regular basis with any of his customers who would listen. But the aged carvings of his face instantly became prominent when she asked him about the caldera. It was as if he himself was part of the earth's violent creation, an igneous rock spewed from the depths of the volcano forming its visage not of its own accord but by the extreme forces of nature. And he leaned into her with even more intensity, his upper body bending forward ever so slightly but enough to alert her to the metamorphosis that was taking place before her. She was neither afraid nor shaken by his transformation. Instead, she found herself intrigued by him and, following his downward gaze, by what lay beneath the worn wooden floor and its foundation of stone, the ancient earth under their feet. His respect for what lay beneath was akin to the respect one would pay while standing at a grave site or on the ancient stone floors of a Gothic cathedral whose worn surfaces within the hallowed interior of the church protected the long dead buried beneath.

He reached for her arm in a fatherly manner to support her, breaking the spell that she had fallen under, and led her to the back of the shop. No words were spoken as she allowed him to guide her, and she was not surprised when she felt herself move closer to him with each step. And within the shadows of the shop, a place where few were invited, he told her, an understanding and appreciation for him overwhelmed her so that she allowed her tears' release. He noticed and reached his gnarled fingers to his own cheek blotting the moisture from the crevices of his skin. She thought that she saw his lips form a paternal smile but was not sure in the dimness. He removed his arm from hers and moved behind a counter, equally as old as her afternoon companion, she mused, if not more so. She stepped toward the worn wooden barrier and ran her hand back and forth on its surface, focusing on its rough texture, a product of so many years of wear. Intermingled with the oils of her hand, the aged wood seemed to pronounce an even stronger fragrance. She breathed deeply of its presence, sensing that she should.

He returned and stood next to her, having placed in front of her rocks whose explanation for existing filled the next hour of their time together and confirmed for her that she was where she was supposed to be, in this tiny shop, alone without her husband, guided by an aged Greek shopkeeper who until a few hours ago had been a stranger to her, but whom she now knew to be important to her, somehow. And she accepted this realization without the need to know why. Some moments in life, she knew, were not to be analyzed.

Outside the shop, having left him alone, perhaps ready to close for the day as the hour had grown much later than she realized, she did not follow her own advice. She found herself contemplating what could only be described as a strong connection between them. Perhaps her attention to him was all that he needed to reassure himself that it was worth his time to talk with this American. Perhaps it was the association of her last name that spurred him on? He seemed convinced that there was a family connection between her husband and Michael Bingham.

She could have stayed in that small, dark shop, missing the ship's departure and not have given it another thought, so comfortable had she been with this gentle man. However, she knew better, and she thanked him for his kindness and time with her. Leaving his place, she paused by the seawall to admire the beauty of the coastline. Purchasing herself against the rugged surface of the volcanic rocks that clung together to serve the village as its protector from a raging sea, she pulled out her notebook and began to write.

        As one foot plodded in front of the other toward the dock, she suddenly realized that she had not thought of Stephen once while in the shop. For a moment, she felt alarmed. After all, leaving on a rather sour note, she had just left him standing alone. She questioned herself as to whether or not she had been too abrupt and selfish in her desire to enjoy this trip. Was she so callous that Stephen's feelings no longer mattered? Had she grown so independent of him that she could have made this trip on her own and still would have had a wonderful time? The thought of having to face Stephen worried her. She could only base this worry on his odd behavior in the shop. She played over different scenarios of which she could have some control once she confronted him. Simply acting as if nothing had happened seemed out of the question but the easiest in her mind. Maybe he had had second thoughts as well and felt badly about his tourist meltdown. She highly doubted that that would be the case, however. Something in his eyes, what she knew she saw, would not let her shove this aside. *Just face him, clear the air, and resolve whatever the issue is,* she told herself, as she climbed the gangway only minutes from their stateroom. That was the only tactic to take.

        She opened the door to their room to find no one there. Feeling a sense of relief as well as disappointment, as she had readied herself for the inevitable confrontation only now to be postponed, she wondered where he might be. It was well into the happy hour on ship, and her immediate thought was that he had probably gone down to one of the lounges. Well, that was all right, as it gave her a bit of time to recuperate from the heat of the day. She took a long shower, letting the cool water refresh her. Dressing in one of the many sundresses she had brought with her, she made herself look presentable. A good drink would be welcomed right now, and if that meant joining Stephen in a public place to do so, then she would. She would have preferred holding off until they were in the privacy of their room, but she knew that the longer she postponed speaking with him, the worse it would become, perhaps for both of them.

She did not have to wait long at all. Deciding to take the stairs instead of the elevator, she saw him at a distance, leaving a lounge. He was heading for the stairs. Eliza debated whether to meet him halfway or just wait for him to come to her. The taste of a good gin and tonic, however, propelled her down the staircase, only to come face to face with him just before reaching the landing. Her new heels were pinching, and the short descent found her toes screaming their discomfort. Chiding herself for wearing them and for choosing the stairs, she looked at Stephen and smiled.

"Hello. I thought that I would come and join you, but it looks like I'm a little late."

Stephen smiled, and his face reflected the Stephen she knew, the one man she had fallen in love with and would always love. "Sorry. I waited for you to return. Then I thought that you would know where to find me. Should have left a note. Sorry. Been saying that quite a bit today, haven't I?"

He still knew how to make her comfortable, to draw her into him so that any concerns she might have had dissipated immediately. Her love for him at that moment outweighed her worries of the afternoon. "Stephen, I'm the one who should be saying sorry. I should never have walked out on you in that shop, much less ignored you for the afternoon. I just felt frustrated and hurt and, yes, I suppose a bit selfish. Were you okay in the shop? You gave me a bit of a fright at one point. You were so distant and..."

She was thankful when Stephen interrupted her babble

by taking her in his arms and whispering, "I love you. I always will, my dear Eliza." He kissed her forehead, taking her arm and leading her back to the lounge. "I sense that a gin and tonic is waiting for you, love. Let's end this day over a couple of them, shall we?"

What had seemed such a disruption in their relationship faded almost instantly, so Eliza and Stephen never did have the conversation that Eliza, at one time, was so determined to face. The evening was memorable as they lingered over dinner and then found themselves on the dance floor in one another's embrace until the band announced the last dance. They danced until the final note was played. Perhaps all that she had read about cruising was really true. You fall in love or fall in love all over again when you are at sea. There is no escaping it, she thought. Something about not being attached to land, being in the middle of a large expanse of deep rolling waters, never ending, as one might imagine it to be, knowing that terra firma is out of reach until the mass of steel and ironworks that keeps you afloat touches shore…it was almost a rebirth to be at sea. This evening and this trip, even the afternoon on her own, was everything that she had dreamed of and had it not been for Stephen, she would never have experienced it. She knew that. She would have been happy to spend the rest of her life pounding out the words, by herself, day in and day out. There was a certain reassurance in the life she once had, a certain satisfaction that she was okay and that she could survive. Would she trade what she had now for her former life? The question always stumped her. Why couldn't she just blurt out, "Hell, no!" Some remnant of independence stubbornly hung on to her and she accepted it. But eventually, the "no" would surface and she would count her blessings.

Chapter 8

The fall in Boston arrived seemingly earlier than usual, although the calendar hanging in their kitchen stubbornly proclaimed that the autumnal equinox occurred on September 22. Eliza could always feel the change of seasons in her bones; the undeniable need to start nesting, to change gears in readiness for the onset of shorter days and darker evenings, to prepare for survival of another winter. Her eyes always noted the subtle changes in light moving from glaring summer sunlight on the environment around her to a subtle golden hue that seemed to bring objects into a defined and glorious existence. It was as though the leaves on the tree outside the front window that had not changed color, shape, or size from one day to the next throughout the long summer months became more defined, their life-giving veins protruding in the dimming sunlight almost pulsating, and yes, their color screamed out its right to own the summer dominion it had enjoyed all the while knowing that it was slowly fading. Its last gasp was that of a brilliance that drew the eyes to the abundance of color created by the leaves that clung to the millions of trees in New England in the fall.

For Eliza, it was a time of satisfying productivity. Her words filled the screen as quickly as she could imagine them, and they seemed to have the power to create her stories while dictating to her fingers to do so. In the warmer days of summer, she had found herself easily averting her eyes from the screen to the tree in the front yard. She had intentionally set up her writing nook, as she liked to call it, on the second floor of the house. She had found an old oak desk, like the ones she had seen so many of her teachers sit behind, at a garage sale and knew that it would serve her well. Stephen had helped her move it in front of the bay window that looked out over the front yard. The window's view was that of a large maple tree's upper boughs, some softly brushing the glass when a light summer breeze blew through the yard. She loved this location. It brought her closer to nature while sitting at an antique desk behind a laptop in a second-story room of a historic home in the city of Boston. All the elements that she had carefully planned seemed to feed her as a writer. Her environment was important to her. After each daily session, the exhaustion was overwhelming, and she found herself working hard to bring herself back to reality. However, there were mornings when she worked through her fatigue because to turn her back on a developing character seemed a betrayal of the creative process; even more so a neglect, like that of a bad parent, of an innocent and helpless child.

It was not intentional that she and Stephen saw less and less of each other as the days of fall wore on. The thought crossed both of their minds that a distance was growing between them. Stephen found himself deeply entrenched at work, requiring longer hours into the dark evenings and earlier rises on the chilly mornings. He never left the house without gently awakening Eliza with kisses and reassuring her that he loved her and would see her in the evening. He always added that perhaps he could "break away a bit earlier this evening." And Eliza responded with sleep-drenched kisses so that he would know that she was aware of his departure. However, she also knew that he would not be home any earlier on any evening but always responded with, "I hope you can, sweetheart. I miss you."

Stephen's departure each morning was full of routine. Having tended to his sleeping Eliza, he went through the motions of readying himself for the day. Once he left the bedroom, he felt the exhilaration of the new day before him. He thrived on his work as an investor, and it had served him well. He owned homes, could travel when he desired, had a network of wealthy individuals who seemed to respect him and his advice, and had a beautiful and talented wife. Family, in the larger sense, was not present. Like Eliza's, his parents were deceased. And like Eliza, he had no siblings, he had told her. She found the similarities of their histories compelling and perhaps a sign that they were meant to have found each other in order to care for each other. The act of falling in love, if dissected for both Eliza and Stephen, could be broken down simply into cause and effect, and had either of one of them bothered to delve deeper, they would have found that it appeared to be the only element upon which their marriage had been created. Two lonely people now partnered, no longer lonely yet still alone.

Stephen arrived home one evening well before the dinner hour and well before Eliza had expected him. She had spent most of the day composing, with short breaks to get up and stretch, to snack and to rub feeling back into her chilled joints. The days were becoming less brilliant and the upstairs window now looked upon an almost leafless tree. The colder air found its way through the gaps of the bare branches and confronted the window with barrages that drafted into the room. She first noticed the change in temperature when her toes and hands began to feel chilled. She had asked Stephen numerous times since then to allow her to run the heat during the day, but he insisted that it was wasteful and that heating the home only in the evening and through the night was better for both of them. "Bundle up, if you feel that cold. Hot cup of tea will warm you through," he would remind her with a gentle squeeze of her shoulder. She sat feeling numb, not only from the cold, but also from his touch. To ask him to rearrange the room so that the old red couch, already starting to fade from the summer sun, could be moved under the window and her writing desk moved to the space vacated by the couch was out of the question. Stephen had grown particular as their marriage aged. Everything had its place and once decided upon, was to remain in its place. She recalled how upset he'd become when she had made the decision to move the contents of the kitchen cabinets around to be more efficient. In doing so, she also filled a cardboard box with items that were duplicates, damaged, or hardly ever used. What had she heard once? If you look in your closet and see clothing that you haven't removed from a hanger in a year, you don't need it, so get rid of it. She applied this thinking to the kitchen. The result, she thought, was a well-working kitchen. She also thought that Stephen would agree and be pleased with his wife's practicality.

Remembering that this wasn't so, she suddenly heard

footsteps on the stairs. Startled, she turned to see him standing in the doorway holding a bouquet of flowers whose fragrance immediately filled the room. His face seemed ruddy, revealing the actual temperature outside, and he was sniffing in place of finding a handkerchief to quell the annoying drip. Eliza could sense his frustration. After all, he was making this grand entrance in order to impress her, but all the while his body had other plans. Embarrassing for him, Eliza thought. To save him from further humiliation, she jumped up from her seat as if she had been counting the moments until his arrival and there he was! However, to go to him, to smile as warmly as he was doing for her, and to find the words that would satisfy him at that moment seemed a challenge.

"Darling, you surprised me! What a treat to have you home so early. And the flowers, sweetheart. They are beautiful!" She leaned into the bouquet to hide in the overpowering fragrance while trying to avoid Stephen's face and wondering from where those tender words had sprung. He released the bouquet to her and quickly dug in his coat pocket for his "rag." Turning from her for a moment, he then turned back and embraced her awkwardly as the oversized bouquet came between them. Eliza had purposely kept it in front of her.

"It's good to be home, Eliza." He seldom used her first name and it felt odd to her. Terms of endearment were the norm for Stephen, and she had learned how to use the same, but it came harder for her. "I have been missing you all day. Couldn't keep my mind off you. Kept going back to the first time we met. Who would have thought that a 'closed' sign would have brought us together? Happy anniversary, sweetheart. I've made plans for a romantic dinner at The Capital Grille for seven. Can you be ready by then?" Seeing Eliza's confused look, he quickly added, "I should have given you a heads-up, right? Completely unexpected, I know, but I really did want to surprise you. You're okay with this, aren't you?" He really couldn't remember the last time he had made such a production of their wedding anniversary, but he knew that ten years together could not be noted with a simple though tasteful anniversary card that contained the same sentiments each and every year. His eyes searched hers for some kind of recognition of his out-of-the-ordinary attempts to connect with her.

"Stephen...darling," she quickly threw in the "darling," "yes, of course. You just caught me by surprise. I've been so involved in my work and was not expecting you home until much later. You caught me by surprise, that's all." Her heart was not beating normally, and her head was beginning to throb with the syncopated rhythm of her rebellious heartbeat. How could she have forgotten that it was their anniversary? It didn't seem possible. Why had she let this slip by? More importantly, what was she going to do so that Stephen would never know of her failure to mark the passage of time with him? How many years had it been? Eight? No, nine. That's right. Or was it? She could feel panic taking over as he stood so close to her. She couldn't think clearly. *Simple subtraction, you idiot. Today's year minus wedding date year. Come on, come on. Oh, my God! It's been ten years!* And she had forgotten.

"Love, don't worry. Let's just enjoy our evening together. I'll put the flowers in water and you get yourself together. We'll need to leave in about an hour or so. Do you want me to make you a drink? I'm going to have one and relax for a bit. Don't get to do this as often as I would like. Would like to see what it's like to be a nine-to-five breadwinner."

His laughter brought her out of her chaotic thinking and she said, without hesitating, "Absolutely!"

"I'll have it ready in no time. Go ahead, sweetheart. I'll bring it up to you."

In the quiet of their bedroom, the fragrance of the flowers remained with her as she remembered to take some deep, deep breaths and to quiet her mind. A quick shower would give her some private time to think. What could she give him? He must be expecting something. Oh God. How could she find herself in such an awkward position? *Stupid, stupid, stupid,* she thought as she entered the warm shower waters. And then it came to her. Her poetry.

Before she had become so consumed with her novel, and

in the first two years of her marriage, she had composed a small group of love poems to Stephen. She had never let him see them, still doubting her talent, and did not want him to give her false praise. She had forgotten their existence until this very moment. For some reason, they came back to her like neglected but loved friends and she could recite each one without hesitation. The words flowed from her gently in a soft whisper while revitalizing her, just as the warm waters cleansing her body enveloped her. A relief came over her and then an excitement to retrieve these love notes from their hiding place. For Stephen, she knew, these poems would be meaningful. After all, her words reflected a time in their marriage when love was the anchor that held them in place. He would recognize that time together and perhaps his unexpected actions of this afternoon's flowers and evening plans would make sense, then, to them both. She had hopes that her gift, even though not as carefully planned as Stephen's had been, would reflect the same need to find that moment in time again when everything felt just right.

After dinner, Eliza reached inside her bag and placed in front of Stephen a very thin leather-bound book. The rich, deep brown leather of the front cover, having no title but only beautifully intricate engravings that continued onto the back cover, caught the reflection of the table's candlelight as Eliza moved the book closer to Stephen. "Happy anniversary, sweetheart." She looked directly into his eyes as he placed his hand on the book. He kept his eyes on the cover for what seemed such a long time for Eliza, who had had numerous afterthoughts about the appropriateness of this last-minute gift. Had she done the right thing or had she created greater discomfort between them? Her hands were damp with sweat as she placed them in her lap and waited for some response from Stephen.

He gently opened the cover and began reading. She glanced at him, hoping to catch a clue as to his reaction, and not seeing one, occupied herself by reading the dessert menu repeatedly. The silence was unbearable while she quietly prepared herself for his false praise and gratitude.

He closed the book of poetry, picked it up, and ever so

carefully placed it in his jacket pocket. Leaning toward her, folding his hands as if ready to pray, he spoke so softly that she missed the first words as she realized he was speaking. She closed the dessert menu now memorized.

"…and I will cherish this book for as long as I live, Eliza Bingham. I love you more than you will ever know."

Suddenly feeling warmth and true affection for him and expecting him to reach for her hand, she extended it across the table to him. However, clearly dismissing the moment, he made no move to hold her hand as he suddenly sat upright. Looking around the dining room, he asked her if she would like dessert. The warmth vanished. In its place, she experienced a churning in her stomach and a flush of confusion, once again, as he waved down a waiter. Her intuition was trying to tell her something but could not make its way through the jumble of emotions tossing about within.

Steadying herself, she made a mental note of how strange life can be. It grabs you and tosses you about as if you were a rag doll, then throws you without any particular direction in mind until you come to a landing place, recognizable or not. It's your problem to get back on your feet and locate a sense of direction. Dessert was the true north for the moment.

"I thought that you would never ask. Of course, and you?" She felt weakened.

"Dessert it is. Try the mousse. It's the house special. You'll love it." Stephen looked back down at his menu.

She had never cared for mousse. It was thick, creamy, dark, slimy, and slid down the throat without any work. For her, it was a reminder of childhood fare. The kind that you can't choke on no matter how hard you tried, all for effect, and certainly can't hide in a napkin at the dinner table while your parents were already doing the dishes. You had to remain in your chair until you had eaten the whole gooey mess.

"Of course. That sounds good. What are you having?" What had she just agreed to? Why couldn't she just order what she really wanted? A cup of peppermint tea.

The waiter approached the table and Stephen ordered for

her. "Sir, will you be having anything? Perhaps a coffee, a dessert wine?"

"No, just the mousse, and only one spoon." He did not look at Eliza. Handing the menus to the waiter, he leaned back in his chair and closed his eyes.

"Are you not feeling well?" She offered this query as she secretively fumed on the inside, anticipating how lousy she was going to feel after ingesting the mousse. He opened his eyes and focused on her.

"Sorry, just realizing how full I am, or should I be more appropriate and say that I am pleasantly satisfied. I really don't understand how you can consume one more bite."

These last words hung in the air and then rung in her ears so loudly, thoughtlessly, and rudely that she wanted to stand up and leave him sitting alone at the table. Intuition was making some progress. Where had she done this before? It felt strangely familiar. Greece—that's right, Greece. Had he purposely placed her in this position over something as meaningless as a dessert? Didn't he know that she would be upset by his actions? What was he expecting as her reaction? Did he want this evening to end badly?

"Stephen, I would have been content with a cup of tea, quite frankly. I thought that you were having something, and I didn't want you to have to eat alone."

"Well, it's too late for that, isn't it? Why couldn't you have just said no to my suggestion? After all, that's all it was. No one's forcing this down your throat."

She wasn't completely sure but for a moment, she thought she saw a familiar darkness in his eyes. Perhaps it was her own anger with him and herself that caused her to see something that was not there. *Get a grip, girl. It's only a meal.* Her true north was beginning to waver, so she was having a difficult time knowing in which direction to go next.

The silence on the drive home only intensified her discomfort with her husband. Sharing the backseat of a cab felt claustrophobic to her, and she fought the urge to open the door and jump out. Anything to be free from him, just until she could clear her head of her growing concern about him. Acknowledging that she could be blowing it all out of proportion somewhat tempered her thinking, but she couldn't ignore what intuitively she suspected: there was something very wrong with him. What was causing his moods to shift so suddenly, so unexpectedly, and seemingly for no good reason?

As the cab pulled up to the curb, she knew what had to be done. She had to confront him about her concern before another incident took place. Having no idea how to begin with him, she realized that she was now calm, breathing easier, and physically relaxing her tense body as the cabbie opened her door. The cool night air slammed into her face, demanding that she take a deep breath of the city's atmosphere, a concoction all its own. Free now from the confines of the cab, a sense of confidence and then urgency filled her. She would confront him as soon as they were inside.

He had stayed behind in the hallway to open the mail that still lay on the small table just inside the entrance.

"Stephen, we need to talk." She had turned to speak to him, waiting for him to look up from the mail and acknowledge her presence. "Stephen?"

"Give me a minute." He didn't look at her but stood stiffly and with a businesslike air, reading the contents of one of the envelopes.

"Do you want something from the kitchen? A nightcap, maybe?" She hadn't planned on delaying the discussion and regretted that she was caving in to his possible desires.

"Bourbon," barely escaped his lips as he mumbled his order, still not looking at her.

"Okay. I'll be in the living room. Please don't take too long there." Without looking at her, without saying a word, she noted a subtle, slow movement of his head back and forth. She tried to ignore what she interpreted as his disgust for her.

She had poured a diluted drink for herself and dutifully placed his on the end table by his chair, just as he liked it. He had not left the hallway and her impatience with him grew. Gripping the glass unnecessarily hard, she remained standing until he appeared.

"Okay. I'm here." He swept into the room as if harried and determined not to stay longer than needed. Lifting his glass, he did not acknowledge her as he usually did. A simple clinking of their glasses. A ritual. Instead, he swallowed the contents in one intentional gesture that he knew would upset her. Putting the empty glass down, he finally looked at her, a quizzical expression on his face, an unmistakable indication that she needed to start whatever it was that she wanted to say. His demeanor at that moment couldn't have been a more appropriate instigator for her. A foul mood or not, she would not let his instability frighten her off.

"I'm just going to say it, Stephen. I am worried about you, and, for that matter, I'm worried for me, for us." She could not pause to let him speak, and so continued despite an obvious change in his expression. His face was stone. "I never know what mood you're going to be in, and I don't understand what causes you to shift from one moment of happiness to the next of...I don't know, whatever." She was not communicating as clearly as she had wanted to. She knew that and chided herself for ruining her chance to address the issue. She would have to do better. "Is it me that sets you off? Because if it is, you have to tell me. I'm not doing anything to intentionally upset you, believe me. If you would just talk to me, then maybe I could avoid whatever it is that gets to you about me. I just don't know who you are sometimes, Stephen, and that scares me." She realized that she was taking the blame. It was all on her shoulders. She was the one who had the problem. *Damn!* Not at all the direction she thought that she would take with him. But it was too late to retrieve her words. She waited for him to respond. Forgetting for the moment that she was holding a full glass, in the silence of the room, she took a gulp and shivered as the liquid slid down her throat.

"I apologize for whatever you think I'm doing. Shifting moods? I'm really not sure what you are referring to. Sure, I have my ups and downs. Who doesn't? So you're telling me that my being who I am scares you?" He had taken a step closer to her.

"I don't mean to scare you, Eliza. It hurts me that you feel this way." Now he was close enough to take her into his arms, but he didn't.

"How do you explain tonight, for example? The dessert fiasco, I mean. So stupid and so unnecessary. One minute you are gung-ho for dessert, leading me to believe that we would enjoy it together. Then you flip to the opposite side. 'Only one spoon.' What was that about?" Her voice was strained and growing louder, and she felt like a schoolgirl in an argument with another girl. Whining, obnoxiously immature. Why couldn't she express what she was truly upset about? Why couldn't she just tell him that she didn't trust him?

"Is that what you're upset about? Really. You've got to be kidding me." He was smiling as he reached for her hand. She let him take it. "Look. I admit that I can be a bit hard to live with. Something I've got to work on, obviously, based on what you've said to me tonight. I assure you, I would never hurt you intentionally. I'm sorry, Eliza. That's really all I can say. Does that help?" He brought her hand to his lips and brushed it with a kiss.

She knew it didn't. She made no headway because she failed to stand up to him. No wonder he blew her off. Dessert? That was the best example she could give? She should remind him about his behavior in Greece. His stinginess and callousness when she asked to turn up the heat. His irritation with her when she tried to make the house her home as well. His sudden coldness upon receiving her book of poetry. All of that mixed, when he felt like it, with his gestures of love for her. Fatigue prevented thinking clearly beyond pulling her hand away from his and she suddenly longed to sleep, the sleep of the dead.

"I'm going to bed. It's been too long a day." She headed toward the stairs and then stopped. Turning to him, she remembered. "By the way, thanks for the flowers and dinner." She did not wait for his response. As she came to the bedroom door, she heard the low rumblings of some late-night television show. She closed the door behind her, shutting out her reality, at least for the night.

Chapter 9

The call came on his cell while Stephen was at work, and he was grateful for that. The years had passed quickly, and all memory of Michael had been buried long ago, as had any memories of his parents. Stephen had made sure that any reminders of his "family" were destroyed. He had forced himself to become someone else, someone who could move through this life independently, cut off from anything in the past that would betray him.

He recalled the panic he had felt in the small Greek shop when his brother's name was spoken aloud and the fear of losing control as his wife and the Greek stranger innocently plotted to reveal all that he could not let emerge. Eliza had proven herself to be safe, however. She had never mentioned the episode again, as if it had never occurred. He found that he could create a new self in her presence and realized that by doing so, he began to enjoy living again. He did feel affection for her. After all, he had married her. Complying with her request, he had taken her on her trip to Greece. And in general, he was satisfied that she was happy with him.

The voice on the other end of the call was grave, distant, hesitant, and unrecognizable. "Stephen, hello? Stephen? Is that you?"

Stephen tried to breathe deeply to quell the pounding pace of his heart, somehow knowing deep within that what he had long feared was coming next. His palm was moist as he clutched the phone to his ear, knowing that this could stop if he just ended the call before it began, but he couldn't take that step. It was as if he was frozen in time and had nowhere to run or hide. The sour bile from his breakfast rose suddenly into his throat, gagging any response.

"Hello? I'm looking for Stephen Bingham. Hello?"

"Yes, this is Stephen," he managed. An audible forced expulsion of air from the caller filled the space between them.

"Who is this?"

"Stephen. This is Michael."

He heard his voice say his brother's name out loud, something he had not done in over forty years. "How did you get this number?"

Did it really matter? What mattered was that Stephen's world had just shattered. His sense of reality was suspended, and he felt angry, lost, and terribly fearful.

The floor under his bed was the only place he could hide and not be found, but only if he stayed very still and didn't make a sound. He knew that his brother would hold onto him as they lay as one body, shivering with fear, waiting for the inevitable. And it would always come. The heavy footsteps on the stairs, the muffled sobs of a woman somewhere in the house as the brothers desperately tried to stifle their own frightened whimpers.

"Stephen, it's good to hear your voice. It's been so very long. I know this must be surprising, huh? I just needed to make contact, Stephen. I didn't mean…"

"No, Michael. No more. Don't ever call me again." He could hear his brother calling his name with an intensity that grew the longer he delayed in ending the call. Through blurred vision, the phone's END CALL red light nestled in the palm of his sweating hand came into clear focus, glaring at Stephen to do what he should have done minutes ago.

"Stephen! Run! Run! He's coming. I saw his car coming down the road. Run!" Michael pushed him out of the swing, toppling him to the ground. He knew that he had no time to complain about his brother's action, nor would he. His big brother was always there to protect him and at this moment, Michael's command to run was to be obeyed. He saw his brother reach out his hand to pull him up, and Stephen clutched it as a lifesaving force. The cabin, set back in the redwoods, seemed to be miles away as both boys willed their legs to move. The need to warn Mama was foremost, and

then they would hide.

He was visibly shaking. He could feel it and see it as he willed his finger to the red light. It was so simple to stop the pain and, with a light touch to the screen, Michael was gone. Stephen sat limply at his desk; any strength left in him had dissipated as he listened to his brother's pleas for recognition. Recognition of the truth. Recognition of who Stephen really was. Recognition of a past life that had not gone away. The realization that he was not in control, that there was something far greater than his desires and his carefully crafted existence, flashed before him and would have sunk its teeth deeply into his conscience if he had let it. But even in his weakened state, he had fought back.

"Get out here, you little shits! Don't go pretending to hide on me, like I don't know where you are." He stood at the top of the stairs only feet from their bedroom door. He was right. They knew what was coming next. Their father was in a drunken state again as he pushed open the door. "First one out is gonna be better off. Who's the brave one of the two of you pain-in-the-ass worms? God almighty, don't make me get down there and pull you out." This time, the brothers simultaneously knew that their father was out of his mind with drink, his words horribly slurred, his voice saturated with hatred. They clutched each other so tightly that their breathing became quickened, heaving breaths of terror. Michael looked directly into Stephen's eyes, silently pleading with him to stay, not to move, not to cry. Be brave, little brother. I have you.

Lighting in his office was important to Stephen and when he designed his work space, he made sure that at all times of the day the lighting was appealing to him, all the while taking advantage of Mother Nature's artful illumination. At this time of year the evenings grew dark quickly, and he often found himself forced to work under artificial light. Because of this, he tried to ensure that his day was productive enough that he wouldn't have to work under those conditions. However, on this day, the day of Michael's call, everything was turned upside down.

He wasn't sure how long he had sat there after ending the call. He didn't know that the desk phone had rung with five calls during this time. He hadn't heard his secretary knocking at the door, calling his name in her professional manner but with growing concern for her boss's well-being when no response was given. He barely noticed her standing in front of his desk when, in desperation, she entered the room without his permission only to find that he had not collapsed from a stroke or heart attack or worse yet, was slumped in his chair with a clean shot to the side of his head, his pistol floating in a pool of dark blood on the floor beside his chair. He didn't see the relief on her face when, not acknowledging her presence with words, but with a simple nod of his head, he rose slowly from his desk, cautiously standing for a moment, his legs feeling like jelly. As if taking a quick inventory of his physical state, he flexed his limbs, one by one, then straightened his shirt and tie while glancing down at his pants and shoes. Running a hand through his dulling hair that had once been jet black and quite full, he took a deep breath as he retrieved his phone and shoved it into his briefcase. He gave her another businesslike nod of recognition and headed for the elevator.

"Mr. Bingham? Mr. Bingham?" she called after him when she realized that he was leaving for the day. She reached the elevator just as the doors were opening and Stephen was entering. "Are you all right? I am sorry to have disturbed you back there, but you were not answering me. Are you all right, sir?" She was concerned for him because this was not the first time that she had observed what she could only describe as odd behavior. In those moments, she found it reassuring to enumerate the many reasons why he might act unusually. What always came to mind first was that he was constantly under pressure, which he seemed to handle well most of the time, but there were moments. She had not forgotten them but knew that the job she held was not easy to come by, and she would be damned if she would let any unprofessional behavior on her part jeopardize her job security. He treated her well and paid well. That was enough for her. Besides, she had convinced herself that if and when she felt that Mr. Bingham was a danger to himself, she would act responsibly and call the authorities. However, there was also a gnawing concern that he might endanger her and as much as she tried to ignore it, she knew that it lay just below the fragile surface of this professional relationship.

"Of course, of course. Just a bit tired and ready to call it a day." He now was focused on her and seeing her look of concern for him he was touched. "Sorry to have worried you, Jillian. Just got plowed under and too engrossed with work. I'm fine. See you in the morning then?"

His smile reassured her that her worries were probably unwarranted, and she stepped back from the elevator. "Of course, Mr. Bingham. All of this can wait," she said, looking down at the papers cradled in her arms. "Have a good evening and please give my regards to Mrs. Bingham, and..." The elevator doors had shut before she could finish.

The cab began its descent, carrying Stephen from the forty-fourth floor to the garage. He prepared himself for the numerous stops, the employees directing an artificial nod of recognition his way and he doing the same as they entered the elevator. What he longed for was a long, quiet, and isolated ride so that he could collect his thoughts about the events of the afternoon. However, as usual, he found himself pushed up against a corner wall as the population in the descending cab grew with each stop.

"Why do you vex me so much? You just asking for it? Both of you together are dumber than all get-out! Get out here!" Stephen could feel his father's strong, callused grip on his ankle as he yanked him out of his brother's arms and their hiding place. With the strength of an angry animal, he threw Stephen against the chest of drawers and ordered him not to move a muscle. He then did the same with Michael, except that Michael, being older and stronger than Stephen, could put up a good fight against the monster who was their father. He never won, though, and found himself

grabbed and shoved into the heap that was Stephen's quaking body. Instinctively, Michael covered his brother with as much of his mass as possible, a futile attempt to protect Stephen, but an attempt that gave Stephen momentary comfort and relief.

"Leave us alone, you creep! Get out of here!" Michael screamed at his father, only to feel sudden burning pain in his head as his father made contact with his fist and then the warm, thick liquid oozing from somewhere above his ear and running down the back of his neck. Unable to move for fear of losing consciousness, all he could do was stay close to his brother so that the same did not happen to him.

"You don't tell me what to do, you hear me, you little shit? And what do you think you're doing hiding behind this poor excuse of a brother?" Feeling his father's grasp on his arm, Stephen could do nothing to avoid the inevitable. It wasn't the first time and Stephen knew that it would not be the last. He could not escape any more than Michael could. Dragged out from under Michael's bloodied body, Stephen couldn't tell if his face was soaked with his tears or the blood of his brother.

Screaming his resistance with words that he knew meant nothing to his father— "No, no, no. Don't, no, don't! Please don't!"—he prayed that someone would hear him. Someone would come and take them to safety. Someone would kill their father so all of this would stop forever.

The well had not produced any water since the drought seven years ago but still held the remnants of dampness and mildew from the winter rains. Their father had dug it himself in his younger days. He had been told by the few locals, who inhabited the area but were separated by great distances, that in order to hit water he would have to dig deeper than he had thought because of the location. The ground was densely rocky and the water table had not been measured here. Probably the reason why he could buy the land so cheaply when he did. However, he thought himself smart enough to have purchased the ten acres of land in the Ventana wilderness. Today, he wouldn't be able to touch it, as the value of the land had skyrocketed. He had no intention of ever selling an inch of it.

The doors opened at the garage level. Tired and overworked, the occupants were polite enough to follow elevator protocol, allowing the human remains of the day to civilly exit into the garage. Stephen made a point of staying in place until the last person departed. "Got it," he nodded to a fellow worker who was holding the doors open for him. "Thanks, though." He stepped from his corner and shoved his arm against the automated motion of closure. Then he stepped back in and let the door shut. Pressing the twelfth-floor button, he focused on the digital numbers crawling to nine, ten, and just before eleven appeared above his head, he reached forward and pressed the STOP button. Somewhere between the tenth and eleventh floors, suspended by an automated system that could be overridden at any moment and then completely out of his control, he slumped in the corner of the elevated enclosure, cowering from what only Stephen saw at that moment. Unable to catch his shallow and heaving breath, he hid his head into his chest as far as he could so that his arms became his only shield against the terror that had joined him in this confined space.

The coarse, twined rope cut into his bare waist as he suffered the weight of his own body while dangling in the dank darkness of the small stone enclosure surrounding him. The stench sickened him but he did not vomit. He feared the pain that he knew would come if he placed any more tension on his exposed skin. This was not the first time he had experienced this enclosure, but it was the first time he had been here without his older brother dangling right next to him, reassuring him that everything was going to be okay. High above him, he could see wisps of powder-puff clouds move across the circular opening against a late-afternoon sky, and he heard Michael's taunts followed by his howls of pain.

He heard his father's laughter, much like the laughter that Stephen remembered one Christmas morning when their father opened the gift that his wife had given him. Holding up the flannel shirt so that they all could admire it, his laughter filled the room. It began sincerely, its source, she cautiously thought, the pure joy that she would have thought enough of him to find just the right shirt with which to surprise him. Not sure if they should join in their father's pleasure, neither boy made a sound but kept an eye on both of their parents, especially their father.

His wife smiled tentatively, all the while sensing pain in her palms as her nails pressed against her skin in her enclosed fists. The laughter abruptly stopped.

"How did you know that I wanted this shirt? How did you know, huh?" He leaned forward in his chair and held his wife captive with his penetrating glare. His voice revealed a growing agitation. It seemed that minutes had gone by while the room and everyone in it froze in time. Suddenly, freeing each one of them from his invisible grasp, he stood, awkwardly holding the shirt against his chest and arms while falsely admiring himself in front of them.

For a fleeting moment, he reminded Stephen of Peter Pan, who tried to press his shadow against his body only to find that it wouldn't stay on. Strangely, Stephen found a moment's relief and comfort in the image of Peter and of Michael reading the story to Stephen very quietly under the covers late into the night when they were supposed to be asleep.

"What man wouldn't want a damn lumberjack's shirt? Hey, you should just fill my closet with them since you think I'm going to wear this. What do you take me for? You waste my hard-earned money to buy me a shirt for Christmas? That's what you think of me? That's what you goddamn think of me? All I'm worth to you is a lousy lumberjack-ass shirt?"

Stephen shut his eyes while covering his ears with his hands, pressing so hard against them that he could almost shut out his father's tirade. When the noise finally stopped, he waited for minutes before opening his eyes, afraid that his father might look in his direction. It was Michael who took Stephen's hands away from his ears and whispered that it was over, and it would be okay.

What he did see was his mother cowered in the corner of the living room, their Christmas tree on its side in front of her, who now was the recipient of remnants of shattered Christmas decorations and broken lights. In the early-morning light of the rising sun, Stephen thought that he saw beautiful red Christmas ribbons adorning his mother's head and face, as if she were their special gift, only to understand upon closer look as Michael and he approached her that the crimson ribbons were not ribbons at all. As she clutched the flannel shirt in her lap, the bloodied stains were absorbed by the soft red plaid only to become invisible to an onlooker at first glance.

Chapter 10

Redialing for the sixth time, Eliza was beginning to worry. She had called the office only to learn that Stephen had left a bit earlier than usual. Jillian had no idea where he was but assumed that he was going home. She would let Eliza know if she heard from him, of course.

He heard his cell but it sounded distant. Removing his hands from his ears, he reached into his pocket and only felt emptiness as the annoying sound continued. As he tried to remember where he had put it, he was startled to find himself sitting on an elevator floor, huddled in the corner. Slowly assessing his situation, he stood up, grabbing onto the railing. Had he fallen? Collapsed? Confused and weak, he became aware that the elevator was stopped between floors. He moved to the panel of buttons and hit G. As the digital numbers above the door descended, Stephen tried to make sense of this. He remembered leaving the office and entering the elevator, the number of people who had joined him, and the sensation of being crowded against the back corner wall. But nothing else.

His cell had stopped ringing. Reaching down for his briefcase, he remembered grabbing his phone from the desk and mindlessly shoving it in the case, something he never did. He began to search for it among the papers and files that filled the case when the elevator door opened and revealed an almost emptied parking garage. How long had he been in that elevator? What time was it?

Now fully conscious, his mind began to race. Eliza. Was she calling him? Once in his car, he pushed the seat back as far as it would go and leaned against it, his head resting on the headrest, eyes closed, breathing slowing. The sensation of peace came over him and he heard himself say aloud, "It's over. It's going to be okay." He readjusted the seat, started the car, and headed for home.

"Eliza?" Stephen was relieved to hear her voice as he

called her from the road. "Hey, hon'. I'm sorry not to have picked up your calls. Must have had the ringer off. Stupid. I didn't mean to worry you. Everything okay?" He couldn't imagine that she was okay, not after trying to reach him six times, not knowing where he was or what he was doing. So he prepared himself for her legitimately frustrated and angry response.

"I'm fine, but what about you? Jillian said that you left the office early today. It's late, Stephen. I was really worried about you. Why didn't you let me know that you were leaving? I could have met up with you for an early dinner, maybe?" Eliza was upset but tried desperately not to reveal this to Stephen. Kindness and understanding were needed here, not a childish rant. She sensed this to be the right thing to do. No. The safe move to make. This last thought she tried to erase from her mind. But where had he been? Wasn't this how extramarital affairs revealed themselves to the innocent wife? An afternoon of pleasure for one becomes an afternoon of agony for the other once the deceit is revealed. And how many afternoons had already taken place? Where? With whom?

"I'll be home in about twenty minutes. I guess you've already eaten? Do you want me to bring in anything? I'm really sorry to have worried you, honey." He had listened to her questions but didn't have any answers. He needed some time to understand what had taken place. He also knew that he could never share any of this with Eliza. Twenty minutes should give him enough time to come up with a plausible story. He had no choice.

"Just come home safely. I don't need anything but you safe and sound. See you in twenty, then. Right?"

"Right. 'Bye. Love you." Stephen added these last words as sincerely as he could without their sounding like a last-minute tag-on to close the conversation.

Chapter 11

The lie was a simple one. He did leave work early and was planning on coming home to relax and be with his wife after what had already been a trying week. He had seen a window of opportunity to do this and took advantage of it. However, he ran into an old business acquaintance whom he hadn't seen in years as he was going to his car in the garage. The guy used to work with him when Stephen was first starting out in business and had been a great mentor to him. He had lost contact with him over time but had not forgotten him. Now retired, Ed had been paying a visit to one of the bigwigs who was one of his partners in a venture years back. "Just catching up with old friends." In running into Stephen, Ed felt fortune smiling on him as he had now encountered another old friend, all in the same day.

He invited Stephen to have dinner with him and Stephen had said yes, somewhat in a daze and without thinking to call his wife. A thoughtless mistake, he knew, and he would apologize.

While at dinner, Ed had reached into his jacket pocket for his cell and had switched it to silent mode. He explained to Stephen that there were a lot of things that "drive me up a wall and one of those is cell phones ringing in restaurants and rude, selfish idiots thinking that everyone is interested in their conversation, albeit one-sided."

Stephen, who always kept his phone on, and certainly fell into Ed's category of idiots, reached for his cell and did the same. They had a great time catching up but, of course, as the evening had worn on, he had not heard or even checked his phone. Out of hearing range, out of mind. It wasn't until the check came that he realized how late it had gotten, and it wasn't until they were in the parking lot having said their goodbyes that Stephen remembered his phone was off as he glanced back to see Ed making a call on his, probably calling his own wife.

"So I called you as soon as I got into the car. Really stupid thing to do, going out to dinner without calling. Can't believe that I did that. Forgiven?" As he sat on the side of their bed, he reached for Eliza's hand.

"Sure, of course. I get it." She put down the book she was reading. She had been so close to drifting off when she heard Stephen come in. With both hands caressing his, she responded, "Must have been quite an influence on you all those years ago that you still feel it even now, and you are probably much more successful than him. Interesting, isn't it, how some people have that kind of power over others? I mean, you move on with your life, you don't have contact with someone like that for years on end until they appear again out of the blue, and all of a sudden, you are back there with whatever baggage you thought you left behind a long time ago. And there they are in complete control as if time has stood still." She stopped when she saw the expression on Stephen's face grow dark and vacant. Had she crossed another line? "So, Ed. Will you be seeing him again?" She changed course in her rambling, wanting Stephen to return to her.

"Uh, no, no." Stephen wanted this lie to be over. "Just one of those chance encounters, not meant to go any farther." The end. He needed to get ready for bed, get away from her insights that Stephen could feel dragging him under. "I'll be with you in just a minute," he said, and he pulled his hand out of hers. "Keep the bed warm."

Placing her book on the bedside table, Eliza suddenly remembered. "Oh. By the way. I almost forgot. You had a phone call this afternoon from a man. Didn't want to leave his name. Said you knew who he was and that it was important that he speak with you. I guess he didn't know that we were married. Sounded surprised. I told him that you were at work and gave him your cell number."

Stephen turned to her, rigidly poised at the foot of the bed. Alarmed by his countenance, she knew that he was not pleased. "Sorry if I blew it. He seemed very nice and grateful that he had spoken with me, so to speak. Did he reach you?"

He was sure that he was visibly shaking and forced himself to regain his composure in front of her. He felt his facial muscles release as he internally vetted what would have been an angry and revealing response. "No, he didn't. No messages. No texts. Just your calls. Did he leave a number?"

"I asked him to but he said that it wasn't necessary, that he would get ahold of you eventually. That was it. Are you angry with me?"

He was, but he knew that he couldn't blame her. How could she be held responsible for something she knew nothing about? But she was the catalyst who threatened everything that he had created and preserved all these years. A simple phone call threatened his very existence. And he could see no way out of what he knew would eventually confront him.

"No, of course not. You did the right thing." Not willing to draw this out any longer, he turned back toward the bathroom. "Turn off the light if you need to get to sleep. I'll be back in a bit."

She watched him close the door behind him, relieved that he was not upset with her.

With hands gripping the side of the sink, Stephen tasted his own tears as he waited for the first strike of his father's heavy hand on his backside. He was frozen in terror. It never occurred to him to let go and run out of that bathroom, run to Michael, who was in the next room. His four-year-old mind did not logically reveal to him that he could run, that he did have the power to escape. He only knew that he was told to grip the sink's edges and to pay for his stupidity. He only knew that there was nothing to do but feel such a fear of his father and to obey his commands.

And then the pain came. Again and again. But he did not let go of the sink as his little legs began to quiver and his knees gave way to the weight of his small body. And when he did find himself on the floor, his arms were still outstretched above his head, burning with tension, as his small hands continued to clutch the sink's edge.

It was only when Michael's hands gently pried his fingers from the cold porcelain that he crumbled into a pile against Michael, who cradled his sobbing, wounded brother on the bathroom floor.

"Stephen, I can't keep the bed warm forever. Honey, what on earth are you doing in there? I'm turning out the light." Eliza had tried to stay awake so that she could give Stephen a kiss and embrace him to once more confirm that everything was all right. She needed to do that so that she could fall asleep and push from her mind the doubts that kept creeping in. His initial reaction about the call disturbed her, the more she thought about it. Where had she seen him like that before? What had caused him to react the way he did? An exhaustion hit her suddenly and with no answer from Stephen from behind the closed bathroom door, the room now dark, it subdued all concerns as she curled into her pillow and bedsheets and let her fatigue drag her elsewhere.

The feeling in his fingers was beginning to leave and then a numbing prickle alerted Stephen. Opening his eyes to see the vice grip in which he held the sink's edges, he slowly released his fingers and turned over his hands to see red indentations in both palms. How long had he been in here? *Just a minute,* he had told Eliza. *Keep the bed warm.* Hadn't he said this to her just moments ago? He turned to the closed bathroom door and saw no light seeping under the threshold. Quickly and quietly, he removed his clothes, rinsed his sweat-stained face, and finished the nightly routine. Crawling into bed without disturbing the covers that Eliza lay under, he felt an overwhelming fatigue. He closed his eyes and heard a voice say, "It's over. It's going to be okay," as he sunk into velvet-warm darkness.

Chapter 12

The first frost of the season had left the remaining plants in the garden wilted and dead. However, within the death of the garden there remained a beauty as the frozen dewdrops reflected miniature prisms that sparkled in the dimming rays of the late fall sun. These cold mornings kept the occupants of warm houses snuggled even deeper under their covers until there was no choice but to get up and start their days.

Anticipation always filled Eliza with the first frost. It meant that the cold, dark days of winter were not far off and that the seasonal celebrations that she so dearly loved were also very near. She also found it even more pleasurable to write each day as the outside was not inviting. She looked forward to snuggling in warm sweats, wool socks, and her favorite rabbit-fur-lined slippers while sipping on a hot cup of tea as she sat in front of her laptop, waiting for inspiration to take hold.

She was currently working on a novel and was having difficulty keeping track of her own imaginings. Inevitably, after each reread before starting the day's composing, she would catch a blaring conflict in the text. It could be something as simple as the number of years since an incident had occurred as stated on page 30 being in direct conflict with a different number of years on page 145. She had even caught herself recreating a character's personality so as to jive with the current text, which was in conflict with that character's identity in earlier pages. It became frustrating for her. She had listened to published authors talk about their process and couldn't remember any of them referring to the problems that she was experiencing. She began to have doubts that she could write a novel that anyone would want to read. Her poetry had been her mainstay, and perhaps she should reconsider the expenditure of energy given to prose. After all, she enjoyed writing poetry because it was so immediate. She never lingered for days, weeks, and months over a piece. Each came to her easily and completely. Seldom, once done, did she find the need to revise, nor did her publisher.

Now, as she sat staring at the most recent text of her novel, she could not bring herself to close it. She had invested months on this project and, if truth be told, she did enjoy working in prose. It was a greater challenge for her and perhaps that was what she needed to face.

As the fall months slipped by, Eliza kept busy writing. She continued to struggle with it but was in a better frame of mind to accept the struggle and to overcome it. She even considered having Stephen read what she had so far and welcoming his critique. Perhaps when she finished the next chapter she would ask him. However, chapter followed chapter, and she made the decision to withhold the draft from him until she was finished. Not that he wouldn't have something substantial to offer. She had no doubt that he would find the flaws in her thinking, but she feared that she would be overwhelmed by his suggestions and would never be able to move ahead as she slogged through the corrections. Better to get it all out and then tear it to shreds.

Christmas was Eliza's favorite time of year. She and Stephen decorated their home in the soft colors and warm haze of Christmases past. The scent of cinnamon and Douglas fir filled the rooms from the small bags Eliza purchased in Oregon one Christmas long ago. She had carefully saved them with all of the tree decorations year after year. The scent was beginning to fade, but if she vigorously rubbed the bag between her hands, she could revive it for yet one more Christmas.

Eliza had kept special decorations from her childhood and made a point of displaying them each year, either on the tree or on the fireplace mantel. The fresh greens bought at the corner Christmas tree lot were carefully laid across the mantel. Stephen wound the small white lights through the scented needles while Eliza nestled miniature Santas of all sorts within the greens. The tree took almost the whole day to decorate because they both took such care to place each ornament in the right place.

The final touch was to hang their stockings. Eliza's stocking was over fifty years old and had been hung each year with care since she was a baby. She had bought Stephen one in the first year of their marriage, as he'd told her that he had no idea where his original stocking had gone. He knew, however, that he had never had a stocking, much less anything remotely resembling a normal Christmas. He had no memories like Eliza's. He was plagued by other memories. For Eliza's sake, his childhood Christmases were fabricated.

When all was done, Stephen would light the logs in the fireplace and Eliza would make warm toddies. With the fire fully established, hot liquid in hand, Stephen would turn out the lights and then light the tree and the mantel. For Eliza, it was magical. For Stephen, it was a tradition that they had established as a couple, and he enjoyed seeing Eliza's childlike wonder each year. Only happy that he could provide for her and allow her to sustain her memories, Stephen was content to sit on the couch with Eliza nestled next to him as the warm liquor slid down his throat. With a second drink, he could begin to imagine what Eliza's Christmases must have been like. And with a third, he relaxed into a gentle sleep filled with the scents of cinnamon and Douglas fir.

In the doldrums of January, when the anticipation of the holidays was far behind, the weather was incessantly cold and snow fell in alarming amounts. Eliza remembered her first winter in Boston as being rather mild. She had imagined that a Boston winter would find her constantly bundled up against the elements, and she looked forward to it. Winters in California were wet and could be cold, but nothing like she knew she would experience in Boston. But the first winter for her came and went without much interruption. The snow fell, but it melted quickly and the few days that it did stay on the ground, it slowly became mushy, dirty goo that froze at night and then wept during the day. Boston was on record that year for having the lightest snowfall in recent history. This winter made up for it, however.

She had never felt so isolated and depressed as she did week after week, feeling like a prisoner in her own home. She went out only to stock up on groceries and necessities, and even that short a chore became a challenging experience. She had never felt comfortable driving on the snow and ice-covered roads and was especially fearful of getting caught in a driving snowfall while out. Stephen had taken the time to show her how to maneuver in the weather, but she never gained the confidence she knew she needed. Upset with herself, she was resigned to limited excursions and hours upon hours in the warmth of their home.

Not all was lost, however. She was glad that she had not given up on her novel, as this self-enforced confinement provided her with uninterrupted hours of composing and the words flowed with ease. Now with an ending closer in sight, Eliza's daily writing brought her satisfaction and a sense of accomplishment. The thought that her hibernation was going to bring forth the completion of her first novel propelled her forward. She realized one morning, as she readied herself for work, that she was the happiest she had been in a very long time. Beginning to think that she really did like these frigid winter days, she could see herself in her later years still finding comfort in writing each day, a cup of hot tea in hand, while the barren tree outside her window, whose gnarled trunk revealed its aging process just as Eliza's crinkled skin would, suffered under the weight of a recent snowfall or of an early-morning freeze encasing each branch and all of its tiniest parts in a crystalline replica of itself.

Chapter 13

Michael had not called Stephen again. He knew that it would be futile. The only way to make contact with his brother was to see him, to confront him finally with the truth. Michael had carried it far too long by himself and was afraid that it might be too late for Stephen. He could only imagine the life his little brother must be living, and he felt physically sick as he recalled their boyhood together.

Now that he was clean again for the first time in years, almost three years to the day, he felt as though he had been given a second chance and had gained the courage to contact Stephen.

The first time, he had blown it by giving in to his weaknesses that he knew he could not control. He had been young and ignorant. The immediate high, the mind-numbing effect of the alcohol, the constant need to feed and thus quell any rising doubts as to who he really was and what he was running from, had thrown him back onto the streets where he had learned how to survive.

During his first clean period, however, he had managed to find odd jobs, with the help of the clinic in which he had been confined for two years and had saved enough to travel. He knew where he wanted to go. While incarcerated, he had reached out to one of his fellow patients in the facility, about his age, in his mid-thirties, who, when in a rare, lucid state, would regale Michael with his memories of Greece. His words filled Michael with images that were so foreign to him, so enticing, that he made it his goal to go there himself one day. Upon his release, with little else than a backpack and enough hard-earned cash in his wallet, he had spent a month in Greece, a time that he would never forget.

But coming back to the States had hit him hard, and all that he had managed to bury deeply in the recesses of his mind would not stay buried. It insisted that he pay attention to it, as if to convey in its most evil voices that he still did not know who he was or what it was that was chasing him. To stop the condescending cacophony that only increased in volume and intensity the longer he tried to hold off from succumbing, the poisons that he once again consumed and that fed his brain dulled the noise, lulling him into the numbing state of absolute denial and a deathly comfort.

His second chance had come because someone, a stranger whose identity he never knew, had rescued him from himself. He had found Michael in some alley, his body curled up as if in the womb, oblivious to the stench of the trash overflowing from a nearby dumpster, some of it haphazardly wrapped around parts of his body to provide some insulation from the cold. He had come to, once again, in a different facility. But the painful experience of rehab and counseling, not unknown to him, had somehow brought him back to life, a life that he swore to his therapist and fellow inmates he would cherish and respect.

He had found work at a publishing firm working as a lackey, all the while absorbing the literary world from the bottom rung, but not a day had passed for Michael even in the deepest drug-and-alcohol-induced stupor that he didn't wake from sleep suddenly under the weighted responsibility for not having protected someone as he should have. Because of this, he had decided long ago never to get close to anyone, never to marry, never to commit himself to another person. The one person who was the exception had been Stephen.

Separated by the system into foster care when they were only four and eight, the brothers were in and out of different homes, only placed together twice, other times separated until one of them ran away to find the other. After numerous runaway events, the authorities finally realized that the connection between these fragile young boys was too strong to purposely separate them from one another.

When Michael turned thirteen, he abandoned the system and his nine-year-old brother. Without revealing to Stephen his plan, he ran away from his final foster home to make his way on his own. His decision had not been easy, but his intentions were well founded. Although naïve, he would find work, earn enough to support himself and Stephen, and then find a way for Stephen to leave foster care so that Michael could finally protect him as he should. He figured it would take a good year to save up enough and he was willing to do it. If he had shared his plan with Stephen, he knew that Stephen would beg to go with him, and Michael did not want to go through that. He knew that it was better this way. He would find a way to keep in touch with his little brother during that year, no matter what.

Out on the streets, completely on his own, Michael secretly thanked his father for his early childhood. After all, how would he have learned to defend himself in the face of danger? How would he have developed the callous shell that encased him so that no emotions from an outside force could penetrate, while any emotions that he felt were kept prisoner within? But deep within, all the while, a fire burned whose embers smoldered painfully in the crevices of his memory. Survival for Michael meant that he would do whatever was necessary. He needed to succeed in order to save Stephen.

With determination but a great lack of street sense, Michael found his way in with a gang who told him that they had his back, that this brotherhood was stronger than any family could ever be, that he owed his allegiance to his "brothers" and to no one else. Michael had assured them that he agreed, but silently pledged his only allegiance to his little brother.

Money was easy to come by and after handing over a percentage of his take on drug deals to his "brothers," he managed to accumulate enough in less than a year to make it on his own. Even though he hadn't spoken with Stephen since he had run away, he knew that it would only be a matter of seeing his brother and reassuring him that they would be together again permanently. Michael wanted that. He really did. However, he found that leaving the brotherhood was not possible, and ridding himself of his drug habits was even more of a locked door. He had descended into the oblivion of drug and alcohol use along with his "brothers," who encouraged him to taste the coke he was selling. He smoked weed, though it cleared his head from the last binge only to leave him craving another snort, and the downward spiral had no end. The money he had saved was gone. His need for a continued high far outweighed his thoughts of Stephen until there was no memory of a little brother somewhere waiting to be rescued by his protector.

Chapter 14

The news came to Eliza as a surprise. She had no idea that Stephen was considering moving out of Boston and back to California. Learning this over a late-night dinner, she found that she could not respond in any intelligent way. She fought off the need to yell at Stephen for trying to destroy this beautiful life that they had built together in Boston, for his callousness in assuming that she would be all right with it, that all that mattered was what Stephen wanted. A million like thoughts spun in her head, and it was all she could do not to blurt them out. Instead, she half listened to Stephen as he tried to convince her that this was a good decision for both of them.

"It's not that big a deal, sweetheart. And it's not like we're moving to a place you don't know."

The words now came. "I haven't known it for years now, Stephen. I thought we had decided that this was where we would make our home, our lives, here in Boston? You have your work and are doing so well and I have my writing. I can write here, Stephen. I have never felt more productive. Remember, one of the reasons I came here was to rediscover myself, to find a new career, but I found that I was a real writer here. I don't know what it is about this place, but I am thriving in it, Stephen. I can't just leave it and expect the same to happen in California. It's different." She heard her own voice and couldn't decide if she was whining or pleading. In any case, Stephen quietly listened, never changing the expression on his face. Almost blank, she realized. Was his mind already made up? Had he already decided for them? "Stephen, we really need to talk this through. Please?"

"I understand your hesitancy…"

Hesitancy? Did he really describe her feelings as hesitancy?

"Look, I haven't told you before because… well, quite frankly, I knew you would react this way." Without changing his expressionless countenance, he leaned forward to engage her.

"I've bought a home in Ventana—you know, Big Sur area."

Eliza felt as though she had lost all control of her senses but tried to pay attention to what he was telling her.

"It's beautiful there, you remember. This place is what we need, what I need. It's a two-story cabin but has all the amenities of our place here. As a matter of fact, I had to close the deal quickly because there were other buyers eager to get their hands on this property. You'll love it, Eliza. It even has a writer's nook just like the one you have now. The only difference is that you look out on massive ancient redwoods with sunlight streaming through their branches, there are no sirens and city noise to disturb you, and you can throw open the window and breathe clean sea air. All year long, Eliza! I've made reservations for next week to fly out so you can see it firsthand. And I've already dealt with our agent about this house, and it's well on its way to finding a new owner. We'll be moving out at the end of next month. Rainy season, I know, back there, but nothing compared to what you've been suffering through here. A lot to absorb, I know, huh?" He grabbed her hands in his. "It's a new beginning, Eliza, for both of us. We're going home."

As she looked up at him from her abandoned dinner, for the first time in a long time she saw her beautiful, younger Stephen, the one who had lingered with her on the sidewalk outside of a closed Gregario's, whose gaze she couldn't escape, whose sweetness she fell in love with. Perhaps, just perhaps, this would be okay. She tried to control her breathing to calm her and to clear her head. He meant well, she knew. And perhaps, going home again now that she was established and comfortable in her own skin as a skilled author, it didn't matter where she composed. There was no need to worry about Stephen's circumstances, as she knew he was smart when it came to business dealings, and everything that he had decided thus far had worked out well. The nagging feeling, however, that he hadn't thought enough of her and their relationship to discuss this with her before he made the final decision would not leave her. But, as in the past, she had learned to conceal her frustrations most of the time and to push into the dark recesses of her mind her real feelings.

"You've done it again, Stephen." This time she leaned in and a slight frown appeared on his forehead. "Surprised me, I mean. There's a lot to digest here, Stephen. You have to understand where I'm coming from. Right?"

"Of course I do, Eliza. Sure. What questions do you have? How can I help clear the air here for you?" He sat back and took a sip of his wine. She saw a slight upturn of his lips that seemed to her to unintentionally reveal his satisfaction with the conversation's outcome. "Well?"

"I just mean that I need time. The decision's made; I get that. I just need to sort it through, for my own sake. For starters, tell me more about the cabin. You know I have a visual of those summer cabins my parents used to drag us to. Please tell me it's not like one of those!" A smile crept across her face at the brief memory of her childhood, and Stephen saw it and knew that she would be all right.

Having now seen the property and returning to Boston to begin preparations for the move, Eliza was excited. She had forgotten the beauty of the area, its smells, its light, its peacefulness. Big Sur was magical, she knew that, and experiencing it now as an adult tweaked her perception of it. She did not remember as a child that she ever took note of something as simple as the feel of her shoes on the forest floor or the endless shades of green that were the forest. She did remember that her father had once commented upon her insightful thoughts, but this was different. It was as if noticing these details would ensure that she appreciated what she saw before her. That she was meant to take it all in and not let it escape her notice this time.

Upon seeing the house for the first time, she was taken aback by its age. For some reason, she assumed it had been built only a few years ago, the way Stephen described it. But even as an aged home, it had modern amenities, just as Stephen had said.

She was especially taken with the second floor. It held two bedrooms, a remodeled bathroom, and a sitting room. This area was what Stephen had referred to as the writing nook. And he was right. It would serve her well. The room was at the end of the hall. There were two windows in it, one facing due east and the other due west. They each rose from the base of the floor to a height of ten feet, ending where the angled redwood beams of the ceiling continued to the roof's peak. The room was full of light. Through the second-story windows, she looked upon the redwoods' trunks and branches as they rose above her and out of sight. She felt as though she were climbing each tree. Both windows, designed to be unobtrusive, opened outward and the sounds of the forests were invited in. The warmth of both the morning and afternoon sunlight kept the room comfortable and welcoming.

She decided that her desk would be in front of the east-facing window, as she did the bulk of her writing in the early hours of the morning. And the red couch that she knew they should leave in Boston, as it was showing its age and wear, would sit in the western window. A lovely place to read in the afternoon, she thought. And best of all, there was wall space galore for her bookshelves. Yes, she was going to love this special place. Stephen had been right, she realized. This would be a home in which they both could find solace and perhaps rekindle a love that was struggling to exist between them.

Chapter 15

The years of abuse to his system had very nearly destroyed Michael, so he appeared to be much older than his thirty-seven years on the earth. Found in the middle of a busy LA freeway, he had somehow managed to wander into the oncoming traffic only to collapse as he reached the median strip just before a semi came barreling down on him. Narrowly missing him, the truck blew past him, and Michael lost consciousness as he heard faintly in the background the squeals of braking tires on the hot Los Angeles pavement.

Waking up in a hospital room, hooked up to tubes and needles, frightened him and he grappled with the restraints that held him to the bed. Someone had taken both wrists and ankles and had tied him down. He tried to yell for help, but no sound came out of his parched and sore throat. He couldn't swallow and couldn't feel his body. It wasn't until he began to regain full consciousness that he realized every part of him was screaming. His agitated state grew worse by the minute as the absence of mind-numbing drugs threw his whole body into rebellion. When was the last time he shot up? How long had he been here? Before losing consciousness again, he recalled a quietly reassuring voice telling him, "It's over. It's going to be okay."

He was discharged from the hospital almost two weeks later and sent to a residential house to clean up his act. The detox was worse than anything he could remember going through. Even his father's most tortured discipline meted out on him day after day did not compare to the misery his body experienced as it was denied the sweet powder that it insisted upon. There was no guarantee that he wouldn't slip back into the darkness that he yearned for, but his living circumstances had suddenly changed, and he now had people in his life who seemed to care whether he lived or died.

Two group sessions were held each day. Michael could not deal with listening to the others' stories; each story, that when put together with the others like a jagged jigsaw puzzle but always with pieces missing, shed some light on how the remnants of what once was a whole person came to be. There were similarities despite the different backgrounds: neglected child, sexually abused child, physically abused child, emotionally abused child, child of an alcoholic, pressured child, abandoned child. The patterns were so easy to identify but not easy to repair as the leaders in each group patiently and, at times, coldheartedly maneuvered the intricate dance steps between the client and the therapist.

Michael met his father head on during one of the sessions. He had been so careful not to sink to the level of those who fell under the spell of the therapist while revealing so much about their personal histories. Determined to ride it out, Michael stayed at surface level, intent on interacting with as limited a response as possible. His emotions intact, too deep within to reach, he thought that he had beaten the system, that he could get out of this "prison" unscathed.

"How about you, Michael? Can you remember a time in your life when you truly were happy?"

He heard the leader's voice, but his comprehension was limited.

"Michael? Did you understand my question?"

He had no idea how long he had sat there between the therapist's questions. What he realized, though, was that the circle of faces was vacantly focused on him, waiting for him to spill his guts. Had he ever experienced true happiness? What kind of new-age question was that? Would he be here if he had? As he fought back a response, needing to break visual contact with these vultures, he pushed his chair back out of the circle, looked down at his hands, which now pressed deeply into his thighs, and kept silent.

"Michael, would you like to pass?"

It was obvious, wasn't it? What did he need to do besides get up and walk out, which would have been futile? Head still down, eyes shut, he refused to speak but nodded. The therapist's voice now addressed someone to his left, and Michael no longer was present as the voice faded until Michael heard nothing.

Battered so badly with eyes almost sealed shut, he tried to determine if his body could move, if it could roll over and find a way to sit up. The pain ran through every nerve in his small body and, for the first time ever at the hands of his father, Michael felt that he might die. The ground beneath him was cold and did not embrace him but worked against him, so he could find no comfortable position as he tried desperately to make himself stand.

It was eerily quiet now. The drunken monster's yelling had stopped, and Michael sensed that he was alone, but he couldn't verify it as his eyesight seemed to diminish by the second. And then he heard it. He lay very still in his anguish, trying to distinguish the sound. He had heard it before, but not when he was as injured as he found himself now. He waited to hear it again. No sound came. And still no sound other than his restricted breathing as he fought to be as still as possible.

Again, he tried to roll over, and this time managed to do so. Slowly, he attempted moving each arm, and he breathed easier when he realized that they were not broken. But it hurt somewhere in his chest to take a breath. He figured that a rib or two suffered from the incessant pounding on his boy frame by adult fists so much larger than his. Without shifting his body any more than he had to, he focused on his legs. Could he move any part of them? His left ankle screamed in pain, but both legs moved. Did he sprain or break his ankle?

He tried to remember what had happened. His father had grabbed Stephen away from Michael's protection and gone to the backyard with him. He remembered his brother's screams for help, calling Michael's name over and over again. Michael tried to help him. He did try. He ran after his father, not having any idea what he would do once he reached him. What he saw next sent such a wave of anger through him that he did not care what happened to him. He would not let his father get away with it this time.

Having knotted one end of the coarse rope around his brother's tiny bare waist and the other to an aged piece of wood, the original beam that kept the stone walls of the well in place, he then roughly hoisted the hysterical child over his shoulder. Michael's rage filled him with adrenaline that propelled him forward so that he reached his father's legs just as he threw Stephen over the edge of the stone prison. Grabbing a large, muscular leg and holding on as he tried in vain to knock his father off balance, Michael felt a sharp pain in the middle of his back as his enraged father punched him with all of his drunken might. And the pummeling continued. Through the pain, Michael found the strength to taunt his father relentlessly, only to bring down heavier blows on what was becoming an almost lifeless pile of eight-year-old bones.

Michael heard his brother's cries as he called for him to help him. He heard Stephen's sobs through his hysteria. He knew what Stephen was feeling and seeing down there. How many times had he been thrown in there by himself? The smell, the unknown in the darkness below him, the solid walls all around him, and the realization that he was suspended between life and death by a rope. The times when they had both been in the well, Stephen, though frightened, had relied on Michael to get him through it. And Michael always had, calmly talking to his little brother about Mama and how much she loved them and would let nothing take them from her. But this time, Michael was not there for Stephen. It wrenched his heart to hear his brother's calls, but there was nothing he could do for him. He was fighting for his own life now against a cruelty that continued to feed itself with each pummel on his now submissive body.

The sound came to Michael again as he slowly regained consciousness. For the first few moments, unable to determine where he was or what had happened, he strained to focus on the sound. It was not intelligible, more like the cry of a wounded animal in the throes of misery. Stephen. Michael tried to call out to his brother. "Stephen?" A pain shot through his chest as he managed to prop himself up on one elbow. "Stephen? Can you hear me? I'm coming, Stephen. Hold on! Hold on." His own voice was nothing more than a coarse whisper as he forced the words from his swollen jaws and mouth. Michael knew that he could not lift his brother out of the well. His own wounded body would not allow it. But if he could somehow drag himself closer and perhaps pull himself up to the edge of the wall so that Stephen could see him, it would reassure his brother that he was not alone.

He had read about heroes in books who, when all looked lost, found the strength to overcome any obstacles in their way, including any injury to their bodies. He now imagined that he was Stephen's hero and made a torturous effort to lift himself off the ground and to stumble to the edge of the well's wall. His ankle screamed its discomfort to him, but he made every effort to ignore it.

What he saw sent dread through his body. At the end of the rope dangled the lifeless body of his little brother. There was no movement, no sound now even as Michael screamed through his own pain his brother's name again and again. A sickening echo was the only response. He reached for the rope and tried to pull Stephen up to him, but his brother's deadweight fought against the agony of Michael's injured body. Slumping to the ground, Michael wept as painful heaves of loss overwhelmed him. He did not see or hear her approach but felt himself suddenly swept up in the comfort of his mother's arms as she, like an angel from heaven, whispered in his ear, "It's over. It's going to be okay."

"It's over, Michael. The session has been over for a while now. Michael? Tell me what you are thinking. You can't disengage yourself like you did, Michael. Please tell me what is going on?"

He looked up and found that he and the therapist were the only ones in the room. The therapist had pulled his chair over and sat directly in front of him, leaning in, searching his eyes for some indication that he was in the present. "Michael, you know that I'm here to help you. You know that, don't you? Was it the group? Are you uncomfortable talking in the group?"

Michael could sense that there was some concern for him from a person he didn't know and didn't want to know. He also knew that the guy was being paid to be concerned, and not just for him but for the rest of the crazies under his care.

"At some point, you need to talk to me. You can't hold the demons inside, Michael. Don't be afraid to open up. What you tell me is between us only. I'm here to help you move on. You do want to move on, don't you? You're too young a man to let your life go to waste. Michael?"

How should he respond? Tell him all the gory details? Tell him of his abuse by a parent? Tell him of the hatred that should never fill a young boy's mind? Tell him of his need to kill his father? Tell him of the fear that was with him every waking moment? Tell him of a mother who was a victim herself? Tell him of the love he had for her but could not be returned to him? Tell him of the agonizing regret, blame, and sorrow he felt each day for the loss of his little brother? Tell him that his ideal of a hero had been shattered long ago? Tell him that he was damaged, broken, an empty vessel? Yes, the man would have a field day with all that information. No, even if it meant getting out of there, away from these prying minds, he would not, he could not face himself.

"Look, I know you are doing your job. I know that." Michael, surprised by the sound of his own voice, had to say something to have this man leave him alone.

"Hey, it's not a job. Not like you think. I care about you, Michael. That's all there is to it. And because of that, job or no job, I can't stand back and watch you sink back into the hell you existed in before. Don't you get it? You can get better. You can be healthy again, both physically and emotionally. But you can't do it by yourself. You have to allow someone to help you through it." He knew he had said too much, too insistently, to continue. He could see that Michael was physically pulling away from him. "Okay, okay. Sorry. I can get too passionate about my work, it's true. I need to get going, anyway." He stood up and carried his chair back into the circle. As he held on to the back of it, he looked up at Michael. "See you tomorrow, then. Looking forward to a good session." And he picked up his clipboard and left the room.

Michael, relieved that he was now alone, couldn't rid himself of the therapist's words. He played them over and over again in his mind. *You have to allow someone to help you through it.* He knew it was true. But he also knew his failure when he'd tried to help someone through it a long time ago. He would rather die on the streets, his mind blown beyond repair, than face failure again. With that decision made, he got up and walked toward the waiting nurse who held in her hand the paper cup of meds that would save him today.

Chapter 16

The house sold quickly, just as Stephen had said it would. His timetable was in place and so far had been kept to with the precision of a fine Swiss watch. Eliza found herself surrounded by help in every matter of the move. All Stephen had asked her to do was go through her belongings and get rid of anything she didn't want to take. He said he was doing the same. Fresh start. There had been discussions between them about some of their joint belongings, including the red couch. At first, Stephen could see no reason for holding on to it, especially considering its condition. But Eliza had insisted on it coming with them and had explained her plans for it, its placement in her new writing nook, as Stephen continued to refer to it. He gave in and seemed to understand her need to have the familiar around her. The movers made a comment or two about the number of sealed boxes listed as "Eliza's Books." Was she planning on opening a library? Never moved so many book boxes before. Had she read them all? She stilled their inquiries merely answering "yes" to their questions.

As the day wore on, the home slowly became a vacant house again. Eliza moved through the rooms after the movers had removed the last bit of furnishings. She stood for a long time in each, recalling every piece of furniture and the knickknacks that she had so thoughtfully placed around the home. She felt a sense of loss as she walked through each room, but it wasn't until she climbed the stairs to her writing nook and stood in front of the window where her desk had been just this morning that she felt the full weight of her sadness.

The tree's branches, still barren as they awaited the warmth of spring to nurture their new buds, appeared as bleak as she felt. Struggling to move beyond this feeling, she recalled the beauty of the tree as she had observed its life span through all four seasons year after year. How many times had she reaped inspiration from its beauty as she struggled with an idea that refused to budge beyond the last word she had written? How many times had she just let herself gaze upon it, no thoughts in mind, only a peaceful rest from the work of composing? How many times had she been distracted by its varied occupants who flew in and out of the branches, sometimes lingering as if to enjoy its beauty as she did? Realizing how much this tree had been a part of her daily writing exercises, she suddenly began to weep. Surprised by her reaction, she quickly rubbed the tears from her face, turned her back on the window, and left the room behind.

As she moved through the last of the upstairs rooms, she could hear Stephen's voice speaking to the movers. He had handled all of the logistics of the move so that she did not have to concern herself. She knew that he liked to take charge, but she also knew that he was aware of her initial hesitancy to leave and because of this, he wanted her to be happy. It was true; he had made the physical aspect of moving very simple, not realizing it left her with too much time to experience it emotionally. However, she was sure that she felt life more deeply than Stephen and found herself in these last moments in her Boston home fighting the urge to become overly emotional. After all, she had told Stephen how she felt about the house in Ventana; she felt deep down that she would love it there and she had let him know this.

At the top of the stairs, she forced herself not to turn around for one last look but to join Stephen in the living room with a smile on her face. He was doing a last-minute check as well, but not for the same reasons as Eliza. Practical and thorough, he informed her that nothing was left behind, that the house was as empty as it was going to get, and that it was time to leave. They had reservations at one of the airport hotels for the evening and in the morning would be on a flight to San Francisco. With luggage in hand, Eliza and Stephen stopped on the front stoop while Stephen locked the doors for the last time.

"Doing okay?" Stephen asked her as they headed down the steps to the waiting taxi. His words were sincere, and Eliza felt his love for her. She fought back the tears that were waiting to spill once again.

"Yes, sure. Just hard to leave, you know. You feel it too, don't you?"

Stephen stopped and put his luggage down as the taxi driver came around and opened the trunk. Taking her in his arms, he whispered something in her ear, but she couldn't make it out as the driver interrupted at the same moment by asking if this was all of the luggage. Stephen released her and assured him that the four bags were all. He opened the door of the taxi and helped Eliza in. What had he said to her? Had he reassured her as she wanted him to? Did she need to have him repeat it, or would that ruin the moment that he'd experienced? Best to leave it alone. She had let him know what she was feeling when she asked the question. Best to leave it alone.

Stephen never said more to her on the way to the hotel. He was completely engaged in a mundane conversation with the driver, who seemed to enjoy having someone in his cab who wanted to shoot the breeze for the thirty-minute ride. Eliza half listened and soon did not hear either one of them as she gazed out the window, watching Boston fly by.

Some of the old brick office buildings she recognized. She remembered walking by them and entering them on business. The eastern houses built to ward off the damage of heavy snow, their fading clapboard sidings revealing the abusive weather that came each year, now passed out of sight. She tried to give each one some attention so that she could imprint their individual details in her mind. She knew that she would forget these places, this town, if she didn't. It wouldn't happen right away, but eventually, she would not be able to recall accurately what had been such a large part of her life in the years she spent here. She knew this would happen because she had tried to recall in vivid details her memories of California. Although she could recall some clearly, so many more were dim, blurring into and invading other unrelated memories. As the Boston harbor came into view, she could smell the water, the diesel fuel of the boats, and remembered the stink of the hot asphalt on the harbor walks that sizzled in the late summer heat. She recalled walking past the many restaurants, each emitting an aroma that begged her to enter and until she did, being bombarded by the blend of these individual aromas nagging at her hunger in stiff competition with each other. She turned her head to the back window to see the city skyline for the last time as a flood of images entered her mind: the alleyways, Boston Commons, the square, the street entertainers, the tourists, the monuments, the history that was to be found around every corner, the energy that was Boston. She would miss all of this.

She turned to Stephen and watched him leaning forward, animated and happy, as he and the cab driver, a stranger, carried on as if they were the oldest of friends. And so she sat, alone, taking in every detail of what was outside her window as she said goodbye to Boston.

Chapter 17

Their plane landed, one of the last of the day, while others were diverted to San Jose or Oakland as SFO became socked in with a heavy coastal fog. Relieved that they weren't diverted, Stephen's mood was even more elated. During the flight, he and Eliza had carried on bits and pieces of conversation about their past and now their future. However, nothing substantial, in Eliza's opinion, had been discussed. She knew it wouldn't be as she took note of how many drinks Stephen had ordered on this flight. He handled himself well, even so, and for the final two hours of the flight fell into a deep, alcohol-induced sleep.

The plan was to spend a couple of nights in San Francisco to celebrate their big move and then to drive down to Big Sur on the third day. Stephen arranged for them to stay at the Ventana Inn for a few days. When the movers arrived, they would be there, ready to move into their new home. In the meantime, absolute relaxation and rest would do them both a world of good and would help acclimate them to their new and very different environment.

Set on the high hills of the Ventana Wilderness, the inn provided all the luxuries while offering a sense of solitude and escape from the world only a few hours away. The views were breathtaking even when the fog hugged the coastline. Sitting above the fog line on most days, the guest rooms faced the Pacific Ocean. A short walk through the meadows and redwood groves that surrounded the property took the visitor to the cliff's edge. Just below its edge, the fog hid the ocean below and stretched to the horizon, while the sun, still untouched by the foaming mist, shone down from a crystal-blue sky. In a moment of rapture, one could almost imagine stepping off the cliff's edge only to walk to the horizon on a bed of foaming mist. This place was as magical as Eliza had remembered it to be from her childhood visits. As she stood on the edge of the western world, she suddenly understood that all would be well. She was home again.

As Stephen took in the best of what was offered during their stay, he felt that his life was working out better than he had ever thought it would. Upon meeting Eliza, he knew that she was his life partner and that wherever he found himself, she would be by his side.

In leaving Boston he'd had his regrets, but they were few and far between. So much so that the nagging urgency he'd felt to return to the West Coast, and which only intensified as time went on, could not be ignored. He couldn't explain it as much as he tried to understand it. Nor could he explain why he was drawn to the cabin. He had viewed so many other properties that most people like himself, with the opportunity and wherewithal, would grab. He could have easily bought any one of them but, instead, chose the cabin.

His greatest fear had been that Eliza would put her foot down and not go with him once she saw her new home. It never crossed his mind that she would take offense when he revealed to her that the deal was done, that they were indeed going, and that their Boston home was on the market. On the contrary, he thought that she would be proud of him for taking charge and taking care of business.

Well, none of that mattered now. In a matter of a few more days they would be settling into their new home. Stephen was determined to make this time memorable for his Eliza. Whatever she wanted, he would provide. Even the old red couch was welcomed as he imagined her curled up against its faded cushions while she pored over one her many books, recently unpacked, as if she had never opened its covers before. He found himself smiling. His beautiful, dear Eliza. Yes, he was happy with the way life was playing out before him.

Chapter 18

Michael had a choice. He didn't have to attend the session. He would feel the negativity surrounding him if he didn't, but he didn't care. He had made up his mind to separate himself from the rest of them. If all he needed to do was make it through the day until the next cup of tiny pills was presented to him, then that's what he intended to do. It was so much better than struggling to survive on the streets. He knew, though, the reality was that he would have to face the group or at least open up to the therapist or he would be thrown out of the home to give room to another in greater need. No, to give room to another more motivated to welcome the help. He couldn't imagine that there was anyone who was more screwed up than he was. And because of that, Michael knew that he was beyond help. The more he thought this, the further he drew into himself so that he was left alone. He didn't know how many days had gone by without his attending a session, but it felt like weeks. Had he been completely forgotten then? Was it that easy to have them leave you alone? Maybe he should have withdrawn a lot sooner to save himself from the agony of listening to the other crazies' problems. To escape from prodding, stupid questions. To avoid having to face himself, revealed and naked to the world.

The knock on his door interrupted his thoughts and he heard himself say, "Come in." When the door opened, he felt the air-conditioned climate of the outside corridors invade the small space of his room. He hadn't realized how stuffy his room was.

"Michael, how are you doing?" The therapist stood in the doorway, looming larger than Michael remembered him to be. "Michael? Boy, it's pretty darn warm in here. Isn't the fan working?" He walked over to the air conditioner unit and saw that the dial read OFF. "Did you turn it off, Michael? Probably not a good idea. Not healthy." He turned the knob to COOL and then moved closer to Michael. "You know, we missed you. Didn't turn up for your last two sessions." He pulled up the one chair in the room and brought it next to Michael's bed.

As he watched the therapist come closer, Michael realized that he had never used that chair the whole time he had been in the room. His bed was his safety zone, the covers blocking out everything and everyone. He wasn't under the covers now. He locked eyes with the leader and started to speak but stopped himself and broke contact.

"Look, you know the rules, Michael, about attending sessions. I won't be able to do much for you when they tell you that your time is up with us. And they will if you miss another meeting. You are not ready to go back to where you came from. You know that as well as everyone here. But you can't stay here indefinitely. You are running out of time, Michael, and I don't want to see you walk out those doors without me knowing that we did everything we could for you, that you did everything you could for yourself. Do you understand me, Michael? You have an incredibly important decision to make about letting me help you.

"You know the rules! Who the hell do you think you are around here? I ain't gonna pick up after you and the more you screw up, the rougher it's going to be for you. How dumb can you get? Worthless piece of shit. Should have drowned you along with the damn cats when I had the chance."

His father pushed by his mother, shoving her against the door jamb, and left the house, slamming his fist into anything he could find along the way. Michael stood in the small bedroom that he shared with his little brother and surveyed the damage his father had wrought in just a matter of minutes. All of his and his brother's clothes were thrown on the floor, some still haphazardly hanging from the corners of the drawers. The only lamp in the room had been slammed to the floor in his fury, and the bulb had shattered into hundreds of shards that now mixed in with the folds of the strewn clothes. Looking around him, he did not see Stephen but could hear his whimpers. Under their bed as close to the wall as he could get, Stephen huddled, trying to stifle his cries. He had taken refuge there as soon as he heard his father approach their bedroom door.

Earlier in the morning, deep in the grove, he and Michael had been playing war with their model airplanes, the ones that their mother had given them last Christmas without letting their father know. She had saved up her extra change from the weekly housekeeping and bought each boy a model kit. When she gave them her gifts, she told them she hoped that they liked them, but that they were never to let their father see what she had given them and were to be careful where they played with them. She suggested going out in the grove away from the house and to keep the airplanes out of the house. The boys did just that. Michael found an old wooden box, and the boys stored their precious gifts from their mother there, carefully hidden under the fallen branches of the redwoods. They spent hours playing under the tall trees, each running with one arm raised to hold the plastic plane now in flight while the free arm flew through the air for balance. They were always careful not to make a lot of noise for fear of waking their father, who had sunk into another drunken sleep.

On this day, however, he had announced at breakfast that he was driving up to Monterey on business and would be gone for, well, he didn't know for how long. They would see him when they would see him. And with that, he left the house and backed the old pickup down the dirt drive and was gone.

Both Michael and Stephen heard the house breathe a deep sigh of relief, or was that their mother? The three of them sat at the table and finished their breakfast in an uncomfortable silence, as if at any moment he would change his mind and slam his way back into the house. But minutes passed, and nothing broke the silence. Their mother looked to each of them and asked if they had had enough food. Both boys nodded. "It's best that we go on with our day. Do your chores now and when you are done, then you can go play. But do your chores first. Check in with me. Do you both understand?"

"Yes, Mama." They got up from the table and took their dishes to the sink.

"I'll take it from here. Now go on now. Take care of business." She turned from them as she dipped her worn red hands into the dishwater.

They cleaned up their room so that it was spotless. The clothes in their drawers were neatly arranged and the two pairs of shoes that each boy owned were sitting on the closet floor, perfectly in line with each other. Michael remembered to button up his shirt that was carelessly hanging from a hanger so that it now sat properly and was ready to wear. They made the bed together so that nothing was wrinkled, and the pillows were placed as they were supposed to be. Nothing cluttered the room, for they had very little with which to clutter it. Knowing that they had done their best, they went to the kitchen. Their mother was still cleaning the morning dishes and tidying up.

They went outside into the fresh, cool morning. Michael's job was to sweep off the porch each morning. During the nights, the redwoods needles would shed from their boughs and the remains would be scattered all about the front of the house. Stephen was too little to do an adequate job of sweeping, so his job was to hold the bucket into which Stephen dumped the boughs' castoffs. Sometimes, if their father wasn't about, Michael would pick Stephen up and put him in the bucket to smash down the fragrant greens so there would be more room. Stephen would laugh out loud, and Michael would join in as their giggles could be heard throughout the grove. Michael would always reach in, grab his little brother under his armpits, and with an exaggerated display of strength heave him out of the bucket. Stephen would then stand on the freshly brushed porch and, without thinking, brush the debris off his clothes onto the porch, and the fun would resume once again.

With chores completed and after having checked in with their mother, they decided to play with their airplanes. Racing to the hiding spot, Michael, who always won, was already digging away the boughs and had uncovered the box when Stephen ran up, heaving for breath.

"Here you go." He handed a small plastic model of a navy plane to Stephen while he reached for his own model F-4. It was the harder of the two to put together, as it should be, but he had helped his little brother make his. He liked helping his brother because Stephen was always so grateful. It made Michael feel very proud of himself and loved by his little brother.

Their play began in the grove, and the numerous enactments played out under the shaded sunlight of the towering redwoods soon found both boys tired and ready for lunch. Hoping that their father wouldn't be back for some time, maybe not until tomorrow morning, they threw all caution to the wind and brought their airplanes with them into the house. They ran into the bathroom to wash up and then into their bedroom, where they hid the planes under their bed until later. Mama would be disappointed that they had broken their word and brought them in, but they wouldn't let her know. Besides, they would be back in the grove after lunch.

During lunch, noticing that the light in the house was dimming, Michael looked up to see that the fog had started to roll in. Seeing the *disappointment on his face, his mother reassured him. "Well, that's okay. You can still play outside for a while. Just bundle up a bit better this time. You know how chilly and wet it can get."*

"Can we stay inside, Mama?" Stephen didn't like the fog, especially if he was out in the grove. When it came down heavily on the land, it soaked everything and hid from sight the dangers awaiting him.

"Well, I don't see why not, but it's really not that bad yet. Better that you get some fresh air while you can." She smiled and reached for his little arm and gave it a gentle squeeze.

"Mama, please. Can I just stay in? Michael, you want to stay in with me?" Michael, forgetting the airplanes under the bed, agreed to stay in with his brother if it was okay with Mama. She relented but asked the boys to help her clean up the kitchen from lunch. The three of them finished the task in no time at all. Mama took off her apron and walked over to the front window. She was looking down the drive and the boys knew why. No sign of their father yet.

"Go play, boys. I'll let you know when your father returns. I, for one, am going to get off my feet for a bit. Maybe read, maybe nap." Her voice was relaxed, and both boys found that comforting but at the same time, disconcerting. They only recognized their mother's constant intensity as the norm. Seldom could Michael remember hearing his mother so relaxed.

Once in their bedroom, they closed the door and remembered the airplanes. "Oh, no. Stephen, we have got to get these out of here. You know what Mama said about them being in the house. Come on."

"No, Michael, please? Just for a little while. We can play in here real quiet, 'cause Mama is going to nap anyway. Just for a little while."

"If the old man comes home early, we're dead meat, little brother. But, okay. Just for a little while." As he said this, he knew that it was the wrong decision, that he should have been stronger with his brother and insisted that they put the planes back in safekeeping. His thoughts were interrupted as Stephen's plane came roaring down onto Michael's F-4 with the fury of a four-year-old boy having the time of his life.

The fog thickened as the afternoon wore on. The boughs of the trees bent from the weight of the dampness, causing drops to fall steadily against the roof of the house as if a soft rain was descending. In the quiet hours of the afternoon, their mother found the time to rest while the boys stayed in their room, completely absorbed in their make-believe world of war. She didn't hear the truck come up the path as she had fallen into a deep nap, nor did the boys, who had shut their bedroom door so as not to disturb her.

The peace and quiet that their mother was enjoying and the childhood contentment that the boys luxuriated in was not to last. Their father had come in with the expectation that there would be the smells of dinner being prepared, that a couple of chilled beer bottles would be waiting for him in the fridge, and that the house was his again. Their mother jumped from her nap, a fear surging through her not yet fully conscious body, and saw him coming toward her. The boys, still oblivious to anything but their make-believe world, continued their play in the precarious shelter of their bedroom.

It wasn't until they heard their mother's screams that they both froze in place. Michael stood up and made a motion with his hands to hide the planes. Stephen grabbed them and scurried under the bed so that the planes and he were as close to the wall and as far away as possible from the grasp of his father. The room was in disarray, the boys' creation of a world that only they could see. They were planning on cleaning it all up before he came back.

Their mother, rubbing her shoulder and upper arm to ease the pain of the blow against the door jamb, entered the room carefully so as not to step on any of her sons' belongings. She had been crying, Michael could tell as he crawled out from the shelter, quickly surveying her face, and he knew that the red splotches would soon turn ugly shades of purple and black.

"Where is Stephen?" She asked it as casually as if she were playing a game of hide-and-seek with them. Michael pointed to the bed and realized that he was shaking, as his arm seemed to wobble uncontrollably in front of him. "It's over. It's going to be okay." She smiled at Michael as Stephen gingerly crawled out from beneath his hiding place, a model airplane clutched in each hand.

Chapter 19

Both Eliza and Stephen woke up in an anxious mood. Stephen had received a phone call just before going to bed to let him know that the truck had arrived and that they would be parked in the lot of the general store in Big Sur. The driver asked Stephen about access to the house. Stephen had known all along that a truck that size could not make it down the drive. His solution was to make numerous trips from the moving van to the house using a smaller rental truck. He'd had the presence of mind to reserve one, even though the closest rental was in Monterey. The movers were fine with the idea, as they were not going to go any farther.

Eliza wanted to be there when the first of the many trips arrived with their belongings. The house would be completely empty, allowing her to visualize her new home and its interior. Once she heard the rental coming up the road, the anxiety she had felt earlier disappeared, to be replaced by a kind of giddiness and excitement that only a new adventure could bring. Stephen jumped out of the cab, as did the two movers, and got to work unloading an assortment of boxes, leaving them outside so that Eliza could do an inventory while deciding on the order for opening each box. Multiple trips were made that day until all their belongings were either in the house or still awaiting prioritization by Eliza.

Tired beyond description, Stephen and Eliza found themselves collapsed on the floor of the main room as the sun was setting. They hadn't eaten all day, too caught up in the business of organizing life.

"I don't know about you, honey, but I don't think that I can lift another finger today. I am really tired and hungry." Eliza believed that Stephen had to be in the same shape and when he agreed, she said, "So, what's there to eat?"

Knowing that nothing was unpacked so that they could begin to create a meal, Stephen slowly and painfully crawled to a standing position and laughed. "I'm up for getting in the truck one more time and heading back to the inn for a decent meal. What do you think?" She was waiting at the door, purse in hand, before he got a verbal confirmation.

The days that came and went in the next few weeks were full. Eliza lost herself each day in creating the environment that would become the perfect home for the two of them. She asked Stephen's advice frequently, remembering their Boston home. But as time went on, he seemed content to let her carry on, and his comments confirmed her decisions.

She was happy. The writing nook took shape quickly, since so many of the boxes were full of her books, which needed to be put on shelves just to relieve them of the clutter of boxes. As planned, the desk sat in front of the east window and the old red couch sat under the west.

Still not believing how beautiful the room was as daylight filled it, Eliza found it hard at first to sit at her desk and get much done. Just as the tree outside her Boston window had distracted her with its activity and seasonal beauty, so did these trees. But it wasn't only the redwoods that captivated her, but also the air, the clean, fresh ocean air wafting from the damp bark of the redwoods, from their sodden mulch, from the gentle lace-like boughs themselves. And the fog never depressed her but took her to a place of solitude and peace as she found the words for her compositions. She spent her days writing surrounded by the natural beauty of the world.

Stephen knew that Eliza was happy. She had said as much, but he also felt a deep and sincere expression from her each time she thought to say something to him. She was different here. The years had passed for them, of course, and they had each grown into themselves and into each other in ways that were not possible when they began their marriage. A comfortable state settled upon them and upon the house. Stephen continued to carry on business dealings and was away more than Eliza liked, but never for long. He always came back eager to be home, eager to be in her arms again.

Eliza had created a kitchen that served their needs while

she continually enhanced it with ideas that she had read about in magazines. She loved the idea of cabinets and not open shelving. The original cabinetry was still intact, and Stephen had suggested remodeling the kitchen. But Eliza had disagreed and with a little cleaning and tightening of screws, she almost had the cabinets looking new. At the end of the kitchen she devised a drying rack for the herbs and flowers that she grew in the sunny areas around the house and by what looked to be the remnants of an old stone structure of some sort. There was always something hanging from the rack, which gave her satisfaction. She had planted it, grown it, harvested it, and now was recycling it for other uses. Her kitchen gave one the impression of an old farm kitchen, always well stocked, practical, and welcoming.

The years seemed to fly by for them and they were the happiest years of their marriage. Well into the fifth year of living in the Ventana Wilderness, Stephen had decided to retire from his business. They were well enough off for him to do so. Eliza had published two books during this time, which had been met with acclaim, and so her income had been added to the family coffers. She was happy for him when he told her that he was going to retire. That would mean more time together, and perhaps more travel, which they hadn't done in years. Together they began planning trips, first short ones and then longer ones. They had no demands placed upon them now, so their lives were their own. However, the plans always stayed plans.

As she observed her husband fall deeper and deeper into a state of selfish contentment, Eliza tried to convince Stephen that they needed to get away for a while; a change of pace and scenery was needed, she felt. Keeping herself busy was harder to do. Working around him was aggravating, and she struggled to fight the urge to walk out for the day, to take her car and drive up the coast to San Francisco just to breathe in the life of the city once again. How long had it been? She had lost track of time as each day melded into the next with nothing remarkable to note.

She recalled taking a weekend trip up to the city with Stephen, and they had been inspired by the beautiful fall weather. Perhaps a year ago or more? The sky was crystal clear, a sharp, distinct blue that seemed to make everything she saw "pop." The varied shades of whites and grays of the city's buildings as viewed from the Marin Headlands did not blend together on this day but stood out as individual structures, even at the distance from which she was viewing them. The bridge's orange rust paint glimmered against the sky and the water taking her breath away. Without discussion, they had headed north again on CA 101 and Stephen had taken charge. Another three hours and they could be in Mendocino. Along the way, they had stopped in Bodega Bay for lunch, had taken a leisurely walk through the town and down to the beach, and then continued to their destination.

The weekend played out before them as if taken from a romantic paperback novel. She would never forget it and wanted to repeat it, knowing that it would be impossible to do. Those moments were meant to be scarce in a relationship so that the memory endured. She knew that pushing Stephen to go with her was futile as well as unwise. And so she lived with Stephen, each day wondering if adventure would develop over a morning coffee but knowing in her heart it would not.

The winters had been wet and cold, not the kind of bone-chilling cold that they had endured in Boston, but damp and lingering. The redwood groves that surrounded the house had kept the dampness and darkness in place as the low winter sun struggled to shine through the towering, full boughs of the trees. In the middle of the day it could feel like late evening, especially if a rainstorm was taking place. On some days, the lights in the home were on from the moment they awoke to the moment they went to bed.

Eliza watched her garden die as it was choked out by the redwoods' droppings. She had, at first, been vigilant about preserving the harvest ground throughout the year, and she remembered the first winter and its heavy rains as both welcome intrusions and the enemy. But she loved the challenge of working with nature, understanding its needs over her own. It gave her a feeling of what it must have been like as a pioneer, trying to tame a strange land and all that supported it. She couldn't help but wonder if she had at some time in one of her lives been a woman on the plains in the 1800s, trying to survive with her husband and children. She felt it strongly as she tromped through the yard in her "wellies," rake and shovel in hand, ready to clear the land once more after a heavy rain or wind so that she might bring order to her labors of the summer past. The garden was still there, just under a bed of soft debris. At the end of the day, she would stand back and admire her work as the boundaries of the garden once more appeared.

Looking skyward, she could only imagine how much more sun could nurture her first plantings of the year if only the trees were less full. During the last two seasons, she realized that her gardening space was becoming more limited as each year passed and the sunlight diminished. When they moved in five years ago, it had been very different. She'd had a difficult time deciding in which sunny spot she would grow her garden.

Deciding to clear the area next to an old stone structure, now a collapsing pile of rocks, she had the idea to include the pile as a rock garden in the planning of the rest of the growing area. Trying to stay true to nature and not disturb what she was privileged to temporarily own, she was satisfied with her decision. Stephen had tried to convince her to plant elsewhere. He had his reasons, none of which held any water in Eliza's opinion. Something about location and how odd it would look, out of sorts with the rest of the landscaping. Better to either leave the rocks where they lay or get rid of them completely. But he eventually left her alone to create her own vision. He had never enjoyed working in the yard and certainly had no clue about the art of gardening. As he was much happier occupying his time with his own interests, they came to an arrangement with which Eliza was happy. She spent hours out in the yard, never watching the time other than being observant of the sun's coming and going. In the evenings, they would come together for meals and quiet nights together. They had fallen into a life pattern that worked well for them both. But now, as she sat across from him at breakfast, knowing that the day would be just the same as yesterday and the days before, she could stand it no longer.

"I've been thinking, Stephen, that we need to get away,

even if just for the day. It's really a lovely morning and we could drive up the coast a bit or down, if you would prefer. I could make a lunch and we could just go and see where the day takes us. What do you think?"

He looked up at her from the book he had been reading, took a sip of coffee, and responded, "What did you have in mind?"

Hadn't she just told him? It was so hard to get through to him at times. "I thought we could take a ride, pack a lunch, and head out in any direction we wanted, and then see what the day has in store for us. That's all. Just a little bit of excitement. I have no detailed plans, but that would be the fun of it. We used to do this all the time, remember? Come on, let's get a move on." She knew what his reaction would be. Why did she even try?

"Fine. When do you want to go?" It was not an enthusiastic response, but it was a positive one, and Eliza, once over the shock, decided that she'd better have a decisive answer to his question or she would lose the moment.

"Does an hour give you enough time to get ready? I'll make the lunch and if you would just make sure we've got chairs in the car and a blanket, maybe the freezer chest—yes, the chest with ice in it—I'll take care of the rest. Are you good with that?" She didn't wait for his response as she opened the fridge, surveying the contents for anything that would make appealing sandwiches. She hated the uncomfortable tenseness that remained in the room, the intentionally unfinished conversation.

Stephen went back to reading his book and sipping his coffee and remained there while she made the lunches. "Want the chest now?"

"Yes, the cold food is ready to go in. Will you be ready to go soon?"

"You gave me an hour and I'll be ready when it's up. I'll get the chest and leave it on the porch." With that, he slowly got up from the table and dumped his coffee in the sink while holding his book under his arm. He looked over his shoulder at Eliza as she was cleaning up the remains of the sandwich makings and smiled. "You, know, this is a good idea. It will be good to get out for a bit. Looking forward to it." And he turned fully to her and kissed her on her cheek.

She stood at the counter, alone, wondering when the change of heart had taken place for Stephen. Realizing that she had no answer and probably never would, she let it be and felt a bubble or two of childlike excitement in anticipation of the day ahead.

Chapter 20

As he left his room to attend the morning session, Michael closed the door behind him for the last time. Careful planning on his part had prepared him for this final encounter. He feared deeply what would become of him once he left the facility with its twenty-four-hour care, which, in some comforting way, he knew he would miss. In the quiet of the nights, he had lain awake fighting the demons that continued to ravage his being. The memories of a childhood of pain, of an adulthood of self-abuse, and of a feeble attempt to help himself when others around him were ready to see him through it but he was not willing to let them. There were moments when he felt so lost in his own thoughts that even then, he was failing—failing to see clearly what others could see. Why couldn't he find his way out? Why was it easier to give in? Why had he failed so terribly? But there were no easy answers—nothing came to him on his own, and he knew that he had sealed the doors behind him when he decided to keep his voice to himself. There was only one person who needed to know the truth, and he was gone. He was gone because Michael could not save him from the system, from their bastard father.

As he turned the corner, the therapist was standing outside the door to the room. Leaning against the wall, one foot propped up behind him resting against it, clipboard in hand, he greeted his clients one by one as they checked in with him. He was a friendly person, Michael had to admit, and he could understand how some of the members of the group felt at ease with him, enough to spill their guts to him. They trusted him to hear their most horrid truths, taking them away and replacing them with any words of comfort that would begin to turn their sorry lives around. They had such hope. Michael did not.

"Good morning, Michael. Good to see you. How are you?" The therapist's smile was genuine, and Michael detected that his ambivalence toward the man was a forgotten matter. A new morning, a new beginning and all that crap, Michael thought as a sudden distaste for the session took him by surprise. He thought he had prepared himself to stomach the next hour with these people, to perhaps even add a comment or two while being extremely careful to guard himself from any real exposure. He was prepared, he thought. He gave the therapist a half-hearted nod and signed in.

"Great. Have a seat and we'll get started in just a little while. There are snacks. Enjoy." The therapist left his position against the wall and turned to point to the back counter in the small room. Michael nodded again, then found the closest seat to the door and sat down. The members of the group were gathered around the snacks. Some were speaking to one another while others just seemed to float in space, mechanically placing food and drink in their mouths, waiting for the next direction to guide them through the day.

As he sat waiting for the therapist to get the meeting started, he ran back through his mind the plan. Why he hadn't thought of it sooner, he had no idea, because it was so simple. He had worried about being formally discharged from the program, because that would mean he would have it on his record. Not wanting to go through the bureaucracy that he would have to face, he decided to take everything into his own hands. The decision, when it came to him, was so very clear. *Walk out. Just walk out of here. Don't look back, don't think twice, and don't be afraid. Just keep walking until you can't anymore.* The few personal belongings he did have, he had stowed on his body earlier in the morning, and he'd worn the bulky wool sweater that was given to him by one of the staff one cold morning so that any unusual bulges would not be detected. It didn't matter if the facility's heating system was at full speed. No one would insist he take off the sweater. After all, he was one of the crazy ones, wasn't he?

"Okay. Let's get started. If you would all come to the circle, please?" The group slowly gathered and once again, Michael couldn't help but feel anxious in these last moments. This was it. All he needed to do was be present and survive on the surface one last time. This time tomorrow, he had no idea where he would be, but he knew that he had to be somewhere other than here.

"We've come a long way together, you know." The therapist was speaking as his eyes moved around the circle, focusing for a moment on each participant. "A longer way for some, to be sure, but for each one of you on your own path, you've made progress. I'm proud of you for that. You need to thank yourselves each day for having the courage to face yourselves and to want to move on to something better. You may not realize it right now, but the strides you've made in these past months can't be dismissed by you. You've proven to yourselves that you want to change, and you can't deny yourselves the opportunities that are waiting for you. So, today we're going to spend our time thinking about the future. Maybe start by measuring how far you've come to where you are now and where you see yourself in a year from now? If that's too far off, think of a month or so from now. But put yourselves on a positive path now. Who do you want to be, where do you want to be, and with whom do you want to be? I'll give you some time to think about these questions—it's a lot, I know. Maybe you can only answer one of them today, but that's okay. It's a great start."

The therapist sat back in his chair, crossed his legs, and focused on the clipboard in his lap. The room's silence weighed heavily on Michael. He tried to keep his eyes down and out of the way of the therapist's contact, but he was curious. How were the rest of them reacting? Were any of them going to speak about their future? Wasn't their future this place? They all seemed so comfortable here, secure in knowing that someone always was there to hear their sorrows, their messed-up life stories. Why would they want that to stop? They thrived on it, on each other's misery. A future without the freedom and assurances that it was okay to invade someone else's space with your crap? Weren't they the same crazies on the streets that confronted you with their senseless babble and supplications for help, any kind of help? Weren't they the ones that you strategically moved around so as not to be subjected to their despair? No, he would be surprised if anyone in this group would jeopardize the security of this place by revealing that indeed, he or she had a brighter future. They were all losers, including himself. He knew that, but he also knew how to take flight when there was nothing else to do.

He had no idea how much time had gone by before the first in the group spoke up. He half listened to her. Something about wanting to have a normal life, a husband, maybe a kid, but she wasn't so sure she was ready to take care of a helpless human being when she still needed to work on herself. But she had hope and could see a future with her family. Then she stopped speaking and sobbed uncontrollably. The therapist and the others gave her words of comfort while those closest to her moved even closer, awkwardly embracing her as best they could.

The hour passed in much the same way as most of the participants unveiled their bright future, some coming to the realization while in midstream that all of it was futile and then the breakdown would hit. The therapist tried to keep the positivity flowing, acknowledging that this was a difficult exercise that would churn up deeply held emotions, the hopes and dreams that had been buried under layers and layers of negativity and damaged minds, not to mention damaged bodies. But it was a part of the healing process and, once again, at the end of the session, he confirmed to them his belief that they had taken another large step toward a brighter future. Painful as it was, it had to be faced. Good for them, he had said. "If you like, take any snacks back with you. There are leftovers by the looks of it and they'll only go stale. Be my guest. See you next session."

And that was it. Michael had stayed afloat. No one had spoken to him, no one. It took him a moment to comprehend that the next step for him was to carry out his plan. Without looking at the therapist or anyone in the group and not taking him up on the offer of the free food, Michael stood up and walked out the door and down the hall to the exit. His legs were not functioning as he imagined they would, carrying his body swiftly down the corridor to freedom. It was as if he were trying to make his way through the bough-laden ground, the wetness left by the heavy fogs of the nights and days before, the slippery ground where wet leaves from the bay trees had been polished by the dampness waiting to betray a footstep. He kept his focus, however, on the double doors in front of him, the light that was waiting on the other side once he pushed them open.

Upon reaching the doors, he turned to see if anyone was watching, if anyone was going to stop him, if anyone really cared. The corridor was empty. He turned, and with both hands extended in front of him, he shoved the door open with all his might. He heard the alarm, which was his wake-up call to move. And he ran toward the light of day, out of the heavy fog, until he could run no more, only to collapse under a grove of redwoods deep in the forest of his childhood.

Chapter 21

They decided that they would head north on Route 1, stop along the way for a walk, and find an out-of-the-way place to have a picnic. The morning was full of promise as the sky was crystal clear, while every growing thing seemed to have a brilliance that was the result of a light rain the night before. The air smelled fresh and was invigorating as they hiked the trail up the coastal hills, careful not to lose their footing, stopping frequently to look back toward the west and taking in the beauty of the sparkling Pacific Ocean below them.

Eliza had packed a bottle of Syrah along with the mundane sandwich makings, fruit, and chips. As they stretched out on the blanket once they had reached the summit of their hike, they could not take it all in. They both felt it at the same time, and as if choreographed, looked at each other with smiles growing on their faces. They had made a good decision to take the time to be together and to be here in the beauty that surrounded them day in and day out. The wine's warmth and taste lulled them both into gentle half naps as they lay next to each other, their bodies touching while the early sun's rays enclosed them in an extra layer of warmth. Far above them, red-tailed hawks played in the thermals while at their sides, insects could be heard busily trying to survive from one blade of grass to another as their small world adapted to the disturbance caused by the blanket's weight crushing their domain. Eliza and Stephen did not move from the spot, nor did they want to. The time allotted them on this day was their own to do with as they wished, and there was an unspoken agreement to let time pass without concern.

Stephen's sleep was deep and velvety, almost suffocating, as if a blanket were pulled too far over his face, suddenly awakening him. He floated, levitated above the blanket, leaving Eliza in a gentle wine-and-sun-induced sleep, watching her face peacefully at rest next to him. He watched her become smaller as he moved higher, and then she was out of sight. He did not feel panicked or alone, but rather taken over by something not in his control that had a firm grip on him and pushed him into deeper darkness.

The pain came suddenly, the gasps for air, while at the same time he was trying not to breathe the foul atmosphere that surrounded him, suffocating him. His skin burned and was wet and sticky around his middle, but he couldn't see in the darkness and was afraid to touch himself. The opening above him was now barely visible. The only light seemed to be coming from the moon, somewhere out of sight but above him. He had no voice, he knew. He could barely work up enough saliva to swallow. As he dangled in the dark, the cold of the evening began to take its toll on his small and wounded body. His shivering began slowly and then became uncontrollable and with each gyration, the rope carved yet again more deeply into the oozing wounds it had already created.

And then he felt it. The rope was tightening around his waist and the pain became unbearable. At the same time, he knew he was moving upward, and then he heard his mother's voice saying his name. He felt her hands grab under his arms as he reached the edge of the well's wall and the strength of her arms ejecting him beyond the stones; then he found himself held tightly against her body while the rope, still attached to his waist and the wooden beam, hung limply on the ground at their feet. She sat and laid his injured body against her as she gingerly untied the knot, all the time whispering, "It's over. It's going to be okay."

"Stephen, honey? It's getting cold. Stephen? Are you awake?" Eliza had woken suddenly from a deep nap, and it took her a moment to adjust to where she was. A cool breeze had come up, and with it the late-afternoon fog was on its march to the land, preceded by plenty of warning. The sun had moved closer to the fog line, and the loss of warmth disturbed her restfulness. Stephen heard her voice in the distance and came to as she started to pack up the lunch leftovers. "Hey, sleepyhead. Sorry to wake you, but it's getting cold. Did you have a good sleep?" She continued to tidy the area as she spoke.

Stephen opened his eyes, which felt moist and fatigued. He wiped the sleep from them and sat up. Eliza watched as he unconsciously wrapped his arms around his waist and moved them as if massaging an ache. "Damn. That was a deep one. How long have we been out?" He dropped his hands to his side and started to help her with the packing.

"I don't know. But judging by the sun, it's been a while. I don't want to get caught in the fog. Are you feeling okay?"

Now fully awake, he did not hesitate in his response. "Feel just fine."

She let her momentary concern for him go. "Let's start back down, then. We could go into Monterey or Carmel for a warm meal. By the time we get there, it will be just about the right time to eat again. What do you think?" She reached for his hand and held it.

"Sure, sounds good to me." Gathering the blanket in her arms, she let Stephen take the chest and they headed back to the car. It wasn't long before they were on the road, still heading north. It had been a good day, Eliza thought, just the way she'd hoped it would be. She sat next to him in the car, relaxed and warmed up once the heater kicked in. He seemed to be just as relaxed as she leaned her head against his shoulder at one point, and he reached with his right hand to caress her face, holding it there until he had to maneuver a sharp turn in the ribbon of coastal highway that lay before them.

Chapter 22

"Michael, come help me, please. I know you are in such pain, so be careful. That's right. He's hurt, and I need you to help me carry him back to the house. Careful, honey."

Michael had been careful to move his body slowly toward his mother and brother to avoid the pain he was suffering. He knew that his mother didn't have the strength to carry the two of them, much less her own wounded body. He had to help.

"Are you hurt badly, Michael?" His mother's voice was still the strained whisper she used so that no one would hear other than the three of them. He fought against the tears, but it was useless. They suddenly poured down his cheeks, a relief that only his mother's voice could provide.

"I'm okay, Mama." He managed to lie to her, knowing that she did not believe him. He crawled closer to her now and could see Stephen's ravaged body nestled in his mother's lap. He, too, wanted to nestle there, but he needed to stay focused on his mother's words. The darkness that surrounded them provided protection from the monster's eyes, Michael thought. He questioned the logic of going back to the house, for he knew full well that he would be there. He would be asleep, having forgotten in his drunken fog the damage he had done, but if disturbed from that sleep he would certainly do more. Michael searched his mother's eyes in the hope of seeing another way to escape.

"Okay. I am going to have you help me stand up so that we can carry him back together. Can you do that for me?" He felt her hand grip his forearm.

"Mama, I don't want to go back. We can't go back. We've got to get away from here. It's dark enough that we could find our way out to the highway without him seeing us. He's out like a light. You know that. If we go back and he wakes up, it will start all over again. Mama, please. We can get away." Michael now had a grip on her arms and with each plea for sanity, he was gripping her harder than before.

"Hush, Michael, hush. I know you don't want to go back. I know it. I don't either, but we can't get out of here on our own like this. Your brother can't be moved far and while you tell me you're okay, I don't believe

you. You are brave, Michael, but we can't do something stupid that will make things worse. How far do you think we can get down that driveway? Who's going to be traveling on the highway who will stop and pick us up? Michael, we have to go back. It will be all right, I promise you."

He couldn't believe that his mother was refusing to listen to him, to take charge and get them out of there. His frustration, growing by the minute, blocked out all reasoning and logic in his eight-year-old mind. He forced himself to stand up and grabbed hold of the closest tree trunk for balance.

"I'm getting out of here and I'm taking Stephen with me. I won't go back there, and I won't let you take him back there either!" His temper was growing, and his voice was rising. He heard his mother's pleas to quiet down, to take it easy. To hush. But he kept on.

Stephen gingerly shifted his weight in his mother's lap as she changed position to reach for Michael. He could hear his big brother's angry words and tried to understand why he was so mad. After all, he was in his mother's arms, safe, and Michael was close by.

It all happened so quickly. There had been no time to think, no time to plan. As Michael screamed on into the night, trying desperately to convince his broken mother to get up and move, he did not hear the cabin door slam. Nor did he hear his father's voice yelling through the night, calling their names interlaced with blind rage and hatred. He felt his mother grab him and pull him down toward her so that he stumbled and found himself painfully pulled to her side. She carefully slid Stephen from her lap and laid him next to Michael's crumpled body.

"No more. No more! No more!" Her voice was foreign to him now, a rush of syllables intensifying with each breath.

In the darkness, his vision allowed him to see her awkwardly come to her feet, standing above her two boys but with her body facing the oncoming threat. She moved a few steps away from the brothers. Two adult figures heading toward one another, both with their own agenda. Michael watched in horror as his father gained ground on them and their mother. He was waving something over his head, screaming wildly like a banshee in the cold night air. Their mother stood her ground even when he was within only a few feet of her. His words were no longer words but a gnarled, hot and frantic conglomeration of unintelligible sounds, like those of an animal in the last throes of death.

"Stop it! Stop it!" As she screamed these words at him, Michael,

terrified, watched with a strange sense of relief as his brave mother confronted the terror before them all. "What are you doing? These are your children! I am your wife! You are full of drink! Stop it! Stop it now!"

She reached for his flailing arm that held a familiar object in its hand high above his head. Michael did not stop to think but moved so quickly to place himself between his mother and father that in doing so, he shoved Stephen's injured body away from him and onto the soft ground beneath them. His father's voice filled the area with such anger and hatred that Michael knew only to save his mother from this uncontrollable monster as she continued to place herself in jeopardy for her children's sakes. Somewhere, deep within, he found the strength to turn to her and push her with all his might away from the imminent threat of certain death. Losing her footing, she stumbled, trying desperately to regain her balance to save her son.

"Michael, no! Michael, run!" But her pleas ceased as suddenly as they had begun as her balance failed.

Michael, in horror, watched his mother's body strike the side of the well's stone wall and wobble to the ground, arms still reaching out, desperately searching for balance. He heard it, even above his father's ongoing tirade. A sickening thud, and then he saw no movement.

Dismissing his father's presence, as time seemed to stand still allowing Michael to absorb the sight in front of him, he stumbled to his prostrate mother's dying body. Even in the darkness, he could detect the rich red liquid saturating the few displaced well stones that now served as a pillow for her crushed head. Comprehending what had just happened, he painfully turned to his father. Pushing himself up to stand and confront him, he recognized the weapon in his father's grip that now hung limply by his side. The demonic vocalizations from the man had stopped for the moment as he stood staring at his wife's limp body.

Then, just as suddenly, he glared at Michael while coming alive with rage once again. Michael's baseball bat was now raised over his father's head as he prepared to lower it onto his older son's body. With only one thought, that of Stephen, Michael stumbled to his brother's side and desperately clasped Stephen to him, all the while trying to shield him from the inevitable. As their father loomed over the innocent huddle, heaving for breath, breathing down upon the boys as if in a fairy tale of dragons and demons, Michael reached as deeply into his eight-year-old body as he could *for the strength to become his brother's knight. And it came to him as he rolled Stephen's body gently away from him once again and drew his father's attention from what was left of his family.*

The sting of the wood on the back of his head and the warm liquid he felt slowly dripping down the back of his neck stunned him as he began to run, not down the road to the escape he had recently pleaded his mother to take, but deeper into the groves, all the while grimacing in pain with each step he took but gaining an inner strength in the knowledge that his brother lay undisturbed by this monster. He could hear his father's heavy breathing and footsteps gaining on him. He would have to outrun him or face him. To face him could end this once and for all. To outrun him would only kill his brother and him eventually. It had to be now, in this moment of panic and flight. In his confusion, he knew he was lost.

Nothing looked familiar to him even though he thought that he knew every inch of the area. But that was in the daylight, not in the darkness and so deep into the forest. He had never been this far from the cabin. Without stopping to think, he dove into the hollow of an ancient burned-out trunk and listened through his own uncontrollable breathing for his father's approach. He could hear thrashing and words of frustration as the monster came closer. But he also knew that his father could not see him in the darkness of the blackened tree.

And then he was upon him, standing just to the other side of the opening. He had stopped and was breathing heavily, hitting the underbrush around his feet with the bloodied stump of the bat. Michael saw the bat push its way closer to the opening where his own feet, pulled up tightly into his body, were exposed. It was then, as the bat was about to make contact with the bottom of one of his shoes, that he reached out of his hiding place, grabbed the sticky wood from his father's unsuspecting grasp, and lashed out, all the while willing his body to exit the safety of the tree's trunk.

He could hear the wood clash with his father's legs, and he continued to hit with all his strength, ignoring his physical pain in his murderous frenzy as he worked his way up his father's body with the bat, until he heard ribs crack. His father's arms flailed in the air and darkness, trying to focus on the source of the beating but still in a state of drunkenness, unable to regain balance once he started to fall back. He landed heavily on the soft ground and felt himself sink into the boughs as the blows continued to cover his body. As he tried to reach for Michael through swelling eyes and bloodied vision, the final blow struck his forehead, pushing his skull down farther under the fragrant dampness of the redwood boughs until he lay still.

Chapter 23

When Michael was picked up by the police, he did not try to flee, nor did he try to explain himself. It was hard enough just to remember his name and why he was not in the facility, much less come up with an elaborate lie or, worse, the truth. He didn't ask how long he had been out there, but he sensed a desperate need for water. Hunger was not a factor in the early stages of his body's awakening. The authorities were kind enough to him, tending to him immediately so that he felt safe. Their words were softly spoken, assuring him that he would be all right now. It did not occur to him that, in this assurance, he had just lost his freedom once again.

Arriving at the hospital, he was met by a team of ER nurses who rushed him into the brightness of a sterile room. All around him was the language of medicine, of trained professionals, of beeps and drips, the hurried comings and goings of his caretakers, the distant intercom voices calling out for attention. He drifted in and out of consciousness, always waking to the same light and sounds and loneliness until someone was standing over his bed, checking on him.

Although he remained confused and out of touch, he couldn't help but feel relaxation and the great need to sleep deeply. But his body would not let him and forced him back to life at odd intervals so that he began to feel agitated. The agitation grew as he lay awake in the foreign bed until he sat up and yelled with all of his strength. The sound was unnatural as it forced its way into the silence. His muscles worked against him so that he began to tremor and to jerk in spasmodic movements that frightened him, and he screamed louder. The injection and drip finally gifted him with sleep and he remained in this state, completely out of his control.

He had no idea how much time had passed when the doctor signed the release papers. Somehow, he knew, though, that he was not going to be released, not in the way he so desperately wanted. He still imagined the freedom that he had very nearly tasted again. Desperately, he longed for it. But with each passing day, he knew that he was farther from it than ever before.

In the new treatment facility, he would have to start all over. Would have to find the strength to play out the game again, to stave off the hounds and their masters. Frankly, he questioned whether he had the stamina to do it, never questioning the desire that lay now deeper within but continued to smolder. How much beating down could he withstand until they broke him free from himself? How willing was he to protect himself, his secrets? He feared that he would break every time the pills were given to him as watchful eyes made sure that he had swallowed what his body still craved. It was in these moments when the chemicals took hold that he felt nothing, that any ability to fend off the enemy did not exist. Succumbing to the numbness that invaded his mind, all fears and insecurities disappeared, and he knew he was vulnerable once again.

The notebook lay on the desk in front of him. It was new, and someone had written his name in black ink across the top. Next to it lay a number 2 soft yellow pencil, freshly sharpened. His name slowly came into focus and his stomach muscles clenched as he recalled a fragment of anxiety when sitting as a young student at his desk, unprepared for the test that he was about to fail. The others around him had already started, and he could hear the lead of their pencils scratching the surface of the blank sheets.

"Michael, would you like to begin?" The voice was female, very soft and kind. It startled him.

"What?" He looked around, trying to find its source.

"You can begin anytime you would like. You don't need to fill the page. Just write anything that comes to you."

The same voice, sweet and unoffending, he thought. He felt her presence before he saw her. She had moved toward him and now stood behind him, one hand on his shoulder while the other gently moved the notebook closer to him. And then she moved away from him. He looked up to see her moving around the room, softly speaking to the others, reassuring them.

And then he began to comprehend. There wasn't a circle; there were only tables that were separated from each other so that he sat alone, as did the others. Not facing in any one direction, they seemed to have been scattered about the room with little concern as to any structure. He realized that he wasn't forced to look at anyone nor they at him, but only to see an obstructed profile as a writer labored over the next words to scribble while resting an angled head on a supportive hand, or the back of a head with neck hunched low over a notebook while an arm moved in a frenzy of writing.

Moving the notebook even closer, he opened the cover. The glare of the white page startled him, but the light blue horizontally measured lines began to dull the sensation. He ran his hand over the blank page and then again, as if to clear it of any debris or flaws it might present to him. The pencil sat in his grasp naturally and comfortably while he flashed again to an older woman's hands gently moving his small fingers into the proper pencil grip. Suspended, the pencil tip patiently waited to grasp the paper's surface.

As the words appeared, Michael slowly focused on their similarity, the repetition, the rapidity of their creation. With each attack, the lead pressed more deeply into the paper's thin texture until he felt the pencil give way under the pressure of his hand and heard a snap. The shattered pencil tip's fragmented wood sunk into the letter that had not been completely formed while Michael held it in place, afraid to remove it. He knew that if he did, he would not return to the notebook. As he sat, unable to move, the lines in front of him blurred and then cleared, only to blur again. He willed himself to focus his eyes by blinking repeatedly and in doing so, regained control.

"Oh, Michael. It's okay. Give me your pencil. I've got another right here for you. Keep going." She did not take the pencil from his grip but waited for him to release it to her before she gave him the sharpened one. She did not stand behind him but to his side and held out her hand to him. He stared at the shattered tip as he dragged the remnants of the exposed lead down the length of the paper until the desk's surface appeared. The line stayed connected to the incomplete letter in the line above, and he imagined the smudged streak leading him to freedom, just at the end of the dirt drive.

Chapter 24

The trip back to Big Sur had been quiet. Dinner had been more than they planned to have, and a satiated state overwhelmed them both as they headed south in the darkness and warmth of the car. Stephen felt the drowsiness come on suddenly and realized that he had shut his eyes momentarily. Eliza had fallen asleep, her head awkwardly hanging over her chest. Rolling down his window, he immediately felt the cold and damp air invade his nostrils and wake up his senses. He readjusted his position, pushing himself upward in the seat, repositioning his hands on the steering wheel while checking his mirrors.

The traffic had been light. Really, no one was traveling the coast at this time of night. If it hadn't been so dark and late, he would have enjoyed the ride more. It always bothered him to travel the highway at night, especially going south. Just to his right only a few feet from the road's surface, the continent ended abruptly in numerous places, with sheer cliff edges sinking hundreds of feet into the blackness of a sea below. Only if the moon were full could the white waters of the breaking waves be seen for a moment as eyes left the road just to get some bearing.

The Big Sur Lighthouse's intermittent beam crossed the horizon and upon approach, the road stretched out in a straight line separating the cattle's pasturelands as neatly as if a ruler had been laid down and a line had been drawn in the sand. It was only at this place that Stephen began to feel more secure with the dark road. He knew that he would continue to wind with the contour of the land, but he found comfort in that. The trees, not all tall and fragrant, but of variety, hugged both sides of the roadway, which he somehow always found comforting. And soon he would see the turnoff to the house and would bring them home safely once again.

Eliza did not awaken from her sleep even as the car made its way up the drive and came to a stop. Not wanting to startle her, Stephen gently rubbed her forearm without saying a word. She opened her eyes and stared forward into the darkness of the night. It took her a minute to realize where she was.

"Oh, wow. We're here already?" She sighed heavily and reached for her seatbelt. "Did I sleep the whole time? I don't remember falling asleep at all." She turned to Stephen, who was stepping out of the car.

"You've been gone since right after we got on the road. The last thing you said was something about being full, and it was la-la land from then on." He came around to her side and held the door open for her. Reaching in, he grabbed her hand and she fell into his arms as she lost her footing. "Hmm. Maybe it was a bit more than the food and the good fresh air of the day. Feeling okay, honey?"

"Sure, sure. Sorry. Just a bit groggy. I hate napping like that. Probably won't get to sleep tonight now. Great!" He could sense that her mood was beginning to wane, and the sooner they got inside and in bed, the better she would be.

The place was cold. He had forgotten to close a window in the bathroom, and it never took long for the outside to find its way in. They both shuddered at the same time as they entered the front room.

Eliza turned on the lights as she moved through the house and took a quick inventory of the state of the home. Everything should be as she left it, she knew, but she was never quite convinced that its location was all that safe. Anyone could venture down the road, and even though the PRIVATE PROPERTY signs were in view on the highway, they really didn't mean much to anyone who wanted to trespass.

Stephen came out of the bathroom and apologized about the open window. By that time, she had lit candles and turned up the heat. Grabbing a throw from the couch, she wrapped it around her and invited Stephen to join her as she stood in the kitchen debating her tea choices for the evening. He smiled and pointed to the closet, where he pulled out his oversized sweatshirt and threw it on.

"Aren't you going to try to go to bed? It's late, you know.

Come on. We can read for a while under the covers." He knew that she was not going to come with him, but he wanted to say it.

"I need to regroup, Stephen. Just for a little while. I feel like I just lost a small segment of my life. Unconscious for the last forty-five minutes, losing time being together. Sorry for that. But I really don't feel tired right now, not at all." She turned to the kettle, whose faint whistle was just beginning to grow.

"Do you want me to stay up with you?" he asked as he fought off another yawn, barely keeping his eyes open.

"No, of course not. I'm fine. You did all the work and you do look tired. Go ahead. I'll be in shortly. I'll just sit up and read for a bit. I'll see you in the morning." She finished pouring the steaming water over her tea bag, put the kettle back on the stove, and turned back to him to give him a good-night kiss. She saw the back of him as he staggered down the hallway to the bedroom. The door shut behind him while she gathered her cup and sank down on the couch in the front room with her book.

Sleep came quickly for Stephen. He knew that he was tired as his head sunk into the softness of the pillow. The darkness of the room always helped him fall asleep even if he needed to do a replay of parts of the day. When he was working, the replay could last a long time, so much time in fact that he would awaken himself from the fine line of consciousness to unconsciousness and then toss and turn until he had to get up. He lost hours of sleep, he guessed, during his working career but somehow managed to maintain his alert presence throughout the days. He chalked it up to being younger and cockier. But lately, sleep came quickly to him until the soft light of the next day penetrated the room.

He used to remember his dreams and would carry them with him for hours as glimpses of a detailed imagined moment would invade his thoughts and then disappear forever. Some dreams were not vivid but left an uneasiness that he couldn't shake soon enough, while others seemed to be imprinted forever on his consciousness. He was frightened by them and fought against their reappearance. He never knew when they would visit him; he could make no connection between an existing event and their presence. But they would come, and he lived in the fear of them. Since moving to the house, they appeared more frequently. He had not mentioned anything to Eliza, of course, and became quite comfortable finding ways to camouflage any indication of a bad night or moment in the middle of the day. It became exhausting for him, but he knew that he had no choice in the matter.

There were some things that could not be said, revealed, or examined. There were moments that were not clear to him but that felt so much a part of him that he couldn't ignore their deep-seated impact on him, somehow, but that he must keep only to himself. He did not understand why, however. Those moments in the past that he had slipped into and sunken to so deeply overtook him unexpectedly, but he had fought his way back. As long as he could find his way out of the darkness each time, he assured himself, he would be okay.

Chapter 25

She knew not to comment on her clients' work as she glanced down at Michael's efforts. She also knew not to show any emotional response. However, the words that filled the first third of the page spoke with such rage as the lead's mark grew darker and darker with each labored stroke, and the size of the words grew as if following the contours of an inverted funnel so that the last letters made before the lead shattered were three times the size of the others on the page. And then the smeared, uncontrolled line that exhausted itself at the bottom of the page as if the hand had just given out. She knew not to do anything but wait until he took from her the new pencil. He released his grip and the pencil fell, resting on the page.

"Michael, would you like another pencil? Would you like to continue?" Waiting for his response, she tried to process what she saw in front of her. She knew that this exercise worked. Having observed others, she found it to be a safe and controlled avenue for them to express themselves. Although some of her clients balked at the idea, it didn't matter to her. If she could reach even one in a day, she had affirmation that it was worth doing. So, she waited for Michael to take the pencil, to respond while the words on the page in front of him begged for completion.

"Yes, thanks."

She barely heard him as he reached for the sharpened pencil. She took the broken one from the page.

"If you like, you can start a clean page. It's your notebook, Michael. Good work. Keep going," she said, and she moved from him to another client.

He watched her move across the room as he turned the first page of his notebook, and again, carefully cleared the new page of debris as his open palm wiped it clean. This time, the pencil fell naturally into his grip as he rested it on the top blue line of the page and began to write.

He began by describing his little brother. The words came slowly at first, but then so quickly that the pages turned one after the other until he felt a nagging ache in his wrist. He stopped then and laid the pencil down on the desk. Rubbing his wrist and shaking out his hand, he repeatedly made a fist to flex his cramped muscles.

It did not occur to him to read back what he had just produced, for now there was no time for that. The urge to fill the pages overwhelmed him as he poured out the pain held so long inside. It wasn't until the moisture seeped into the detailed graphite testimony and the letters smeared under his hand that he realized he was crying. Not sobbing, but with a continuous shedding of tears as he remembered Stephen. He suddenly felt spent, and a fatigue took control of his body and mind so that all he could do was lay the pencil down and close the notebook. His head fell onto his chest and the last bit of moisture still clinging to his cheeks crawled down, only to drop gently on his folded hands in front of him.

Once back in his room, he slept for what seemed hours. He did not dream. The blackness of his sleep and the freedom from any intrusive thoughts that could disturb him allowed him to lose time without any reference. He awoke feeling hungry and thirsty. When he looked at the clock, he realized that he had slept almost three hours and that he had missed lunch. The attendant entered the room and came over to him. He was smiling and carrying a tray of food as well as two Dixie cups containing the real sustenance that Michael still needed.

"We were starting to worry about you, Michael." He laughed as he said this, as if Michael would not understand that he was saying it in jest. "That was one good, long rest. How are you feeling? Got to be hungry, huh?"

"I'm okay. Yeah. I'm really hungry." Sitting up and trying to get his bearings, he watched the attendant place the tray on the small table.

"You know the routine. Got to see you down these before I go, then you can eat and…" He held the Dixie cups out to Michael, who consumed the contents before the attendant could finish.

"Okay, then. Go for it. I'll be back to pick up the tray later. *Bon appétit.*"

The food went down quickly, his thirst quenched with continuous gulps. Starting to feel better, he began a replay of the morning's events. He looked for the notebook, only to remember that she had it. She held everyone's for safekeeping, she had said. She had promised them that no one ever saw the contents other than the writer. He believed her. He wasn't sure he could find a reason not to. She had been only patient and kind to him. She hadn't tried to question him in front of anyone, hadn't tried to make him come up with some stupid response to an even more ridiculous question that had nothing to do with who he'd been and still was. She had only put a notebook in front of him with a sharpened pencil. He had done the rest. He felt a satisfaction in what he had done but, at the same time, a need to complete what had just begun.

As he sat in his room, staring at the remains on his tray, he fought the urge to find her, to find his notebook and to open the pages once more. More than Stephen had appeared in front of him this morning. So much more that he feared if he didn't write and write now, it would dissolve back to where it originated, so deeply hidden that he would never find it again.

The pills prevented the agitation from starting, the physical reaction that would never allow his mind to clear. But he had been taking the pills now for such a long time, it felt. Why was it only now that he saw more than ever before? Where was this taking him? Why wasn't he afraid to go back? Why was the present not as important to him? How far back into his childhood would the notebook require him to recall and to examine? "Why am I not afraid of you, all of you?" He let his spoken words linger in the room with no one there to hear them.

Chapter 26

The winter set in heavily along the coast and the days offered little sunlight. The dampness of the air permeated everything so that to walk barefoot on the floorboards of the house left the soles of the feet chilled and damp. The dark, rich wood of the redwoods grew even darker as the moisture deepened the brown and red hues of their soft trunks. Where bark was exposed, fungi took hold and displayed a variety of shapes, textures, and colors. There was no other natural aroma in the forest than soft dirt mulched by the fallen branches of the trees. The fog sometimes came in during the night and clung to everything through the day and into the darkness. On other days, a storm would hit with high winds and heavy rains, only to clear to a fog-enshrouded sky so that even then the sun could not penetrate to the forest floor.

This winter seemed worse than the others, Eliza noted, and she began to long for the spring once again. From her windows, which had held such promise of inspiration as she tried to compose, she no longer saw the beauty of the season but only felt its heavy weight and endless darkness. Its effect on her she was not prepared to face. She fought the negativity that surrounded her—one of her own making, to be sure—but could not shake it. She knew perfectly well why she suffered but could do nothing about it: her need to escape from the darkness and the awareness that in trying to do so, everything only became darker. Stephen had begun to take notice but kept to himself about it.

Together, in the cabin day after day, they unknowingly choreographed their movements so that they were aware of each other's presence but expertly avoided any unnecessary contact. It wasn't because they did not love one another nor, at times, long for the other's touch; it was more so out of convenience of routine, a continuation of an expected flow of life—no surprises, nothing to debate, nothing to resolve.

At one point, the thought crossed Eliza's mind that she might be suffering from depression. She knew that her environment wasn't conducive to a positive outlook. She longed for warmth, for the sun, for the forest in front of her, all around her, to suddenly dry so that the aromatic scent of heated redwood balms and warm soil filled her lungs with hope and newness. She longed to place her hand against the tall windows' glass surfaces and to feel the sun's radiant heat tingle her skin. She sat at her desk and tried to recall the sun's play on the floor as the beams spread from one side of the room to the other and the crystal that hung from the ceiling caught the rays and scattered them against the walls to create miniature particles of rainbow light. In these moments of recall, Eliza sensed an uplifting of her spirits and told herself to hold on. Spring was coming and with it, another year of wonder and life.

She began to make plans for the "spring cleaning" of the yard. Each year the garden patch, overgrown and deeply covered with a winter's worth of nature's debris, had to be tended. The satisfaction that she felt when she uncovered the rich earth below always filled her with joy and excitement. She would, upon seeing the first glimpse of dirt ready to be turned over, start planning the garden plot. In her mind's eye, the garden was completely planted by the time the last clump of debris was cleared.

The days and weeks passed uneventfully. Stephen spent much of his time reading and doing very little else. Eliza kept to her writing, faithfully producing even on those days that nothing seemed to be worth saying. Infrequent outings up the coast and, once, down to Cambria for the day broke the monotony of their combined lives. They both enjoyed leaving the house and always, on the way home, one of them would comment that they should do it more often, but they never did. And that seemed to be all right for them both.

The official first day of spring brought one of the worst storms the coast had seen in years. Huddled together in the living room, listening to the groans of the saturated giants surrounding their home and the howls of gale winds, Stephen and Eliza, for the first time since living there, were terrified. All it would take was one of the redwoods to lose its grip on the earth and tip with its mighty weight in the direction of their home. It would wipe the house out and probably them as well. There was no place safe to hide. They had waited too long to leave the area, as trees had already fallen along the drive leading to the highway.

For three days and nights they waited out the storm, until Eliza awoke in the middle of the fourth night to an eerie silence. It was so very quiet that she thought she was dreaming, that this was what sudden deafness must be like. Then she sat up and heard Stephen's deep breathing but nothing else. Going to the window of their bedroom, she opened the curtain. The moon's light filled the sky, illuminating the trees' branches. She strained to see deeper into the night sky, searching for the remnants of storm clouds, praying that there were none and that this storm had passed. Unable to take the night sky in completely, she left the bedroom.

Standing in the center of her writing room, she was surrounded by the bright moonlight that saturated the room. Even though the high boughs prevented her from a clear view of the sky, she could tell that the clouds had moved on away from the coast and that, if she could see out to sea, the horizon would appear clear and crisp in the reflection of the moon's beams. At once elated while dreading the cleanup that awaited them outside these walls, she surprised herself by letting out a pent-up sigh that seemed to last unnaturally long. It was only then did she realize how tense she had been for these past few days and now how relieved. She hadn't noted the time when she left the bed but upon returning to it, was surprised to see that it was only 3:10. She crawled in next to her sleeping husband, who seemingly hadn't moved all night, felt a sudden chill under the sheets as her body adjusted to the warmth of the bedding, and fell back asleep.

Stephen was up before her. He had slept well and woke feeling anxious for the day ahead. Not aware that the storm had passed until he came fully awake and conscious of the silence outside their door, he also felt relief from the weight of impending disaster with no escape. He had never experienced such weather in this place before and, momentarily, he wondered if it was worth staying here another winter. With no choice in the matter, he knew, he shrugged the thought off and decided to get on with his day. The cleanup would be labor intensive. The fallen trees in the drive had to be moved so they could get out. Checking the property immediately surrounding the house was imperative. He only hoped that Eliza would be willing to help him. He had little doubt, but it was going to be tough going for her. Digging over dirt for her garden was one thing; lifting and carrying storm-drenched logs was quite another.

As he prepared breakfast, he heard her get up and shower. Yes, this would be a good workday and at the end of it, they could nest in again over a couple of drinks, soothing their sore bodies, and cuddle up by the fire. Slowly, he could feel the beginnings of excitement, of anticipation for the day he had planned for them.

Eliza, still feeling sleepy, entered the kitchen and gave him a gentle "good morning" peck on the cheek as he placed the last of the pancakes on the warming dish. "Sorry. I didn't hear you get up. I would have been out here to help you. Smells good."

"How was your sleep?" He didn't look at her when he asked this but concentrated on balancing the dish of pancakes with one hand while gathering the syrup and butter container with the other as he moved to the table.

"Fine. I did get up in the middle of the night. Don't know what woke me, but it was beautiful. The sky was clear, and the moon was so bright. I think we must be over the storm, don't you?"

"It looks that way. We have a lot to take care of today out there. Eat up because we're going to need all our energy just to clear a way out of here. I figure we start with cutting away the trunks of the downed trees in the drive. You up for that?" He didn't look up at her but shoveled in the pancakes as if he were a wood furnace that needed to be continually stoked.

"Sure, I am. I don't know how much real help I can be

with the lifting and all, but you know I will help you, honey. Have you checked any other areas around the house yet?"

"No, not yet. Thought I'd take a quick look before we started on the trees. But there's no question that the drive has to be done." He cleaned his plate of the last vestiges of pancake and syrup and took it to the sink. "Will you be ready soon? I can get out there and get the equipment. You want to meet me up there, then?" He looked back at her over his shoulder as he rinsed his dish.

"Sure. Give me a few minutes and I'll join you." The pancakes were good and warm, and she wanted to savor every bite. Once they were out working, the hours would fly, and they would ignore the hunger pains just to get one more thing done. She knew how they worked together. "See you up there."

The morning's work took its toll on them. Cutting and moving logs was one thing, but saturated with water, they became almost impossible to move, and both Stephen and Eliza strained under the labor. The area looked like a battle zone, with fallen trees and debris everywhere. It took all morning to clear just enough blockage to get their car through a narrow opening. In the distance, somewhere, chain saws could be heard. Distant neighbors, well out of sight and usually of hearing, were now joining in the cacophony of noise that the sharp teeth made as they tore into the wet wood that littered their lands. Stephen commented at one point that it was good to know that they were not alone, and he wondered what the extent of the damage had been to them.

By mid-afternoon, with the drive cleared enough to be passable, they gathered their equipment and headed back to the house for a bite and some rest. Eliza felt a sense of satisfaction in the work they had accomplished together and knew that Stephen was feeling equally satisfied. She could tell by his demeanor; even though exhausted, he looked more relaxed as he trudged through the layers of wet soil mixed with tree debris. His face, no longer showing the stress of worry, glistened with a fine film of dirt and sweat so that droplets balanced on the stubble of his whiskers and within the crevices of his skin, dark channels of dirt gathered while others ran slowly down his neck and into the collar of his flannel work shirt. Eliza, walking beside him, took note of his appearance and felt a sudden warmth for him that took her by surprise. And in her own exhaustion, she realized how much she loved this man.

There wasn't much left of the afternoon when they headed back out to the yard. Eliza had asked Stephen if he would help her with the clearing around the garden beds. He seemed to hesitate before answering her. When he said that he would, he suggested that it would be better to start by looking up. He had meant that if there were any limbs or branches that were about to fall, that they should take care of them first. The last thing that he wanted for either one of them was to be surprised by a painful blow to the head by a precariously hanging limb. What they could reach, they needed to be rid of. She had agreed, knowing that common sense prevailed.

Once the area around the garden plots was safe from any threats, Eliza was grateful to have a shovel and rake at hand to start the clearing process. Stephen started at one end of the plot farthest from the house while Eliza worked on the other. The plots had been measured out carefully when first established so that they were ample growing areas for their needs. Stephen had even included a raised bed in each area. However, uncovering the boundaries was becoming more difficult each year and after this storm, it seemed that they would never get to the bottom of the storm's wrath.

Chapter 27

Michael woke up earlier than usual, long before he could hear any movement or sounds in the hallways. Lying in bed, he chose not to get up yet. After all, he couldn't go anywhere until the door opened from the outside only to allow the attendant to check on him to make sure he was still in the land of the living. A quick "good morning" was all that was required of him in response. Then he was left alone to get up, dress, and take care of personal business. He had grown accustomed to this routine, and it gave him great comfort to have the personal contact at the beginning of his day. The door would remain locked from the outside until a second visitor came with his daily dose and stood over him until convinced that the chemicals were now in Michael's system. Then the door would shut one more time until, once more, he would be visited by the first attendant, informing him that he should come to breakfast. Every day, the same dance. Every day without fail. There was something to be said for routine, Michael thought, as he headed to the dining hall on this morning.

As he joined others in the hallway, he found himself wondering what had woken him so early. Trying to replay those last moments of sleep before regaining consciousness, he could find no reason, but it lingered with him and stayed on his mind throughout breakfast. Had he been worried about something that he wasn't aware of? Had he been woken by a sudden noise or disturbance that he didn't register at the time but that had thrown him from his slumber? Normally, he would not wake until the attendant entered the room for the first greeting of the day. But this waking was sudden. He woke without feeling tired or numb. He woke alert and ready. Ready for what? The chatter around him at the table did not break into his rambling thoughts but seemed to buoy him on an invisible ocean so that he floated and bobbed with the rising and lowering of tidal voices, completely alone, treading water on the surface of a vast sea.

"You aren't going to finish this?" He didn't hear the question. "Hey, if you're not going to eat those pancakes, do you mind if I do?"

He saw a hand reach for his plate and start to move it away from him. Without much thought, he held onto the plate's edge in a tug-of-war with the intruder.

"Aw, come on. If you were going to eat them, you would have done it by now. Come on, don't let them go to waste." It was a whining voice that began to creep into his awareness.

He held tightly to the edge of the plate and focused on the hand that was not his. With his other hand, he lifted his fork and quickly, before either could stop it, the fork sank its tines into the soft skin of the intruder's just below the last row of knuckles. The whining stopped only to be replaced by a howl and moan that filled the room, bringing everyone to a standstill.

As he pulled the tines from the wounded hand, he felt an arm reach across his chest grabbing the fork from him and then another set of arms lift him from the chair and drag him across the room and out to the hall, all the while the screams of his victim continued with growing intensity. Even though he knew he was not free as the arms grew tighter and heavier around him, he was free of the noise as they moved him back to his room. He wasn't sure how long he could have withstood the screaming. Grateful to be behind his closed door and now sitting on the edge of his bed, he waited. He knew there would be consequences. He had seen others act out and then hadn't seen them for days. Not having any idea what those consequences were, he could only imagine, and the havoc wrought by his imaginings drew him deeper into himself.

He did not know how many days he had been in his room after the incident. He vaguely remembered people coming in and out, administering meds, hovering, attempting to communicate with unintelligible sounds, and then leaving him alone again. How many times this occurred, he had no idea. Perhaps only once? They probably figured that he was a lost cause, a bother, a broken and irreparable mess of a human. He understood that.

How long had he been here? How long had he been in facilities like this? Where would he go from here? If stabbing someone in the hand was offensive enough to have him thrown out of the facility and on to the next one, he was prepared for the message. He wondered who would deliver it. Maybe no one. One day very soon, he would find himself in an ambulance or maybe the van on his way to God knows where. And they would mumble something like, "It's going to be okay, Michael. You're going to be okay." And he would numbly hear their words and numbly dismiss them. And the damn game would start all over again.

He had forgotten the notebook. She entered his room to find him sitting by the one small window that looked out onto the back gardens. With his back turned to her, he prepared himself for the attendant's approach with the cup of meds in one hand and a cup of water in the other.

"Michael? Good morning." Her voice startled him as he turned to see her across the room, standing just inside the doorway. "How are you, Michael? Did I surprise you?" She knew that he did not fully comprehend the present moment because she knew how the drugs in his system kept him just on the other side of reality. In remembering how that felt, her empathy momentarily overwhelmed her as she gazed upon him. "Michael," she moved closer to him but kept what seemed to be a safe distance, "would you like me to stay a bit? We've missed you at our sessions, and I thought that you might be missing us too. I brought you something." She held out his notebook and moved closer. "I was thinking that maybe you would like to have this for a while. They're telling me that it might be too soon for you to join the group again, but I didn't want you to feel that I had forgotten you. Would you like me to leave it with you?" She moved to the only table in the room to lay it down next to him.

The sound of her voice was distant, but he understood her. She moved closer to him as if a gentle breeze had lifted her just off the ground and floated her closer and closer. He was not afraid of her, this apparition that knew his name. He tried to remember where he had heard that voice before, but his mind was still shut down from the meds lingering in his system from the night before. He watched her lay something on the table but couldn't bring it into focus.

"You know, you were making great progress, Michael. The number of pages you filled is impressive. Sometimes, people have a very hard time writing. But you...you have a lot to say. And I think there is more." She waited. Not sure that he would respond to anything she had said, she picked up the notebook and walked toward him. "Here. Maybe you would just like to start by reading what you have written so far. Sometimes that helps so that you can go on."

She held the notebook out to him, secretly saying a prayer that he would look up at her, maybe respond with eye contact, and take the notebook from her. After what seemed an interminably long time, she withdrew the notebook from him.

What had she really expected? She knew going into his room would be a violation of her own rules about her clients. It was their territory, their private space, and only a very few clinical types could enter it unscathed. She had set herself up to be the woman in the sessions room, the woman who waited for him twice a week, the woman who was responsible for creating a safe and welcoming environment for his crushed psyche, the woman who would not force him to reveal deep-seated memories in front of anyone else, the woman whose main goal was to help make him well. Had she just violated all of that by coming to him, by assuming that she had the magic touch with him just because he liked writing in a notebook? After all, did she know what he had filled the pages with? It could be unintelligible nonsense. The one thing she did know was that she had remained true to him and had not read a single word of his writings. Wanting to tell him this, to defend herself, and fighting a twinge of anger toward him, it was all she could do not to as she suddenly felt uncomfortable in his presence.

Unresponsive and further withdrawn since she had come into the room, her client sat. She laid the notebook on the table once more, gave it a motherly pat as if to say, "You'll be all right," and turned toward the door. Just as she reached for the handle, she turned back to him. She thought that she had heard something, a movement that would affirm her presence. Nothing appeared any differently than a moment ago. "Michael, I will see you soon," she said in barely a whisper. Then she opened the door and entered the hallway. The door silently shut behind her.

Chapter 28

With the two garden plots cleared and a pile of debris waiting to be dispersed into the surrounding forests, Stephen watched Eliza as she knelt and ran her hand over the newly exposed soil. Its rich aroma was intensified and released as she reached under the surface and turned over the soil with her bare hand while crumpling the dirt between her fingers, examining its content.

Smiling, she turned to Stephen. "Nature has a way of taking care of its own, you know? All of that," she pointed to the piles that they had just created as they cleared the area, "was for a reason. And here it is. This soil is rich and beautiful, ready for us to work with it. Thanks, Mom." She laughed as she looked up to the sky and then gestured to the giants surrounding them.

This was what Stephen loved about Eliza. She appreciated life, the simple things that most people overlook day in and day out. Eliza was in tune with her surroundings, something that he wanted to be but never felt as deeply as she did. There was an innocence and childlike quality to her that was not always evident, but in moments such as this, that was all there was to her and that was more than enough for Stephen. He felt such contentment and love for her as he moved toward her.

Kneeling on the ground next to her, he took her hand, which still held remnants of the dark dirt, and brought it to his lips, gently kissing it.

"It's been a good day, hasn't it?" She looked into his eyes as she said this.

"Yes, it has. Although my body is telling me that kneeling down was a mistake."

They laughed while Eliza reached out to him to help him get up. In doing so and losing their balance, they both fell back onto the warm soil and found themselves on their backs, looking skyward through the branches of the trees. Neither said a word for some time as they individually took in the beauty of the moment.

"We are lucky, you know? I think about that a lot, how lucky we are." Stephen turned on his side and reached for her as she did the same. The soil and bodies became one for a time as they made love for the first time in months, while the only interlopers were the jays that scolded at each other high up in the treetops.

In the weeks that followed, they felt as though their relationship had begun all over again. The excitement and discovery of one another filled their days as they continued to work in the yard and area surrounding the house. They found time to talk more revealing details of their lives to one another that either hadn't seemed important earlier in their courtship and marriage or had been so long forgotten that had it not been for the magic of the present moment, whatever that was, would still lay dormant in their memories. Laughter and sympathetic tears often filled their conversations as they ended their days of labor over a fragrant glass of wine and a warm fire.

Eliza knew that these days were special in their relationship, were meant to be, and were meant to be appreciated and remembered. She fought the urge to dig deeply into questioning why they were coming about now after all these years together, and she wondered if Stephen was questioning this as well. He must be aware of the strangeness of it. What had brought them so close to one another? Wary of it disappearing as suddenly as it appeared, she woke each morning fearful that this might be the day that Stephen would step away, that what they had experienced before these magical days was back to stay.

The unsettling part of it all was that she did not know how to hold onto the magic. She did not know how to hold onto the Stephen who had given her such joy and contentment most recently. She feared more than anything losing him to something that she did not recognize and could not control.

Chapter 29

As she shuffled through the paperwork on her desk, the strong cup of tea that she had purchased two hours ago on her way to work, although now tepid, still held a welcome distraction from the business at hand. Pushing herself away from the desk while grabbing the paper cup, she leaned back in her chair and debated, after a quick taste, whether it was worth the effort to go to the microwave and warm the remnants of her breakfast. She felt the familiar twinge of hunger as she wavered in her decision. No eating until at least one, she reminded herself. Liquid sustenance was sufficient, cold or warm. The energy it would take just to walk down the hall and up the stairs to the staff room might encourage the hunger she was feeling and so she pulled herself back in place, swallowed the remains of the tea, and got back to work. The backlog of cases on her desk would keep the pangs at bay.

Engrossed now in reading Michael's most current case study, she jumped at the sound of her name. Looking up, Jared stood just to her side, leaning over the cubicle wall.

"Hey, Allie. You're at it early."

She liked Jared as a co-worker; nothing else even entered her mind. He did the same job as she but came at it with his own style, one that she did not always agree with or understand. But he had successes as she had, and for that she could not hold any ill will. The people whom he touched were now leading different lives than when they first entered the facility. He never boasted about these accomplishments; it wasn't deemed professional, even though there were two other "professionals" who never let Jared or Allie forget their victories in the hard-won battle against mental illness. Because of this, Allie and Jared had formed a solid alliance to keep their own sanity in a residence for those on the periphery of saneness.

"Yeah, I guess I am, but it wasn't easy. Something about reams of paper greeting you in the morning just as you left them the night before. No headway being made here, I'm afraid."

"Do you meet with clients today or can you slip away to somewhere quiet and get ahead of the game?"

He was sincere in his question, she knew. There really wasn't an ounce of negativity in this guy, she thought. A breath of fresh air, if she consciously did not take him for granted.

"My afternoon is booked with three sessions, one right after the other. My only relief from the printed page. What about you?" She had reached for the cup of tea, taking a sip only to remember that she had already emptied it. Not wanting to appear the fool, she continued to sip at the bone-dray cardboard. It served as a distraction, something to do as she began to feel uncomfortable and vulnerable. She knew this feeling and how it could creep up on her, and she also knew that she didn't understand it and her reactions to it. She half listened to Jared's response as she tried to fight the growing agitation that her mind insisted upon entertaining.

"…is not that bad, really. I like working with my clients in the morning. Gets my day off to a solid start and gives me time to reflect on them for the rest of the day. I guess the opposite of your routine." He laughed gently as he said this.

What had he said before she was tuned in? Was she expected to respond in some fashion? Oh God, she hated this about herself. How could she stay engaged with her clients but not with a "normal" human being?

"Okay, I'm off to get started on my day. Hope you have a good one, Allie. See you around the campus." And then he was gone.

Holding the cold, empty cup in her right hand, she pushed herself away from her desk and shoved the cup into the wastebasket underneath. How long it would take for her to regain some semblance of normality, she couldn't gauge, but focusing on her paperwork, especially Michael's, would get her there sooner than trying to understand what she just experienced. Some professional psychologist she was, she couldn't help thinking.

As she began to read Michael's history and her work with

him thus far, a sense of accomplishment swept over her as she remembered his notebook, with its pages, at first, filled with unintelligible markings but recently with his fervent writings. This last setback for him had disturbed her, and she questioned whether her techniques were valid in the long run.

She had made a promise to her clients that she would never read their notebooks without their permission and then, would do so only in their presence. She preferred that they read aloud to her their own words so that she could remain an objective receptacle for their pain. She had kept her promise over the years and intended to continue to do so. Some of her clients would allow her entrance into the pages between the notebook's covers, while others never did. She considered these her failures, even though she had many other tricks up her sleeve to get through to them. They were failures because she loved to write. She had done so consistently throughout her childhood and into adulthood. It served as her way to release some of what was bottled well inside of her. She also knew how painstaking the process was for most writers, not to mention those whose mental health was at risk. For that, she admired those who took their notebooks and spilled their fragile selves upon the thin blue-lined paper. Especially, now, Michael.

As she reminded herself of his early history with drugs and alcohol, her heart hurt for him. She remembered reading somewhere in her graduate studies that to be a good healer, one must be able to empathize. In her early twenties, this seemed to her to be requiring too much of people in training and, frankly, rather unrealistic. After all, she could not accept the idea that to be good psychiatrists and psychologists it was necessary that their lives parallel, in some way, those of their clients. In her first years of practice, working in a group with older doctors, she was sure that their success was not due to a troubled childhood or adolescence suffering abuse, neglect, or depression.

But now she understood. Allie had confidence in herself and in her natural ability to empathize without having suffered. She was told that she was a good listener and that her responses were appropriate and productive for her clients. With each positive appraisal given to her by her mentors and colleagues, her confidence grew, as did her initial opinion about empathy. Perhaps she was just special that way. God's gift and all that. Whatever the reason, she knew that she was in the right profession and that she was awfully good at it.

However, the cold, objective words lunged at her from among the thousands that filled the pages of his file. And as she continued to read about her newest client, these same words remained in the forefront of her thinking. The names of the drugs rushed in circles, colliding with one another, separating into syllables, and then pulling their separate pieces back together, somehow, so that his drugs became her drugs, his pain became her pain. So that she could not convince herself otherwise. What she was feeling was real empathy.

She remembered very little of the accident. Mostly the pain that followed, only to be relieved by the gifts of medication that were pumped into her body for weeks. She knew it was weeks only because her mother had been her calendar. The doctors' decisions to keep her under their care for well over a month in the hospital room was out of her control, completely. She could not communicate to them a single syllable, could not move her body, could only hear the clinical noises and serious voices that hovered all around her as she slid in and out of sleep. Her mother's soft, caring voice, often choked off by tears and gulps of air to gain control of her emotions, was her only reprieve during this time.

She had lost sight of who she had been before the accident as she lay under the sheets that smelled of burnt cotton left too long in an institutional-sized dryer. Her memory was not gone, just stunned so that the present dominated her thinking.

And the present was physically painful. The tears welled constantly while she fought to remain sane and not scream out as the drip, in full sight, came to an end and the suspended bag of magic caved in upon itself. And just as she felt that she could control herself no longer, someone would appear at the side of her bed and with dexterous movement, replace the bag with one that was full and fat of the magic juice that she welcomed into her starving veins. Sweet relief from pain, and then sleep would come quickly.

In the weeks that followed her release from the hospital, her mother had been insistent that Allie stay with her so that she could give her the care needed. Besides, it would be financially beneficial for Allie to do so, as her monthly budget left no room for anything other than the roof over her head, food on the table, and an occasional movie.

When the accident occurred, she was only a few months away from earning her PhD in Psychology and was eager to enter the professional world, opening her own practice. The accident was a setback, but it did not conquer her dream. It did, however, hold tight to her psyche as she struggled to erase the flashes of memory from her mind. The sickening sound of the cars colliding into one another, the whipping of her body around and around while confined by a seatbelt that grabbed hold of her torso with such force that she still carried the remains of discoloration from both the external and internal bruising, her head jerking in every direction until it collided with the caved-in windshield with an impact that not only shattered the glass into a million crystal fragments that abstractly reflected the dying beams of the yellow headlights and someone else's brake lights but also instantly snuffed out any awareness of what followed. She replayed these final moments before she awoke in the hospital bed repeatedly, somehow trying to move the memory forward to fill in the gaps during unconsciousness. Not knowing the details still disturbed her. She needed completion of the incident.

She was told very little by the paramedics who came to visit her during one of her lucid moments, other than that she was lucky to be alive, that removing her from her vehicle was tricky, but the Jaws of Life had done their job, and that transfer to the hospital went smoothly and quickly. Frankly, she did not know what questions to ask. No, that was not true. She did know one, but she found herself stopping each time before asking. She felt that she knew the answer already, not based on any facts or observations but a gut instinct that plagued her painfully both physically and mentally. If she was correct, then she would have to bear the responsibility of killing someone.

She recalled being questioned by officers while in the hospital. Their questioning was gentle and, she felt at the time, reassuring. She couldn't remember any feeling of suspicion on their part, any indication that she was to blame. More like gathering information from her to help them understand. It wasn't until she was in her mother's home that she was told the truth. She had woken the first morning in her mother's guest bedroom surrounded by so many familiar objects. Not wanting to put away some of her more precious memories of her daughter's childhood, her mother had tastefully displayed them so that a guest might feel the impulse to ask about their significance but not enough to overwhelm a visitor with memorabilia.

When the bedroom door opened, she hadn't been awake longer than it took to roll herself onto her back, carefully maneuvering her body to inflict the least amount of pain.

"Good morning, love. So glad that you're awake. How are you feeling? Did you rest well? If you need more pillows or blankets, I don't want you trying to get up to find them. I've done a lot of rearranging since you left, so you would be looking for who knows how long. You need to let me be the mother again."

She stood over Allie by the side of the bed, her right hand reaching down to her forehead to gently sweep her damaged child's disheveled hair away from her eyes, keeping her hand in place as though never to lose contact again. Allie made no attempt to move nor to ask her mother not to do it. It was too comforting and so familiar. She welcomed it.

"How long have I been sleeping, Mom?" There was no clock by the bed now. Arranged elsewhere, she thought.

"Thirteen hours, if you can believe that. I woke you once to give you a pain pill, but that was it. Obviously, your body is trying to heal itself. I was a bit concerned each time I checked in on you. You hadn't moved an inch in all this time. Must have something to do with the residue of all the medications they gave you in the hospital. And you still have prescriptions to fill to help with the remnants of pain."

Remnants? She almost let out a laugh, but the thought of how painful it would be to do so stopped her. The pain was alive and well, certainly not like it was in the hospital, but she would never consider herself suffering from the remnants of pain. And as this thought swam around in her brain, she realized that the pain was indeed intensifying as she gradually moved out of the sweet state of slumber.

"I need something, Mom, for the pain. Did they give me something?" She turned her head gingerly toward the bedside table, searching for any amber plastic bottle that might hold relief.

"Here." She saw her mother's hand pick up a bottle and put it down, doing the same with others until finally she held one up to read the print. "This is the one for pain. I'm not so sure that I should be giving this to you already. It says here…"

"Mom, please. It's okay. I need something now. It's only going to get worse if I don't take it now. Please." She reached for the bottle, but her mother held it firmly.

"Okay, but we need to keep track. I worry about how much you're taking into your system. That's all." She placed the bright blue horse-sized pill into her daughter's palm and then poured a glass of water. Carefully handing the glass to Allie, she sat back down and watched her baby medicate herself.

"Thanks, Mom. Don't worry." Alison could read her mother like a book, sometimes too well. "I'll be fine."

As if surprised by her daughter's concern for her, her mother sat up and leaned her body toward the bed, resting her forearms on the edge of the mattress, hands folded as if ready to give a recitation. Alison, through the beginnings of a mental fog bank moving in to relieve her pain, saw her mother's face loom in front of her, its age revealed more so at this moment than she had ever remembered it to be. Drying skin was drawn tightly around the mouth and hundreds of creases moved with her expressions, marking the strain of living and the passage of time. Her mother's face frightened her momentarily until she heard her sympathetic voice, soft and distant. She tried to reconcile the incongruity of the two impressions but couldn't hold onto the effort long enough to do so.

"Darling, you need to understand something about the accident. It worries me that you may not know." Her mother paused before continuing. She unclasped her hands and fidgeted with the bedsheet that had pulled away from underneath the mattress. Gently tucking it back under and then reaching to smooth the sheet across her daughter's chest, she let her hands pause over Alison's heart, gently resting there as if to make this connection before going on.

Alison tried to fight off the dimness that was surrounding her vision and the heavy fatigue that was slowly shutting out everything but welcomed sleep so that she could stay present with her mother. She recognized, even in her drug-induced state, that this was a special moment between the two of them.

"Nothing that happened is your fault. Nothing. He caused the accident, and he will have to live with that for the rest of his life. You are going to recover, get on with your life, and grow to be a wonderful old woman, just like me."

She couldn't be sure, but she thought that she heard her mother laughing gently and lovingly as Alison could keep her eyes open no longer.

Chapter 30

His cell phone rang shortly after four in the morning, but he wasn't conscious enough to answer it, much less remember where he had left it the night before. Moments later, he heard it again, and this time he automatically reached for it on the nightstand where he always put it before bed. Without forcing himself to fully awaken, he answered. "Hello?"

As clichéd as it seemed to him, the heavy breathing on the other end both humored and angered him. He hit the END icon and silenced it. With no thought beyond rolling over under the covers, it was not long before he was in a warm and dark space.

At breakfast, Eliza sensed that Stephen's mood was off. Unwilling to start her day with a confrontation, she made a concerted attempt to ignore it. "How did you sleep?" A courteous and nonthreatening query, she thought.

He looked up from his paper and then back down. "Fine."

As he refocused his attention on the article and away from his wife, he suddenly recalled the early-morning interruption of heavy breathing. Dropping the newspaper, he quickly left the table to retrieve his phone from the bedroom. Forgetting he had silenced it, he corrected that move immediately. Concerned that he might have missed important calls, he started to check voicemail and his recent history only to see that the single call thus far on this day was from an unknown number and area code, placed at 4:06 a.m. Whoever the heavy breather was had been stupid enough not to realize that the recipient of his early-morning gag would now have his number. Stephen had no patience for some people's lack of simple technological knowledge. He deleted the history.

Eliza had observed him with curiosity. She played back the last few minutes of breakfast with Stephen. One minute, limited bland verbalization just to fill up space; the next, he was completely distracted and had left her without explanation. She waited for him to return.

"Sorry about that. Did you hear my phone ring around four this morning?" He held it up in front of him as if it were a foreign object he had never seen before.

His voice was warmer, kinder, and she internally sighed in relief. "No, but I do remember you pulling the bedding over you and leaving me with a sliver of quilt to keep me warm. I'll get you for that, my little pretty." She surprised herself as she morphed into the Wicked Witch of the West for a moment. Stephen recognized, thank God, the reference, took a double take in Eliza's direction, and finding her eyes locked on his, they both burst into laughter. "Not to worry," she said as she reached her hand across the table to Stephen, "my broom has been out of commission for quite a while, so it's going to take some creative thinking to get you."

And the morning was under way for them. They both, in their separate moments, reflected on the morning's mixed vibes and they both, separately, wished deeply that the lightness of mood would continue as the day progressed. Yet Stephen found himself replaying the sound of the phone call and fought a growing agitation. It was only a crank call, he reasoned, but what if it wasn't? No. Crank call by a crank. Simple. End of story. Put it to rest, now. Although he should have noted the number. Maybe called it? Maybe not. But at least he would have had the number. *Should have noted the number. Why? Don't be crazy about this. A simple crank call. Period.*

When Stephen had asked her about the early call, Eliza had been curious as to who had called him, but the thought passed as quickly as it came. Even this far into the forests of Central California, the solicitors found them—not as often as when they were living in the city, but enough to become frustrating at times. She could only assume that Stephen must have been upset when the call woke him. It probably explained why he tugged the warm bedding from her sleeping frame this morning. But she thought better of suggesting that he silence the phone at night.

Stephen's agenda for the day did not include her, for which she found herself grateful. She had been longing for time to herself in the day to do some writing and when he told her that he had an appointment in San Francisco with an attorney regarding some of his real estate back east and then banking business, she feigned her disappointment that he would be away for the day while inwardly thanking God for this little gift of time. He reassured her that he would be back in the early evening but told her not to wait on dinner for him. He'd get something along the way. Still trying not to reveal her excitement at the prospect of a day to herself, Eliza pushed it a bit too far. "Couldn't you cancel it? Try to arrange another time? Maybe we could make a day of it the next time?" She could see in Stephen's face that she was convincing and felt alarmed for a moment that she had been too convincing.

"Why not come with me today? The only reason I didn't tell you about the appointment before now is that I didn't think you would want to go that far only to have to sit around and wait for me while I take care of business. I have no idea how long I'll be with the attorney or with the bank. But, sure, if you don't mind hanging around, come with me."

"You know, you're right, honey. I really don't want to go up to the city only to sit and wait most of the day for you to be done with your business. I can get some things done around here, maybe write." How hard was that to tell the truth, she thought? She relaxed and continued. "Don't concern yourself with me. We can plan another day up there when the time is all ours to do with as we choose. Hope the meetings go well for you. Are you planning on selling property back there, then?" Stephen seldom discussed his business deals with her and she was fine with that. He provided for her and was more than generous with his monies when it came to her comfort and security. She had surprised herself with the question.

"That's a topic of discussion with my attorney and the bank. I'm playing with the idea of letting go of the house in Maine. Real estate right now is hot, especially on the shore. We haven't used the house since we moved here, and I don't see us doing it in the future. Want to find out if moving on a sale now is the smart thing to do. We could build our nest egg by a healthy amount, you know."

He was including her in his thought process, which she appreciated.

"Sounds as though it should be researched a bit. Perhaps by the day's end, you'll have a good idea about the direction to take, Stephen. Does sound like a day of business, though. You're right about that. Have I ever said thank you for looking out for us as well as you do?" She gave him a kiss on the cheek.

"In many, many ways, Eliza. Just don't go planning on spending the money before we have it." He wrapped her in his arms as he said this, and she could feel the strength of not only his body but his mind as he chuckled at his owns words. "Well, let me get ready to hit the road. Is there anything you want me to do before I head out?"

What she wanted to say was, *Yes. Don't let go of me. Hold me like this for the rest of my life. Let me feel as though I have sunk into your physical body so far that we become one in every sense. Yes. That is what I need you to do before you go.* "No, sweetheart. Can't think of a thing. Go ahead. Get ready. Do you want me to do anything for you while you're gone?"

"No, just want you to have a good day and I'll see you later this evening. I'll call you before I head home. How's that?"

Smiling, she nodded while desperately trying to understand why she was suddenly fighting to hold back tears, why her heart was beating overtime, and why she felt an overwhelming sadness. He moved away from her to the bedroom, leaving her alone in the kitchen, clutching the cold tile counter, trying to slow her body's rebellious behavior.

She heard his car's tires grate against the gravel of the drive as she watched Stephen head up the drive and out of her view when he turned the corner onto the highway.

She stood for a long time at the door, taking in the fresh morning air. Her emotions once again intact, she stepped onto the porch, taking time to survey the grounds and all the work the two of them had accomplished recently after the heavy storms of winter. The last storm of the season at the beginning of spring had done the most damage but had not convinced either one of them that they might be better off elsewhere. She realized how much she loved this place, with its beauty as well as its surprises. She couldn't imagine herself anywhere but here. Admiring the tamed and well-kept garden area, she took a sip of hot tea while wrapping her hands around its ceramic warmth. The morning air was cool and the longer she stood there, the chillier it felt.

About to go in, her eye captured movement in one of the plots and she tried to focus on the object. Too small, of course, to be the deer who loved to challenge the boundaries that protected the enticing greens just on the other side of the netting, the thought of rabbits finding the garden's treasures set her into action.

Carefully setting the teacup on the railing of the porch, she didn't think twice but headed down to the garden. Cursing herself for wearing her slippers, which quickly absorbed the dampness and the cold, wet soil, she continued toward the intruder. Yes, he had been busy. The new greens were nibbled almost to the earth's surface, and not in any consistent pattern. As a matter of fact, not one of the plants had been left unscathed, though some were in worse shape than others.

As the mumbled curses continued to escape her lips, she saw out of the corner of her eye a white cottontail scurry under the fencing and into the forest. Mourning the remnants of what were to be future salads and veggies, she looked around for scat. How many of these little monsters were there and how was she going to keep them out? Not finding any traces of scat, she surveyed the damage and gently kneeled in the soft garden soil, speaking reassurances to her wounded plants that she would protect them at all costs and that it was their job not to give up on her but to grow.

The fencing of fine netting that she and Stephen had surrounded the plots with was advertised as critter resistant. She remembered when they were putting it up and, in her sometimes-negative state, had commented to Stephen that she would be surprised if the so-called critters would not be smart enough to find a way around the supposedly smarter humans. Then it dawned on her that they had not thought about rabbits, who are wonderful burrowers and who don't give a second thought to a netting just above their dirt-soiled snouts and paws. Their only concern is to reach the plant, right along with their buds, the gophers. The deer had become the least of their worries and seemed to have found greener pastures in the last few months. She couldn't remember seeing one since the fencing went up.

Knowing that it would take some time to think this one through and that Stephen would come up with a solution as he always did, she turned her back on her suffering patients, realizing that there was little she could do for them now. As long as their roots were intact and the shock of being abused by hungry rabbits didn't kill them, she would have to wait until tomorrow to attend to them. She said a little prayer that they would hold on until then and turned to head back to the house.

As she started back, she remembered the rock garden on the far side of the house and decided to visit it, almost afraid to see the damage that might have been done to those plants. She was so proud of this creation and thought that her mother would be proud as well. A gifted gardener, her mother had convinced her husband when they moved into their first house in the Santa Clara Valley in the late 1950s to gather as many good-sized stones as he could find so that she could create a rock garden like the one she'd seen in an article in *Sunset Magazine*, her gardening bible. Her father, of course, obliged his wife by not only finding good-sized rocks on their weekend excursions, but many more than she had envisioned. That did not stop her from building a structure that not only included each rock thoughtfully delivered by her husband, but also expanded to include a wide variety of plants that found themselves happily sharing the company of each other and the warmth of the protective rocks that surrounded them. Her neighbors would always comment on the beauty of the garden, and it was at times like this that Eliza felt close to her mother and missed her terribly.

Most of the stones for Eliza's rock garden had been collected from the debris of a stone structure that had been part of the property when the house was built many years ago. Stephen had told her that the original house dated back to 1875. It appeared that over time, the stone structure had crumbled to the ground, and now it was impossible to determine what it had been. Eliza had asked Stephen if he had any idea, but he hadn't and was not interested in pursuing the subject. The only interesting aspect of it, Eliza thought, was that the stones, even though seemingly indiscriminately scattered about as one approached the area, formed a pattern the closer one moved to the center of the remains. In fact, the almost perfect circle of stones, precariously perched upon one another and cemented by time's application of mud and fallen redwood debris, intrigued Eliza. It looked to her to have been a circular wall that now stood only a foot tall at its highest point. Its diameter was at least three, maybe four, feet. Perhaps a place to store crops, something like a silo that she remembered seeing on her travels with her parents? Perhaps part of another structure whose remains had long been removed by former owners?

Intrigued as she was, she was more captivated by the thought of building her rock garden, and so she and Stephen had proceeded to remove the loose rocks from the area and haul them to the other side of the house, the perfect place for a successful rock garden.

As she came around the corner of the house, she immediately sighed in relief to see that the rock garden stood in front of her undamaged. In fact, it was flourishing from the warm sun that found its way through the branches of the few trees that were on this side of the home. Some of the stones' surfaces had imbedded quartz, whose veins reflected the sun's light and proved to be a brilliant contrast to the dark soil and rich hues of green vegetation that seemed to be standing up straight while giving thanks to the earth for sustaining their precious lives.

Comforted by the fact that at least one of her accomplishments was thriving, she headed back to the porch and her cup of tea. How long she'd been out there, she wasn't sure, and it really didn't matter. The day was hers, she remembered, but best not to waste it away. Besides, her feet reminded her that the thin soles of her slippers were no protection against the earth's chilled surface.

Upon reaching the porch and her cold cup of tea, she respectfully glanced one more time at her damaged plots, sighed, and thought how frustrated Stephen would be when she told him about their visit from Peter Rabbit.

Chapter 31

Feeling satisfied that she had made good headway on the paperwork that filled her desk, Allie sat back and checked the time. She had just about an hour to regroup, get something to eat, and then meet with her clients. If she was efficient with her time, she could grab a salad at the deli across the street, get in a walk, and be back by one. Enough time then to do a quick review of her clients' histories and updates.

The fresh air immediately revived her as she exited the building, and she felt her spirits lift upon entering the deli. It was the same lunchtime crowd as usual, familiar faces who shared her culinary desires. After a few greetings and with salad in hand, she decided to go back outside to eat. The day was comfortably warm and if she didn't take advantage of it, she knew that she would regret it once in sessions throughout the afternoon. Seeing that all the tables were full, she decided to take her walk first with the destination of the park in mind. There she would find a quiet place to eat and relax.

As she watched the time and ate her meal, she willed herself to slow down and breathe. *Listen to your own breathing,* she kept telling herself. *Slow it down, breathe deeply, enjoy the warmth of the sun on your face. Don't ignore the moment.* The mantra began, and she was proud of herself for staying focused on taking care of herself. The desire to shut her eyes and to sleep came and went as reality reminded her of the time. *Forget the self-absorption,* she thought. *Did you really think that you could escape?* She snapped the lid of the plastic salad container shut, finished her drink, sighed taking one last look at the outside world, and pushed herself off the bench and back to work.

Checking her appointment schedule, she noted the first two clients' names and did a quick review of their files. They both suffered mental distress but were extremely different in their history and responsiveness to her therapy. Sometimes, she could overlap some of the therapy applications or even duplicate them to save her time in preparation. She would never admit this to any of her associates, but saving time was the bottom line.

Her third client, Michael, was her challenge. She knew that she would have to find ways to break through to him, and him to her, to keep from losing him forever to the system. She had decided that she would succeed, that he was worth saving. Not that the other clients weren't. However, there was something that drew her to him, and she had no idea what it was or where it was coming from. It had nothing to do with sexual attraction. She knew that. Perhaps it was all in the mystery of him. She opened his file to the first pages to read once again what she had read many times before, not wanting to overlook any details that might help to piece together this damaged human being.

Born Michael Edward Bingham in 1946 to an Althaia (ne) Zabat Bingham and a Robert Stephen Bingham in Big Sur, California, on March 4, he was delivered at home without any complications. His medical records indicated nothing of note, just the normal childhood ailments. He had been immunized properly, suggesting that his parents were responsible ones. Both were now deceased. Records indicated that he'd had a sibling who died in childbirth, no name given. A third sibling, male, home birth as well, survived. No name given. Placed in foster care from the age of eight, Michael had run away at age thirteen. He had been educated in California but had not completed high school. His work record was sporadic. He'd never held a job longer than a few months at a time and seemed to have worked at odd jobs just to survive.

The more disturbing facts glared from the page, and she had highlighted them in red. He was an alcoholic, now recovering, had abused drugs in large quantities, had come very close to losing his life because of them, and had been in three facilities, including this current one. He was considered a flight risk at all three facilities, having successfully "escaped" the confines of the first two, if only for a short time. She had been told by her supervisor that his admittance to this facility was his last chance, and he trusted that she would work her magic. If not,

Michael would find himself a ward of the state in an institution from which he would never be free. She hadn't bothered to read through his admittance records, so struck had she been not only by the supervisor's apparent confidence in her abilities but also by his threat. One or the other, or maybe both combined, piqued her interest in her new client, and she was determined to save him. The notes that she had added to his record since working with him were detailed but not revealing. She believed, though, that given time, she would be able to complete this file on a positive note.

The three meetings today were individual ones. She looked forward to these sessions even though she enjoyed the group work. Today would be the first time that she could spend an uninterrupted hour with each one of the clients with the goal of moving forward with them in some way. Michael's appointment came at the end of the afternoon. She had purposely scheduled him so that, if she needed to, she could extend the hour, which she hoped she'd do.

Michael had been told earlier in the day by one of the attendants that he would be meeting with his therapist later in the afternoon. He digested the information without any consideration until the attendant added that it would be by himself this time and that he would be going to a different room for the meeting. The attendant kept his concern to himself but feared that Michael might act out when he was taken to a new location. He had witnessed this scenario with others too many times.

Michael had been through this before: the group, then the doc, then back to the group and so on and so on. He found it just a bit humorous that the attendant thought it necessary to prepare him for the unknown. He wondered, though, if this meant that he would not be given his notebook, if it was going to be one of those sit, stare, and wait-for-a-response sessions. If that was the case, then they might as well leave him right where he was. He was not inclined to "talk" to anyone about anything. However, he longed for the notebook and the empty pages that needed to be filled. It had surprised him when the floodgates opened in him. He hadn't meant to reveal anything about Stephen, but he had appeared right in front of Michael as Michael had last seen him, and he had begged Michael to bring him back. How could he not? He had failed him before but would not do so again.

As he waited out the afternoon hours for his session to begin, he began mentally composing all that he would tell his notebook. The details were easy to recall but uncomfortable to reveal. The facts were imprinted solidly in his mind. But his feelings were a jumbled mix, and he found it difficult to assign the correct emotion to a detailed incident. There were too many emotions clamoring to be noticed, to be affirmed. It never occurred to him that they could also be negated. Each one was real and permanent, in his mind.

"Are you ready, Michael?" The attendant stood in the doorway, holding the door open, inviting Michael to come with him.

"Yeah, but don't take me to a padded cell. Been there, done that." He gave the attendant a wry smile. "Promise?"

"No worries, Michael. I promise. The room I'm taking you to *is* padded but not called a cell, for Pete's sake. Took that lingo out a long time ago." He stopped, watching Michael to see if he picked up on the humor. He thought it funny. Maybe Michael didn't. He was relieved when Michael said, "Funny. Real funny."

"Just trying to keep it light, my man. Just trying to keep it light. You okay?"

"'Course I am," Michael said as he brushed by the attendant. "Are you?"

The attendant gave him a pat on the back, laughed, and said, "You're all right, man."

Together they walked down the long corridor and entered the room. She was waiting for him. There was a table, two chairs, and a window. Stark but practical, he thought. Comfortable-looking chairs which was a good thing. He noted no padding on the walls and turned to make a snide remark to the attendant, but he'd already left. Disappointed that he couldn't keep the repartee going, he decided that he would pick it up with him later. It would give him more time to really think of a zinger. Besides, he liked the guy.

"Hi, Michael. It's really good to see you again." Allie moved from the window and pointed to a chair. "Have a seat."

He noticed it before she sat down. She had nothing with her but a pad and pen. Where was his notebook? He had been half joking earlier about another sit-and-stare session, but now it seemed that it was no joke. He made no move to sit.

"Michael? Would you please sit down?"

She was already comfortably occupying one chair and had placed her pad on the table between them. Her smile was lovely. He liked that about her. It put him at ease most of the time, but right now he only felt betrayed. It was illogical, he knew, to feel this about her, but he couldn't help it. Hadn't she been the one who was so excited that he had filled pages? Wasn't she the one who visited him, uninvited and unethically, in his private room with the notebook, hoping that he would take it from her and write? He remembered that meeting even through the drug-induced haze he had been experiencing. So why wasn't the notebook here? What was she up to? Did she really think that he would carry on a conversation with her after all this time without one? *Get real lady,* he thought.

"We have an hour together, Michael, and I think that you would be more comfortable sitting than standing. Anyway, I have an inferiority complex about being short and you're not helping it right now by towering over me. Come sit." She laughed gently as she said this, hoping that her attempt at humor would put him more at ease.

"Did you bring my notebook?" He did not move. He needed to know.

Allie smiled again. "Of course, I did, Michael. Of course. Come sit."

Chapter 32

Eliza sat back down for one last go at it for the day. The story that she was working on now seemed to come in stops and starts, unfortunately more stops than starts. She wasn't frustrated by it, however, for she knew that this was part of the process. But the story line itself still seemed vague to her and almost an insult to her intelligence. How many stories had she written over the years that just poured onto the page without any hesitation? Perhaps she was slowing down, had lost some of the enthusiasm and creativity she'd possessed in her earlier years as an author. She had heard of writers who were so prolific at one stage in their career but then stopped even though, from an objective standpoint, they had plenty of productive years ahead of them. She always wondered what that would be like, to have it one day and lose it the next. Her fear now was that she might be falling into that category.

Reason took hold of her as she fumbled through her negative thinking, and she came to believe that she was not writing fluidly because her mind was not 100 percent in the zone. She knew why. Stephen kept appearing, shoving his way in between original thoughts that never came to completion because of his interloping. Her mind would then dwell on him, accompanied by an uneasiness that she couldn't identify. And so, it went like that all morning. The breaks from her work were her way to clear her mind of him before she continued. But he always returned, insisting upon her full attention.

Looking at her watch and realizing that she hadn't eaten since breakfast, she backed up what little she had accomplished and shut the laptop down. *Enough of that,* she thought. Not hungry and knowing she had done nothing to work up an appetite, she decided that fresh air and a bit of exercise before it started to cool down with the late-afternoon fog would be good for her. She knew she still had time before Stephen even called, much less arrived home.

Passing the garden plots whose damaged occupants looked no better than they did earlier that morning, she decided to head toward the rock garden, but this time went deeper into the forest, an area that she had never bothered to explore. She had no fear of becoming lost as she had a good sense of direction and, if she was careful not to stay out after the fog came in, she could always note her position by the sun. Even without it, she was confident that she could find her way back to the house. She glanced at her watch, noting the time, and decided an hour outside was all that she needed. She determined that she wouldn't go that far anyway—thirty minutes out and thirty minutes back, just far enough to find something new.

The redwoods shaded her for most of the walk. The numerous groves that shared the land with Stephen and Eliza were constantly producing offspring that in another hundred years would shade another wanderer in these woods. It never completely sunk in that some of these trees whose tops were not visible because of their height were well over three or four hundred years old, probably older. All she could do was touch their bark and hold her hand there as if expecting the tree to share its history and for her to suddenly see images of times past in which the tree stood still, strong, and observant.

Forgetting her self-imposed time constraint, now completely absorbed in the natural surroundings, an excitement grew as she blazed her trail deeper into the groves. She felt a bit like an explorer of long ago, stepping onto land that no one before her had trod. She was treading on virgin earth, she imagined, and everything that lay ahead would be seen for the first time by her and only her.

Her imagination was in full swing when she felt her shoe catch, breaking her stride. How quickly the earth came up to greet her and how slowly she realized that she had fallen, landing so that her hands, knees, and face took the brunt of the impact.

The dark, rich soil's fragrance filled her nostrils, as did the dirt, and she quickly turned her head and through her nose breathed out with force. The jolt of the fall would not be felt until later, she knew, and at this moment as she found herself in a crawling position on the forest floor, her good sense kicked in and told her to sit up and do a check of her body. Rolling to a sitting position, wiping the forest floor from her hands, she shoved up her pants to check her knees. They had let her know that they'd been as shocked as she by the unwelcomed impact on their intricate workings but upon examination, all she could see was a bit of redness and, after straightening her legs out slowly and repeating the motion a few times, nothing seemed damaged. The palms of her hands were just as red but also functioned properly.

What did hurt were her forehead and her nose. It wasn't until she touched this area that she felt wetness on her face. Her fingers came away sticky and red, with bits of redwood bark and dirt clinging to the moisture. She delicately touched the bridge of her nose and could feel some pain as well as swelling beginning. With no way to see the actual damage, she wiped what she could of the blood from her face with her shirtsleeve and continued to sit.

Trying to replay what had just happened, all she remembered was that she tripped. It must have been over a branch or rock, though she was trying to be so careful with each step that she took. She knew it didn't take much to trip when walking through an area like this. What was she thinking? Must have lost her focus for a minute. That's all it took. Stupid. How was she going to explain this to Stephen? It was bad enough that he worried about her in the garden, much less wandering around the property to parts unknown without him by her side. Well, she would have to face the music, but perhaps by the time he came home she would be in better shape, and with a little makeup and the low lamplight in the house, might be able to get by without having to explain herself.

She felt it before she looked up and saw the fog starting to wisp its way through the treetops. The air was colder, suddenly, and the dampness was almost palpable. In another thirty minutes she would be surrounded by the low, moist clouds, and she knew that she needed to make her way back. Checking the time, she could not believe that she had been walking for two hours. As she stood, she felt the stiffness in her knees that had lied to her about their condition. With a couple of good hand rubs to them and a talking-to that they'd better not fail her now, she turned to head back the way she came. This time she would look down and watch with eagle eyes what lay in front of her.

Because the ground was now her focus, she saw it. Unable to make it out clearly but realizing that this was the culprit that had tripped her up, she stopped and with her boot, tried to knock away the soil that buried most of the protruding object. Not comfortable kneeling on her injured knees, she leaned over as far as she could to pull it from the ground's grasp. As she did, she stopped as the last of the porous bone revealed itself. Dropping it to the ground, she stepped back, surprised. Was it an animal's rib? Deer most likely, poor thing.

Finding no remnants of fur or skin as her boot continued to excavate more of the loose soil, she hit another object, and this time she did crouch down and painfully moved to her knees, finding the least nagging position against the soft ground. Her hands, now sunk in the soil, worked together to expose yet another bone whose structure was that of a rib and then another and another, until she'd uncovered an area of forest floor that was strewn with what looked like the partial remains of a mature human being.

Her shock, fear, and revulsion were overridden by her curiosity and excitement. An adrenaline rush had taken control of her reasoning, which was telling her to stop, to flee. It wasn't until she uncovered the remains of a human skull whose position in the soft ground caused the eye sockets to make complete eye contact with her that she shot up and screamed, a scream heard by no one other than a jay who had been observing her grave robbing. He anticipated many good meals imbedded in the newly turned soil and eagerly awaited her departure.

She did not know how long she stood there staring down at what had once been someone. The body's bones were not all there as they would have been in life and the skull seemed damaged. She had no idea what had gone through her mind as she froze in that spot and wouldn't be able to recall much of anything that had taken place prior to finding the skeleton. Lost in a trancelike state, she realized that her surroundings were darker than before, colder, and much wetter. The fog was in and had found its way to the surface of the earth, clinging to everything, living and nonliving. She was cold and tired, and ached from the shock both physically and mentally.

Knowing that she needed to get back, she debated as to covering the bones out of respect or leaving them so that she could find them again with Stephen by her side. Common sense kicking in, she turned and as quickly as her sore knees would allow, headed for the house. The sun's intermittent and almost imperceptible light through the fog was, thankfully, enough to keep her going in the right direction. After what seemed endless hours within the forest's grasp, the house was now in sight, though still a painful distance away.

As she struggled up the path and to the first garden plot, she saw him. He saw her at the same moment, took one last nibble knowing he had time, and then looked up at her, pricking his ears as if to learn all about her adventure in the woods, then turned and was gone.

Chapter 33

She had left him by himself, leaving the notebook and pencil within reach on the table. The only thing she asked of him was to pick up the pencil and write. She would return in thirty minutes to check in on him. Her smile of encouragement lingered with him, even though he did not acknowledge it at the time.

The stillness in the room allowed him to relax. He hadn't realized how tense his body had been all the while that she was present. Releasing his fists so that his fingers slowly straightened themselves, almost one by one, then straightening his legs so that his knees unlocked, taking the pressure off his thighs, he was able to readjust his position and to reach for the notebook. How long he held it in his lap before opening to the first page he didn't know, but he had not even picked up the pencil to write when he heard the door open.

She stood in the doorway, not making any attempt to enter, but looking at him, taking in as much as she could of his progress without interrupting him. He didn't dare look in her direction but fought to stay focused on the open page, as if in deep thought as to what to write next. The pencil's original position on the table betrayed him and she noted it. However, she never said a word about it other than, "Another thirty or so, Michael." With that, she quietly closed the door and was gone.

Having read what he had already recorded, he fought to hold back the tears that were so very close to spilling. Wiping his moist eyes with the back of his hand, he then reached for the pencil and began. He knew not to think about how to begin; he just needed to record what came to him. An objective observer might assume that this man was possessed as he began feverishly scratching at the notebook pages. He did not slow down nor come to any stop as the minutes passed by. He was completely absorbed in his thoughts. The pages filled quickly, turned rapidly by his left hand so that the right hand could continue with ever-growing speed and intensity.

He was not frightened. He had invited Stephen to appear again. His little brother found his way onto the pages easily and, with a sense of joy and relief, Michael filled the first few pages with memories of Stephen as his playmate and confidant. As if trying to communicate with his brother, Michael surprised himself when detailed conversations revealed themselves to him, happy memories that had been so long ago suppressed by the reality of their young lives. He felt that Stephen and he were back in the redwood groves deep in boyhood play, running and hiding from each other, digging in the soft soil, exploring the thick undergrowth, imaginations on fire as their worldly innocence served as the kindling. Moments were recorded that caught him by surprise, and he could feel his jaw relax while a smile crept slowly into place. How he loved his brother, his best friend!

He stopped suddenly. The pencil dropped from his hand. Overwhelmed, he closed the notebook and nestled it against his chest, feeling his upper body rocking back and forth as he held tightly to the bound papers in his grasp. He did not stop the tears this time, for he wanted desperately to be blinded by them so that he could not see the small, tortured body of his brother deep in the darkness, swinging helplessly at the end of the rope, back and forth.

Chapter 34

She couldn't eat and each time she sat down to read while waiting for Stephen to return, her mind would not focus on the print but, rather, on the vivid image of the overturned earth that unveiled its secret to her and that stubbornly persisted in blocking everything else out. Trying to will time to speed up so that she could be with her husband and tell him what she had discovered, her frustration at his absence began to mount. She watched her mother's mantel clock slowly tick away the time and when nine chimes filled the living room, she could feel panic beginning. She hadn't heard from him yet, and he said he would call before leaving. It was a good three-hour drive and if he hadn't left yet, he would not be home until after midnight. How could he be so thoughtless as not to let her know what was up? She had tried to call but only reached voicemail each time, which fed her frustration and growing anger with him. Not wanting to upset him, she left only a brief question each time with a simple request: "Where are you? Please call me."

Perhaps it was because of the afternoon's disturbing discovery, the dull yet persistent aching of her body's injuries, her growing frustration with her husband, and her anger that she found herself unable to keep her eyes open, fighting an overwhelming fatigue that seemed to descend upon her much like the dense fog that had settled on and all around the exterior of the house. The urge to climb into bed, pull up the covers, and fall into a sweet cocoon of darkness fought against her need to stay awake and wait for the call, no matter how late it became. She prepared a mug of black tea and stood in the kitchen, afraid to sit down, afraid to succumb to her body's demands. By ten thirty, she had rearranged the dishes in the cabinets and sorted through the utensil drawers, ridding them of the duplicate bottle openers, peelers, and an unexplained number of plastic funnels for cooking, as well as the odds and ends that had no right to be there in the first place. And still no call.

Now her anger had given way to a growing fear of disaster. It was like him to forget to call and just start home. He had done that before. Just gotten sidetracked. But she couldn't help but worry this time as the drive home in the dark on this highway could be an accident waiting to happen, especially if he was at all tired and had had a few drinks. She had read of so many fatalities that had taken place on the coast road, with cars not being found until days later when someone put two and two together and called the police to report a missing person. One minute the driver had been maneuvering hairpin turns with ease and the next, for whatever reason, had left the roadway as if to fly off across the Pacific, only to have gravity win by drawing him with growing force to the rocks below the steep cliffs.

Forcing herself to dismiss this thought, she remembered that he had a list of attorneys and legal contacts in his desk drawer. She chided herself for not remembering this earlier. Stephen had made a point of telling her where it was and giving her the information she would need if, God forbid, anything should happen to him. She rifled through the drawer in a panic, trying to find who she thought he might have been with earlier that day. He had told her the names, but they had not registered with her, so she could not recall them. Perhaps if she saw a name, it would ring a bell.

None of the names listed sounded familiar to her, though. How could that be? She knew that she wasn't that dull. As she looked through the list again, it dawned on her that all the addresses and area codes were on the East Coast. Not making sense of this, she dug deeper into his files but could find no San Francisco attorneys. Wanting to give him the benefit of the doubt, she reasoned that he had not updated the list since they had moved back to the West Coast. It made some sense but did not ease the urgency she felt to contact someone, anyone, who might have been with him earlier in the day.

With her hands tied and realizing that the best she could do at this point was to wait it out, she decided to go to bed and read until she fell asleep. After making sure the house was locked up, she shuffled to the bedroom clutching a mug of hot milk and stopped to grab the book that she had left on the couch. Two perfect companions to keep her company in an otherwise empty bed.

Gingerly climbing in, as her sore knees complained, she immediately felt relieved to be off her feet, to welcome the end of a long day. She adjusted her body under the sheets and comforter, arranging the pillows just the way she liked, propped her book open upon her tummy, and then reached for the milk.

For a moment, she felt that all was right with the world and that she had earned this luxurious moment before her eyes would fall shut. She embraced the feeling of the warm liquid sliding down her throat and could feel its heat fan out into her chest. How many times had she fallen asleep with a cup of milk? As far back as she could remember, as her mother had taught her to do and as Eliza could still see her mother doing in her own bed or in her chair, sipping her milk and reading. It was so very comforting to do as her mother had done. It brought her closer to her in these late-night moments, as if they had prepared, together in the kitchen, their nightly cocktail and perhaps shared a giggle about something that struck them as humorous at the very same time. She did miss her mother but sensed her always around her each day, at times seeming so present that Eliza found herself looking around for her, perhaps standing by a tree or kneeling in the dirt across the garden plot as she prepared for the new plantings. Her mother was always present in the garden.

She could feel the milk's sedation at work and had dozed off a couple of times, only to have the book start to fall enough to jolt her awake. Trying to finish one last paragraph, she attempted to keep her eyes open but finally gave in. She marked her place, closed the book, and placed it on the bedside table. Turning off the light, she slipped down under the covers, rolled to her side, and closed her eyes.

The uneasiness revisited her and caught her by surprise. It was the same uneasiness that she'd experienced in the kitchen this morning in front of Stephen. It had frozen her to the countertop, had sent her heart into abnormal rhythms, and had brought stinging tears to her eyes. Awake now, she turned on her back and felt the moisture slowly find its way down and around the contours of her face. The sadness was present again, not fear but such grief that she could not control the sobs that began to form deep within and that, in the stillness of the room, almost choked her as she released them. Sitting up in bed, her body convulsed as some primordial angst insisted upon freedom from its unknown depths. And she succumbed to it.

How long she suffered she was not sure. It might have been minutes; it might have been all night. All she knew was that her whole body awoke in agony, as if she had been beaten where she lay. The light from the rising sun appeared through the lace droplets of the bedroom curtains, casting delicately parceled beams across the room and onto the disarrayed covers of her bed. From her half-shut swollen eyes, her fatigued and embattled brain somehow was able to calculate that the previous day and night's fog had lifted. In realizing this, Eliza experienced a brief instant of relief until the reality of her situation sunk in.

Stretching her hand to the vacant space next to her, she reached for him. She stretched her arm farther, only to find no one in bed with her. Although she had shoved covers up and down all night, it seemed, Stephen's side of the bed indicated that it had gone untouched. Not willing to accept that he was not there, she lay back down, quietly listening for his familiar movements in the bathroom, and when not heard, she focused every ounce of her hearing on the kitchen sounds. She thought that she could smell his coffee brewing. However, she heard nothing that would indicate Stephen's presence. Afraid to get out of bed and to confirm her suspicions, she called out his name. "Stephen? Stephen?" With no response, she knew. Her stomach felt squeamish, and her heart's controlled rhythm once again was interrupted. The reality of the evening before, when she had fought against her emotions during Stephen's unexplained absence, once again filled her mind with worry. Climbing out of bed, she stumbled to the bathroom, threw up, and proceeded to clean up to face the day, whatever it would bring.

Chapter 35

He held on to the bat, clutching it with such ferocity long after there was no reason to defend himself. How long, he had no idea. He then loosened his grip ever so slightly and held it as one might a cane to aid one's weakened legs as he kneeled to see better whether his father's chest was rising and falling. Standing up slowly as pain began to intensify throughout his body, he willed his arm to raise his weapon to his waist as he gingerly kicked his father's side, ready to attack again if the monster should suddenly stir. He could not look at the face that no longer held any resemblance to the man who had ruled their lives for so long. It lay mashed, bloodied, and almost buried in the sweetness of the forest floor as the once green and fragrant redwood boughs, now coated with a crusting crimson liquid, suffered the unwelcomed intrusion of death.

Then he remembered. Mama. Stephen. Still holding on to the bat, he backed away from his father's body, slowly and with a growing fear that he had not really ended his father's life. The fear that if he turned his back on the body in the forest, it would be upon him before he could think and would surely take its revenge on him. The fear that had been well nurtured for the last eight years of his life and that had become an integral element in his makeup. Without that fear, he would not know how to survive.

Out of sight now, he turned and tried to run to his mother and to Stephen, but everything hurt him, and to take even one step toward them sent excruciating shots of pain through his body. But he had no choice. With tears streaming down his face, he tried to cry away the pain and heard his own voice produce unfamiliar sounds that gave him away. Any beast in the area would stay away from this wounded animal, at least until the death throes had ended. He was frightened, not only by the pain and what that surely meant, but also by the thought that he would not reach his family, that he would collapse somewhere deep within this forest. He knew that he would die as his mother, father, and Stephen had. He needed to get to Stephen before then. He needed to hold onto his lifeless little brother while he, too, became lifeless. He wanted to be near his mother, who had tried to protect them but who was too weak. He wanted to whisper in her cold ear how much he loved her even if she had failed them all. And he wanted them both to know that he had ended the fear that had kept them captive. That now in death the three of them could peacefully sleep in each other's arms.

Chapter 36

"Oh, Michael." Her voice was but a whisper and filled with sadness as she stood in the doorway, watching her client in such pain. He was not aware of her presence. It was all she could do not to run to him, to kneel beside him, and let him rock gently in her arms. She knew better.

As she waited for his sobs to subside, she silently congratulated herself for bringing him the notebook. Obviously, it had opened doors that had been locked tightly within him and that the group sessions could never gain entrance to. She had done one thing right. She also knew that once the doors were unlocked, her client would experience a reaction, one that would be upsetting to be sure not only to the client, but also to her. It was one of her weaknesses, she knew, that she felt too deeply their pain, and because of that, she struggled to gain detachment so that even a small amount of objectivity could help wipe out her need to be too close to them. In some cases, this came much easier to her, as she didn't like the person to begin with. Another secret that she needed to keep under wraps. So far, she had done well in not revealing to herself or to her colleagues her real feelings about her more objectionable clients. She did not want to betray her own standard of professionalism.

But here was Michael. And here she was unable to decide, fixated on the process that she had established for him and that seemed to be working. Observing him now, his emotions, raw as they were, revealed a damaged human who in the privacy of this small space, with nothing but a pencil and paper, was beginning to see what he had chosen not to see. And if she was careful and patient with him, perhaps he would share in his revelations. Indecisive about whether to close the door behind her and leave him alone or go to him, she felt as though her feet were cemented to the floor. *Come on, girl! Make up your mind. Do your job!* She snapped to as her internal reprimand sunk in. Taking a step into the room, she let the door close behind her, while taking a long, deep breath and then letting it out slowly to calm herself.

He looked at her as tears ran down his face, dripping onto his shirt, the collar and front absorbing most of the moisture. The edge of his notebook was also absorbing the dampness, and puckered streaks of cardboard had begun to appear on the partially hidden front cover. He had stopped rocking now and sat sniffling as he continued to stare at Allie. She thought that she heard his silent plea for help. Was it his eyes that sent the message to her? Was it the slumped body still clutching the object of his pain? She saw in him at that moment a need for connection. She was sure of it. Because of this, she turned and pulled up a chair, placing it in front of him, and then sat facing him.

"Can you talk to me, Michael?" she asked, forming her question so as not to belittle him. No response came. She glanced around the room for tissues or paper towels, something to offer him so that he could begin to regain some sense of composure. Seeing the tissue box, she retrieved it from the counter and brought it to him, holding it out to him. She could see that his grasp on the notebook was strong and that releasing one hand to take a tissue might not happen. He would become vulnerable even for a short moment. Taking a tissue from the box, she laid it on top of his clutched hands and smiled at him. Then she stood up and moved to the far side of the room. She could hear his movements, grabbing the tissues, one after another, quickly. He was trying desperately to clear his nose, to wipe away what had served as his curtain hiding what he could not bring himself to see. She knew all of this and so waited patiently until he was done.

"I'm sorry. I...I am sorry." She turned at the sound of his voice, exhausted and tense. "I think I ruined the book." He had laid the notebook on his lap and was running the palm of his right hand over its surface as if to wipe away the damage he had caused to it.

Moving toward him, she reassured him. "It's all right. It's nothing to worry about. It's what's inside that counts, and that is still safe in your keeping." She was standing in front of him now and, without thinking, placed her hand on his and softly told him, "It's over. It's going to be okay."

Chapter 37

Stephen had lied to her. He had truly lied to her in the most hurtful way he could imagine. He knew that she would be worried sick, that he was putting her through hell. He also knew that he could not work his way through this one as easily as he had done in the past. The way things were going between them, he wouldn't be surprised if this was the last straw for her. She would leave and never have contact with him again. He deserved whatever decision she made. He also knew that she loved him, and he loved her. How far could that love sustain them on this ever-tightening thread that they called their marriage? He had done an awfully good job of weakening the thread; he knew that. She had done just as good a job in repairing it each time. Waiting for it to snap was becoming unbearable for him, and he wondered if Eliza felt the same way. Everything was just a matter of time, he reasoned. He could see no future with her and he had tried to. He had pretended to be a part of her life with as much enthusiasm as his lying heart could contrive. Did she suspect him? He wondered and tried to recall any moment together in which she had been transparent but could think of none. No. This was all his doing. He had brought this on himself and now on Eliza, and he would have to find a way to end his betrayal to her.

She would never understand. *He* didn't understand. How could he try to explain anything to her if he didn't understand it? Driving away from the house the day before, he'd struggled with leaving. He had nowhere to go but knew that he could not be with her another day, although he didn't know why. He needed to figure himself out. And he would need time to do it.

Ever since the second phone call, the one with no one on the other end, he had been plagued by a feeling of approaching doom. Not doom in the sense of death, but more like the end of something. The calls prompted him to be on the defensive, to be on guard, because the enemy was ready to destroy him. This thought had begun to permeate his thinking recently. Getting away, he could take an accounting of his life. He could hear himself think without the pressure of sharing or having to justify his behavior to her. He loved her and because she seemed to love him, he knew why she showed concern for him. But he didn't need it, didn't want it, and now had realized that he didn't want her. Did he really love her?

The highway wound its way through the coastal landscape as he headed south. He wasn't conscious of how far he had driven while wrestling with his thoughts until he noticed that he was in the red zone on the gas gauge. Taken by surprise, he chastised himself aloud while banging his fist against the steering wheel. How stupid could he be? Where was he going to find gas around here? Probably not for a good fifty miles or so. Had he passed a station within the last thirty miles? He tried to recollect the scenery he had just come through. Cambria. He had come through Cambria and it hadn't even registered with him at the time. Checking his GPS, he breathed a sigh of relief. Only twenty-five miles behind him.

Making a U-turn, he headed north. This time, he would pay attention. He needed to keep his eye on the gas gauge, anyway. To keep his mind from wandering, he turned on the CD player and turned up the volume. Opening the driver's-side window, he forced himself to take in the good sea air and to relax. He was not going to run out of gas; he could control his thinking and by doing so, block out any thoughts of Eliza.

He pulled into the first station that he came to and whispered a "Thank you, God" to no one. Cambria was not a big place, but it attracted tourists with its interesting shops and unique restaurants. It always seemed to have a good number of visitors on its sidewalks, and it felt like a tiny metropolis hidden away on the coast between Monterey and Santa Barbara. He liked Cambria, just hadn't had the desire to see it again and again as Eliza would have liked.

Eliza. She was waiting for him. An uneasiness swept over him as he removed the nozzle from the tank and placed it back in the pump. The need to distance himself from her consumed his thinking as he approached the exit. Without hesitation, he turned south on Highway 1, leaving Cambria with the intention of never seeing it again.

The beaches were more inviting and easier to get to the farther south he traveled. Not like the coastline around Big Sur. You had to be a billy goat, he thought, to access some of them, the ones that were special. And that was okay because once on the sands of these beaches, you were literally between a rock and a hard place. The rock being the towering cliffs that you had just descended and the hard place being the roaring Pacific Ocean that hid from view the undercurrents, the rip tides, the sharp drops into oblivion, and the real power of the waves. The smart ones would never venture into this water and would never turn their backs on it. They would be conscious of and mark the times of high and low tides. And that was the beauty and intrigue of the place. But the southern beaches were wide expanses of sand and the water was warmer. The waves were gentle compared to the Central Coast and were usually populated with surfers and swimmers. The beaches were colorful canvases of umbrellas, bodies of every shape and size, beach towels and blankets, and beach paraphernalia that cluttered while serving as borderlines for spots that families had carved out for their day's stay.

He decided to pull over and stretch his legs. Taking his snacks and water, he headed out to the warm sands. How far he would walk, he hadn't a plan in mind. Stretch, breathe, eat, and rest a bit. Not many people populated this beach, he noticed. Mostly mothers with infants and toddlers too young to be in school, and boogie boarders and surfers who probably should be in school. He found a spot away from the sunbathers and the noisy children and settled into the sand. Having finished his food, he took off his shirt and rolled it up, placing it under his head. Lying back, he closed his eyes and focused on the sun's warmth on his bare chest and face. The heat from the sand and the sun's rays bathed him in comfort, and he could feel himself falling deeper and deeper into a welcomed sleep.

Chapter 38

It wasn't distinguishable at first. A sound like the wind howling through the trees on a stormy night. He had always crawled deeper under the covers of his bed and covered his ears when the howling began. He knew it would go away eventually but in his four-year-old mind, it seemed to take forever. And now he tried to listen but could not stay focused. Drifting in and out of consciousness was his only brief relief from pain. And the cold. The cold was all around him. Not able to move even to curl up his body to keep warm, he started to shiver uncontrollably, so the gentle relief of unconsciousness was kept at bay by his own body's gyrations. But the sound continued to grow now. It moved closer to him, he could tell, and he was afraid but couldn't move his hands to cover his ears. He cried silently and the wetness stung his small face as the salt found its way into his wounds.

The voice was not his mama's nor his father's nor Michael's. It was muffled and he couldn't understand what it was saying to him. Other voices joined in and they, too, were muffled. Someone was leaning over him, touching him gently, and saying something. He struggled to make his mouth form words so that he could make a connection but all he could verbalize were cries and sobs and with each one, the pain increased. He thought he had called out for his mama, but she had not come. Perhaps he had called out for his brother, but he was not there either. Then he felt hands lift him from the ground and lay him on a bed in a very bright room that flew through the night, while the howling, now deafening, continued as he lost consciousness one more time.

The sand hit him squarely in the face while the earth seemed to rumble below him. He heard the voices before he opened his eyes. Upon doing so, he rose to his elbows and took his bearings. Wiping the kicked-up sand from his face, his attention was drawn to the water where a small group was gathered. A rescue had caused quite a stir among the beachgoers, who watched with growing concern as the medics tended to the three still bodies sprawled on the beach just at the water's edge.

Another ambulance had arrived, its siren blaring and then winding down with a sickening wail. The first two were already in the parking area.

Stephen stayed where he was. He hated to be one of those people who fed on someone else's misfortune. He could imagine what was going on and the possible outcome. He didn't need to see it up close and personal. Looking at his watch, he calculated that he had been asleep for over an hour. He felt rested, clear headed, and relaxed. Something had woken him, though. He had been dreaming. He knew that, but he couldn't remember anything about it other than sounds and something covering his face. Must have been the sand. But the sound he just couldn't place. It didn't matter anyway. How many times had he dreamt without being able to recall a single detail? Though he was always uncomfortably aware of a lingering dream shadow, Stephen had taught himself not to pay any attention to it. It was only a dream, after all.

He left the beach without looking back at the growing crowd at the water's edge. He was not the least bit curious to see who would part the crowd, who would be carried off the beach to a waiting ambulance. Whoever the poor souls were, they were in good hands. And that bit of knowledge freed him from joining the group who were feigning concern over perfect strangers.

As he reached for the car door handle, his phone vibrated in his pant pocket. He did not answer it and let it go to voicemail. The number was not one he recognized, nor was there a message. Sighing with relief, he deleted this call and put his cell back in his pocket.

No reason he could think of not to continue south. He would reach Santa Barbara in less than an hour if he got started now. Knowing he was getting a bit too close to rush hour on Route 1, he prepared himself to crawl into town with the rest of the vehicles on the road. That was all right, he thought. No deadlines to meet, no one waiting for him. The freedom he felt now caused him to smile while his whole body relaxed into the driver's seat as he turned back onto the highway.

Chapter 39

The 911 call should have been made earlier in the day, she knew, but she held onto the false assumption that she would hear his car come down the drive any minute now. But with the sun lower in the sky and the day coming to an end, she panicked. No matter how absentminded he had been in the past about things, she knew that this excuse was no longer holding water. Something had gone wrong. She tried to keep at bay the thought that he was in trouble. If he'd had an accident coming home last night, he might not be discovered for days. Who would know to look over a cliff unless she alerted them?

The voice on the other end of the call was calm and straightforward while it requested all the pertinent information the authorities needed to do their job. She had forgotten Stephen's license plate number, but while stammering over this volunteered information was reassured that it wasn't needed. They had the information. Someone from the police would be coming out to speak with her. Upon hearing those words, all of it became too real and it was all she could do to control her voice and not to release her constricted throat and the sobs that lay just behind it. She couldn't remember everything that she had said, and she was frustrated that she had not asked how long it would be until an officer arrived.

As the hours grew later, the sun's light was only hinted at while the high clouds transitioned from white to shades of rose as the fog crept in below them. She watched for the police from the front window, afraid to move away in case she should miss their approach. Silly, she knew, but her longing for someone to come down the drive was now overwhelming. She willed the arrival. Then she saw the headlights flickering through the trees as a car slowly approached and stopped in front of the house. Both the passenger and driver's doors opened simultaneously as two officers got out and took a moment to readjust their waist-belt gear, as if needing to regain the correct balance before taking a step forward. She went to the door but did not open it until she heard a knock.

"Good evening, Mrs. Bingham?" The younger of the two greeted her with a kindness that warmed her. The older one stood a bit behind him and nodded his head. "I'm Officer Cormack and this is Officer Vance. You called in an emergency about your missing husband? May we come in?" She stood back and motioned them into the room.

"Thank you for coming, officers. I'm sorry that you had to come so far out of your way. We're off the beaten track but we love it here. Have been here for..." She stopped in mid-sentence as she heard herself speak. *They're not here for a social visit, you idiot. Stop gabbing on.* Feeling her face heat, she secretly thanked them for not reacting in any way other than to wait patiently for her to finish. "Sorry. Can I get you something?" She had already started for the kitchen, praying that her embarrassment could be forgotten over a good cup of tea.

"No, thanks, Mrs. Bingham. We wanted to let you know that we have located your husband's car down in Santa Barbara. Haven't located him yet, but we have a missing person's out on him. Do you know if he has any connections there, any family, someone he might be trying to get to? Anything that you can think of, the smallest details, will help us."

He's not at the bottom of a cliff crushed against the rocks. He made it through the night. These thoughts repeated themselves again and again in her mind. *Thank God. Thank God.*

"Mrs. Bingham? Do you think you have any information that can help us? Ma'am?" The younger one was speaking to her.

"I'm so sorry. I'm just grateful he's alive. I mean...I was worried he had had an accident coming home from the city. He loves to take the coastal route, but at night I always worry. What did you ask me? Sorry."

"Information, Mrs. Bingham, is going to help us find him sooner. Does he have any connections in Santa Barbara? Family? Business?" The younger officer had his notebook open and pen ready.

Did he? She tried to remember if he had ever mentioned

anyone and no one came to mind. Santa Barbara? Odd, because he had told her so many times that he wouldn't be caught dead— a bad choice of words, she thought—in the overpopulated and overdeveloped areas of Southern California, not even for a visit. She remembered this because she could never convince him to take a road trip or, for that matter, fly there. But now they were telling her that he was in Santa Barbara? She couldn't compute it.

"No, no. Not that I'm aware of. He never liked the idea of going much farther south than Cambria. Are you sure you wouldn't like something? Please sit down. Should have offered when you first came in. Coffee, tea?"

"You did offer. We're fine, but thanks," the older one answered, leaning forward. "We have a description of him and an image from the DMV, but can you give us any distinguishing features that would help us identify him? What was he wearing when he left?" He looked at his partner, who nodded his head as if to reassure him that appropriate questions were asked.

"No, not really. Nothing of note, but he was wearing a blue dress shirt and khaki pants. I think he had a sports jacket with him. Casual business attire. I do have a better photo of him than what you have, though. Would that help?"

"Sure, that would be terrific. Do you mind if we borrow it? Won't lose it. Promise." For a brief instant, Officer Vance reminded her of her father. He had always made promises to her and had kept them.

"Oh, of course. It's right here." She pointed to the side table next to the fireplace as she moved to take it from its place. Removing it from the frame and handing it to the older officer, she managed a smile. "I'll keep you to your promise."

"Of course, ma'am. Wouldn't have it any other way," he said. "There is one more question. Did anything occur between you and Mr. Bingham before he left? An argument, perhaps?"

Had anything occurred? No, other than she did not want him to leave. But she had never said this aloud to Stephen. And there was no possible way she could explain her feelings to the officer. She couldn't explain it herself.

"No. As matter of fact, I almost went with him but decided against it. My choice. He left assuring me that he would call before leaving the city and would be home that evening."

"Pardon me for asking, but would you say, then, that you are on good terms with your husband and he with you?"

"Yes, of course." She saw his facial muscles relax, and she dismissed her fabrication as quickly as it appeared.

"Good. Always need to ask. Do you have anyone you could stay with, Mrs. Bingham? Or are you all right being out here on your own? Could we call someone for you?"

Thinking that he must be a father with grown kids who never stopped worrying about them, she was touched by his kindness and concern. "No. But I am perfectly fine. Please don't concern yourself about me. Just concentrate on finding Stephen. I've been out here for years and would feel uncomfortable being anywhere else, frankly. I'll be okay knowing that a search is on. Can I ask you one thing, though?" She took a step closer to them.

"Sure, of course," the younger one encouraged her.

"Will you be sure to keep me informed? The one thing that I know will get to me out here is not hearing anything at all. If I can be reassured that you will stay in contact with updates, I'll be just fine."

"We can make sure that that happens. Of course. But we want you to be sure to let us know if you hear from him or learn or remember something that will help us find him sooner. Will you do that?" As the younger one finished his request, he reached into his pocket and handed her his business card. The older officer did the same.

"Yes, yes, of course. I can't thank you enough. You know, I wouldn't think too much of him going missing like this if he had headed north. We've spent time up there, I mean, in the city, San Francisco. It would make more sense to me, I mean I think that I could accept it easier, but Santa Barbara?" She let the city's name hang in the air.

"Understood. Hopefully we'll get to the bottom of this soon, Mrs. Bingham. Lots of folks go missing every day. Some just want to drop out for a bit. They aren't missing in their minds.

Just on a vacation, if you will, from their lives." Seeing Eliza's look of surprise, he quickly added, "That's not saying anything about Mr. Bingham, you understand, but most of our missing person's reports end with a happy reunion. Keep that in mind, all right?" He didn't expect her to respond, nor was she going to. She just smiled at the young officer, who probably was still wet behind the ears and had not lost his optimism about life.

"Well, if you're sure that we have all that you can give us and that you're going to be all right on your own, we'll leave you. Thank you for your help, and we'll be in touch with any information that we get. Have a good evening."

She watched the headlights illuminate the drive, and the brush and trees on either side of their immediate path, as the car headed away from her, leaving darkness in its wake. She locked the door and began to close the curtains across the living room windows when she remembered the overturned soil, the remains, and the urgency she had felt to show them to Stephen. Why such a disturbing find had not come to mind a few minutes ago when the conversation with the police about Stephen took place she found it hard to imagine. She'd completely forgotten it, sidetracked by a missing husband. If she had remembered, would it have been a mistake not to tell the police? No, she had to tell Stephen first. She had to show him and depend on him to guide them in the next step. He would know what to do, and that would be to call the police. She knew that speaking to them without his knowledge was wrong. It was between Stephen and her for the time being.

The thought of not knowing when she would see him again hung in the air all about her. Oh God! What more could happen today? Uncomfortable with that question and certainly not entertaining an answer, she finished closing the house for the night, warmed her milk, and headed for bed and what she hoped would be some sleep if only for a little while. "Good night, Stephen, my love," she whispered turning her body to the still vacant space that remained undisturbed while her tears ran freely onto the pillow.

Chapter 40

1953

The area's residents began hearing about the death at the Bingham house. Even though they enjoyed their seclusion from one another, the community was still, for the most part, connected, so word spread at the village market, then reached the deepest recesses of the Ventana Wilderness. Nothing like this in living memory had ever occurred, and it created a blemish on the idyllic environment they had created for themselves.

The family was not well known as they tended to keep to themselves, but the owner of the market knew the wife as a regular customer coming in about twice a month. She was warm and friendly, always talking about her boys. Even though she didn't know her neighbors, she would always ask for any updates on the locals. It seemed to the market owner that she was a lonely sort, and the two trips in to the market were her way of staying in touch.

He had never seen the husband. Wouldn't know who he was if he walked right up to him. The wife never spoke of him, he realized, as he tried to give the authorities any useful information that could help them with the case. He was awfully sorry to hear about her death. Had he been killed too?

"We're trying to locate him," was all the officer offered.

The market owner prayed that they wouldn't ask about the children. What he had heard was horrible, and he had boys of his own about the same age. As a matter of fact, the older kids probably all went to school together. Funny, neither he nor his wife had ever made connections with the family at any of the school events. Couldn't remember even seeing them there. For that matter, they hadn't come to any of the community events, and there were not that many.

"Everyone comes!" Both arms opened wide as he turned his body from left to right as if to include the many miles that surrounded his little store while sweeping everyone up from the forests in his embrace. There wasn't anything more that he could tell them. He wished he could be of more help, he offered, as he shook hands with the two detectives. They reassured him that he had been helpful and appreciated his time. But he had to ask before they left, even though he was afraid of the possible answer.

"Should we be scared? I mean, do you think that there is someone out there ready to do more harm to us? I got a wife and two boys. Do I need to be ready to protect them from some crazy on the loose?" He did want an answer, he realized. "Not saying that I would take the law into my own hands, but if my family was threatened, I'd be God damned if I would let the same thing happen to them as happened to those poor bastards." He immediately felt ashamed of himself for referring to this family in that way and quickly corrected himself. "Sorry. I didn't mean it that way. Can't imagine what they must have gone through. Just don't want anything like that to come our way or to any of the folks down here."

The detectives responded by saying that they didn't have enough information to say one way or the other at this time but reassured him that if the community needed to know more, they would be told. With that, they left the market.

The call had come in to their office that morning from a woman who lived not far from the house. She had never met the family who were the closest to her, but she had heard them, on and off. Sometimes, if the fog was low enough and the air was real still, she had explained, sounds traveled farther than normal. No, she had not heard conversation. Rather lots of yelling, on occasion. Always a man's voice. Occasionally, she heard a cry like an animal in distress. Lots of animals out here. Little critters that fall prey to the cats, and she would always say a little prayer for the fox or deer whose life was being extinguished by the hungry jaws of a predator. She never thought much about the yelling.

She had lived in the area since birth and knew that some of the folks who lived here were real individuals.

"I mean, think of crusty old farts who don't want to be bothered by anybody. Made a point of being out here so they could do as they pleased, for the most part. There was one fellow, he's dead now, use to walk all over his property every day and yell at the top of his lungs. Couldn't really make out what he was yelling about, but I heard from others that he was just plain angry. Lived angry and died angry is what I heard. Lots of interesting folks out here."

The officer who had received the call listened patiently and waited for her to take a breath before interrupting her. "Ma'am? What is your call concerning?"

And she proceeded to tell him about the night before that had kept her awake and that she couldn't shake the feeling that there was something wrong up there at the property next to hers. The man's yelling was familiar enough, but then she was sure that she heard a younger voice screaming and a female voice as well. Definitely some kind of domestic problem, she added. Not like she had ever heard before. She tried to listen as long as she could, but she'd fallen asleep and woke up remembering this morning. Living by herself, she wasn't feeling comfortable to take the hike up to their place to check it out for herself, but she couldn't ignore what she was sure she heard, either. That's when she decided to call the police.

"Do you have an address, ma'am?" She had no idea but gave them hers, and said she'd be glad to show them the drive off the highway as she passed it all the time going to the market. "I think we'll be able to find it, ma'am. You have been very helpful. If you think of anything else that might be pertinent, give us a call back, please. You can ask for me, Sergeant Durst. Okay?"

She assured him that she would and offered, once again, to show him the place if they should get lost. "Number right there on my mailbox, big numbers and fluorescent so that you can see them easy," she added. "Don't have hardly any visitors, but when I do they never have trouble finding me in these forests." Then she suddenly burst into laughter, surprising the sergeant on the other end of the line. "Don't be looking for the box on the right side of the road, you hear? I don't live in the ocean and if you turn right going south, that's where you'll end up, in the sea. More likely, on the rocks. You be careful now."

The sergeant shook his head, wondering how much longer he could maintain his courtesy with her. "Know that highway well, ma'am. Don't you worry about it. South, ocean on the right; north, ocean on the left. Have a good day." And with that he ended the call.

Entering the drive, the officers took it slowly down the rough, narrow road. Eyes surveying the surrounding forest and brush as well as what was directly ahead of them, they were never sure what they were driving into on these calls. Most folks in these parts were law-abiding citizens who just wanted to be away from the chaos of the world. Wanted their privacy and some peace and quiet. But that did not mean that they weren't a close-knit community—just not on top of each other all the time. They were there for each other when needed.

In learning about this family, however, the warning signs had been revealed. They only hoped as they drew closer to the house that they were not walking into a tragedy that could have been prevented. Left unsaid but simultaneously in their thoughts, better to be greeted by some angry husband standing on his porch with his rifle nestled in his elbow, muzzle pointed at them with cowering wife and kids in the background, than the alternative. This was not the first time for either one of them to deal with the stresses of domestic strife going awfully wrong.

They saw it at the same time. Parking a respectable distance from the bodies, they gathered their gear and slowly, with weapons raised, got out of the car. There was no movement anywhere, but the lights were on in the house and the front door had been left open as if someone had just stepped out for the moment. One of them, upon seeing what they hoped they would not, called for backup and ambulances before they exited the car.

"Mr. Bingham? Mr. Bingham, this is the police. We are entering your house. Put down your weapon and show yourself. Now!" There was no response. "Mr. Bingham. This is the police. Put down your weapon and come out!" Still no response. The officers separated to survey both sides of the house, trying to get any visuals. What they saw indicated no struggle, nothing out of the ordinary. They saw no one in the main rooms. As they came together at the front door, with guns raised, one entered while the other followed right behind him. Surveying the front room and then moving through the house, they found no one.

"He's not here," the taller of the two announced, his voice expressing relief as well as disappointment. The backup and ambulances had arrived while they were in the house. Coming out onto the porch, their line of vision was interrupted by the ambulances' positions so that the horrific scene that had greeted them was now out of sight. They holstered their guns as the newly arrived officers approached them.

"No one in the house. Haven't searched the grounds yet," the taller of the two informed their counterparts. Before he could say more, his partner and the other two officers nodded and headed toward the garden and then behind the house. He headed toward the ambulance and to the bodies that lay about two hundred yards away.

The woman's head rested on the scattered stones that were now stained with rusted blood. Her arms, stretched out from her sides, indicated that she had fallen while trying to gain her balance. One leg lay bent under the other. Not far from her, a crumpled boy not much older than the officer's own young son lay half naked, his upper body exposed to the elements. The paramedics were working on him as they gently shifted his frail and ruined body to examine the deep trench of broken skin that encircled his waist. The officer knelt on the ground and holding a blood-soaked rope in front of him, shook his head in disbelief as he made the connection to the child next to him.

The woman was removed from the area first and placed in one of the waiting ambulances. The child, who was unconscious and barely alive, was gently placed in the second ambulance while paramedics continued to monitor him. Both mother and son disappeared down the driveway while howling sirens could be heard as they entered the highway heading north.

Chapter 41

How much farther he would go, he didn't know, but he did know that he had made a mistake from the moment he lied to her about the meetings in the city to his decisions to keep heading south. He had really made a mistake in not making any contact with her for the last two days. Even though he knew that he couldn't go back to her, to the house with her still in it, he owed her the courtesy of facing her in person. Why this rational thinking had invaded his thoughts he could not say. It came so suddenly, so unexpectedly, that he had to pull over to the side of the road to hear himself think clearly.

What was he doing? What the hell was he trying to accomplish by running away? More importantly, why was he running from her, from the place he loved, the place that he had brought Eliza to, the place that compelled him to it? He had left her alone, probably out of her mind with worry. With no thought as to her well-being, he had made a decision, a rash one that had no explanation. How could he face her with nothing to say, no way to explain himself?

He would need to call her and let her know that he was okay. He'd tell her that he would explain everything to her when he saw her, but that the most important thing was that he was okay, and was she? He would apologize repeatedly to her while trying to get her off the phone so that he could get back on the road and back to her. That would be easy enough to do, to make the call now and worry about the rest later. Reaching for his cell in his jacket pocket, he did not notice the car pull up behind him.

When he did see it in the rearview mirror, he did not panic or frantically start searching for ID and registration. A calm prevailed, and almost an audible sigh of relief escaped his throat as he put the window down and waited.

The verbal exchange was brief. They had been searching for him from a missing person's report filed by his wife. It had been a little over forty-eight hours and they were just glad that they had found him so quickly. He needed to step out of the car and come with them.

Placed carefully in the backseat of the cruiser, a partition between the front and back seats blocking his view, they asked him a series of questions determining his identity as that of Stephen Bingham. A call was placed to his wife to inform her that he was found and seemed to be all right. She was told that it was not within their rights to force him, as an adult, to return. He was asked if he wanted to speak with her. He declined, not ready to make contact, not yet. They informed him that they had no legal way of making him return but that his wife was distraught, and that he needed to tie up loose ends in the husband-and-wife department. Once found and determined to be of sound mind, there was nothing the police could do to an adult other than give him or her their strong advice.

Stephen listened, then told them that he understood, without going into the reason he had pulled off the highway to begin with and the decision he had made just before they arrived on the scene. They released him, wished him good luck, and admonished him to take care of business for everyone's sake. Leaving him standing by his car, the dust from their tires kicked up and encircled him.

It was too late to start back today. He didn't want to arrive in the middle of the night and then try to explain himself to an overwrought, exhausted wife who had waited up for his arrival. His text message was short and clear. "Heading home tomorrow morning. See you late afternoon." He felt better. She could finally relax a bit, and he could try to unravel his latest faux pas in the next twenty-four hours before turning into their drive.

Chapter 42

"I want you to read my notebook." He handed it to Allie while searching her eyes for any recognition that she understood how hard this was for him. He saw it not only in her eyes but also in her smile, and he felt her warmth as she reached with one hand for the notebook while the other rested on his shoulder and did not move.

"Michael, thank you. Are you sure?" She was conscious of her tone, not wanting to appear excited to have been given this precious permission by her client. Her hand remained on his shoulder, deepening its grasp just enough that she became suddenly aware of his bones. He was thin, but not as thin as when he entered the facility.

"I want you to read my notebook," he repeated. "I have more to tell. I... I don't know if I can go on without some help. Maybe if you read this," pointing to his book now in Allie's hand, "well, maybe you could ask the right questions. I mean, that's what you're trained to do, right? Ask the right questions?"

"I'll read it, Michael, of course. Yes, I can ask questions that I hope will help you. But you do realize how far you have come, Michael, just by handing me your book? It's a step that not many can take, and I want you to know how much I appreciate your trust in me. You do trust me, Michael, don't you?" She regretted immediately her last question. How foolish to question his trust when what she'd hoped for had finally happened. He had trusted her with his damaged life and now she was questioning his decision? She started to apologize when he reached up and gently took her hand off his shoulder.

"Just read it, please. And would you mind leaving me alone now? I'm feeling tired. Want to take a nap. Okay?" He stood up and waited for her to open the door so that he could go back to his room.

"Oh, of course. Of course. Here, let me get the door." She moved faster than she wanted to toward the door, partly out of embarrassment for her ill-phrased words and partly from the excitement she felt for her success with him and her work.

"I'll see you on Thursday for our regular session, Michael. And I'll bring your notebook with me then. You okay?" She could not feel at ease with him in his state while hers was bordering on ecstatic.

"Sure. Sure. I am now," he reassured her as he brushed by her into the sterile, bright hallway that led to his room.

His script was almost unintelligible for the first eleven pages. She remembered the first day when the notebooks had been handed out. She could now see and touch the agony up close that Michael had gone through that day. The words were disturbing enough, as they were forced onto the page by some hidden demon within him, but the thick, dark black line that wandered on its own, escaping any letter formation, to the bottom of the page and beyond disturbed her now as much as it did so many weeks ago. She placed her index finger on the first letter of the first word that repeated itself until the lead broke free of formation. Tracing the lines of the S then to the T to the E followed by the PHEN, she paused at the end of the first entry. STEPHEN. A place to begin. A first question to ask. She took notes on her yellow pad.

"You need to go home. You don't live here, you know. Although I'm beginning to wonder if I'm just plain wrong in my assumption." He leaned over her cubicle as he always did, dropping by to check in on her. Not having heard his approach, she jumped at the sound of his voice.

"Whoa! Didn't mean to surprise you. Sorry." His smile was always so welcome.

"Yeah, you did surprise me. Just a bit involved here. I guess I lost track of time. Your assumption is correct. I don't live here but sure feel like I do sometimes. How are you, Jared?" Coming up from the depths of Michael's tortured life, she really was sincere in asking him this, as it brought her comfort to be speaking with a healthy soul. She marked her place and closed his notebook.

"Doing fine. Thanks for asking. I'm taking the next two days off for a long weekend. Want to go somewhere quiet and free of demands on me, you know? Just need to be able to breathe a full breath for a change. I've forgotten what that feels like."

"Sounds wonderful. Where are you going?" A long weekend. What a thought! She couldn't imagine breaking away for even the regular weekend without carrying with her the files of concern she had stored in her brain's file cabinets.

"Going hiking. Maybe some fishing along the way. Thought that I'd head somewhere east of here. Maybe Whitney area. I used to go there all the time with my parents when I was a kid. They loved to hike and introduced me to it while I was still in my mother's womb. But it wasn't until I was out, obviously, that I got to hang tight on her front in one of those baby carriers—you know, the ones that swaddle the kid real close to its mother? Then you're old enough to turn outward and see where you're going instead of seeing nothing but darkness while snuggled into your mother's shirt and breasts. Anyway, I'm looking forward to getting back there. Ever been?" He almost seemed out of breath as he gave a great sigh while still resting his elbows on the edge of the cubicle's wall.

"No. Do you mean Mount Whitney? That area?"

"Yup. Never climbed it, though. Maybe one day. Who knows?"

She had seen pictures of the mountain and surrounding terrain. Not a hiker, it didn't appeal to her in that way, but she appreciated the beauty of the peaks and could understand why Jared would want to return there. "Well, maybe after this trip you'll be inspired to do it. Something to aspire to, Jared. Talk about getting your mind off this place."

"You interested in maybe joining me this weekend? I mean, I'm not trying to be forward or anything, but just two friends enjoying some time outdoors, getting away from it all?"

He was sincere in his invitation, she knew, and thought him sweet to even consider another person invading his private space. If she were not entering her fifth decade in a month, an unsettling reality, and was twenty years younger, she could see herself with Jared. After all, he was a good person and not hard on the eyes. But she reminded herself that she was old enough to be his mother. If he really wanted to take his "mother" along, she might consider it.

Glancing down at Michael's notebook, reality interrupted her musing. She had made her promise to Michael to be ready to meet with him and she also knew that, the deeper she moved into his writings, the harder it was going to be for her to get through them. Even now, after having read only the first section of the notebook, she felt completely exhausted, not so much physically but emotionally. She hadn't realized the impact of his words on her until she was forced to stop and change gears, to come back to the world as she knew it, and to engage in a perfectly normal conversation with Jared.

"You know, on any other weekend, I would consider it. It's just that I have a lot of work to do to prepare for one of my clients. I think that I've made a wonderful breakthrough with him and I can't jeopardize the moment by ignoring what I have promised to do. It's not an excuse, Jared. It's just important for me to focus completely on this client and bring him farther than he's ever gone before. I can't miss this opportunity with him. You understand, don't you?" She looked up to see him smiling broadly at her.

"Hey, completely. Of course. I'm just kind of happy to hear you say, 'any other weekend.' I can live with that, no problem. So, I'll take you up on that when I get back. Depending on whether my body holds out and I don't get lost in the woods, maybe we could plan something for a couple of weeks from now. What do you think?" He had moved from his perch and now was standing next to her.

She regretted her "any other weekend" response, realizing she needed to slow this down a bit. "We'll see, Jared. We should start out slowly if any hiking is involved. Not a pastime that I've experienced." She thought to add, "Maybe a morning hike so that I can let this aging body recover before work on Monday."

"We'll talk when I get back. Great. Well, try to take the work home with you, if you have to, but get out of here soon. Don't like the thought of you here by yourself slaving away while I'm packing my pack. Promise?" He stepped back and turned as if to leave, then turned to her again. "I'll say a little prayer for you somewhere along the trail. Be good to yourself, Allie, you hear?" And with that he headed to the exit.

Chapter 43

The text from Stephen was cold and unloving, she thought. He hadn't called her to hear her voice, or for her to hear his. He wouldn't speak to her when the police had her on the line. He hadn't made that gesture, she knew, for a reason. She'd expected the worst. To hear that he had been found dead somewhere. That's what she had prepared herself for, not a simple message that confirmed his existence but little else. The police had told her where they'd found him and what condition he was in. They couldn't confirm, though, that he would come back. That was out of their jurisdiction. If she had any further problems, she shouldn't hesitate to call.

She knew that she should be feeling relieved that he was alive. She wanted to feel excited that he was returning to her, or at least to the house. He had said "coming home," not "coming back to you." It didn't mean the same thing in her mind.

She fought off the rise and fall of nausea that plagued her throughout the day while she waited for his car to come down the drive. She had no idea how she would behave; she feared that she would really lose it with him this time. She could not fathom how she would gain control of the situation, whatever it would be. He was in control now. He had been all along, she knew, but now the reality of it was too much to bear. All those times when she had silently questioned his behavior suddenly overwhelmed her, and as much as she tried to occupy herself with anything but Stephen, she failed miserably.

The years with him had gone by so quickly. She tried to remember their happier moments, and there had been many. Confusion entered her thinking as she thought about the most recent days with him and how content they were. But she also remembered raising her own disturbing questions about Stephen and whether he was as content as he seemed. The shadow in their marriage that had always been there had resurfaced for a short moment as she wondered about her husband's state of mind, but she had shoved it back as far as she could, refusing to allow it to destroy her own fragile contentment. And then he needed to leave her for a day. On business. Taking care of their future. Taking care of her. Now, nothing but a lie darkened her thoughts and beyond that, she could think no farther. His betrayal had ended their marriage. She was prepared to say that to him.

He didn't say anything when he entered the house. Neither did she. If he had expected her to run to him, embracing him so as never to let go again, he was mistaken. She had made up her mind that the only way to control the situation between them was to hold off and to wait for him to make the first move. After all, he was the responsible party for the last two days that she had sleepwalked through. She could control her own behavior.

He walked past her with his head down and into the bedroom, shutting the door behind him. As difficult as it was, she forced herself to go to the kitchen and to look busy. With no appetite and with a stomach that would not accept food even if she forced it down, she gave up and went back into the living room. Sitting on the couch, she reached for the book that she had almost finished and tried to keep her eyes focused on the words in front of her. Not digesting anything on the page, she closed the book and stood. She could not go to the room and write. Not in this condition, nor would she contaminate it with the sour aura that surrounded her. She needed air. Grabbing her jacket from the hook by the door, she went out, closing the door behind her.

The air was fresh and chilly, and she stood straight while taking in deep breaths of its cool sustenance. The garden plots had been ignored during the last few days, and she wondered if there was anything left of her tender young growth. Resigned to the fact that more than likely there were numerous overstuffed rabbits just out of eyesight, she moved down the porch stairs and, in no hurry, casually walked to the plots.

Indeed, the once leafy veggies now were no more than sheared-off stubs of traumatized green. It looked as though a mower had made its way through each plot, leaving as little behind as possible. At any other time, she would rage against the Peter Rabbits of the world, probably shed some rage-filled tears of disappointment and sorrow for not being a better caregiver to her babies, and then sit in the plot out of exhaustion and frustration until her better senses came to her. But now, she felt nothing. What was the point? Nothing seemed to be permanent right now. Even here, among the remnants of what would have been, she had no control, not really. She turned to leave but took a moment to kick the ground, not once but numerous times, almost as if burying the young dead.

His footsteps made a heavy sound on the porch stairs as he moved toward her. She was afraid to look at him, afraid to finally face the inevitable. He approached her and stopped in front of her, blocking her path. Neither of them said a word for what seemed a long time. She knew that he was looking at her, waiting for her to raise her head, to acknowledge his presence. Her body was producing such heat that she felt that she might faint right in front of him. She found it suddenly hard to breathe. And it was getting so cold outside.

"I am so sorry. Look at me. Please, will you look at me, Eliza?"

He did not touch her, but she knew that he was waiting for her to release him from his own created hell. How long could she stay in control?

"Eliza, you have every right to be angry with me. Please, please look at me. I need you to see me." His voice was pleading, asking her to acknowledge him.

"Don't, Stephen. You have nothing to say to me that can erase what has happened. Nothing."

She started to move to one side of him so that she could escape his presence. He stepped in front of her again, taking her shoulders in his hands.

"No, you're right. I have nothing to say that would make any sense to you. But I need you to see me, please. Look at me!"

Fear. She suddenly felt fear as his voice was raised and strained. Looking up at him while trying to release herself, she saw a face that she remembered to be his while the rest of his body was acting out in a way she had never experienced before. Her shoulders were starting to ache from the pressure of his grip on them, and she felt anchored into place as their weighted strength grew.

"Stephen, let me go. You're hurting me."

She struggled and then he released her. Stepping back from her, he reached for her hand, but she drew it away from him.

"I can't deal with you right now. I don't know what to say to you. I don't want to hear your excuses, your lies yet again."

And then the tears came so quickly that she was overcome with sorrow. He moved quickly to her and took her in his arms, and she let him.

The words that he needed to say to her came easily and quickly, and afraid to pause for fear that they might slip back into the deep recesses of his mind, he ignored her growing sobs. He had wanted her to look at him when he told her that he was leaving. He needed that final connection with her while he destroyed their life together. Feeling her body grow tense against his, he released his embrace and stepped away from her. He knew how much he had hurt her just now but, as he looked at her searching for her reaction, he felt nothing. No pity, no regret, no love.

Eliza could not speak as her mind swirled with the vivid as well as foggy details of their marriage. What had just taken place was the moment she had seen in the shadows that had plagued her all these years. The foundation of their marriage, although never solid in her mind, had dissolved in less than a minute as Stephen's revelation struck it down. In one sense, she felt an odd sense of relief and clarity. She had been right all along about him. Her intuition had served her well, but she had refused to act on it while trying to create a life with him. It surprised her, the sudden rush of anger that she felt. Not just because of him but because of her stupidity, her willingness to be dominated by him, to allow him to be the stronger of the two of them. His strength was not visible, not physical. It was insidious, gentle, but persistent as it manipulated her into a state of acceptance. Acceptance of this man who now stood in front of her, ready to leave her forever for no reason other than what he deemed reality. His reality that she had no desire to deal with anymore.

A greater feeling of relief swept over her now as she looked at him. She almost felt sorry for him because she had found him out.

"You and I need to take care of ourselves, Stephen. We can't do it together. I don't think that we have ever really taken care of ourselves as we should have. You're right about one thing. You leaving me is the best thing that you could do for me."

Her words were meant to sting him, to draw him into the conversation so that they could both feel they had had their final say. She watched his face react in surprise. She had turned the tables on him, she knew, and she didn't care if he felt anything, really. All she knew was that she now was in control.

"So, the sooner the better, I guess. Get your stuff and leave. You might as well keep going and consider your visit today just that, a visit."

Where was the anger to accompany these words? Her voice was calm and steady. She could see that her words had penetrated as he raised his hands up, almost like praying, then dropped them by his side and walked away from her to the house. Had he given in to her that quickly, so resigned to finish what he had started but now on her terms? Elevated by this small victory, she took a deep breath and turned back to the plots. She could not go in the house with him there while he packed. She would give him the space needed, not just for him but for her own sake as well. Not sure how this newly acquired strength would hold up, she could not afford to subject herself to any show of weakness in front of him.

Then she remembered her find two days ago in the forest. She had waited to tell him instead of going to the police. Would it matter if she didn't tell him? But it was still his property and if anything came of it, he would find out anyway. She thought better than to keep this from him, as much as she wanted to. Not for any reason other than that the clean closure she had just performed with him would no longer exist. She would have to open the conversation. Yet revealing the disturbing news would keep them together a bit longer, she knew. And she was afraid of what might happen during that time. Everything suddenly was going backwards. She would intentionally be working against herself, but she had no choice.

She entered the house to find him coming toward her with two suitcases in hand and his backpack slung over his shoulder. Since she was standing directly in his path, he stopped mid-stride. "Excuse me, but these are a bit heavy. Do you mind?" He nodded toward the front door.

"I have to speak with you about something important, Stephen." She waited for him to put down the bags, but he started to shift to her right as if to move around her. "No, Stephen, this is not about us. You need to hear me out on this. Please."

He put down the bags and let out an audible sigh of frustration with her. "Okay. I'm listening."

"Can we sit down?" She motioned to the couch and sat down, being sure to sit at one end.

Sitting down on the opposite end, he remained on the edge of the cushion, feet flat on the floor as if ready to jump up at the least possible opportunity. He said nothing but waited for her to continue.

"The day you left to go up to the city…" She paused and corrected her misstatement. "The day you left, I spent a lot of time in the garden. But I also took a walk into the forest farther than we've ever gone before. I wasn't really looking where I was going and tripped over what I thought was a root or a rock. But it was neither of those, Stephen. I…I tripped over a bone. My first thought was that it was an animal's and I don't know why, but I began to dig about a bit and found several bones, what looked to me like rib bones. Still thinking that it was the remains of a deer or something, I uncovered a skull, Stephen. A human skull!" She stopped here and waited for his reaction.

"What do you mean, a human skull? What are you talking

about?" He had responded with doubt in his voice and she knew that he did not believe her.

"Just what I said. I was staring into the eye sockets of what had been someone! I couldn't believe it, Stephen. I kept on uncovering various human bones of a skeleton. It looks as though animals have had their fill and have carted away some of the major bones, as it's not a complete skeleton, but it's there, Stephen." She could now detect his interest as he turned to face her. "I didn't tell the police when they were out here—you know, the missing person's report—because I wanted to tell you that night when you got home. I figured you'd know what to do. I waited, Stephen."

"Okay, so you waited and now you've told me." Eliza was taken aback by the sudden coldness of his voice. The meanness just below the surface. She tried to ignore it.

"Don't you want to see it? We've got to do something about it, Stephen. Let me take you to it before it gets too dark, before you leave."

"Sure, take me to it. You should have told the police, you know. That would have been the smart thing to do. Anyway, let's do it." He rose from the couch and went to the door. Opening it and looking out, he turned to her. "Come on. You're right. It will be dark soon." He held the door open for her as she passed by him into the fading light of the late afternoon.

Chapter 44

She had heeded Jared's parting words and was proud of herself as she stood in line at the deli. Planning on grabbing something to take home along with her work, she was looking forward to shutting herself up in her apartment, warm dinner in hand, a glass of wine, and the notebook. He was right, she knew. Getting out of there would help clear her mind so that she could focus on Michael.

Settling into the notebook, thoughts of Jared persisted in filtering between Michael's tortured words. She smiled when she thought of him hiking the steep trails, cooking his own meals, maybe the fish he had caught. Every time she saw his face, his smile seemed to be larger than life and she realized that she loved that smile. It always put her at ease, even now without him present, she could bask in its warmth.

Putting aside the notebook, she filled her glass a second time while scrounging around the cupboards for some forgotten sweets she had hidden from herself. Feeling pure joy at finding a small box of See's that a family member of one her clients had given her as a thank you, she pulled up a DVD—a love story that she had been avoiding viewing, not really her cup of tea in subject matter—grabbed the throw her mother had given her for Christmas, and with a full glass of wine in one hand, a box of dark chocolates in the other, settled into the comfort of her couch and home.

The sleep had been dark and deep and had buried her in its protection. She remembered being aware that she was sleeping but unable to remove the blanket of darkness that covered her, so she gave in, once again. She also remembered sinking. There had been no bottom to this sleep as something invisible pushed her farther and farther down. She had felt no panic, no fear of being so far below the surface. In fact, the feeling was one of surrender and peace. And she had stayed there, not moving but fully absorbed in the palpable darkness surrounding her and buoying her up, then releasing her farther downward and then, again, buoying her up, but never to the surface.

As she crawled off the couch, the See's box fell to the floor, scattering the empty dark-brown paper cups onto the surface of the throw that lay at her feet in a small pile of synthetic fabric. Her head hurt when she stood up. Eyes barely open, she saw the glow of the screen in front of her, long done with the love story whose details she had already forgotten. My God, she felt lousy. What had she done to herself? How could she have gotten so off track? A good long, hot shower and a healthy breakfast would set things right, she reasoned.

The warmth of the water felt good on her body. She was beginning to feel half human again. She did some of her best thinking under the shower's spray, but this morning she fought the haziness that still lingered from her sleep. Now recalling how deeply she had slept, she worked her brain even harder to wake up. What did she need to accomplish today? The weekend, great. Then Jared's face loomed in front of her and she remembered what he was doing. She recognized a hint of jealousy, on her part, of his optimism, his spirit, his freedom, and his age. It vanished as she realized how much she needed to accomplish in just a few days. And with that, she was back on track, just not on all four wheels yet.

Settling into Michael's notebook was easier than it had been the night before. She was now in her work mode, and all other distractions were kept at bay with little effort. She had trained herself, over the years, to focus on what mattered now, and Michael mattered to her most now.

She took a minute to review her notes on what she had read so far. She tapped her pencil on the first notation: *Who is Stephen?* Her second notation was related closely to the first: *Reason for emotional state?* Surprised that she hadn't gotten any farther with her notes, she thumbed through the first few pages of the notebook. Some of it seemed familiar, and then she remembered that she had put it aside prematurely last night. Why? Jared. Wine. Dark chocolates. Love story. Sleep. Well, that would explain her absence for eight hours or more, she calculated as she looked at her watch. Time to get to work.

My little brother was four years younger than me. Even so, he was my best friend. Before I turned eight, we were never apart, not really, except when our father was drunk. Sometimes, he would take Stephen, but he always brought him back. Even when he was a baby, he would look at me as if he already knew me. His eyes wouldn't leave mine and I would be the one to break contact first, every time. We started playing together while he was still in the bassinet. I can remember flying my toy airplane over his head, imitating the engine's roar as I made it soar high above the bassinet, disappear out of sight for a moment, then pilot it back over his head and onto his blanket for a perfect landing. He would laugh that baby laugh, a signal to me to do it again, and I did. Once, when I had crept into our bedroom while he was napping, I stood watching him sleep, while leaning on the edge of the bassinet. Suddenly, he opened his eyes and smiled at me. Then he did something that I will never forget, never. His tiny arm reached up toward me while his even tinier fingers stretched out to me. I gently took his hand in mine and held on, smiling right back at him. I'll never forget that. It was the first time that he had done that, but it wouldn't be the last.

When he started crawling, I would crawl on the floor with him and for a minute, I could escape to a time when I was just as helpless as he was then. It wasn't hard for me to pretend I was a baby, but those moments never lasted long. I taught him how to walk. He would sit on the floor of our room, and I would tell him to watch me as I took big steps across our small room. He would crawl right alongside me instead of watching, and I would pick him up and put him back down on the floor, telling him to stay put and watch me. And he would do the same thing again. Until one day, we were playing, and he crawled over to the chest of drawers and proceeded to grab the knob of the second drawer, pulling himself unsteadily to his feet. I remember freezing in awe, not really believing what I was seeing, but there he was. Standing on two legs, wobbly to be sure, but upright, until he turned to me with a smile so big, so proud of himself. Then, forgetting that he didn't know how to stand by himself yet, he let go of the knob and tipped back on his behind. I could have told him that that was going to happen, but he had to find it out for himself. It wasn't long after that that he was staggering around, falling, and staggering around until, it seemed overnight, he could walk right alongside me, holding my hand as we explored the house from his new eye level.

Now that he could walk and keep me company, we could go outside and play. Had to stay real close to the house, of course, but being in the forest where we lived, we didn't need to go far to feel like we were miles away. We had a favorite spot where a grove of redwoods hid us from view of the house but that only our mama knew about. So, if she needed us real quick, she knew where to look. But when we were left to our own devices, the grove was our home away from home. It took on the shape of an airfield, then morphed into the open ocean, and that dried up to become a desert island, only to dissolve into a battlefield. Sometimes, we would just lie together on our backs and watch the high clouds changing shapes through the fragrant green boughs that seemed to grow high enough to meet them. When the fog came in, we could feel the chill in our bones long before the first wisps formed above us and began to penetrate the forest with its life-sustaining moisture. Sometimes, we would brave it and stay in the grove, our bodies shivering next to each other, until Stephen would start to cry that he wanted to go back to Mama. So, I would grab his cold little hand and guide him back to the house.

Once inside and if it wasn't too close to dinnertime, we would go in our room and play until Mama came to tell us that he was coming up the drive. Then we knew it was time to clean up the room and ourselves so that we would be ready. We never knew ahead of time what for, but that didn't matter. It wasn't our place to know, just to be ready.

Mama would always have the dinner ready on time. But once, when she wasn't feeling well, she fell asleep on our couch and didn't wake up until he came in the door. Stephen and I were hard at play in our room, so we didn't know that Mama was still sleeping, or we would have wakened her so that she could get the dinner started. Even though Stephen was little, and I wasn't much older, we knew that there would be some kind of trouble if things weren't like they were supposed to be. But we failed Mama by not checking on her. I thought about it at one point, but I was worried that she would be upset with me if we disturbed her. She never got enough rest as it was. I was only trying to help her by letting her sleep.

Then he came in our room and the yelling began. He was always drunk or just plain angry at everyone and everything. We were too little to know what drunk meant but we did know that whatever it was, a lot of yelling followed. We knew that would always come. What we never were prepared for was what he would do to Mama and us. Sometimes, he would just yell and call us names and mess up our room even more than we had, just to be mean. Sometimes, we could hear him yelling at Mama. She never yelled back, but we always knew when he made her sad because we could hear her crying. One time she came into our room after he quieted down. I remember her face was really red and we both could see that she had been crying hard. She kept holding onto her shoulder. But what I remember most was the beautiful smile that she managed to give us even though she was sad inside. And she'd always tell us that everything was going to be okay, that it was over, and everything was going to be okay.

But sometimes, he didn't stop at the yelling. Sometimes, he hurt us. Stephen was so afraid of him that he would always hide under our bed, thinking that he was safe there. Sometimes I would join him and push him up against the wall while I faced the outside so that I could see what was coming and maybe save my brother. Other times, I would just stay on the floor of the bedroom right where I had been playing and take what came. I think that he liked that I tried not to be afraid of him because he became even meaner with me, and if he thought of him, also with Stephen.

I didn't know where Mama was when he was with us. I wanted her to be there to help us, but she wasn't. Maybe she was too afraid to get in the way and make it worse. Looking back on it, maybe that was the reason. I just don't remember her anywhere around, even in the other rooms of the house, as he dragged one or both of us out the front door. Maybe she was too afraid. Maybe.

Now I wonder where she thought we had gone with him. Did she know? Did she know what he was doing to us all that time? She knew that we were hurt, because I remember her coming to us after he would bring us back into the house and shove us in our room, telling us not to come out until he said we could. Then the house would become so quiet. It seemed like Stephen and I were the only ones left in it. We would sit huddled together on the floor, holding onto to each other, careful not to touch our middles as they were so sore. Stephen would start crying after he left us alone, not because he was scared but because he hurt so much. I would do my best to comfort him until his cries became just whimpers, and then he would fall asleep in my arms.

I never knew how long it was until the door

would open and there would be Mama. She carried some kind of ointment, bandages, and some wet washcloths every time and would gently take Stephen from me and lay him on the bed. She always said to me, "You're next," while she carefully removed Stephen's shirt and pants. I knew what she was going to do because she would do the same for me. Like an angel of mercy, she carefully wiped his wound, that wound around his tiny waist, until she was sure it was clean. Then, applying the ointment, she would reassure him that it would make the pain go away. Finally, she would tenderly lift him to a sitting position and wrap the cloth bandages around him, covering the irritated skin. Then she would lay him back down and draw up the quilt, tucking him in with a good-night kiss even if it wasn't night-time yet.

Turning to me, she would ask me to help her get my shirt and pants off. She would do the same for me as she did for Stephen, but I was big enough to crawl into bed by myself while she gently moved Stephen over so I had room too. Then with the quilt now covering both of us, she would kneel and give each of us a kiss on our foreheads, whispering to us something that I didn't understand, almost like a foreign language, and then stand over us for a little while. Closing the door behind her, we would not see her until the next morning. It never occurred to me that I was hungry and that we would miss dinner. I think that the kindness our mother tried to give us as she tucked us in was enough to sustain us until we had to face the next day together.

Once, I asked her what she was whispering. She said that it was a prayer that her mother had taught her a very long time ago. Did I want to know what she was saying? She taught me the prayer and to this day, I remember her words, although I didn't understand, at the time, their significance. "O Christ, who alone art our defender: visit and heal Thy suffering servants, delivering them from sickness and grievous pains. Raise them up that they may sing to Thee and praise Thee without ceasing, through the prayers of Theotokos. O Thou Who alone lovest mankind. Amen."

Allie turned the next pages eager to hear Michael's voice continue, but he had stopped here. Still sitting with the notebook open on her lap, her mind raced. She began to jot down notes that, if approached carefully with him, would continue to open what was still locked deep inside of him. She sensed that his words, as difficult as they must have been to record, were only the tip of the iceberg. However, what he had revealed to her so far gave her a place to begin to understand him. "Dysfunctional family," she wrote as she began to organize the few notes she had in front of her. "Younger brother, Stephen, mother, father"; "No mention of other siblings"; "Physically/emotionally abusive father figure"; "Victims: wife/children"; "Wife dominated by husband"; "Children confused"; "Children resilient"; "Very strong brother bond."

Eager to be with Michael again, she closed the notebook and slid it into her bag along with her notepad. Thursday. She would be sure to give him his notebook then and ask him to continue. She would let him know that she had read every word, and she would thank him for allowing her to do so. She would be sure to tell him that before he began to write again, however, they needed to talk about what he had already shared with her. Most importantly, he needed to understand that the words still unwritten would not be easy to write and perhaps to share, but that he had already cracked open the locked door and that it was both of their jobs, together, to open it as far as it would go. To reassure him; that was her most important mission, she knew, for not doing so would only slam the door, possibly forever. She was not willing to let that happen to either one of them.

Chapter 45

The idea of approaching the site of the remains again had not bothered Eliza when she spoke with Stephen. In fact, because of Stephen's jolt to her reality that the marriage was over, she had not given her secret find any thought. But now, leading the way as they walked farther away from the house through the undergrowth and densely populated groves of towering redwoods, uneasiness came over her. At first, just a twinge with the reminder that they were entering an area that was completely foreign to either of their realities. What secret these remnants of one human being held she did not know, nor would Stephen. This brought her a moment of comfort, as they would still have this in common.

He had not said one word to her since they had left the house but only steadily followed her, keeping a good distance between them. She wondered how he would react upon seeing the bones. He could be so cold and detached, at times, as she recalled the roller coaster of his emotions taking her for unwanted rides so many times in their marriage. Perhaps he would respond with disgust or fear or sadness. Perhaps he would take on his all-business persona that she had initially been introduced to in the early days of their marriage and would insist that the authorities be called immediately. She hoped that the latter would be the case; the burden of this find by itself had been enough for her to bear and no matter what the state of their current union was, it was only fair that he take over from here. It was the least he could do before he left her.

Coming through the last bit of undergrowth, Eliza stopped short. The distance from the house to this spot was much farther than she recalled. On her initial walk, she had been lost in her own imaginings until she fell, and the emotional and physical trauma of the return trip wiped out any concern about distance covered.

Catching her breath, she could hear his footsteps coming

up behind her, but she did not turn to him. She waited until he was closer, and then indicated with her head that the site was right in front of them. "Over there," she said, her voice barely above a whisper. Was that her way of paying respect? She wondered. They were, she realized, the first words that had come from her at the site since she had stumbled over it two days ago.

He moved past her without uttering a word. The area was as she had left it. Nothing had been tampered with. She wondered if her presence when she first came across it had left traces of scent that disturbed any foragers or predators. After all, she had not even thought about lifting the bones from the earth with her bare hands, kneeling into the soft soil, and digging with the toe of her boot against the ground that had hidden for who knows how long the dead. For a moment, she questioned who she had been at that moment to be so inquisitive and disrespectful. A sudden sadness overwhelmed her as she felt now a trespasser, a grave robber, a callous living being who was only one breath away from the bones in front of her.

Her thoughts were interrupted as she realized that Stephen was standing among the bones. His right shoe's heel was resting on the midsection of a rib bone, and she was about to say something to him when, in horror, she held her breath as he ground the bone into the earth. He methodically moved from bone to bone, boring the earth with what seemed to be a growing intensity as now both shoes took turns or worked together to send the bones back underground. He never used his hands but remained erect, seemingly taller in stature than Eliza had ever noticed before as now his legs joined along with the movement of his hips to lend greater force to the work at hand.

She was afraid to speak, to cry out. All she could do was be the observer of his macabre dance. He did not look at her, not once, but stayed focused on what little lay now under his feet. Then he came to the skull, whose sunken sockets' ghostly sight had also observed him and now seemed to widen in the knowledge of what was to become of them as Stephen bent down and lifted it in front of him. With both hands clutching the sides of the skull, he drew it closer to him, at eye level, and did not move. As if communicating with the bone structure in his grip, Stephen's face contorted into grimaces as if suffering great pain, while his eyes welled with tears whose density could not be held back, only to cascade down his face to the ground below with no obstacles blocking their descent.

No sound was produced. Eliza froze in place, waiting for him to release what was within. Still no sound as he now seemed to writhe in front of the bone, a weird gyration of his own making; he was twisting his torso from side to side and then back to front, only to repeat the motions again and again, all the while his face grimacing and soaked with his tears.

She could stand it no longer, and the sound of her voice startled them both. "Stephen! Stop it, Stephen!" She could not make herself move toward him. It was as if she were cemented in place and could only watch what was unfolding in front of her from a distance. The intensity of her command further frightened her, as she had no idea what she would do if he obeyed her. It was at that moment that she was hit with the idea to turn and run. She was so far from any known reality in which she could find comfort. Her legitimate fear of him now took over any hope of ever finding him again.

His movements slowed down as his face relaxed under the mysterious strain that she had just witnessed. He did not look at her, though, but continued to focus on the skull. The tears still flowed, and she thought she heard him mumble something but could not make out the words. Even with his slow return to normalcy, Eliza stood frightened and unwilling to communicate with him. She just wanted to be away from him now, to put all of this behind her, whatever it was, and to leave him here, alone in the forest, to deal with his demons on his own. She felt no sympathy, and her words spoken to him moments ago had been nothing but her immediate reaction to her own fear. She knew what she had to do, and she knew that she needed to do it now.

She shifted her frozen stare from him so that her eyes now focused on the trees all around her. She willed herself to turn her back on him, on them, and to stay focused on the trees, the undergrowth, and the now nearly trodden path that lay before her and that would bring her back to the known. As she took the first few steps away, she was shocked to feel her body betraying her as her tightened muscles shook uncontrollably when she tried to use them. She had no idea that she had been so tense and fought the urge to stop until she could relax her muscles. No, the need to distance herself from him now was stronger and she began to run, willing her legs to perform, unaware whether he was in pursuit.

Finally coming to the opening, she could now see the house, the garden plots, and her rock garden. Out of breath, lungs burning, she slowed to a brisk walk as she kept moving to safety and the known. She had thought, at one point in her flight, that she heard his heavy footsteps coming up behind her, but she could not afford to lose ground by turning to confirm her fear. Now, as she stood in the clearing, she forced herself to look back into the forest. Nothing. No one appeared, and she inhaled deeply the coolness of the evening air while the quiet of the thickening fog encircling the trees above her dampened her fears for the moment.

How quickly the turn of events had come, she thought, as she entered the house and saw his suitcases by the front door waiting patiently for his return. He was the one on the way out the door when she stopped him. Now it came to her what to do, and that was to be the one gone before he returned. She had to escape whatever he had become in the last moments in the forest.

Feeling a shiver of fear once again, she did not grab anything but her purse and his keys to the car. Her warm fleece, hanging on the hook by the door, begged her not to forget it, and she pulled it from the hook as she opened the door to leave. With no time to regret her decision, she bounded down the porch's stairs to his car, parked a farther distance from the house than usual. Not in any frame of mind to consider why this was so, she took one last look at the house. She had no idea when she would be back, if ever.

Chapter 46

How many times had he swung from the bottom of the knotted rope? How many times had he panicked in the darkness surrounding him? How many times did his small frame shake uncontrollably from the cold and the shock of the wound once again opened by the wiry hairs of the coarse shipyard rope? How many times had the pain been so excruciating that the only way to make it go away was to surrender to unconsciousness? How many times? He could hear no answer as he screamed silently at his father's skull.

The bones that once were the monster of his dreams and awakenings now held no resemblance to the figure that had ruled his young life and that of his brother and mother. The same bones whose intact skeleton enabled his father to drag his four-year-old body from under the bed, that allowed him to clench his fist and to hit his mother so that she was helpless, unable to come to his aid or that of his brother, that supported his small body's weight as he lifted him off the ground after cinching the rope around his torso and then tossed him over the edge as if a bag of garbage into the darkness below. Even now through his tears, Stephen began to see in the vacant bone structure staring back at him the threatening, drunken face of his father. He had never been so close to it in life as he was now in death. And he couldn't let go, unaware of the intensifying grip of his fingers against the sides of the skull.

To bury any traces of him once and for all would send him far away from Stephen, farther than he had ever been before. To physically trample him into the ground, all that was left of him, came naturally to him. He gave it no thought. For that matter, what had just taken place came from somewhere so deeply hidden that he had no say over his actions. It raged within him as it boiled to the surface, an eruption of such intensity and destruction, and he still had no say, no way to stop it, no desire to do so. It needed to be over and he needed to be freed from the grasp of the truth, as well as his own invented history.

Her voice, familiar yet strident as it broke through to him, lingered in the stillness surrounding him. He felt great fatigue as his gyrating body slowly came to a gentle sway. Still holding his father in his grip, he watched in horror as the cruel face dissolved in front of him and the stark recesses of the hollowed bone eye sockets came into focus. His throat tightened so much that he feared he could neither breathe nor swallow as a gurgling sound rummaged its way forward to his mouth's opening. Barely spoken, hardly intelligible, and known only to Stephen, his brother's name escaped him, not once, but many times as the unacknowledged brother of Stephen was resurrected.

Unaware of her departure, he turned to Eliza. He could hear her movements through the undergrowth, and he realized that she was moving away from him. He needed to explain. Clarity. No, he needed her to keep all of what she had seen to herself.

As clarity quickly caught up with him, he became conscious of the scene in front of him and below his feet as his vision revealed his recent rampage. He had, once again, come out of it back into the light but this time, everything had changed. He could not go on as he had been doing, could not continue with one more act of his mortal play. Nor would he allow her to exist in his life. He had already taken the necessary step to end their relationship, but he was dimly aware that it was not enough to protect what little he had left of his pathetically screwed-up life. If she were to learn about his history, that of his childhood, his father and mother, and of Michael, she would never separate from him but would insist on staying with him to see him through the bad times ahead as he would be forced to face reality while strangers prodded and delved in their clinical ways. He would die before that took place.

And then he remembered how close she had come to learning of Michael all those years ago in Greece. He had been so successful in burying him, but at the mention of his name back then, he recalled feeling a disturbance within, though nothing came of it. Now he imagined that disturbance to resemble a hardly perceptible quivering, like that of loose soil disturbed by a footstep.

Releasing the grip on his father's skull as if a poisonous element threatened, once more, to harm him, he thrust it to the dirt and watched as it rolled into a resting place, eye sockets turned into the churned-up soil of the rich forest floor. He was barely aware of the sudden gust of wind that encircled him as the trees above shed dry brown growth that descended to the earth only to find a temporary resting place on the back of the skull.

He felt his legs carry him forward as he tried to gain ground on her. She was far enough ahead that he couldn't see her, but he could hear the forest react to her movements. His senses seemed fine tuned as he pushed through the underbrush and the low-hanging branches. Somewhere in his brain, he heard his apologies to the innocent lives he was crushing underfoot. The strangeness of this thought lingered with him as he came into the opening just as she was entering the house.

Moving forward, his breathing stressed, he knew that no matter what, he had to find a way to stop her from leaving. Was it too late to talk with her, to make her understand what he barely understood himself? Could he find the right words that would convince her that he was right in asking her to do what he needed to be done? To destroy any remnants of the dead? To never reveal what was now the only thread in their ravaged relationship that they shared? Could he trust her if she agreed? He knew that she did not trust him. And that was the breakdown of their relationship now. It was futile to think that he could have it his way. Too much damage had been done between them. Too much had been observed by Eliza that could never be explained and, he determined, never would be.

He heard the front door open as he approached the rock garden. She was hurrying, he could see, to get away. Her fleece was dangling from the strap of her purse as she struggled to gain her balance after missing the last step of the staircase. He knew that she couldn't go far, as he had the car keys. No, he had left them on the kitchen table! And then his voice came to him as he yelled for her to stop, to wait.

"Eliza! Please, just wait. Wait for me! Eliza, please. I need to talk to you. Wait!"

He watched her turn to him and then turn to the car, but she did not move. "Eliza, yes. Just wait for me, please."

Then she turned back to him. Neither made a movement, as if a crevasse had appeared in the earth between them, barring them from moving any closer to one another. He couldn't go forward, not having any words to say to her that would make sense. He couldn't go forward and take her in his arms to reassure her that he meant well. The thought repelled him, surprisingly. He knew that she would never allow it anyway. Now that he had her attention, he was at a loss as to what to do next.

"Eliza?"

She did not acknowledge that he had said her name but turned in the direction of the waiting car.

The stone came out of the earth with ease and left behind it a disturbed tangle of bright green succulents whose foothold had just been torn away from them. With it now in his hand, he moved quickly toward her so that he was upon her before she knew it. She heard him, but it was too late to defend herself. And even if she had heard him in time, she would not have believed what was to take place next. With arm raised and fingers tightly grasping the cold stone's rough surface, he called her name out one last time as the stone found its mark on her unsuspecting forehead. He watched, frozen in place, as her body collapsed to the ground.

He stood waiting as the minutes went by until he saw no visible movement. The ground around her head supped on the rich fluid seeping from her wound and he, upon approach, was careful not to step in it as he knelt by her side.

The familiarity of this moment surprised him. At first, any regret, disbelief, anger, or fear were strangely absent. The woman now in front of him whose life he had taken almost instantly was nothing more than something known, something already seen, a déjà vu moment. He sat back on his heels, one hand resting on her chest, the other still clutching the stone. He struggled to understand what he was feeling, trying to justify why this was so familiar to him. And as quickly as the feeling washed over him, it was gone.

With its absence, his mind now focused on the reality of what he had done. His body's muscles shifted him to an upright position as he found himself repelled by the corpse at his feet. Feeling the weight of the stone in his hand, he turned it around to see a faint red stain brushed upon its surface from the impact against her soft flesh. Then he dropped it so that it landed just to the side of her outstretched fingers.

Unable to think clearly, he started back toward the front steps, slowly at first, then at a run. As he reached the first step, he doubled over and retched. His mind was swimming as he tried to climb the steps to the front door. Fumbling with the door handle, he pounded on the wooden panel as though, if he knocked hard enough, someone would come to answer. The door had locked behind her, and it came to him that she must have taken his keys, all of them. She must have had them in her hand when she was trying to leave quickly. Realizing that they were still in her possession, he turned and headed back to his dead wife.

As he came upon her, he noticed more details about her than he had before. Now marred by drying blood as the gash above her nose and across her forehead above her right eye was starting to coagulate, her beautiful face lay on its side, as it had sleeping next to him each night for so many years. But her body was arranged as though it had been a dishrag that fell to the hard ground. Her legs were splayed so that the right one bent under the left. Her torso was neither on its back nor on a side but propped somewhere in the middle while her arms, spread out away from her body, served as makeshift struts holding her in this precariously balanced position.

So engrossed was he in his fallen love's last moment that he had forgotten why he'd returned to her. A sudden urge to lie next to her once again, to feel the warmth of her body next to his, to be secure in her arms as she murmured love words to him, and to fall asleep without remembering he had done so only to wake in the morning light to her sweet face resting next to his overcame him, and it was all that he could do not to act on it.

Slowly, he became aware of what he had done as he drifted back to reality. *My keys. My keys. That's why I'm here. Where are the keys?* He saw nothing in either of her hands and as he looked more closely at her body, it occurred to him that they might be under some part of her. A moment ago he wanted to lie beside her and caress her. Now her body repelled him, and he felt physically ill again while he gingerly shoved her over from one side to the other, still finding no keys. The only other answer was that in her fall she had let go of them and they had landed far from her.

He began to search the ground around her body, and it was only then that he noticed how dark it was getting. He really couldn't see much without a light. Why hadn't he noticed the oncoming nightfall before? He remembered the Maglite in the car and knowing that he never locked it because they were off the beaten track, so to speak, he started to feel more in control as he retrieved the light from the pocket of the driver's door.

The beam's broadcast illuminated the ground in front of him as he returned to the body. Moving away from her, he methodically began searching the ground as the light revealed its surface content to him. He began to doubt that she ever had the keys as he continued to move farther away, covering a much wider circumference than he had thought he needed. With one final sweep over the scattered stones that lay on the perimeter of the area searched, his eyes caught the reflection of the silver fob peeking from below disturbed leaves and dirt. Carefully maneuvering over the rocky surface, he reminded himself to clear this area of these obstacles that served no purpose other than to trip him up when he wasn't paying attention. Saying a quiet "Thank you, God," he reached down and retrieved the keys from their hiding place.

As he turned to head back to the house, the wide beam of his light crossed more stones, but these were not scattered on the ground but carefully piled one on top of the other. Curious, he walked closer, keeping the ground illuminated while he watched his step through the uneven bed of stones under his feet.

When he came upon it, he could see that it was not a pile of stones but the remnants of a circular wall. He recalled that Eliza had pointed it out to him once, but he'd had no interest in it. He stood next to it and measured it against his leg. About a foot high, he guessed. Upon closer examination, he could see that there had been another layer or more of stones upon what remained as he ran his fingers over the jagged surface of broken stone and cement. Standing back, he wondered how high this structure had once been and then wondered what it was. Judging by the many stones scattered all around the area, it must have been something of importance. He moved closer to it again, somehow drawn to it. Standing next to it now, he cast the light into the center of the circle. He couldn't really tell what he was seeing; it was filled with dirt and debris from the trees on the property.

He felt them before he remembered them. The keys in his hand. *God! Get it together, man!* The feeling of control that he'd experienced just moments ago was leaving him again, and he knew that this was no time to lose focus. He needed to get to the house, get his bags into the car, and get away from here. It was clear and simple to him. Not much different than the times that he left her for the day or longer. He knew, though, that he couldn't leave, not until he figured out what to do about Eliza.

As he threw the last bag into the backseat of the car, it came to him. Again, so simple. So clean. So easily explained, if needed. He opened the trunk to find that she had not cluttered it with anything and that its contents remained just as he had arranged them years ago. Only necessary items to aid in any vehicle emergency neatly organized in one container and ready at a moment's notice. He took time to congratulate himself on being prepared as he pushed the container even closer to the back of the trunk.

In the house, he grabbed the throw that Eliza had always cuddled under in the chill of the day or night. Oversized, as she had insisted upon, it would serve his purposes well and perhaps give her some afterlife comfort.

Returning to her body, he carefully laid the throw on the ground next to her. He wasn't comfortable with what he needed to do next, but he had no choice. Leaning over, he carefully lifted her unresponsive body just enough to clear the outer edges of the throw as he lay her in the center of it. Wrapping her securely within its now uselessly warm confines, he left her there while he brought the car closer to her. He was using his head, he thought. *Good for you. Smart, because you can't carry her up to the car without dropping her. Not in your condition.* He slipped her into the clean trunk and pulled the throw's edges tightly around her once again, as they had fallen away to reveal small glimpses of his Eliza.

The traffic was surprisingly light on the highway and with the darkness now fully upon him, it was difficult to see much on either side of the road. He hadn't realized it at the time but was now grateful that the moon was in its darkest part of the monthly cycle, while the fog that had reached down to the earth's surface hindered vision even more. He knew the road and the turnouts well. For a stranger to the highway traveling at night, the challenges were many, and the knowledge that steep and unmarked cliffs lurked just within feet of the road's boundary in some parts was enough to dissuade many from traveling this stretch of the continent's edge ever again.

After maneuvering through the hairpin turns that dug deeply into the lush gorges of the Ventana area only to end in a rise to the top of a hill and then back down again, he exited the roadway, crossing against traffic to pull into a small and somewhat hidden turnoff. Carefully steering the vehicle, he backed into the area, keeping a good eye on the sides of the hill to gauge his distance from the edge of the cliff. He immediately turned off his headlights. No need for the Maglite this time.

He got out of the car and waiting a few minutes for his night vision to kick in, he took deep breaths to fill his lungs with the salty moisture that swirled about him. The wind that pushed the whiteness inland felt refreshing against his skin and he opened the palms of his hands that, until now, had been hot and sweaty. It dawned on him that he had been clutching the steering wheel with an unusual amount of strength. As the darkness gave way to grayish images whose outlines began to look familiar to him, he moved to the back of the car. Glancing toward the highway in front of him and watching for telltale glows of illuminated fog, he saw nothing on either horizon.

Quickly, with no thought as to what he was about to do, he reached under the throw and lifted Eliza from the trunk. About to turn toward the vast darkness behind him, he stopped and gently pulled a freed edge of the throw that had slipped from its place back tightly over her head, then turned, stepping carefully forward, lifting her ever so slightly as if making an offering to the heavens with arms outstretched, muscles beginning to burn and quiver from her dead weight, and let go.

Chapter 47

Anxious for her arrival, he found it hard to wait in the room alone. He had prepared himself during the last few days. The knowledge that he was in control had strengthened his resolve to approach her reactions carefully, to protect what still needed his protection while offering her scraps of his life, enough to keep her at bay. He had spent the last two nights sleepless as he relived his young life numerous times and considered what he had not told her. The words had come easily as he let the pencil slide over the blank sheets. Somewhere deep within, he felt contentment as he wrote, a familiarity with the process. His thoughts untangled easily before him and lay clearly on the blue lines, which begged for more. But he knew that the subject matter going forward held unconscionable details whose roots were so complexly entwined in his memory that disturbing them, even slightly, could destroy it all, could destroy him.

As she entered the room, she looked to him like an angel. The lighting had caught her outline as if she were carrying an aura about her while her arms, bent and extending from her sides, seemed to him the shape of folded wings. He had never seen her wearing all white. As she drew closer, the angel faded into the stark reality of this woman whom he had carefully allowed to enter his life. Her wings dropped their load on the table in front of him, and the crisp white sleeves straightened and fell to her sides as she placed each hand in a waiting pocket of her jacket uniform.

"Good morning, Michael." Her voice was cheerful, upbeat. He wasn't surprised. "How are you?" She waited for his response.

He reminded himself, *Stay in control. Stay in control.* "'Morning. I'm okay," he said, not revealing any hint of emotion to her.

"Good. Good, I'm glad." She meant it. Anticipating this moment had caused her to imagine every scenario as he saw her for the first time since allowing her to read his notebook. The one fear that plagued her during her days away from him and in possession of his words was that he would have regrets about letting her in and would shut down in front of her for good. However, she tried to push that thought aside each time by remaining positive in her thinking. She relied on the fact that this process had been successful with others, so why not him? What she did know quite well was that the path ahead with him must be trodden lightly and sensitively. She could not let her own selfishness get in the way of his progress. Admitting to herself how much she wanted to dig more deeply into his psyche, especially now that he had given her permission to do so, it would be her challenge to hold her reins intact at all costs. She was aware of how easily she could lose him.

Michael watched her take her hands out of the starched pockets and extend them toward him but then drop them gracefully, one holding onto the edge of the tabletop while the other gently, and with what seemed to him the greatest respect, rested upon his notebook.

"Thank you, Michael, for letting me read this." She cast her eyes upon the notebook. Looking back up at him, she said, "I know that this was not easy to tell, especially to someone whom you don't know that well. I want you to know that I appreciate your trust in me." Had she forgotten anything else that she wanted to say to him? *Think. Every word.* She had read every word. Was it too late to add this? Would it sound too patronizing? *Yes. Don't continue. Give him some credit.*

"Did you read every word?" He was looking at her now, eye contact made.

Her eyes gave her away as she worked hard not to reveal the smile her muscles were straining to form. Had he just said exactly what she had been thinking? She was not aware that her laugh lines, the few that she had produced over the years in this profession, were evident even while she fought to keep the smile from the surface.

"Are you laughing at me?"

His question startled her. "Oh no, Michael. Not at all.

It's just that your thoughts were the same as mine just a moment ago, and I was happily taken by surprise when you asked if I had read every word. You see, I was going to add that, but you spoke it before I could say it to you."

That sounded reasonable. Had she just saved herself and him? Her heart was letting her know how nervous she was as she stood defending herself before him. Searching his eyes and aware that she was leaning forward too far over the table toward him, she straightened and took a step back.

"Michael? Do you understand? I would never laugh at you or anything that you said in your notebook or to my face. You know that, don't you?"

Was that desperation she heard in her voice? She could not let Michael see how much she was weakening her stance with him, that she was pleading for him to continue to accept her. Not to lose trust in her.

"So, you read every word. Where do we go from here?"

Now he was in control; he had heard it in her voice. Yet he did not want to cause a chasm to form between them, not now. He needed to put her at ease. He needed to go forward, not waste time.

"Well, it's important at this point, Michael, that we talk about what you have shared so far. You write beautifully, by the way."

This time the smile broke free. She thought that she saw a hint of one on his face as well but if it had been there, it was gone in an instant.

"Are you willing to talk with me? I have questions, as you probably have figured out, and before you go forward with the notebook, I would like you to hear them and do your best to answer them for me. You do remember me mentioning this to you the last time we met?"

He didn't respond to her but had remembered.

"There's a reason for this, Michael. It's like when you move from one house to another. You have so much to pack that you need to stay organized. Think about what goes in which box. Take the time to think about each object, especially if it has any sentimental value, and decide whether to keep it or get rid of it. Sometimes, while trying to decide, you remember details about its history that may only be known to you that help you decide what to do with it. If you do decide to keep it, you carefully wrap it up and place it in the box. Once sealed you don't open the box again until you are ready, but you know that the contents of the box are important to you and you understand why. It's bringing closure to moments in past and present times so that you can be open to the future moments. What do you think?"

As usual, she had said more than was needed and could tell by looking at Michael, whose whole body had, at some point during her weak analogy, turned in its seat to stare out the window.

"I can deal with that. Where do you want to begin?" he asked without turning toward her, but his voice could not hide the pent-up relief that escaped him as he thought he saw a glimmer of what could be, just waiting for him to latch on.

"To start with, is Stephen your brother?"

She knew what she had read, but she wanted him to say it aloud. This might be too abrupt a way to open the gates, but she had decided that it was the best approach. It would either shut him down or set him on fire. She hoped for the latter.

"He *was* my brother."

He had turned now and although not directly facing her, his tone of voice indicated to her that she had not made a serious error by asking the question. In fact, she understood his response to be the invitation to open the gate all the way. She was finding it difficult to submerge her growing anticipation of what the next hour would reveal.

Carefully arranging the words in her mind, she forced herself to go slowly with him. "Michael, can you tell me about Stephen?"

She feared that his reaction to the question might be one of frustration, as he had already told her about him in his notebook. She wondered if she had made her first blunder so soon in their conversation. When she was about to retract her question, Michael interrupted her thoughts.

"If you read my words, as you say you did, then you know about my brother." His statement was surprisingly matter-of-fact in its delivery, and she could detect no frustration or anger with her.

Relieved, she continued. "I did read every word, Michael. Is there more that you wanted to write about Stephen that you couldn't?"

His eyes were now focused on hers and, not wanting to lose the contact that he had offered, she willed herself not to glance away from him, not for a moment.

"Do you want to tell me, or do you want the notebook?"

Why had she asked if he wanted the notebook? Stupid. If so, the conversation would be over. She forced herself not to look down at her watch. It felt as though only minutes had passed from the precious hour that she had for him and now she worried that she had unintentionally closed the gate, at least for this day.

He was first to break away, but not from the task at hand. "If you give me the notebook, then you won't be able to ask the questions that you need to, will you? If you want to talk to me, then let's talk. You forget that I'm not so far gone that I can't carry on a conversation. Meds in my system, yes, but I've grown accustomed to their poison and can ride above them."

Leaning back in his chair, folding his arms across his chest, he knew that he had taken her by surprise when she unnecessarily cleared her throat and awkwardly reshuffled her papers. He also knew that he was still controlling their interaction.

"I can tell you more about Stephen, if that's what you want me to do. But I am warning you," his face seemed to grow darker, as if a shadow had fallen across it, "that the forest primeval is my only home."

Chapter 48

He felt the need to think of something, to perhaps whisper to the night sky some good wishes for her journey to eternity. But nothing came to mind other than a welcome relief. He had accomplished what he had set out to do three days ago. However, he had to admit that he had not foreseen the end to be quite like this. He had been content to ride off into the sunset, leaving her behind on the porch stairs. He had worked it through numerous times and was at ease with his decision. But it would take time to digest this act of finality, as well as to plan how to cover his guilt, if anyone should approach him.

Remembering that the trunk was still open and that he had not paid attention to any oncoming traffic during the last few minutes, he felt panic, and quickly shut the trunk and got in the car. A growing concern that someone might have driven by and that he had not noticed, had not heard the engine while ridding himself of the most recent part of his life, overwhelmed him with an urgency to move. Starting the engine but not turning on the headlights, he slowly moved forward onto the highway and drove for a brief time before he turned on the lights.

Now, heading north, he needed to distance himself from her, from the house, from his past. However, as his thinking cleared, he realized that he couldn't just walk away. That it would not be long before someone would inquire as to her whereabouts. That he needed to cover himself now and not later. No, he had to return to the house and in a few days, call the police. He would do what she had done: file a missing person's report and come up with some logical explanation as to why she was missing. Perhaps she was distraught over his walking out on her? Perhaps, when he was heading back to her as the police had advised, she became distraught? Perhaps she never received his text message saying that he was coming home. What was she to think? He could never imagine that she would do anything but wait for him and be there when he got home. He rehearsed these questions as the miles passed by. Yes, he would be the one who was now distraught, fearing the worst for his wife. He would beg the police to find her and he would offer to help. A few days, then he would begin the play.

Her phone? He had to find her phone when he got back to the house. Destroy it and any evidence that would lead to him and negate his story. He had time, he figured, to do this before he allowed the outside world in. Had he missed anything? The darkness of the night, illuminated by the beams of his headlights before him, comforted him and calmed his thinking so that he was able to push aside the last hour and focus now on the past day. He saw her face loom before him with its wounded forehead, and then the stone. The stone that had traces of her blood on its surface. What had he done with it? Did he drop it, or did he hold onto it? Where was it? He added that to his list of to-dos.

The oncoming headlights startled him, their high beams blinding him for a moment until the driver remembered and shut them off, flying by him into the dark. But the intensity of the light lingered in front of him while he forced his eyelids to blink repeatedly, as if to wash away the offending brightness.

As though he had been awakened suddenly, he saw it. It filled the windshield so that the road in front of him, still there, was invisible to him. The soil overflowed onto the dashboard and the strewn, crushed bones lay visible and telling. Slamming on the brakes, he felt the machine that enclosed him swerve out of his control while he frantically tried to steer the car away from the cliff's edge. The railing met the car's metal and did not give way but cuddled the passenger's-side door while Stephen corrected and slowed the two tons of metal structure so that it found its way back into the lane where it had been only moments ago. He was breathing heavily as he tried to calm himself. The realization that he had come so close to his own death sent a shudder through him, and he fought off the thought of karma.

The dirt drive to the house seemed to him uncomfortably longer than usual. Still reeling from his brush with death, he parked closer than he had before as the house came into view. It was now early morning, he guessed, somewhere around one or two. He was surprised when he checked his watch to see that only a couple of hours had passed and that it was not even tomorrow yet. There was nothing he could do now about cleaning the area. What he needed was to get a good night's sleep, and in the first hours of the morning he would take care of business.

As the sun shone through the curtains, he could feel the warmth of its beams filling the room. He lay there, enjoying the sensation until reality interrupted. Everything that had transpired over the last three days now rushed in and scrambled to be the first for attention in his overwhelmed mind. Bloody stone, Santa Barbara, argument, the crushing sound of metal against metal, missing person, oversized throw, kind police, finality of a relationship, crushed unearthed bones, a partial glimpse of her. None of it would fall into the right order, nor would it go away. He closed his eyes and tried to will it all out of his mind. Yet its pressing urgency to be addressed was resistant to any efforts on his part to make what was so wrong have the slightest semblance of right.

It was apparent that there had been some sort of scuffle where Eliza had fallen. The dirt revealed unnatural markings, especially the now pooled dried fluid where her head had fallen. He felt strangely at ease as he relegated the task before him to the bottom of his list. What he needed to do first was locate the stone and get rid of it.

It lay there, right where he had dropped it. Its unblemished surface was exposed to the light and it could easily pass as one of the many scattered stones in the area. But he knew this to be the one as he now clearly saw her outstretched hand and fingers within inches of it. He thought that he had been ready to face what lay before him, but his mind began to insist that he see what he did not ever want to see again.

Fighting away the images that began appearing, he quickly leaned down and picked up the stone. Turning it over, he saw that dirt clung to the thick, still moist fluid that had been preserved in the dark and damp earth. With the stone in hand, he looked around him for the perfect place to rid himself of the evidence. Should he wash it off and place it back where it had so conveniently left its long residence with the others? Smarter might be to take it with him and at a turnoff, throw it into the ocean, where it might sink or perhaps land far below the roadway's edge onto the rocky debris of a cliff's constant erosion. This last thought appealed to him. He found a plastic bag in the kitchen, placed the stone in it, and put it in the trunk of the car. All he needed to do now was recreate the natural state of the disturbed area.

The bones were more of a challenge. To rebury what remained and to cover the surface with debris as it must have been before Eliza kicked up the undisturbed soil would take longer than he could afford, but he had no choice. Even though the site was far enough away from the house that it would probably never be discovered again, he couldn't take the chance of leaving it in its current state.

With the equipment needed, he headed back through the forest, this time without any anticipation. He knew what awaited him, but when it came into view, he was taken aback at the destruction committed upon the site. Had it been this way when Eliza showed it to him? He would have remembered, surely. It looked as though wild animals had come upon it at the same time and while attacking one another, wreaked havoc upon what once had been an animal himself.

Still unsettled by the sight, he began to dig a hole large and deep enough to hold the bones, including the skull that lay face-down in the dirt. With each intrusion into the soft earth by the shovel's sharp edge, a satisfaction settled upon him as the uninvited and unwanted burden of memories long ago buried were diminishing in their clarity and insistence to come to light. With each shovel of dirt thrown to the side, the hole in front of him grew larger, while the pungent aroma of freshly exposed forest firma seeped into his nostrils. He took deep breaths of its aromatic goodness and innocence. Turning to the trespassed bones, he used his shovel to lift them from the ground, balancing the unwieldy pile in the shovel's depression. He moved slowly, not out of respect, but out of necessity. He did not want to be here any longer than needed.

With the last fragments of partially crushed skeleton deposited deep below the earth's surface, he moved to the skull. With a gentle dig below the ground, he lifted it from the darkness that had held it in place. Not willing to examine it any more than he had done with the rest of the skeleton, he dropped it on top of its own remains. He hadn't paid attention to its placement, but if he had, he would have seen the ghostly stare of what were once his father's eyes looking up at him as he buried him in the darkness from whence he came.

As he had planned, the stone fell far below him into the welcoming ocean, now a nondescript rock that would find its resting place washed clean each day by the ceaseless movements of the undulating salt water. As he stood in the sunlight that shone against a crystal-blue sky, he was startled when his body suddenly shuddered, releasing a sigh of relief that was long and deep. He accepted the feeling of freedom that overwhelmed him as he stared out onto the vast expanse of ocean in front of him. His senses seemed heightened as he listened to the distant gulls scolding each other while in flight over the water; the redwing blackbirds sitting upon the very tops of grasses and shrubs, as if to have the better view while singing their distinctive songs; the waves crashing upon the scattered stones below, only to tow some of them back out to sea, grinding their surfaces against one another in the process; the heat of the sun finding its way below the surface of any exposed flesh while injecting its nutrition into his frayed system; and the aroma of warming vegetation all around him, releasing its essences into the heated air. He realized that he felt alive for the first time in a very long while.

The drive to San Francisco gave him time to think again, but this time not about making any excuses to anyone. This time, he would begin to plan his future. There were unresolved issues, but he would do as he had always done: categorize, prioritize, and take care of each one in a timely manner. Once that was accomplished, he would be free to do and go wherever he chose and this thought, alone, excited him. Perhaps back to Europe?

Someplace that was familiar, for the time being. If he planned it well, he could venture out as time went on. What was there to keep him anywhere anymore?

The house in Ventana was placed under a real estate management company that Stephen had directed to rent the place out when he gave them the okay to do so. He had no intention of ever living there again but felt compelled to hold on to it for nothing other than its value. He would keep both East Coast homes.

As for Eliza, he had followed his plan to report her missing after a few days' absence. He returned to the house to make the report and to meet with the police. He gave them no indication that he would no longer live there, that he had wiped his hands clean of his and Eliza's history in the house. On the contrary, he played the grieving husband's part well, while staying put for what seemed to be an acceptable amount of time until the search for her had come to an end, and the case of "Missing Person: Eliza Bingham" was now on the books as a cold case. Understandably, they all agreed, his decision to move away and start anew was to be expected and they wished him well with, yet again, condolences tagged on for good measure. It had all played out so well, he thought, as he purchased a one-way airline ticket to Paris.

Chapter 49

Michael's statement was meant to be disturbing, she knew, but she also knew that she had been at this mind-game business longer than he had. She accepted his challenge while inwardly congratulating herself. She had been careful with him, enough so that he was ready to let her farther in. He trusted her. Looking directly at Michael, she pushed herself back into her chair and crossed her legs while casually putting her hands in the pockets of her white coat, leaving the papers and pen untouched on the table between them. She had managed this maneuver without losing eye contact, and by forcing herself into this outwardly relaxed posture, she felt anything but relaxed. It was her job to sustain her appearance no matter what he said to her, but deep within she felt unprepared for the darkness he would share. Had she shut her own darkness far enough away?

"Stephen and I were separated by the authorities when he was four and I was eight. Different foster homes. Only twice did they put us back together under one roof; the first time lasted less than a month when the foster parents complained that we were too damaged, individually and especially as a pair, for them to feel comfortable with us. They returned us like they would the wrong size shirts. The second time and the last time was when Stephen was eight and I was twelve."

His words stopped and the silence that followed could not be filled, not right away. She waited, formulating her first question, at the ready if he chose not to continue.

"Did I tell you that I thought he was dead?" He was focusing on his left pant leg, following a crease in the material with his right index finger, up and down across the worn fabric.

"No, Michael. You didn't tell me that. Why did you think that he was dead?" She again was on guard not to push, not to ask too many questions at once. This one would further their conversation, she was sure.

"Because I was there. I saw what he had done to him, to

them." His finger had given way now to his whole palm as it rubbed the crease now from right to left, only to repeat the motion as the stubborn crease remained.

"Michael, you saw them? Who was there other than Stephen?"

She could feel him drawing her into him now, ever so slightly. He would not look at her, so completely engrossed in the futile attempt to rid himself of the flaw in the pant leg.

"They were together. She was holding him and me, but he wasn't alive. But she kept holding him like he was. I knew he was dead. I knew he was dead even in the darkness. I guess that she thought if she held him long enough, he would stay alive. I guess. But he was dead. My mother; she was the other person. My mother."

"Michael, can you look at me for a moment?" She was afraid that if she could not calm him down, he would leave her. "Look at me, Michael, please?"

His head slowly moved up and now his eyes, once again, were upon hers.

"Michael, would you tell me more about Stephen? How did he die?"

She fully expected him to hesitate in answering her and had barely finished her question when he sat upright and leaned toward her. His voice was strangely strong.

"He killed him. It was only a matter of time before his little body would give out. I knew that, and every time he took Stephen outside, I guess I prepared myself for him never coming back. But he did, every time. And Stephen and I would keep playing and pretending that everything was going to be okay because our mother kept telling us that while she tried to heal us. But she never understood that the wounds that we both suffered were not only physical but so deep within us that no matter what she said or how much balm she applied, nothing was going to stop the seething infection inside of us. I guess I can't really speak for Stephen about that. He was too young to get it, but I knew what was happening to me."

"So, he physically abused you both?"

His body relaxed, and he sat back, as she noted the almost imperceptible slouch.

"Yeah, oh yeah."

She couldn't equate the response with the sarcastic laugh that accompanied it.

"You know. You must work with a lot of patients that tell you about their abusive childhood. I'll bet nothing surprises you anymore. Am I right?"

He was tottering on the edge of being flippant with her, he knew, but he couldn't help it. She was getting so close to him. He had given her permission, but now the anxiety grew in him and he longed for a double dose of any kind of med to quell what he could not control on his own.

"Michael, I am only interested in helping you right now." She wanted to take back the previous question and punished herself for being obviously redundant and unnecessary. *Wounds. Idiot. Think!*

"Okay. I have your full attention then. Right?"

His slouched body began to irritate her. "Of course."

"What would you think if I asked for my meds right now?"

The smile was not genuine, she knew, but manipulative. She had seen it so many times before in her career.

"You've had your meds already this morning. You know that."

She chose not to go farther, then thought better of it. She sounded like a mother scolding her child. She needed to soften her words. "Sometimes, medicine is not what is needed. Sometimes, if you can, fighting through the urge can be the best medicine, Michael. What you have been sharing with me this morning is painful to remember, to bring to the surface. I know that. And because you are doing this, your mind and body are fighting against your better judgment, trying to scream at you that the meds are the easy way out of an uncomfortable situation. You can't listen to them. Michael, I am right here, and you can lean on me. Okay?"

"I don't know if I can go on."

The tone of his voice had done a 180. His vulnerability filled the empty spaces of the room.

"It is up to you, Michael, but I think that you can."

Indecisive about whether to touch his hand for reassurance or to retain her professional distance, she felt a thin layer of moisture forming above her upper lip.

"Michael, what do you want to do?" she asked as she deftly wiped her index finger across her wet skin, leaving it there as she rested the elbow of her now raised arm on the chair's own arm. A waiting stance that concealed her own insecurities.

"Can I at least get a drink of water?"

She smiled at him as he returned the gesture. They both needed a break, she thought. Bringing the cup of water to him, she remained standing while she removed her clinical coat. She realized that she might be more familiar to him without it, less of a threat. Besides, she reasoned, the warmth that had crept up on her was probably because she was wearing that extra layer of unbreathable fabric. Already, she felt more at ease and couldn't help but laugh inwardly at the comment her father used to make all the time: "Clothes make the man." Some truth in that, she reckoned. Michael stood and walked to the window. He slowly drank, seeming to savor every drop as if it were his last.

"Would you like more?" Without looking at him, she heard the paper crush in his grip.

"No, no thanks. I'm good."

"So, let's continue for a bit longer, Michael. You tell me when you want to stop, okay?" She stretched out her hand toward his chair, indicating that he should sit. *Stupid. You're not a theater usher. He knows where his seat is. Stupid.*

Throwing away the cup, he circumvented the direct route to the chair while taking a leisurely stroll around the perimeter of the room, finally coming to rest in front of her.

"After you." He gestured toward her chair.

"Thank you, Michael."

The session was running its course, she knew, and for the first time during the hour, she worried that they had not gone far enough. She would need to focus carefully from now on so that every word spoken by him and every question asked by her moved them farther into his darkness.

"May I ask you a question, Michael?"

"Fire away but be gentle." She felt a strange warmth toward him when his humor appeared.

"Of course. You were talking about your mother trying to heal your wounds, both yours and Stephen's. Can you tell me more about how you got the wounds? What did your father do to you both each time he took you out of the house?"

She was conscious of holding her breath as she waited for his response. Hoping not to be obvious, she allowed herself to take a replenishing deep breath.

"What he did to us? How detailed do you want me to get?" He didn't wait for her answer. "Do you know the nursery rhyme *'Ding Dong Bell'*? Probably not. Let me tell it to you.

'Ding Dong Bell
Pussy's in the well.
Who put her in?
Little Johnny Flynn.
Who pulled her out?
Little Tommy Stout.
What a naughty boy was that,
To try to drown poor pussy cat,
Who ne'er did him any harm,
But killed the mice in the farmer's barn.'

"Funny how that came to mind. I haven't read nursery rhymes since I was a kid. My mother gave me a book of rhymes when I was five and told me that they were very old rhymes that she had learned when she was my age and that her mother had taught her and her mother before that. I remember her telling me that even though they were sometimes referred to as nonsense rhymes, their origins were steeped in real life. You know, like *'Ring Around the Rosie,'* which refers to the Black Plague in Europe and how the flower bouquets were placed to overpower the stench of death. 'Ashes, Ashes, We all fall down!' God, how many little ignorant kids have sung about death while getting dizzy and having a good time?"

"I know I did," she interrupted.

Not acknowledging her statement, he continued. "Anyway, the well. That is what you want me to talk about. When we lived there, the well had long dried up. We were told not to play around the area, so we always went into the forest. The only time we found ourselves near the well was at the hands of our father."

He was surprised to hear how calm his voice was as the images began to gain momentum and clarity, like a slide show speeding up uncontrollably.

"We would try to hide from him when he was drunk. That's when he became loud, ugly, and mean. Stephen would scramble under our bed every time, somehow thinking, I guess, that if he pushed himself as close to the wall as possible, he would not be found. He was only four, after all, and I guess, now that I think about it, every time was like a first time for him. Never occurred to his four-year-old mind that our father knew where to look each time." He paused and slowly shook his head. "Poor kid. But we really didn't have anywhere else to go. I would join him, keep him hidden behind me knowing full well that I couldn't do anything, really, to protect him. I think that he thought I could. But I never could, and most times, we both would be dragged out from our hiding place. Our father was a strong son of a bitch, I'll give him that. He carried both of us out to the yard while we screamed and fought against his grip. And we knew what was coming. Sometimes, I wished I didn't. Sometimes, I just wanted relief, for both of us. Especially for Stephen. He was such a skinny little kid. There wasn't much there to begin with, but that didn't matter to our father. So, the pussy in the well. Stephen was the pussy, and I joined him when the SOB was in the mood."

He could see the well as clearly as if it had just dropped through the ceiling and now sat between the two of them. Then he saw the rope. "Did I tell you that it was a dried-up well? No water?"

She nodded. She could not produce any words, her mouth cotton dry, but waited for him to go on.

"So, you can safely assume that he didn't try to drown us, unlike the pussy in the rhyme. I know that would have been the kinder thing to do to us, though." He paused again, rapidly blinking his eyes as if to absorb any indication of the raw sadness rising from within.

"There was an old rope, big and thick. I remember wondering why it was so hairy, like the chest hairs I'd seen on his body when he would sit around the house shirtless. It was left over from the days when they used it to haul buckets of water to the surface. Pretty old, I'd guess. But it still served its purpose, just in a different way with us. When he got us to the well, neither one of us was brave enough to run away because we knew that when he caught us, everything would be worse than it already was. So, dropped on the ground like two bags of garbage, we would huddle together waiting. He always took Stephen first, grabbing the end of the rope and wrapping it around his waist that was hardly there. In order for the rope to hold, he would pull on it as hard as he could, and Stephen would cry but not loudly because with each breath he took, the rope carved even deeper into him. Then he'd pick him up and hold him over the well's opening, and looking back at me, would drop him until the rope became taut against the wooden beam that held the pulley in place. I could hear Stephen screaming until all he could manage was to whimper. I can still hear him."

He stopped speaking, and she watched his eyes lower their focus to the floor between the two of them. She knew that he was seeing something that she could not.

"Do you want to go on, Michael?" she ventured. The question really was could she go on listening? This is what she had hoped would happen. However, she was not prepared for how dark the darkness was.

"I have to. Pussy's in the well. Never did him any harm, never."

Suddenly, it wasn't clear to her that he was still fully present. He seemed to be drawing inward as he mumbled his thoughts to no one in particular. His hands came up to his face and he leaned forward, rubbing his temples gently at first and then with growing intensity.

"Never did him any harm, never did him any harm, never did him..."

She was not prepared for the tears, the great heaves and sobs that she had seen before when he didn't know she was there. But even having been a witness to his emotional collapse once before, she fought the urge to turn away so as not to be pulled into the vortex that had suddenly entered the room. He needed her to be there, right now, she knew. All she could do was reassure him that he was not alone, that she was right in front of him. All he had to do was reach out or let her reach in.

"Michael, I'm right here. Right here. You are safe. I'm right here."

The volume of her voice was raised to be heard over the unnatural sounds he was producing between his sobs, all the while trying to catch his breath.

"Michael, you are okay. Breathe now, slowly."

She reached out and placed both hands on his shoulders, gently rubbing them, hoping that the human contact would be felt. As his rebelling body slowly calmed itself, she let go of him, grabbed some Kleenex, and offered them to him. Before he came fully back to her, she wondered in amazement how an eight-year-old boy could, after all the years gone by, be sitting in front of her, reaching out for her hand.

Chapter 50

Leaving all his past behind him was his intention as he boarded the Air France flight at SFO. He had not felt this good about anything in such a long time. A sense of adventure consumed his thinking as the world seemed wide open to him now. He had purchased a first-class ticket, as he used to do in his younger years when it never entered his mind to do otherwise. He'd had the means. Now, at sixty-four, he was living off his retirement savings, which had many sources.

He had tapped a small amount of it to purchase a country home in the small village of Tigeaux just outside the city so that, when the desire presented itself, he could take the train and be in Paris in less than thirty minutes. He knew that he had provided for himself the best of both worlds. How long he would live there, he couldn't say. Nothing would hold him there, certainly. He would be sure of that. His life was now all his own and he had full control of it. He would be cautious and pragmatic in his later years. After all, the things he was leaving behind were enough to fill a few lifetimes, all of them, he prayed silently, things he would never encounter in any way again.

Congratulating himself on his wise financial decisions early in life as he made himself comfortable in the soft leather seat, he nodded to the steward's offer of French champagne, served to him in a tall glass flute and accompanied by a presentation of caviar, cheeses, and crackers. Toasting himself and his achievements, he looked out the window to see the plane begin to pull away from the gate and distance itself from the country that he had decided never to see again.

Chapter 51

Both drained emotionally and physically, they sat quietly facing each other, though neither was able to look at the other until each had regained some control. Holding his outstretched hand, Allie tried to follow her own advice that she had practiced so many times before. *Focus on your breathing. Listen to the sound of the air going in, going out. Visualize your lungs filling, then releasing, then filling again.* She needed to regain her control so that she could guide Michael through and out of this traumatic episode that he had revealed to her in which he, alone, experienced the truth. Her vicarious involvement was only that, and she knew that he had relived it all in front of her but without her seeing the vivid images that filled his mind. How steep a climb it would be this time for him to reach her, she wasn't sure, and this thought frightened her.

"That's better. Good. Keep breathing, Michael." She could feel the muscles in his hand relax as the bone-crushing grip began to lessen around hers. "You are doing just fine."

Her voice was soft and comforting, and she couldn't help wondering if she was, in fact, speaking to herself. She thought that he would pull away from her, but he continued to hold on, gently and tenderly. Not willing to lose this contact with him, she did the same.

"Thank you."

It was barely a whisper, but his voice seemed to fill the silence of the room. As he raised his head to look at her, she drew her face up as well and met his eyes. She realized that she was fighting the need to draw him to her, to comfort him, like a child who needed to know everything would be all right and that he had done nothing wrong.

"I have never told anyone."

"I know, Michael, I know. Are you all right?"

Leaning toward him but careful not to trespass into his space, she waited for his response to a question that was meant for the immediate moment but after having verbalized it, sounded ludicrous. Of course, he was not all right. Before she could rephrase yet another blunder, he squeezed her hand as if a signal that she was still in good stead.

"Other than completely wiped out," he said, his other hand's open palm wiping the remaining moisture from his eyes and face, "I think I'll live to see another day." Then he smiled at her, a smile that she had not seen before but that she knew reassured her that she was all right as well.

Still holding his hand or was he holding hers? She wasn't sure at this point but did not let go.

"I think that we've done enough good work today and we can continue next time. How do you feel about that, Michael?"

"Sure. Agreed. About the notebook?"

She had completely forgotten that it was present in the room with them. She sat up and gently released her hand from his. Reaching for it, he put his hand on her arm.

"No, leave it there." She stopped and turned to him. "Don't bring it again."

His voice was not requesting but commanding. She had just lost him. All the work that she had done and all that they had accomplished was gone with his simple command. Somewhere, she had stepped over the line with him and only he knew where that had been. Feeling the warmth of her blood rising and the heat of her body intensifying as a toxic blend of nerves, disappointment, and fear swept through her, she held herself against blurting out an apology for whatever she had done to him.

He could sense her reaction. Could see it in her face, as much as she was trying to hide it. He could see her.

"You don't understand. I don't need it because I can talk to you. Do you have any idea how many sessions I've had to sit through before finding you? Do you know what it's like to sit in a room full of wrecked human beings whose only reason to exist is so that they can have their moment in the spotlight while some shrink nods up and down, but nothing changes for them? Do you understand that I knew all along that I wasn't one of them? That I had plenty to say but was not ready, even though I was made to believe that I could say it? That I should? That if I didn't, I would be medicated and threatened with transfer to another facility? Maybe, now that I consider what I've just said, that was all good because if I had given in and told them whatever they wanted to hear, I would not be sitting here with you right now. Silver lining?" Another smile, but this one reached up to the corners of his eyes.

She smiled right back without hesitation. "If it's a silver lining, Michael, it's both of ours, isn't it?" She didn't try to hide her relief. "I am happy for you. The notebook was my attempt to reach you. You know that, don't you?" She didn't wait for his response. "It was a tool that you have no use for anymore. That's fine. However, I will keep it safe so that if ever you ask for it again, you will have it." Now she waited. His smile remained.

"That's good to know. You do that. Keep it safe. But between you and me and the lamppost, it's as good as gone, gone forever. The next time I put pen to paper, the result will be an autographed edition of my first book arriving on your doorstep, with me as the carrier."

If that were true, he thought, he wouldn't recognize himself. But for a moment, in her presence, anything seemed possible.

"I will look forward to that, Michael. Now, how about you and I pack up this session? I don't know about you, but I am famished. Good work builds a good appetite, I guess. Can I buy you lunch?" She was as surprised by her question as he seemed to be. "I mean, that we could go down to the cafeteria and get something. Would be a change of pace, right?"

Standing now, he moved behind her and placed his hand on the back of her chair.

"Allow me. After you, please."

She lifted her body from the chair as he gently moved it away.

Chapter 52

The months passed at a leisurely pace for Stephen while he took his time to settle into his home and the surrounding area. With each passing day, confirmation that he had made the right choice in leaving was evident in his mood. The neighbors had reached out to welcome him, and he was comfortable in the home that he now occupied. Days could go by where no thoughts crept in from his past and when they did, they were infrequent and always took him by surprise. And as quickly as they arrived, he would dismiss them into the oblivion that he had consciously created for them. With each dismissal, he felt himself one step farther removed from his past and recent history. He prided himself in the fact that he had done such a good job of cleaning up his messes before moving on, before possibly creating any new ones.

He did not speak much French, true. He had dabbled in classes when in high school and college but never took it seriously enough to become fluent. However, he was always amazed that he could understand the written word and had found his way around the area because of this retention. His efforts did pay off in retaining the textbook phrases that would allow him to confidently verbalize if he should ever travel and find himself in a situation that called for the location of bathrooms, train stations, police stations, or a market, or if he needed to tell someone that he was hungry or full or had a headache. Beyond those needs, he was very limited and prayed that English was easier for the French than French was for him. Introductions were simple enough. Wasn't that the first phrase that had been drilled into his head? *"Je m'apelle Stephen."*

That had served him well recently as he ventured out into the village. He was pleasantly surprised by the warmth that the French extended to him, inviting him into their homes for meals, having him join them in celebrations, making sure that he felt welcomed. He had always had a different impression of the French. Something to do with leftover biases from an older generation whose memories were concrete and unwilling to change.

He found it easy to impress these strangers, to allow them to know only what he wanted them to know, no more, no less. Recounting to them his achievements as a businessman in the States during his working years, thus allowing him the ability to travel and live among them, for instance, he discovered that he had a captive audience. They accepted each word spoken while he carefully recreated his image to accommodate his current circumstances. And with each thoughtfully woven detail, any truth was submerged deeply under the cover of his lies.

When the end of his first year in Tigeaux was a month away, there were, of course, the widows of the area who were patiently, as proper etiquette demanded, waiting to make their advances toward him. An American, and a rich one at that, who was single and established. It was as though the heavens had opened and gifted these women with a second, or in some cases, a third or fourth chance at happiness. Stephen was aware that they lurked behind the walls of their homes. He had met all of them at some point or another in the initial rounds of introductions as he became acquainted with families. However, he was prepared if any should broach his privacy. He knew how to be a gentleman and he also knew where to draw the line. He would do it kindly and with consideration of their own circumstances. The grieving widower would be in full play and would insist that it was much too soon for him to engage in any kind of romantic relationship. They would understand—he would make sure of this—that his now deceased wife's long and drawn-out illness had left him empty and drained, and that only time would help to ease the pain and sorrow that had consumed him. That was why he'd had to leave, had to come to someplace new with no reminders of the past. At least the latter had some truth to it.

The envelope had arrived on a Friday and carried two postmarks. Noting their different dates, it registered with him that it had been in the mail for over two weeks. FORWARDED was stamped to the left and above his current address, which had been hurriedly scribbled in childlike penmanship by someone who had thoughtfully admired and preserved what Stephen couldn't also help admire. Who did he know who could write in a script that he had last seen reproduced on the Constitution? It was something out of the past, European to be sure, but still from a distant time. Examining the envelope once more, he noted that the stamp was Greek. He did not recognize the handwritten return address. Further confusing him, since he knew no one in Greece, and remembering that his mail would be forwarded for a year, he debated whether to open it and expose himself to further confusion and possible unwelcome difficulties that might muck up his comfortably established life.

Foolish, he thought, while his curiosity outweighed any further thought. Slipping the letter opener under the sealed thin blue tissue paper, he carefully pulled out the folded sheets. In the same glorious hand, the writer had filled the pages. In the lower right-hand corner, the salutation read, "Eagerly awaiting your reply." His eyes were impatient and had slipped to the bottom of the letter in order to discover the identity of this stranger. The name, "Adrastos Metaxas," meant nothing to him. He sat down and drew the parchment closer to the lamp. The greeting was indeed meant for him as he began to read.

Mr. Stephen Bingham,

I write to you today with a saddened heart but a responsibility to my father weighing heavily upon my mind. I am fulfilling his last request to me and so ask your patience as you read this communication to you from a stranger. I can only understand your hesitancy and possible confusion. Please allow me to explain.

My name is Adrastos Metaxas and I am the firstborn son of Achaïkos Metaxas. My father recently fell ill and after a short struggle to survive was unable to sustain his life. He lived long and was well loved by all who knew him. In our small village of Oia, he was known to all and lived long enough to welcome three generations to his family as well as so many of his countrymen to our village. When very young, he began following in his own father's footsteps and when of age, took over the small shop that my great-great-great grandfather had established. It began as a place for women to purchase goods for their homes but soon grew into more than that so that in the last three decades, my father took pride in his inventory, which now appeals to the frequent tourists who visit our village from the cruise ships docked in our beautiful Aegean waters. Forgive me. I am sounding like a travel agent, which I assure you, I am not.

It seems that you were one of those visitors accompanied by your wife many years ago, but my father never forgot your wife nor you. In remembering you both, he would recall how engaging she was with him. Please excuse me to say, I think that if my father were not happily married then, he would have pursued Mrs. Bingham. He spoke so highly of her even though he was the first to admit that his acquaintance with the two of you was brief. Please understand that she left an indelible impression upon him.

It is because of this that I write to you. In my father's will, he has left to you both items that he wanted you to have in your possession. They were valuable in his estimation and memorable, he was sure, in your wife's. In fact, he told us over and over again how much he wanted her to have them the day she came into his store, but it was not meant to be. But now they belong to you both, given with my late *father's regards.*

May I send them to you at this address? You may wonder how I found you. Your wife had left your names with my father, perhaps in exchange for his? Perhaps another trip would bring you both back to our village might have been their thinking? My father did mention something about the coincidence of serving another Mr. Bingham but had been told by you that he was not a known relative of yours. My apologies for the intrusion. My work does not offer me the opportunity to search for persons who, for reasons many times known only to themselves, have chosen to keep their current location unknown. I took it upon myself to seek the assistance of a gentleman who does this professionally. Again, my apologies, but my intrusion upon your privacy carries with it no more than a dying father's request to grant his final wishes to someone who, even though briefly, left an impression upon him.

I do hope that this communication finds you and your wife well.

Eagerly waiting your reply,

Adrastos Metaxas

He read and then reread the letter before putting it down. He had purposely distanced himself from his past but now, in the privacy of his home, he felt that the enemy was at the door. Which enemy? All of them, he thought, as he rose, shaking uncontrollably while reaching out to the wall for support. How long and how successfully had he kept them at bay? His life now was one of familiarity and comfort. His creation had served him so well until this moment. In a matter of minutes, in the time it took him to absorb the contents of this stranger's letter, he was conscious of the façade beginning to crumble around him. And it took only one person, one stranger who seemingly had no interest in him other than to satisfy his father's request. But he had found him. He had known how to find him. And his father had mentioned Michael and in doing so had pricked Eliza's interest. That didn't matter now. She had taken that with her. He made sure of that.

Who was this "professional" Metaxas alluded to in his letter? How much more did he know about him than his address? The questions came at a rapid-fire clip as he moved about the room in no certain pattern but seemingly propelled to move so as not to stop and collapse. Should he respond? What would be the point? It would only open the door wide to invitation, no matter what this man had written. What was his father referring to when he mentioned the shop and Eliza? A vague memory of a cruise appeared as he struggled to make sense of it all.

Eliza. She was now in the room with him, he was sure of it. Watching him, waiting for him to recognize her presence, to linger until he did. Searching now, he tried to bring the memory forward, afraid to do so but without a choice, he knew. It came to him slowly at first, and then the images invaded quickly and with such force that he spun around sure to see her in the shop, her questioning face, her embarrassed stance because of him, and her departure from him because she had no other choice. All because of him. And the man appeared just as he was then as he tried to give them space to talk.

Oddly, Stephen remembered that now but knew he was not conscious of it then. What was his name? He picked up the letter to read *Achaïkos,* a name whose pronunciation eluded him. He had never asked his name, but Eliza must have, and now, even in her absence, they were again connected after so many years.

He would not reply, he decided. There was no point. He

had no desire to receive anything from the past and, besides, it was meant for Eliza. No, he had made up his mind.

He could feel his mind clear as those who had been present in the room with him were now no longer there. He looked around to be sure and saw the only intruder, the letter, lying on the desk where he had placed it. Had he again managed stay out of harm's way? Yes, he reassured himself, because it was still within his control to do so.

The winter evenings in this small village sent the occupants into their houses early as the darkness fell. As an observer left out in the cold, one might marvel at the quaint stone homes built generations ago, one after another, whose chimneys emitted fireplace smoke only a shade lighter than the night's own blackness. The air filled with the burning wood aroma while the almost invisible soot fell softly back onto the roofs of their origin and of others. It was upon one of these roofs that the ashes of a life almost revealed found their temporary precarious lodgings, only to be dissolved forever in the rains that soon would come.

Chapter 53

She was still riding high on the success of her last session with Michael. It had been a difficult one, to be sure, but the outcome had been more than she had hoped for and now, having crossed one painful hurdle for him, the next of how many she had no idea would certainly follow.

During their shared lunch in the cafeteria, she saw glimmers of what he must have been like at some point before his tortured past took its toll. Their conversation became easy and they both worked at keeping the topics light. No mention of family, of course, or of any history connected to either one of them. Just an airy back-and-forth of observations of their immediate surroundings and a bit about her work. Silly questions about favorite pastimes, to which Michael had limited input. Comments about the quality of the food in front of them, favorite foods, and a promise from Allie that when Michael was released, a dinner would be waiting for him at the restaurant of his choosing. Her treat, of course. And then they parted as she closed the door of his room and headed back to her desk.

"Been looking for you. Someone said that you were at lunch. Do you have a minute?" Jared's tanned face beamed down on her from his usual perch as he leaned over the partition. She couldn't help but notice his hands, as they were the only other skin exposed. Strong and muscular, she thought. They were the same golden hue as his face. And then she remembered his weekend trip.

"Oh. Hi, Jared. Sure. What's up?" Something about his appearance was making it hard for her to take her eyes away from his face. That rugged outdoor look, she guessed. It made his blue eyes even bluer.

"I have something for you." His hand disappeared back over the partition as he moved to the side of her desk. "Thought of you as soon as I saw it."

He placed the box on her desk. A simple wrapping of

brown paper held together with brown twine and anchored in the middle of the simple bow was a flower. Not one she could identify, but she was taken with its beauty as it lay against the dull background.

"Go ahead, open it."

She felt its weight as she gently unwrapped the gift. The flower's scent reached her suddenly and she stopped and brought it close to her nose. "Oh, that is the most wonderful scent! What is it, Jared?"

"Simple jasmine blossom, that's all. Doesn't take much to let you know it's there."

She could tell that he was not interested in her take on the flower but wanted her to reveal the contents of the box. She put the box back on the desk, gently unwrapped the paper, and opened the lid. Resting on a bed of what looked like straw, a rock sat. She stared at it for what seemed forever, trying to elicit the appropriate response. What do you say to someone when he gives you a rock? The heat crawling up her neck would soon reveal to him her discomfort and embarrassment. She had to respond.

"Well, I think that it needs some explanation, right?" He was gently laughing, not at her but about the situation that he had assumed would take place once she saw the contents.

"Jared, I appreciate your..."

He interrupted her. "I decided to climb it. All the way to the top."

He waited for her to connect the dots, but her blank stare made it obvious to him that their conversation before the weekend really held no meaning for her. She had forgotten, which sent him the immediate message that he did not want to entertain. Too deep into it now, he had to close this conversation and get on with his work.

"I met a guy who hadn't climbed it either but talked me into it. I guess we were lucky to make it up and back because we weren't really prepared. Passed plenty of folks who knew what they were doing and looked like walking advertisements for REI. Anyway, I thought of you when we got to the top. Just wanted to bring back a souvenir for you."

Her perplexed expression made him feel anxious and ready to vacate this place, the sooner the better.

"You went to the top? Oh, Jared! That's amazing! I read a bit about Whitney after our chat last week and the picture of it was beautiful, but it looks so rugged and unfriendly. I can't believe you went to the top! And this," she reached into the box and lifted the rock from its nest, "this is so thoughtful of you. I'll treasure this, Jared. You know as well as I do that I'll never be able to pick one up on my own, not at that elevation. I can't believe you did this!"

She had surprised herself with her response, which had not been anywhere near the surface of her thinking a minute ago. More surprising, she realized as she rolled the rock in her hands, was the fact that she meant every word of it.

"Never say never, Allie. Glad you like it. Got to get back to work. See you later."

He turned and headed back down the hallway. She had remembered, he thought. She even looked up the mountain. He silently took back the negative thoughts about her interest in him and felt the grin coming on an instant before it covered his face.

Setting the rock on the shelf over her desk, she found it hard not to keep looking up at it as she focused on the emails that had invaded her screen. And each time she did, she saw Jared's face. Just as she was about to read the last email before giving herself a break from the next barrage, a message from him popped up. She skipped the last one and opened his.

"Hey! Forgot to tell you why I brought you a rock. Metaphor. Allie=Rock/Rock=Allie"

Another popped up. "Take it the right way, OK?"

Another. "Should have brought you the mountaintop!"

She couldn't respond. His words seemed to fill the screen while she coped with trying to understand why this person, a workmate only, had latched on to this impression of her. Was he saying what she thought he was? Was she supposed to be his rock? And why? What had she ever done for him that would place her in the category of dependability? Wasn't that what his metaphor was all about?

Now she feared that in some way she had led him on. She felt guilty at the thought. Old enough to be his mother, the idea that he might have a crush on her terrified her. Had she, without realizing it, given him the impression that she was interested in him? The banter about a weekend trip, her exuberance about a rock, and her revelation that she had followed up on his destination last weekend without her; had that been enough for him to think that there was hope? She needed to straighten this all out, which meant that she had to talk with him, face to face. And she would do it when the next opportunity arose. Not now. She had a full day ahead of her and knew where her focus must be. To do that, she reached for the rock, returned it to the box, and shoved it into the bottom drawer of her desk. The jasmine blossom, however, took its place on the shelf. That was okay, she thought. It had no permanency. She would enjoy its fragrance until it withered and was thrown away.

Chapter 54

This session, he knew, would require him to hold on no matter how he reacted. Knowing that she would be right next to him gave him the strength that he would need to rely upon. He found great peace in the knowledge that he no longer had to face his past alone. What he had longed for deep within had finally become a reality: ridding himself of the memories and the burden that had been preventing him from finding himself again. He had to admit that, even though he had been dismissive of this therapy mumbo-jumbo, there was something to it. The something was not a thing but the one who had unlocked the door. Gratitude was an emotion that he had not felt in such a long time, but he welcomed its appearance and made a note to himself to keep it in the forefront of his mind. Maybe this was what coming to Jesus was all about?

He knew, however, that he was not a completely changed man. Too many ghosts still hiding within prevented him from fooling himself. Once, he could stay fooled by ingesting the variety of poisons at his disposal, floating beyond his own reality, oblivious and disconnected. Now, with his life on the verge of being fully resuscitated, each day freer of poisons than the last, his mind clearing as he began to release himself from his past, he woke each morning rested and ready to move forward.

"I brought it, just in case." She pointed to the notebook on the table.

"Good to know, but no need." She looked a bit preoccupied, he thought. Maybe a session before him had not gone so well? "How are you?" She was usually the first to greet.

"Michael, thanks for asking. Sorry. I'm just fine. What about you?"

She moved to the chair next to him and sat down. He did the same.

"I'm good. Sleeping better."

"Sleep is a gift, isn't it? Changes your whole outlook."

She wasn't looking directly at him as she fiddled with her glasses, trying to set them right upon the bridge of her nose. "Well, we have work to do this morning, don't we?"

He suddenly felt as though he was a child in school, sitting behind a desk too big for him while the teacher towered over him, waiting for his response. Was it her words, the intonation of her voice, her distracted behavior? She was acting as though their last session had never existed, that the lunch that followed with its ease and warmth had not occurred. Fighting off these negative impressions, he smiled at her, but she did not smile back.

"Let's begin where we left off, okay?"

"You'll need to remind me. I would rather not repeat myself, if I don't need to."

"Understood. Of course. Your brother, Stephen. The well. Pussy in the well. The rhyme? Your mother? Do you remember telling me about that?" He nodded. "Good."

It never took long for the images to appear, nor did it this time. His mother beside him, then pushing him gently off her as she struggled to stand.

"My mother. I remember that it was the first time that she had come out of the house to see what he had done to us. She was the one who pulled Stephen out of the well that day. I wanted to help her, but she wouldn't let me. She could see that I was hurting."

He stopped and rubbed his thighs as if working out cramps. As the rubbing intensified, she feared that she would lose him again.

"Why were you hurting, Michael?"

Pulling his hands away from his pant legs and now crossing his arms in front of him, he leaned back and extended his legs in front of him.

"Why was I hurting? Because of him. Because of my father. I wasn't going to let him get away with it this time. I ran after him. He had Stephen and I knew what he was going to do to him. If anyone was going in that hole, it was going to be me and not my brother."

256

As he sat forward again, he drew his legs in and curled his feet under the chair. His arms stayed crossed.

"I was too late. I tried to stop him but was just too late. I can still hear Stephen calling out for me. God, he was so frightened, so alone."

She detected a slight rocking back and forth of his body.

"What did he do to you, Michael?"

Her now familiar and caring voice helped block out Stephen's pleas. He could go on.

"I grabbed at his leg just as he let go of Stephen. He turned on me. I remember that with each hit of his fists, I was growing weaker, blinded by the blows and my body screaming with pain. I must have lost consciousness because I remember waking up thinking I was hearing Stephen call out to me. But I was hurt so badly that I was afraid I was close to dying. Somehow, though, I managed to crawl to the side of the well and pull myself up far enough to look down and to tell him that I was there and that it was going to be okay."

Again, she sensed that this might be the end of the session. She waited only as long as she dared before she spoke.

"It's okay, Michael. Keep going. You told me that you thought that Stephen was dead. Do you remember that?"

"He was so still at the end of that rope. He just dangled there, like a rag doll. No sound. I tried to pull him up, but there was no way that I could do it. I never got him out."

"But he did get out, didn't he, Michael? How did he get out?"

"She must have pulled him up because the next thing I knew, she was holding both of us next to her on the ground."

"She, meaning your mother?"

"Yeah. I remember feeling so safe with her. But then she wanted to take us both back to the house. She didn't understand what would happen this time if we went back. He was out of his mind with drink, and she thought that we would be okay walking into that?"

He was shaking his head in disbelief, as if hearing those words spoken to him about someone else.

"She made me angry because she wouldn't listen to me. I wanted to get out of there, but she wouldn't let me. I threatened to take my brother with me even if she wasn't going to come with us. I remember how much I hurt just yelling at her to do the right thing. It was like a nightmare where you can't make any headway no matter how imperative it is that you do so. Nothing made sense at that moment. I must have thought that my mother was losing her mind thinking that she could keep us safe from him. I knew that I was angry with her. I remember that so clearly."

Again, a pause. He shifted his position so that his now uncrossed arms rested in his lap, finger loosely entwined with each other. He uncrossed his ankles and anchored his feet to the floor, flat on the ground directly under each knee, as if ready to withstand a sudden jolt from the earth below.

He continued after taking an unnaturally audible, long deep breath. "I didn't hear him come up from behind, but she did. I remember that she suddenly grabbed me so that I was now on the ground next to Stephen. And then she left us. It happened that fast. She was screaming at him. I had never heard her scream like that. Never heard her scream at all. She yelled at him. Stood right between us and him and yelled at him. I don't remember what she said, but I knew that she was trying to protect us. All I could do was protect Stephen, so I stayed next to him."

As if all verbal ability suddenly abandoned him, Michael stopped speaking. But Alison watched his eyes and mouth as they betrayed him. She knew that there was more that he was only allowing himself to hear, to see. Tears flooded his eyes and he fought to keep his mouth still by tightening his lips so that they seemed to disappear from his face. He dropped his face as if searching for the words on the floor at his feet while gravity released the moisture from his eyes, wetting the tops of his shoes. His ravaged voice startled her.

"And then she was on the ground. I remember seeing my mother lying on the ground and the blood coming from her head. She wasn't moving, and I knew she was dead. I don't remember making any conscious decision, but I do remember pushing myself up and somehow running away from him so that he would follow me and not come near my brother. I don't know how far I ran or how I even managed to get away from him, but I did, and he was not far behind. I had the advantage, I guess, because I was not full of mind-numbing booze, just functioning with a broken body. His brain was having plenty of fun with his bodily functions, that's for sure. So, I hid from him knowing all along that Stephen was safe. I remember finding a grove of redwoods, one of which had a burned-out trunk. I ducked into it and pulled my body up, trying to become invisible. I still can smell the burned bark and feel its coolness on my sore back and head. It occurred to me as I sat in its embrace that an old fire's damage could still be lingering within the moist red fibers of this mother tree. I remember drawing comfort from that." He stood. "Do you mind if we take a break, just a short one?" He started to walk toward the window.

"Sure. Sure. That's probably a good idea. Can I get you some water?"

"No, I'm okay. Just need to stretch a bit. Sixty-five years spent on this planet, and I'm not getting any younger, you know."

The mention of his age prompted her to silently calculate the numbers. He was eight years older. Not such a wide spread in ages. Not at this stage of the game. Dismissing these thoughts, she stood as well but did not move toward him. Instead, she walked to the door, as if expecting someone to enter at any moment. Peering through the rectangular glass window into the bright artificial light that filled the hallway, an idea came to her and before vetting it, she blurted out, "Got an idea, Michael. Let's take a walk. It would do us both good."

Looking at the back of his head, she suddenly realized that she probably couldn't do that and get away with it. She would need an attendant to accompany them, certainly. What was she thinking? Before she could correct her error, he had turned to her and was heading toward the door.

"Great idea. Only thing is that if we're going for a walk, it's straight out of this building and into that!"

He pointed to the window as she, for the first time today, focused on the environment beyond the confines of this building's walls. The window revealed a bright patch of blue sky while letting in the warm rays of the sun that slid across the floor, covering her shoes and continuing somewhere behind her.

"What are we waiting for?"

What was she waiting for? That seemed a good question, and one that she would not answer with the obvious reason. At that moment, the decision was made as she opened the door and stepped into the hall. He was right behind her.

"We'll just head straight out that exit."

She pointed down the hall to the overhead exit sign. The short distance to the door suddenly grew to a nightmarish length. Then she felt his open hand on the small of her back, gently shoving her forward.

"Let's do it then," he whispered in her ear, and she found her hand pushing the exit door open sooner than she'd expected.

The sun was much warmer than she thought it would be as they walked the paths that meandered through the grounds. She tried to take in the moment. So, this was what it must be like to have time to take care of yourself. Always too tired to do it first thing in the morning, she seldom had any time at lunch—really, what was lunch? And she was unable to move a muscle at the end of the day as she staggered into her apartment. Her exercise regimen consisted of getting in and out of bed, brushing her teeth and hair, and walking the few steps it took to get to her car and out of it again into the office.

When she thought about it, she was alarmed that she led such a sedentary lifestyle. The only part of her body that really got a workout was her brain. And even that she questioned as she walked with a patient on the open grounds without an attendant accompanying them. How many rules had she broken so far today? What could she possibly do to prevent this adult male who outweighed her from breaking into a run, one of escape? But so far, nothing had happened, no one had come running after them. Perhaps they had gone unnoticed for the time being. And with that thought, she thought better of them staying out any longer. It was going to be difficult enough to go back through the doors without someone questioning where they had been. Then she remembered. What was she thinking? She had her keys to the side entrances reserved for employee access. Easy enough, then. But still, it was time to end what she realized had been a special moment in her day.

"Let's head back in, Michael. Don't want to ruin a good thing here, but I'm not supposed to have you out here without supervision. Let's go." She turned around and waited for him to do the same.

"Am I going to get you in trouble? You can always blame me for forcing you out the door." His voice was serious, but his smile revealed otherwise. "Okay. If we must, we must. But this has been a gift. Thank you."

He was now next to her, so close that their shoulders touched briefly. She moved away, providing an acceptable space between them as they headed back down the path.

"You're welcome, Michael. And thank you for the shove."

Back in the room, he took his seat and readied himself for what was to come. Feeling more relaxed now, he gazed out the window as if to draw in the light and air that he had left behind moments ago.

"Are you ready to continue?"

She knew what he was thinking as he turned and gazed at her. She hadn't wanted it to end either.

"Yes. I need to."

"Good. You were huddled in the burned-out tree. That's where you stopped, Michael. Do you want to go on from there?"

He nodded. "The tree, I thought, in my eight-year-old mind, would protect me. And it might have. But I could hear him getting closer. He had my baseball bat in his hand, the one that he'd hit my mother with, the one that he hit me with as I tried to run from him. I could hear him hitting and thrashing the ground, the undergrowth in his way. He was so drunk that it took him forever to reach me. He was upon me but didn't see me in the darkness of my hiding place. I reached out and grabbed my bat. I guess I surprised him because he let go of it so easily. And then I jumped out of the tree and laid into him wherever I could. I could feel the wood contacting his body." He looked at his hands as he turned the palms face-up. "The vibration."

Her eyes followed his arms as they rose above his head, fists clenched around an invisible wooden bat's neck while he motioned downward furiously again and again. Alarmed for the first time in working with him, she felt a sudden fear of him. However, she stayed in her seat, waiting out the battle that he was waging. For some reason, she knew that she was safe with him, that the fear she felt was only a knee-jerk reaction.

His movements subsided as he released the invisible object that only he had seen so vividly in his grip. As though nothing had taken place, his hands found their previous resting place in his lap and he sat back, turning to her.

"I saw him fall; he was trying not to, but he couldn't do anything else. But he was still alive even after all the bashing I had tried to do to him. That's when I did it. Just like he had done to my mother and tried to do to me. I didn't care if he was facing me. I knew that I had to end it for all of us. So, I made a final blow to his head. He didn't move after that. Just lay still, finally."

"Michael, you killed your father out of self-defense. You are not to blame yourself for any of this. Do you understand me?"

Not surprised by the outcome of his revelations, she was able to remain calm and professional. The words imprinted in her brain, the responses that she had carefully memorized and properly applied during her training and internships, slid off her tongue. So easy to step back, isn't it, she thought. Separate yourself from the clients when necessary so as not to be drawn into their emotional drama. Stay in control. Your job is to guide, to delve, but only enough so that the client does all the work. She waited for him to affirm this.

"Blame myself for my father's death? Is that what you think I am doing?"

Now that he was fully engaged with her, she held on tight to the edge of her chair.

"The blame is not mine. I won't begin to own any blame for his death. Not his."

His words were heated. His hurt was evident in them because of her reliance on retreating to a clinical place of safety, and it broke her heart. And now they poured from him so quickly and with such intensity that she had to remind herself to breathe, so suffocated was she by his barrage.

"He deserved every blow. Every broken bone. His death. No. I accept no blame. Not for him. But do you care at all about my mother, my brother? For God's sake! He took my family away from me. He tortured us for his own amusement. Over and over and over again. And did she do anything to stop it? Not until it was too late. Not until after I let my brother die at the end of a rope. Not until I was barely alive enough to try and reason with her. Blame. Who do I blame?"

His voice was angry and loud, and she expected that at any moment, the door would fly open and attendants would race toward him and wrestle him to the ground. She tried not to think about that, however. She tried to stay with him, to keep eye contact, to somehow let him know that she was where she said she would be. Right by his side.

"Michael, Michael..."

"I tried to blame her. For years I blamed her for everything. God, I was only eight and saw only what I knew as reality. She was supposed to protect us. She never did. Always came in after the fact. After the damage had been done to us. Carrying her bandages and her balms into our room and thinking that soothing the wounds would be enough each time for us to believe what she always said? That it was over and that it was going to be okay?" He paused, and then almost imperceptibly shook his head as he continued. "I never understood what she must have gone through. I knew that he yelled at her and that she cried a lot but always seemed over it when she got to us. And in my mind, each time, I would believe that it was finally over. That's how she would make me feel. That it was finally over. But then it would begin again. And the play would continue, with her acting her part with him and with us. I tried so hard to blame her, but she was caught as badly as us. It's taken me a lot of years to figure that one out." He had lowered his voice now, almost in a reflective manner, as if it didn't matter that anyone was in the room with him.

This time, she waited, without the need to interrupt him.

"I do blame myself, but not because of them. Stephen would be alive if I had kept my promise to him. He knew that I was supposed to protect him. There was no one else. Who else could do it? No one knew about what was going on at our house. No one. I was his protector and that's what he depended upon. I failed him when I should have been the one in the dark, not him. I never should have let our father take Stephen out of the house. I could have somehow stopped him and none of this would have happened. But I didn't."

He paused, with no acknowledgement of her presence. He was elsewhere, she knew. Then he shot up from his chair, startling her. She willed herself to remain calm. The sudden intensity and anger in his voice shattered the brief silence.

"And I can see him! I can hear Stephen's cries even now after so many years. He won't speak to me now. Wants nothing to do with me. But he won't let go of me and I can't let go of him. Not this time."

He was done. She knew he was finished. She sat quietly, watching him as he lowered his body, now visibly relaxed, into the chair. He had allowed her in. She felt no urgency to respond to him but let his words linger between them so that she could attempt to absorb their meaning.

Back at her desk, she recorded her notes, which came at a rapid speed. Interspersed with questions, the document in front of her continued to grow in length as the screen automatically reeled new empty pages. Surprised by the energy that she felt, her fingers flew over the keyboard, and she was suddenly aware of her rapid breathing. She understood that she had brought him to the light, clichéd as it sounded. Now the work would begin. The real work of helping Michael understand and accept all that had happened and then all that could happen. He needed to know that he was so close to starting again. To living a life that he had accepted as never possible. Whatever that life might look like was not for her to decide. All she needed to do was walk him up to the door so that he could open it for himself.

"Time to pack it up."

The familiar voice and message brought a satisfied close to her day as she watched Jared saunter down the hall out to the light.

Chapter 55

Sleep eluded Alison. Exhausted and mentally spent, she had looked forward to crawling into bed and leaving everything behind for a few hours. Her body had demanded it of her. Some quick microwaved leftovers had been about all she could cope with, and they had satisfied the need for an evening meal. Her wind-down time each evening was usually spent reading or watching TV, but she had forgone both activities only to have taken an early shower and a couple of aspirin before sliding under the covers. She could not remember falling asleep, but its sweet relief came quickly.

An hour later, she awoke suddenly. Checking the clock, she saw that it was 12:25. She rolled over, determined to sleep through the night and sleep came once again. But it didn't last. Interrupted sleep was not uncommon for her but had grown in frequency in the last few months. She could never pinpoint what it was exactly that had stirred her but once awake, her mind clicked on at an accelerated rate so that a myriad of unrelated thoughts shoved their way in front of each other, vying for her immediate attention. And she would find herself trying to solve unsolvable issues repeatedly. She had read somewhere that the worst thing to do when this happened was to stay in bed. Get up, move around, have a warm cup of milk, read a bit; do anything but lie there exhausting yourself trying to get back to sleep.

She stumbled into the kitchen, debating about the milk remedy. Not a fan of milk in the first place, she decided to read instead. The room was chilled by a window left open a crack. In her fatigue, she had forgotten to close it. She shut it and went back into the bedroom to layer herself a bit better. With book in hand, she headed back to the living room, plopping down on the couch unceremoniously while grabbing the throw. Warm and almost too toasty, she wedged herself into the cushions and pillows, propping the book on her stomach, and began where she thought she had left off. The bookmark had slipped out in her maneuverings.

It came to her, an intruding thought that made her sit straight up and drop her book to the floor. Stephen, the brother. Was he dead or alive? He couldn't have died at the well. Michael had revealed to her that the brothers had been placed in foster care. If she remembered correctly, the last time they were placed together was when Michael was twelve and Stephen was eight. Yet, Michael insisted he was to blame for his brother's death. That Stephen *was* his brother. But didn't he also say that he, Stephen, wouldn't speak to him now? Wanted nothing to do with him? Confusion swallowed any clarity in her thinking. She struggled to refocus on what she knew was his confusion, not hers. Michael believed that his brother died there along with his mother. But his most recent words betrayed him. His brother had survived, at least long enough to be in foster care with Michael. The records could easily confirm this. Did he know something else? Something that he had come to terms with at some point and that struggled to survive as a reality that Michael could accept?

Now, fully awake and ready for the day to begin, she moved off the couch. Pulling her notepad from her briefcase, she started to put into writing the confusion that had just visited her. If, indeed, Stephen was still alive, two important and suddenly pressing issues presented themselves that both she and Michael needed to tackle. Finding his brother and bringing them together would be the first challenge. Not a difficult issue on the surface, but perhaps a rather dangerous one if Michael's confusion over his brother's fate was real to him, the imaginings of a tormented and much damaged mind. What had happened at that scene so long ago that had led him to create his own reality? The second challenge did not come as easily as the first for her. If he was alive and Michael knew it, then her work had just become even more complicated. She felt blocked in her problem solving. How to confront him with this possible truth frightened her, and she suddenly felt inept. He was fragile, and she would be the one to shatter him completely and finally if he wasn't ready to face it.

It dawned on her that she might be in over her head. How quickly she had come to this state as she thought about Michael and the last few days with him! Had his good progress inflated her thinking that she was the only one who could reach him, who could help him find his way out of this maze? She would need to seek some advice, clarification that she was on the right track. More importantly, how should she proceed with him?

Laying the notepad down next to her unread book, Jared's face loomed in front of her. No, he was much younger than her, and she was sure that his experience in the professional world did not yet amount to much. He would only confuse her because she would never be able to accept his advice. She mentally listed her professional contacts including past professors, as well as the two doctors with whom she had interned while finishing her PhD. Of these, Allie decided to contact Dr. Ellen Forbes, whom she had admired from day one. Dr. Forbes had been a wonderful mentor to her and had given her the greatest encouragement about her God-given gifts in psychology. If anyone would understand and give appropriate advice, it would be her.

Feeling as though she now could begin the tasks at hand, Alison felt sudden hunger pains. She smiled, realizing that she had just consumed plenty of food for thought but now needed to pay attention to other parts of her body, which were complaining loudly and clearly to be fed. *This I can do without any help,* she thought, and headed into the kitchen.

Chapter 56

He hadn't forgotten about the letter. He had tried to move beyond its arrival in his home. However, physically destroying it had not removed the contents from his mind. When he closed his eyes, he could see the elegant lettering loom from the stationery, which seemed to scream to him that he could not avoid the inevitable. As the scream grew in intensity, the letters became horribly distorted in front of him, yet inexplicably still legible. Fear did not slowly creep up on him but pounced its terrific weight upon him so that he felt momentarily paralyzed by the reminder that, after all these years, his brother was still alive.

And this reminder was not welcomed by Stephen. No. He would not let this most recent event destroy what he had created for himself. After all, Michael was no longer his brother. He had stopped being his brother when he left Stephen in a home that had not been theirs, one of the many in which he had found himself, all without the companionship of his brother. However, he could no longer deny that Michael existed, considering the phone calls and now the communication from a stranger who unwittingly reintroduced Michael to Stephen.

All of this was inescapable, so he found himself accepting this truth, but he vowed to seal it away forever. What he was unable to do was acknowledge the other truths, so deeply buried in his subconscious, that of a four-year-old boy. And because of this inability, he carried on with his life as though he had only recently appeared on the earth but as a grown man in his sixties whose time here was growing shorter with every breath he took.

Chapter 57

A part of her felt such relief to have come to a decision regarding Michael. To accept that she could not proceed on her own felt good. She felt a twinge of disappointment in herself, but she could deal with that. She had scheduled to see Michael later in the afternoon but knew that it would be a mistake to do so without the ammunition she needed. One of the attendants would let him know of the change. As she opened her briefcase, she remembered the notes that she had taken the night before, which she would need in front of her when she spoke with Dr. Forbes. She could only hope that the good doctor would be receptive to her call and willing to listen to the history of her complicated client. More to the point, that she would have the sound advice that would arm her as she and Michael climbed yet one more mountain together.

The voice on the other end of the line was comfortably familiar to Allie. She had been prepared to introduce herself to the woman who had guided her so carefully and well but who, by this time, had done so with many predoctoral interns. Allie would be surprised if her name sounded at all familiar to the doctor.

"Good morning, Dr. Forbes. This is Alison Lawler. I was an intern with you twelve years ago. I am sure that you do not remember me, but you left such an impression on me. I'm practicing now here in Los Angeles."

"Alison. Of course. I remember you, which must say something about you, don't you think?" The laughter that accompanied this question relaxed Allie.

"I can only hope that it communicates positively and not the other way around."

"My dear. I purposely force myself to forget the negative contacts, of which, I must say, there were many. You were a rare one to come along. How are you?" Her tone was sincere.

"Thanks for your kind words, Dr. Forbes. I'm fine. I am

sorry to disturb you, but I wondered if I might speak with you regarding a difficult case? I'm stymied as to how to go forward and thought that if you had time either now or at your convenience, I might be able to present to you my dilemma. Perhaps get some advice?" Allie was conscious of holding her breath as she waited for a response.

"You know, it's been an awfully long time since we last saw one another and right now is not a good time." Allie's heart sank. "However, are you free tomorrow sometime in the afternoon? Perhaps over lunch? You name the place and time and I will be there."

Had she heard her correctly? Was it that easy to find her way out of her problem? Did people like this really exist? Allie became uncomfortably aware that she had gotten too used to the other side of human behavior.

"Oh, that would be wonderful. I can't thank you enough, Dr. Forbes. I certainly don't want to intrude on your busy schedule, but lunch would be lovely. How does twelve thirty sound? I'll make a reservation at Café Stella."

"Good. I look forward to seeing you then, Alison. And it's so good to hear from you. Until tomorrow, then."

Buoyed by such a positive interaction, Allie felt relief from the worries that had plagued her over the last twelve hours. Wanting to make a good impression tomorrow, she would need to organize her thoughts. After all, Michael's history was not straightforward. However, she knew that she could not reveal too much. She knew the ethical boundaries. She would not shy away from referring to her notes, word for word if necessary, so that she would not waste Dr. Forbes's time. Her goals were to walk away with answers and to gift Michael with yet one more open door for him to walk through.

Waiting outside the restaurant's entrance, it dawned on her that she might not recognize Dr. Forbes. She wondered if her mentor had changed at all. Allie knew that she had. If nothing else, she had gained weight and knew that her face, haggard and

and drawn, was no longer the youthful visage that Dr. Forbes remembered.

"Alison?" She turned, and Dr. Forbes approached her, holding out her hand. "How good to see you." Her handshake was firm and reassuring.

"Dr. Forbes. Thank you for coming. I wondered if you would recognize me. It's been a while, and this profession has taken a bit of a toll on me."

"You look no different than the last day I saw you. Well, a bit more mature. Aren't we all?" Her smile was friendly, and she reminded Allie of her mother.

"Yes, I suppose we are. Well, let's go in. I hope you have an appetite. Have you been here before?"

"Oh, yes. Many times. I was pleased that this was your choice, Alison. After you." She gestured toward the entrance.

As they sat down, Allie worried about the timing. She had played it over in her mind. To get through her questions, she would need to talk right through the meal and then after. She only hoped that Dr. Forbes was amenable to this approach.

After ordering and as the glasses of wine were being poured, Dr. Forbes leaned forward. "Why don't we get down to business, Alison. We can catch up at another time. I would like to reestablish our acquaintance as professionals."

"I would certainly like that, Dr. Forbes." It was so easy, she realized, to speak with her, to practice the professional interaction that she now realized she had been missing and longing for. "I hope you will forgive me for using my cheat sheet, but I was afraid that I would overlook some of the questions I have for you. Do you mind?" She held up her handwritten notes.

"Of course not. It just reinforces my memories of you as such an organized and intelligent intern. Go ahead." She sat back and sipped her wine, never taking her eyes off her former student.

Alison began by reviewing in as general terms as possible the history of her client. Her excitement was evident to Dr. Forbes as she revealed her small success with him and her approach through journaling. When Allie took a breath and looked up from her notes, Dr. Forbes was smiling. Not a "good girl" affirmation but one of insight, unspoken wisdom. Almost identical to the expression her own mother used only when she knew more than Allie but patiently waited for her daughter to understand on her own. Allie continued.

"I've come to a sticking point. My concern is that I will ruin all the good progress we have made to this point if I go at it without some sound advice. His fragility is just below the surface. But now I need to question him about the truth, and I don't know how to do this so that I don't destroy him. He has one foot in his reality and the other in ours."

She could feel the weight of this burden suddenly descend upon her, and the promise of relief that Dr. Forbes might hold seemed impossibly out of reach.

After all the facts were presented, Allie sat back, fatigued by having gone through Michael's journey again. The woman across the table from her appeared to be equally burdened. Allie prepared herself for her response, lifting her untouched glass of wine and letting the warmth and fragrance of the liquid fill her mouth before swallowing. She noticed, as she lowered the glass, that Dr. Forbes's glass was almost empty.

"First of all, it appears to me that you have handled this client very well." Her words came slowly and intentionally as if the recipient might struggle with their meaning. "I must commend you for that. You were right to stop when you did. The ground in front of you is rocky and treacherous. It means a great deal to me that you have asked me to advise you." With this last sentence she moved her lunch plate to the far edge of the table, leaned forward, and resting her arms on the table, folded her hands together. "I am going to ask you a question which you may or may not be able to answer right now. If you need time to think before you respond, please say so. I have no agenda and my time is your time in this case. Do you understand?"

Alarmed and caught off guard, Allie sat a bit taller in her chair. "I do, yes, of course." She had not foreseen the conversation taking this turn, and she hoped that her current discomfort was not apparent to Dr. Forbes.

"Have you developed a relationship with your client that is not strictly professional in nature?"

One question. Yet it lingered between them as if a loaded gun had fired numerous bullets across the table and, as if in some science-fiction matrix, they hung suspended in air, waiting only for their release to continue in the spectrum of reality. Dr. Forbes had not moved but focused her eyes on Allie with such intensity that Allie could do nothing to break the contact.

"Remember, no need to answer immediately. But I want you to search deeply and then not be afraid to speak the truth to me."

Slowly, she leaned back, her body seemingly melting into the chair so that the distance that had, a moment ago, felt suffocating now allowed the air to return to Allie's starving lungs as she realized that she had been holding her breath.

"Dr. Forbes, I...I..."

"No need to answer. I have taken you by surprise, haven't I?" She reached for her glass, holding it up but away from her mouth. "I'll tell you a secret. It's a question that all of us have had to answer at some point in our careers. For some, more than once." With that, she tipped the glass as she drew it to her lips and emptied it of its red liquid.

Allie was thankful that she had been given a temporary reprieve. But only temporary, she knew, as she frantically tried to generate something, anything, to say. What had she said that would cause the woman sitting across from her to ask the question? Nothing. She was sure of it. Had she gotten anywhere? She was about to end this meeting without any kind of support. She would walk out the door with no more than she had before she entered. Feeling shortchanged and a bit miffed, she worked a smile into place.

"Thank you. I would like to respond to your question."

What was she doing? Was she trying to sabotage this relationship by responding to her loaded question? No. She knew the answer. She knew it before the doctor finished speaking. What she wasn't sure about was where her response would take her in her relationship not only with Dr. Forbes, but also with Michael. But she had asked for the meeting, the advice, and she knew that she was in capable hands. For a moment, she sensed a glimmer of a client-therapist relationship between them. *That's my own inexperience casting a shadow over reality*, she thought. Suddenly aware that she had been holding her glass of wine just above the table's surface as if to drink from it, she once again let the liquid slide down her throat before responding.

"I would edit the phrase 'developed a relationship.' I feel as though there is the possibility of one developing. Truthfully? There have been moments, most recently, in which I sensed something more. I'm not sure if it's my interpretation or if it's reality. Frankly, I think that there could be something there, but only when he is able to receive it. Have I really gone too far astray? Have I crossed the line?" Another sip.

"Not at all. Not yet, anyway. You have recognized the situation and have verbalized it to me. Allie, understand that in this work, when one human being is fully engaged and invested in another, it is only natural for feelings to emerge that take you by surprise. The trick is to determine why the feelings are there. Once you do that, you will know if they are real or just an empathetic reaction. That's when the work begins for you."

Okay. Now she was sure. This was turning into a session and she was the client. How could the table turn so quickly? She was going to leave and go back to work with the extra burden of examining herself before she could continue with Michael. She had no one to blame but herself. She should have taken the doctor's advice and given her response some thought. That way, at least, it would have given her time to work through her options. Perhaps, permanently burying the truth that she had known all along.

Chapter 58

"I just wanted to thank you for seeing me yesterday, Dr. Forbes. You gave me food for thought."

Her voice was strong and in control. She had spent much of the morning rehearsing her words before she called the office, and she felt prepared for Dr. Forbes's reaction. She knew that she would advise against Alison's idea, but that was all right with Allie. She needed to separate herself from this new set of eyes that had peered too closely. Not yet sure about how she would proceed with Michael, something within her reassured her that she would be better off on her own at this point. She had just had a moment of doubt about her own capabilities; that was all. Regretting that she had ever contacted Ellen Forbes, she hurried to finish her memorized communication before she forgot it.

"I appreciate your advice and have decided to continue my work with my client, who, after careful examination of my own intentions, holds no attraction to me whatsoever. I want to complete my work with him so that he can function independently and successfully outside the confines of these walls. That, alone, will bring me great joy and satisfaction."

There was no response—none.

"Dr. Forbes? Are you still there?" Still no response. Thinking that she must have lost connection, she debated whether to call her back or wait for her to do so.

"I'm here."

Allie put the phone to her ear once more. "Oh, good. I thought that we had lost connection."

"What I am about to say to you might sound rather ethereal, and for that I apologize. However, I will say it, and then this conversation will be over. We have not lost connection, but I fear that you, my dear, have. It is apparent to me that my words have fallen on deaf ears. So be it. I wish you all the best in your decision to proceed. Again, it is your decision, not mine. Take care." The line went dead.

She had no idea how long she sat at her desk holding her cell to her ear. She thought that she had been prepared for any response just because she had made up her mind so strongly about her lie to the doctor. But she had read right through Allie's verbiage and her insecurities. Allie felt a twinge of guilt and experienced a childhood memory of an adult's reprimand that generated sadness in disappointing someone whom she respected. Grown up enough to recognize where the feeling was coming from and why, she shoved it from her mind as she lay her cell on top of a pile of paper.

She remained satisfied with her decision even though stung by Dr. Forbes's accusation that Alison had not heeded her advice. She had answered the question twice: once to Dr. Forbes and once to herself. And she knew which one was the truth, as did Dr. Forbes. Allie knew that from this point on, the rules had changed and that she had changed them. Michael, a victim of his own history, could easily become a victim of her own selfishness and desires. She was about to cross another line, one with the potential for life-altering damage to them both. The realization that she held not one but two fragile lives in limbo shot through her like a bolt of lightning, temporarily paralyzing but miraculously enlightening. The way was suddenly clear to her and any hesitation in acknowledging her feelings for Michael vanished. And clearer still was the need to include Michael. How and when she would do this was not as clear and weighed heavily on her as she tried to refocus on the paperwork that awaited her attention.

The afternoon seemed interminable. She had gone over her words so many times that she began to doubt their meaning, not to mention their sincerity. But she had no other way to express what she felt and, considering that the recipient of her communication might be in a mental state unable to receive them, she could not veer from their practiced order. Her thinking was plagued by the thought that she was breaking every rule in the book. But she didn't care. She needed to move this whole thing forward so that both she and Michael could come to terms with their lives, together or apart.

She entered the room. He had not arrived yet. It was stuffy and smelled stale. She opened a window and felt the cool air envelop her upper body. Taking a deep breath, she detected a hint of some spring blossom somewhere on the grounds, its fragrance lifting her spirits momentarily until she heard the door swing open. Turning to greet him, she was surprised at Michael's appearance. He looked disheveled; he had misaligned the buttons on his shirt so that one hem was easily three inches lower than the other, he wore no socks, and his pants sagged around his hips, which barely protruded enough to keep the waistband in place; he had not snapped them at the waist and the fly was only halfway zipped up. He smiled at her.

"Good afternoon."

"And to you, Michael."

She was surprised that she managed to produce those words, considering his shocking state. Unsettled, suddenly, she took another deep breath to void herself of a sudden unknown.

"You seem to be unusually ready to go. Anything that I should be aware of before we get started?"

The words hung between them, both waiting for one or the other of them to state the obvious.

"Not a thing. Just eager to see you and to close my life story, as it has played out so far, for good. That didn't come out quite right. I mean, I feel different since we last talked, like a burden has been lifted and the way seems much clearer to me. I forgot what being relaxed feels like. And I have only you to thank." He kept on smiling, never taking his eyes off hers. "So, I'm thinking that we should get started."

This was not expected. She was thrown off and uncomfortable in his presence. He had taken control before she could open her mouth. Had she been thinking clearly, she would have rejoiced in his positive frame of mind and said something that would let him know that she had recognized this achievement. But nothing was making sense to her, and the only response she could generate was physical. Turning away from him, she headed toward the door.

"Whoa! What's going on? Why are you leaving?"

He stood up and was moving toward her too quickly. Now standing behind her so close that she could feel his breath on her neck, she reached for the door handle but failed to turn the knob as his hand enclosed hers in the duplicate act, the strength of it preventing her own hand's movement.

As suddenly as she had made her decision to leave, she turned to him and with his embrace, she fell into him. The wash of relief that consumed her blocked out every thought that should have been reasonable, logical, and acceptable. None of it mattered now. The world, her world, had changed in a matter of minutes. There seemed to be nothing but silence and warmth encircling her as Michael's embrace grew stronger.

The session never took place, at least not the way she had wanted it to. Instead, their lives, once so separate, seemed to be weaving together in a partnership that neither of them had thought possible. Careful not to draw any attention to themselves as a pair, Alison consciously worked with Michael in every session with professionalism. An observer would suspect nothing other than a client-therapist relationship in progress. Both Michael and Alison harbored safely their growing passion for one another. The work that needed to be done was exhausting enough without the added exhaustion of giving in to their undeniable desires.

As the weeks passed, Michael's progress continued. Alison felt that she had been able to guide him through the horrors of his early childhood. It had been disturbing for her to comprehend that such cruelty could exist in a family, and she did not linger on his nightmare any more than she had to. It would do neither of them any good. The only productive approach was to move beyond his darkness.

Three months had passed when news came early one morning to Michael. Alison had recently presented her report and findings to her supervisor, who seemed pleased that she'd had such success. Michael's release would be within the month once all files were reviewed and all paperwork submitted. Arrangements would need to be made for an outside contact for him and for a place to live. With ongoing support, his prognosis for a successful transition into the normalcy of life was good.

She knew, however, that he would need his space once on his own. They both might. The confines of the clinic that held them both in check had also aggravated their need to be together. Now, with nothing to prevent them from exploring each other as a couple, Alison felt exposed and afraid. She had not voiced these feelings to anyone but knew that they could be the catalyst that would threaten any happiness she could imagine with Michael. And she had spent hours upon hours imagining the two of them as one. For him to transition into his new life, she had to leave him alone. She would, of course, be there for him, but not in the way that she knew they both wanted. Not now. Not yet. Once again, she found herself torn and unsure of how to proceed with him, but she knew that she must confront him before his release so that he would have time to prepare. There was nothing she wanted more for him than a smooth transition, free from any relationship that could jeopardize all that he had accomplished. She would find a time to talk with him, perhaps in the garden, with the sunlight and its warmth bringing them both a familiar comfort.

Chapter 59

It came out of nowhere. And it lingered so that for each night of many nights in a row, sleep was interrupted with its arrival. Never at the same time and never in quite the same scenario, and always with a slight change in detail. However, the message was clear even as Stephen, awakened by it, hot and agitated, tried to calm himself.

By the end of the second week, he found that he could roll over and go back to sleep. Now that he was no longer taken by surprise nor struck by its disturbing content, the subliminal intrusion began to lessen in its intensity as the images, at first presented with such clarity, appeared disjointed and blurred, watery details that held less and less meaning to him. It was almost as if his brain, which had caused the disturbance to begin with, had thought better of it and was methodically erasing its most recent efforts.

As with everything that had not worked out well for Stephen in his life, he masterfully ridded it from his presence. He congratulated himself upon awakening one morning, realizing that he had finally slept straight through the night and that he had conquered yet one more unwelcomed interloper into his comfortable existence. But he had not considered that the daylight hours were no less congested with the interlopers of his own making; he had forgotten those moments of terror that had consumed him, that had debilitated him occurring during his working days when least expected, and of their consequences that had wreaked havoc on his relationships, on his life.

His life right now seemed a million miles away from the east and west coasts of America. He was happy, content to live in a foreign country, left alone as he chose to be, and to his own devices that had now found a comfortable and frictionless existence. Recently, however, he had reached out to a few people in the village so that he would not be considered unfriendly and a loner. He did not want to draw unnecessary attention to himself by purposefully alienating himself, even though that was what he truly desired. He knew better than to conduct himself in such a manner. The widows kept their distance and were cordial in their greetings, as was he. He had no desires, sexually or emotionally. And he thought nothing of it.

However, he missed the camaraderie of his fellows, perhaps spurred on by his memories of his working years. He missed the conversations that were always unnatural as each guarded his words so as not to seem too caring or concerned for the other. A man's way of communicating, he thought. He was under the impression that men could read between the lines much better than women, which explained why men's conversations appeared very limited in their content while women could never run out of words. Even though the French language remained a bit of a barrier for him, Stephen made the effort to engage in conversation with the local shopkeepers, the men especially, and was comforted to realize that there were really no differences between them and their American counterparts when it came to "manly" subjects. A universal language existed where none had been recorded.

In particular, Henri had reached out to Stephen in the first days after his arrival in the village. Born here as a sixth-generation Benoit and following his father's, grandfather's, and great-grandfathers' footsteps, Henri ran one of the two cafés in town, his family's being the oldest establishment. He was close to Stephen in age and was taken by the American's history, especially as a successful businessman. Knowing full well that it was never meant to be for him to become as successful nor did he really want that, Henri still could not get enough of Stephen's background, entranced by this man. He had no idea, however, that what little Stephen told him was carefully vetted. Too much was at stake, Stephen knew, to make a foolish mistake that would unravel his identity as Henri knew it to be now.

And, if truth be told, Stephen enjoyed Henri's company, his easy way of seeing the world. He found himself regretting, in some way, his life as he had created it long before coming to France, somewhere back in his earlier years when he was consumed by the energy and desire to become someone. He had some regrets, he realized, in falling prey to the world of business, the pressures, and the enticements that were momentary but that led him through doors whose thresholds he had gladly crossed each time. However, he did not regret the benefits that followed and that he skillfully managed. Had he not, he would never have been able to relocate to his current home nor leave little trace of himself in his abandoned country.

"*Bon jour,* Stephen. You are looking well today, *mon ami.*"

Henri leaned forward so that the upper half of his body cast a shadow across the sunny window table that Stephen had claimed as his own. Carefully reaching across the table, Henri rearranged the small glass vase of yellow rosebuds that had been pushed up against the windowsill and not in the center as intended. He took great pride in not only the food, but also his establishment's presentation and first impression upon his guests.

"I was just thinking about you this morning, hoping that you would come in today, and here you are!"

He stood back from the table and with a wave of his stubby right hand, needlessly indicated Stephen's presence there. His command of the English language was quite good. He had spent a few years in New York City, he had told Stephen, to better his culinary skills. All he knew previously he had learned from his father. Wanting to experience more than fine French cuisine, he had saved and gone without when he was younger to make the trip to the States.

Even though Stephen had not lived in the city, he felt he knew enough about it to carry on a light conversation with Henri when the topic surfaced. Other than careers, the two of them did not venture farther with new topics. It never felt necessary.

"Ah, I think that after all this time here I have finally settled into a sleep routine. Slept right through last night and I awoke feeling as though I slept for days. Guess I am finally catching up with everything, huh?"

Henri's laughter added to the lightness that Stephen had been experiencing since he first opened his eyes, and the flashing thought that this feeling must remain with him caught his attention and then vanished.

"My mama used to say that sleep is the magic pill that can cure anything, you know? I suppose it helped, but I never believed that the case of chicken pox I suffered from as a young boy went away because I slept. But bless my mama in her wisdom." Henri glanced toward the ceiling and made the sign of the cross upon his chest. "Well, the chickens have laid beautiful eggs this morning, and the rosemary bread will be out of the oven in moments. What do you desire to begin your day?"

"Perhaps two of the beautiful eggs scrambled with two pieces of warm bread and butter. My mouth is watering in anticipation, Henri."

"Yes, yes. That is fine. It won't be but a moment. Coffee?" He was already walking toward the counter as he spoke. "Very fresh, just made before you came in the door." An empty cup in hand, he filled it for Stephen and brought it back to the table. "I already know your answer, don't I?" He smiled, proud of himself for knowing his customers so well.

"Yes, you do, Henri, and thank you." Stephen hoped that Henri did not notice his amusement. Henri reminded him of a little boy so very proud of a first and simple accomplishment, hoping to hear that he was such a good boy and that his parent was very proud of him.

The first sip burned the tip of his tongue, but the pain was quickly dismissed as the aroma of the beans filled his nostrils.

"Ah, this is a good cup of coffee, Henri, a very good cup."

Henri had disappeared into the kitchen and may or may not have heard Stephen's compliment, but it mattered little to Henri. He knew that he made good coffee. Stephen wasn't the first American to tell him so.

Chapter 60

"Word travels slowly around here. I just heard that one of your clients is being released tomorrow? Good for you. That's really good news. Is it true? I guess that should be my first question. By the way, how are you? Sorry, that should have been my first."

Jared did not bother to hover over the cubicle but had come up from behind and startled her. Her head shot up and she swiveled her chair simultaneously at the sound of his voice. She had been engrossed in paperwork that still needed to be completed and was due today. Last bits of info that would free the man she had fallen in love with and who felt the same for her. She had completed these same forms numerous times before but now, because of the client, she was taking every precaution to be exact in her wording as she filled in each blank. They never made the lines long enough, she was thinking, when Jared interrupted her.

"Oh, hi. Sorry. Deep in thought here. You startled me, not that you haven't used that tactic before." Her smile confirmed that his intrusion was welcome. "Just need to get this done before noon today. You know how it is. Last thing I want to see in my mail is the same form with a note telling me I blew it and to start over. God! I don't need that." She had already turned her back on him as she picked up her pen to continue.

"Yeah, no worries. Understand where you are coming from, my friend. I'm sure I've got something urgent cluttering up my desk as well. Well, as I was saying, congratulations. You do good work, Alison."

She did not look up at him, and he wasn't sure if that was his signal to move off or not, but he didn't want to upset her. Moving toward the front of the cubicle with one hand placed on the top of the partition, he leaned over as far as it would allow him to.

"Okay, see you later, then." He waited for her response,

only to catch an imperceptible nod of her head in reply.

There was little left to do but wait. He had gathered the meager amount of his belongings into one place on the table in his stark room. When the word came down, he would be ready to move them into the small cotton bag provided to him by the facility. He had entered with nothing but the clothes on his back, and they were confiscated right on the spot, only to be replaced with the "uniform of the inmates." Very soon, he would trade it for nondescript donated articles, enough to cover him to look normal when he exited this place.

She had given him his notebook and pencil. He would take that with him for no other reason than to reassure himself in some darker moment in the future that his life had been fuller than it might appear. He chose not to flip through the pages reminiscing his past. He knew what was on each page, each line of the tattered notebook. He knew who was between the worn cardboard covers. Not afraid to encounter any of them again, he dismissed this excuse as to why the book would remain closed. More to the point, he promised himself that the book would stay closed just as he had closed the multiple chapters of his life that had led him to this place, confined behind these walls for almost three years now.

He knew that had it not been for Alison, he would have had no future. He owed her his life. The thought of her overwhelmed him, and he was no longer surprised to feel the moisture roll down his cheeks, clinging to the day-old stubble. He had never felt such an emotional need as he felt for Alison. He would be free to love her for the rest of his life in just a matter of days, and this thought produced further tears.

Why she hadn't paid better attention to his admittance papers, she couldn't say. But as she reviewed his whole file one last time before submitting the final paperwork, her eye caught a phrase imbedded in a lengthy paragraph on the fifth page. She must have read it multiple times before she sat back in her chair and fought waves of nausea. Her head, more specifically, the right side of her forehead, insisted on hammering at her temple so that she became suddenly aware, as the nausea rose and subsided and rose again, of her heart and of her pulse, both seemingly betraying her at the same time. Her hands clenched the edge of her desk as she tried to take deep breaths to slow her body's reaction to what her brain had just decoded from the information in front of her.

Willing herself to take back control of her rebellious innards, the nausea subsided so that she no longer anticipated the next wave, all the while slowly and with hesitation continuing to breathe. The banging in her head prevailed, however, and her eyes burned and her vision blurred as she tried to focus one more time on the printed catalyst. She needed water, to rinse her face, to readjust. The restroom was at the other end of the corridor, and the only path to it forced her to pass multiple cubicles, all occupied by fully engaged employees who, she hoped, would pay no attention to her.

The cool water seemed to cling to the sweaty film covering her face and, at first, she could feel no relief. With paper towels in hand, she wiped the water from her face and started over, this time saturating the towels and laying them against her burning skin before wiping herself dry.

The result should not have been surprising as she looked in the mirror, but it was. Her mascara now streaked under her eyes while rivulets of black ink meandered in numerous directions over her cheeks, some north to her eyebrows, and ink-black flecks were captured in the miniature crevices near the bridge of her nose and her eyelids. Any makeup that survived was no longer evenly placed upon her skin but mottled and smeared, seemingly clinging for dear life within the minute pores. In short, she was a mess.

As she stared at her image, a mix between a circus clown and the horror flick's disturbing "Chucky," she began to laugh. Just a small laugh to begin with, but it grew in its volume and intensity as she found humor in the moment. Perhaps it started with her furtive, seemingly never-ending walk past all the cubicles until the female icon appeared on the door in front of her; after all, if one counted the number of cubicles, there were only four between hers and the safe-haven behind the restroom door. Perhaps the humor became apparent when she realized at some point the absurdity of her waking up half an hour earlier each day just to apply her makeup so that she could feel normal and well put together before appearing in public. After all, a single tear generated by a cold early-morning breeze could begin to wreak havoc on the perfectly applied eyeliner and mascara. Perhaps the humor grew to greater proportions as she continued to view herself and the disaster of a face that laughed back at her.

Could she possibly make it any worse? Yes. The lipstick had stayed on her lips except for a smear that elongated the left side just where the top and bottom lip met at the corner. All she needed to do was take a swipe at the smear and drag it farther down her chin. And she did.

Chapter 61

Brought quickly to her senses by the door swinging open, she dashed into the closest stall and waited until the bathroom was empty again. The best she could do was to use the soap in the dispenser, a pink foaming solution, and paper towels to scrub the damage from her face. The result, acceptable enough to see her back to her cubicle where she could try and recreate some vestige of her earlier appearance, she took a deep breath and opened the door. She felt relief as one after another of the cubicles held no occupants. Glancing at her watch, she realized that it was already lunchtime, which explained the abandoned desks.

Now more relaxed, she slipped into her chair and dug for her purse in the bottom drawer of her desk. The short, thick strap caught upon something toward the back of the drawer, and her tugs were unsuccessful in releasing it. She leaned over and reached beyond the bulk of her purse, feeling along the strap's length until her hand hit the obstacle. The box. She had forgotten about the box that contained the heavy rock. She lifted it with one hand while the other slid the leather strap under it, freeing her purse. She shoved the box farther back against the end of the drawer's back siding.

Regaining control as she applied the last bit of blush to her cheeks, she leaned back in her chair and let the fatigue that suddenly surfaced take command as she closed her eyes and fell asleep, head nodding forward until it rested upon her chest.

She awoke to the sound of voices and footsteps all around her. She had slept right through the lunch hour and as she came to, she felt the beginnings of hunger pains. Her purse, still lodged against her belly and the desk, reminded her of all that had transpired only an hour ago. Dropping the purse to the floor, she pushed it under her desk with her feet as her focus fell upon the documents on her desk and the deadline that she could not miss.

She knew that what she had read in Michael's file could not be ignored, but all that mattered now was to send the file forward. After all, as disturbing as the content was to her, she knew that ethically there was no reason to hold back his pending release. The matter that she would have to deal with did not impact her decision. It was personal, something between them and only them.

With a final review, she signed off on the paperwork, placed the two-inch-thick pile of paper neatly into a manila envelope, and walked it over to her supervisor's secretary. Once it was placed in her hands, Alison walked away feeling some of the burden lifted from her. She knew her footsteps were lighter and the stressed muscles in her face suddenly released their tautness. On a whim, she decided to treat herself to some fresh air. Reaching under her desk, she grabbed her purse and flung it over her shoulder. Perhaps she would find somewhere interesting and new while treating herself to a real lunch for a change. She needed to clear her head so that she could focus on this new hurdle that had unexpectedly appeared.

The cool breeze caught her by surprise as she exited the building. She had been inside all morning with no way to tell what was happening with the weather. Each day was like that, she realized. Too much containment and not enough exercise. She made a vow, softly mumbling aloud, that she would begin a healthier regime. Well, she had to be honest with herself. She would begin *a* regime, as she had not entertained the thought of one at all until now. She decided to leave the grounds of the facility. She would not venture far, she told herself, as she checked the time on her phone.

The walk out led her down the long drive and past the entry gate, where the guard on duty who noted her employee badge waved in greeting. Waving in return, a sense of well-being came over her, and she smiled at him.

Her walk took her through neighborhood streets whose houses dated back to the forties, she was sure. She remembered that the facility had been built on the grounds of an old army base long demolished. It was like stepping into the past as she admired how well each home was preserved and how established the gardens were that surrounded and, in some cases, overwhelmed the small post–World War II GI houses. Many of them were enclosed by picket fences to indicate the boundaries of their property. Each fence was a slightly different shade of white or gray and showed signs of aged boards among the replacement slats. The urge to pick up a stick and run it along the slats as she passed the fences made her smile. She was surprised by the thought, taking her back to Tom Sawyer and Huck Finn, and their antics as young boys. She was astounded that she would recall such distant and dusty memories when her mind was so cluttered with the present, an affirmation that she was freeing herself of the past three years of investing herself in someone else's life. Only now was she beginning to recognize how deeply invested she had become as she breathed the cooling air into her lungs, taking long, deep breaths, and then slowly releasing her lungs as her mouth formed a slight "O" so that the poison could escape. Much the same process that she had advised her clients to do, she thought, as her feet carried her farther and farther away.

She heard the sirens before she saw the ambulances and fire trucks. Instinctively, as if she were in her car, she stopped walking and looked around her trying to determine from which direction the sound was coming. It was behind her. She realized that the noise was becoming louder in its intensity as it drew closer to her location. And then they were upon her, flying by, emitting ear-piercing wails of urgency to all within hearing range. It couldn't have been a block from where she stood that within seconds the wails wound themselves down to silence. While struggling with going forward or turning around, her curiosity got the better of her and she continued her walk with more urgency. She knew that she wouldn't be able to help in any way as the authorities had arrived, but she wanted to know what incident had occurred that had interrupted her peaceful venture.

Coming around the corner of the next block, she caught

herself and stopped abruptly. Three cars, as best as she could determine, were entangled so terribly that it was difficult to know where one began and another ended, as though they had been lifted high in the air, thrown into a blender, and then poured out onto the asphalt below. A plume of black smoke was escaping from the melded wreckage as the rescue teams and fire personnel quickly moved into action. A small crowd of spectators was forming on the other side of the street while police shoved them farther away from potential danger.

She crossed the street to join them. This was not like her, she thought. What do you call those people who feed off others' tragedies? Looky-loos? Ambulance chasers? Rubberneckers? Did she fall into any of those categories? Such an odd time to feel self-conscious, but she did. At the same time, she could not draw her attention to anything or anyone other than the scene before her.

And then she heard the cry. A female's voice, she could tell, as its pitch seemed unnaturally high. The medics heard it as well as the fire personnel signaled to them to assist. The plume of smoke, now only small, intermittent puffs escaping the steel pile, reminded her of smoke signals.

A sudden chorus of audible gasps from those surrounding her interrupted her irreverent thoughts. A man standing directly behind her pushed her forward as he tried to get a better look. Thinking better of standing her ground, she shifted slightly to her right while feeling the girth of his body shoving itself against hers.

"Oh my God! Oh my God!" he repeated over and over. Carrying his oversized body forward, he struggled to break through the police line, arguing and crying aloud as three officers tried to contain him.

The words that escaped through his anguished cries were not clear, at first, until she heard, unmistakably, two words: "My daughter!" She heard no more; not the sound of the crowd, not the noise of the rescue machinery, not the wails of more emergency vehicles approaching, not the verbal commands given in directing the rescue, and not the father's lamentations for his "little girl" as he collapsed in the arms of the three officers who tried to turn his back from viewing the body as strangers gently and carefully laid her, battered, broken, and lifeless, onto the waiting gurney.

She awoke in bright light. Artificial and cold. Lying still, she tried to focus on her surroundings: the décor of the room, the sounds so close to her and farther away. Her body seemed detached from her head and only very slowly did it start to gather itself together so that she became aware of the warm sheet and blanket that covered her bare legs and feet.

"How are you feeling?" A soft female voice. She turned her neck toward the sound to see a nurse standing next to the bed at her shoulder. "Alison?"

Her jaw and mouth, strangely unresponsive to her efforts to voice a response, remained motionless. Could her thoughts be heard?

"You took quite a spill. You are feeling the effects of the medicine we gave you. Can you nod your head if you understand me?" Her voice remained soft and kind.

Her head cooperated and by the reaction of the nurse, her affirmation had been noted.

"Good. I know you must have questions, but I don't want you to worry right now. The meds will wear off shortly and you'll be feeling better. I can tell you that you passed out. Do you remember being in a crowd of people at an accident scene?"

Once again, a nod. She did remember, vaguely, a crush of people.

"We're running a couple of tests just as a matter of precaution. Doctor's orders. Have you had fainting issues in the past?"

No, not that she could recall. It took some effort for her to move her head left to right.

"Good. I'll let the doctor know that. You are in St. Vincent's Hospital and under the care of Dr. Walter Goodwin. He's a great doctor and so caring. You're in good hands. He'll be in to see you later today. In the meantime, you need to get some rest, so don't fight the sleepiness that you might feel. Your body is healing from a shock to its system. Let it do its work." Then she laughed gently while placing her hand on Alison's shoulder. "The meds are helping out as well. If you need anything, just push this button and we'll come running."

The nurse reached into the side of the bed and placed a cool plastic object into Alison's hand while maneuvering her thumb over the button.

"There. Do you feel that?" A nod. "Great. So just push the button if you need anything, anything at all. Okay?"

A final nod as she felt the approaching fatigue carry her under and into darkness.

Chapter 62

He stood next to her cubicle wondering where she was. He had passed by four different times since coming back from lunch, only to find the items on her desk in exactly the same place each time. Knowing that she always cleared her desktop of papers when she was with a client or in a meeting, Jared was becoming concerned as he observed the clutter of paperwork strewn across the surface. Walking past the other cubicles, he asked each occupant if he or she had seen Alison during the afternoon. No one had. He called her numerous times on his cell but only got voicemail. Leaving a message to call him, he had done just about all he could think of. There was one more thing, but he felt reticent about doing it. His boss was busy enough. However, Jared's concern was growing as he felt he knew Alison well enough, at least here at work, to know that something was off.

"Hey, not a bother, Jared. As a matter of fact, I just this minute got off the phone with her mother. Seems she collapsed while out on a walk sometime after lunch today. She's okay but is in St. Vincent's until they complete some tests. She'll be able to have visitors tomorrow, if you're interested. I think someone from the office should check in with her. I would, but am up to here in paperwork, including a hefty ream from her concerning one of her clients. Go ahead and get some flowers from all of us and save your receipt for reimbursement. Appreciate it, Jared. If I hear any more, I'll let staff know. Anything else?"

Okay. He would be the emissary. Not one to favor the hospital atmosphere, he generally steered away from this kind of mission. There was always someone who was better adapted to representing the group in the sympathetic manner that was required for this chore. Well, not a chore. Wrong word. However, when it came to him, he did see it as a chore.

But this was Alison he would be visiting. This was the woman whom he always said hello to each day, most days numerous times. This was the woman he'd thought of when standing on the top of the highest peak in the contiguous United States. This woman, for whom a mere granite rock as a present was not enough, not really. And this was a woman who understood him. He was sure of it. Beyond all of this, she was suffering. Of course, he needed to be there.

"No. I'll take care of it," he responded with the assurance of someone who did this kind of thing all the time.

It was the smell that got to him first, long before he found his way to her room on the third floor. He'd found himself in a hospital only once in his life and that was long ago; he'd had his tonsils removed when he was five, and he was unable to remember a single moment of that ordeal other than the smell.

Clutching the cellophane wrap that enclosed the cut stems of flowers he thought Alison would like, white and yellow blossoms whose scent unfortunately was not strong enough to camouflage the hospital smell, he fought a rise of nausea beginning somewhere deep within his core. *Come on, Jared. Get it together, man.* It was a half whisper, but enough that he heard himself through his clenched teeth as he pushed the door open.

She was looking in the direction of the open door as he struggled for a moment to adjust to the dim light of the room. Unaccustomed to hospital room layout, he slowly moved down the stunted hallway that led him past the bathroom on one side and a countertop on the other. He couldn't take it all in, not at first. Her eyes were following him, he could finally see, and his audible sigh of relief brought a slight smile to her face. He stood at the foot of the bed, unable to speak. He had a sudden flashback to his first real date to the prom when he was fifteen. He was clutching a plastic box in front of him holding the corsage that his mother and he had picked out for his first love. He was so afraid that it would slip right out of his sweaty hands before he could present it to her. And so, silently, he held on for dear life until she stepped forward and reached for the box.

"Hi, Jared."

Brought back to his senses, he saw her lift her upper body slowly up to reposition herself on the pillow.

"What a surprise to see you. Are those for me?" She lifted her arm toward him, and it was at that moment that he was fully back in the present.

"Oh, yeah. I didn't know what you liked but thought these had a great smell." He moved around to her right side.

"Can I get a whiff, please?"

Her smile was growing, and he sensed that she was enjoying his discomfort but not in a mean way. He felt as uncomfortable next to her in this setting as he would have felt if she had consented to going with him on that weekend hike to Whitney. This was all pretty stupid. He knew he was the wrong person to be visiting her.

"I can smell their fragrance from here, but how about one good noseful?" She reached out and took the bouquet from him. If she felt the moisture clinging to the wrap, she never indicated it.

"Oh my. So beautiful. Fills my brain with peace. You know that, Jared? Just fills and relaxes me."

Now he was smiling as he watched her bury her face in the delicate petals once again.

"Glad you like them. It's from everyone in the office, Alison. Everyone's concerned about you and told me to tell you hello. So that's what I'm doing."

He shifted his weight from one foot to the other repeatedly. He had no idea why, as he realized his own body's movements. Consciously putting a stop to it, he took a step back from the bed and sat in a rather worn upholstered armchair strategically placed for a visitor.

"Do you want me to put them somewhere?" He took a quick survey of the room.

"Sure. On the counter over there, okay?" She nodded toward the dark, stunted hallway. "I'll ask the nurse to put them in water when she comes in. Thanks, Jared. Really thoughtful of you to come." She had turned to him now. "I'm feeling much better, by the way. Crazy thing. One minute upright, the next, face down on the ground."

"Do you want to talk about it? I mean only if you want to."

He placed the flowers on the counter next to a kidney-shaped plastic bowl and a box of tissues. Fighting off the visual that the bowl triggered, he walked back to her bedside.

"I've got to tell you that I was really worried about where you were. I came by your desk so many times and asked others around you if they had seen you. So weird when no one knew anything. Like something out of a sci-fi flick, you know, unexplained disappearances. People who are always where you expect them to be, then they're not. Weird, I got to tell you..."

"Jared, I am really sorry to have put you through that. I had no idea. You're the first person from work I've spoken to. God, I'm really sorry." She lifted her arm once again and this time reached for his hand. "Really sorry, Jared."

It took him a moment to digest that the hand suspended before him was meant for him to grasp and he did. He felt her soft, warm flesh press into the recesses of his palm and her fingers naturally and comfortably entwine with his. He would never let go, he thought.

"No worries. Just good to know where you are and that you're okay."

She didn't let go either. It was something about feeling grounded. That's what she was feeling. A balance had come back into her life. She knew that it was because he didn't know what had caused the imbalance in the first place, and she also knew that he could never know. It would ruin everything that she found so comforting about him.

"So, do you think that you just fainted? The fall, I mean. That's what Nick told me, that you collapsed. In a crowd? Do you remember where you were?"

"Yes, I collapsed, fainted, whatever they want to call it. And yes, in a crowd. Guess I hit my head in just the wrong spot." She gingerly touched her forehead. "I went out for a walk just to get away from the paperwork, deadlines, the office. You know. Just needed to get some air."

He squeezed her hand and laughed. "Didn't get the right air, obviously. Need the high peaks' air to keep you upright."

"Right. But that wasn't available just then."

Her response, followed by a gentle giggle, confirmed for him that they were back on familiar ground.

"So, I went out through the gate thinking that I needed to get a good walk in and still get back in plenty of time to finish the day. There was an accident. I'm not sure how far into the walk it was, but I came upon it as the sirens flew past me. It was horrible, Jared. A tangle of cars and smoke. So many of us watching someone else's tragedy unfold. I remember feeling uncomfortable for a moment, like I shouldn't be there, shouldn't be gawking. It felt like I was invading their privacy, whoever they were. I remember some big guy trying to get in front of me and I let him. But that's it. That's all I remember. The next thing I know, I'm awake in a hospital bed. The doctor is coming in sometime this afternoon to fill me in. You know, I feel okay right now. Really need to get back to work and…"

Her words ended abruptly. Startled, he stood up and leaned over the railing of the bed. "Alison? You okay? Alison?" He tried to stay calm while unconsciously squeezing her hand.

Michael's face loomed in front of her and then seemed to float above her, waiting for recognition of his presence. She shut her eyes tightly as if to squeeze the image out of her sight. When she opened them again, she could hear her name and saw Jared's face instead.

"Alison? Hey, I'm right here. Come on, Alison. Don't scare me like that."

"Can I get a drink of water, Jared?" Something to distract him until she could get her bearings once again. "Over there, on the counter. The pitcher and cups."

"Yeah, sure. Of course. You okay? Do you want me to call the nurse?"

"I'm fine, Jared. Really. I just remembered some important documents that I left on my desk. Not for public viewing. Do you know if someone has been at my desk?"

She knew that she had not left anything of importance

before she went out for her walk, but she needed to lead Jared away from her truths.

"I don't think so. I mean, I was the only one who kept visiting your empty cubicle. And each time I did, nothing seemed to have been moved. Do you want me to take care of something for you?" He was more than willing to help her out. If nothing else, he could just slide it all into a box for her to sort through later.

"I expect I'll be out of here today after I speak with the doctor. I can come by later tonight if need be." She paused. "On second thought, I guess, if you have the time, you might just shove what I left out into the bottom drawer of the desk. Maybe that would be the smart thing to do, just in case. Would you mind?"

"'Course not. Anything else? Your apartment? Anything there?" He wondered if he was being a little too forward now. "I just thought that maybe you'd need some fresh food or something...?"

"Sweet of you, but that's okay. I'll be fine."

He felt it before he saw it on her face. She was slowly pulling away from him again as he watched her face turn away while she pulled the covers up to her chin, submerging her arms deep within the sterile bedding.

"I'm feeling a bit sleepy, Jared. Sorry, but do you mind? Really sweet of you to bring the flowers from the office. Please let them know I appreciate their thoughts, would you? I'll see you at work. I mean when the doctor says so. Thanks for coming to..." and she drifted down into the welcomed darkness once again.

"Okay then. Sure. See you soon, and don't worry about a thing." His words fell on sleep-numbed ears, so the only person he was reassuring was himself.

Chapter 63

He had reassured her correctly. Nothing had been moved on her desk. It was as if it stood alone somewhere in time instead of in the middle of a busy office. He sat in her chair and thought he felt the contours of her body imbedded in its worn fabric. Or did he just want to feel it? The view from her chair as he rotated it in a slow 360 was limited, and he now understood her need to be up and out of this area as often as possible. At least his desk faced a large window with a view to another world. Then he saw himself leaning over the cubicle's edge as he always did when visiting with her. What a strange perspective she must always have of him: shoulders, arms, neck, and head.

If he had read her recent signals correctly, the ones she gave when he gave her the flowers in the hospital, he had now freed himself from the barrier and would be able to come around to her desk each time so that they would have complete views of one another. But then he recalled the feeling of losing ground with her and her turning her back to him to sleep. It was all too frustrating. Better that he just get on with what he had come to do. What he had told her would be no problem.

He considered organizing the scattered documents into neat piles and then one big pile to be placed in the bottom drawer as she had requested. But that consideration passed almost as quickly as it had appeared. He felt a twinge of guilt for not taking better care of a co-worker's stuff, but that, too, passed. Gathering it all together into one pile, he leaned down and opened the bottom drawer. Grabbing both sides of the pile, he carefully lifted the papers from the desk and dropped them straight down into the dark opening. But they didn't fall into place as easily as he imagined they would. His first thought was that not only did she have a lousy desk location, but they also gave her a lousy older desk with shallow drawers. No way could she put hanging files in this drawer. He wondered if she had ever put a request in for a better desk or if it even occurred to her to do so. No, what he knew of Allie was that she was patient and solid, putting up with whatever as long as she could get her job done. He would have to mention requesting a new desk when he saw her next.

In the meantime, he needed to finish the job. The papers, now sliding into the drawer instead of neatly stacked as he had planned, were uncooperative as he tried to lift the pile from its precarious position. A paper escaped, sliding under the desk and out of sight, and more followed in its path as he failed to hold them all tightly in his grasp. The cockeyed edges of multiple sheets created a monstrous uneven border on all four sides of the pile. He slammed it down onto the desk's surface, agitated that such a simple task could take so long to complete. Kneeling, he reached under the desk's surface and ran his hand over the floor to find the renegade sheets. He wasn't sure that he had captured them all as he placed them in the open drawer.

Still on his hands and knees, he caught a glimpse of something toward the back of the drawer. He reached in and felt the edges of a box. So that was the problem. He took out the loose sheets and placed them on the desk's surface while the other hand reached for the box. He was surprised by its weight until he had pulled it out far enough to recognize not only the box but also its contents, sight unseen. Silently he prayed that it was anything but what he knew it to be. That she had taken the gift home and placed it in one of those special places that women like to create for themselves. A very special place that served as an altar to the past and sometimes to the present. He had hoped that the future was included on her altar.

Without opening the box, he could tell that he had made a mistake. He had wanted her to understand him as only he could express himself at the time and maybe even now, given what he had just discovered. The familiar weight had traveled with him all the way down the mountain, torn from its natural setting for his selfish purposes only to be hidden in a box at the back of the bottom drawer of a crappy old desk. He couldn't identify what he was feeling, but it was all he could do to stand up and walk away.

With the box firmly held in his left hand, as an afterthought, he turned back to the desk and with his free hand, swiped at the precarious pile of papers as he detachedly observed them all take to the air, each on its own flight path. He did not wait to see where they landed.

Chapter 64

When he questioned the orderlies, they shrugged their shoulders and reassured him that they didn't know where the doctor was. Hadn't seen her for a couple of days. They would check into it for him. But they hadn't. It wasn't their business. Their job was take care of his immediate needs. What the "docs" did was their business and their business alone. You could lose your job if you tried to come between a "doc" and a client. Michael was left in the dark about Alison's absence,

"Michael. Hello. I'm Doctor Klein. May I speak with you for a moment?"

Michael had been accompanied to the doctor's office by two of the closemouthed orderlies. No explanations given. As he was left with Dr. Klein, he tried to take in his surroundings, this strange office, and this stranger who wanted to speak with him. With no knowledge of Alison's situation, he felt suddenly adrift, and the seas under his feet were harboring unseen dangers as each moment passed.

"Have a seat, Michael, please."

Dr. Klein's voice, masculine and deep but strangely soothing, started to put Michael at ease. He had learned over the years not to react immediately to the unknown, but to ride it out slowly and carefully so that he didn't miss any telltale signs of a threat. He sensed nothing of the sort, yet.

He waited while the doctor took his seat behind an overly large and ornate desk. Michael couldn't help but think that this guy was not a shrink just by the size of the desk. What shrink in his right mind would separate himself from his patient by such an ungodly distance? Talk about insecurity. Michael sized him up immediately as having major insecurities and fear. It was almost comical to him until he thought better of going there with that thought. He was still within the confines of the facility and under the direction of people like this Dr. Klein. He would behave and play the game.

He waited for the doctor to adjust himself so that his white jacket's sleeves were pushed up enough around his chubby forearms for him to rest them on the desk, extended from the rest of his body, with hands folded almost as though if he didn't take this stabilizing position, he would fall out of his chair. Again, Michael fought the urge to smile. He quietly and surreptitiously enjoyed the visuals that he was creating.

"Can I ask you something?" His question felt like the first serve in a Ping-Pong game waiting to be volleyed.

"I would prefer it, Michael, if you would allow me to open our discussion so that you understand why you are here, who I am, and what will be happening next for you. Is that all right with you?" He didn't wait for Michael's response. "If I don't answer your question, then, by all means, you need to ask it. But let me begin."

He never changed position but held his hands outstretched even farther toward Michael as if shoving ever so gently an invisible object his way. And then, as he sat up straighter, his arms and hands, still entwined, retreated closer to his white chest.

"What I can tell you, Michael, is that you have been approved to be released. It's official as of this morning. Why am I the one to tell you? Because I am the head of this facility and Dr. Lawler works for me. Generally, she would be the first to give you the good news. However, she is not available to do so. It then falls to me, a duty I happily accept. It is my understanding, as I have reviewed your files in the final step of this process, that you have made great strides. We are very proud of your accomplishments, Michael, and want to make sure that you reenter the world on solid footing. Three years with us is a long time, and even more so when I think of what the world out there looks like now, just the changes that have taken place in so many areas of daily life. You will not be left to your own devices, Michael. Not until we feel that you can survive and maintain a healthy and secure lifestyle."

The words rushed over Michael like hundreds of mosquitoes just set free from an incubation jar. The urge to slam them to the ground before they sucked the blood from his system was growing quickly, and he fought to stay focused and in the reality of the moment. There was nothing the doctor was saying that was harmful to him; on the contrary, it was good news. He was being taken care of as he deserved to be. All he wanted now was what the good doctor was describing to him. He wanted the normalcy that others experienced every day. He wanted to land on his feet and stay upright. He was ready to do it. Most of all, he wanted to be with the woman he loved. She would complete him, as clichéd as that sounded, he thought. But he knew it to be the truest idea he had ever known.

"Michael? Are you following me? Do you understand what I am saying to you?" His voice was calm, almost monotone as it broke through and into Michael's thoughts.

"I...I...of course I do. Thank you. I'm sorry to seem distracted. It's just that I have finally heard what I've been hoping to hear for so long. But you have to know that it's difficult to comprehend it all."

He was looking directly at the doctor, who now unclasped his hands and pushed himself away from his desk. He sat back in his chair and swiveled it to one side, giving Michael his profile. Dr. Klein slowly leaned his head back as if to carefully take in the view in front of him, floor to ceiling, pursed his lips, and breathed in, heavily and at length, then exhaled slowly through his nostrils. Had Michael offended him in some way? He waited for the doctor's response, praying that he had not damaged any chance of experiencing freedom just outside of these walls.

"Do you know that I have worked with hundreds of clients? Hundreds. Perhaps thousands in my career. I can remember most of them fairly well, Michael. Maybe not immediately, but something will come to mind like a flash that brings that human to the forefront for me, and it is as if we are working together once again and that time has not passed, not for a moment. It's a gift and a curse, I think."

He chuckled, turning to give Michael a full view of his face, which comforted Michael in some strange way as the doctor continued.

"I regret that you and I did not meet when you first arrived here. I regret further that you were not my client. You see, I only take on a very few clients nowadays, what with my position. I know myself well enough to know that I can't stretch myself thin. It's not fair to my staff, to my clients, or to me. But I wish you had been brought to my attention sooner. Why do I say this?"

Michael shifted in his seat, trying desperately to be appear comfortable in front of this man even as his discomfort grew.

"Because I can detect a genius in you, sir. Untapped, stymied too early in your development because of a multitude of circumstances not within your control, but it is there. Just below the surface. Do you feel it, Michael?"

The tables turned so quickly that Michael felt squeamish, feeling the dizzying effect of the doctor's words. Was he complimenting him or was this a shrink's pitiful attempt at humor, sarcasm?

"Michael, I know about your journal."

The concrete ton block he imagined suspended above his head now fell on him as he felt what little bit of air he had been taking in rush up his windpipe, explode from his chest, and forcefully project into the stale air of the room.

In seeing Michael's reaction, the doctor rose from his chair and came around to Michael, standing close by his side. He placed his hand on Michael's shoulder, a tentative move on his part, not knowing how Michael might react to the contact. There was no reaction. Michael's shoulder felt tense under the doctor's sympathetic hand, not a surprise and something that he knew how to handle.

"Sorry to upset you, Michael. I am sorry. I only meant to say that Dr. Lawler told me of your success with journaling and that you worked through so much of your experiences by recording your thoughts." He could tell that these words were not any reassurance as the muscles under his hand tightened even more.

"What is it, Michael?"

"Did you see it? Read any of it?"

Simple questions. He needed a truthful answer to each one. Michael was strangely calm suddenly as he waited for the doctor to speak.

"Ah, I really am not doing a very good job communicating with you, am I? Leaving out the most important information, what you need to hear, of course. Michael, I have not seen nor read a single word of your journal. Whatever you may think of us doctors, I am sure I, for one, respect all our clients' rights and abide by the regulations that we are expected to follow. Doctor/client privilege is to be observed always. I can assure you that that is the case here and with my staff. If it makes you feel any better, you should know that Dr. Lawler was very clear about not revealing anything that was in your journal to me or to anyone. What she did tell me was that you used it as she had hoped you would and that had you not, you wouldn't be where you are right now, sitting in front of me as I hold your release papers on my desk. You have nothing to worry about, Michael. Let me assure you of that. Dr. Lawler has been nothing but professional in her work and interactions. You are very fortunate to have met her and to have had her be your guide these past few years."

And then the body below the doctor's hand seemed to dissolve into itself, losing its height and stature in an instant. Sensing that no more needed to be said to Michael about the journal, he sat in a chair next to Michael's that also faced his desk. He knew that he needed to be close to this man if only until he recovered himself.

"Michael? How are you feeling? Can you talk to me?" He waited.

She had not betrayed him. That thought would not let go of him as it swirled in every direction in his brain. His genius brain! Isn't that what he heard? This stranger next to him had reassured him that the woman he loved, he loved for the right reasons. Betrayal was a thing of his past, not his present. And he was a genius. He had to be smart enough never to let it happen to him again. Never. The news of his release, of his love's commitment to him, and of his healthy sanity and untapped mental prowess was almost too much to bear.

But he had heard the doctor ask him how he was feeling. How was he feeling? As smart as he must be, the words would not form, his thoughts so inflated with positive feelings, feelings that he had not felt since he was a little kid, feelings so infrequent as to make the few memorable.

In an instant he was feeling the soft ground under his feet, the cushion of moist soil mixed with dry redwood fronds; the cool droplets falling on his face while he watched the blue sky above change as puffs of fog formed a gray ceiling that enclosed him safely in its mist; the aromas of the forest filling his nostrils with its varied pungency; the sensation of flying with his arms outspread to catch the updrafts and thermals as he imagined the red-tailed hawks felt when they hunted for prey far below them; and finally, his little brother's shivering body next to his as they stubbornly refused to end their play when the air's cooling moisture seeped ever so gently under their young skin, reaching their developing bones, as they huddled together in the solid ancient's ashen shelter.

Chapter 65

Her mother's calls were unending, it seemed. Alison had been released from the hospital late Friday afternoon after two days of observation and tests. She felt fine and the weekend would give her time to get back to normal before work on Monday. Yet her mother would not accept the idea that there was nothing the matter with her. She had experienced a physical blip on the screen that had been checked out thoroughly, finding nothing wrong. Had her mother even considered the worst part of all of this? The costly medical bills that would soon follow and that insurance might or might not pay for, at their whim? If anything was going to have her relapse, it would be the sight of the numbers on the bills. They can't get wine out of a raisin, she thought, or whatever that phrase was. She could let it roll off her shoulders right now, but not her mother's nagging attention.

"Mom, I'm just fine. Please stop worrying. There is nothing wrong with me. Nothing. I keep telling you, it was because I hadn't eaten anything for breakfast…I know, I know. I usually have breakfast; I was just running late that morning. Thought I'd grab something at the office but got busy. Didn't even think about it when I decided to go for a walk. Just plain stupid of me. I didn't even take water with me. I learned my lesson, Mom. I know…" All she could do now that she had returned her mother's most recent call was stop talking, hear her mom out, agree with her, and then hang up. Same routine each time. She had no idea what would make her mother happy and satisfied.

She had been out of the office for two days, and she was ready to return, if for no other reason than to be free of her mother's calls. More importantly, she needed to contact Michael. She could only imagine what he must be going through without her there to reassure him. She had heard from Dr. Klein about his conversation with Michael and he'd made sure that she understood that he had acted in the utmost professional manner with her client. In fact, he was rather proud of himself that it turned out as well as it did. Her client's reactions were to be expected, but he'd skillfully brought Michael back down to normalcy so that he could understand all that the doctor needed to tell him.

He sensed the alarm in Alison's voice as she continued to ask him questions about Michael's well-being, not convinced that the good doctor had been as successful as he would like to think. However, he left her with assurances that Michael left the office a new man. Someone ready to take on the next stage of his life. It had seemed to the doctor that Michael had had an epiphany right there in his office that changed his outlook completely. Did she know that this man was a genius? That someone whom she had been working with for three years had so much potential for success? Alison thanked him for seeing Michael and for his guidance. She would take it from here; as he'd reminded her, it was her job after all.

He was led to the front room just next to the receiving room, a place that three years ago he did not have the ability to take in but now, as he waited in his adopted clothing with nothing in hand but a small bag in which his journal rested, he tried to commit to memory every detail of that room and then turned to the room in which he was standing. Again, determined to commit to memory details that resounded in him of contrast. However, the rooms themselves were almost identical in structure and décor. It occurred to him that he was wasting valuable time seeking out the contrasts. There were none. But then it occurred to him that there *were* contrasts, just not ones that were visually apparent. He needed to focus on what he was feeling, not seeing. And the rush of feelings could not come quickly enough as he consciously imprinted them to revisit them some other time.

The entrance and the exit to two very different lives. And a third life. The one that followed him into this place and plagued him and took hold of him for three years within these walls; the one that screamed at him not to leave, not to abandon it for the unknown; the one that was finally crushed under the weight of his own making—no, not of his own making. The life that was given to him with his very first innocent breath, whose path was already laid out for him, the realities of that life slowly and carefully revealed to him because of one who did care about him. Yes, he realized that he had crushed his former self, painfully and traumatically but at the same time with a determined stab at renewal, a new life, leaving everything else behind so that he felt weightless and free.

"Today's the day, Michael. Can you believe it?"

She came up behind him with barely a sound made upon entering the room. She had startled him, she realized, as his body seemed to jump in place.

"Oh, sorry. Didn't mean to surprise you." Her words held laughter and hope.

"No, no. I'm okay. Okay, yeah. You surprised me, but what a lovely surprise. I was hoping that you would be here."

He wanted nothing more at that moment than to reach for her and draw her to him but knew better. He sensed that she wanted the same.

"You know that I wouldn't miss it for the world. We... you have worked too hard not to have a proper farewell, Michael. I'm your bon voyage party, all one of me."

Her smile filled the room with warmth. He'd never felt so happy and alive as he did at this moment.

"Anyway, this is certainly not goodbye. You'll be seeing plenty of me in the coming days and weeks. Got to get you on your way and settled in."

She looked directly into his eyes as she said this, the hidden meaning of her words comprehendible to only the two of them. She fought the urge to wink; it would be much too obvious and possibly detectable as the room's cameras continued to record them for posterity.

Neither one of them realized that Dr. Klein had stepped into the room until, from the corner of his eye, Michael detected him moving toward them from behind. He saw Alison's reaction deep within her eyes as the moment they had just shared evaporated with this man's presence.

"Good morning to you both. Alison, so glad that you are here as well." He moved quickly as he positioned himself almost between them, seeming to form the third angle of a triangle.

"Yes, hello, Dr. Klein. This is a surprise."

She didn't mean it to sound as it did, sarcasm seeping into each syllable. There was no reason for it, but he made her uncomfortable as he appeared to want to dominate what should have been a very private and meaningful departure for the two of them.

"I…uh, well I thought that…"

"Ahh. I see. I only thought that it would be fitting of me to bid Michael good luck as he and I made such a good connection during your absence. You don't mind, do you, Michael?" As he spoke, he did not look at her but kept his eyes on Michael.

Struggling for the right words to appease them both as he could see the strain this man was causing for Alison, he smiled, offered his hand to the doctor and said, "Thank you." He then turned back to Alison. "Shall we, then?" He motioned to the exit.

"Of course." No further words were spoken between the two of them while in the presence of Dr. Klein. Easily and confidently, Michael opened the door, stepped aside waiting for Alison to exit, and then followed her, letting the door silently close behind them.

The walk off the grounds was familiar to Alison as she recalled her recent adventure, but this time it was so very different. The waiting taxi was just at the end of the drive beyond the guard, who recognized Alison and gave her a nod and smile as she passed with her companion.

"Good luck to you, sir!" he called after Michael, who turned and gave him a thumbs-up.

Once in the taxi, he left the door open so that she could see his face and hear his words. She did not dare move any closer but stayed a sensible distance from him, focusing on him as if he were in her arms.

"Thanks for everything, Doc. I won't forget you and everything you did for me. I owe you my life."

The power of his smile seemed to lift her right off the ground.

"You are welcome, Michael. We'll be in touch, you know. I'll call you in a day or so to see how you are settling into your new home. We'll all miss you."

What else could she say that was generic and suggested nothing other than a therapist/client relationship? She was satisfied that they had played the scene out well. He gave her a nod and shut the door.

She gave a slight wave as the taxi moved out of the driveway and off the grounds and then turned, smiled at the guard as she walked past, and heard him call out, "Another success story, huh? Good for you, Doc."

As she came closer to the building, she suddenly was aware that she was smiling so hard that the muscles around her mouth were beginning to ache. She didn't care. She had the sudden urge to walk right off the grounds herself, not to follow Michael but to revel in the freedom that he was experiencing right now. Just a quick about-face, that's all it would take—but then she became aware of the strap of her purse digging into her shoulder and remembered that in her excitement of this morning's event, she had gone straight to the room in which Michael was waiting, passing the hallway to the office cubicles without giving her desk a second thought.

Chapter 66

The ground underneath him was hard and cold. He tried shifting his weight, only to be held in place by a force that was stronger. His head, lying on its side with eyes half open, could not move either, so what little vision he had was focused on the small segment of the world before him from the ground up. The minuscule grains of dirt and bits of shattered stones created a maze for the ants who struggled to maneuver over and around what were miniature obstacles to him but, he knew, to them mountain peaks. He saw the billows of dust first followed by the fragments of rock suddenly shoot up from the earth's surface, precariously falling into new positions as more dust and shards flew skyward in front of his eyes. Coming into view for a moment, he recognized her worn, scuffed leather shoes, with soles barely separating the ground from her foot's bare skin. No sooner had he somewhere in his mind's eye identified the images than they disappeared, only to be replaced by smaller bare feet not much bigger than his own.

He lay there, entranced by the quick steps as if watching a young dancer practicing the steps that someone was teaching him. Perhaps his mother's instructions? And then a third pair of shoes—no, boots. Massive in size and in disrepair, they stomped toward the small bare feet that now pivoted so quickly to face the worn leather shoes.

Captivated by the choreography that was playing out before his eyes, he focused too late on the sounds above. A gruff, loud, and angry voice muffled female yelling so aggressive in its tone that he wanted to cover his ears so as not to listen any longer, but his arms would not cooperate with his brain's command as his hands lay twisted underneath his wounded body. Eyes now forced wider open, he took in as much as he could see of the three pairs of feet as they continued their strange dance.

And then it happened. The bare feet in the middle leaped from the ground, only for an instant, then landed, one in front of the other, with such force that he shut his eyes to avoid the earthen shrapnel that exploded from the impact. He felt the second ripple of the earth's quaking before he opened his eyes. No more than three feet away from his head, he suddenly viewed his mother's face on its side staring at him, eyes wide, her mouth gently opened as if to say something comforting to him while the tangled loosened strands of her thick brown hair, serving now as the only cushion she had between her and the earth, crisscrossed her face in bizarre pathways going nowhere. The beginnings of tiny red rivers blended with one or two strands as they made their way to the edge of her cheek, forming slow, dark droplets at the tip of each strand that fell and seeped into the ground from an unseen source only to form a pool under and around her head. It grew larger and larger until, suddenly, it filled his eyes with its once life-giving liquid so that, with eyes wide open, he was now completely blinded.

Stephen felt terrible. The longer he lay in bed while the early-morning light began to creep across the ceiling of his bedroom, the worse he felt. He knew that he should get up, but he couldn't, not until he could account for his condition.

He hadn't awakened, not once, not even to use the bathroom, which for him was becoming a nightly routine of at least two trips to relieve himself. He had purposely cut back on liquids of any kind before bed, but he realized that he was probably fighting an uphill battle whose summit was never meant to be reached. Age. He knew that was what he was facing with each passing day. But even on the evenings when he got out of bed, was awake and conscious of his actions, he could wake in the morning fairly well rested. Not this morning. This fatigue was almost restricting his movements as he tried to make his body react enough to assure him that he wasn't dead. God! How he longed for his youth, or even his fifties.

Forcing himself to sit up, he shoved his body back against the pillows that were oddly strewn about the bed. It shocked him when his back, expecting to be buffered by his down sleeping pillow, slammed against the wooden headboard. He allowed himself a moment to understand the sign that he must have had a restless night: fatigue, pillows out of order. Did he dare move off the bed only to discover that the floor beneath his feet no longer existed? Shaking his head in disgust with himself, he swung his legs over the edge of the mattress, planted his bare feet on the hardwood floor, stood up, and tried to stretch out his body before taking the first step of the day.

The fall was returning earlier than usual, he thought, as the coolness of the wood under his feet caused him to shiver momentarily. He found his slippers nestled together half hidden under the bed frame, as if trying to find shelter for the night. Reaching down, he quickly placed one after the other on his chilled feet. He continued with his morning routine as he had done for so many mornings. This morning, however, a strong cup of black coffee was calling his name, the sooner the better.

He tried not to hurry but must have, since he felt the nick before he saw the effect. The prick of the blade against his chin sent a slice of pain to his nerve, lasting only a moment but long enough to alert him that he needed to be more careful. Grabbing a tissue, he blotted the droplet of blood that had come to the surface of his skin. Keeping a piece of the tissue in place, he continued, this time with care, to finish his shave.

Leaning over to rinse the shaving cream from his freshly mowed face, he forgot the fragment of tissue covering his minor wound. The cool water felt refreshing as he doused his face repeatedly until he had unconsciously rinsed four times, the same number of times that he rinsed each morning. However, if it were brought to his attention that he never strayed from four rinses each morning, he would deny it immediately and contend that the observation was ridiculous. There was no set pattern, he would argue. It was just until the cream was gone, and his face felt clean. End of story.

Looking in the mirror as he dried his face, he saw that the nick had not finished oozing. Once again, he tore a small section of tissue and, holding it in place over the wound, waited for it to stick. Removing his finger, he watched in amazement and then in horror as the blood continued to saturate the small white paper so that it now was a pinkish red in hue and completely saturated.

"What the hell?"

He pulled his magnified mirror closer to his chin, thinking that perhaps what he thought was a nick was something more. Had he cut a mole? Gone deeper than a normal nick? Nothing indicated anything to him other than a pinprick of a wound, but the blood continued to flow. It dripped onto his white T-shirt, forming spots here and there as he moved about trying to stem the flow. Head held back, he placed heavy pressure on the wound with his finger pressing down on more tissue layers, but to no avail. Frightened now, not sure what to do, he felt the warm trails of liquid run onto his lips as his head, still held back, allowed gravity to take over. He panicked as he tasted the salty liquid finding tiny crevices in his lips whose microscopic deep channels provided free passages into his mouth's cavern and onto his tongue. At the same time, the warmth ran down and around his neck, tickling the skin between his shoulder blades as it continued its course.

Frozen in fear and disbelief, he forced himself to find his cell phone. He knew where it was; on the bedside table, where he always kept it at night. He needed to call for help. Dripping blood along the floor as he made his way to his cell, he suddenly took a moment to realize that he was losing blood, a lot of it, and that he should be feeling weak and faint. He did not. In fact, his energy level seemed to grow with each step he took.

This is all so unreal, he thought as he picked up the phone. 911. No. That was in America. *Come on. Think.* Parisian emergency number? Did he even know it? *Oh my God! Call someone. Anyone!* And then it came to him: 112. How did he know it? It didn't matter. "Just make the call," he said aloud. As he called up the dial pad, the glaring white light from the phone's small surface seemed to fill the room with its brightness, so much so that he had to blink his eyes multiple times to see clearly. The numbers emerged from the depths of the cell and waited for him to engage them. *112. The number is 112. Do it! Do it!*

He held the phone in his left hand while with his right hand keeping pressure on what was now an impossible gush of red warm liquid saturating everything around him. The thumb of his left hand heeded his command as it moved over the 1 as if waiting for a magnetic connection to pull it into place. Simultaneously, he felt it, the liquid no longer willing to stay below the midway point of his pained face. The liquid poured into his nostrils, over his cheeks, and filled his eyes so that the brightness of the cell was obscured as darkness blinded him completely.

His scream awakened him as he forcefully rubbed his eyes, trying to clear his sight. Slowly, he became aware that he was in his bed, caught in the rumple of sheets that had somehow twisted around his body as if holding him in their tightened grasp. He could hear his heart loudly beating double time, it seemed, as he tried to take inventory of his present state. The light in the room was not the same light that shone in the early-morning hours. It felt later. Eyes now fully functioning, he looked at the clock on the bedside stand. Already ten thirty in the morning! How could that be, he wondered.

A vague memory began to appear to him as he wandered back through the night and the evening before. Had he gone to bed later than usual? Eaten something that was disagreeable? Nothing out of the ordinary, he thought. He remembered feeling good and tired when he did go to bed and looked forward to a good night's sleep. Yet, something was nagging him and wouldn't let go. The night. He must have been so restless to find himself caught up in the bedding as he did. The pillows, however, were just as he had placed them before getting into bed, undisturbed and obedient. He kicked at the sheets while maneuvering himself free but did not get up.

Alarmed now by his heart's rapid beating, he rested the palm of his hand on his chest as he tried to breathe slowly and deeply, making a conscious effort to slow his pulse, to bring it back to normal. He could feel his body slowing down as he continued to breathe. Feeling better, he allowed his body to remain reclined for a while longer. How decadent, he thought, to be still in bed halfway through the morning. He hadn't done anything like this in years, not since he was a younger man recovering from a very late night. His body, he remembered, could bounce back then so quickly time and time again. Not so this morning.

He tried to recall what he had dreamed about, for that

was the only explanation for his rude awakening. The answer lay just beyond his ability to acknowledge its content. It was futile, he realized. A waste of time to worry about the tricks his subconscious was playing on him in the dark. *Leave it and get on with your day*, Stephen admonished himself as he ran his hand over the night's growth of stubble, then swung his legs over the side of the bed, placing both feet on the soft, caressing surface of the carpet.

Chapter 67

She would have a busy afternoon, she knew, just getting caught up with everything that needed to be done because of her absence. Yet her mind was still reeling from the morning and thoughts about Michael. She tried to imagine where he was at this very moment. Perhaps just entering his new apartment? Trying to visualize his expression as he opened the door to his new home, the beginnings of his new life, she closed her eyes and saw his face, now free from stress and worry. She could hardly wait to see him and share in his happiness. Knowing that she needed to give him some space, she would not call him today, but she felt that he knew how close she was to him, even without contact. She was with him right now, she knew, just as he was with her.

Cubicle occupants took a moment to look up as she passed to say hello and welcome her back. She was surprisingly touched by their efforts and felt suddenly buoyed up, enough so to face her workload with a positive outlook. She made a note to herself that she should probably reach out to her colleagues more often than she had before. Then she rounded her cubicle wall and froze in place.

Her first thought was that she must have been in a real rush to get out of here. But she knew that that was not the case at all. Besides, she never left her area until she had tidied it.

"What the...?"

Her words escaped her lips and hung in midair. She looked behind her as if expecting to see the whole office staff standing right with her, shaking their heads in disbelief. No one was in her cubicle or anywhere near it.

Papers of all sorts were strewn across her desk, while others had perched on the seat of her chair or on the floor. A few, she suddenly noticed, lay cockeyed, half in half out of the bottom drawer. The drawer was pulled out as far as it would go. Both cubicles on either side of her were vacant, she remembered as she considered questioning the occupants as to whether they could shed any light on the condition of her desk.

Still disbelieving, she began gathering the papers as her hands began to tremble. Was this fear? Of what? Perhaps intimidation? By whom? She understood the embarrassment that she felt. There was no way to explain this to anyone. They might listen politely and sympathetically, but she knew that they would walk away shaking their heads as they conjured up all kinds of scenarios to help explain their strange co-worker. No, she needed to clean this up quickly before anyone was aware. Bring things back to order.

Once she'd restored a semblance of order to her space, she turned to the bottom drawer. Those papers she gathered and added to her small and organized stacks. The emptiness of the drawer, now cleared of the paper clutter, stunned her for a moment. Had she always had this much extra drawer space? *Of course not, you idiot. Your purse, remember? Stuff it in there.* As she did, it slipped back with ease into the recesses of the drawer. Something was off. She always had to stuff it in just right so that it fit because of the box at the...

She didn't remember seeing the box when clearing the drawer of the loose papers. Lifting her purse from the drawer, she ran her hand along the back wall and surface. Nothing. No box. Just an empty drawer. Had she taken Jared's gift home with her and forgotten? She would have remembered, she was sure. She took one good look at the top of her desk just in case she had thought better of hiding the gift and placed it somewhere within eyesight. No rock anywhere.

All of this was starting to get to her. Had someone ransacked her desk and stolen the box with its contents? Who and why? It made absolutely no sense to her. She sat back in her chair and tried to retrace the moments leading up to her departure, searching for some clue. Had she insulted someone unknowingly? Had one of her clients taken a bit of revenge? For what? She knew that this was an impossibility. They had no way to access the office area. Besides, she had no sense that any of her patients were upset with her. She knew herself and she knew well each relationship that she had developed with her clients. She was running out of possible solutions and suddenly felt fatigue gaining on her. *Enough. This is ridiculous. Just report it and let someone else worry about it.* Easy enough and with that, she dropped her purse into the drawer and shoved it closed.

Applying herself to her work, she paid no attention to the time until she realized that there was movement all around her. People were closing for the day and heading home. She glanced at her cell and was surprised to see that it was already 5 p.m. She hadn't put in a full day, she thought. Well, she had, really. The morning seemed so far away now. It had been part of her work, just much more enjoyable and fulfilling than what she had labored at all afternoon. She decided that she would put in an extra hour so that she would be completely caught up and could start fresh tomorrow morning.

Pulling up the last caseload that needed her attention, she regained her focus as she updated the file. She looked forward to seeing her clients and realized how much she missed the one-on-one contact. Tomorrow afternoon she would begin seeing them again. That made her smile as she caught a blurred reflection of herself on the screen in front of her. Finishing the last entry of the file, she pushed her chair back while saving her data. It felt good to move away from the brightness of the screen, to look around for a moment to stretch the eye muscles a bit and to flex her fingers. Good. She felt satisfied with the success of her reentry into the mundane routine of work.

Calling it a night, she straightened her desk, recalling the unsettling image she had seen only hours ago. *Report this. Don't forget,* she reminded herself. *Tomorrow. Don't forget.* Opening the bottom drawer, she pulled out her purse. Jared. She hadn't given him a thought since the discovery of the missing box but suddenly he filled her thinking. Jared. She hadn't seen him all day. He hadn't dropped by as usual, just to check in. Not even as the day ended for everyone. No Jared to tell her to pack it up. Strange, she thought.

As she stood, slinging her purse over her shoulder, then sliding her chair under the desktop, she remembered the last time that she had seen him. In the hospital. He had been there. Brought her flowers. Stayed with her for a while. She strained to remember what had transpired while he was there. Had they talked about anything? Was she at all coherent? She couldn't remember him saying goodbye. Holding on to the back of her chair, fingers tightening their grasp on the upholstery as she played back all that she could remember of his visit, it came to her. He had asked her a question. What was it? Something about helping with…her desk! That was it. He was going to straighten her desk for her.

Now even more confused, she pulled the chair back out, allowing her body to collapse into its contours. What was going on? She could make no sense of it. Yes, she had given Jared permission to straighten up her desk. She was beginning to remember clearly the conversation. She had said to put everything in the bottom drawer. It was that simple. He had been so generous with his offer to help her out. Wasn't there something else he had offered to do? She couldn't recall it. The sickening realization that he was the only one who had any business to be at her desk and whatever took place in the aftermath froze her to her seat. Unable to do anything but replay the hospital scene again and again, she tried desperately to make sense of this. Jared. The box. The rock. They were gone. Had he done all of this? And if so, why? His absence today only reinforced her conjecture.

Then she remembered that she was going to speak with him about her concerns that he might be misinterpreting her intentions. She was going to confront him so that if she was leading him on, completely innocently, she thought, then she had to set him straight without hurting him. That was before all of this had taken place. She tried to remember how long ago she had decided to speak with him.

Unable to remember, she grew angry with herself for not taking care of business when she should have. Now she was dealing with—well, she wasn't sure with what or with whom. Had she caused Jared to act out? It was not possible, she thought. He was such a grounded and happy person. She had admired that in him. The rock, though. Hadn't that been his gift to her? The metaphor that he felt so strongly about? That he thought of her as his grounding point? Had she somehow shattered this undefined relationship so that his actions screamed loudly of his hurt and anguish? After all, she had shoved the rock into the deepest recess of the drawer and out of her sight.

Chapter 68

The key slid into the lock with ease and with a simple turn of the wrist, Michael opened the door to his new home. He had worked at getting his bearings as the cab driver maneuvered his way through the busy LA morning traffic. He had begun to recognize familiar storefronts and gas stations along the way. He had the address on a card in his pocket, and he reached for it now as he entered the living room. 19260 Stern Ave., # 8, Los Angeles, CA. His new home.

It was a modest one-bedroom, built sometime in the 1950s, he guessed. New appliances, a small breakfast nook that faced east so that the morning sun filled the kitchen, a living room large enough for his needs, already furnished with a couch, a coffee table, an easy chair, and a small bookcase. The décor was a Goodwill mix of various decades, but he didn't mind. In fact, he felt comfortable with it. Not that it reminded him of home, but more of the era in which he grew up. A single bed, a chest of drawers, and a bedside table filled the bedroom space. He opened the closet and laughed out loud. No hangers, but it didn't matter. He would have nothing to hang on them if there were any. The bathroom had a tub and shower. He surprised himself with his delight in the bathtub. He couldn't remember the last time that he had treated himself to a long, satisfying soaking. Someone had thought to place a new bar of soap, a toothbrush and toothpaste, and a towel and washcloth on the counter. It was at that moment that he realized how little he had to call his own. Fighting back tears, he said a little prayer of thanks to the thoughtful stranger.

Not sure what to do next, he put his bag with his journal safely inside in the top drawer of the chest in the bedroom. The kitchen was stocked, he discovered. The fridge had the basics, enough for him to get through the first week on his own. Silverware, dishes, glasses, and two pots and a frying pan were all neatly placed in the kitchen drawers and cupboards. A coffeemaker sat in the corner on the counter. Had he found the coffee yet? He could do with a cup. Yes. The cupboards held more basic dry goods, including ground coffee. Another laugh escaped him as he congratulated himself on his first attempt at making a cup of coffee in years. He realized that he hadn't needed to raise a finger for the last three years. Always, food awaited him, drink was brought to him, pills were doled out....

He quickly shut the thought down. He was starting over, clean and healthy. His life was finally what others called good. Alison. She would be calling in a day or so, he remembered. He would talk to her but this time away from cameras, away from the sterile confines of the facility. He would talk with her like men and women talk to one another. And then he would, when they saw each other again, embrace her, drawing her as close to him as humanly possible, and no words would be necessary. The thought of her lifted his spirits as he sipped the freshly brewed coffee.

He heard the phone ring, startling him. He had not used it in the three days since his arrival to his apartment and it took him a moment to locate it. There, hanging on the wall just inside the kitchen. He hesitated in picking it up until he remembered that it could be Alison. Her voice on the other end was a breath of fresh air as he pulled on the cord, stretching it to the kitchen table, where he sat down and tried to calm his nerves. He felt like a kid talking to a girl for the first time.

"Hey there. Hi. How are you?" His voice did not give away his temporary insecurity.

"I'm fine, Michael. It's so good to hear your voice. How are you doing?"

"I'm doing just fine. Finding my way around my mansion. No, really. This is a great apartment. It's all I need right now. I mean, you know. Sometime in the near future I'd like to move into something a bit bigger, but that's putting the cart before the horse, isn't it?"

"Maybe, but you should be looking toward the future,

Michael. I like hearing that from you."

Always so positive, he thought. One more reason this woman was the one. "When are you coming by? I can make one mean cup of coffee and whip up some lunch or dinner. Really would love you to see what I've done with the place."

He smiled as he took a quick survey of the kitchen and living room, which looked just as they did three days ago. He'd get around to making the place more his own.

"That's what I was calling about. I'm here at the office until five today but thought that I could stop by on my way home. I'll bring dinner as a housewarming gift. How does that sound?" She congratulated herself on her professionalism as she controlled her emotions that, inwardly, were spinning out of control. "Do you have any requests?"

"Wow. No. None. Dinner sounds great. My dinner experiences have been rather blasé for the last few years, so whatever sounds good to you will be great for me. What time can I expect you? Want to straighten up the place a bit." Again, a smile crossed his face. What was there to straighten up?

"How does six sound? I can't stay too long. Just enough to share a meal and make sure that you are doing okay." She hoped that he could read between the lines, as her words were meant now only for him.

"Sure. Six it is. I want to assure you that I am doing fine, thanks to you. Well, to all of you. The apartment, my health. You know, my well-being. But we can further that conversation when you arrive. Appreciate the call."

"Of course, Michael. See you soon then." She ended the call.

He sat there for some time replaying the sound of her voice as if committing it to memory, just in case he might lose it forever. It was difficult to comprehend that she would be sitting here with him in just a few hours. Only the two of them, free to share what was pent up inside. He wanted this to be the perfect evening but in viewing his surroundings, realized that even though the apartment was welcoming to him, bland and scarcely furnished, it might not be so for her. There needed to be a feminine touch. Maybe a tablecloth, and certainly flowers for the table. No candles. Not this time. If all went well tonight, next time. Flowers on the coffee table. Yes. Those touches would make all the difference.

He had been given a weekly allowance until his Social Security payments began. It was generous enough and he appreciated the state taking care of him, temporarily, he decided. Checking the cash on hand, he took only enough to cover the expense of a few flowers and a cheap tablecloth. He figured he wasn't breaking the bank. The excitement he felt at the thought of shopping amused him. Then he remembered what he had heard others say to him. "It's the simple things in life that make it worth living." No truer words had been spoken, he thought, as he turned to lock his apartment door.

Chapter 69

Before she saw Michael as planned for dinner, she promised herself that she would speak with Jared. She could not let the incident drop as she became surer about him, his juvenile lashing out at her, the missing box, and his convenient absence from her life for the last few days. It didn't take a genius to figure this one out, she thought, even as she forced her disappointment in him from her thinking. What she needed to do now was what she should have had the courage to do before. Confront him, clear the air, and if a friendship should survive, wonderful. If not, she could live with it. The thought of Michael provided her with the advantage. Before him, she would have been sick at the thought of losing a friend, a connection to the world, for she had very few to begin with. But with Michael there to catch her, her bravado kicked in as she found her way through the office and to Jared's desk.

He didn't see her approach and she was glad of that, because she knew that he would try to find a way of avoiding her if he had. Pretty much his MO lately, she thought.

"Hey there."

The sound of her own voice surprised her, briefly, as she had been in deep thought throughout the morning, speaking to no one other than Michael. She stood next to him as he lifted his head from the work in front of him. He did not look at her immediately. It seemed to Alison that he was searching for an escape but found none and seemed frozen in place like a frightened animal whose instincts had failed it miserably.

"Just wanted to stop by and say hello." *Fool. That's not the reason you are here! Say what you need to say and leave. Do it. Now.* "I need you to…"

"Don't need to say anything to me." His voice was almost a whisper. "I should be apologizing to you. Acted like a lunatic. I should know. I work with enough of them."

Normally, she knew, he would laugh at his own humor,

but she detected none in his voice.

"I guess I was just kind of upset. Really stupid. Sorry about it all."

He still hadn't made eye contact or, for that matter, looked in her direction. Instead, he lifted a pencil from his paperwork and began to make markings in the margins as if taking notes on his comment to her.

"Jared, I didn't come here for an apology. As a matter of fact, I wasn't sure that you were to blame. I just put two and two together, what with the box missing, and realized that if you did mess up my desk and take the box that you only did it because you were upset about something. I know what it is, Jared. That's why I want to talk with you. If any blame should be cast, cast it my way."

She hoped that he was listening and that she wasn't "beating about the bush," as her mother used to say. She prayed that he would look at her, just for a moment, enough to throw her the anchor that would hold her in place long enough to get this over with.

He stopped his note taking and, gripping the pencil at its middle point between his index and middle finger, annoyingly began manipulating it so that the pencil now resembled, in her thinking, the wings of a hummingbird hovering in midair. He continued this, even as she began again.

"Jared, I wish you would look at me. It's hard to talk to you like this."

She heard the faint twinge of a whine in her voice, which was upsetting to her as she wanted to remain in control. After all, he really was a child in this relationship, and she would not stoop to his infantile behavior.

"Would you stop that and give me a moment?" She detected no whine this time.

Without looking up at her, he let the pencil fall onto the desk and watched it roll over the edge and onto the floor between them.

"Yeah, okay. Go ahead. I'm listening."

"Would you look at me?"

She had not moved from her position but now took a careful step toward him.

"You and I have a friendship that was formed here at work, Jared. I've missed you not coming by, cheering me up, getting me out of my funk, and reminding me to pack it up. I miss that."

She paused, unexpectedly, as her throat started to tighten, an indication that she was becoming emotional. Overcoming the surprised reaction to her own words, she continued.

"That day when you invited me to go with you for the weekend? Well, I think that I may have misled you then. I think that you may have thought that I would eventually take you up on something like that. The truth is that I wouldn't. Not because I don't like you. You know I do, Jared. But not in the way I think that you like me. Now I'm sounding pretty sure of myself. Sorry."

She did not give him time to respond. She couldn't. She was on a roll.

"When you brought the rock to me, I didn't get it at first. I was confused by its meaning until I got your email that day. It was then that I realized that we were on different paths. I knew that I had to talk with you so that I wasn't leading you on, but I kept putting it off. And in doing so, I've really made things worse. I can imagine what you must have been thinking when you found the box in that drawer. I never meant for anything to hurt you, Jared. I was just not thinking about any consequences. I don't blame you for being angry with me. But I need you to understand that our friendship is important to me and I don't want to lose it. Will you forgive me?"

She quickly stepped back as he pushed his chair away from his desk and stood up. Turning in her direction, he reached out his hand to her.

"No worries. Friendship stays intact. I get what you're telling me. Kind of figured that was the case anyway."

The distance between them was no more than a simple handshake away, but to her it felt as if a mile-wide chasm had formed instantly. She forced a smile but saw no indication of one on his face as she reached her hand toward his to bridge the gap that was now impossible to close. The brief contact with his hand lightly forming around hers lasted no more than a second before he sat back down.

"I've got stuff to do here. So..."

He glanced in her direction and then back down to his desk. She got the message.

"Sure. Okay. Of course, Jared. See you around the office, then?"

She said this as she backed away toward the cubicle entrance. Still in his view, she waited for his response, only to notice a weak nod of his head. Better than complete avoidance, she thought.

Feeling better, some of the weight lifted, at least, she approached her work and two of her patients with a lighter air about her. She had thought about Jared's reaction, the intentional distance that he was creating, and had settled herself knowing that his response was that of a younger man, still with one foot in adolescence and the other tentatively trying to find purchase in the adult world. There was no more that she could do to repair any wounds that she had caused. He would have to learn to deal with them, just as everyone else in this world had to do. All part of growing up.

She reminded herself, as she finished the work on her desk later that afternoon, that she needed to buy a housewarming gift for Michael as well as a dinner. Time was getting short. She had worked a bit longer than she'd wanted to and, with the time out of her day for Jared, she now felt the urge to move. They had agreed on six o'clock for dinner and she couldn't be late, but it was already four thirty. There was no time to go home. She would have to make do with what she had on. Just needed to spiff up her appearance before leaving the office. With everything taken care of as far as work was concerned, she opened the bottom drawer and took out her purse. A quick stop in the restroom would take care of business.

"Much better," she said aloud. She stood back and gave

one final look in the mirror at her freshened face and tamed hair. Not bad, considering, she thought. However, she knew how the lights in this room played tricks on the viewer. Who knew what she really looked like in the light of day? Gathering her makeup and brush, she shoved them into her purse and headed back to her desk.

As she made one final pass over its surface to assure herself that everything was in its proper place, she froze. There, pushed back under the bottom shelf directly in front of her, was the box. Not sure that she even wanted to acknowledge its existence, she hesitated in reaching for it. However, she couldn't let it remain there and as she picked it up, she forced herself to scan her surroundings suspecting that he would be lingering in some part of the office, eager to observe her reaction. He was nowhere in sight.

As she placed it in the palm of her hand, surprised by how light it was, she felt something attached to the bottom of the box. Lifting the unfamiliar weight high enough to see what was attached, she tore it off the cardboard surface. A small white piece of paper folded carefully into fourths, she unfolded it to reveal a pencil-scrawled note in a juvenile handwriting. Every instinct screamed for her to crumple it and throw it away. Not to read it. Not to give it the time of day. But she was weak, she knew, and would not be able to rest if she did not know what he had wanted her to read. She was surprised as the paper in front of her trembled in her grasp.

"No metaphor. Rock is metamorphic. Definition: Rock that was once one form of rock but had changed to another under the influence of heat, pressure, or some other agent passing through a liquid phase..."

She opened the box. Inside lay a rock that she had never seen before, not the one that he had brought down from the mountaintop for her but an intruder that, even though she had no intention of keeping it in her possession, had almost instantly imbedded itself in her conscience with no intention of being displaced. As she picked it up to examine it closer, a flake fell off, dropping to the bottom of the box. There, where it landed, she saw a small sticky note upon which he had written, "Schist—look it up."

She felt the heat of her face intensifying as if he were standing directly in front of her, her embarrassment and discomfort growing by the minute. Still trembling, she carefully lay the rock back in the box, shut the lid, and dropped it in the wastebasket. As she moved away from her desk, she checked the time, only to find that it was now close to five. She needed to move, and silently, while recognizing a growing distaste in her mouth for him, she swore at Jared for possibly ruining what she had wanted to be the perfect beginning of the rest of her life. Yes, she decided thoughtlessly, as she unlocked the car door, a bottle of wine, maybe two, would be on her list.

Chapter 70

It was cheap. However, as he unfolded the fabric and laid it on the kitchen table, it looked to him as though he had purchased it from the finest linen shop in LA. The deeply embedded creases of the folds, however, were a problem. He remembered seeing an ironing board behind the kitchen door but not an iron. Common sense told him that there must be one somewhere in the kitchen or what good was the ironing board? Finding it pushed far back in a bottom cupboard, he got to work.

Everything he did now he found surprisingly satisfying. Activities as simple as making his own bed each morning, preparing his own meals, tidying up after himself, and now filling the iron with water; all of what most people considered to be mundane, he found exciting.

The cloth lay on the table, perfectly pressed. He hadn't laid a table properly at any point in his life and worried that she would notice this deficiency. Making educated guesses as to where the silverware should rest on either side of the plates and trying to recall on which side the napkin needed to be, he experimented a few times. Standing back from the table each time, he made his decisions on placement based on how he thought it should look. He said a silent prayer that he wasn't too far off base. The few drinking glasses in the cupboard were water glasses. They would have to do.

Finally, the touch that he had wanted to be sure was in place was the bouquet of flowers. Within its clear wrap, it held a variety of common blooms, some fragrant. The hues of yellow had caught his eye and he had thought of Alison. Perhaps it was the brightness, the lightness, the warmth that the blended blooms generated. He wasn't sure exactly what drew him to this bouquet of the many stuffed into water containers in the display. All he knew was that he saw Alison's face, her smile, her warmth, her love for him. He found a tall glass, filled it with water, and after releasing the delicate stems from the rubber bands, carefully placed each stem, one after the other, into the glass. Seeing that they were too top heavy for the glass, he readjusted the stems, some of which he broke off to shorten them so that the weight was better distributed. Once again, he stood back and this time, admired his handiwork as he placed the glass in the center of the table. The simple things, he thought. There was little else to do now but wait for her. He checked his watch. Five forty-five. Enough time to freshen up, yet again.

She arrived right at six with three bags of Chinese take-out from one of her favorite places. She liked to think that it was the best Chinese food in town but knew that her favoritism could easily be negated, as she had not ventured into many of the numerous Chinese restaurants in LA. It didn't matter, though, because she knew that Michael would enjoy the change in cuisine from the bland foods he had been offered for the last three years. If nothing else, the aromas would knock him over as soon as she entered the room.

He greeted her at the door as if he were on top of the world. She had never seen him so happy, so peaceful. Everything about him was different, and in a good way. She couldn't keep her eyes off him as he took the bags from her grip and directed her into the living room. Their greetings were simple and respectful of one another, almost as if they were meeting for the very first time.

The apartment was sparsely furnished, she noticed, as she inconspicuously surveyed the rooms in front of her. For a moment, she felt sorry for him. She realized, however, that she was comparing her place to his, which was ridiculous. He still had a long way to go to establish himself, she silently acknowledged. She also knew, somehow, that he would and that this moment in time was only temporary.

She followed him into the kitchen and stopped short when she saw the table. Noting that he had gone to the trouble of setting a table and adding flowers to complete the presentation, she smiled and commented to him how beautiful it looked. He laughed, appreciating her noticing and saying something.

The conversation during dinner remained polite and guarded. He commented on the food, and she promised to bring the same the next time. Probably more convenient for her anyway since the restaurant was on the other side of town, closer to her apartment than his. However, he told her that he wouldn't invite her back unless he could do the cooking the next time. It was not hard for her to agree.

As she had warned him, it was to be a shortened evening this time. She had made sure to say this on the phone so that he would not be disappointed. One step at a time, and her worries continued to plague her about professionalism even outside the confines of the workplace. All her imaginings of them being together in a "normal" man/woman relationship would come to be, but her better sense came into play. They had time, she reminded herself. What was that expression her mother had always used when she was overly anxious about something? "You're putting the cart before the horse?" Something like that.

Michael hadn't shown any signs of wanting to go any farther than share a meal with her. And for that, she was grateful. She knew that had he done so, all her willpower would be out the window. Perhaps it had been the same for him, she thought, as she drove off promising to call him in two days. On the seat next to her lay five stems from the table's bouquet. Michael wanted her to take them so she would remember their first real grown-up dinner together. She laughed at the idea and he did as well, but she took them and told him that they would greet her each morning from the center of her dining table, reminding her of their evening.

As the weeks passed, Alison was dutiful in her reports regarding Michael's progress and was able to convey that he had found a job in a local bookstore and was keeping the apartment in good shape. Her weekly visits, usually dinners now that he was working, were for the most part all business, but the meals were now more leisurely and an after-dinner beverage, always tea for them both, was becoming the norm.

They continued to surprise each other as they discovered how much they had in common. Based on their likes and dislikes about music, food, modern culture, and history, it would appear to a stranger as if they were made from the same mold. Their shared sense of humor enhanced by their repartee. Alison recalled someone mentioning to her that Michael was a genius. Who was that? The good Dr. Klein. Right. She'd been uncertain, but now she was beginning to think that he might be right. And she was wondering if she could keep up with this man whose love for her and hers for him continued to grow deeply, though still undercover.

It had been five months to the day when Alison decided that Michael was well on his way to being successful on his own. He had been promoted to assistant manager of the bookstore, had opened checking and savings accounts, was paying his bills on time, and had managed to budget his earnings so that he could continue to add to his apartment's décor. Dinners now were always provided by him. He wouldn't have it any other way. One small way, he had told her, to pay her back for everything she had done for him. More importantly, for everything that she was to him.

Never was the topic of addiction brought up, even though somewhere deep in the recesses of her mind, his file's detailed history lingered behind every glass of wine she shared with him. She was alert to any signs and had seen none, but that did not quell an underlying worry that something could trigger the need once more. However, each time they were together reassured her that his life had changed for the better, that the man admitted almost three and a half years ago was now a very different man. She found it difficult, at times, to even remember him then, how destroyed he was, balancing on the brink of oblivion. But she would remember and, momentarily, felt frightened for him, for herself, and for their future together.

And lying just below the surface of her concern was an unresolved issue that needed to be addressed and that she had, once again as she had with Jared, put off. But Michael wasn't Jared. She had too much at stake in this relationship to jeopardize their happiness. The contents of the paragraph in his admittance papers had thrown her completely off balance when she first read it and, even now, the implications were unfathomable but, she knew, the truth. And that was what she needed to confront Michael with: the truth. He would not accept it at first, she was sure, but if anyone could convince him it would be her. There was no right time anymore to approach him, as she had run out of time. For their relationship to go any farther, this final obstacle had to be confronted.

This time, dinner would be at her place. She had thought the evening through and all the possible ramifications of her talk with him. Knowing full well that she needed to give him the advantage of an escape route, it was better for him to leave than for her to do it. Saving face. Wasn't that what she should allow him to do? He might need to remove himself from her presence. She could imagine his face, the expression, his agitation, his embarrassment, his disgust. She needed to protect him while, at the same time, possibly destroying all that they had together.

He picked up on the first ring. "It's time that you paid me a visit. Dinner at my place tomorrow?" She kept her voice as uplifted as she could, a strain though, given her intentions. "I promise a home-cooked meal this time. Just to prove to you that I can turn on the stove and mix things in a pot. Not guaranteeing any taste treats, however. How can you turn an offer like this down?" The more she blabbed on, the more relaxed she became.

"Sure. I'd love it, but I do have to go to work the next morning and need to be reassured that I won't be up all night suffering from food poisoning or some other gastronomical ailment. Can you assure me of this?"

She loved his sense of humor and the mood he always managed to create because of it.

"Don't make me sign anything. I have a better idea. How about we make the meal together? That way, there will be a built-in checks and balances going on. Pretty clever solution on my part, don't you think?" This was going much better than she had anticipated.

"I can agree to that as long as you let me help you with supplying the ingredients. How about that?"

She could hear his smile in his voice. "Okay. You bring

the salad makings. I've got all the rest here. You okay with that?"

"I'm okay with that and have to say that you negotiate well. Same time?"

With every word that he spoke, her heart grew lighter and the anticipation of being with him again grew.

"Same time, then, Michael. I am looking forward to seeing you, salad and all. Take care."

"You do the same."

And with that, all the months of procrastination had now dissolved. There was no turning back, and she found strange relief in accepting this.

Chapter 71

She remembered the file, but only after she was heading for her car. Turning back while mumbling something about her stupidity, she checked her watch to make sure that she had time to run copies. Stuck in frustratingly unproductive meetings all morning and busy with clients all afternoon, she had somehow, maybe conveniently, forgotten Michael's file. But tonight, she would need it in front of her so that they could both see together what the fine print stated. She needed to rely on this backup and not just her jigsaw-puzzle-pieced memories.

Taking a moment to refresh her thoughts, she sat back down at her desk, conscious of the passing time but unwilling to meet with him tonight without having a plan in place, much like she always tried to do when dealing with him as her client. Comfortable in going forward after having reread the revealing passage, she stood up, gathered what she needed, and headed home.

The preparation for the dinner went smoothly as she and Michael naturally, as if having done this for years together, moved about her small kitchen in what appeared a beautifully choreographed movement. She found herself strangely at ease, even with the intention of the evening just a thought away. He made her feel this way and she could tell by his mood that she was creating the same feeling for him. At one point, they both turned at the same time to come face to face within inches of each other as he held a tomato in one hand and a head of butter lettuce in the other, while both of her hands clutched two freshly rinsed and dripping chicken breasts. Their eyes met with intensity, but the awkwardness vanished between them as they each, at the same time, broke eye contact, excused themselves, and carried on with the preparations. There was laughter and some comment that the kitchen wasn't big enough for the two of them.

With dinner now over, she could tell that Michael was

concerned about getting home and the next day at work. His dedication and commitment to his job impressed her and she was happy for him. A good deal of the dinner conversation revolved around his job; he talked about the people whom he met each day, some regulars, some travelers whom he would probably never see again, and the great variety of books. He had told her about the slow times during the day and the opportunities to read. He was reading three books simultaneously and loved the idea of traveling back and forth between the different worlds within their pages. She couldn't help but notice how his face changed when he talked about the books; he looked younger somehow, eager, and innocent—an explorer of worlds unknown, of his own intellect's capacity.

"Don't worry about the dishes, Michael. I've got all evening and I know that you need to get home soon."

She said this after he had collected the dishes and placed them on the kitchen counter. She knew that he would do all the cleanup if she let him. He was just that way.

"If you can give me just a bit more time, there is something that I need to talk to you about."

Turning to her, he said, "Sure. But I really don't want to leave you with *our* mess." His hand swooped around the kitchen counters to indicate what was, indeed, a mess but that held no urgency for her right now.

"It's really okay. This is more important. Let's sit in the living room. At least that way we won't have to be reminded of our mess. Please?"

"You've got my attention, but can I tell you that I am feeling a little ill at ease? The last time your voice had that tone was when you were in a white coat and I was a captive."

He was smiling, but she sensed a genuine concern growing on his part and she needed to quell it, and quickly. He moved to sit next to her on the couch and as he did, he saw on her lap a file folder. He turned to her.

"Is that me in there? This is a bit too déjà vu for my liking."

"Michael, yes. There are pages in here that I wanted you

to read. I know that this seems like something that should have stayed behind locked up within those walls, but this...this is something that both of us need to talk about. It's not just about you this time."

How much more of a mystery could she create? This was exactly what she did not want to happen. She needed to get to the point.

"Do you remember anything about the day that you were admitted?" The look on his face startled her. She saw a growing fear in his eyes. "Michael, please try to remember, if you can. Anything about that day?" She had to ignore his reactions, at least until she said what she needed to say.

"What are you talking about, Allie? That was over three years ago. I mean, no. I don't remember that day. What I do know is that person doesn't exist anymore, and I'm not sure why you are trying to drag him up again. I thought that we were done. Where are you going with this?"

He could feel growing anger deep within but couldn't understand why. Or was it fear? He realized that he hadn't felt these emotions in some time and was not about to permit them now.

"Okay. Maybe if you read what I read in your admittance papers, it might make more sense than me trying to tell you. Michael, I missed this information when you first entered the facility and it wasn't until I was closing your file and was sending my report forward that I noticed it. We need to talk about this, just you and me, and then we can bury it as you have done with the old Michael. Would you just read this section? Please, Michael, just read it." She pushed the pages onto his lap and waited.

She had highlighted the sentences in a bright yellow that now seemed horribly offensive to her. He stood up, taking the pages with him as he moved to the far side of the living room. Having trouble focusing on the print, he moved toward the lamp by the door. Holding the papers so that he took full advantage of the illumination, he forced himself to concentrate on the yellowed words. He did not look up after the first reading, nor did he lower the papers as an indication to her that he had completed the task she had given him. Instead, he felt frozen in place, unable to indicate anything to her. He returned to the beginning of the paragraph and reread and reread it. He had no memory of the event, none. He could easily deny that this was even his report, but he knew that was ridiculous. He knew Alison well enough to know that she was sincere in her request and in her intentions.

There were certain phrases that loomed from the page, escaping their yellow bath. His focus revisited them repeatedly. "Unauthorized release... Admitted to ER... Found unresponsive on inside lane... Intoxicated. Blood level... Substance abuse... Vehicle collision... Sedan and semi-trailer... Female survivor... Male survivor... No victims...

"I can't make sense of this." He looked up to find Alison standing next to him. She took his arm.

"Michael, come sit with me. I think I can explain this to you. It's okay. Come sit with me."

She was gentle with her wording, almost motherly in her actions. He let her lead him back to the couch and dropped his full body weight onto the cushion next to her. She had planned carefully how she would get through this with him so many times and now the moment was here. *Please, dear God. Don't let me blow this. Not this time. Please.*

"Michael, let me explain and then you can ask questions. I am afraid that I might not be able to say everything I need to say if I'm stopped in my tracks. Is that okay with you?" It would have to be, she thought. It would just have to be.

"Go ahead, but don't ruin us, Allie. Please don't do that." His eyes were moist and pleading as he kept his head down, waiting in anticipation of the unknown.

"Oh, Michael. No, of course not. Nothing will ever ruin us, never."

She waited for him to look up at her, but he didn't. She needed to go on. Focusing on the open file resting in her lap, her eyes quickly scanned the print to find her starting point.

"You came to us three years ago from a rehabilitation

center upon referral." Her eyes left the printed line momentarily, finger kept in place, as she turned to him. "When I met you then, so much work had already taken place in your two years there by both the doctors and therapists and you that everyone felt that you were just on the other side of the substance abuse that almost took your life. You were still not in the clear from your dependencies, but all the heavy lifting seemed to have been done already, leaving me with the task of giving you the tools to successfully survive."

He did not respond, seemingly numbed and distant. She refocused on her finger's resting place.

"Before that, you were in and out of detox facilities for a period of over five years. And there are no clinical records for you between the ages of thirteen and twenty-five."

She looked up from the printed Michael to the real one sitting so very close to her. His countenance had not changed. She continued.

"It appears that you were out of the country at some point because you had a passport. Do you remember that?"

She did not look at him this time but waited for his response. Nothing.

"No? Okay, it's okay."

She took a deep breath, not concerned about how it would appear to him as she heavily released the air and tried to identify any trace of relaxation in him, only to detect none. She needed to get to her point, the whole point of this conversation.

"According to your records," her finger now moved under each word with the determination to finish the task she had created, "your first detox admittance occurred when you were twenty-five. Between the ages of twenty-five and thirty, you struggled with detox, cleaning up and the falling back."

She waited, heard nothing, afraid to look at him, and continued.

"It says here that you left the last detox facility without permission."

She made a point now of pressing her finger even harder against the paper as his history unraveled before them both.

"It appears that you were on your own for a few days while others were looking for you and, during that time, you fell back on your dependencies on drugs and alcohol. I can't imagine what you must have been going through."

Her words fell from her mouth into the otherwise suffocating silence. She silently scolded herself for going off course, letting her emotions interrupt what needed to be stated factually. *Almost there,* she thought, as her finger began to plow through the last few sentences on the page.

"There was an accident, a car accident with a truck." She paused, not for effect, but to ground herself for what was to come. "It appears that you were the cause of the accident."

She stopped here and knew that if she didn't look at him, and make him look at her, she would lose the little control she had as her own emotions and memories started to rise to the surface.

He did look up and at her. She was taken aback by his expression concerning what was incomprehensible to him. He really did not know, she realized. No clue at all. No memories? Wanting him to respond so that she would not have to continue on her own, she took his hand in hers.

"Michael, talk to me. What are you thinking? Talk to me."

Remembering that she had asked him not to interrupt her, here she was trying to force him to do so. She was afraid, not of him but for him, for them both.

"What do you mean, 'the cause of the accident'? What are you talking about?" He pulled his hand out of her grasp as he moved farther away from her on the couch. "Tell me! For God's sake, what are you saying?"

His voice no longer controlled, upset her and she hurried on.

"You couldn't help it, Michael. You were not yourself. You were high on drugs and drink. That's why you have no memory of it. They found you in the roadway. The driver of the truck was injured slightly but remembered everything. He told the police that out of nowhere, someone stepped out into the lanes and that he had to swerve to miss the guy. In doing so, his truck hit another vehicle, Michael. The sedan mentioned there." She pointed to the page. "Michael, that sedan was mine."

The silence that filled every space in the room was so heavy that she felt that she might suffocate. How much time passed before a word was spoken, she had no idea. But relief came as he moved closer to her. He did not reach for her, did not comfort her in any way. He just sat and waited for something.

"Michael, I don't know how else to tell you other than give you the truth. I was inside the sedan when that truck rammed into me. I had no idea that there was someone else at the scene other than the truck driver and myself. Even in the hospital after weeks of recovery, no one said anything about you. I was kept in the dark, Michael, even by my mother. My memories are limited, thank God, but I'm all right."

Again, she took his hand, which fell into hers easily.

"I want you to know that I do not blame you for anything. Nothing. It was not your fault. You were not in control. Do you understand what I'm trying to tell you, Michael?"

She could feel her own tears welling quickly behind her eyelids and prayed that she could keep her control just for a little while longer. She had hurt him, she knew. Had thrown his life into confusion. But she'd had no choice, and all she could do now was try to make it all right.

"Allie…"

It was a whisper, hardly perceptible to her ears, but she heard him.

"It's okay, Michael. It's okay." She reached for his other hand and held onto them tightly. "You don't have to say anything, not now, not ever. I just had to tell you, Michael, because there is more to it than just the facts."

Now she was completely off track and, finding herself in uncharted waters, she took a deep breath and began.

"Michael, for a long time I carried the fear inside me that I had caused the death of someone at the accident scene. I remember the sirens, the voices, the smells. What I could never remember was what had really happened. No one told me. Nothing came of it other than what I have already said. I guess it was a matter of protecting me, but it backfired and continued to do so for years. My addiction to any pill that dulled the pain, both physical and mental, almost killed me, Michael. I fought help for a long time but when it came, I couldn't believe what darkness I had been in for so long. My sleep stopped being peaceful long ago. But when I read the admittance papers on you just recently, everything came to light. When I read, 'No victim,' I was freed. And then it all started to make sense. I knew that I could not keep this from you, that you needed to know no matter what the cost." She could feel him grasping her hands more tightly and now his eyes were upon her. "But here's the thing."

Was that a change of emotion coming through, almost akin to blissful joy? He was sure of it as he struggled to gain some emotional footing.

"You and I? We came together because of the accident. We would not be sitting here right now if it had not happened. Michael, do you see? As horrible as it was for both of us, it was meant to be. It was for a reason."

Her tears could not be held back any longer and freely fell down her face and onto their clutched hands.

"My God, Allie. I am so sorry, so sorry to have put you through everything. Oh, God, I am so sorry."

His tears joined hers as they collapsed into each other's embrace, releasing their shared pasts forever.

Chapter 72

The registered letter sat on his kitchen table all day long. He purposely ignored it by leaving the house after signing for it. He would find something to keep himself occupied for the day, beginning with a morning meal at Henri's. It was becoming a habit of his, he noticed, and he enjoyed spending time in the café. Henri was never one to lack conversational tidbits, which seemed to flow together easily and comfortably. His range of trivia as well as local gossip interested Stephen, a surprise to him. Perhaps Henri was growing on him. In the past, he had lacked the patience for small talk, especially gossip that was nothing more than someone's exaggeration of the truth, if truth were ever to be found upon closer examination.

Henri chatted on between the arrival and departure of his regular customers and a young couple visiting from Canada, and Stephen lingered long after his meal was done. Not only Henri but also his coffee was growing on him, he thought, and he suddenly remembered Boston and Gregario's. A flood of flashbacks appeared, so many that they began to meld together. He took another long sip as he tried to focus on anything but the past. He longed for Henri to come over and regale him with chatter at that moment, but he was suddenly nowhere to be seen. Leaving ample money on the table, Stephen left the café without saying goodbye, something he had never done to Henri before and now felt guilty about. He would make up for it next time, he thought.

The air helped clear his head as he headed up the narrow street toward the open fields that surrounded the village. His pace quickened as they came into sight. A good walk would do him a world of good and the day's weather promised to be beautiful. He breathed deeply as he strode off through the first open field that he reached.

The day was late as he entered the road leading to his home. He wondered at how quickly the time had gone. He had walked for many miles, he was sure. His feet and hips were starting to complain during the last few miles, and he was grateful that he had listened to them and had turned around. As it was, he hoped that he could hobble down the last stretch to his front door. He would need to treat his unhappy appendages to a good, warm bath this evening while he downed aspirin with his supper.

Telling himself that he would not venture that far again without proper preparation, he reached his front door just as the last rays of sun extended themselves across the dusky sky. He stood for a moment, taking in the beauty of the sunset as it forced the sky to change hues one after the other. A sudden sharp pain in his right hip pulled him back from the light show and he turned the key in the lock.

He had not forgotten that the letter was on the table as he walked past it into the bedroom. He knew that he would have to acknowledge it eventually, but fatigue and hunger were screaming at him, drowning out the inevitable. He drew a warm bath while preparing a light supper of leftover vegetable soup. Two days ago, Henri had gifted him with a fresh loaf of bread straight out of the oven and it now waited on the countertop, carefully wrapped to preserve freshness. He felt the sensation of saliva rushing onto his gums and between his teeth as the aromas began to fill the room. He hadn't realized how hungry he had become. His own foolish fault, he thought, heading off like that not prepared at all. But he was home now, and his creature comforts were ready for him.

Perhaps because of his age, now closer to his seventh decade than the sixth, he enjoyed the idea of nestling in for the evening. A good book always waited for him on the small table by his easy chair and another on his bedside table. Inevitably, he would fall asleep mid-sentence no matter where he read. Another disadvantage of the aging process, he noted. Couldn't stay awake and read for hours as he once did. Tonight, however, the book remained on the table as he eased his tired body into the chair. In its place he held the envelope.

This time he recognized the elegant cursive, the tissue-thin blue paper, and the postmark. Tempted when he received the letter to crumple it and send it to the heavens as he did the first one, something had held him back. He couldn't identify what it was but was compelled not to ignore the feeling. Not that he was greeting an old friend by revealing the contents of the letter. He knew better than that. Even though the author was no enemy, what the letter most certainly held was.

He slipped the letter opener carefully under the sealed sheets and unfolded the papers. He had been right. It was almost identical in appearance to the first letter but not as lengthy, he noted. Reaching for his reading glasses, he sighed deeply as if resigned to the fate that awaited him.

Mr. Stephen Bingham,

It is my hope that you recall my first correspondence with you now well over a year ago. I write to you today with the hope that you will be so kind as to respond to my request. It is my intention to carry out my father's wishes as best as I am able. I know that he would understand if my attempts to fulfill his last wishes fail through no fault of my own. So, it is with that said that I will hold onto these gifts of my father to you. However, as you may well understand, I would like to bring closure to my late father's affairs as soon as possible. I do not dare to presume that you have suffered such a loss, but in the event that your fate relates to mine in such a way, you must therefore understand my need to bring peace to my father's soul.

Would you allow me to send these items to you at this address? If not, do you have another way in mind of receiving them? Forgive me, but we are not that far away from one another at this time, geographically. I do not foresee my travels taking me to France, but

352

perhaps you would like to come here? Again, I do not mean to presume. Please know that you are always welcome.

I will await your response to this, my final letter to you. If I do not receive your response within the month, I will dispense of these gifts in another manner. They hold no meaning to me and I know that my father would understand. I hope that you are both well.

Sincerely,

Adrastos Metaxas

In reading the letter again, Stephen was surprised at his reaction. Very little of one. Perhaps it was because of the familiarity of the hand, the repetitive message, the polite stance taken by this Adrastos. Whatever it was, Stephen was not outwardly upset. For that matter, he felt settled, much more so than before opening the thing. If he did not respond, the matter would be resolved by this man. If he did respond positively, the only disadvantage would be the receipt of two undisclosed items into his home. In either case, he did not have to maintain communication with Adrastos nor Adrastos with him. He should have tended to this when he received the first letter, but he understood his reaction very well. Now, settled and comfortable in his life, this letter was no longer a threat to his existence. He could see no reason not to respond this very night. He would post it first thing in the morning. Yes, let him go ahead and send whatever it is that his father so desperately wanted her to have. It would be of no importance to him anyway. He had never been a part of their conversation to begin with all those years ago. And, besides, he knew how to throw unwanted items away.

Part II

Catalyst

Chapter 1

He lay beside her deeply saturated in a peaceful sleep, one arm stretched over her, bringing her an indescribable comfort. She did not move, afraid of waking him, but turned her face toward his, completely absorbed in its beauty and tranquility. It was a face that she had never seen before, yet she had seen his face time and time again. Each of those times, however, his expressions hid what she witnessed now. This was Michael, the Michael who she'd known had been there all along and the Michael she would be with the rest of her life, if he let her. She felt the warmth of the bedsheets, which held the combined heat of their bodies throughout the night. She listened to the even rhythm of his breathing and found her own matching his. She tried to recall every detail of the last hours with him, as she did not want any of it to fade away. She replayed his lovemaking over and over again: the slow, gentle movements of his hands, his exploring fingers and tongue, the strength of his embraces, the sensual touch of his mouth against hers, and the frenzy of climax followed by pure exhaustion as she thought for a moment that she was levitating with him, so weightless and free of burden were they both, until they both slipped into the deepest sleeps of their lives.

And now, in the morning light with him at her side, there was nothing to do but rest with him until his eyes met her gaze. Truth be told, she was tempted to invade his space, slowly and lovingly, as she felt a familiar twinge between her legs, its throbbing insisting on attention. But she also wanted him to rest. To get caught up with his life. They had time.

When she awoke next, two hours had passed. This time, he was the one doing the gazing. He had taken his arm off her body and had propped himself up on his pillows so that he was facing her.

"Good morning, sweetheart." She heard music in his

voice. "I won't tell you the time, but you had one heck of a good sleep." His hand now rested on her exposed shoulder. She would not share with him her earlier awakening.

"Oh, gosh! It's so bright! Michael, what time is it? Don't you have to be at work?"

"Called in sick while you were sound asleep. We have the whole day to ourselves." He slid down from the pillow and snuggled his head against her shoulder. He was intoxicating. But the thought of work made her resist his advances.

"I have to go in, Michael. I need to see my patients. I have so much..." His kisses, one after another, prevented her mouth from forming any words other than "I love you" as he responded with the same.

Her apartment was bigger. It was that simple. With all the proper steps checked off, Michael was free and clear to continue with his life, but now on his own terms. Free from the structure that had imposed its boundaries on them, their lives were rapidly blending into one. Living together was easy, easier than Alison had first thought it might be. They'd had long conversations about going too fast, especially when the topic of moving in together came up one evening two months ago over a quiet dinner at his apartment. They were both happily surprised to hear the other say yes to the idea.

His work kept him busy and happy while she plugged away at others' problems and pain. Their mornings together flew as they prepared for work, but they made sure that once both were home in the evenings, every moment counted. And that same thinking followed them into the bedroom. Never regretting a moment, they still had those mornings after a night of lovemaking when the world was spinning much too quickly. To get one foot out of bed, not to mention two, seemed to take every bit of effort left in their weakened and fatigued state. However, night after night, the moments counted and morning after morning, there was hell to pay.

He had a donut halfway in his mouth when he turned to her and said, "Wait a minute. Don't go out that door yet."

"I'll be late and so will you, honey. What is it?" She never knew when he was serious or ready to send forth his quirky humor. It better be a good one, she thought as she glanced at her watch. "I've got two minutes, then I'm out the door." She waited.

He put the donut on the counter, leaving her standing by the door, one hand on the doorknob.

"Michael, honey. Come on. I've got to go!" she yelled after him as he ran down the hallway into the bathroom.

"Yup. Know that. Right with you, sweetie."

And then he appeared from the bathroom, walking toward her slowly and deliberately with an expression she could not read. She thought that his eyes were sparkling in the morning light and noted that to be such an odd observation.

"Michael, what is going on?" She started to turn the doorknob.

"I wouldn't do that if I were you." It sounded like more of a tease than a threat.

"Well, you don't have a group of unhappy individuals waiting for you to fix them, do you?" She wanted to take back her words as soon as they left her mouth. However, he seemed unfazed by her remark.

"Okay."

She barely heard the word muffled in his intake of air and then he was down on one knee. His eyes had locked on hers and she stood frozen in place, hand still on the doorknob.

"Alison, will you be my wife?"

His eyes were sparkling through his tears and now through hers. He held the ring up to her as she let him place it on her extended finger. He did not get up as she fell to her knees and they remained in one another's embrace, her initial "yes" multiplying into a hundred yeses. He rocked her in his arms as the front door, now ajar from her unintended turn of the knob when she had sunk to her knees, revealed two young neighbor boys watching the unusual display, all the while giggling and punching each other in the arm, uncomfortable but entranced by the spectacle in front of them.

A simple wedding was desired. Her mother and a couple of their friends were the only people in attendance. The ceremony took place in a small chapel, officiated by an ordained minister of uncertain faith; it didn't matter to them as long as the marriage certificate was official. Money was not abundant, so they took a road trip north to Central California, spending nights in cozy little bungalows and bed-and-breakfasts along the way. Their destination was San Simeon, William Randolph Hearst's massive estate, now a treasured relic of an opulent time long gone.

Returning home to LA was hard as they approached the growing traffic jams along the Pacific Coast Highway the closer they came to the city. But they calmed each other by reminiscing about their honeymoon and planning their future together.

The months passed quickly into their second year of marriage, perhaps because they both found such happiness in each other, enough to buoy them up when apart. Alison's caseload had grown to its capacity, and she dragged herself home each night thoroughly exhausted. Michael was always home first, just as tired but in a different way. However, he never failed to start the dinner and welcome her home with every ounce of love in his body. She felt guilty, as her response was never quite so heartfelt. He never once commented on it but took everything she had to give him, good, bad and ugly, in perfect stride. She had to pinch herself, wondering how she deserved such a person in her life.

"I've been thinking, sweetheart, about a trip."

He waited for her to look up before he continued. The salad he had prepared had a new dressing of his concoction that he had drizzled over the variety of fresh greens that filled her mouth, and she was relishing the exquisite flavors. As she swallowed, he continued.

"I've saved enough, and I thought between both of our savings we could afford to treat ourselves to an adventure."

"Okay, I'll bite. What kind of adventure?" She jabbed her fork into another mouthful of greens, knowing she'd have time to enjoy another bite while he continued his thought. She was a good listener, after all.

"Well, long before I met you…long before my former life, the one that you were unfortunate enough to come upon, I traveled a bit. I loved the idea of seeing in person what I had only been able to see in the textbooks. Especially ancient history. You know. Places like the Acropolis, the Coliseum, the Pyramids. I only got to one of those places, Greece."

"Wow. Okay. That explains the passport."

His quizzical look reminded her of his confusion over three years ago when she last mentioned it to him. She let it go as quickly as the words escaped.

"I was under the impression that your life fell apart when you were fairly young and really hit the skids when you were a young man. I'm impressed that you were able to do it. I have never been anywhere outside of this country." Her tongue played with a piece of lettuce that had adhered itself to the back of one of her molars. "Sorry. You were saying?"

"I want to take us to Greece. I want you to see what I've seen. It was long ago, granted, but I would bet a dollar to a nickel that the changes are few in the places I remember. It's a beautiful place, Alison. I know you'd love it."

He looked so happy, excited like a little kid at the prospect of parents finally saying "yes" to a Disneyland trip. How could anyone ruin this moment?

"You really want to do this, right? This is something that means a lot to you?" She put down her fork and pushed the dish to the side. Leaning forward, she reached for his hand.

"I couldn't mean it more. We could do it, honey. So what if we don't eat for the next few months. What's that phrase? 'I've got your love to keep me warm'? Guess that doesn't solve the hunger issue, does it?"

His laugh was his way of transitioning to the next level, the one that he had prepared himself for: her yes or her no.

"As a reward for creating such a delectable repast for this weary body, I will say yes to your proposal. Hail to Caesar and all those other guys!"

She held up her wineglass and waited, amused, for his

jumping up and down to cease before they toasted one another on their next adventure.

Alison had only two weeks of vacation available to her and when she let Michael know this, she could hear his disappointment even as his words reassured her that the trip he had in mind could easily be accomplished in that time. Still, she could only imagine that the freedom he was enjoying now had to be overwhelming and enticing, as so much of his life had never been in his control. Without voicing this to her husband, she forced herself to accept his words as heartfelt, no matter the intention. She was surprised when he told her that his boss had no problem with him taking the time; however, because of his short tenure with the bookstore, he would be paid for only one week of the vacation. At first, Alison questioned him on whether they could really afford to go. The cost seemed prohibitive when they started researching their options online. But he reassured her that once over there, they could do things on a tight budget. He had researched this as well. There were lots of deals out there. She was not as convinced but went along with his planning, having neither the time nor, if truth be told, the desire to do it.

As the days passed, she grew excited about the trip to places she had only dreamed of seeing, but she could not free her mind of the work and the needs of her patients. She worried for nights, right up until the day of the flight, about her clients and the paperwork that would be waiting for her when she returned. Dr. Klein had reassured her that her caseload would be well cared for and that any paperwork that could be done without her would be. He would see to it. Of that, she was sure, based on his interaction with Michael during her stay in the hospital. The thought crossed her mind that she was easily replaceable, which caused further sleepless nights. None of this would she share with Michael. *Anyway,* she thought, *it's my insecurities, my guilty conscience.*

"So, what do you think about this?" He was working at the computer while she was cleaning up the kitchen after another delicious dinner.

"Umm. What are you up to now, honey?" She didn't turn

in his direction but continued to rinse the dishes.

"About the trip. Remember that I told you that I had been to Greece years ago, right?"

"Uh-huh."

The trip again. He was on a different plateau right now than she was as she placed dripping utensils into the dishwasher, all the while playing back her emotional day at work. As a matter of fact, there were no plateaus in sight for her as she found herself abandoned in a deep valley populated by those who depended upon her to keep them floating face up in each of their turbulent oceans.

"I think I've figured out a way to save some money while we're there. It's a long shot, but worth the effort to do some more research. Are you intrigued by my thinking, my sweet?"

He had not left his chair but had turned to her, and she felt his eyes upon her even without turning herself.

"Well, are you?"

Placing the last of the utensils in their plastic nests, she wiped her hands on a tea towel and turned to him. She smiled seeing her husband's excitement.

"You have my undivided attention, sir." She shoved the dishwasher door shut and came over to him.

"Good. Sit right here."

He pointed to the small stool that he had pulled from its nook. She couldn't remember the last time she'd used it to for anything. It had caught her eye at a thrift shop, and she'd brought it home just because she liked the looks of it. It had character, she'd thought, as she imagined just how many people had used it in past years. Nicked and worn, it brought her comfort.

"So, here's what I'm thinking. On that trip—God, it would have to have been when I was in my very mid-thirties—I spent some time in small villages in the southern part of the country. I wanted to experience the people and surroundings without the crush and razzle-dazzle of tourist traps. On foot or by bicycle, if you can believe that, I managed to see more than I had imagined. Anyway, in one of these villages, I met a family who ran a small shop with odds and ends and, of course, staples for the residents. The fellow's name just isn't coming to mind, but I know I would recognize it if I did research on the village. That name I do remember. I thought that I would try to contact the family. Obviously, the man I met, who was in his later years, is probably dead by now, but I'm guessing that the next generation, my age about, might still be there. Might even still run the shop."

"That was a long time ago, Michael. No offense, but it seems to me quite a long shot." She wanted to support him but worried that he might not be thinking clearly.

"No offense taken. But to your comment about a long time ago. Yes, but that shop had been in the family for generations and it might still be. I get that this current generation might snub its nose at it and want more for themselves, but I'm talking about my generation. Maybe, just maybe, we might be in luck. The point is, when I met this man, he offered his home to me as if I were his son or brother—anytime, he told me. We spent hours in conversation and I really grew fond of him." He paused. "It was hard to end that trip, to say goodbye."

"I guess I don't have to ask but will anyway. Were you able to keep in touch when you got back to the States?" She knew the answer.

"Downhill slide from that point on until I met you."

"Of course. But that's ancient history, isn't it? So, finding out the family name is your next mission. Is there anything I can do to help you?"

She meant it. His thinking was beginning to wear off on her—his enthusiasm, his sense of adventure. It was what she needed right now, and she stood up and gave him a bear hug while planting tiny, breathless kisses on his ear.

"This may just be the trip of a lifetime, Michael, not only for you but also for me." More tiny kisses. "It's romantic, don't you think?"

He turned to her and without saying a word, stood up and swooped her into his arms so that before she knew it, he was holding her in the air and gently but intentionally carrying her to the bedroom.

Chapter 2

Only a few weeks had passed when Stephen found the note in his mailbox. It simply stated that a parcel was waiting for him and that he needed to sign for it. It would be held for three days and then returned to the sender if not picked it up by then. It was still early in the day. He had made plans to shop for food, take a walk, and do some reading. He added this chore to his list.

The parcel was wrapped in brown paper, overly taped, he noticed. He would have recognized it among all the parcels in the post office just by the script that covered the top of the box. It did not escape him that, on the surface, this package resembled something from another era as he observed the postal worker's look of admiration when checking the written address against Stephen's ID.

"It's beautiful, no?"

Before handing the package to Stephen, he ran his fingers over the inked art as if hoping to visualize the sender or perhaps a time that no longer existed.

"A thing of beauty. It is art, you know."

He finally passed the package to Stephen, who understood the man's admiration but was well over it.

"Be careful, it's quite heavy. Can you manage?"

Indeed, the weight took him by surprise, even with the kind warning. He secured it in both hands, shifting his own weight to accommodate the added burden. Needing to carry on with his day's plans, he had no time to engage in conversation. A nod and a mumbled simple response would do.

"*Oui. C'est vrai. Merci.*"

As he approached the house, he could feel in his legs and back the consequence of trying to carry too much. He had placed his groceries in one of his many hemp bags and had slung it over his shoulder. Usually, he would carry the bag by the straps in his hand, if carrying more than one bag, alternating between the two, but both hands had been quite occupied with the heavy parcel.

Had he known how heavy it was going to be, he would have made a separate trip or possibly asked for someone to deliver it to him.

Only a few more steps before he would be relieved. His back screamed now, the result of too many tense muscles in his right shoulder, all of which tried to compensate for his obstinate dependency on only one side of his muscular structure. Once started, he had not stopped to put down the box and to switch shoulders for fear that he wouldn't be able to stand back up. Better to just get on with it, forcing himself to take one measured step at a time. He was old but not that old, not yet.

Carefully placing the heavy package on the kitchen table, he turned from it to empty his bag of food. Living alone had some advantages, he thought, as he placed his freshly purchased goods in their proper places. He had grown very finicky about his surroundings. Each shelf in the refrigerator had been designated for certain foods and those foods only. Not only did each type of food sit on the proper shelf, but it also occupied the correct area of that shelf.

Perhaps it was just a habit he had gotten into or, he thought, he might be losing his grip on life and its priorities. In either case, he could not sit down and rest until every item was purposely and safely placed in its appointed spot. The process seemed to take longer each time, as he found himself checking and rechecking to be sure that all was well within the confines of the appliance. Then he would move to the dry goods, and the same attention was paid to these items. By the time he felt satisfied with these chores, the fatigue set in as if to paralyze him right where he stood.

He turned from the kitchen, passing the waiting unopened parcel, and shuffled his way to the bedroom. A quick nap. That was all he needed, and then he would feel himself again. He momentarily thought of the box and silently cursed the persistent sender, but then remembered that it had been his own fault. He had accepted the request to mail it to him. *No one's fault but my own,* he thought, and as he lay down on the bed too tired to take off his shoes, welcome sleep evaporated any further ruminations.

The light in the room had changed. He noted this as soon as he opened his eyes. He gauged that mid-afternoon had arrived while he slept in darkness. Looking at his watch, he was taken aback by the passage of time; he had been sleeping almost three hours! Never had he taken a daytime nap that lasted any longer than half an hour. He was lucky if he could sleep that long, even when his body communicated to him that it would enjoy a longer rest. He was appalled when he realized that his shoes were still on his feet. He would need to launder the coverlet, as its minute fibers now harbored who knew what kind of germs and dirt from his wanderings.

Careful not to shed any more filth where his feet lay, he lifted them gently from the bed while simultaneously pushing himself up to a sitting position. Seated on the edge of the mattress, he waited patiently for the rest of his body to join him. He could feel the rapid pace of his heartbeat for a matter of minutes and took a series of long, deep breaths to calm it. It occurred to him that he should see the doctor sooner rather than later, as the frequency of these events could not be ignored. He had prided himself for a very long time that he had kept away from the medical world, whose grip he could no longer escape from at his age. There would always be something wrong with him. He would be told that each time he visited. Still, he had decided that unless he was on his deathbed, he would not say yes to any medical procedure.

Reaching for his glasses on the bedside table, it dawned on him that he had never taken them off. He said it aloud purely out of frustration. "Stupid idiot. You'd probably lose your head if it wasn't so well attached." And then he chuckled as he visualized what his neck would need to look like for his head to become detached from it. Cartoonish in his visualization and very far from reality, he could laugh at his cleverness. However, as he rose from the bed, the comical neck and then the dependent head, his own, in all its weird distortions was overtaken by a more gruesome image, so real in its composition that for a moment he felt the urge to lash out at it, to throw it to the ground and destroy it. But as quickly as it appeared, so did it vanish.

Shaken, he sat back down on his bed. Visibly trembling, he willed himself to stop. Part of a leftover nightmare? Something was out of sync. Was he having a heart attack? Stroke? None of this thinking was helping him as he tried desperately to calm down, to take an account of his real state of being so that he could return to normalcy.

He heard the phone ringing in the kitchen. He should answer it if for no other reason than to reassure himself that he could speak and comprehend. He had heard that stroke victims could have difficulty doing any of this. But he was too late, as it stopped ringing when he reached the bedroom door. Now standing, he felt better. All he needed was something to eat and drink. He had skipped his regular light lunch, not intentionally, as sleep had dismissed any hunger pains.

Passing the box on the table, he paid little heed to it other than thinking that it was one more thing that he needed to take care of. He would eat first. Not willing to lift it to another location, he sat down to his meal, his only dining companion a stranger patiently waiting for his full attention.

Chapter 3

"You're not going to believe this one, honey." Michael could hardly contain his excitement in sharing his find. "Look at this." He dropped a small black pocket notebook, the size of a business card, on the table as she was finishing up her breakfast.

"Okay, I'll bite. What is it and why wouldn't I believe it?" She did not reach for it but left it right where he had dropped it.

"It's kind of unbelievable, really. I had forgotten I even had this." He appeared to be deep within his own thoughts as he reached for the notebook, bringing it to his chest. "You know where I found it?"

"I have no idea, honey." She finished the last bite of eggs and wiped her mouth. She looked up at him. "None."

Michael pulled up a chair and shoved it close to her while pushing her breakfast dish to the side. He laid the small notebook in front of her. "Inside my notebook. That's where it was, stuck deep between the pages!"

She struggled to understand what he was referring to and then it hit her. The notebook. Of course, his notebook.

"How did it get there, Michael? I thought that you had nothing on you when you entered the place, and the only thing that you took out of there was your notebook. Did you have this," she pointed to pocket-sized book in front of her, "the whole time you were in there?"

"I guess so. I just can't remember ever seeing it then. But the thing is that this is the notebook I had with me when I visited Greece—you know, when I traveled eons ago. I can't believe it's in front of us now."

"So, can you tell me what's in it? Please don't tell me it's an alphabetized listing of all the females you met along the way."

Silly as that was to voice, it caused them both to catch a quick breath.

"Sorry, that was a stupid thing to say. Have no idea where that came from."

"With a steel-trap mind such as mine, that list is permanently imprinted up here, my dear. Not to worry."

He tapped the side of his head and waited for her to react to his humor. And she did. With a playful, quick swipe narrowly missing his forearm as he reached for the notebook, she feigned anger. He ignored it.

"Okay. Here's what's so exciting. The shopkeeper? His name is in here. I don't remember writing anything about him, but it's here. Full name, name of the shop, the village, the date. It's just plain weird to me that, even reading this again, I have no recollection of recording it. Must have been a reason for doing it, though."

"Are there notations in there about anything else?" She was becoming curious.

"Yeah. A couple of notes with dates all about the same time as the Greek visit. But my penmanship was—still is—a mess. I think they have something to do with an itinerary, you know, like the places I might have wanted to see. But I never did. I think I must have cut the trip short. Anyway, I have the info we need to make this trip worthwhile."

"So, who is the shopkeeper and where is he in Greece? Or was he?"

"It looks like it's an 'Achaïkos Metaxas.' Probably slaughtering the pronunciation, but that was his name. The only thing I do remember is him talking to me about his family and how he was following in the footsteps of his father and grandfather before him in keeping the shop open for so many years. We hit it off, I guess. Anyway, may be long gone, but he talked about his children. There might be a chance that his shop is still there and, hopefully, for his sake, is still in the family."

He stood staring at the small page that contained so much vital information about a long-forgotten past.

"Michael, the village? What's the village's name?" She was eager to help him begin the search and had already moved to her laptop.

"Right. Oia. Not sure that's the right pronunciation. I'll spell it. Ready?"

He didn't need to ask the question as her eager fingers were resting on the keyboard.

"Go."

"Okay. O-i-a. Got it? It appears to be part of the island of Santorini. That much I can make out."

"Yup. Here it is. It's pronounced 'EE-ah.' Sound familiar?" She did not look up but continued to pour through the abundance of information about this place that appeared before her.

"Vaguely. What have you found? Let's see." He moved behind her as she continued to scroll through the text.

"Boy. It's beautiful, Michael. Look at these photos. How could you forget a place like this?"

She regretted the question. The pained expression in his eyes revealed what she knew, what she should have considered before speaking.

"Sorry, Michael. Of course, that was another lifetime, I know. Sorry." She reached her hand behind her, searching for his.

Taking her hand, he gently squeezed it. "No worries. Yes, another lifetime to be sure. But let's focus on the present, okay?" Another squeeze and then a release.

"Pull up a chair, honey. There's plenty of information here. Might take a while."

Comfortable now as he leaned in to view the screen, he began to read about a place that had not let him go. The more he read, the clearer the memories became. Ignoring the beauty sitting next to him, he helplessly felt that he was distancing himself from her, from the apartment, from the present.

He began to feel the warmth of the sun as it beat down through the scattered high clouds forming above the South Aegean Sea. He vaguely visualized the village, now, as he walked along the cobblestone road. Clean white buildings hugged one another, their sea-blue roofs and balconies reminding him of the country's symbol, the clean, stark white-and-blue flag.

"How interesting. The village was built along the northern edge of a caldera that forms the island of Santorini. And below it is a small fishing village. It appears the only way to get down to it is by climbing down steep steps from Oia. I guess that whole area was created because of volcanic activity, right?" She didn't look up at him but kept reading.

"Yes, that's right. I forgot that it was a bit above sea level. I can remember certain images, but the rest is a blank. I mean, I can't even picture the shop, much less Mr. Metaxas." He was focusing on the page in the little black notebook as he tried to pronounce the name more clearly.

"There is so much here to learn about this area, Michael. Are you getting excited? I am. It looks and sounds as though it would be a difficult place to say goodbye to. I suppose you don't really remember any feelings you had about it, do you? Just the need to return to it, which I think speaks reams about your time there." She was now looking directly at him, waiting for his response. "Am I right?"

"I'm not sure about the reason for wanting to go back, Allie. Really, I can't pinpoint it at all. But there must have been something about the place, the conversation, perhaps, that after all these years hasn't left me. I figure finding this notebook was a sign. Don't really believe in stuff like that but right now, feeling the way I do, I'm a believer. What are the odds, huh? This bit of bound paper should have lost itself a long time ago. But here it is, and I must have put it in the notebook. Man, it's getting too confusing and a bit spooky for me right now." He stood up and headed toward the kitchen counter. "Want some tea or something? I'm going to make a cup of coffee—you know, the kind that you can walk on? Got to clear my head for a while."

She watched him open the cupboard and pull out two mugs. His last remarks lingered, preventing her from refocusing on the material in front of her. She tried to ignore them, not wanting to fall into client/therapist mode, but it was difficult. His words were revealing. Memory loss. Why? There could be so many reasons, and she convinced herself at that moment that because of the traumas, disruptions, and abuses in his life, it was only natural that times long gone could easily have been unconsciously Xed out, those happier times that "normal" people registered instantly for the long haul and that can be accessed with ease by them in boring detail over a cocktail.

She knew, though, that sometimes memory is lost purposely, through a premeditated effort on the client's part. A contradiction in terms, she thought, as there was no loss of memory at all. Their memories were as clear as could be; nevertheless, artfully and with a good amount of cleverness and skill, patients submerged them just below the surface to be hidden from everyone else. Wasn't that what "triggers" were all about? A word, an object, a smell, a sound, or a touch could trigger a memory in these people.

She continued to watch him maneuver his way through the kitchen as he ground fresh beans. Was it stressful for him to be on alert? To be vigilant of his feelings and, at the same time, the uncontrollable elements that surrounded him, knowing that at any moment, his well-guarded other self could be discovered and then misunderstood?

Her eyes were growing moist as her throat began to tighten, and she physically blinked back the onset of emotions that had everything to do with her husband. *Pull back, you fool*, she told herself. *Why are you getting worked up over nothing? Shut it down, including the third party in the room, and join him for coffee. Move!*

"Change your mind?" The aroma of the beans filled the area where he was standing. She nodded to have him pour her the sacred dark water.

Chapter 4

Even he could appreciate the script so that he carefully cut around the sample of written communication that was, for most of the world, a thing of the past. He would save it, he thought, along with the beautifully designed stamps. He wasn't a collector but couldn't bring himself to throw them away. As he cut through the transparent tape loosening the brown wrapping, he carefully lifted the paper away from the box within, tilting the weight of it just enough to slide the paper out from underneath.

He played a mental game with himself for a few moments. This package was meant for Eliza. It felt, in some way, that he was trespassing, breaking the law by opening what was rightfully hers. But then again, she was not here, and he was. Whatever was in the box would have meaning for only her. He tried to imagine what could be so important that the contents would have been included in a will. Possibly something of great monetary value, he conjectured, as he'd had to sign for it to be sitting in front of him. But its weight. He tried to remember what he had seen in that shop. Just another tourist trap, as far as he could remember. Nothing came to mind. He purposely stopped his musing so that he would go no farther in remembering.

Enough of this, he thought. Removing the lid, he peered inside only to see bubble wrap swelling to all corners and now rising above the edge of the box as it took advantage of its sudden freedom from the lid's restricted space. There was more transparent tape to deal with. Reaching in to lift the contents from the box, his fingers betrayed him and weakened. He could not get a good grip; the contents' shape was awkward, heavy, and unforgiving. It wasn't until he turned the box on its side while slowly and gently shimmying the contents, left to right, that the objects began to appear freed from their cardboard captivity.

Before him lay two bubble-wrapped objects, still not identifiable until he attacked the plastic wrap with his scissors. Growing weary with this chore and angered by the difficulties it was presenting to him, he cut into the wrap at many different angles, trying to free the mysteries inside.

And once done, he sat staring at the two objects, one larger than the other but of the same substance, consistency, and color. He left the remnants of bubble wrap under each one of them so as not to mar the table's surface. Sitting back, he shook his head in disbelief and disgust. What a fool he had been to succumb to the request to begin with! And now he sat with two rocks in front of him. They were volcanic, to be sure. He had seen enough volcanic rocks in California to know one when he saw one. But as he thought about it, he remembered that volcanic rocks, the ones he was thinking about, tended to be lighter, more porous. These did not follow his thinking. Upon closer inspection, as he leaned toward them, he noticed that these rocks appeared darker in color. They were porous, but each tiny angle that led into and away from the shiny surface of the rocks caught the light of the late-afternoon sun. The smaller one was almost identical to its larger counterpart, but its pockmarked surface held fewer recesses and the edges of the tiny pockets were sharp, like the edges of a painstakingly carved miniature arrowhead.

His first thought was to be rid of them. What was he going to do with rocks? He had never had an interest in collecting them and certainly was not going to start now. He had nowhere to put them other than in the small plot by his front door that was considered a garden. Certainly not by him, as he had not laid a finger to it since he moved in. He was not concerned about what anyone thought as it slowly succumbed to his inattention.

He stood and reached for the box to throw it away. As he did, something fell from its recesses, slid across the table, and landed on the wooden floor. He dropped the box back on the table and tried to locate the item. *Please, not another rock.* He stood back and glimpsed a corner of white paper resting on the threshold of the kitchen floor. It was folded neatly and as he unfolded it, a somewhat familiar hand came into view. It was not that of the author of the last two communications, however. He determined that quickly. His curiosity piqued, he hoped that there was an explanation for these interlopers staring at him from their nests of plastic bubbles.

My dear Eliza,

I want you to have these rocks for your garden. Do you remember? I am not a gardener, but I remembered that you built one of rocks. My son has given you another paper that explains these rocks. You will understand better when you read my son's paper.

My regards,
Achaikos Metaxas

He had forgotten all about her rock garden, consciously avoiding the memory. He did not see another paper. He hoped that he had just overlooked it. Perhaps stuck in the box or with the now mangled plastic? He lifted the box only to find nothing but emptiness. As he stared at the rocks, it dawned on him that he had not picked up either one of them. He chose the smaller one first, finding nothing. The larger one took both of his hands to lift and as he did so, he carefully tilted it so that the bottom of the rock was revealed. There, attached to its uneven surface by some sort of adhesive liquid, a second folded paper waited for him. Not wanting to destroy the contents by ripping it carelessly, he very gently maneuvered the paper until it was free in his hand. Placing the rock back in its nest, he sat down once again. This time, no manually produced letters appeared but the crisp, clean print of computer font. Taken by surprise by the time-travel moment, he now felt comfortable as he welcomed the familiar print.

Dear Mrs. Bingham,

These rocks are sometimes called volcanic by the untrained eye but, in truth, are plutonic rock. They derive their distinction by their formation. To be clear, both volcanic and plutonic rocks are igneous (there are three types of rock: igneous, metamorphic, and sedimentary). But scientists have divided igneous rocks into the two categories that I mentioned above. These categories are based on where the molten rock was solidified. The rocks that my father has given you are plutonic because in their formation they were solidified below ground. We call these intrusive igneous versus extrusive igneous, which are formed on the surface. Volcanic rock is fine-grained while plutonic rock is coarse-grained. To the uneducated eye, it may be difficult to make the distinctions that I have mentioned, and there is much more about these rocks that I cannot present in this note to you. That is not my intention.

However, my father was given the rocks you now have in front of you by his father and his father before and before him, and so on. They are considered invaluable and rare to have in our possession. He must have thought very highly of you to gift them to you. Please understand that I hold no umbrage toward you as you are now the recipient and not me. My father's wishes are to be obeyed, and it is not my place to question his decision. He would rather that you enjoy them as a memento of your short time with him. Perhaps one day we will meet one another, Mrs. Bingham. It would be my honor.

One more detail that he wanted me to convey to you and I apologize for not including it above. My father was not a superstitious man. However, he paid close attention to his father and, through his father, all fathers before him in his lineage. Their words were meant to speak through all of time, even before ancient time. During ancient times, the gods ruled our land, and my father's fathers of those times. They understood messages and signs from these gods that we cannot begin to understand in our modern world. In fact, we scoff at the thought now. The rocks now in your possession do not come to you without meaning. They bear a message as to their creator. My father insisted that you would understand their meaning. It is this: Plutonic rocks are called this because their name comes from Pluto, the Roman god of the underworld. I can only imagine that your interaction with my father, as only you know of it, bears the reasoning behind these gifts.

Most Sincerely,

Adrastos Metaxas

Stephen's eyes lingered on the last two sentences: "…of the underworld…" "bears the reasoning behind…" He wrestled silently with their implications while she appeared in and out of his thinking, more clearly each time. He was drawn back unwillingly to the shop, to the old man, this Achaíkos Metaxas, who had connected with Eliza in a way that he would never be privy to or be able to understand. He knew that it was futile to even try, especially after so much time had passed. But now he was confronted with a truth that frightened him. That this old man had seen through him; no, into his soul. What else could he have meant by specifically calling upon the underworld in his note? It was too convenient, too coincidental. But he had not physically harmed Eliza at that point. He had not become the devil yet. Had the old man seen beyond? Had he warned Eliza about him?

It was all too much to consider as he stood up from the table and turned his back on Eliza's gifts. Foolish meanderings! He chastised himself. None of it mattered at this point anyway. The old man was dead. Eliza was dead, and if he could, he would kill off the memory of all of it. He had done so well ridding himself of his past so many times before and now, still angry with himself for weakening and thus allowing his past transgressions to reenter his life, he needed to complete this task yet again.

The obvious place to start was by removing the rocks, valuable or not, from his possession. Not only would he be putting an end to his personal demons, he thought, but he would also be responsible for ending the chain of inheritance that he couldn't care less about. This thought gave him great satisfaction.

In fact, now that her gift had been received, there was no reason for any further contact with the son. Perhaps his weakened moment of decision had not been his undoing but his recreation.

Folding the notes, one inside of the other, as he had so efficiently done once before, he threw them into the fireplace where they would wait to ignite as paper kindling, nestled in among their unmanufactured brethren.

The rocks presented a dilemma. He did not want them in his sight, so placing them on the property was not a solution. Even though he rarely gave a thought to the grounds surrounding his home, he would know that they were there, just outside his door. No, he would need to take them somewhere away from the house, away from him. The heavy sigh that audibly escaped Stephen's lips surprised him as he realized that he must, once again, lift the heavy burden and carry it elsewhere.

Chapter 5

Allie, careful not to step on his toes, wavered about her possible suggestion. It only made sense. After all, how disappointing it would be for Michael if they traveled all that way, not to mention the expense, only to find that what Michael remembered no longer existed. She knew, somewhere deep within her being, that even though he now appeared to be secure and happy with his life, and with her, all of it was resting on thin ice. Upset with herself every time she doubted his stability, she quickly found reasons why her thinking was twisted. She needed to accept what was in front of her, what she had with Michael, what they were building together, what their relationship meant for them both. In doing so each time, she put a finish to her doubts by mouthing a silent "thank you" to God or the gods, just to give herself extra insurance.

"I've been thinking, Michael, about our trip and wondering if it wouldn't be a bad idea to contact the shop in Oia, just to be sure, you know, that it still exists? I guess we could look it up online, but the way you described it, that might be a long shot. Either case, it would be a shame to go all that way to be disappointed. What do you think?"

He was deep in another book that he had picked up at the bookstore. He'd told her that everyone in the store had read it and that it came highly recommended. She noticed that he had spent hours at a time lost within its pages. A novel, he had said, about human interactions and the numerous crises that were the inevitable results. That's all he would tell her. She would need to read it. He didn't want to spoil it for her.

"Sorry. Hold on a minute. Almost finished with this chapter. Just another page, honey." He didn't look up.

Yes, she was blessed, she told herself. By even the smallest of moments, such as this, with her husband next to her but blissfully detached in a world that captured him like a child lost in a picture book, too young to read the words yet but perfectly capable of understanding the plot as he examined thoughtfully the artist's colorful renderings. She couldn't help but smile.

"Okay. Thanks, honey." He placed the bookmark between the pages of the tome on his lap and closed its cover. "So, what were you saying? Something about our trip?"

"Yes. I was just thinking that it might be a good idea to contact this store in Oia before we get there. You know, just to be sure it still exists? I'd hate for you to be disappointed if we found nothing or worse yet, some apartment building where it used to stand."

"I thought about it, actually, but then decided, no. No need. If it's there, it's there. If not, so be it. There is still plenty to see and do once we're there, Allie. I'm not being foolish here, just practical. Both of us understand what the passage of time can do. I'm not going into this with blinders on, you know. I guess, now that I think about it, it makes the adventure better. Are you still up for an adventure or are you having doubts?"

She could tell by the tone of his voice that a sudden concern invaded his nonchalant response.

"No, no doubts. As long as you've thought about the possibility, that's all I care about, Michael. Sounds as though you have and that we're going to experience a trip of a lifetime one way or another, right?"

"One way or another, yes, of course." He hadn't removed the book from his lap and was resting his hands on its cover. "Okay, then. Anything else on your mind?"

"No, that was it. Do you realize that we are leaving in less than a week? I guess I'd better start organizing my thoughts about what to take." She was struggling to find a closing remark that was innocuous as she observed him reopen the book but not start to read it. She knew that he was waiting patiently for her to find something else to do other than interrupt him again. "Okay, then. I'm heading to work. See you later." She leaned down to kiss him as he lifted his head to meet her lips.

"I'll be going in too, in about an hour. See you tonight. Have a good one, sweetheart."

She nodded and was walking to the door when she turned back to him and said, "I just remembered. The meat. Take it out to thaw, would you?" He did not look up but gave a nod as he fell back into the waiting pages.

Chapter 6

The weight of the rocks took him by surprise as he lifted each one from the table and, one at a time, took them outside and dropped them in the dirt plot in front of the house. *For the time being,* he thought, as he mulled over the fact that they seemed to weigh less than when he brought them home. He remembered now how tired he was from the long walk back from the post office and that he'd not only carried the package but groceries as well. No wonder these rocks felt like bricks then. Dealing with them now, one by one, they seemed to him less offensive. However, they could not and would not stay on his premises. On his next trip to the shops he would take the larger one and deposit it somewhere along the side of the road. He would do the same with the smaller one on a following trip.

Satisfied with his decisions and rid of their presence inside his home, he closed the front door. Out of sight, out of mind. The adage seemed quite appropriate. As he finished pouring the boiling water from the teakettle into the waiting mug, his nostrils filled with the scent of the peppermint leaves reacting to the heated water. He always enjoyed the first whiff of the various teas found in his pantry. It soothed him and somehow, if only momentarily, made everything feel right. Like waking up to a rainy day whose chill seeped in between the unseen cracks of the house so that the only logical stance to take was to hunker down with a good cup of tea, a warm blanket, and a good book. He had given up coffee recently, concerned about his health. The only thing missing as he carried his book and mug to the living room was the inclement weather. Instead, after placing the hot mug and book down on the end table, he moved to the front window and pulled down the blind to shield himself from the bright morning sunlight.

Knocks. Knocking. His eyes shot open as he quickly came to. Knocking on the door. His brain was trying to get through to his sleep-soddened state. He had fallen asleep holding the mug causing him to spill his now tepid tea onto the book that lay in his lap. Some of the liquid had found its way onto his pants. Swearing at the tea, the book, himself, and the knocking on the door, he called out, "Coming, coming. Just a moment, please!" Carefully setting the mug on the table along with the now ruined book, he stood up and straightened his tea-soaked clothing. "Coming, coming." He shuffled over to the door, still not completely alert and smelling of peppermint. The bright sun blinded him for a moment as he opened the door. He had trouble making out the image standing in front of him.

"*Bon jour, monsieur. Comment allez-vous?*" The voice was cheerful and somewhat familiar.

"Ah, yes. *Oui. Excusez-moi, monsieur. Très bien, merci. Et vous même?*" Stephen recently had decided that he should learn the simplest of greetings as a newcomer in this country. It was the least he could do. But his French was limited, to say the least.

"*Oui, oui. Très bien aussi, merci. J'ai une enveloppe pour vous.*" The postman reached into his bag and handed it to Stephen. "You, how you say...*ecrire*... *vôtre nom?*" He held out a pen while writing in the air and then pointing to the envelope in his hand.

"*Merci.* This is unusual," he commented while slipping back into familiar lingual territory. "To write my name? *Oui.*" A registered letter. Stephen scratched his signature on the small green label. "*Merci, monsieur,*" he said and handed it back to the postman.

Stephen turned from him and shut the door, not waiting to hear a response. The dampness of his pants reminded him of the mess he had made a few minutes ago. It was only after he placed the envelope on the table, setting it next to the mug and the dampened book, that he felt a slight twinge of remorse for shutting the door on the poor man. After all, he was only doing his job and in such a small village as this, it was not unusual for lengthier conversations to develop or, at least, civility to be practiced with each encounter.

He changed his clothes while prioritizing his next moves. He needed to check the couch for any spill and clean that up. Then he would attend to the pages of the book. Dry them out so as not to seep into the pages below on either side of the binding. Wash the mug. Perhaps make another cup of tea, as he had just wasted the last one. Yes. That was the order of things. The envelope still waited for his attention, he knew. He hadn't even bothered to look at the front of it. Not having any idea as to whom it might be from or why it was registered, he played a successful mind game, always pushing the blue parchment farther and farther away from his present state. Whatever it was, whatever it contained could wait a little while longer. He'd had enough surprises since yesterday's package.

When all was back in order and he'd poured his second cup of tea, he stood in the kitchen, back to the table, waiting for the leaves to steep. Now thinking more clearly, a registered letter meant that whoever sent it would know that he had received it. Without a thought, he had signed his name, a consent to someone that he existed. He knew only a very few people who knew where his life had taken him and none of them did he want to hear from ever again. But here he stood within feet of an impending intrusion, once again, into his life. It dawned on him that he could throw the letter away without opening it. That perhaps he could claim somewhere down the road, if he had to, that the signature was forged and that he had never received the envelope in question. He had a choice; he was still in control of his life, he told himself. He had managed to rid himself of the other letters and he would do the same after he read this one, he decided.

He sat at the table and placed the tea mug so as not to knock it by accident. Silly, he thought, but he felt better, remembering that unwanted things always come in threes. Now he focused on the address, and his heart seemed to thump loudly and irregularly. He recognized, once again, the script. "Shit!" He shook his head in disbelief. Slipping the letter opener under the seal, he slowly and cautiously unfolded the paper as if he expected at any moment something lethal to pounce on him.

The script was that of the son. Stephen's heart quickened as he noted how brief the text was this time. He took a sip of tea and began to read.

Dear Mr. & Mrs. Bingham,

I have neglected one last request of my father as it has only come to my attention. The gift that you have received is only one half of the complete gift to you both. It is at my father's insistence that the second part of the gift be claimed by you both in person. I know that this is asking much of you. I will obey my father and keep it in my possession until we meet. I would appreciate a response when you are able.

Regards,

Adrastos Metaxas

No! There would be no meeting. What gall to expect that they—no, he—would consider the demands of a dead man whom he had no intention of ever appeasing, even in death. Enough! As he had done with the most recent notes included with the unwanted package, he crumpled the sheet and dropped it into the fireplace. It did not matter to him that this Metaxas fellow would know that he had received his letter. Perhaps, with no response on his behalf, he would finally leave Stephen alone.

And then he remembered the rocks just outside the door. The urgency to remove them from his home could not be ignored now. All of this needed to be over with and removed completely from his life. This last correspondence spurred him on to complete the task today.

He decided that he could not carry them both with him. As much as he wanted to and as much as he thought that their combined weight was not as bad as he once thought, his better judgment reigned. The larger of the two rocks would be the first to go, as he had originally planned, while he had energy and incentive. Grabbing the canvas bag from the hook in the kitchen and making sure that he had his house key in his pants pocket, he went outside. Lifting the larger of the two, he awkwardly managed to place the rock in the canvas bag while resting it on the ground. Too heavy to hold in one hand, with both he lifted the bag, holding tightly to the canvas straps while hugging it to his chest. *Yes, one at a time,* he thought. He decided that he needn't go far, just far enough that they would be out of sight and not in an area that he would regularly pass.

The morning was late, and he could feel the heat of the day beginning to build. He had left the house without a hat, something he had taken to wearing recently as his age and ability to withstand the heat as he had done when a young man no longer seemed to exist. *No matter,* he thought. *Just a short walk and then find a spot somewhere off the roadway.* He would do the same for the second rock waiting patiently for him.

He had not gone far when he saw a dirt path leading from the road into an open pasture. No fences blocked his way and the terrain looked welcoming. His concern for solid footing was yet one more consideration that belied his age. When had he become old, he wondered? Even though the bag's content had not become burdensome yet, he would be relieved to be rid of it, the sooner the better. He just needed to be aware of his footing. *Like an old man,* he thought, as he cautiously made his way through the pastureland. Any place was good enough now as he looked back to the road. He leaned over and laid the bag on the ground, lifting it a bit at a time as the rock found its way free. *Good,* he thought. The rock did not really blend in with the terrain, but it didn't matter. If someone should come upon it, it would be a genuine mystery as to its presence and would supply someone with hours of interest and possibly research. He smiled as he imagined this scenario. He might be doing some real good here after all.

His second trip went much quicker as he decided to deposit the smaller version within spitting distance of its companion. *That should keep someone occupied for a while,* he thought, as he headed back across the pasture and on to the roadway. The canvas bag dangled from his right hand, its weightlessness bringing him an unexpected sense of relief. If he had been younger, he would have broken into a jog, he thought. As it was, his pace quickened ever so slightly, and his thoughts raced with optimism.

Arriving at the front door, he stopped and took a good look at the plot of dirt, now empty of his recent burden. It was, he estimated, no more than three feet by four feet. With an unexpected change of heart, he visualized the barren spot filled with flowers. He would buy some plants, water them, and enjoy the fruit of his endeavors. A small garden, very small, but a place in which life would spring, life that he had nurtured.

Not a gardener by any means, he sought the advice of the woman who owned the small nursery nearby. All he wanted was a variety of flowering plants that would take very little skill to grow. Her smile did not break into laughter, but it lingered on the edge of her lips. She was patient with him as she asked pertinent questions about location, soil condition, and preference in the flower choices. Stephen was not afraid to admit that he knew really nothing about growing a garden, and so opened the way for the woman to take him under her wing and all but plant the garden for him. She would have the plants delivered to him the next day, along with some good soil and fertilizer. Did he need help in planting? She could send her son to do the work if he would like. Stephen's first reaction to her suggestion was absolutely no. But he held his tongue and thought better of it. Why not have someone do it for him and do it right? He agreed to her proposal, paid her a bit more than he had budgeted for, and thanked her for her help. He looked forward to tomorrow, he told her.

He heard the truck come up the road as he was finishing breakfast. Good. An early start pleased him, since it would leave the rest of the day for him to enjoy without interruption. He got up from the table, leaving his dishes, and went out to greet the boy. He was surprised at his age. No more than twelve or thirteen, he was sure. But he was driving a truck and unloading bags of soil and fertilizer as well as the potted plants with the ease of a grown man.

"*Bonjour,* Monsieur Bingham!" He waved from the truck as he lifted the last of the plants and placed them on the already full cart.

"*Bonjour. Bonjour,*" Stephen called, waving his hand in greeting. The boy pushed the laden cart up the walk and stopped just short of the planting area.

"*Je m'appelle Jean-Pierre. Je...* I...I am happy to meet you, *monsieur.*" He stretched his hand toward Stephen. "*Pardon, pardon.* Hands dirty." He withdrew his hand before Stephen could shake it.

"That is all right. I do not speak French. Only a bit, *un peu.*" He held up the thumb and index finger of his right hand, placing a very small distance between them to indicate just how much French he knew. The boy laughed, and the simple response put them both at ease.

"Mama say I to help you." He pointed to the cart and then to the vacant plot. "I do this today for you." He smiled at Stephen.

"Yes, *oui. C'est vrai.* Do you need my help?" He knew he had paid well for this job and would not expect to offer his help but as he studied the boy, Jean-Pierre, he grew concerned. He wasn't quite sure how he would be able to sit inside in the comfort of his home, sipping tea and reading a book, while a child was laboring for him just on the other side of the wall.

"*Non, non, monsieur.* I do it fine. You like when I finish. Now I work." And with that, he gave a slight bow to Stephen, turned to the cart, and began his labors.

At one point, Stephen could not stand it any longer and opened the door to offer the boy some food and water, but Jean-Pierre was nowhere in sight. However, what he had accomplished in only a few hours was, to Stephen, miraculous. Not all the plants had found a home in the plot, but those that had were placed artistically so that the taller ones were closer to the wall of the house while consistent tiers of color were being created by this young boy's creative vision. Even the turned-over and fertilized soil smelled good to Stephen. As he gazed on what would soon be his garden plot, he did not hear the boy come up behind him.

"Do you like? I not finished, but soon." He now stood next to Stephen, barely reaching Stephen's chest.

"It is beautiful, Jean-Pierre. Just beautiful. I came to offer you some lunch, something to drink, but you were not here."

"*Oui, merci.* I eat with Mama. I am good." He rubbed his stomach comically as his grin grew. "*Très bien!*"

"Good then. I will leave you to finish your work. Do you want some water?" Stephen could feel the heat of the afternoon sun burning the top of his head and worried about the boy.

"*Non, merci. Je suis bon.* I okay." He was already removing the last of the plants from the cart, indicating to Stephen that enough conversation had taken place and it was time to work.

"I am right in here, if you need me." The boy nodded. Stephen closed the door and went back to his reading.

The tap on the door was barely audible. Jean-Pierre, appearing tired and sweaty, was grinning and pointing to the plot. Stephen's gasp was loud enough for them both to hear as he admired the finished product of the child's labors.

"Do you like?" Jean-Pierre waited patiently for Stephen's response.

"Oh my. It is lovely, Jean-Pierre. Just lovely. I can't thank you enough." He had a momentary urge to place his arm around the young boy's shoulder but held back.

"*Bon.* Good. You welcome. I go now. *Bon soir,* Monsieur Bingham." He turned from Stephen and pushed the empty cart back to the truck. As he drove off, one arm out the window waving, Stephen noted how small he appeared in the truck's cab.

Left by himself, Stephen did not go directly into the house but lingered in front of the newly created garden. He could not help but marvel that only this morning a barren, ugly plot of dirt was now transformed into the wonder in front of him. Even in their transition to their new home, the plants and their blooms seemed to embrace him with their fragrance and beauty. He turned to the roadway, smiling, as if to point out his beautiful garden to anyone passing by. With no one in sight, he turned back and leaned down to the tallest of blooms. Gently pulling the red and white carnation's head to his nose, he was stunned by its cinnamon scent. How wonderful, he thought. How wonderful. He would take good care of his garden, he reassured himself. Somewhere in the deepest recesses of his memory this all felt very familiar but too distant to recall.

Chapter 7

Michael didn't mean what he said to Alison. It did matter to him. The more he thought about it, the stronger he felt about the shop, although he didn't understand why this was so. Playing the partial memories of the visit so long ago over and over in his mind did not reveal any clues as to why he felt so drawn to revisiting it. With each recollection, however, he was able to see one more detail of the shop's interior quite well and if asked, could probably sketch out these details with some accuracy. The outside of the shop in his memory revealed only a small front window whose glass exposed the passerby to a myriad of odds and ends that were meant to intrigue. He remembered that he had stumbled upon the place and had been one of those casual tourists who couldn't resist what waited inside. Once in the shop, he remembered, even now, the musty odor that attacked his nostrils—years of collected dampness and dust; various scents given off by plants and some of their dried companions; garlic bulb strings, some of which had been hanging from the low ceiling long before he was born, he was sure; and the sickly-sweet fragrance of cigar and tobacco smoke that permeated everything in that space.

And then there was Achaíkos Metaxas, the shop's owner. Michael had never really forgotten his name. He had written it down in his newly found notebook so long ago and seemingly committed it to memory without intending to do so. He loved the sound of it, but more importantly, he had been taken by the man himself. Metaxas had sat behind a counter in a darkened corner of the shop. Upon entry, Michael had not seen him, and he would not have seen him at all if he hadn't wandered over to this corner, carefully maneuvering through all the clutter so as not to break anything, all the while drawn to a display of rocks that hid in the shadows. Even now, he could not explain why the rocks had caught his attention. He had never had any interest in geology and had only recently discovered a book on rockhounding in the bookshop somewhat by accident as it fell from its precarious purchase, probably dislodged by a careless customer. He'd kept it at the counter with him, oddly drawn to its contents, captivated by how many rocks existed and their colors, textures, metamorphosis, origins, and names. He had stolen free moments between customers to learn all that he could, but he still could not tell one rock from another.

Now visualizing the display of rocks in the shadows of the Greek shop, he remembered touching their cold surfaces— some rough, catching on the callused skin of his hands; some smooth as glass, whose edges were sharper than a knife but when illuminated, gleamed while playing with the surrounding light. The appearance of the rocks belied their weight. When lifted, some felt featherlight in his grasp, while others, so similar in appearance, called on extra strength to keep them aloft.

He recalled holding a dark, lightweight rock in his hand when he first heard Achaíkos's voice. Although weakened by age so that the vocalizations seemed to crackle, fade, then crackle, there was a detectable rich and deep tone struggling to make itself heard. It was not hard for Michael to hear what would have been the younger man's voice in this stranger's greeting. Michael did not see Achaíkos until he stood and came around the corner to stand next to him. Remembering nothing of the conversation about the rock that he had held or about the rest of the collection for that matter, he could recall with stinging clarity the ancient fragrance of the older man by his side. And he remembered that this shop was very special, having been in the Metaxas family for generations. He remembered how genuine Achaíkos had been, how welcoming. The pride he had taken in the shop that had belonged to his father and his father's father and all the fathers before him was evident to Michael then and even now. As he tried to remember all the details about the visit, this one memory continually fought its way through his hazy recollections time after time. Michael had envied Achaíkos. To have a family history as he did—Michael could only imagine what that would have been like. Then the moment of envy passed as suddenly as it had appeared. He could not identify its source. He had submerged any clues through the abuse he had done to his body. Frankly, he was surprised that he could remember anything about the trip, considering the altered state he had been in for a good part of his life.

Yes, it did matter that the shop still stood. It mattered that the father's son and his son and all the sons to come would be found in the shop, ready to greet the casual tourists who continued to arrive, curious and full of anticipation.

On the flight over, Alison had spent most of her time reading about the island of Santorini and all that there was to do there during their visit. She filled her head with images of this beautiful place and was anxious to finally see it in person. As with most of the area, its history was rich, and she found it fascinating that so many places in the ancient world had withstood the ravages of time to survive and prosper in the modern world, thanks in some part to tourists such as herself.

She wanted to share all the details of her travel book with Michael, but he had slept most of the way there and when he did wake, he excused himself to use the bathroom, carefully maneuvering his body around her legs and the seat in front of her so as not to disturb either passenger any more than necessary. He would always time it so that upon his return, food was being served. She smiled inwardly at his flying savvy. She couldn't sleep no matter how hard she tried. Excited and full of anticipation, her brain stayed wide awake as if on guard, ready and alert. It had crossed her mind numerous times that she would need to be prepared if the point of the trip did not pan out. It was such a long way to come without knowing, she thought. But she had allowed Michael to take the lead and although she did not believe him when he told her that it didn't matter if the shop still existed, she knew him better than that. And because of this, she needed to prepare herself for his reaction, whatever it might be. Her deepest unspoken fear about her husband was what she did not know herself, what she could not identify: the line that separated him from the discomfort of reality and the blissfulness of an induced state of unreality. Where the tipping point was continued to plague her subconscious when she thought about Michael, her husband, her love.

Oia was as beautiful as depicted in all her travel books. Situated on the northwest edge of Santorini within the Cyclades, the village stretched for a little more than a mile along the northern edge of the caldera that formed the island, sitting about 330 feet above sea level. Their small guesthouse, once a simple seaman's house but now attached to another small dwelling, overlooked the sea, the caldera, and the ancient remains of the volcano that created the island. She had read about the homes but was stunned by their brilliance; the blue roofs that topped the gleaming white walls seemed to melt into the blue of the Aegean skies above. Breathtaking!

Michael was eager to complete the task that had brought him here. It was evident to her from the moment they stepped off the small excursion boat. As if stepping on the volcanic ground transmitted an electrical charge through his body to propel him forward, he was now wide awake and curious. Holding his arm as they made their way to the waiting car that would take them to the guesthouse, she noticed the tenseness in his muscles and, for just a second, thought that she felt a shock, a tiny jolt transmitted by him to her.

They arrived late in the afternoon and were treated to a wonderful evening meal by the owners of the guesthouse as a welcoming gesture to their village. Afterward, they sat on a pristine whitewashed terrace and watched the orange sun as it closed the day behind it, disappearing below the South Aegean Sea's horizon.

Before going to bed, Michael sought out the proprietor of the guesthouse, anxious to ask him if he knew the Metaxas family and whether the shop still existed. If he could have an answer now, he would be able to sleep. Alison wanted to say something to him about his not really caring one way or the other about its existence but knew better to keep it to herself. She knew she had been right all along. Michael had just confirmed it. And because he'd unknowingly revealed this to her, she felt a sudden queasiness in her stomach. The beauty of the last few hours on this island seemed to evaporate in front of her as images of what might await her flooded her thinking. She forced herself to think clearly. She told Michael that she wanted to go with him, if for no other reason than to formally meet the proprietor and to thank him personally for the comfortable accommodations and for the wonderful meal. Fortunately, he seemed to have assumed that she would accompany him.

"I am sorry to bother you, but could you direct me to the owner?" Michael had gone back to the dining room and was asking the young woman who had served them.

"Yes, of course. Is there a problem?" She had placed the hot dishes she was carrying onto the shelf by the door.

"No, not at all. I needed to ask him a question about the village. I don't want to bother him if he is busy." She nodded and slipped behind a divider.

A moment later the owner appeared. An older man with a ruddy complexion that surprised Alison, he looked as though he belonged on one of the fishing boats anchored in the harbor below the village, not in the office of a guesthouse.

"Yes, may I help you?" His smile put them at ease, and the urgency that Michael had felt to know the answer dissipated under the man's kind demeanor. "Mr. Bingham, is that right?"

"Yes, thank you. I am Michael Bingham, and this is my wife, Alison." He turned slightly and gestured toward her. Alison nodded and was about to greet him, but Michael continued almost as if not taking a breath. "I wondered if you might help me—us," he said, again with a nod in her direction. "I visited Oia many, many years ago and met a shopkeeper, a Mr. Achaïkos Metaxas. It was a wonderful visit, and I wondered if the shop is still here. It's likely that he has passed, as he was elderly then, but he spoke of the shop being in the family for generations. Perhaps it still is here with another generation running it?"

In his urgency to express himself, Michael did not detect what Alison observed: the owner's acknowledgment of the name as soon as Michael spoke it. The owner's grin only grew wider, still unacknowledged by Michael.

"Mr. Bingham, yes, the shop is here and much like the way you saw it, I expect. Achaïkos passed almost two years ago, bless his soul, but as you had assumed, his sons have taken their responsibility seriously and now run the shop. It is as Achaïkos would have wanted, and I know that he is happy." He looked up at the ceiling as if waiting for Achaïkos to agree with him.

"That's good to hear." Michael looked at Alison, who was smiling even more broadly than he was. How he loved that she loved him so much!

"Yes. Yes. Good. You would like to know the son's name, the one who is really in charge of the shop? His brothers help, but Adrastos is the one you must meet. Adrastos Metaxas. He will be so happy to meet you."

"And I him. Could you help me remember where the shop is located? My memory is not very good about its location." Michael reached for the small notepad and pen in his shirt pocket.

"Let me, if you do not mind. I will write out the directions from this place so that it will be easy to find." He waited for Michael to hand him the pad and pen. "You know, we are not very big to begin with, but the pathways that wind through these homes and shops can play tricks on one who does not know where his destination lies. I will draw the paths as well?"

"Yes, of course. That would be most helpful." Michael handed him the pad and pen. "I can't thank you enough for your help." He squeezed Alison's forearm like a little kid excited to be the next to go on an amusement park ride.

The owner finished, silently mouthing the directions to himself as he traced the meandering lines on the notepad before him. "No, no," he said aloud, but in a voice only meant for himself to hear. "Sorry." He looked up at Michael. "I start one more time so that it is easier to follow." Then he began again, this time slowly and thoughtfully imagining the way to the familiar establishment. "There. That is better. Let me explain it to you, okay?"

When both Michael and Alison had reassured him that they understood his instructions, Alison spoke up. "I am so sorry, but we have been quite rude in not asking your name."

"Of course, of course. I should have introduced myself to you already. I am the first of four sons of Achaíkos Metaxas, the older brother of Adrastos Metaxas. My name is Artemidoros Metaxas." He extended his hand to Michael, who, not disguising his surprise and delight, did the same in return.

Seeming to ignore Michael's reaction to this revelation, he continued. "I would take you there myself," Artemidoros offered, "but my feelings tell me that you need to seek our father's shop on your own. Besides, my map, if you can call it that, will guide you. If you lose your way, just ask anyone you see from our village. They will help you. Okay?" He held his arms out in front of him and gestured for them to be on their way. "Just turn left as you leave this place. If you go right, well, I only pray that the gods watch over you." His laughter filled the small room as he held open the door and gently guided them through it. "I will see you again soon."

And with that, he closed the door behind them.

"So, do we go now? What do you think?" Alison knew his answer well before she finished the question. She was surprised that he had stood still for as long as he had.

"I can't believe this. That we should be sleeping under the roof of one of his sons. What are the odds?"

"Well, I think that they're pretty good, honey. We're not in LA anymore. People tend to stay put in places like this, is my guess. And now that you know there are four sons, I wouldn't be surprised if we run into another along the way." She added this as an afterthought because it had fallen on deaf ears. Michael had already headed down the cobblestone road on a journey of his own making. "Hold up!" she called, and she said a little thank you that she'd had the sense to wear her walking sandals as she gingerly gained her footing on the worn, rounded stones.

Chapter 8

The evenings began to send a chill through the house and alerted him to the change in season. Even though the month of October had not yet ended, the fall air was warning of the coming winter. He could taste it as well as feel it. This evening, as he sat to read, wrapped in a warmer blanket, he decided that a fire would add the right touch. He hadn't used the fireplace since last winter, and it dawned on him that he should at least clean out the old ash left by previous fires.

On his way out of the house to retrieve a broom and dustpan that he kept in the little shed next to the house, he glanced at the flower garden, now only a shadow of its former late-summer splendor. He had promised himself that he would take care of it, that he would nurture its growth and help it through nature's transitions, but now as its ugliness rudely assaulted him, he chastised himself for not carrying through with his intentions. He could only imagine what Jean-Pierre must be thinking if he passed the house and saw the demise of his handiwork. The boy had come to the door weeks ago offering to replenish and tend to the garden for him, but Stephen had politely told him that it was not necessary, that he would like to do it himself. He told the boy that he had been doing some research into becoming a successful gardener and hoped to be half as smart as Jean-Pierre one of these days. No, he would take care and practice his gardening skills. He had thanked him sufficiently and closed the door as he watched the boy head toward the roadway, pausing to take a lingering look at his suffering plants.

He had forgotten about the paper he had thrown into the ash, but he recognized it immediately without having to examine it. The blue tissue, at first, seemed to blend in with the grayish-blue ash that had, over the last few weeks, blown onto the paper, covering much of its surface as the colder winds of fall had found their way down the chimney and into the living space. He was careful not to sweep it into the dustpan for his intention had been, all along, to destroy it, all of it. Pushing the fragile papers to the side of the fireplace away from the ash, he managed to sweep most of the ash into the pan without too much escaping onto the hearth. He took a moment to straighten his aching back, another sign, he knew, of the aging process. The simplest of chores was becoming unpleasant. He sighed heavily as he leaned forward and swept the last of the ash into the dustpan, whose lid now shut on the offensive remains of once fragrant cedar logs. Careful not to spill any, he slowly and methodically moved one foot in front of the other until he reached the front door. Once outside, he felt relief as his tense muscles relaxed, and he quickened his pace while carrying the dustpan to the trash. The ashes fell slowly and in a cloud to the bottom of the trash can, leaving a thin deposit along the sides and against its inverted rubber handles. He was careful closing the lid, moving far enough away to avoid having the ash fly back in his face.

Placing the dustpan and broom back in the shed, he moved to the other side of the house, where he had neatly stacked split oak logs. He'd had the sense not to try to split them himself two years ago, instead hiring men to deliver logs and split them for him right on his property. He wanted to stack them himself, he had told them. They tried to talk him out of it, perhaps concerned about his age or perhaps wanting to complete what they knew to be part of the job. He was left with a healthy amount of wood, enough to see him through a number of winters before he would need to restock. Slowly, over the days that followed, he came out to the pile and little by little, stacked the logs as neatly as if he were building a wall, each log precisely lined up against its brethren to create a solidly smooth facing wall of exposed cut timber. He remembered, upon finishing the task, how proud he was of his endeavor. He was beginning to think now, as he observed the aged stack, that this dead wood would probably outlast him. Pushing the thought away, he began lifting the logs from the stack, three at a time, and taking them into the house. After four trips, he had certainly enough to provide a warm fire for the evening, with more in reserve on the hearth. Before lighting a match, he reached for the blue tissue papers and crinkled them in his hand, then shoved them between the waiting logs. He had brought kindling in along with the logs and had prepared the pile as his fire starter.

Striking the match, he held its long stem toward the kindling, waiting for the first of the flames to appear. As they did, he gently leaned forward and blew upon the flames, igniting more of the slim wood until the fire sparked the dry oaken bark and crawled its way along the dead wood's surface. Had he looked away for even a moment, he would have missed the instant inflammation of the blue tissue as it momentarily held its shape until its fibers gave way under the intense heat so that a deep blue, then black, remnant of what had once been threatening now disappeared in purple smoke and ash.

The evenings that followed during the closing days of October and into the very early days of November were comforting to him. He enjoyed the idea of hibernation with each passing year, and he had read more in his time here than in all his life, he guessed. The rains had begun, and with them came the familiar dampness that seeped through any crevices it could find in the woodwork. The evening fires helped to warm only the front room. He had pulled out of his wooden chest at the foot of his bed extra bedding, including a down comforter that he had splurged on when in Paris for a weekend visit. There were times when he missed the big city with every comfort known to man, if he had the wherewithal to acquire it. But even if he didn't, the city, any big city for that matter, provided the options of less expensive versions that generally were just as good. However, what the city could not offer him was what he had here in his small home in the countryside: peace and quiet, privacy and anonymity. He cherished these qualities in this village, in his home.

The fall soon turned into winter, one that was quite tame compared to the last few. There was good rainfall, of course, but the freeze that had descended upon the area last winter did not come this year. In all, he thought that it had been a temperate winter season, with enough rain to saturate the ground and enough cold to invite all living things to hibernate while waiting for the warm sun and winds of spring. He had read in a gardening book, when he thought he was serious about becoming a gardener, that bulbs needed the cold, dark winter to get ready for the spring blooms. Had he planted bulbs in his yard, he would have enjoyed their colorful and fragrant greeting. But he hadn't. He had nothing, really, other than the plot outside his front door, now completely ignored and finding its own way back from whence it came. However, he had long stopped feeling badly about it and about the boy. In the bigger picture, which he continually reminded himself was becoming smaller for him each passing year, a dead three-by-four garden plot was a dot on the continuum. And so, the winter passed into a beautiful spring whose lukewarm days soothed his aches and pains and cast a glimmer of promise on the year ahead, if he bothered to pay attention.

Another weekend trip to Paris was planned for in the middle of April. His excitement grew slowly as the urge to be in the city once again could not be ignored. This time, however, he would try to find something different to do, something away from the hordes of tourists that flocked to Paris in the spring. When he had first arrived in the country, like any newcomer, he had explored. The city was well covered, he felt, as he had taken in as much as he could. The countryside, however, still held its charm, and the house that he lived in was a testament to his succumbing to its charm.

He decided he would take the train in and perhaps, as he followed the map, get off when he was drawn to do so. He had no real agenda, no one to meet, no companion who might have different ideas. He was on his own, free to go at his own pace following his own desires and was now at an age where he couldn't care less what anyone thought of him. How wonderful!

But he found himself in Paris without having gotten off the train at any of its many stops along the way. Once aboard, he felt as though he was captive to the car's comfort, its gentle rocking as the countryside flew by in bits and blurs, never decipherable unless one was familiar with the area. He had slept, had done some reading, and certainly had enjoyed the onboard meals and drinks. And, strangely enough, he thought to himself, he had no regrets. As if invisibly drawn to the frenetic pace of this city, he knew that he had no choice in the matter. Never had.

The taxi took him directly to the hotel, one in which he had stayed before. Without a reservation, he worried about where he would finally rest his head for the night, but he was in luck. Two rooms were left. Did he prefer a view of the Arc de Triumph or of the Seine and Notre Dame? He chose the water view and could not believe his luck. Although the expense of the room was much more than he had planned on spending, something told him to do it. Not to worry about tomorrow. After all, how many more visits did he think that he would make to Paris? He needed to be a bit realistic.

Indeed, the room was comfortable, well appointed, and the view was lovely from the tenth floor. The bed begged him over to it as he kicked off his shoes, one by one, removed his overcoat, and promised himself that he would only take a catnap to recover from the trip. He would be refreshed and ready to eat again while exploring the city in the early-evening hours.

The phone by his bed was ringing and as he came to in the darkness of the room, he tried to adjust his eyes to what had been visible to him seemingly only moments ago. Reaching blindly for the phone and the bedside light switch, he brought the receiver to his ear. The voice on the other end was unfamiliar to him but greeted him by name. "Monsieur Bingham?"

"Yes," Stephen managed to vocalize and then cleared his throat. "Yes, this is Mr. Bingham."

"*Oui.* Yes. I am sorry to bother you. I am the concierge and am calling on behalf of our front desk. You had inquired upon your arrival about sights to see here during your stay. Unusual ones, you had requested." Stephen had forgotten this. "I wanted to let you know that I have put together a list for you, *monsieur,* of what I think you will find interesting. Shall I have it delivered to your room for you to review? Or I could meet with you tomorrow morning to go over it with you in person. I am sure that you will have a question or two." Stephen looked at his watch. He checked it twice, not sure that he saw the numbers correctly. Nine fifteen!

"*Merci, merci.* I appreciate you doing that. I fell asleep upon my arrival and forgot all about it. I am sorry. I am having trouble believing that it is past nine already." He stood up and walked over to the window.

"It happens," laughed the stranger on the other end of the line. "Please do not apologize. Travel can take the best out of us, *non*? I will say that the comfort of our beds is a testament, as you fell so soundly asleep." He laughed again at his effort to be humorous as well as loyal to his employer.

"Yes. You are very kind. I would appreciate having the list sent up to my room. If I can schedule a time to meet with you tomorrow morning, that would be best. How early will you be on duty?"

"Of course. Why don't we meet as early as you would like? I am here beginning at seven thirty."

Stephen knew that he would not be ready by seven thirty, not after sleeping some of the night away already; who knew what time he would fall asleep now. He was afraid that he would be up half the night only to fall asleep just before dawn. "I will meet you at nine, if that is all right?"

"*Oui, bon.* I will send up the list immediately and will see you tomorrow morning at nine. *Bon nuit,* Monsieur Bingham."

"*Bon nuit. Merci.*"

As he stood on the small balcony admiring the lit pathways along the Seine and the lighting of the cathedral, his stomach suddenly reminded him that he hadn't eaten since early afternoon, the last full meal served on the train. The city, he knew, would take care of him, as the evening was still young for those who knew her. He recalled a small café not far from the hotel that would welcome him and happily sustain him. He washed his face, ridding himself of the grime of traveling and the cobwebs of sleep. Putting on a clean shirt and pants, he placed his wallet and a map of the city into his overcoat's outer pocket and headed into the Parisian night.

The café was small and intimate. Finishing his meal, satisfied and content, he paid his bill, put on his overcoat, and left the café. He was not surprised that fatigue had not come yet. The environment that he had just left was stimulating, even though he had eaten alone. The maître d', pleasant and friendly, had continually checked on him throughout the meal. Small talk ensued, but never a conversation of any substance. The boundary between clientele and employee had remained intact. However, he had enjoyed eavesdropping on the couples who surrounded his table. He had been the only single in the room, he'd noted. But he had not felt uncomfortable. In fact, he couldn't help but admire himself, an older man, independent, out later than his counterparts of similar age who were deep in fitful sleeps, and an American in a Parisian café. And the young couples were equally uncaring of anyone's opinion. They laughed loudly or, softly, or muffled their happiness behind cupped hands over unwrinkled lips. They reached for one another's hands, holding on tightly as if to let go would send them separately flying into space in opposite directions. And they kissed, as one would lean over the half-devoured plates while the other followed suit. Long, passionate kisses that seemed never to end and from which he was compelled to avert his eyes out of politeness.

He realized, once out onto the boulevard and turning in the direction of the hotel, that the pain he was feeling was emanating from his jaw, from the smile on his face that he could not relax, nor did he want to. Suddenly, there was another pain, sharper and persistent, but he could not recognize its origins until he was aware that his right hand had slipped under the overcoat's left lapel and rested heavily over his heart.

**

The hand-drawn map was surprisingly accurate. Artemidoros had recorded every twist and turn as if he had laid a large sheet of tracing paper over the village's roadways and minimized it for their use. Michael was a bit in awe of its accuracy, although if someone who had lived here all his life couldn't be accurate in giving directions, who could? He laughed aloud as his answer came silently to him: his phone could.

Turning the final corner, which led into a wider cobblestone street, a moment of déjà vu struck him so strongly that he stopped abruptly. "I remember this place, right here, this corner. Alison, I can see myself here so clearly. Weird, huh? After all of these years it feels like I was here just yesterday." He had actually, for the first time since they'd left the hotel, taken notice of her. She had barely managed to keep up with his pace throughout the maze of streets, consistently behind him by a few yards or more, and now thanked God that she hadn't lost sight of him, since he had the map. "Are you okay, honey?" He came to her and touched her arm. She knew it was out of genuine concern as she tried to regulate her audible breathing, one breath at a time. *When we get back home, I'm signing up for an aerobics class,* she thought.

"Sure. Just give...just give me a minute to catch...catch my breath." She rested her hand on his, which had not let go of her arm. "Are we close, then?"

"According to this," he waved Artemidoros's map in the air, "we're on the right street. The name of the shop is interesting. It wasn't called this when I came, but that was so long ago. Change can be a good thing, right?" His smile was more than a smile at that moment. It was, in Alison's mind, his confirmation that all was right with his world now and that she was an integral part of it.

"It's the best, sweetheart. It's the best." Her breathing had adjusted but her heart was pounding in her chest—not from overexertion, she realized, but from the love she felt at that moment for the man standing in front of her. She stepped forward and kissed him so intensely that both, for an instant, lost themselves to one another; none of it mattered as long as they were together.

"Do you have any idea how much I love you, Allie?" He held her in his arms a moment longer as he whispered the question into her ear. "Do you?" He did not release his hold on her.

"I love you, Michael Bingham, and I always will, because you love me so much. I know, sweetheart." If this moment ended now, it would be enough, she thought.

Still holding her as he stepped back to see her face, she was shocked to see the dampness on his; the remnants of tears clung to his skin. "Just can't help it," he laughed and wiped them away. "That's what you do to me."

"Well, this is no way to spend a vacation. We'll both be emotional wrecks before the trip is over at this rate. Come on." She now took the lead. "Show me the way." She pointed to the map dangling from his hand.

"Right, right. Okay. We're looking for a shop called The Line's End. Interesting name. Looks like, if we came the right way, it will be on our right. Shall we?" She waited for him to retake the lead. After all, he needed to be the one to find it first even if she had already noted its location just up the street.

Michael entered the store first, as Alison had wanted. She lingered behind him as they stopped just inside the entrance. Both were taken aback by the clutter. Flashes of recorded memory attacked Michael, coming quickly and with an intensity that he was not prepared for. He remembered now the smell, the darkened corners of the shop. He tried to clear his mind in order to focus on the present as he moved forward. Alison stayed close to him.

"Good evening." The voice was familiar to Michael, and he knew he was hearing Achaíkos's voice as a younger man. However, the man now standing in front of them appeared to be Michael's age; if not yet seventy, very close to it. But in his face, through the dim lighting that filled the shop, Michael saw a shadow of Achaíkos as Michael remembered him. Alison sensed that Michael was struggling. He didn't respond to this man, only stood as if transfixed and senseless.

"Good evening," she said. "You have an interesting shop. Are we here too late? Are you closing soon?" Michael seemed to have stopped breathing as he stood quietly next to her.

"My brother told me that you were coming. I am glad that you have found your way. He can be forgetful lately and could have easily sent you down to the dock." His laugh was kind, gentle as he recalled his older brother. "I am Adrastos Metaxas, the fourth and youngest son of Achaíkos Metaxas. And you are Mr. and Mrs. Bingham? Am I correct?"

At the sound of his name, Michael seemed to come to. "Yes, that's right. I...we are so happy to meet you. Frankly, I'm finding it difficult to believe I am standing here after so many years have passed. I'm sorry for the loss of your father. My condolences to your family."

"Thank you. You are very kind. We lost him almost two years ago. It doesn't seem possible. I can still see him clearly behind the counter, right over there." He pointed to the still darkened corner where the countertop nearest to them protruded into the light. Michael felt his throat tighten ever so slightly and fought his emotional reaction to the finality of that man's life.

"I remember. When I came into the shop so long ago, I remember thinking that no one was in here. And then, suddenly, he was by my side having come from behind the counter hidden from view."

Adrastos smiled in remembrance. "He had a knack for doing that. Do not feel that you were the only one. He would not come from behind the counter until the visitor crossed my father's imaginary line in the shop. If they crossed that line, he was willing to engage them. It meant that they were curious and interested in his products. See, here."

He had moved to the rear of the shop, perhaps five feet away from the counter that had concealed his father's presence and pointed to the floor. Michael directed his eyes to the spot indicated. There, faded but still visible if pointed out, was a crude drawing of what looked like a mountain. Its base faced the front door of the shop while its summit pointed to the darkened corner. Michael was intrigued as he knelt down to examine it closer. It was then that he began to make out the worn details of the drawing. Along the mountain's side, he traced his fingers over dulled reddish streams that flowed down its surface. Moving his eyes to the peak, he saw what he had begun to suspect. Now barely visible as the original shades of gray and black were almost gone, worn into the surface of the wooden floor by who knows how many shoes, a plume of smoke rose from the mountaintop. A volcano.

"Our father had strong beliefs, first, of course, in God, but he was not timid to teach his sons that God's power was to be seen in everything and to be revered and respected. You know that this village sits on the edge of an ancient volcano? That we build our lives on the caldera of this mountain?"

Alison, having also knelt to observe the image on the floor, stood up. "Yes, I read about it on the flight over. It's amazing, and the village is beautiful. Is it dormant or extinct?"

"We would like to believe that it is extinct, but that is not what we are told. We experience a rumble or two frequently, which reminds us that we humans are at the mercy of the gods." He laughed again. "But I suspect that you will be quite safe during your visit with us. Hades has been taking a very long nap and, like all of us, has fitful stirrings but falls right back to sleep." He said no more, as if waiting to observe their reaction to his attempt to lighten the atmosphere that he had unintentionally created.

"Tell me, then. Is this drawing of the volcano that forms this island?" Michael was fascinated by the image at his feet. "Is your father's drawing?"

"Yes, in answer to both of your questions. This caldera is filled with the sea, but she has not reached the summit of all its walls. We have been living on this northern exposure for centuries. If you look at a map of the area, you can see more clearly how large the volcano's summit had once been. Now, all that is left above the Aegean's surface is us and a few smaller islands that the sea has allowed to exist."

Michael slowly nodded, seemingly accepting Adrastos's mini geology lesson, but Allie could tell that he wanted to move on. She could see the intensity in his face. The need to justify his presence here as well as to the spirits who lurked in the shadows.

"You understand," Michael continued with his train of thought, "that I must have walked on this image years ago as I crossed the line. I had no idea, none. Amazing to me, it really is." Alison watched as her husband tried to deal with the past, present, and now, she feared, the future. "So, I was fortunate enough to meet your father because I crossed the line?" He shook his head slowly in disbelief. "And because of that meeting, I find myself back here almost 35 years later? And for no reason other than I was drawn back by memories?" Now he looked at Adrastos and their eyes engaged in the dusky light. "There is no other reason, am I right?"

"It was not my intent that you should find us again, no. But there is something that you need to know and that, not possessing any of my father's sixth-sense gifts, as I like to call it, seems to explain your presence here this evening. Come with me." He moved carefully around a cluttered tabletop of odds and ends and led them to the front of the shop. Just to the right of the front door, he disappeared into a small compartment that served as an office. "Please, come in." They followed his voice.

He sat behind a small desk surrounded on two sides by file cabinets and bookshelves. The room's appearance was a stark contrast to the shop's interior. Everything had its place and his desk was neatly appointed, even including an antique inkwell and a quill pen. Current time in space, however, was marked by the laptop that he had set to the side of his desk as he opened the desk drawer and withdrew a file folder. He motioned for them both to sit.

"I am perplexed that you sit across from me now. There is more at work here than simple memories. You are here because my father wanted you to be here, Mr. Bingham. He must have known the difficulty that I would have in contacting your brother. My father was wise."

All Michael heard was "brother." None of this was making any sense, and for a moment he felt as though he was losing control. Alison took his hand in hers and squeezed it to let him know that he was not alone. A voice somewhere in the background of the cacophony of noises in his head fought its way clear, and he was able to refocus on the man sitting across from him.

"Excuse me, but you did say 'brother'? Did I hear you correctly?"

"Yes. Mr. Stephen Bingham. It seems that he and his wife came to this shop not long ago, perhaps ten years ago now, I think. In any case, that does not matter. What is important is that my father and Mrs. Bingham, Eliza, made a strong connection, so much so that my father never forgot her."

"Wait, wait a minute. My brother and his wife?" The words escaped his mouth before he realized that he had confirmed to this stranger what this man's father must have known somehow.

Too much to take in, thought Alison. *He will never survive this.* Could she? She gripped his hand tighter.

"Yes. That is what I said. Please let me finish. You see, my father, upon his death, had dictated that Eliza, Mrs. Bingham, would inherit cherished objects held in my father's possession for all of his life and all of the lives of his ancestors as far back as can be traced of this family. I do not know the content of their conversation or the importance that it held for my father. But I do know that he would not have made these arrangements if it had not been so important to him. I had to honor my father's wishes."

Michael could find no words. He sat as if dumbstruck.

"I have contacted your brother three times to let him know of his wife's inheritance. The first time, I received no response after one year had passed, so I wrote once again. This time, he responded by letting me know that I could send the gifts directly to the address that I had for him. I did so, and…"

"Excuse me, but may I ask what the inheritance was?" Alison knew that she had not only interrupted but had spoken for her husband, who did not seem to be registering anything.

"I will come to that, of course. Mr. Bingham, if that is all right with you?" His question confirmed her faux pas. Michael nodded.

"So you see, I sent the items to Mr. Stephen Bingham at

his address outside of Paris. I did not hear from him that he had received them, but I can only assume that he had. It wasn't more than a few days later that I found the second half of the inheritance. You can imagine my surprise as I came across a box tucked away on a shelf where my father used to sit in the dark. The other side of the line, remember?" He waited for a response, but neither Alison nor Michael had caught up with his revelations. "Well, to continue. The box was tied with simple twine and underneath the knot was an envelope. The note inside was in my father's hand. It indicated that the contents of the box were meant for Eliza—Mrs. Bingham, excuse me—and that she was to inherit it along with the first gifts. Somehow, it was never formally written in his will, but his intent was clear. However, and this is what I find so strange about our meeting this evening, my father was very clear as to how this second gift should be delivered to her. As a matter of fact, he specifically indicated that both Mr. and Mrs. Stephen Bingham should receive it in person, here in this shop." He stopped as he sat back and observed the couple in front of him. "Oh my, this is too much information at one time, I think. May I offer you warm tea? Something to drink?" He was pushing his chair away from the desk. "Perhaps something stronger?"

Alison let go of Michael's hand. She leaned forward and shifted her weight in the chair. "For me, no thank you. I am fine. Michael?" She turned toward her husband, whose hand still rested where she had released it. "Michael, honey?"

"Uh, no thanks. I apologize. You have caught me completely by surprise. Completely..." The word drifted into the still air of the stuffy room.

"I should explain." She was doing it again. Stepping in where she should not. Why couldn't she keep quiet? She knew that Michael had now turned to her, and she was afraid to look at him as she began. "Michael and Stephen have not had contact with each other for a very long time. This all comes as a surprise to Michael and to me. To comprehend that his brother's connection with the shop is the same as his own not only shocks him, I am sure, but also mystifies him...us." She knew better than to continue, as Michael's gaze seem to pierce her side with its intensity. She fought the urge to explain to this stranger all that she knew about her husband, to defend him, to be his protector.

Finding his voice, Michael turned from her and addressed Adrastos. "How did you know that Stephen and I are related? I really don't understand how you made the connection."

"Ah. I see your confusion, I think. In my father's possessions, we found a notebook. We were very surprised by its content. He had kept a diary, I suppose you could call it, of every day that he spent in this shop. The weather, his own state of health, his family's well-being, his inventory, his 'things-to-do' list. But to answer your question, he also recorded in exacting detail his interactions with his customers. Some description of their appearance, but more so how he interpreted their…well, I do not know how to put this other than to say 'their soul.'" He paused, expecting either one of them to ask for explanation, but they sat still as if spellbound by his words. He continued. "As I said, our father had a gift that we cannot understand but must accept as fact. We, as young boys and now grown men, and now you both, have witnessed something of his workings. Not to be explained, but to be accepted and respected. To your question then. You, Mr. Bingham, my father wrote at length about. Not only did your brother's wife leave a lasting impression on him as he has recorded, but you did as well. He writes about your visit with him in the shop and how interested you were in him and in some of the items that you admired. Upon our first reading of this entry, I must tell you that my brothers and I were a bit jealous of you. Our father wrote about you as if you were another son to him. You would always be welcomed under his roof." He sat back and smiled, expecting that Michael would respond to this information, but there was no reaction. "Perhaps this is too much information? Do you have any questions?" He waited patiently.

Michael's voice, not angry but impatient, startled Alison as the stillness in the room was suddenly broken. "How did you know that we were brothers?"

Adrastos was taken aback. Hadn't he explained this already? "I am sorry. Did I not tell you?" He was sure that he had.

"No. Does it have to do with his notebook?" Michael was aware of Alison's body shifting in her chair as if trying to get closer to him without getting up to do so.

"Yes, in a way. I will get right to the point."

Michael braced himself, fully expecting another rambling explanation, and this time was ready to interrupt if Adrastos did not stay on track.

"On the last page of his entry about his visit with you, he had taped a small, lined piece of paper as if torn from a small notebook. And on it, written in a hand that we did not recognize as our father's, was your name with a phone number and below it, the name Stephen Bingham and a phone number. In parentheses under Stephen's name was the word "brother." It was not until we were reading through our father's will and last wishes that we began to understand. For whatever reason, and only known to our father, your family was important to him."

Alison sat frozen but her head was roaring. Nothing was making any sense to her and her thoughts were unintelligible amid the persistent noise between her ears. She couldn't look at Michael. She was afraid of what—no, who—she might see.

"Does that answer your question?" Adrastos was not oblivious to the impact his words were having on his guests. He knew better than to go on.

Michael, now standing as if to stretch, moved behind his chair and rested both hands on its back. "May I see this notebook?" The face seated across from him indicated that Michael had crossed the line with this request. "I mean, not the whole notebook, but the page that you are referring to? Please?"

"If it will help you to understand better, of course." Adrastos courteous response could not be construed as anything but forced, but Michael did not care. He needed to see what he knew to be a truth. That he had indeed been here before was obvious to all in the room, but what had not been obvious to him until this moment was that he had known the truth about his brother, even as long ago as his first visit here. He had written his brother's name down and given it to a stranger. A definite confirmation that Stephen existed. More than that, a contact number. He was sure the same one that he had used when he tried to contact Stephen but had been rejected by him.

Adrastos reached into his desk drawer and withdrew the notebook from its confinement. Its rich leather jacket testified that it had been well used, had been at times carelessly shoved back into an already stuffed drawer, judging by the scratches that gently and, in some cases, deeply gouged the soft surface of an animal's tanned hide. He held it up, as if to prop it in place to begin reading, but instead laid it back down on the desktop and started to thumb through the pages until he stopped about midway, thumbed a few pages backwards, and finally opened the book to let it rest open on the page in question. Michael had moved from the chair and, without thinking, had come to stand behind Adrastos, looking over his shoulder.

There, as if he had just finished writing it yesterday, lay his few words to Achaïkos written in haste so many years ago. And he was suddenly there with Achaïkos, seeing him bring out the notebook and asking for Michael's information. Seemingly so harmless, so normal a gesture to leave with this new friend his contact information. But even in the brilliance of this memory, Michael could not remember offering—no, admitting—that Stephen was a part of his life then. How could he have blocked so much out? How could he have been so confused during his work with Alison? He felt the familiar beginnings of a kind of panic somewhere deep within and fought now to contain it, to restrain it in whatever hellhole from which it was trying to escape. He heard her voice in the distance, as if years away.

"Michael. Michael? Sweetheart?" Her arms reached around his own, which were clutched against him as if holding him in position. "Sweetheart, it's okay. It's okay. Come. Come sit down." And with her touch, he felt his body relax within his wife's gentle embrace as he let her guide him back to the chair across from the startled shop owner.

"Can I get you a glass of water?" was all Adrastos could manage to say. What had just taken place between the notebook and this Michael Bingham was a mystery to him, and something he did not want to know. It was between his father and this family. He had done his duty, he was sure.

Alison answered for her husband. "Yes. That would be lovely. Thank you." She watched Adrastos move from his desk to the door and then into the shop, seemingly relieved to be away from the two of them for a moment.

"Michael, are you doing okay?"

When he looked at her now, the glazed appearance that only moments ago alarmed her had dissipated and his face was relaxed. "I'm really sorry. I didn't mean to worry you. He must think I'm a nutcase." He couldn't hold back his smile as he realized the impact of his words between them. She smiled as well and at that moment, the world seemed all right again. "I'm okay. Really. Just in too much of a shock to make all these connections. I guess I'm having trouble believing what I'm seeing. But it's there and it's beginning to make sense. This visit, this need to return. I just…"

Adrastos's entrance interrupted his thoughts. "Here you are, Mr. Bingham. Is there anything else that I can get you?" He waited before sitting down.

"No, thank you. You have been most kind, especially with your time. Thank you."

Pulling his desk chair out, Adrastos eased himself into the worn, comfortable grooves of the aged wood, grateful that he could now bring this meeting to a close. What more could come, he wondered? He hoped nothing. He ventured forward. "So, you now understand how we became aware of you and your brother?"

His question reminded Michael of the third-grade teacher who used to ask him over and over again if he now understood how to multiply.

"Yes. It makes sense to me." Not the same response he gave Miss Wheatley in Room 3, but close enough.

"Good. I am happy that we have cleared that up." As if

he had just remembered to do something important, Adrastos sat up straight in his chair. "Should we continue then? I mean about my father's wishes for your brother and his wife?" It seemed to all of them in the room that this part of the conversation had taken place days ago, so caught up had they been in the crisis that just passed.

"Of course. Yes. You say that he has a Paris address?"

"Yes—well, no, but a village just outside of Paris. Tigeaux. I have it right here." He started to shuffle through the papers in the file folder. "Yes, here it is. I know that he receives his mail there, but I do not know if that is where he lives. I have just received notice that he signed for the most recent letter I sent him by registered mail." He did not offer the piece of paper to Michael but kept it in the folder.

"And that most recent letter? Can you tell me the contents?"

"Under the circumstances, I am compelled to do so, don't you think? It was very short and to the point. Simply put, I let him know of the second gift from my father and that the only stipulation was that both he and his wife must receive it in person. That I would keep it in my possession until we meet. I awaited his response."

"Have you heard from him?"

"No. And now I am wondering if I am meant to." Adrastos was now standing and moving toward the small opening to the shop. "I will be right back."

About to ask Michael again if he was all right, Alison held her words back as Adrastos reentered the office. He was holding the box. Setting it down on the desk, he reached for his chair, sat down, and pulled himself forward. Hands folded in front of him resting on the worn wood's surface as if ready to pray, he stared at the box. "You say that you have not been in contact with your brother for a long time, is that right?"

"Yes." He looked straight ahead as he responded, but his affirmation was not lost on Alison as she silently apologized to Michael, sensing his disappointment in her. He could speak for himself and she needed to let him. "I had no idea until now."

"It seems to me that my father's wishes will not be honored unless I take into my own hands this problem. Under the circumstances, I know that he would approve." He looked up to the ceiling and made the sign of the cross three times over his chest. "I had thought to give you this box to deliver to your brother and his wife, but that I cannot do. However, I am wondering if you could contact your brother, if I am not being too presumptuous, and convince them to come here, perhaps in your company?"

"Considering that I have not seen him or spoken with him in a very long time, it might not be as easy as you suggest." Now Alison recognized her husband. He had regained his footing and, she could tell, was thinking clearly. "It is really none of my business, is it?"

"I only thought that your relationship as brothers carries much more importance than mine. Again, I do not mean to presume anything." He started to move the box away from the center of the desk as though it had suddenly become threatening and destructive to any solution to his problem.

"No, you are right." Michael paused and after a moment asked, "May I have his address? I will make contact with him and let him know about this." He gestured toward the box, now shoved to the side. "I will do my best for you and for your father."

Everything was suddenly happening so quickly that Alison could only sit and absorb what had just transpired. Had Michael really offered to see his brother? All because of a box whose contents were still unknown? Had he taken the time to understand the risk involved in doing so? A myriad of scenarios filled her thinking, none of which had a happy ending. How could he not see what she could see so clearly? The possibility that a disappointment greater than he had ever experienced would not only destroy him but them both. She knew, somehow, that even though their marriage was strong, it would never be strong enough to withstand the destructive forces lurking within them both. Aware that she was the only one still sitting, so deep in thought, she looked up to see Michael shaking Adrastos' hand.

"I am most grateful to you, Michael." Alison noted that this was the first time that he had addressed her husband informally. "Please keep in touch as to your progress, okay? In the meantime, I will safely store this until its rightful owner crosses the line." He smiled, managing to synchronize with it a wink directed at Michael. He then turned to Alison. "It was a pleasure to meet you, Mrs. Bingham. I hope to see you again sometime?"

Alison shook his outstretched hand. "I must say that not only has it been a pleasure but also quite an experience. Thank you for your kindness and for your help. You...your family has a lovely shop."

"My best to you both, then."

Now standing together, arm in arm, on the cobblestone street in the growing darkness of the evening, neither of them said a word. Michael pulled out the map and moved them under a streetlamp. "Okay, are you ready to backtrack? One streetlight at a time, my love."

**

"You have suffered a small episode, Monsieur Bingham. Your heart, you see. You were fortunate to have suffered the attack in front of the café. So many people came to your aid and called 112 quickly. A matter of rest now, and later we can discuss further a plan for you so that this does not happen again, yes?"

The voice was intelligible, and the meaning was clear. As his eyes tried to adjust to the hospital's lighting and his ears worked overtime to hear the clinical background noises, he fought to speak, but his mouth remained shut and to swallow seemed unbearable.

"*Non, non.* Do not try to speak yet. You have medication in you that will make you sleep, so let it do so. We will speak again when you are feeling better. Tomorrow."

He felt himself drifting farther away from the light of the room, the noise of the hospital, and the sounds of voices all around him until darkness engulfed him.

Chapter 9

Now back in their room, Alison could not contain herself any longer. She knew that she would regret what she was about to say to him, but it was a matter of their survival. She had convinced herself of this as they found their way back to the hotel. "Michael, I..." He had just stepped out of the bathroom and didn't hear her.

"So, this is the plan." He stated it loudly, as if he were instructing troops into battle. She was facing him and tried to begin again.

"Michael..."

"I am going to Paris tomorrow morning to surprise this long-lost brother of mine and bring him back with me to Oia, fulfilling the wishes of a dead man, and then...well, I don't know what will happen next." He was removing his clothes, obviously ready to call it a day.

"Michael. Please. Will you just listen to me? To what I have to say?" Did that sound like a plea? She fought to keep control of her voice. "I understand that you want to do this. But could we slow down just a bit? Our life together is about to change, Michael, and I am not so sure it will be for the best. Have you thought this through, I mean, the possible implications, the consequences?" She hoped that she had said enough so that he would comprehend her fears that didn't need detailing. "Michael?" She watched him throw the decorative pillows to the floor, pull down the covers, and punch the sleeping pillow until it appeared to meet his liking. Then he climbed into the bed.

"I think that you should come to bed." He patted the mattress. "Come to bed."

"Michael, why aren't you taking me seriously? This is not a conversation about what to have for dinner. God! Do you realize what this all means?" She recognized that she was losing control and didn't care. "You have to understand what you are about to do to yourself and to us." Now the tears that she had forced back broke through, and she became angry with herself for appearing so emotional.

"Allie." He had gotten out of bed and was now holding her against him. "Allie, sweet Allie." His hand reached up to her head and he gently ran his fingers through the length of her bedraggled hair, repeating the motion to soothe her. She wanted to pull away, to stand her ground, to have him respond to her questions, to hear him assure her that everything was going to be okay. But she couldn't, and the tears came now freely as she sobbed into his bare chest.

He had lifted her off the ground and gently laid her on the bed, leaving room for him to cuddle next to her. A wave of fatigue washed over her suddenly and the temptation to shut her eyes and block it all out was strong. "Alison, don't fall asleep. Not yet." Michael was leaning on one arm, gently shaking her. "Let me get you some water." She felt him leave the bed and then return with the glass half full. "Here. Here you go." She took it from him and the first swallow seemed to revive her. "Okay. Let's talk." His voice was gentle now; all authority had disappeared from its tone as he slipped in beside her.

"I am worried, that's all. I'm worried about you, Michael."

"You have nothing to worry about. Nothing. I know that you think I haven't thought this through, but I have, and yes, I get what you're afraid of. But you have to know that nothing is going to come between us. We've both waited too long to find one another, and I would do nothing to jeopardize this relationship."

The words were satisfying to hear, but she couldn't shake the foreboding that cast a shadow on them. "What will you do, Michael, if he won't see you? Are you ready for that possibility?"

"What difference would it make at this point? It would be no different than it is now. No harm, no foul. It's not like I'm going to miss him any more than I do now."

"Then you are prepared for his rejection?" She was sitting up now, facing him.

"Hadn't thought of using that term, but I guess it fits the

situation. Yes, I am okay with that."

"And what if he welcomes you with open arms? What then?" She couldn't let up now.

"I don't think that's going to happen. I mean, it's more likely to take heavy persuasion on my part to get him to come back here. After that, I'm pretty sure I won't see him again. It's not like he's been missing me enough to seek me out."

"You seem very laissez-faire about this, Michael, and maybe that's what worries me the most. I think that I know you pretty well now. After all, revealing your past to me was painful for you, so I know what's at stake here. I want you to reconsider, for me…for us."

"You are not understanding me, Allie. Okay. I've reconsidered, and the decision is the same. This is not within my control. Do you get that? There is too much going on that I don't understand and neither do you. The coincidences can't be ignored any more than Adrastos can ignore his father's wishes. I'm not superstitious. You know that, but…well, let's put it this way. I'd like to live to see the morning sun with you."

"What on earth does that mean?"

He smiled. "I'll be the last one to make the gods angry."

"I'm off. Catching the early flight out, sweetheart. Are you awake?" She felt him nudge her gently enough to shake off the last remnants of sleep.

"You're leaving so early." It was more of a groan than a statement of fact. "What time is it?"

"Just after five. Sorry to wake you, but I'm not leaving here without a kiss or two." He leaned down and kissed her lips, over and over again. "I won't be gone long, hopefully. Just overnight. If he agrees, we'll come back either tomorrow night or the following morning. If he says no, I'll be back in time for bed tonight. And don't worry, okay? I know what I'm doing. I'll keep in touch."

She reached out for him as he rose from the bed. "Michael, I love you so much. Travel safely, sweetheart."

He turned to her, leaning into her sleepy body, and kissed her cheek. "Will do. Don't forget. I've got the gods on my side, right?"

She heard the door close quietly behind him as her heavy eyelids shut out the reality of the moment.

Chapter 10

He was informed of his pending release by the doctor after spending four days in the hospital. Just a matter of finishing the release paperwork, then he was free to go. However, he would be leaving with specific instructions for how to live the rest of his life. With daily medication, a dietary plan, and an exercise program accompanying him, Stephen felt as if he had narrowly escaped slipping into the darkness for good. He made a vow to himself, the warm sun caressing his face as he sat waiting in his wheelchair for the taxi to pull up, that he would take better care of himself. It seemed that if he wanted to live into his next decade and perhaps beyond, he had no choice. Not being a spiritual man, he did not give thanks; he just thanked his lucky stars. Simply not his time to go.

The taxi delivered him to the front walk of his home. The driver, noting his fare's situation, offered to walk with him to the front door, just in case. He thought that he might be of help to Stephen, who had been on his back for four days straight, as Stephen had revealed to him; an extra pair of legs would help balance him. Stephen refused the help, politely and with gratitude; he wanted to do it himself. After all, he would have no one in the house to help and the sooner he regained his old self, the better. The driver reluctantly acquiesced but remained by his car after opening the passenger door for Stephen. He would not leave until Stephen had entered the house, he insisted. With a slow and what looked to the driver a half-masted wave, Stephen indicated his thanks once again, then turned and unlocked the door. He heard the taxi drive away only after closing the door behind him.

Now inside, he noted how musty the place smelled. For an instant, he was overcome by the stillness of the house, the subdued lighting that filled the front room, the loneliness. An adjustment, he knew, from the 24/7 artificial lighting, the cacophony of unfamiliar noises and voices, the unannounced awakenings by nurses and doctors, the ongoing human contact of which he'd had no control.

As he moved into the room, he remembered the plastic bag that he had stuffed into his overcoat pocket and reached for it. Placing it on the kitchen table, he tried to recall the instructions given to him by the discharge nurse. There had been so many. He relaxed as he recalled her telling him that everything he needed to know was written out for him and placed in the bag along with the medications he would need to take starting today. He remembered that he had been given something, a small white pill, as one of the last requirements before leaving the place. But now, free of the eyes and ears, the probing and poking, he decided that he would not bother with the bag's contents until he'd had some decent food, a good cup of tea, and a bath. He needed to feel as though he was really in his own home, with his own established structure and comforts.

As he made his way to the bedroom to change from his shoes to the welcome softness of his slippers, he noted that he was moving slowly—not cautiously, just slowly, as if moving through thick mud. With each exertion of his legs, one after another, the fatigue that he felt alarmed him. Perhaps, he thought, the nurse was right in telling him that he would need to take it easy, not to expect that he would be at 100 percent right away. At that moment, he was thankful for the recollection of her words as they subdued his alarm. Yes, all right. He could accept that, but a good meal and a relaxing bath would move him closer to normalcy.

He found himself staying within the confines of his home for the next three days. He had no need to go anywhere, and, if he was being honest with himself, no desire. His strength was beginning to return as he found small, less taxing chores to do to keep himself occupied. If anything fatigued him, it was trying to follow the new regimen that had been dictated to him by the hospital staff. The exercise included gentle walks at first, to be followed by more sustained exercise. They had strongly recommended that twice a week he attend the Healthy Ways exercise classes that were offered at the outreach clinic in

Tigueax. Instead, walking from room to room, again and again, he checked off the list "gentle walks." The food requirement, however, demanded that he change some of his habits. Although not an overeater by any stretch of the imagination, the foods he did eat proved to be one of his two enemies, the second being his lack of and aversion to exercise. The kitchen cupboards and refrigerator were a nightmare, he realized, when it came to so-called healthy foods. He had called the local grocer and asked for a delivery of some of the foods listed. Enough, he planned, to get him through the next few weeks until he could make his way to the shop on his own. Never once did he consider how good it would be to have neighbors stepping in to help.

Two weeks had passed since the episode, as it was identified officially, and he was beginning to feel cabin fever setting in. Now, on the thirteenth day of waking to the prospect of very little, he decided that he would try to walk into the village and do some light shopping. What he could not carry back, he would have delivered. The thought of opening the front door and closing it behind him lifted his spirits. Yes, it was what he needed, what the doctor had ordered. He spent the early-morning hours, until just before ten, making a list of food and supply needs. He might, if he wasn't too tired, even look in on the bookshop. He was in desperate need of new reading material, having consumed all that was available to him on his own bookshelves. He noted, at one point, a lightness in his being, just for a moment, as if he were a young boy excited about life.

Remembering to take his pills, bring his canvas bags, and stuff the list into his shirt pocket, he opened the door to the brilliance of the morning awaiting his arrival. Closing the door behind him while reaching for his key to lock it, he noticed them. He hadn't paid any attention to anything other than the confines of his home for the last two weeks. Having difficulty comprehending what was in front of him now, he descended the front step and backed away from the sight so that he was now off the front walk and standing rather gingerly in his neglected dried weeds and dirt. There, in the long- abandoned garden plot, now nestled within new lush green plantings that clung to their sides, winding their tender tendrils around and over the tiny crevices to reach for neighboring rocks of different consistencies, shapes, and sizes, lay two volcanic rocks. The three-by-four area had been expanded to take in another foot, which reached into the front yard away from the house. As he began to understand what was in front of him, he recognized the whole area to be a rock garden. Its presence confronted him as if the devil himself stood before him. He forced himself to shut down the image of another rock garden, somewhere very far back in his past.

Shaking with a growing rage and fear, he turned back to the house. Upon entering, he threw the canvas bags to the floor. Grabbing the phone, he called the nursery. He was aware of the heavy and rapid beating of his heart and tried to take some deep breaths as he listened to the ringing, while no one picked up on the other end. Just as he was about to end the call and try again, he heard a male voice greet him.

"Jean-Pierre? Is that you?" The effort he was making to stay in control was painful as his whole body seemed on fire.

"*Oui, c'est moi.*"

"This is Mr. Bingham. I am calling because…" He was cut off by the young man's excited voice.

"Oh, *oui*. How are you? I hope that you well now. Do you like my gift?"

Stephen was taken by surprise. His gift? The innocence of this child's efforts suddenly dawned on him, and he felt his body's initial rage slowly subside as he sat down in order to fully comprehend the boy's meaning. "I do not understand. What do you mean by 'gift'?"

"I watching your garden for long time now. I feel sorry that it died. Mama told to me you went to hospital for your heart. I wanted you come home to beauty again. It is gift to you from me."

Jean-Pierre had no idea. An innocent gesture on this young boy's part. That was all it was. But the rocks. He did not understand the rocks, their placement, their proximity to the house; no, their proximity to his secrets, to everything that he had never revealed to anyone. And yet, they were with him once again, this time well imbedded within something as nonthreatening and, indeed, quite beautiful as a rock garden. He could not respond to Jean-Pierre. So immersed in thought and confusion, he let the phone drop from his hand, and it landed on the wooden floor, bouncing across the hard surface until it lay still somewhere in the small room.

A matter of minutes had passed, it seemed to Stephen, since he had abruptly ended the call to Jean-Pierre. The knocking on the door startled him. Not the inquisitive knock of someone politely interrupting the occupant but the invasive, aggressive banging of someone on the other side insisting on entering his home. He stood abruptly, catching the edge of the table with both hands for balance as his head's interior seemed to slip and slide back and forth like a child's swing slowly coming to a stop. He heard his name repeatedly called out through the door, alternating and sometimes simultaneously with the loud banging.

"Coming! Coming," he managed to call out.

Standing now in front of him was Jean-Pierre, breathing heavily and very red in the face. Stephen thought that he saw tears on the boy's cheeks but couldn't be sure.

"Oh, *monsieur.* You are okay, *non?* You okay?" He did not move forward toward Stephen but respectfully kept his distance.

"Of course I am okay. What is the matter? I am fine." As he spoke these words, he knew that he was lying to this child and to himself, for that matter.

"I only worry. You stop talking to me on the phone. I hear a banging noise. I thought maybe your heart kill you. *Mon Dieu! Merci!* You okay." His grin covered his face.

For a moment, Stephen felt a warmth for this child, something akin to a connection with him, but he refused to let the moment develop into anything at all. In fact, he was beginning to feel just the opposite, and he let this feeling take control of him.

"When did you do this?" He extended his arm past the

boy's shoulder and pointed to the garden. "When? And who gave you permission? I certainly did not." He now stared at the boy, seeing past him to avoid having to make real eye contact.

"I do when you in hospital. I tell you that on the phone. I want to make gift to you." Stephen could see that the boy was visibly shaken by the adult standing in front of him, accusatory and ungrateful. He did not care. He, too, had been—no, still was—shaken, by the child's gesture.

And then it occurred to him. The rocks. He wanted to know about the rocks. "Where did you find the rocks? These rocks." He took a few steps past the boy now as his hand indicated which rocks he was referring to among the many that had been placed so carefully.

"From the pasture, *monsieur,* down the road." He turned and pointed in the direction that Stephen knew well. "They are different, *non*? I like them with the plants." Now the boy had moved closer to Stephen as he admired his work. "The plants, the new growth, I like against the darkness of the rocks. Mama tell me like dark against light, good against evil, or maybe like life against death. It hard for me to tell you the right way, like Mama tell me."

Stephen had stopped listening. As much as he wanted to look away, to turn his back on the boy, and to go inside, shutting the door on what he would never be able to shut from view, he eyes continued to rest on the blackened ancient rocks that, he suddenly realized, were meant to be a part of his life. His laughter took him by surprise, beginning as a giggle but quickly building to a volume that frightened the boy who, still unsure of this man's intent, covered his ears with his hands and turned, breaking into a run before he had cleared the property.

Chapter 11

Landing shortly before mid-morning, Michael was grateful for the easy flight into Charles de Gaulle. He only hoped that the rest of the trip would go as smoothly. He remembered Alison's sleepy face as he had told her goodbye just a few hours ago and wondered what she would be doing at this moment. He would remember to call her once out of the airport and on his way to Tigeaux. He smiled as he said a silent thank you for her presence in his life. A life, he knew, that could be altered within the next few hours. He set his mind on a positive track, though, so that any disappointments, imagined or real, would not burden him.

Having no checked baggage, he moved quickly to the transportation hub and hailed a taxi. He had not figured out the mileage from Paris to the village of Tigeaux but was willing to pay the fare. He had not bothered to look into the trains, something that he should have done before leaving Oia. A vague memory of traveling through Greece on trains tried to make its way forward in his memory but faded as quickly as it appeared.

The taxi driver's eyes lit up when Michael told him his destination. All he said to Michael without turning his head from the roadway in front of him was that it was not far. He had not given Michael the opportunity to respond as he stepped on the accelerator and moved swiftly away from the crunch of airport traffic.

"How long, *monsieur*?" He might need to rethink this. He leaned forward in his seat as he spoke through the Plexiglas partition.

"No more than an hour, *monsieur*, about fifty kilometers." The driver hoped that the conversation would not continue, that this passenger who would pay him almost a whole day's wages in one fare and possibly a bit more would not change his mind. A rich American, he thought, as he tried to hide his excitement at the prospect of extra euros in his pocket.

Michael sat back in the seat. Was it worth it? Yes, he would not stop the driver. Perhaps he might engage him in more conversation once out of the city's traffic and learn something about this country. It might be quite interesting, he told himself.

Once on the toll road, Michael addressed the driver, who was listening to a French talk show. "*Excusez-moi, monsieur?*" Michael had pushed the Plexiglas barrier to one side.

"*Oui?*" The driver kept his eyes straight ahead as he maneuvered through the morning traffic while adjusting the volume.

"I wonder if you know this village, Tigeaux? If you know anything about it?"

"*Oui, mais…*I mean in English. Sorry. Yes, but if you are looking for an exciting and, how do you Americans say? A 'happening' place? Well, *non, non,* Tigeaux *n'est pas pour vous.*"

"Actually, I am meeting someone who lives there. I just thought it might be nice to know something about it before I arrived. I did give you the address, didn't I?" Michael suddenly panicked as the reality of his mission sank in. He searched his pocket, not waiting for the driver's reply.

"*Oui,* monsieur. I have it written down right here." He was pointing to a small notepad that lay on the dashboard.

"Ah, yes, of course. Sorry. My mind was elsewhere."

He saw the driver look up from the road in front of him as he caught his image in the rearview mirror.

"Do not worry. I know what travel is like. At least, *monsieur,* you have an address. So many times I drive people, tourists, out to towns and villages just because the concierge at their fancy hotel tells them that they must see it. They have the name of the place but no more. I drop them off, collect my fare, say *au revoir,* and wish them well."

"I will ask you to stay until I am sure that the person I am going to meet is there. It will not take long, and I certainly will pay you for your time."

"But of course, *monsieur.* Not a problem."

"So, I was wondering. What do you know about this village?" He sat back now, feeling a bit more relaxed.

"It is a small village, *monsieur*. A little water runs through it, the Morin River, and once the mills helped in producing wheat and lumber for the bigger city, Paris. Now it is sleepy, with tourists visiting it often. It is very old, I think."

The road made a sharp turn to the left, and he stopped talking to make his way across the oncoming traffic. Then he settled back in his seat, adjusting his body as if to create a different and more comfortable cavity in the worn seat cushion. He drove on in silence for some minutes until Michael's curiosity demanded attention.

"So, you said it is very old? Do you know how old?"

"No, I am not sure, *monsieur*. But I remember my papa telling me about Tigeaux when I was a child. He frightened me." The driver paused and then laughed. "I was such a little boy then that I did not know not to be afraid. It is a legend, I think you say?"

Michael was drawn in now. "Yes, a legend. Go on, please."

"*Oui, oui.* Long ago there was a saint known as St. Leu. In our language, *Français,* our older language, the word *loup* means 'wolf.' His name came from this word. And there is a reason for this, you see." He again looked away from the road and into the rearview mirror, catching Michael's attentive face in his sight. "He traveled the countryside, always preaching to all he came across about charity and morality. It is said that he could cure convulsions and fear. In this village and some of the surrounding villages, the people, from the time that they could understand their parents' words, learned to be very afraid of wolves. Their fear never left them but grew with them as they became adults. It was like this until the end of the nineteenth century. By then, the children who became educated at university changed the thinking." He paused for a moment. "But there are many who are still fearful. But to St. Leu. He was fifty years old when he died. If I remember correctly, he died in the early sixth century. During one of his visits to Tigeaux, in his later years, he blessed a well in the town whose waters now have the power to cure maladies of the eyes and to cure fear. I have not seen the well, but I think that I will visit it someday soon. My eyes are not as good as they used to be. Perhaps, on this visit, while I wait…"

Michael had stopped listening to the driver. Not because he had lost interest but because he was internally doing battle with a barrage of images that he could not identify one by one. They were collage-like in their appearance and each one did not last longer than a second. But they were pounding at his consciousness, relentless and determined.

Then his vision saw clearly the startled and disbelieving eyes of his father staring up at him from the forest floor, growing large and then receding into tiny openings only to lunge at him once again, larger than before. His own eyes had remained open but unaware of his surroundings. He now shut them tightly, leaning his head down toward his chest while bringing his right hand up to cover them both. The darkness that he had created did nothing to quell what would not leave him alone. In front of him now, he saw the well's stones that pillowed his mother's head as she lay dying in front of him. The stones that once had served a good purpose but that had fallen away from neglect and age, innocently strewn by gravity to catch his mother's fatal fall.

"*Monsieur, monsieur!* Are you not well? Shall I stop?" The driver's voice cleared the images from Michael's mind as quickly as they had arrived. He lifted his head and opened his eyes, taking a moment to let their pupils dilate as the late-morning sun shone directly into the side window.

"*Monsieur?* Do you need to get out?"

Michael wiped the film of sweat from his upper lip and forehead. "No, no. Thank you. I am fine now. Must have been something I ate on the plane." He hoped that this would be sufficient to satisfy the driver's concern. "Really, we must almost be there, right? I am fine. Please, keep going." He felt suddenly tired and a short nap was unavoidable. He leaned his head against the back of the seat and gently closed his eyes.

The driver had averted his eyes from the road numerous times during the last few minutes and, upon seeing Michael through the rearview mirror comfortably asleep, he checked the time and sighed deeply and thankfully that the only thing wrong with his passenger was travel fatigue and maybe a bit of French cooking that did not agree with him. The quiet little village was no more than twenty kilometers away and would be a welcoming place for his passenger to rest and revive, thought the driver, smiling as he felt the imagined weight of the extra euros in his wallet.

Chapter 12

Three weeks had passed since the incident with Jean-Pierre. Stephen had not spoken to him since then but was daily reminded of the boy's good intentions. Each time he left the house, trying to follow the doctor's orders to take in more exercise, he made no attempt to ignore the invasive rock garden that continued to grow voraciously, consuming the exposed sides of rounded stones with new light green tendrils reaching for a holding place on the smooth surfaces. In fact, he had taken the time to water the area and was somewhat taken aback at the success of his limited efforts. The darker, larger two rocks still looked out of place, he thought, but even those were beginning to blend into their surroundings. Hadn't it been Jean-Pierre's vision that there should be such variation in the rock garden? He would need to say something to the boy if he ever saw him again. He knew that his behavior during their last encounter had frightened the boy off.

On this particular morning, as he slowly headed down the front walk to the road, he took a moment and turned toward his house. Yes, he would indeed say something to Jean-Pierre. What he had done had made such a difference to the home. He needed to apologize.

He did not intend to go directly to the nursery. He had intended to bypass it in the hope that Jean-Pierre might be out working elsewhere, and Stephen would casually run into him. But finding himself standing at the door to the shop, he had no choice. Especially as he heard the boy's voice calling out to him from behind the closed door.

"*Bonjour,* Monsieur Bingham." The boy held the door wide open to Stephen and stood to the side to give him room to enter. "How are you?"

Passing the boy as he entered the shop, Stephen turned to him. "I am very well, Jean-Pierre. Very well. Thank you."

"That is good to know, *monsieur*. We are glad that you so good." He turned to indicate his mother's presence as she came forward.

"Oh, Monsieur Bingham. I am ashamed that I have not come to visit with you since your return from hospital. Please forgive me."

Stephen was startled. Forgive her? "Madame, it is I who should apologize. To Jean-Pierre. For my behavior, you remember?" He looked down at the boy, who nodded his head. "I behaved badly. And I apologize."

His mother came to him and put her arm around her son's shoulders. "I do not understand. You said nothing to me about this, Jean-Pierre?"

"It was nothing, Mama. It is fine now. *Merci, monsieur*. I understand." He reached for Stephen's hand to shake on it. Stephen reciprocated, feeling at once relief as well as uneasiness with the mother's concern.

"Madame, I misunderstood Jean-Pierre's good intentions. I may have been upset with him, you see. I had just come home from the hospital and was not well. You have a good boy here." He nodded in Jean-Pierre's direction. "He did nothing wrong. Nothing at all. As a matter of fact, I have been thinking about a short trip to Paris again, just for a weekend. It has just now occurred to me that perhaps, Jean-Pierre, if you would like to earn some extra money, you could work on the other side of the front walk while I am gone?" He had been thinking about getting away now that he was feeling better and could walk for longer periods of time without terrible fatigue setting in. *Apparently*, he thought to himself, *I have made the decision.* "What do you think? Of course, if it is not a good time for you, the weekend I mean, anytime would be fine." He waited for the boy's response.

Jean-Pierre looked at his mother for guidance. "I would agree to my son doing more work for you, Monsieur Bingham, of course." She looked at her son, whose eyes had not left hers. "However, it is my son's decision, not mine."

Stephen could sense the strong connection these two

shared as mother and son. He had never thought to ask if there was a father, a husband. It appeared to him that that was not the case, but he knew that one could never assume something like that.

Jean-Pierre turned from his mother and faced Stephen. "Okay. I can do it for you. This weekend?"

"No, no. This weekend is too soon. It is already Thursday. I haven't made any plans. But will you come next weekend?" He wanted some time to think about how he would spend his two days in the city. Perhaps find something different to do. Yes, he would have to think about it. The only sure thing he knew was where he would stay: the same hotel that he had always stayed in. He would need to remember to ask for a room with a river view. The tenth floor. The same room, if he could remember the number.

"*Bien sur, monsieur.* I will start next weekend for you. *Merci beaucoup, merci.*" As he had done earlier, he reached out his hand to Stephen.

"Wonderful, wonderful." Stephen shook the boy's hand, tipped his head toward his mother, and turned to leave. About to take a first step, he appeared frozen in place, then turned on his heel, facing the two. "By the way, only one thing to remember, Jean-Pierre. No more rock gardens, okay? Anything you like but no rocks, *s'il vous plaît?*" He smiled warmly at the boy, remembering how frightened Jean-Pierre had been by his reaction weeks ago. The boy, understanding now Stephen's gesture, smiled in return.

"*Je comprends, monsieur.* No rocks."

As he slowly walked along the side of the road on his way back home, this time carrying a lighter load of only one bag filled with fresh vegetables while the other dangled empty in his left hand, Stephen reflected on the last hour or so. He had found himself on the doorstep of the boy's home, unintended, had apologized for his bad behavior, had verbally contracted for more work to be done on the front of the yard, the yard that he had not really cared about, and had committed himself by doing so to a weekend in Paris. He had not really been thinking about a trip when he said that to Jean-Pierre, but he'd spoken it aloud so that two other people now knew of his plans. He supposed that that was not a bad thing, but he wondered when he had become more receptive to others. Had he felt badly for the boy? Enough to encourage him with more work? Had he spoken carelessly just because he'd had a weak moment in his presence and that of his mother? He'd read about people who had suffered near-death health situations and who, upon full recovery, had vowed to change their ways as what was left of their life awaited them. He hadn't made any vows that he could remember. In fact, his episode hadn't been a life-or-death one. It was a minor episode but enough, he had admitted to himself, to wake him up to the fact that he was not as healthy as he had assumed all these years. A weekend in Paris. The idea of it began to feel good to Stephen as he looked up from the road to find himself only a few steps from the front walk and not out of breath.

"This is the name of the hotel and the phone number, if you need to reach me. I am leaving this morning and will be back late Sunday night or maybe early on Monday morning. Is there anything that you need from me?" He watched as the boy held the paper in front of him while focusing intently on the information that Stephen had just given him.

"*Non, monsieur.* Today is Friday, and maybe I can start this afternoon?" He folded the paper and placed it in his pants pocket.

"That is fine with me, Jean-Pierre. I have been thinking, however, that I do not want you to do more than you did already. I mean, you do not understand, I am sure, not at your age, but my income only goes so far, and I must be careful how I spend it. Do you think that your plans could cost no more than what you have already done for me?" He heard himself and would be surprised if his confused request would make sense.

About to clarify his meaning, the boy replied, "Certainly.

I have plan for you—beautiful colors but not much money. I understand."

"Good. That is good. Well then, I will see you in a few days, and remember to call me if you have any questions. Okay?"

"*Oui*, okay. I will call you."

Stephen stood in his doorway, waving to Jean-Pierre, as the young boy broke into a gentle run and was soon out of sight. Closing the door behind him, he checked the time. He had less than an hour before the taxi would arrive to take him to the station. He had packed the night before and had little to do until then. Puttering around the house, he straightened anything out that was amiss, wiped the kitchen counters yet one more time, made sure that all the windows were locked and that he had turned off the lights, and checked that he had his keys, his money, his pills, his extra set of glasses, and the thrice-read book that he still enjoyed (he had forgotten to buy a new book the week before.) He was tempted to make one last cup of tea but thought better of it, knowing that his bladder would find an inconvenient time to remind him of its contents and its urgency to be emptied.

"*Bon jour, monsieur.*" The taxi driver held the passenger door for Stephen. He reached for his one small bag and waited for Stephen to enter the car.

"*Bon jour, monsieur. Merci.*" Stephen sat back in the seat, fastened the seatbelt, and felt through the vibration from the thump of the trunk's lid as the driver slammed it shut.

"To the station, *non?*" The driver spoke facing forward while turning the ignition switch.

"Yes, please. I have an eleven o'clock departure to Paris."

"*Oui, oui.*"

Stephen took one more look at the front of the house as the taxi pulled away. He had no idea what Jean-Pierre would create next, but it did not matter. He trusted the boy, he realized, and did not question himself as to why.

Chapter 13

Alison had not heard from Michael. She was surprised that he had not called or at least texted her from the airport once he'd landed safely. Disappointment consumed her thinking and she found herself in a sour mood. She would need to rid herself of it, though, as she had said yes to Artemidoros's dinner invitation in the hotel's dining room this evening. He had taken her under his wing, it seemed, as he had made a point to check in with her throughout the day. Was she all right? Did she need anything? Could he accompany her anywhere? With her husband gone, he wanted to be sure that she was okay, he'd said. She couldn't help but feel grateful that she wasn't left alone in such a foreign place. So when he asked her to join him for dinner in his own hotel, she could not refuse. In fact, she was looking forward to it.

She had planned to get an early start to the day and explore the area. However, Michael's early departure had awakened her and even though she knew that her body was not ready to get up, her mind would not let her relax and fall back to sleep immediately. She lay in the empty bed, trying to imagine where he was as each minute passed. She imagined him checking in, then sitting at the gate, anxious to board. Then she worried that she should have gone with him if for no other reason than for moral support. Having had this internal conversation with herself already, she knew what the right decision was and she had made it. Still, it nagged at her that she was not there with him.

After getting up to use the bathroom, she forced herself to return to the bed when she saw that it was only 6 a.m. She recognized the jet lag that still lingered, and she hoped that a little more sleep would bring her back to normal. Rolling over onto her side, she shut her eyes, waiting for the darkness and fatigue to work together so that she could slip away.

Something had awakened her. Experiencing an instant of confusion as to where she was, she lay on her back replaying her last waking hours. Quickly regaining her sense of place and time, she sat up and retrieved her phone from the bedside table. Nine fifty! "How could it be almost ten o'clock?" She voiced the question aloud, alarmed at the passage of time and then upset with herself that she had already missed half of the morning. There were no messages or voicemails from Michael. She had thought that he would send a quick "safely boarded" or "on my way" or "I love you" text, but nothing. She knew that his mind was focused on Stephen and she understood, perhaps, that "out of sight, out of mind" might apply here. She also knew that there was no ill intent on his part to neglect her. If anyone should understand the workings of the mind, it should be her, she reminded herself.

Too late for breakfast and not really all that hungry, she stopped by the small café within the hotel building and ordered a cup of tea and a pastry. It would be enough to tide her over until a mid-afternoon meal. She was excited about getting out on her own and seeing the village of Oia firsthand.

"Ah, good morning, Mrs. Bingham. I hope that this beautiful morning finds you well." Artemidoros had seen her from across the hallway. "You are eating lightly, I see." He pointed to her pastry, untouched, as she had just sat down.

"Oh, yes, good morning, Mr. Metaxas. I am a bit embarrassed, having slept in longer than I had intended. Saving some appetite for dinner."

"The jet lag." His laugh was meant for the two of them but to her, it seemed to fill the small room.

"I wasn't prepared, I guess. Michael got up quite early this morning to catch his flight to Paris and I fell back asleep after he left. So, I sit here with my tea and pastry ready to explore this lovely place." She was beginning to feel herself again as a sense of calm came over her. She sat back, relaxed and content.

"I would be happy to accompany you for the rest of the morning, if I am not being too forward. The needs of this place demand that I not leave for long, but for an hour or two I can show you much of the village. We are not that large, after all.

May I?" He gestured toward the chair on the other side of the small table.

"Yes, of course. Please." Struggling with the idea of this stranger sharing her adventure, she tried to come up with a reason as to why she wanted to be alone. Nothing sounded convincing to her other than the easiest approach—the truth. After taking a sip of the tea, she took a breath. "I appreciate your kind offer, Mr. Metaxas…"

"Please, if you don't mind, call me Artemidoros."

"Of course. As I was saying, I do appreciate you offering to show me around. It is very kind of you. However, I was looking forward to exploring on my own. Something that I would like very much to do. I would welcome, though, any suggestions that you might have as to what to see and do. Or should I speak directly to the concierge, then? I do not want to inconvenience you."

"I do not mind and understand your desire to be on your own. We are a good village. No worries about your safety here. You will find everyone most helpful. I have some places that I would recommend to you. Here, let me write down the names and you can ask the concierge for more information." He pulled out one of his business cards from his shirt pocket and dug for a pen in his pants pocket. "There, there you are," he said when he had finished writing and handed her the card. "You must take some time to admire our natural environment. I mean the caldera, the volcano that long ago created this island. From its natural violence so long ago, a place of beauty has appeared." He looked out the window and fell silent.

"This is great. Thank you, Mr. Met…sorry, Artemidoros. I will be sure to take time to do so. And thank you again for offering to accompany me. I know that Michael will appreciate your kindness." She pushed her chair away from the table, while balancing her cup of tea and pastry dish in the other hand.

"Is he in Paris now?" He had turned back from the window as she spoke her husband's name. "I would expect that that is the case, yes?"

Looking at her watch, surprised again that time had gone

by so quickly, she looked back at him as he rose from the table. "It's eleven thirty. He was due to arrive half an hour ago." Not wanting to be rude, she held off checking her phone in front of him for any messages.

"I am sure that he has had a good flight. He will be back soon?"

"If all goes well with meeting his brother, he is supposed to be back no later than Monday. However, it could be as soon as tonight. He did not check in advance as to whether or not his brother would be there. He liked the idea of surprising him, I think." She did not want to reveal too much about this dysfunctional relationship between siblings to a stranger, the little that she knew of it herself. A little fib would steer him in a different direction, she thought. "So, we will see. I may have an extra day of sightseeing in store."

"Yes, that would be good. You are getting a bit of a late start as it is, but our evenings are long and our sunsets worth waiting for. I wonder. May I invite you to eat with me tonight? Here, in the hotel?"

His smile was so kind, she thought. "I would like that, yes. What time would you like me to meet you?"

"I will have my finest table waiting for your arrival. Let's say seven?"

"Yes, seven is fine. Thank you, Artemidoros. The company will be lovely. However, if Michael comes back tonight, I may have to cancel at the last minute."

"If that is the case, then the two of you can join me for dinner. It is not a problem. So, we will see one another, then, tonight, with or without your husband." He nodded to her and pointed toward the concierge's desk. "Right over there. Have a good day, Mrs. Bingham."

She watched him disappear into the hallway and around a corner. Still standing with her tea and pastry, she sat back down and hurriedly consumed her meal.

Chapter 14

Still deep in a heavy sleep, Michael did not feel the car come to a stop. Nor did he hear the driver repeating *"Monsieur?"*. It was only when the driver's door slammed shut that he woke up suddenly, as if hit in the chest by an unknown force. The cool air embraced him as the driver held open the passenger door. *"Monsieur*, we are here. *Monsieur?"*

Michael, coming to, looked out the open door while the driver opened the trunk and removed his bag. The familiar thump through the seat as he closed the trunk motivated Michael to get out of the cab. He stood by the open door for a moment, trying to gather his dulled senses and memory.

"This is the address, *monsieur*. Do you still want me to wait?" The driver was motioning Michael away from the cab so that he could close the passenger door. "You slept for the last twenty kilometers. A shame. The countryside is so beautiful. But the body had other plans, no?" He was not trying to hurry Michael but if this passenger did not need his services, he needed to be back in circulation. There was still more of the day in which to earn his much-coveted euros. "So, I wait for you here?"

Michael had turned away from the car and started to take in his surroundings. A country road lay ahead and behind him, bordered on both sides by pastures of tall grasses and wildflowers. He noted that there were no fences, no walls, nothing preventing one from leaving the road and wandering into the sea of gentle green and pastel waves, urged on by the unhampered breezes. The beauty of the area was soothing to him and he suddenly felt at ease. "Yes, please wait. Is this the house?"

As he took his small bag from the driver, he indicated the house that stood by itself among the pastures. As he asked the question, he felt idiotic and was about to say something to the driver to cover his remark when the driver opened his door and politely responded, "It is the address that you gave me, *monsieur*." Michael secretly thanked him for his diplomacy.

"Of course. Thank you. I will just see if my friend is at home."

The driver nodded his head, got in the car, rolled down his window, and checked his fare meter to make sure that the minutes were passing while the fare continued to grow.

As Michael started up the walk to the house, the nerves that he had kept in control only moments ago were now playing games with him. He began to doubt himself. The thought that trying to connect with his brother was a bad idea pushed its way past the doubting stage and was gaining momentum in becoming a fact. Yet his feet moved forward, one in front of the other, with no hesitation, no leaden weight holding him back. As he came closer to the front steps, he first noticed the freshly overturned earth on the left side of the house suggesting a gardening project was underway. The smell of the newly exposed earth filled the air and, for a brief moment, another earthen aroma tried to make its way forward but disappeared as suddenly as it had appeared. To his right, a beautiful garden clung to an assortment of rocks carefully placed as part of the design. He was taken by the artistry of the rock garden and by his little brother's obvious green thumb's talent or, perhaps, that of his wife. He smiled. A small detail, but enough to comfort him. He knew something about the adult Stephen before he knocked on his door.

Standing on the top step, he felt the rough wood under his knuckles as he knocked, at first gently, then with more effort. He stood back and waited. A myriad of feelings collided with each other as Michael anticipated the sight of his brother after so many years. Would he even recognize him? Would Stephen recognize his big brother? The anger and dismissiveness that Stephen had revealed to Michael when he had tried to contact Stephen years ago was fresh in Michael's mind now. He suddenly felt caught between a rock and a hard place. Behind him was an escape, to be sure, as the cab sat waiting for him. In front of him, on the other side of the door, was a future that he had not foreseen before coming to Greece. But now, here he was, ready to jeopardize all that he had ever wanted in his life: a future that was known, still intact, full of promise, love, and companionship.

No matter what was about to happen when the door in front of him opened, it would impact Alison and him in ways that he did not know, could not know, but he knew somewhere deep in his heart that nothing would be the same again. As he forced himself to knock once more, he could only hope that his reality and that of his brother would not clash but find some traces of a time so long ago, when their imaginations had protected them, had buoyed them from the darkest places of their youth as they piloted their hopes and dreams through the scented undergrowth while flying in and around the massive protection of the giants in their own forest.

"*Excusez-moi, monsieur?*" Jean-Pierre's voice startled Michael as he turned to see a young boy standing behind him, dirty with the remnants of freshly turned earth clinging to his pants and the sleeves of his shirt. In each hand, he was holding two large, leafy plants whose root beds, just having been released from pots, still held their imprisoned shape. The boy moved to the left of the steps and gently placed the plants on the soil, moving them slowly back and forth until he found a balanced place for them.

Michael waited for the boy to face him again. Jean-Pierre wiped his hands free of the loose soil and, for good measure, wiped each one on the sides of his pant legs before extending his hand in greeting. "I am Jean-Pierre Lenot. I am working for Monsieur Bingham making his gardens." He pointed to the rock garden and then to the waiting plants that he had just placed. "You are looking for Monsieur Bingham?"

"Yes, *oui*. I am. Is he here?" Michael was struck by the fact that he was suddenly talking about his brother as if he had never lost connection with him, as if he were just stopping by to borrow a tool from his brother's garage or confirming a time to get together for a family barbeque. It seemed so casual, so real.

"Oh *non, monsieur*. He has left for the weekend. That is why I am doing the work now. It is a good time for me to finish my job." Again, he indicated both sides of the walkway as he spoke.

Feeling a mixture of disappointment and relief, Michael

knew that he could not go back to Greece now that he was so close to making contact. "I understand. Do you know where he went?"

"*Oui, monsieur.* To Paris, to..." Jean-Pierre stopped. He was not sure that he should tell this stranger where Monsieur Bingham had gone. He had not told Jean-Pierre to keep it to himself, but he also knew that Monsieur Bingham liked his privacy, and that lingered in his decision-making. He wished that his mother was here to take over. She would know the right thing to do.

"To Paris? Do you know where in Paris?" Michael hoped that the exasperation he felt was not coming through.

"Oh, *monsieur.* I am not sure to tell you. I am not sure that Monsieur Bingham wants me to tell."

Michael could see that the boy was uncomfortable. "I understand, and you are very good not to tell a stranger. But, you see, I am not a stranger to Monsieur Bingham." He thought twice about telling this boy that Stephen was his brother, for he assumed that Stephen had never revealed that he had a brother to anyone. "I am a very dear friend of Monsieur Bingham's and I have traveled from the United States via Greece to see him again. He does not know that I am coming, as I wanted to surprise him. Now, I realize that I should have let him know."

"Oh, a friend from America!" The boy's eye lit up and his demeanor changed instantly, his voice a register higher. "I want to go to America when I am older. To New York City and to Hollywood. Have you been there?"

A child's anticipation, excitement, innocence. A flicker of memory momentarily connected him to this boy. "Yes, I have, and maybe one day you will as well. So, I wonder if you could tell me where in Paris I might find my good friend. I do not want to leave without saying hello to him but must fly back home on Monday or I would wait for his return. Do you have an address?" Michael, convinced that the boy was now on his side, waited patiently. He knew that the cab driver would be happy to hear that a return fare to Paris was his.

"*Oui.* I have his address. He left it with me." Reaching

into his pants pocket, he pulled out a folded, wrinkled paper and handed it to Michael. "I need that, *monsieur*. You cannot keep it." The boy had become serious and concerned as he handed the paper to the stranger.

"No, of course not. Let me just copy this address down." He did so and handed the boy's precious paper back to him. "You have been a great help and I thank you."

"It is good that you will see Mr. Bingham. He is alone here in this house. My mother and I try to help him when we can and she worries about him being here alone. He only comes to the village when he needs groceries. But now I am here planting his garden for him. I see him many times now."

Alone? Had Michael understood the boy correctly? "Do you mean that there is no Mrs. Bingham?"

"I do not know this, *monsieur*. But he is the only one who lives here."

Michael thought better of pursuing this any farther. Aware that the cab driver was waiting, he quickly changed the subject, although this turn of events left an unsettled feeling in him.

"You are doing a very good job. Well, I need to go. It's a long drive back to Paris. Thank you for your help, Jean-Pierre, is it?"

"*Oui*, Jean-Pierre Lenot, *monsieur*. May I ask your name?"

Michael hesitated. "Yes, of course. I am Michael...Stone," he responded as his eyes moved from the rock garden back to the boy. "It has been good to meet you."

He turned toward the cab, then stopped and turned around to wave goodbye to the boy, who was now kneeling beside the two plants. Michael watched him pick one up and with a gardening tool, gently prod loose the encumbered roots, one by one, from their earthen prison. He did not look up from his work to notice that the stranger had not moved, but lingered, almost as if cemented in place. His glance had moved from the boy and was held captive by two black stones that rose above all the others.

Chapter 15

She was exhausted as she entered the lobby of the hotel. If there was some way that she could politely excuse herself from dinner tonight with Artemidoros, she would. Without Michael's presence as a valid reason, she had committed herself and would need to see it through. Perhaps, after a long bath and quick nap, she would have a brighter outlook on the prospect of dinner with a stranger. Making her way through the lobby to the elevator, she heard Artemidoros's voice somewhere in the distance and moved herself along so as not to run into him. She was in no mood to chitchat, not until she had recovered from the day. Besides, she realized that her mood had been growing sour again, as she had not heard from Michael at all. Not angry with him but disappointed, she had weakened and texted him sometime in the afternoon but still had no response. She had left two voicemails, both unanswered. As the elevator rose to the second floor, she decided that she would try one more time before dinner. After all, she could only imagine what her husband might be going through at this moment and her heart ached for him.

His text came just as she was about to step into the warm, soothing waters of her bath. "Sweetheart. Sorry not to have contacted earlier. On my way back to Paris. He's spending the weekend there, not at his home. Will try to make contact with him tonight. Possibly tomorrow morning. Everything is okay here. Are you okay? xxxooo"

Without pausing, she texted right back, in hopes that he was holding her in the palm of his hand as well. "Darling, sooooo good to hear from you. I was worried. Sorry that you did not meet up with him yet. All is fine here. Spent the day exploring and tonight dinner with Artemidoros. He's taking care of me in your absence. Hurry back, sweetheart. I miss you!!!!! xxoo" The ping was always satisfying to her as she imagined her words mysteriously flying through cyberspace and into his waiting palm. Placing her phone on the floor next to the tub, she stepped into the welcoming warmth, then submerged her body as the waters held her down and out of harm's way.

  Six forty-five. She had been ready since six. A glimmer of guilt invaded her thinking as she tried to decide which necklace to wear of her favorites that she had added to her luggage at the last minute. It had been hard enough to settle on an outfit for the evening: a light sundress that was revealing and comfortable to wear with her husband present or the linen pants and top that was a bit more conservative in appearance, but that she regretted purchasing as all it took was sitting once for hundreds of wrinkles to appear. She really had not packed as well as she thought she had. On the other hand, the notion of being invited to dinner by a stranger without her husband present had never occurred to her. She would make do with what she had and decided to be wrinkled and conservative, which was why, for the last forty-five minutes, she had avoided sitting down. Looking at her watch, she decided that she would leisurely find her way down to the dining room, perhaps arriving a few minutes early but not too early since she did not want to appear eager.

  As she approached the elevator, she decided that she would take the stairs, slowly to avoid working up a sweat and to slow down her arrival. With each step, she tried to make a mental list of topics for discussion. She would certainly fill up her share with details about her day, questions she would ask Artemidoros about the village, perhaps about his family. Then she made a list of what she knew she could not speak about. A short list, to be sure. Michael's life. It was off limits.

  From the first-floor landing, she could smell the enticing blend of aromas from the kitchen. She could hear voices of patrons already enjoying their meals, their laughter, and music somewhere in the distance. Taking a deep breath while running her hands down the front of her blouse and the top of her pants, just in case a wrinkle had somehow found its way into the fabric, she pulled back her shoulders, adjusted her evening bag, and moved in the direction of a table set for two.

Halfway through the meal, she began to relax. Artemidoros had been nothing but a gentleman, greeting her at the entrance to the dining room, seating her as if she were a queen, allowing her to lead the conversation, never prying deeper than what she had offered as a topic, paying attention to her every need, and responding to her with smiles and gentle, knowing laughter. She had, she realized, dominated the dinner with her chatter about her day, and he had responded to her with details about the history of the place as well as minutia about the inhabitants of the village. Had she been a writer, she would have cherished every one of his utterances as fodder for her next novel, so detailed was he in sharing with her the images that he was seeing in his mind. They had not spoken of Michael once as the evening came to an end. Not until he saw her to the elevator. She felt uncomfortably warm and quite full. She had not yet gotten use to the Grecian food and expected that she probably wouldn't. *Thank God for antacids,* she thought.

"When do you expect Mr. Bingham to return?" He pushed the button for the elevator, not looking at her when he asked the question.

Startled by the mention of his name, she remembered her promise to herself. "I expect that he will be back sometime tomorrow or the following day." Hadn't they had this conversation before? She was about to explain to him that it all depended on Stephen and his whereabouts but caught herself. The less said, the better, she reminded herself.

"I am sorry that you have been left here on your own. I would be honored if you would share dinner with me tomorrow night if he has not returned." He slipped his hand under her elbow, leading her into the waiting elevator. He did not let go.

She moved away from him and pushed the button for the second floor, unnecessary on any other occasion as the elevator was tiny but necessary now so that his hand dropped back to his side. "Thank you for the evening. It was a lovely meal and very good company, but I think that I will want some time alone tomorrow evening, if you don't mind. Besides, I am crossing my fingers that my husband will be here tomorrow and that we can share at least one meal together before we leave this beautiful place."

"Of course. Whatever is best for you. But if you change your mind, I will be here. It is my pleasure. Good night then, Mrs. Bingham. Sleep well." If he had been wearing a hat, she thought, he would have lifted it from his head, swept it down in front of him holding it over his belly, while deeply bowing to her. He did all of this without the hat and remained in this position until she could no longer see him through the decreasing gap between the doors. While the elevator moved upward, she leaned against the back wall as the effects of the rich dinner started to work their magic.

Chapter 16

The trip into Paris had been pleasant, but Stephen was more than ready to exit the confines of the train. Sitting for long periods of time bothered him much more than he remembered. He had gotten up a few times to stretch his legs, use the facility, and stretch his legs again. But even with these breaks, the sitting was uncomfortable. He sighed with relief as they pulled into the busy station.

He gave the address to the cab driver, who welcomed him back to Paris upon learning that Stephen was not a first-time visitor but a resident of his country. Stephen said very little as the taxi maneuvered its way through the Paris streets and boulevards. Yes, he had made the right decision to come here for the weekend. He could feel his energy returning as he imagined his blood flowing through his damaged veins more forcefully now in anticipation of the two days that lay before him. He had remembered to take the list that the concierge had created for him during his last eventful stay. This time, he would be sure to check off as many of the sights as possible. He would not waste his time this weekend.

Paying the driver as he exited the taxi, he was greeted by a bellhop, who took Stephen's bag from the driver. Stephen followed the young man into the lobby of the hotel, paid him a pittance for his gesture, and took the bag from the boy. Yes, they were expecting him, were so happy that he had returned, and had the room he had requested ready for him. As a thank you for returning to them, the registration desk informed him that he would have an amenity sent to his room shortly.

The same room that he had occupied weeks ago welcomed him home. The drapes were open and the thin veil of curtains that deflected the afternoon sun were drawn so that upon approach, the blurred images of Notre Dame and the Seine came into clearer perspective. He pulled back the curtains, unlocked the door to the balcony, and stepped outside. From the quiet of the room to the explosion of noise below him and all around him, he took in the Paris that he had come to experience once again. He stepped toward the railing but stopped short, remembering that the outside corner of the iron fixture had felt loose on his last visit when he leaned against it. He had forgotten to report it to the management. Well, no. He would not blame himself, as his visit last time had been unexpectedly interrupted. But he would need to remember to say something. He moved to the railing and gingerly tried to move it. It did not take much effort for him to feel the railing give in his grip, even more so than during his last stay. He wondered how many unsuspecting visitors had stood on this balcony in his absence. Either the management had been neglectful in repairing the railing or no one had leaned against its cold iron surface and complained. Lucky for them, he thought.

The late-afternoon sun cast elongated shadows of bridges, tall shade trees, and buildings across the river's darkening surface. He loved this view, this time of day. He would freshen up and with his list in hand, begin his weekend. A feeling of delight overwhelmed him as he moved from the balcony back into the quiet of the room. A memorable weekend was in store for him. He knew it, somehow.

Chapter 17

The taxi driver, pleased by his growing wealth, had leisurely driven Michael back to Paris with no complaint from his passenger. Michael was surprised, and upon arrival, he commented on how quickly they seemed to have arrived in the city as compared to the ride to Tigeaux.

"Going home always goes faster, *monsieur*. It is just the way it is." The driver shrugged his shoulders.

Handing Michael his bag, the driver patiently waited while Michael dug into his pants pocket for his wallet. He was not surprised by the amount of the fare but now wished he had taken a bit more money with him. He had wanted to be sure that Alison had enough and had left her a little over 150 euros on the dresser by her phone. He would make do and, if need be, withdraw more from their savings. Once he'd handed the driver a handful of euros, they ended their acquaintance by simple nods.

Approaching the registration desk, Michael took in as much of the hotel's lobby as he could without stopping to gawk. The building was old, he thought. Not unusual for this city. Architectural touches led him to believe that it was probably built in the early nineteenth century. The preservation of these buildings had always impressed him no matter where he'd traveled in Europe. He regretted that the United States, with all its wealth and wherewithal, did not have the same priorities. A building in a large city in the States that had managed to survive for two hundred years or more was a rare find. He recalled coming across these buildings once or twice and always pitied them, standing in their original stature but now mere spots on the skyline as towering, glass office buildings encroached upon them on three sides, casting overwhelming shadows. Passed by quickly, they would go unnoticed.

As he moved forward, he focused on the request he was about to make. Not certain that the desk would give him the information that he wanted, he began to feel unsure of himself.

If he couldn't locate Stephen, what then? Not only had he convinced himself that this was the right thing to do, but he also had a Greek stranger depending on him to meet his obligation to his own father. And then there was Alison, who had not been convinced, he knew, that this was the best idea for either of them. But he was here now, and the desk clerk was waiting for his response.

"*Monsieur,* how can I help you?"

"Yes, I believe my brother is staying with you, Mr. Stephen Bingham. If you would be so kind as to let me know his room number?"

"It is our policy not to release that information. I am sorry. However, I can call his room and let him know that you are here. I will need his permission to release the number. Would you like me to do this for you?" The young woman was all business, Michael thought. He did not want to forewarn Stephen. He was sure that Stephen would not allow him to see him. This was all going so wrong.

"You see, I am here to surprise him. We have not seen one another in many years, but I found out through a family member that he was visiting Paris and staying in this hotel. It is a pure coincidence that I, too, am visiting for a short time in your beautiful city. I don't have any of his phone numbers or would have contacted him sooner. Is there any way that you can help me here?" He heard a hint of desperation in his voice and immediately regretted his far-fetched lie.

"I am sorry, *monsieur,* but I am not allowed to release this information without the guest's permission. Perhaps one of your family members has a recent number for him?"

He knew that she was not going to budge, and he begrudgingly admired her for it. "I see. Yes, perhaps. Thank you, *merci.*"

He sank into an overstuffed chair in the lobby. *This really can't be happening,* he thought. To come this close, only to be stopped in his tracks. He would need to figure out something. He had no idea what his brother looked like. The image that he had carried with him for so very long was that of a young boy.

Six decades ago. What was he thinking? Perhaps Alison had been right. Did it really matter if he couldn't keep his commitment to Adrastos? Feeling suddenly weary and defeated, he slouched even farther into the seat cushion, not sure where to go from here.

"*Excusez-moi, monsieur,* but I thought that you would like to know." The voice was angelic as he looked up to see the desk clerk standing in front of him. "He is over there, your brother?" She was discreetly pointing to the elevators when he saw him. "I hope that you have a good reunion." And she walked away. Just like that. He sat for a moment trying to comprehend what had just happened but did not waste any time getting up from the deep depression his body had made in the soft, oversized cushion. As he moved toward the elevators, he watched his brother move slowly toward the concierge's desk.

He looked old. Michael was taken aback by how old he appeared. Only sixty-six, he seemed to move like a man of eighty or older. Slow, careful steps, one after the other until he reached the desk. Michael watched him as he leaned against it, holding on with both hands to its thick wooded edges. His hair, almost fully gray, was sparse and could have done with a trim. Seeing only the back of him as he moved closer, Michael noticed that his brother's body was bent forward not because he was leaning in to hear the concierge's voice, which he imagined he was anyway, but because nature had had her way with his skeleton over the years. A fleeting image of a young child cowering under the protection of his brother and then another of him dangling in the darkness, his little spine contorted to ease the pain of the rope, stopped him in his approach. He could feel his heart breaking as he waited for his brother to finish.

Stephen glanced in Michael's direction as he turned from the desk but did not recognize him. He moved slowly toward the doors of the hotel, passing Michael within a few yards. As much as Michael wanted to move, he felt paralyzed, not physically but mentally. Too many voices suddenly filled his head, uninvited and all speaking at the same time. Voices familiar to him, but he could not identify their source. As they became louder, his pulse rose and he realized that he was experiencing panic. Once, he would have popped a pill and they would all go away. So simple. So numbing.

As Stephen approached the double doors being held open by a young bellhop, Michael felt himself lurch forward while hearing his own voice over all of the others yell out his brother's name. "Stephen, Stephen, please wait!" Before he knew it, he was standing by his brother's side for the first time in fifty-seven years. The voices were silent.

Startled and confused at the sound of his name, Stephen, unsteady on his feet, stopped suddenly so that the bellhop reached for his arm to steady him while letting the oversized glass doors swing shut.

"*Merci, merci,*" Stephen managed to say as he gently moved the boy's hand from his lower arm. He turned toward the stranger standing next to him and saw in his eyes something familiar but could not remember what it was.

Michael, seeing Stephen's confusion, knew that he would scare him away with the wrong words spoken, so fragile was their connection, almost nonexistent. "Stephen. It's me. Michael." He did not touch Stephen's arm as he was tempted to do, to draw him close to his body, to hold him once again. Instead, he stood his ground, waiting for his brother to respond.

Stephen did not say a word but turned from the doors and slowly moved toward the seating area where Michael had just been. It was as if Michael did not exist, as Stephen seemed to ignore the presence of this man next to him. Finding the closest seat, he sat down heavily and indicated to Michael with a slight movement of his head that he sit in the seat across from him. Michael did so and waited for his brother to say something, anything to indicate to him that Stephen comprehended who it was that was sitting across from him. Unable to contain himself any longer, as it seemed minutes had slowly crawled by while he suffered his brother's inability—or was it unwillingness—to acknowledge him, Michael sat forward in the chair.

"Stephen. Are you going to speak to me?" He did not sit back but remained rigid and tense, unable to relax until he heard his brother's voice. The heaviness of the silence generated by Stephen felt suffocating to Michael. Not knowing what to do, he waited. As the moments passed, he fully expected his brother to slowly stand up and walk away without uttering a sound, so distant he seemed, Michael thought, from the importance of the moment.

"Why are you here?"

Michael barely heard the mumbled utterance but understood it enough to know that what had seemed an impenetrable barrier a moment ago had now been breached. With his eyes focused on Stephen's, he did not lose a second in response for fear of losing him once again.

"I need to say so much to you. To apologize, to explain, to ask your forgiveness. So much has happened since then. So much." Michael looked down to avoid Stephen's questioning gaze, trying to prevent Stephen from seeing his own vulnerabilities and fears so close now to the surface. He was sure that Stephen could detect them even as Michael fought to drive back the moisture collecting under his lower eyelids. He was surprised by the strength of his emotions suddenly taking control so that all of the rehearsed mental script that he had prepared dissolved instantly. He knew that if he opened his mouth too soon, he would not be able to halt the deluge of thoughts and memories that crowded and pushed against his weakening control to hold them back. He had been so sure of himself when Alison expressed her concerns for him. He had brushed her off so easily. *Not a problem; what happens happens.* So easy to say. So ignorant, he thought now as he took a deep breath and looked up to see Stephen's gaze had not changed but seemed even more intense.

Stephen's brother sat across from him in a Parisian hotel, in his getaway, assuming that his uninvited appearance would be welcomed with open arms. This brother who he could barely recall as the nightmares that had plagued him for so long had now diminished, so infrequent that he could not remember the last time he suffered from them; a brother who'd succeeded in reconnecting even as Stephen had spent his life avoiding precisely the situation he was now facing. Watching Michael fight the demons that Stephen knew they both shared, he marveled that he felt no emotional tug, no desire to comfort his brother; instead, a disgust rose from deep within Stephen so that the crumpled human being across from him meant no more to him than a stranger passing by on the street. But he knew that Michael could not be ignored, even though he longed for the convenience of that act. He also knew that his brother could not, would not, be allowed entrance into his life at this late stage of the game. How had he handled intruders when younger, when making his way up the social and financial ladders? Carefully, with some diplomacy, while artfully employing deceit and illusion. The suckers never knew what had hit them when he was done with them. He inwardly smiled at the recollection of his successes. He could handle this now. He would have to, he thought, no matter what that meant.

"Michael, it has been a very long time. A very long time." He struggled to find the words that used to come so easily when younger, the right words to entice his subjects to believe in him. He paused, but not long enough for Michael to respond. *Be gentle,* he reminded himself. "Perhaps, as you have come a long way to see me, we should find a quieter place to talk?"

Upon hearing his brother's suggestion, Michael could not hide his relief. "Yes, please. That would be great, Stephen." He did not ask the obvious, as he assumed Stephen had a place in mind.

"I frequent a place just around the corner. Very good food and they know me there. We can stay as long as we like, I am sure. A drink or two, perhaps, to start with? I expect that you might be hungry. A bit early for dinner, at least in this city, but we will break the rules, just for tonight. What do you say?"

Michael thought that he saw the beginnings of a smile on his brother's face, and suddenly the memory of Stephen's grin flashed in front of him as he saw his little brother swoop from behind the tall stand of redwoods, arms extended from his sides while he became an imagined airplane soaring through the moist, thick air of their childhood playground.

Breaking from the warmth of the memory, Michael agreed. "Good, I could do with a bit of something. Until you mentioned it, I didn't realize that I was hungry. Thank you, Stephen. I mean, for seeing me, for taking the time to talk with me." They were now both standing.

"This way, then." Stephen pointed to the large glass doors. "You will have to forgive me, as I do not move as quickly as you might remember me to do."

Michael stopped in his tracks as they slowly moved forward. Had his brother read his mind? Was their connection still that strong? He was about to mention to Stephen what had just occurred but thought better of it. Pure coincidence, he thought. That's all it was.

"Are you okay? Having trouble keeping up with my lightning speed?" Stephen turned to his brother. "I can slow down, not a problem at all." Michael could hear a lightness in Stephen's voice.

"Sorry. No, I'm fine. Just remembered something that I need to do later. Nothing important, but you know how the memory at our ages works. Probably will forget it by the time we get to those doors." He laughed as a reassurance to himself that he had trod softly in his brother's stead.

The restaurant was as promised. Michael was enchanted by its quaintness while still maintaining its place in the tour books as one of the finest restaurants in Paris. As he perused the menu, noting its limited but delectable offerings, it was obvious to him that this establishment had kept up with the culinary times. It also became suddenly clear to him that his little brother must have done well for himself in order to afford these meals as often as he implied he did. Currently, the euros in his own wallet would cover a quarter of one appetizer, he realized. He would need to offer to pay for their meals, he knew. He just hadn't planned on such expensive ones. Alison had insisted that he take their one and only credit card with him, even though he had thought differently. They had worked hard to free themselves of credit card debt and, never saying it aloud to one another, were nevertheless quite proud of their achievement. He wanted to keep it that way. But now, she would again prove to be right, even in her absence. Silently, he thanked her for covering him once more.

"This is my treat, Stephen. Please." *Get it out of the way right off the bat.* He knew that Stephen would insist on paying, but he would not back down.

"Thank you. Kind of you." Stephen was sitting back, menu never touched, waiting for Michael to come up for air from behind his menu. "Have you decided? I would be happy to offer my suggestions, if it would help you."

Recovering from Stephen's unexpected response and then reassuring himself that he would pay off the balance next month, he laid the menu on the table. "I appreciate that, but I have decided. I am sure everything is excellent."

"It comes down to a matter of taste. Always a matter of taste, really. Will you join me in a drink before dinner? The wines are spectacular. But whatever you desire, they will prepare for you."

Michael paused before responding to his brother. He could have one, very light, he thought. He would nurse it until another glass was offered with dinner. And that would be his limit. Even that might drag him to a place he never wanted to visit again. He would be careful, he thought.

They did not wait for the drinks to arrive after they ordered their meal. Michael felt a sense of urgency in speaking with his brother. He wasn't sure why, now that Stephen seemed more comfortable with him. In fact, Stephen gave him the impression that he had nothing but time to be with Michael. Yet although it shouldn't have, something gnawed at Michael about his brother's acceptance of him. Michael pushed it from his thoughts so that he could focus on what needed to be accomplished.

"You have a lot to say to me? Is that my understanding?" Stephen broke through Michael's concentration.

"There is so very much to tell you, Stephen." He leaned forward, spurred on by his brother's invitation. Where to begin? A deep breath. "I wonder what you remember about when we were kids? You were so little. Do you remember anything?"

Of course he remembered. How could Michael ask the question? But he would not give Michael the satisfaction of filling in any blanks for him. No, Michael had come to him, had indicated that he had to communicate with his little brother. Certainly, not the other way around.

"I remember very little, if anything really. I often wonder what is real and what is imagined. There was no one to help me know the difference, you see." He let these words suspend in midair as if in limbo, a purgatory from which he could free himself but not his brother.

Stephen's words were not lost on Michael. If anything, they served to propel him forward. "I wanted to be there for you, Stephen. I was there for you until they took us away. Do you remember? They took us away together but then they separated us. Do you remember that?" He tried to control a voice that was filling with uncontrolled emotion.

"You were there. That is correct. I remember very little of when I was small. How old was I? What were you? I forget our difference in age."

"You were four and I was eight."

"Right. A long time ago." He paused for just a moment. "Michael, I know that you want to explain yourself to me, your absence after all of these years. Why don't you just get on with it?"

Michael was taken aback by Stephen's question. It reminded him of being reprimanded at school for some minor incident in which the principal knew the truth but wanted Michael to confess it on his own. Was it impatience he heard in his voice? Frustration? Anger?

The drinks arrived, and Michael said a small prayer of thanks for the good timing. He wrapped his hand around the cool glass and began to lift it to his mouth.

"No toast? This is an occasion to remember, I think." Stephen had lifted his glass and reached halfway across the table to Michael.

"Of course. Sorry." He wanted to tell his brother that he

was nervous and unsure of the person sitting across from him, as if he were on an amusement park ride in the dark, not knowing what lurked around the next bend but sure to be unpleasantly surprised by it.

"Better. To an unexpected reunion." Stephen did not elaborate, nor did he make contact with Michael's extended and waiting glass. Instead, he took a sip and then another, resting the glass on the table while admiring the growing legs that began to coat its insides. "A beautiful wine, you see?" He pointed to the miniature streams of wine whose appearance reminded Michael of slowly moving raindrops caught upon the glass window of a house in the woods as he and his brother cheered them on in a race to the sill.

"So you need to start, Michael. I promise to listen." Stephen waited, sipping slowly on his already half-empty glass.

Michael took a sip of his and placed it in front of him, holding onto it with two hands, fingers entwined around its stem. He felt centered. "We were separated after having spent a short amount of time in foster care. I ran away to start a new life on my own and when I was settled, to come back for you. I couldn't tell you any of this because you were so little. There was no way that you would understand, and I didn't want to frighten you. I thought it was better just to go. I knew that I would be back, so I guess it didn't seem to me the end of everything. But I was wrong, as you well know." He waited for Stephen to respond but he sat silently, so near to Michael that he could smell the wine on his brother's breath as he shifted in his seat and heavily breathed out. Why did he seem so distant? Michael continued. "I got caught up with people I shouldn't have. Promises of getting rich, of having anything that I wanted. All I had to do was push poison on innocents, just like they were doing to me. All I could see was coming back to get you and the two of us living together again once I was rich. That was all I could see." Again, he waited, only to be greeted by silence. "I failed, Stephen. I failed both of us miserably. I got so lost in alcohol and drugs that nothing mattered but the next fix, the next drink. I was living only for the poisons, nothing more. I was in facilities but never saw any of them through. And then I found myself in a hospital and went through detox and therapy. I also found the love of my life, who is the reason I am alive today and here with you."

Stephen had emptied his glass and was gesturing to the waiter. "Another, *si'l vous plaît, monsieur*. Michael, more?"

Had Stephen heard a word of what he'd just said? Was he listening? Did he care? "No, *merci*. I am fine."

"Sorry, go on." Stephen sat back again, readjusting his weight against the wooden chair's well-used contours, certainly not the same as his own.

Michael could not fathom that Stephen had not reacted in any way to his revelations. However, he had come this far and needed to finish for no one's sake but his own, it seemed. "Stephen, do you remember our mother? Our father?"

Stephen, as much as he tried, could not keep hidden the recognition of these words from Michael. And he knew that Michael had seen his reaction. "I have some memory, yes."

Michael waited for him to continue. He knew that he had broken through. But, again, Stephen sat stoically, having regained his composure and now in control.

"Do you remember what happened to our mother? Anything at all?"

"I know that she is dead, Michael. I know that our father is dead. When you left, I was told later by my foster family that they had died in an automobile accident." His words were spoken as a matter of fact, void of any emotion.

"Stephen, that is not the truth. What they told you was to protect you from the truth. I am sorry that you have lived with that lie all of this time."

"You will need to explain yourself, Michael. What is the truth?" As much as he tried, he could not help but show some interest in what Michael was saying.

"Our father was a coward, a drunk, and an abuser, Stephen, of our mother and of us. He did terrible things to us, Stephen…" He stopped, realizing that his voice might carry to tables close by. Beginning again, leaning in to his brother and lowering his voice to almost a whisper, he continued. "He was a monster that we were deathly afraid of every day. Don't you remember? Our mother could never protect us from him but was always there afterward to help heal us. And she had no one to help heal *her.*" He saw now that Stephen had engaged with him, though silently, and Michael assumed that this was all too much to take in. "Stephen, are you okay?"

"Of course. Go on."

"Do you remember how he hurt us? What he did to you and to me, but mostly to you?"

Stephen shook his head.

"The well. There was a well, or part of one, on our property. Do you remember that?"

Again, a shake of the head.

Michael suddenly realized that he was in too deep for them to come out of this still whole. If his brother had no recollection of the horrors of their childhood, he should not be the one to try and prod the memories. He knew enough from his own experiences in therapy what worked and what was taboo. Frightened now that he could not back out without dragging Stephen deeper, he tried to regroup his thoughts. *Slow down,* he thought. *Enough has been said. Back away. Back away.*

Stephen found himself enjoying this, not acknowledging that he knew anything that his brother was revealing. His brother who so wanted to make everything all right, who wanted Stephen to forgive his leaving him alone so that he was forced to survive and to create his own life—no, lives; who had no idea who Stephen really was and what he was capable of doing. What he had done. And he would never know, Stephen decided. He would hear him out, could bear the details that he knew Michael would spill if there was enough space to fill in the conversation. None of it would shock him. None of it. Michael's problem was that he didn't understand that he was in this alone and always would be. Just as he had forced Stephen to be for all these years. Nothing would change for himself, Stephen realized. But his big brother had just opened the wrong door and there was no turning back for him.

"Stephen, it doesn't matter, that part. What I need to tell

you will matter. You need to understand the truth about what happened to our parents. Our father…" He stopped. The waiter had arrived at the table with the dishes, whose aromas collided above their heads and filled the space between the brothers.

"*Pardon, monsieurs. Voilà!*" He carefully centered each plate in front of the brothers.

"*C'est bon. Merci. Merci.*" Stephen ordered another glass of cabernet while indicating to Michael that his glass needed replenishing.

"No, I am fine, thank you." Michael's concentration was diminishing as the warm food with its enticing appearance and penetrating aromas took control of the moment.

"So, my brother, *bon appètit!*" Stephen did not wait for Michael to say the same but had begun eating as if ravenous. "*Mange! Mange!*"

"Yes, this looks amazing." There was no more that he could say as with each mouthful, he fell deeper and deeper into the incredible culinary creation in front of him with no thought beyond the next taste.

As they finished, Stephen well ahead of Michael, Stephen addressed his brother as if coming out of a coma or some other brain-inhibiting event. "Ah, Michael. Yes. There you are." He was smiling at his brother now, a full grin. The ruddiness of his cheeks as the thin film of sweat clung to his pores betrayed Stephen's consumption of wine during the meal. Michael had kept count, if for no other reason than for every glass his brother consumed, he did not. Pleased that he had remained true to himself, he lifted his glass and swallowed the remaining liquid as he took one last bite of his meal.

"I've been here all along." Flippant but true. "Shall I continue, Stephen?" The dishes were cleared, the table scraped of its crumbs, and the dessert menus laid in front of each of them. "I will have to beg off of any more food. But, please don't let that stop you from enjoying your meal."

"I, too, am feeling satisfied. I will order an after-dinner drink, though. And you? Something to quell the ugly beast that will attack us both, especially you, as you are not used to the richness of this food as I am. Even so, at my age, I do not have the wherewithal to fight it off as once before."

Perhaps one drink to end the evening would be appropriate, Michael thought. After all, he had maintained the course throughout the last hour. Yes, an aperitif would do no harm. "Yes, I will have what you are having."

"Fine. A wise decision, you will see. So, continue then. You were saying, if I remember, something about our father?"

Michael would not prolong the rest of what he had to say to Stephen. Details could be revealed later, if ever. It would depend on Stephen. "Our father was responsible for our mother's death." Was that right? It hit him hard, the flash of blurred memory, and suddenly he found himself caught between the adults' bodies, fighting for his mother's life.

"What do you mean? What are you telling me? That our father killed our mother? Michael, is that what you are telling me?"

He found himself free of his parents as the sound of Stephen's voice shattered the image. Michael took notice of Stephen's tone in asking the questions. Stephen had remained remarkably calm, he thought, much like a prosecutor who skillfully inches closer to the climactic moment in the trial as he questions the defendant knowing perfectly well that the answers will seal the defendant's fate, thus adding one more victory to the attorney's name.

"I, I...yes. He killed our mother, Stephen. I tried to stop him. I tried so hard to stop him from hurting you, too." He had lied. He knew the truth, but he could not tell his brother. He had told Alison but this person in front of him, his own blood, would now never know the truth. He could not go back. He focused on Stephen's face, hoping to read some sign as to what he was thinking. Nothing. Nothing more than a passive appearance that, for some unexplained reason, began to frighten Michael.

"You need to finish what you have started." Stephen spoke softly now and slowly as he leaned farther forward, almost knocking his drink over. "Finish what you have to say."

Michael was now physically shaking. He noticed it as he

lifted the glass to his lips and let the heavy, warm, and smooth liquid glide across his tongue and down his throat. He took a second and then a third sip without pausing. Placing his glass in front of him, Stephen called the waiter to the table and ordered a second round for them. Michael did not protest. The drinks came quickly but Michael did not touch his immediately. He watched Stephen bring the glass to his lips. Feeling the beginnings of the amber liquid's effect, his gaze fell on Stephen's fingers that caressed the cut glass's angles so that for a moment, the distortion of his fingers through the glass and liquid startled him.

"Michael, please. Go on." Again, Stephen had brought Michael back to the uncomfortable reality that he now wished he had never entertained. It was all becoming too hard; he had lost control by lying and now he was frightened. Not of Stephen but of himself. He was not ready for this. Alison had been right; he knew that now. But his brother was not going anywhere, caught up now in Michael's revelations.

The untouched glass touched his lips as he let the alcohol linger in his mouth, his tongue gently blending the liquid against the roof of his mouth, his teeth, his gums, and then drawing it all back to rest on his palate before swallowing. Its warmth relaxed him. He sat back for a moment as if to rest after a long hike and then sighed, gathering his courage to go forward. Readjusting the chair so that it now sat closer to the table's edge, he leaned on its surface, careful not to knock the cutlery and glass in front of him, elbows resting near the edge while both forearms overlapped one another and looked up at Stephen.

"You were hurt, Stephen. You couldn't do anything to help yourself. Just too little and frightened. I wanted to stay with you but I was scared of him and ran as far into the forest as I could to get away from him." He could smell the musty undergrowth now and remembered the softness of the ground beneath his shoes that seemed to spring him forward, away from harm. "I hid in a burned-out tree. I remember trying so hard not to breathe, not to move, but to be as still as the giant that I was temporarily inhabiting. Then I heard him coming toward me. He was carrying our bat." He stopped here so as not to let Stephen know the cruelty that their father possessed. No need for these kinds of details, he reminded himself. "He was standing right next to me, so close that I could smell him, the alcohol on him as he tried to catch his breath. Stephen, he was drunk, always was drunk, when he tried to hurt us."

Stephen was emptying his third glass while his eyes remained on Michael. Then he turned and again ordered one more round. Michael put up his hand to indicate he'd had enough, but Stephen ignored him. "I'm done, Stephen. Don't waste money. I've already had three too many."

"Money is not a problem for me. Aren't you buying? Besides, if you don't drink it, I'll finish it off. You feeling all right?" Stephen knew the answer. It was obvious to him that Michael was not a drinker and was fighting his body's opposition to the poison. *Too bad,* he thought.

"To be honest, no. I'm not feeling that great. Would you excuse me for a minute?"

"Of course. Right back there and through the double doors on your left. Do you want me to come with you?"

"No, no. I just need a few minutes. Would you order some water for me while I'm gone?" The idea of clear, harmless liquid entering his body sounded good as he pushed himself back from the table and stood. His head seemed to be on a separate agenda from the rest of his body as the spinning got in the way of his mobility. All that he had forgotten about being plastered out of his mind came rushing back, so part of him wanted to enjoy it and give in to it while somewhere newly ingrained in him, he tried to fight it off. Wobbling imperceptibly toward the bathroom as he worked to control his movements, he left Stephen at the table.

Stephen smiled as he watched his big brother crumbling in front of him. And he was not the only one. The maître d' looked up from the reception book as Michael passed and slowly shook his head in sympathy, or maybe disgust. It was hard to tell, Stephen thought. A waiter in the back coming from the kitchen moved to the side of the hallway as Michael tried to maintain a straight path to the waiting double doors only to lose his footing, once to the left, then once to the right, as he reached for the walls to stabilize himself, missing the waiter by inches.

When he came back to the table, a pitcher of water and a full glass greeted him. "Thanks, Stephen. This is going to help." He drank the glass of water before he sat down. "I'm feeling a bit better. God, this is not the way I had planned the evening.

"Sorry that you are struggling there, Michael. I probably shouldn't be pushing drink on you. My mistake." Stephen's words were sympathetic but, again, the tone of his voice led Michael to believe otherwise. Still feeling unsettled both physically and mentally, he longed for this evening to be finished.

"I've got to tell you the rest while I still can." His feeble attempt at humor fell on deaf ears. Stephen's expression did not change; his demeanor was that of a mannequin, Michael thought. The only thing that the mannequin couldn't do was lift its arm to its mouth and drink. Stephen had perfected that.

"Fine. I'm listening. You were telling me about our drunk father?" The intention of Stephen's question was not lost on Michael. And he felt an anger growing toward his brother. He had no idea. He didn't know him and all that he'd been through. How dare he compare him to that monster? Fighting to calm himself so that he could go forward and finish what he had started, he breathed slowly and deeply while his body reminded him that it had not cleansed itself of the poison in its system. A wave of nausea crept up his chest and then subsided. He swallowed hard and then continued.

"I killed our father that day. Right where he stood waiting to kill me. And I left him there to come back to you. To take care of you and to get us both out of there. But I was too late. You were already in an ambulance and being taken away. They took me too, but separately. We were placed together in a foster home. Do you remember any of this?"

"I'm afraid not." So matter-of-fact. So infuriating to Michael.

"They separated us shortly after our first placement. Then placed us back together. I think I was somewhere around thirteen when I left. I ran away so that I could find work and then be able to come back and get you. I wanted to take care of you, Stephen."

"Interesting. I don't remember you ever coming back." Again, that voice. That tone now, with a hint of accusation.

"I didn't. I couldn't. My life was a mess for years. I got caught up in bad stuff, Stephen. Nearly ended my life with drugs and alcohol. Now I know why, but then I had no clue what I was doing to myself. I didn't care about anyone, just when and where my next fix would come. Numbed myself with alcohol when the drugs weren't there, but most of the time mixed the two together and was lost to the world."

"So you are here now and appear to be on the straight and narrow, aside from tonight." He smugly gestured toward the still filled glass in front of Michael.

"I'm here. Yes. But there is a reason that I'm not dead in some gutter. I married the woman who saved me from my own destruction. I owe her my life."

"As I owe you mine?" Stephen could not resist, knowing full well that Michael would be offended and hurt.

"No, Stephen. You owe me nothing. It was my responsibility to protect you. I failed to do that. And for that, I am sorry." How many times had he rehearsed these words before this moment? And each time that he had done so, he'd had to fight off the tears that refused to dissipate until they flowed down his cheeks. Having spoken the words aloud now to Stephen, Michael became aware that he felt nothing other than a growing dislike for the man seated across the table. Had he expected Stephen to break down and sob uncontrollably while embracing his long-lost brother? Had he expected him to understand and to commiserate with Michael? Had he expected any thanks? Yes. He had, and none of his expectations were fulfilled. Instead, he felt as though Stephen saw him as the enemy; not his father, not his mother, not the system, but his own brother. Another wave of nausea, this time stronger, grabbed hold of his innards. *Oh, my God,* he thought.

"Do you have anything else to say, Michael?" Stephen

could see that his brother was still fighting the drink and waited patiently for the moment to pass. "Why don't we go up to my room? You can lie down and sleep this off. You should not be traveling back tonight anyway. It's late, and your condition will not allow it."

His words made sense to Michael, and the thought of stretching out and losing consciousness for a while, escaping the misery he was now in, was welcome. And then he remembered. It came to him so suddenly that he turned in his seat, expecting to see Adrastos standing patiently behind him.

"Are you all right?" Stephen, still enjoying watching his brother's discomfort, was curious. "Don't tell me you are seeing things now. Well, are you?" Michael did not immediately respond but slowly turned back to face Stephen.

"There is something else I need to talk to you about."

"Please don't tell me there are more ghosts hidden in your closet."

"No, not the ghosts that you would be interested in hearing about." Michael felt a moment of triumph as he chalked one up for his side. "Alison and I...oh, I didn't finish what I was telling you. Alison is my wife, also was my therapist, and is my angel. We are on vacation now. Not here, but in Greece." He stopped and purposely focused on Stephen's face for any hint of recollection. Nothing. "It turns out that you and I have more in common than bloodline, Stephen." Another deep intake of air to fend off another nauseating wave. "Years ago, sometime during a short lucid period before my final descent into the netherworld of chemical abuse and after I left you, I traveled in Europe. Not for long, I don't think. I just don't remember it all that well. But I did go to Greece and spent some time there in one little village. Oia. Does that ring a bell to you?"

Stephen remained silent and then said, "Go on."

"There was a shopkeeper whom I met and we hit it off. The thing is, on this trip, right now, I decided to go back to that village and to see if the shop was still there. I don't know why I was drawn there so strongly, but I was. And it is still there, and the same family still runs it." Again he stopped, searching his brother's countenance. Still nothing. "To make a long story short, the son of the man whom I met is running the store. When he heard my name, he recognized it immediately. It seems that you and your wife visited the old man years ago as well and your wife left quite an impression upon him. So much so that she is the recipient of some of his inheritance." The words were falling from his mouth now, and any hint of his internal distress had been shoved aside as he concentrated on completing his task for Adrastos. "Putting aside the chances of us both being in the same place, years apart, no contact between us, I promised Adrastos, the son, that I would find you and deliver the message to you. The catch is that for her to inherit the gift, you both must come to Greece, to the son, who is obeying his father's wishes. The gift is to be personally handed to you both. I offered to bring it to you, but he would not hear of it." He stopped to catch his breath, only just aware of how few breaths he had taken in the passing minutes. Reaching into his overnight bag, he retrieved two airline tickets and held them up. "We have a flight for tomorrow morning at ten. Your tickets are round trip, so don't worry about expense. It is all taken care of. I figured that you both might want to spend more than a day there with us, you know, getting to know Alison and me?" He became suddenly aware of an imagined chill that had descended upon them. Placing the tickets back into his bag, he looked back at his brother, whose expression had not changed. "I am sensing that I might have overstepped the boundaries here? I only thought that this would all work out to both our benefits. After all, you are my only brother. Sorry if I have upset you, Stephen." He pushed himself back in the seat and dropped his arms to his side as if to surrender to his own defeat.

"I will not go to Greece, Michael. Not now, not ever again." His words were spoken as if each one held equal importance.

Michael was taken aback by the intonation of his response. "I don't understand. Is it the traveling? What do you mean, 'I will not go.' What about speaking to your wife? After all, she should have equal say, if you don't mind me saying so."

And then he suddenly recalled his brief conversation with the young boy.

"My wife is no longer with me. She died years ago. I have no need for any inheritance." Stephen heard all that Michael had said and, with each word spoken, fought a gathering darkness somewhere within. He consciously made the effort to remain calm, unscathed by the growing presence of what he had laid to rest long ago.

"I'm sorry about your wife, Stephen. It was foolish of me to presume anything about your current life. I would have liked to have met her." He paused, recognizing a feeling of regret and loss for what could have been. "I only thought that the two of you and I could travel back together. I would love for you to meet Alison. I know she wants to meet you. And, if you choose not to accept the gift, at least you could let him know in person. He will be sorry to learn of your wife's passing, as I am, Stephen." He knew he meant these last words. He could not imagine losing Alison.

Another, stronger wave of nausea swept through him, a combination of drink and the unimaginable. He forced himself to fight through it. "If nothing else comes of it," he said, managing to organize his thoughts as the prickling points of perspiration coated his forehead and upper lip, "it would give us time to properly catch up. Fifty-seven years is a long time, Stephen." Again he paused, giving in to the waiting linen napkin as he drew it to his face and dabbed the moist skin as if he had just rinsed it. He looked at Stephen, who remained stoic and, apparently, unobservant. Fighting his rebellious body as well as his brother's negative stance to his suggestion, he laid the napkin down, a feeling of utter despair that the evening had taken this turn and that he had allowed it to happen. "You know, if this is the way it is to be, then I accept it."

His announcement of defeat seemed to fill the room, to bounce off the walls, and to slowly fade in a diminishing echo. He hadn't meant to give in. He had wanted to stand his ground, to make this work, to fulfill the wishes of a dead man whom he had never met but, for some reason, was an integral part of both of their lives. He wanted Stephen to meet his wife. He wanted his brother in his life. And now none of this was to become reality. About to excuse himself from the table and from his brother for what he knew would be the last time, he barely heard Stephen's voice. But he had said something, and Michael leaned forward. "Sorry, did you say something?"

His face indicated no emotion, but his voice was now audible. "Perhaps you are right. I have my reasons for not wanting to go back to places with memories, as I am sure you can understand." Stephen was leaning forward as well, as though to keep the communication between them private. "It is hard for me to make this decision. Very hard." Knowing that he must stay in control, he chose his words carefully in order to elicit the desired sympathy from Michael that would keep him subservient to him. Stephen couldn't help feeling a sense of accomplishment and a sudden surge of excitement as he watched his brother's facial reactions to his well-dramatized unrehearsed script. "If I agree to go with you, you must promise me that you will not place me in an uncomfortable situation by insisting that I accept whatever this man wants to give me. I want nothing to do with it. It must be understood, Michael." He did not wait for a response. "And you must also promise me that you will not persist in your need to 'catch up,' as you say, if I indicate that I no longer want to 'catch up.'" He purposely marked the air with the invisible quote marks, emphasizing his point. Taken aback by one of the few movements made by his brother all evening, Michael worked at refocusing on his brother's conciliatory words. No. His demands. "Is that acceptable to you?"

"I understand, Stephen. My sudden presence in your life is, I am sure, disruptive and uncomfortable. Perhaps we have waited too long to ever be brothers again." He heard his own words; what he had feared to be the truth all along. He had not wanted to accept it, though, not after all that they had both been through. Not now, after having spent the last couple of hours with him still not knowing him while only scratching, unsuccessfully it seemed, a callused and hardened surface.

"You have not answered my question. Are you accepting

my requests? If not, our evening, I am afraid, must end here."

"Yes, of course. I accept." Michael suddenly felt small and threatened. Bullied. Stephen was smiling now and his whole body appeared relaxed, as if melding into the chair. Was he imagining this?

"Good. We leave tomorrow morning? Is that what you said?" Stephen's voice was light and suddenly childlike in its expectation of an exciting outing as he pointed to Michael's bag resting beside him on the floor.

"Yes, that is what I was hoping to do. I didn't plan on staying any longer in Paris than the weekend, depending on your decision. If things had not gone as I hoped they would, I would be returning to Oia tonight. As it is, it is late and a good night's rest will have me feeling better in the morning." Another wave, this time not as strong but an unpleasant reminder that he had done damage to his body. The thought of stretching out on a bed and riding the remains of his own foolishness out until a welcome and deep sleep caught up to him lightened his spirits. The worst was over. Stephen was coming back with him; he had convinced him to do so. What would transpire once he met Artemidoros was out of his hands. So far, the gods had been good to him, other than enjoying his discomfort while imbibing too heavily on the grapes' juices. All he could do now was trust that wherever his life was taking him, it was meant to be.

"Do you have a room? I only ask because it is very hard to procure a room here at the last minute. I have been told that one must reserve months in advance. Not only that, it is ridiculously expensive." A lie, he knew, but one that would serve his purpose. Stephen was moving his chair away from the table and slowly standing as he spoke. He stood, not erectly, but balancing himself comfortably while holding onto the table's edge with one hand. He turned to Michael.

"No, I am afraid that I didn't think ahead, or perhaps I did." Had he subconsciously determined that he would be returning on his own that very night? He felt like a fool in front of his brother.

"It is not a problem. Would you consider staying in my

room tonight? There is a very comfortable couch that would serve your needs, I am sure. You could take a long shower, bath, whatever you desire, and I am sure that you will sleep well. It is very quiet when the windows are shut. And in the morning, you will be delighted by the view."

"I don't want to impose, Stephen. Perhaps there is a room available. Let me see." Michael was now standing.

"No, please. Accept my offer, Michael. After all, it is only for one night. I do not mind telling you that I will be hurt if you don't." Stephen threw this last thought in to ensure that Michael's subservience was still intact.

One night. Sharing a room with his brother again. Only for one night. Lifetimes apart brought so intimately together in a matter of minutes. The gods were present, Michael couldn't help thinking.

"All right, then. Yes, thank you, Stephen. I really do appreciate it." He took a step away from the table and felt the room spinning around him. Grabbing on to the back of the chair, he tried to steady himself.

"The sooner we go up to my room, the better. You do not look well." Stephen slowly stepped around the edge of the table and stood in front of Michael. "I would take your arm, but I am afraid that I would be a danger to us both. Do you think that you can walk to the elevator?" He pointed in the direction of the waiting doors.

"Sure. Just give me a minute." He reached for the pitcher of water and poured another glassful. Its cool and harmless liquid slid down his throat, and he imagined its magic flooding his system as it washed away the poisons within. "Okay, lead the way."

The room was well appointed and large. Enough room to accommodate them both. Michael was grateful that Stephen had offered him a place to stay. There was no possible way that he could have headed back tonight, not in his condition. With a good night's rest, everything would look better in the morning.

He was actually looking forward to tomorrow and the trip with his brother. What they both needed was time. Time to become acquainted. He knew that the connection they once had was gone forever, but he felt sure that they could begin again as aged adults with an abundance of history to share with one another. In time, perhaps, if all went well between them, the first part of their young lives could be revisited, thought Michael. Not to seek the connection that no longer existed, but to seek closure so that acceptance of who they were now could be accomplished. His thoughts were interrupted as Stephen turned to him.

"I haven't slept on the couch, of course, but it looks comfortable enough. What do you think?" He moved to the plush cushions and ran his hand over their surfaces. Michael put down the small overnight bag that he had packed at the last minute. He sat on the indicated cushions and immediately felt his body sink into their well-worn innards while sensing the couch's wooden frame catching behind his thighs. Stephen didn't seem to notice the awkward position in which his brother now found himself, nor his effort to push himself up from the couch to a standing position.

"It's great, Stephen. Just fine." He tried to sound sincere but worried that his brother knew better.

"Good. There is an extra pillow in the closet and a blanket. Plenty of towels in the bathroom. I see you have your own toiletries with you," he said, pointing to Michael's overnight bag, "but if you need anything, just ask me."

"No, I'm fine. Thanks, though. Wait—maybe a cup of coffee. Do you have any? A coffeemaker?" He looked around and saw nothing of the sort.

"No, but I will call for room service. Are you hungry?" His voice indicated incredulousness that hunger could be an issue after the meal that they had just shared.

"God, no." His sarcasm was not lost on Michael. "Quite full, but coffee sounds so good right now. Let me call them. Do you want anything?" He had his hand on the receiver of the in-room phone.

"You know, maybe I will have a nightcap. Will it bother

you if I do? The thing is that it relaxes me and helps in the digestion of the food, especially the rich food we shared tonight. Yes, have them bring your coffee and a bourbon, neat." He was already removing his shoes as he moved into the bathroom. "Sorry. Are you okay with that?"

"Of course."

"I'll only be a minute and then you can use it. Make yourself comfortable."

Stephen shut the bathroom door behind him. Leaning against it, he forced himself to take deep breaths, one after the other, to calm himself. He hadn't notice that his body was on edge, not until he was alone and could hear his heart pounding in his head, his ears, his temples, all warning him of his life-sustaining muscle in distress. His pills. He reached into his jacket pocket and felt for the small medicine container that he was told to carry with him always, for the rest of his life. The cool, hard plastic met his groping fingers, giving him sudden assurance that he was one pill away from "normalcy" again. The water washed the pill into his system while he moved to the toilet, sat down, and waited for relief.

On the other side of the door was his past, in the form of a man whom he did not know and did not want to know. Yet, that man was in his room with him, invited no less, and would be spending the night. He shook his head in disbelief at all that had transpired during the evening. And tomorrow. He had agreed to travel to Greece with this stranger to meet more strangers, all of whom had the strong potential of destroying him. Would this battle never end? Would he ever be left alone to live as he chose to do, as he needed to do? His head began to ache, a dull thudding behind the right temple. Not because of his malfunctioning heart but a different ache, a tightness that with every pulsing thud drove home yet one more concern, one more thing to worry about, one more threat to his existence.

And then it occurred to him. Why he hadn't entertained the thought before, he couldn't say. He was still in control. He had always been in control. He could make things happen and he could prevent things from happening. He did not have to go to Greece. No one was forcing him. He was not obligated in any way to act on his brother's wishes. He could do as he liked. To hell with his brother! To hell with them all!

Standing now, he moved to the sink and turned on the water. Rinsing his face over and over again, he suddenly felt renewed with a clarity that was blinding to him. It was the same clarity that he had experienced in the past. The times when he knew that he had to end what had begun and that had become a threat to him. As if gaining back thirty years of his life in an instant, he stood staring at his gray visage in the mirror but in his mind's eye, it reflected a middle-aged man, successful, powerful, domineering, and resourceful. No problem was a problem, he heard himself say softly. And he repeated it again and again until it became a mantra, now voiced silently. There were no questioning voices confusing him, no deep-seated doubts fighting their way to the surface of his conscience. Nothing. He knew what to do.

He heard Michael thank room service as he closed the door to the room.

"Stephen, when you're ready, the drinks are here." Michael's muffled voice spoke through the heavy wood door.

"Yes. Good. Be right with you." Breathing deeply, he opened the bathroom door. "Sorry to have taken so long. It is all yours." He moved across the room, noted where Michael had placed his overnight bag, picked up his drink, and sat down in one of the two chairs whose backs were toward the balcony door.

Michael was slowly sipping the hot liquid. "Boy, this is what the doctor ordered. If nothing else, I am waking up. God only knows how my stomach will welcome it, but it can't be any worse than what I've just been through. It's been years and years since I've felt this rotten. Oh well, it was for a good cause." He looked over to Stephen, who was smiling ever so slightly. "I mean, that you and I have had this opportunity to be together." He took another sip.

"I understand, of course. If we were younger men, the evening would still be young, but as that is not the case, I expect that, even with coffee, you must be feeling tired. I know that I am." Catching himself, he continued. "I don't mean to imply that we should be going to bed right away. Not at all. Just a comment on what I think is the truth?" He waited for Michael to agree with him.

"A bit tired, to be sure. I don't want to impose upon your kindness. Please tell me when you are ready for the lights to be out." Feeling the effects of the caffeine starting to kick in, he hoped that Stephen could stay awake a bit longer.

"I will nurse this," Stephen said, holding the glass filled with amber liquid up to Michael, "so as to lengthen the evening. Tell me about Alison." The imperative statement surprised him as much as it seemed to surprise Michael. He would need to pay better attention and maintain his control. Having said it, it was too late to retract. And perhaps he was genuinely interested in exploring the subject, but he had no time to analyze his actions since Michael responded almost immediately.

"Alison. Thanks for asking about my wife, Stephen. You took me by surprise for a minute, but I am always happy to talk about the love of my life. How much time have you got?" Clichéd and not funny, but Michael forced a half-hearted laugh to disguise his insecurity.

"Please, go on. Tell me how you met." His voice was calm, inviting, almost like the beauty of nature's brush upon the fragile petal of a tropical flower whose tiny symmetrical markings lure the innocent into the end of life.

He'd already alluded to the fact that he had been in therapy, Michael recalled. But just how detailed he wanted to get with Stephen was questionable. All that he had experienced in his life was a direct consequence of their early childhood, and to draw upon those memories at this moment in order to explain his later behaviors would negatively color the evening's conversation. He might inadvertently shut the doors that, for the moment, seemed wide open. He wasn't sure who would shut them first, however. It was too much of a risk, he decided. Given time, he was sure that they would be on more solid ground to dig deeper into their shared past.

"She was my therapist. That's how we met. I was a mess. As I told you, I had abused my body with alcohol and drugs, had been in and out of facilities that housed me, got me off of the streets, and kept me floating just above ground so that I wouldn't be a problem. Each place attempted to help me, in its own way. I know that now. But then, I thought I knew better and I ran." He paused and shook his head. "Always picked up again and the same 'help,'" he punctuated the air above his head, "was given until I found a way out again." He glanced at Stephen. Any reaction that Stephen might be having was indecipherable. He wondered if he should continue. Was he boring his brother? Disgusting him? Was he saying too much about himself and not enough about his wife, as Stephen had requested? Had he already blown it? "But Alison," he began while forcing these thoughts out of his mind. *Stay focused, you fool.* "She saved my life. Somehow she sensed something about me that I had never discovered for myself."

"Ah. Yes. She knew that you had 'self-worth.' Am I right?" Now it was Stephen's turn, whose punctuated gesture and sarcastically flavored words cut through Michael's thoughts, sharper than a butcher's blade so that the cut was swift and clean.

Michael recovered quickly. "I suppose that is the bottom line, isn't it? Without it, you can be damn lost." He knew that this was true and for some odd reason, he suddenly felt superior to his brother as though he had risen to a higher plain and could see his life, all life, from a clearer perspective. Even so, he couldn't help but feel a twinge of anger with Stephen for having made light of his revelations. Ignoring his anger, he continued. "To make a long story short, she found ways that helped me to climb out of the darkness that I had been wallowing in for so long. And in my doing so, we grew closer to one another and, as they say, the rest is history." He would never tell his brother about the accident and how that incident bound them together. And he would never tell him about Alison's reticence about him making this trip. He owed more to her than to his brother. This realization had been affirmed by his brother's sarcasm.

Stephen's glass was almost empty, and Michael inwardly

remarked that his "nursing" the drink meant nothing. It wouldn't surprise him if Stephen suggested another round of nightcaps.

"Tell me this, Michael. Does your Alison know anything about us?" He had listened to his brother's answer to his question while letting the liquid gold warm him through. He was aware that he was becoming more relaxed now, his thoughts flowing fluidly in a premeditated direction. Still in control, he thought.

"She is my wife, Stephen. She knows I am here, with you." He wasn't answering his brother directly, he knew. Not with the answers Michael knew that he wanted to hear. What harm would it do to give him something of the truth? But he would be careful, remembering Alison's concerns. "I have told her about our parents, Stephen, and about our time with them. Yes, she knows that both of our young lives were hell because of them. And I can't speak for you but as for me, I lived in that hell until I met my wife. Did I tell her all the details, those I could remember? No, not all, but enough so that I could find my way out. She helped lead me out, Stephen, and for that I will be eternally grateful." He needed to stop. The rush of words that poured from him were defensive, he realized. He did not need to defend himself in front of his brother.

"I only ask because I will be meeting her tomorrow. I will feel more at ease in her presence knowing what she knows about me, about us. You do understand, don't you?" He waited for Michael to agree with him while emptying the glass and placing it on the small table between them. He had enjoyed his brother's defensive move.

"Yes, I understand." He didn't. Not really. If Stephen had cared about Michael, about his life and those now in it, why hadn't he responded to Michael's attempts in the past to contact him? Why hadn't he been the first one to seek a reunion? And what did it matter that Alison had been privy to the brothers' past? He knew his wife well enough to know that she would never reveal to anyone, including his brother, all that he had confided in her. Stephen's comments made him uncomfortable and he wished he hadn't said anything. The higher plain upon which he had momentarily enjoyed solid footing now seemed to be eroding under his feet.

"So, that is good. I look forward to meeting her." Stephen stood and moved to the phone. "Another? Perhaps you should stop drinking the coffee. It will keep you awake, you know. Let me order you a nightcap. You can join me in my final one for the evening. It will help you sleep. May I?" He held the receiver in the air, waiting patiently for Michael's response.

"No, not another of anything." He raised his right hand in the air as if trying to halt an oncoming freight train. "I am still feeling the effects of the evening. As a matter of fact, some fresh air would do me good." The thought of anything else entering his system at this late hour added to the rising nausea, once again, that he had thought had ended earlier.

"Just a moment, then." Stephen dialed and turning away from Michael, ordered two bourbons. He turned to see Michael rushing to the bathroom, slamming the door behind him. Moving to the balcony doors, he opened them both wide, and the cool breeze blowing from the river's surface was a stark contrast to the stuffy, dulling air within the room. He imagined it consuming the room's stale air in its clean jaws. He did not move onto the balcony but deeply breathed the air and then turned as he heard the knock on the door.

Setting the two bourbons on the small table, he sat back down and waited for his brother as the muffled retching reached his ears. It was unclear to him just how much this stranger, his brother's wife, knew about him. He knew that Michael was holding back. And he knew why. Stephen could feel Michael's fear of him. That was good. That he feared him, Stephen thought. It kept the stars hanging in the firmament as they should be. But it also did not allow Stephen in, this fear. And he needed to know what this woman knew. No one, other than Michael and she, as far as he knew, had any idea about who he was, from whose loins he had sprung, and into whose monstrous grasp he had fallen. Even if she knew little, it was too much. As his thoughts continued to collide with one another, fighting for the right to be the only one that he should concentrate on, he could feel the familiar pounding beginning in his head. He didn't wait for Michael. He lifted one of the glasses to his mouth and drank deeply. The effects of the alcohol immediately soothed him. And Michael. He had betrayed Stephen. He had, in his selfishness, let someone in. Everything that Stephen had done in his own life to prevent anyone from knowing him was now for naught. Michael had innocently confirmed it. The clarity that Stephen had experienced less than an hour ago now seemed to be taking on a life of its own. It made him feel wonderfully good as he reached for another swallow from the half-emptied glass.

The bathroom door opened, and Michael gingerly moved around the bed to the dresser, where he emptied his pockets of his wallet and keys. "Do you mind if I kick off my shoes?" he asked, already in the process of doing so as he made his way to the chairs where Stephen waited for him. Stephen thought that he looked worse now than when he had stumbled into the room initially.

"How are you doing?" He was satisfied with the convincing tone of concern in his voice.

"Sorry for that." Michael indicated the direction of the bathroom with his head. "If I haven't got rid of it all, I can't imagine what is left." He hugged his stomach for a moment before sitting down. "Oh. That feels good," he almost whispered as he leaned his head back on the chair and let the cool air wash over him.

"Yes, it does. It's coming right off the river. Did you want to walk?"

"Well, it had crossed my mind, but I'm feeling a bit better, actually, and the fresh air is helping. I think that I will stay put. That is unless you wanted to venture out?"

"No, no. Not with these legs. There was a time when I would spend hours walking, but no more. Besides, as you have implied, this is pleasant." Without pausing, he changed the subject suddenly. "Remind me about this shopkeeper. His name? You said the village of... I am sorry, but I do not remember what you said." He was standing now, moving to the desktop. Bringing the complimentary notepad and pen back to the table, he sat down heavily. "This time, I will ensure that I have the information, the old-fashioned way." He held the pen over the blank paper. "His name?"

"Okay, you are one step ahead of me here. I have no idea how to pronounce it, not really. And spelling it is out of the question. However," now Michael was up and moving toward his overnight bag, "my good wife knows me too well and had me write everything down, just in case." He was smiling as he remembered her caring touch. "So, here it is. The current shopkeeper's name is A-d-r-a-s-t-o-s, first name, last name is M-e-t-a-x-a-s. Got it?" He waited for his brother to stop writing.

"The village again, please?" Stephen had not lifted the pen from the paper.

"Right. It is pronounced 'EE-ah' but spelled O-i-a. Strange one, don't you think?"

Stephen nodded. Not looking up from the paper in front of him, he asked, "I suppose you do not know the father's name, the one whom, it seems, we had both met?"

"As a matter of fact, I do have that right here." He remembered the conversation that he and Alison had had with Adrastos about his father's wishes and Adrastos's attempt to reach Stephen. Michael could only presume that in the letters he had sent, Adrastos's father's name would have been included. Perhaps, as Stephen had never responded, his desire not to have anything to do with this family made sense. Why would he remember any of their names if he had chosen to ignore them? "His father's name was Achaíkos. Sorry, A-c-h-a-i-c-u-s. I, for one, had not remembered it but had it in one of my notebooks from the original trip there. That was one of the ways I was able to find my way back there. Anyway, what other information do you need?"

Stephen had laid the pen down, torn the paper from the pad, and was folding it neatly. Placing it in his shirt pocket, he looked at Michael. "Nothing more. Thank you. Must be something from way back in my professional days. Just want to be prepared when I meet this man. First impressions and all of that, you know?" Michael watched as Stephen's hardened face, which had been kept in place most of the night, now seemed to be softening. "Tell me one thing. You must have been fairly sure that I would say yes to you. Airline tickets are not inexpensive, I know."

"I was hoping, Stephen. If you decided not to come, it still would have been worth the price of the tickets to make this connection." He was surprised by his sincerity. Now that he was beginning to feel better, everything had a different lighting to it, including his brother.

"I will pay you for them, of course." He could see Michael's physical appearance changing; a relaxed expression was taking the place of the earlier tense and uncomfortable visage. Perhaps, with a bit of convincing, he would not have to drink alone.

"If you would like, but it is not necessary. After all, none of this would be taking place had I not initiated it. It was my decision and I am happy to take care of it." Again, he marveled at his own generosity, both financially and emotionally.

"I thank you, then. Here, I ordered you a nightcap. I know, I know. You can't touch it, not after tonight. But I can assure you that sleep will come quickly and will be sound with a few sips in your belly. I have been where you are, Michael, a few times, and this is the wonder cure, I have found." He held the full, untouched glass up to Michael. "It will not hurt to try it."

Michael started to say no but found himself sliding the cool, hard glass into his grip and now in his possession, he lifted it to his mouth. He could taste the richness of the liquid before it touched his lips and its fragrance filled his head as he anticipated the first swallow. He did not hesitate but drank one and then two sips. A chill ran through his body, like a shiver that produces an unearthly pleasantness and the desire for it to repeat itself. He closed his eyes so that the darkness prevented the feeling from finding its way free.

Knowing that his brother's willpower was fragile now, Stephen did not waste time. He shifted in his chair and then leaned closer to him. "Michael. I am wondering. What do you remember of our childhood?" The question was simple and stated clearly, yet he knew that he had shattered Michael's contentment when he watched his brother's eyes open, a frown appearing above them as he focused on Stephen.

Michael, without hesitation, brought the glass to his mouth again, but this time swallowed the remaining contents before responding. He couldn't make out the words that were forming somewhere deep within his mind, but he identified an urgency about them that demanded that they be recognized. His brother was waiting for his response, sitting across from him, curious. No. Not curious. Interrogating. He was delving into Michael's thoughts. Michael could feel him as he imagined his brother's long, aging, sinewy fingers reaching deep while attempting to untangle the overgrown roots of his memories. Whose voice was he hearing? The urgency grew but the voice remained distant, garbled, distressed.

"I only mean that you were the older one. My memories are limited, I am sure. Now that we have this time together, I would like to know what you remember. If they are the same memories that I have. I assume that you have already shared them aloud with your therapist... your wife, forgive me. It should not be so hard to share them with your brother, I would think. Shall I start if that would help you?"

Michael could feel himself being dragged into his brother's grasp. Stephen's voice, calm, soothing, and reassuring, washed over him from head to toe. It was louder than the voice in his head but softer somehow. He lifted the glass to his mouth, only to find a drip left that rested on the very edge of the glass. He licked it and let it rest on the surface of his tongue.

"Shall I order us each one more?" Stephen was watching his brother slide deeper under the influence. Michael nodded, and he heard his brother's voice speaking to someone on the phone. It did not register with him that Stephen had only ordered one and not two.

"So, I will tell you what I remember, Michael." Stephen was still standing, moving slowly around the room. He would be careful to remain on the surface; to recall only the inconsequential details of a four-year-old's memory, those that were inviting to a listener whose own memories were similar. A safe place to begin, and for him, to end. He would then sit back and let his big brother continue into the darkness, all the while revealing to Stephen the depth of their darkness that Michael had carelessly shared with his wife.

"I have vague memories of very tall trees and of our bedroom. I remember the underside of the bed, the slats that kept the mattress in place. They seemed so wide and strong over my head. Funny, that memory." Stephen paused for effect. He did not look toward Michael but kept moving back and forth through the room. "But the trees, Michael. You and me. I remember running through the forest of trees. I would be running behind you, but you would never be out of my sight. You remember that, don't you?"

Michael half nodded as his brother's voice continued. "Didn't we play airplanes? I vaguely remember something about airplanes?" He had moved closer to Michael now. The knock on the door startled both of them.

Stephen laid the fresh drink in the center of the table. Michael, without thinking, reached for it and slid it closer to him.

"Yes, airplanes. We pretended to be airplanes." The memory was clear.

"You know, I don't remember much else. Well, that's not really true, now that I think about it. I can't remember our mother's face, but I do remember her hands. I can see them now as clearly as I did over sixty years ago. Always with some kind of rag in them." He would go no farther. Enough had been said. He moved to the empty chair and sat down. It was Michael's turn. Stephen had opened the doors a crack or two, enough, he hoped, that Michael would fill in the gaps. And beyond.

"You really don't remember anything more?" He hadn't meant to sound disbelieving, but he had. How could Stephen not remember? Had he blocked it all out or was being four years old then the best thing that could have happened to him?

"I really don't recall. Chalk it up to an old brain, perhaps. But then I didn't recall even in my younger years." And here he lied. "I tried to remember, tried to see my mother's face, my father's, to see more than the underside of a bed, the place that held all of those trees, to see you more clearly." He watched as Michael sat up straighter in the chair, reaching for the glass. "I never sought anyone to help me see. Not like you."

"I never sought it. I told you that. I had no choice but to face it. And I am glad that I did. I can't believe that you don't remember what happened to us, Stephen. Nothing?" He swallowed the drink. Was it going to be left up to him?

"Sorry, I just don't. Please don't misinterpret what I am about to say, but I find it interesting that your wife knows more about my past than I do. So, I will ask you again. What have you told her about me, about us? You see how in the dark I am?"

"Stephen, she knows about our father's abuse of us and of our mother. All right? She knows that he was a bully, a drunk, a monster of a husband and father, and a child abuser. She knows that we were lucky to make it out of there with our lives. There is no point in going into details if you don't even remember what I just told you. You are better off leaving it all alone. And I'm better off not having to repeat it." He was angry now. Angry that his brother had enticed him even this far. And now he recognized the distant voice. Alison's. He told himself to pay attention. To heed her.

"I am not so sure that I am better off, Michael. Do you have any idea what it has been like not knowing where I came from? So many people came into and left our lives when we were growing up. I remember that you were there and then you were gone. I don't remember names, places. Just that I knew no one, not really. The only person that I knew was you." His intent had been to belittle Michael. To shame him into defending himself, thus revealing everything he had shared with his wife, but as he spoke, he suddenly realized that what he was saying to his brother was the truth coming from somewhere deep inside, untapped until now. "And I do remember pain, Michael. So much pain. Do you remember?" He was so close to Michael now that the alcohol on his breath sickened Michael as it invaded his space. "Did you tell her about the pain?"

Shocked by his brother's sudden emotional outburst, he

did not know how to respond. This was not going as planned. Somehow, Stephen had manipulated him, he realized, and there was no clear path leading him to safety. "I...I...yes, I told her, Stephen. She knows what he put us through. What he put our mother through, what he..."

Stephen's voice interrupted him. "I used to have this dream, sometimes. I will call it a dream because I don't know what else to call it. The funny thing is that I dreamt it while wide awake. I never knew when it would come and, when it did, it paralyzed me, Michael." His voice was calmer and uncomfortably soothing as Michael found himself once again drawn to his brother. "Her eyes. I would see her eyes staring right at me. But the strange thing is that they were not side by side horizontally but vertical in their positioning, as if one was resting above the other." Sensing his brother's voice rising in pitch, Michael intuitively prepared himself. "And they were red, a crimson kind of red, not the irises but the whole eyeball, each one was this red..." He paused as if deep in thought. "Well..." The pitch diminished suddenly. "That's all I saw. Were those our mother's eyes, Michael?"

God! Give me a way out of this! He had never wanted to go back there, not after closing the book on it with Alison. But he felt himself being pushed closer than he had ever been before. He knew why, and he knew that Stephen knew what he was doing. It hadn't been easy telling Alison and had felt very real at the time, but this was different. He was going back there with the only other person in the world who had experienced the horrors he thought he had left behind. He was going back into the darkness with the only person in the world with whom he had hung there, small and frightened, his brother even smaller and more frightened but assured by his presence, the only person whom he had ever betrayed.

"There is so much that I don't know that she does. Tell me, Michael. Tell me. Were those my mother's eyes?" Startled by his brother's hand upon his arm as it rested on the table caressing his drink, Michael drew away from Stephen's grasp. He stood quickly, spilling the drink onto the floor at his feet. "I think you owe me an answer."

"I don't know what you saw, but our mother died by his hand, Stephen. He killed our mother, he killed her, he killed…" Alison stood in front of him, her eyes pleading with him to stop. He reached his arms out in front of him as if to push her away, only to foolishly gesture into thin air.

Stephen observed his brother's farther descent into a hell of his own making and wasted no time. "Go on, Michael. What happened to our father? You have to finish what you have started. What does she know about our father?" Controlling his sudden urge to shake his brother until all of the unknown spilled out of him, Stephen moved closer to stand in front of Michael, in the place where Alison had just stood.

Without hesitating, the words sprung forth. "I killed our father. I hit him over and over again, Stephen, until he was still. You never saw his eyes, but I did. Wide open and staring up to the sky, questioning me. Questioning why I had so much hatred for him that I would end his life. I can still see his eyes, Stephen. He had intended on killing me first, but I killed him and came back for you. But you were gone. All I saw was an ambulance drive off down our driveway into the night."

"So that is all she knows? That our father killed our mother and that you killed our father? And she knows about our pain, our suffering?" She knew so much, Stephen thought. He did not believe for a moment that there wasn't more that she was privy to and that he would never learn. "Well?"

Michael knew that Stephen was angry just as he had been, and a fear seized him. He knew that he had lost control. It had happened so quickly. He had been aware that he was slipping. He could blame it on the alcohol, the second drink, or was it the third? *God! What a fool!* Once again, Stephen was attacking him, breathing down his neck, insistent and relentless.

"Yes, Stephen, yes." He fought through his fear, a fear of his brother now as well as a fear that he was lost. "She knows no more than you do now. Please, can we stop this?" A faint memory of pleading for the pain to cease crept forward. "There is no point in doing any of this. Please, let's just put it to rest."

He turned and bent down to pick up the glass.

"You are right, Michael. I apologize."

Michael stood up and placing the glass on the table, turned to his brother. As if the heaviness of the last hour had instantly dissipated, Michael felt that he could once again breathe. His brother's changed expression indicated the same to him.

"No need. We both need to step back from the brink, my brother." The casualness of this statement did not sit well with him, but the words had already been spoken and the inference made clear. Michael tried to recover. "What I mean is that I understand your need to know. I knew that coming here. What I didn't realize was that I would react as I did. And, if truth be told, perhaps you were not prepared for your reaction either? Like I said earlier this evening, we need time." He watched Stephen's face for any sign of conciliation. None appeared. But unafraid now and thankful that the worst was over, he went on. "Maybe we just need to start over at our tender, youthful ages, and enjoy what we have left of our lives whether that means we choose to be a part of each other's or not. I will understand your decision. And tomorrow we will have a chance to start." Looking down at his watch, he was shocked to see that it was well past one in the morning.

About to suggest that they both needed their rest, Stephen walked toward the balcony doors. "I need some air." He entered the balcony and turned to Michael. "Do you good to join me."

Michael agreed. He owed his body a bit of love after having deluged it with poisons. A few deep breaths of fresh air couldn't hurt. Joining his brother on the balcony, he realized that he hadn't noticed the view. It was beautiful. The lights from the streetlamps dimly lit the pavement, casting halos of mustard-yellow light onto the darkened surface below. Notre Dame's spotlights twinkled just in the distance, while the clear night sky served as a backdrop for its own constellation's light show. For some reason, he thought, the stars seemed so bright on this side of the world. "It's quite something, isn't it?"

Stephen had moved from one side of the balcony to the other. "Yes. That is why I always ask for this room when I come to the city." He moved forward to stand by his brother's side. Gently leaning on the railing, he pointed to his right. "Do you see that light in the distance? The bright one?"

Michael leaned over the railing, trying to follow the angle of Stephen's arm as he stood next to him. "What am I looking at? There are a lot of bright lights out there. Where is it again?" He stepped behind Stephen and moved to the farthest corner of the balcony to get a better view. "Show me again, please."

"Sorry. Right over there. If you look north, you will see it. It stands out among all the rest. You don't see it?"

Michael could see nothing that was being described to him as he vainly sought out the bright light. He knew that Stephen was now standing behind him and felt embarrassed that he was unable to see what his little brother saw.

"There, Michael. Keep looking. It is a famous marker that lights up the night skies. I don't understand why you can't make it out." Stephen had moved from behind Michael and had taken a couple of steps to the side of the balcony.

Michael sensed his brother's movement and did the same, leaning against the railing all the while.

"Okay. I give up. I'm going to have to take your word for it." As he turned from the corner railing, his weight still upon it, he suddenly felt his brother's opened hands upon his chest, striking with such intensity that he felt the wind knocked out of him as he struggled to regain his balance. And then another strike, this time with an unnatural force that lifted him slightly off the ground so that regaining balance was not an option now. He felt the hard iron railing slam into the middle of his back, pain shooting up and across it in all directions; a second, heavier vibration of iron struck against his body as the unidentifiable sound of a thud, then another, reached his ears, the iron now giving way as the weight of his upper body turned him upside down, his legs being lifted by an unseen force that, in doing so, released his whole body to the darkness below.

Breathing heavily, the exertion of his body taking its hold

on him now, Stephen closed the balcony doors behind him, and moved slowly to the phone, pulling down the cuffs of his sleeves and tucking in the loose shirt that had been released from the constraints of his belt. Remembering his brother's overnight bag, he picked it up, unsnapped the opening, and emptied the contents onto the bed. The tickets lay under a change of clothes that he quickly stuffed back into the bag. With the tickets in hand, he slipped them into his pants pocket. Satisfied that each step thus far was completed, he lifted the receiver and dialed the desk to report an accident.

Chapter 18

He heard the hysteria in her voice as he told the desk clerk what had just happened. Moments later, alone in the elevator as it descended ten floors, Stephen used the time to prepare himself. As the doors opened to the lobby, he took a long, deep breath and moved as quickly as he could to the street. A small group of people had already surrounded Michael's body before Stephen could get there. He heard distant sirens quickly approaching the hotel. A gendarme was now moving the curious away from Michael, as a second stood over his brother's body, all the while talking to someone on his radio.

"Let me through, let me through!" he screamed at the onlookers while shoving against them. "Let me through!" The gendarme heard his yelling and moved toward Stephen.

"*Non, monsieur. Arretez! Arretez! Maintenant !* He had grabbed both of Stephen's arms and forced him to stop.

"*Non, non! Vous ne comprendez pas! S'il vous plait. Il est mon frère.* Oh my God! Michael!" he cried, and he collapsed in the arms of the gendarme.

Stephen explained to the detective at the station what had happened on the tenth-floor balcony: that his brother had had too much to drink, that he had wanted to get some fresh air, that they had both been on the balcony when Michael leaned too far over against the loose railing. He blamed himself repeatedly as he gave his statement. He had meant to report the loose railing on his last visit but had completely forgotten. It wasn't until he turned to see his brother's body falling away from the balcony that it even occurred to him. If only he had remembered! The detective taking his statement assured him that he was not to blame. He had silently noted that Stephen was on the elderly side, not very sure on his feet, and might be suffering from memory loss. He was not all that surprised that he had forgotten.

Sensing the detective's support, Stephen made sure to reveal that it was all the more tragic as the brothers had just spent the evening together, after almost sixty years apart, over a wonderful dinner and were planning on traveling together tomorrow morning. Tickets had been purchased and he was excited to meet his brother's wife, who was awaiting their arrival in Greece. He then became increasingly upset in front of the detective, worried about his brother's wife and what would happen now. He had no idea where in Greece they were going, no address. He wanted to make the trip anyway, to personally meet and speak with his brother's wife. Did the detectives retrieve any of Michael's personal possessions? Perhaps a wallet or something with the information that Stephen needed? He was told that the police were holding any possessions until the next of kin picked them up. In this case, as he was his brother, they would be released to him. He was also reassured that their department would contact the wife for him. What he chose to do after that was his own business. The detective was sure that, in the days to follow, Stephen would have enough to deal with as it was. He was reassured, however, after taking witness accounts of those in the restaurant tonight and checking the room service log, that Mr. Bingham had been inebriated. An autopsy would support this, he was sure. He was also told that there had been a complaint made by another customer to the hotel management about the loosened railing on that balcony just days before this incident. For whatever reason, there had been no follow-through. The hotel would be held accountable.

As Stephen entered the taxi to go back to the hotel, he had already begun planning what he would say to this Alison, how he would console her and speak nothing but platitudes about his lost brother, her dead husband. He would be sure to give her Michael's personal items that he had collected from the police. On his body he had carried a watch whose worn leather strap had seen better days, a wallet that contained some cash, one credit card, and some loose change. He had searched through the wallet for Alison's contact number and had found an "In Case of Emergency" card tucked down in the billfold that had obviously been created by Michael or perhaps his wife, its laminated size a fraction of an inch too large on all four sides to fit into the standard wallet pockets. That didn't matter, as it contained the needed details. Both of their cell numbers, a home number, doctors' names and numbers, blood types, and any allergy considerations. Michael's small overnight bag contained clothing, none of which he could imagine Alison wanting back, but he would be sure to hand it over to her. What he really needed he had already retrieved from Michael's overnight bag: two airline tickets to Greece, specifically, Santorini, with a connection in Athens. Michael must have been confident that his long-lost brother would agree to come back with him, Stephen thought.

Watching the almost vacant early-dawn streets of Paris rush by him as he stared out of the passenger window, he found himself lost in thought. He didn't hear the driver tell him that they had arrived. Stephen had not noticed the car slowing down, the scenery changing.

"Monsieur, we are at the hotel."

Hearing the stranger's voice break through his thoughts, he quickly paid the fare and let the hotel bellhop open the door for him. The reality of the last few hours struck him hard as he heard the bellhop's young voice extend his and the hotel's deepest sympathies and their request to please accept their condolences. Ah, yes. The sympathy would suffocate him, he noted, preparing himself for more of it as he passed through the double doors.

Safe now in the room, having managed to avoid the staff in the lobby as they were busy registering arriving guests, he gathered his personal items. He was not alone, however. A detective was taking notes as he stood on the balcony.

"*Excusez-moi, monsieur.* I am sorry for your loss. I am just finishing here. Be gone in a moment." He turned back to his note-taking.

Stephen closed his bag and took a second look in all the drawers, the bathroom, and the closet, now satisfied that he hadn't left anything behind. Shifting the lighter of the two bags, Michael's, into his left hand so that he felt properly balanced, he left the room without saying a word to the man on the balcony.

"Are you sure that you want to check out now, *monsieur?* We have already secured our best room for you for the rest of your stay." The desk clerk, he thought, had tears in her eyes. So young, so sweet, so naïve, he thought.

"Thank you, but there is no need. I intend to keep our…my flight to Greece, which leaves in less than four hours." He checked his watch as he said this. It was now six a.m. He was anxious to leave. "You have been very kind, but I am ready to settle my bill, please." He reached in his coat pocket for his wallet.

"Oh, *non,* Monsieur Bingham. You are to pay nothing. The hotel's compliments and sincere condolences are extended to you and your family." Now he was sure that the tears were there as he watched her dab her cheeks with a tissue.

"*Merci, merci, mademoiselle.*" He said nothing more as he folded the statement and shoved it in his pants pocket. Asking the bellhop to hail a taxi for him, he stood on the sidewalk, bags in hand, waiting for the cab to appear. Once inside and settled into the worn seat, he felt the beginnings of a smile form and confirmed its presence as he saw his reflection in the Plexiglas divider of the taxi. About to rid himself of it because of his own paranoia that the driver might know about the last hours and would note the unusual expression of one who had just suffered a great and tragic loss, it remained in place as the driver slid the glass to one side and Stephen heard him say, "Such a beautiful day it will be, monsieur. Where can I take you on such a glorious morning?"

"To Charles de Gaulle, Air France, *s'il vous plait.* I have a ten o'clock departure, *monsieur. Merci.*" He noted the driver's quizzical look reflected in the rearview mirror as he started the engine.

"I hope that you have enjoyed your visit in our beautiful city. I can see that you have, as no one leaves our city without a smile on his face." He laughed loudly and sincerely as he drove away from the hotel and into the awakening streets of Paris.

Chapter 19

Reaching for the alarm, she knocked over the glass of water that she had set on the bedside table before turning out the lights, having downed an extra amount of antacid, just to be on the safe side. The liquid running over her hand startled her, bringing her closer to an awakening that her body was not ready for. The ringing, though, did not stop as she fussed with the radio alarm, poking, pushing, and sliding every button she could feel in the darkened room. She forced herself to prop her sleep-saturated body up on one arm to reach the bedside light's switch. Although it had seemed a poor reading light last night, it now blinded her vision for a moment. It was not the alarm, she realized, but the phone in the room. An old-fashioned ring, not unlike one of the choices she had on her cell, she thought. She threw the covers off and hurried to the phone. How long it had been ringing, she couldn't say, but it might be Michael and she couldn't miss his call. Lifting the receiver to her ear, she managed to produce as bright a greeting as she could, given the ungodly hour of the morning. She had checked the clock twice in her battle with it, once not believing what she saw and then, upon a closer look, angered by the red digital numbers showing it was 5 a.m.

"Hello?" The voice was not Michael's and she could not hide her disappointment. The male voice was French, the accent strong as he introduced himself to her in broken English. "Madame Bingham?"

"*Oui,* yes?"

"Please, pardon this interruption. It is early, I know. My name is Detective Claude Sagan of the Paris Police Department."

She needed to sit down. He continued speaking, but she did not comprehend any of what he was saying. Collapsing onto the floor, she held the receiver tightly to her ear, unaware of the sharp pains that its hard plastic was causing to her flesh. Trying to catch her breath as each one now, shallow, came rapidly, she suddenly felt her whole body rebelling against any likelihood of regaining her composure. His words poured over her as if someone from a great height had tipped a barrel full of hot liquid directly on her. The pain was unbearable, the intensity of its impact crushing her, holding her down, preventing her from fighting her way out of its torrent while she struggled for breath. She dropped the receiver and it dangled next to her, swinging back and forth, a slowing rhythmic beat against the table, and then brushed her shoulder as if gently tapping her to remind her that it was still there. She thought she heard his name, only to hear it once again, this time loudly and clearly.

"Monsieur Stephen Bingham."

Something about him coming to see her. Michael's possessions? Lifting the receiver to her ear, she wanted to say something to this stranger on the other end who had just announced the end of her life. But her throat was constricted, aching, and the sobs that had come on so suddenly could not be controlled.

Huddled on the floor, exhausted and disoriented, Alison opened her eyes. The carpet had served as a bed, leaving imprints of its worn threads on her face and arms. As she lay on her side, she was convinced that she had fallen through the rabbit hole. The room, from this angle and perspective, was a jungle of tall beige woolen stalks that seemed to go on for miles in all directions. She would never find her way out, she thought. Somewhere in the distance, she could hear the guns booming; the enemy was approaching and, panicking, she pulled herself up into the tightest of balls so that she would not be found. *Hold still! Don't breathe! Hide!* The booming became louder and more frequent as she lay there, sickened with fear, every part of her body throbbing in pain. Voices were yelling at her, calling her by name. How did they know who she was? What did they want from her? What had she done? And then it was too late. They had found her and were looming over her, crouching next to her. She closed her eyes, praying that she would never have to open them again.

"My God, my God, Alison. It is all right. It will be all right." Artemidoros's voice was soft and slow and she sensed his flesh against hers. "Alison? Here, let me help you." He was sitting next her now, his arms lifting her upper body off the floor so that she sensed her body sagging against his. "I am so sorry. I am so sorry." Was he rocking her? The sensation of gentle movement, as if she were a baby in her mother's arms, was soothing and welcoming. "I am here. I am here." And then his words were foreign to her as Artemidoros, in his mother tongue, and as his own mother had taught him to, prayed softly. "O Christ, who alone art our defender: visit and heal Thy suffering servants, delivering them from sickness and grievous pains. Raise them up that they may sing to Thee and praise Thee without ceasing, through the prayers of Theotokos. O Thou Who alone lovest mankind. Amen."

These words, whispered into the tangles of her hair, somehow found their way to her aching heart.

Chapter 20

The Metaxas brothers spoke to one another shortly after Artemidoros received the call from Paris. He made certain to let Adrastos know of the tragic accident as soon as possible. Still stunned by the news, and even more so that they had his number and thought to call him, he could not take his mind off Alison— how he found her in her room, how distraught she must have been all alone when she got the call and what would become of her now. How could he help her?

The detective told Artemidoros that he found Madame Bingham's cell number, the hotel number, and the private number that he was now calling on in Monsieur Bingham's possessions. When he called her cell, she did not answer, and he did not want to leave a message. Certainly not in this case, of course. That would be unacceptable.

He then called the hotel and was connected to her room by the front desk. His concern was that she did not respond to him as he gave her the terrible news. In fact, it sounded as if she dropped the receiver. He asked Artemidoros to check on her and to let him know about her welfare. It bothered him, he said, to give such information over the phone, impersonal as it was. It was not the way he liked to operate. But he had no choice.

Artemidoros let him know that he understood and been anxious to end the call so that he could go to Alison. He started to thank him for contacting him when the detective interrupted him with "one more concern." He was told that Monsieur Bingham's brother, Monsieur Stephen Bingham, would be arriving shortly and that he would have Michael's possessions with him. If he could make sure that Madame Bingham was in receipt of her husband's belongings, they would be most grateful.

Of course, he would see to this. And then Artemidoros remembered that Adrastos was holding the inheritance gift for Stephen. It had been such a concern of theirs, the brothers, that their father's wishes were respected, but now it seemed diminished by the current event in all their lives. Michael had meant so much to their father, as did Stephen and his wife. To lose any one of them was unthinkable, considering the unlikelihood that their individual life journeys had now found their way to the Metaxases' doorstep.

Chapter 21

Somehow, they had been informed of Stephen's loss but not the circumstances. Only that the passenger in seat 5A had just lost his brother the day before and was returning to Oia to be with family. The details and their accuracy were not important, it seemed.

He took offense that his privacy had been tampered with, but he repeatedly reminded himself not to reveal this. In fact, he had a choice in the matter. He could play the part of the grieving brother, which left a bad taste in his mouth, or he could remain silent, withdrawn, only nodding when necessary and managing a mumbled "thank you" should anyone approach him with condolences.

He chose the latter, of course, and was relieved that each of the two stewardesses addressed him only once regarding his loss and did not annoy him with unnecessary or unwanted attention. He had slept for a little while, but upon waking could not ignore the seething anger somewhere down deep that someone had betrayed him.

As the plane made its final descent into Athens, the reality of this trip struck him unexpectedly. He was about to meet his brother's wife, a grieving woman who would need to rely upon him for everything, he was sure. After all, she had been on a trip far from home in a strange place when tragedy struck. He would be expected to take his brother's place, only insofar as certain responsibilities were concerned, of course. He would need to be a gentleman in this new theater of life that he was about to enter.

On a positive note, sighing with some relief as he watched the ground drawing closer and closer, the people he was about to meet in the next few hours were perfect strangers to him, no matter what the past connections to them had been. It would not be difficult, he reassured himself, for them to remain so. He would, though, need to take care of the necessary business of meeting this woman and arranging for her safe return to the States. Rehearsing the interaction that he would most likely have to engage in with her, he knew that he could play his part well. In front of her, he would have no choice. After all, Michael was his brother, no matter how separate their lives had been. She would expect no less, he was sure. The art of grieving was familiar to him.

There was also the other part of the trip that he had, at one point, considered ignoring completely, just as he had done when the written communications found their way to his door. But this time, the sticking point would be his brother's wife. Surely, she must be aware of Michael's reason for coming to Stephen in the first place? It would stand to reason that she had met this Metaxas fellow, as Michael would have made a point of introducing his wife to him. It would be just his luck that, even in her current state, she would make sure that Stephen carried out Michael's and the deceased Greek's wishes. There was no avoiding the inevitable. Not if he wanted to return to the comforts of his own home free of any further "family" connections. He found himself longing for his home now, its simple comforts, quiet, and solitude. He would even welcome the persistence of the young French boy and was surprised to, momentarily, contemplate what awaited him in his front yard. Stephen remembered his admonishment to Jean-Pierre— "No rocks"—and he expected him to keep to his word.

"Pardon me, sir, but do you mind?" The man was half standing, half leaning over Stephen. "Do you mind?"

Stephen looked up to see a young man indicating with his hand toward the aisle. The seats in the forward section of the plane were almost vacant, with the exception of one or two passengers still struggling to organize the various belongings that they had strewn about their area.

"Oh, I am sorry. Of course, of course." He unbuckled his belt, reached into the seat pocket in front of him just to be sure he had not placed anything in it, and then slowly unbent his body into a standing position, all the while grabbing onto the back of the seat in front of him and the arm of his own seat so as not to fall back down. Gingerly stepping into the aisle to free the eager passenger from his confinement, he thought he heard a "thank you" from the young man, but in turning to say "you're welcome," he only saw his right hand extended in the air just at shoulder height as it displayed the universal gesture that even Stephen could interpret. *Smartass,* Stephen mumbled to himself as he reached into the overhead to retrieve his and Michael's small carry-ons.

The ferry ride to Santorini revived him as he took in the beauty of the surrounding area. Standing on the deck all the way over, holding tightly to the railing, he breathed deeply the saltwater air, and the cool breezes seemed to penetrate his fatigued and stressed body. The warmth of the afternoon sun caressed his head and wrapped its healing heat around what little of his exposed skin it could find. He leaned his head back as if to let the sun's rays smother his face. There was something about the heat, the water, the motion of the craft cutting its way through the sea. It was comfortable, this gentle rocking as the ferry moved through the South Aegean waters.

He gave the driver of the small car the name of the hotel. Within minutes, he was left standing in front of the building as he watched the mini vehicle turn down one of the many narrow roadways winding through the village. He took a moment to take in his surroundings and was taken aback by the beauty of the architecture, the cleanliness of the area, and the glimpses of the blue sea that peeked through the spaces between the gleaming white buildings whose aqua roofs blended into the pristine skies above. He had not expected such sights, or had he just not noticed the first time? Turning to the entrance of the hotel, the reality of his visit loomed in front of him. Readjusting the bags in his hands, he opened the door and walked directly to the front desk. He would need to concentrate now on what had to be accomplished. "Stay focused," he thought he heard himself say aloud and looked around to make sure that no one had heard him. The few people in the lobby were not paying any attention to him, he noticed.

The young woman behind the desk was on the phone

when he approached her. She looked up at him and smiled, mouthing the words, "Just a moment, please." He nodded in confirmation and set his bags on the floor next to him.

"Good afternoon. Welcome. How may I help you?" No more than twenty-five, he guessed. Was it a universal rule that hotel desk clerks had to be young and beautiful?

"Yes, thank you. I wonder if Mr. Metaxas is available?" He had debated whether to see the manager before seeing Michael's wife. It made more sense to him to speak with the man first. He would be less emotional, detached even, than she would be, of course. And he would be able to fill Stephen in on any background information that might be necessary to have before making connections with the wife. After all, the original reason for coming here did not involve her, not really. It was really between the men, and the sooner he could finish the business between them, the better. Dealing with the wife would involve only practical matters, nothing that he could not handle with ease no matter what her emotional state might be.

"Yes, I believe he is. May I have your name?" She held a pen ready to write.

"If you would let him know that Stephen Bingham is here to see him, I would appreciate it. He is expecting me." He watched as her hand stopped in mid-writing, then began again.

"Of course." She did not look at him when she said this. "I will be a moment." He watched her as she turned from the desk and headed through a passageway.

Suddenly feeling tired, his legs, he realized, the source of his fatigue, he looked around for a place to sit but then thought better of it. Once down, he knew that getting up would be even more difficult and painful. Better to remain right where he was. At least he had the counter's edge to hold onto and lean against.

"Mr. Bingham. Hello." Artemidoros extended his hand, which Stephen clutched in greeting and, for a moment, used to stabilize his body as he released it from the security of the counter. "Please accept my deepest sympathies in the loss of your brother. I am so sorry." His words slowly swirled about Stephen as if they were feathers gently riding the invisible air currents until each one found its way to the ground.

"Thank you." He was happy with the self-control that he consciously kept in the forefront of his interactions. "I am assuming that you and I have some business still to take care of and that you will take the lead here in making sure that it is accomplished?" He was surprised by the ease with which the words fell into place; after all these years, had he still left within him the skills he had possessed and employed so successfully in the business world? Gaining confidence with each passing minute, he did not wait for any response. He could not afford to. "I am aware that Mrs. Bingham is a guest here and I will need to see her. However, I would like to take care of our business first." Now he waited. The man standing in front of him had not lost his sympathetic expression. In fact, it began to disturb Stephen that this stranger to him could appear so caring. Frustration was growing within him as he resented this man and all that he represented. An obstacle. Yet one more.

"I understand. But I must tell you that I am worried about Mrs. Bingham. The news has devastated her. It might help if you saw her sooner rather than later. This is only my suggestion."

Had he taken a step closer to Stephen? Was he reaching out to take his arm? Taking a step back and away from him, Stephen remained outwardly calm. *A gentleman at all costs,* he reminded himself. "Your concern is appreciated. However, I will want to give her all of my attention and to make all the necessary arrangements needed then. So, to take care of our business first will afford me the time needed to devote to Mrs. Bingham. I am sure you can understand this?" Even if he couldn't, it was of no concern to Stephen. He had determined that he would do just as he wanted to do, with or without this stranger.

"Of course. Perhaps you have a good point. Will you be staying with us tonight? I can provide for you a comfortable room at no cost to you. It is the least I can do considering the circumstances."

"Considering the lateness of the day, I will take you up on your generous offer. Thank you."

"And then tomorrow, we will go to my brother's shop to complete our business."

"No, not tomorrow. I would like to go today. Now. No need to wait. Besides, I will need tomorrow to attend to Mrs. Bingham. So, if you will let me know how to find your brother's shop, I will be on my way." Stephen noted the confusion in the manager's face.

"I...I...Do you mind if I take you there? I had thought that you would want me to do that for you. I can introduce you to my brother properly, and perhaps help you in answering any questions you may have. I am sorry if I am being presumptuous."

Stephen was enjoying this game and he was satisfied that he was still ahead. "There really is no need for you to take the time away from your establishment, but I see no other reason for you not accompanying me. It is most kind of you to do so."

"Good, good. Just give me a few moments. I will contact Adrastos, my brother, that we are on our way. Can I offer you something to drink or eat before we go?"

"Some water, please. That is all." This time he would sit down, just for a moment, before the next act.

Chapter 22

It would have been an easy walk for a man younger than himself, he thought, watching the buildings pass by as Artemidoros slowly drove through the village toward his brother's shop. A short distance by car, hardly worth the gas, but he'd had no choice. His legs, in fact, his whole body was complaining to him, reminding him that this day was coming to an end. And his companion for the moment was wise enough not to suggest anything but the car. The conversation was limited, thankfully, so that Artemidoros's only contribution was something about Michael—how he had enjoyed meeting him and his wife, a beautiful couple, so tragic an ending for them, for everyone, he was sure, who knew him. Stephen had responded with something akin to a grunt meant to affirm. From that point on, silence until Artemidoros turned the final corner and pulled the tiny car into a space in front of the shop.

"So, we are here. My brother's shop. Is it as you remembered it?" He was opening the door for Stephen, whose legs had begun to cramp somewhere between the hotel and their destination. Such a short distance, but they were unhappy about the limited space the passenger side provided, for it did not allow them to stretch out. He was not so sure that getting out of the car would be all that easy and reached for the edge of the roof with his left hand to give him some support. "Here, let me help you." Artemidoros reached in to Stephen, who changed his tactic and let his body's weight rely on the younger man's strength.

"Thank you." Now out of the tiny prison and standing on his own two feet, he waited a moment before moving forward. As if mentally preparing himself for the first two steps, he looked down at his feet and willed them forward. A shooting pain shot up one leg and then the other as he moved across the walk toward the door. And then it was gone. As if his legs were remembering their youth and what it felt like then to move without giving it a second thought, he took the lead and entered the shop as Artemidoros held the door for him.

From the late-afternoon sun's light into the darkened room before him, Stephen was suddenly blind. He could make out only vague images surrounding him. He stayed where he was as he felt Artemidoros move from behind him to his side and then farther into the darkness.

"Yes, I know. It takes a minute for the eyes to adjust. He keeps it this way so that it stays cool in here during the day. I have had no luck in convincing him that some modern lighting and air conditioning would be more attractive to his customers. The old ways are hard to leave behind, I think. Just a moment, please. I will let him know we are here."

Stephen watched him move into the shadows as he tried to focus on the images right in front of him. Slowly now, he began to make out the edges of display tables, then the items upon each one of them. A clutter, he thought. A vague memory splashed across his mind. Something about falling—not him, but things. Catching them, but still they fell. As quickly as it appeared, it was gone. His perception had improved considerably, and the blacks and grays were now changing into colors. He moved slowly forward, weaving his body carefully through the maze of tables and shelves. This was a place that he would never have entered on his own, he thought. He had been brought here this time because he needed to be here, to draw to a close something not of his own making. The first time, he knew no better. Along for the ride, so to speak. He shook his head as he lingered on the awakening memory. Bits and pieces, images, words began to appear. None of them in any order that made sense, and he couldn't help but note a growing discomfort, an unquestionable urge to get out, to leave while he still could.

"Here we are!" Artemidoros's voice, overly excited and annoying, shattered Stephen's contemplation so that he visibly jumped as the brothers' approach surprised him. "Oh, sorry. I didn't mean to startle you." His gentle laughter dissipated as he realized that Stephen had not found anything to be funny.

Standing next to Artemidoros, Adrastos was shorter than his brother and appeared to be more worn down by life than his older sibling. Stephen guessed that he was in his late fifties, maybe. It was hard to tell age in a man. A woman was easier. They tried so hard to hide their age through disguises whose grotesqueness always gave them away. And he had a slight lean to him, a bit toward the left of center. Stephen thought of the Leaning Tower of Pisa. And then it dawned on him that this same tired figure of a man had been responsible for intruding on his life, not once, but three times. And now he had somehow managed to bring him to a tiny village on an island in the Aegean Sea. Remarkable, he thought. If he were wearing a hat, he would have tipped it to him. Had he, perhaps, met his equal?

"Mr. Bingham, may I introduce you to my brother, Adrastos?" Artemidoros took a step to the side so that the two men were now facing one another, like a priest having just pronounced them man and wife and then giving them permission to kiss.

"I am very happy to see you in person, Mr. Bingham. I feel as though we are not strangers." His words were delivered slowly and intentionally. He did not extend his hand, nor did Stephen. Not that he wouldn't have if the other had offered, but the small man across from him was in charge, Stephen realized. Not him. This thought unsettled Stephen for a moment. Reminding himself as to the purpose of his being here, he was suddenly aware that he was lifting his shoulders up and straightening his spine so that, imagined or not, he had gained at least an inch in height over the shopkeeper.

"Certainly not in correspondence, but strangers still." Had he meant his response to sound this cold? Unfriendly but truthful? Yes. It was a matter of survival. Plain and simple. *Business is business,* he thought.

"Of course. Perhaps that is what is meant to be. So, let's take care of what has brought you here." He had turned from them both and was moving toward the back of the shop. "Oh, excuse me. I am forgetful and foolish." He had stopped suddenly and turned toward Stephen. "I am deeply sorry for your loss. To lose a brother, I cannot imagine." His eyes fell upon his own brother and then back to Stephen. "We have remembered him in prayer and will continue to do so. May his soul rest in peace." He did not wait for Stephen to respond but turned and continued through the clutter. "Please, come." He didn't turn around but gestured with his arm to follow him. Artemidoros, seeing Stephen's hesitation, nodded to him and extended his arm toward his brother, who had disappeared around a corner into the shadows of the shop.

"I will wait outside for you to conclude your business. There is no need for me to be here. Please, go ahead. His office is back there."

"Thank you. I can't imagine that this will take very long."

Making his way through the shop, he came around the corner to find an opened door that led into a dimly lit smaller room. The contrast from the shop itself to the office struck him as odd, and he felt immediately comfortable in the neatly kept smaller room. How the shopkeeper could make any kind of profit based on the customer's perspective, which he assumed would be one of repulsion, was beyond him, but there he was. Sitting behind his desk, clutter free, as was the entire office. And his shop was still open and he was running a business. Stephen had seen strange things during his lifetime, but this might top them all, he thought.

"Please, sit." Adrastos pointed to one of the two seats across from him. "So, as you have received my correspondence regarding my father's wishes, I am very glad that you have come to me. Michael was not so sure that you would, you know." He was leaning on the desk now, elbows resting with hands folded. "He has done me, both of us, a great favor. My father is happy and smiling." He looked up at the ceiling for a moment and then focused again on Stephen. "However, how do you say? A mixed blessing? This is a mixed blessing, as Michael is no longer with us."

At the mention of his brother's name, Stephen detected a tinge of resentment deep within. *This is not about Michael. Let's just get on with it.* He wasn't sure how long he would be able to maintain his composure with this man. He breathed deeply, unconcerned as to how this physical rebalancing might appear to

Adrastos. "Yes, it is that. In your letter, you said that the second part of the inheritance was meant for Eliza." He caught himself at the mention of her name. When was the last time he had uttered her name aloud? "And…and that we were to receive it together. But as you can see, she is not with me. I lost her some years ago. It has been difficult for me, all of this. It brings back what I can no longer have. Do you see?" If he could have, he would have patted himself on the back. The poor widower, the sadness and all that came with it. *Have pity on me….* He watched the man across from him unclasp his hands and sit back in his chair. If he was sympathetic to Stephen, his face did not reveal it.

"Yes. Of course. I am sorry about your wife. I would have liked to have met her. My father must have thought very highly of her to include her in his will and had a reason for you both to be present to receive his final gifts. I do not know the reason and am not meant to. However, as you are still in this world, it falls to you to receive this." He reached down somewhere under his desk and brought to the surface two boxes, one a bit larger than the other, but neither one as large as the box that he had carried home. Carefully placing them in front of him, he looked at Stephen as if trying to decipher his initial reaction. What he saw, he had expected. A trace of disappointment to be sure. And was there frustration as well? Yes, he knew what he saw. For a moment, he reconsidered handing them over to this man. However, his father's wishes were to be followed, no matter what the son felt.

Stephen did not immediately reach for the boxes but studied them, as if the plain unmarked brown paper wrap held within its fibers an invisible message that was decipherable by only one person and she was not here. He knew that once he laid his hands on them, they were his to do with as he pleased. Whatever their content, he had decided that he would have nothing to do with them. But he was ahead of himself, he thought. No need to waste any more time here. He reached for them and was surprised by the ease with which they slid across the desk's surface in his grasp. It was only then that he became aware of his suspicions, which had now been proven false. No rocks! He had been worried about rocks. Foolish!

"If you don't mind, I will not open them here."

"I do not expect you to do so. Here, let me give you a bag to carry them back with you." He got up from his desk and opened a deep drawer in the bottom of the shelves that covered one side of the office. Holding open the canvas bag, he motioned with his head for Stephen to place the boxes within its folds. Once Stephen had done so, Adrastos moved to the door, still holding the bag. "And so it is. Our business is done. Please, come this way." He had left the room before Stephen could stand.

Following him back into the shop, he noted that the shopkeeper was taking a different route through the room. Not a direct path to the door that would take him back to the real world, but a meandering one for no apparent reason. Not wanting to prolong this afternoon any longer than necessary, Stephen didn't say a word and followed the bent man as if he were a puppy on a leash.

He suddenly noticed a long counter that ran halfway along one wall of the shop. It was barely visible until one was practically on top of it, as this corner of the shop was darker than the rest of the room, if that was possible. Adrastos was standing behind the counter, the canvas bag resting on its worn surface oddly collapsed on itself as if mimicking the bent man standing behind it.

"I'm sorry, but what are we doing here? Is there more to the gifts than what is in the bag?" Stephen was truly confused and fighting to regain some sense of balance. Something was terribly off.

"It is too long a story to tell. Let me only say this. I stand here, where my father, and his father, and his father, and all of our father's fathers have stood. To me, it is a sacred spot and it is here that I feel my father's and all of our fathers' presence the strongest."

Stephen wanted to say, "Nice, so can we call it a day?" but something was preventing him from speaking. Instead, he moved closer to the counter.

"What is in these boxes, I do not know. That is between…was to be between your wife and him. I can feel the connection between them even as I hold this bag in my hands. Perhaps that is why my father wanted you both to be here, to share in this connection that is beyond our understanding." He paused, looking now at Stephen with an intensity that surprised him. "I am hesitating, I know. Forgive me." He stepped around the end of the counter, disappearing momentarily into the blackness of the recessed corner, and then reappeared, holding the bag in one hand while reaching with his other toward Stephen. "We have not properly introduced ourselves, not really." His open hand waited for Stephen to reciprocate.

Reaching for the bag, Stephen ignored the man's gesture as he clutched the handles and gently pulled them out of Adrastos's hand.

"I think that it is not necessary at this point." He stepped away from Adrastos. "I will be on my way, then. I believe this to be the end of the line in our correspondences as well. Good evening."

Feeling the conqueror, his legs cooperated with his inward command to reach the door without failing him. He did not turn around as he opened the door to the fading evening light. If he had, he would have seen a bent and rugged man somewhere in the shadows of the dimly lit shop, staring intensely at the floor while tracing with the toe of his shoe a horizontal line on the worn wooden planks, not once, but over and over again as though frozen in time and place.

Chapter 23

The room was not comparable to the one in Paris. Though it was small and musty, he would have to make do. After all, he could not really complain, since he hadn't paid a cent toward the expense of this trip. Nor should he have, he reminded himself. Very little exchange had occurred between Artemidoros and him as they wound their way back to the hotel. As a matter of fact, Artemidoros seemed quite sullen and had only asked Stephen if all had gone well. Not sure where he stood with the man, Stephen thought better than to strike up any kind of conversation. Besides, this trip was coming to an end and the smoother the ending, the better. He still had to deal with Alison. It would take some careful consideration before he met her. Understanding what the possible expectations would be on her part, he had resigned himself to do his best for his brother's wife. Of course, everything would depend on her preferences, but for him to close this final chapter forever, he would need to wield some influence over her. The trick was to do it well. Not to create any more difficulties than was necessary.

He considered calling her room before going to bed in order to make the first connection, to let her know that he was here and settle on a time to meet in the morning. It was getting late, much later than he had thought, and he worried now about disturbing her. However, not wanting to miss the opportunity to make the first move, he lifted the receiver of the room phone and dialed the room number that Artemidoros had given him. About to hang up after the eighth ring, he heard her voice. He changed ears so that he could hear what sounded like a distant and weakened greeting.

"Hello?"

In an instant, his commitment to her became real. "Uh…yes, hello. Am I speaking to Mrs. Bingham?" He knew full well that he was but suddenly felt unsure as to how to begin the conversation.

"Yes. Who is this?"

"Alison, this is Stephen, Stephen Bingham?" Why he responded as though he was questioning his own existence he could not fathom. *Get a grip. Focus!* As he expected, the pauses between the opening lines were dramatic, so much so that he wondered if she was in any condition to carry on a conversation with him. "Alison? Are you all right?" He heard a muffled sound like the clearing of the throat.

"Stephen? Where are you?" A logical question, he thought.

"I am right here, in this hotel. I was hoping that we could meet before I head back to Paris? That is, if you are willing to do so." Another pause, longer, it seemed, than the others. Perhaps this was not going to go as well as he'd thought it would.

"I don't know if that's a good idea. I mean, I'm not sure why we need to meet."

Her voice suddenly gained strength, and he thought that he detected a resistance that had the potential of becoming a barrier for him. He would need to tread lightly and carefully.

"I understand your hesitancy. You don't know me, but I would like to assure you that after meeting with Michael, I feel that I know you. He spoke so lovingly of you. You saved his life." He waited for her response. Nothing. "I just thought that I could help you through the next few days or longer, if you would like. I don't presume that you have no one to do this for you, but if that is the case, I want you to know that I am here."

"You spent time with Michael? I never heard from him. I had no idea if he had made contact with you or not."

"I did. As a matter of fact, we spent many hours together. I can't help but think that all of this was meant to be. A precious gift to both of us."

"Perhaps."

He ignored her remark. "Would it be possible to meet, then? If for nothing else than to make this connection?" He controlled his voice so that a hint of nonchalance with a heavy portion of sincerity ran through the questions.

"Yes, it would. I'll meet you in the lobby at nine thirty in the morning, by the seating area."

"Good. That is fine. Thank you, Alison. See you then. Good night."

"Good night."

Fatigue hit him squarely; his whole body suddenly insisted on sitting down. He dropped onto the bed, slouched forward, and clutched his head between his hands. How had such a short conversation taken so much out of him? He waited for the wave of relief to overtake him. He had expected to feel it. One more step taken as closure was drawing nearer. Yet, if anything, he felt drained. Perhaps he had fought a good battle without even realizing it. Or was it the other way around? Had she won? Was she in control? He needed sleep. That was all that was wrong.

And then he remembered where he had been most of the afternoon. Dealing with another stranger who insisted on interfering with his life. Yes, that was why he was unusually exhausted now. He would wake early, clear headed and rejuvenated. Over a strong cup of coffee, he would be able to see more clearly the path he was about to embark on with her.

He forced himself up from the edge of the bed, stumbling into the bathroom. A warm bath would be wonderful, he thought, but it was all he could do to undress, rinse his face, and stumble back to the waiting bed. Turning off the light on the bedside table, he sank low under the covers and allowed the sweet relief of sleep to numb him.

Chapter 24

Sleep evaded her throughout the night. Not unlike the night before but for a different reason. She had exhausted herself in grief the first night and had fitfully slept throughout the following day, the only interruptions being Artemidoros checking in on her. But Stephen's call and the prospect of meeting him in the morning would not let go of her as she played out numerous scenarios of what she now regretted agreeing to. The more she worked it over in her mind, the less she wanted to meet this man. All she wanted was to have Michael in the bed with her. And each time she saw him lying next to her, the tears and sobs, the gasping for breath, paralyzed her in grief once again.

But this night, an unknown disturbed her restlessness. Faceless, a man's image continued to loom in front of her, taking up all the space available within her mind's eye. And with it came a million questions, none of which she could answer with numerous possible choices, so many to consider. All unknown, all conjecture, but all supporting her deepest instinctual feelings about this man and his impact on both her and Michael. She blamed herself for not being firmer with Michael. No, she'd had no choice. He needed to go alone. But she could have forced herself to go with him. She should have been there, period. He would be with her now. She felt this to be the truth, so much so that there was no one to blame for his death other than herself. She could have prevented it.

And then there was Stephen's call that had taken her by surprise. She tried to be guarded as she spoke with him, unsure of his own stability. After all, Michael was not the only one who had gone through hell. What if he was even more damaged than his older brother? It would explain his unwillingness to connect with Michael over the years. She knew nothing of him. Who he really was. What path his life had taken. Had he gotten help along the way? Was he in a healthy state of mind? He hadn't sounded grief stricken during their short conversation. As a matter of fact, he'd never really shared his sorrow with her, if he had any at all. It was more businesslike, more like an agenda that had to be met. No, she was growing more certain as she lay awake that she had made a mistake by saying that she would meet him. How could she be so stupid? She couldn't even follow her own advice that she tried to give to her husband.

She would not meet with him. She would ignore his advances, his offers of help. There was nothing to do that she couldn't do herself or with the help of Artemidoros. She smiled slightly when she thought of him and all that he had done for her so far. A gentleman whose sincerity she could feel each time he was with her. Yes, he would be there to help her.

Her mind now made up, she tried to fall asleep but sensed that the light seeping into her room through the open space between the heavy drapes signaled that the day had begun. Looking at the clock, she sighed heavily. If sleep chose to come now, she knew that she would sleep right through the morning and she didn't want that to happen. She wanted to get on with what she knew she must face. Making arrangements for Michael's body to be flown back to the States. Funeral plans. All of it. The return-trip tickets for Michael and her were dated a day from tomorrow. She wasn't so sure that she could take care of business so quickly, not being familiar with the process in France, and their return was from Greece. But she decided to hold onto them, just in case everything worked out.

She called for breakfast in her room, not willing to run into Stephen in the lobby on her way to the restaurant. He would be waiting for her and she would not show up. Not naïve in her thinking, she fully expected her phone to ring with him on the other end, wondering if she was all right. Pressing her to meet with him. She would not answer it. No. That would send someone, probably Artemidoros, scurrying up to her room again to check on her. How could this person threaten her so? Was she being foolish? Was her instinct just fiction? A product of too many damaged minds sharing their woes with her, their paranoia? Had all of these interactions melded together to create who she was now? Could she even begin to hear her own mind's thoughts without the cacophony of patients she had thought she'd long forgotten?

There had been no phone call. Their meeting time had come and gone. She hadn't enjoyed the food, too anxious to relax. The coffee slid down easily, however, and she finished the carafe, enjoying the unfamiliar buzz that it provided. Perhaps he had thought better of it as well. What would be the point anyway? Maybe he'd embarrassed himself. Thinking that she would want to contact him, the brother who wouldn't even make contact with his own family?

For the first time since his call, she began to relax. The coffee, though, kept her alert and focused, for which she was grateful. She needed to get started with working out all the details. Later, when she was sure that Stephen was gone, she would go down and see Artemidoros. All she would need to do is call down to the desk to see if he had checked out. If not, well…she would cross that bridge when she came to it. The idea of a shower beckoned her, a good, long soak, she thought. Between that and the caffeine buzz, she would be refreshed enough to last a few hours before she hit the brick wall.

It startled her. The knocking. At first a gentle tapping, a hardly perceptible sound against the wooden door. Then louder and with greater rapidity. *Artemidoros,* she thought. *He hasn't checked in on me this morning, bless his heart.* Good timing, as she had just finished dressing. Hair still wet but combed, she felt almost presentable. But he had seen her in her worst state, and a lovely familiarity accompanied her to the door.

He stood in front of her, no words spoken, but waited for her to begin. He was younger than Michael. She knew that, but his physical appearance surprised her. Had she expected someone who looked like Michael? Gray hair, stooping posture, and a face that held no expression other than complete weariness. She could find no hint of her husband in his brother's face.

"Stephen?"

"I was worried about you. Forgive my intrusion. When

you did not appear at our arranged time, I waited, understanding that everything must be quite difficult for you right now. I did not sleep well, so I can imagine that that might have been the case for you?" In fact, he'd had a wonderful sleep, but he needed to commiserate with her.

The words were not coming to her. She knew where she wanted to be, what she should be saying to him, but their formulation was escaping her.

"Are you all right?" His question helped her to focus. A simple answer was all that was necessary. A perfectly good little lie.

"Yes, sure. I overslept. I should have called the desk to let you know. My apologies." His smile led her to believe that he understood how that could happen. Somehow, he was putting her at ease, she realized.

"I'm not at all surprised. You have gone through unbearably difficult days and with more to follow, I am sure."

Now she recognized the source of her ease. He was more like a grandfather than a brother-in-law, a term that she had never used before to describe Stephen. "I am being rude. I would invite you in, but I need to finish up here." She pointed to her wet head, implying more than that.

"Of course. I am the one who should apologize. I wonder if we can still meet today? I have nothing planned and would be available to you."

She knew that she was about to go against her better judgment but did not give herself the time to debate the issue, other than to acknowledge that the sooner she met with him, the sooner he would be gone. "Yes. If you can give me about thirty minutes, I'll meet you in the lobby?"

"That would be fine. Again, I am sorry to have interrupted you but very happy to see that you are fine. In half an hour then?" He turned and headed to the elevator.

Closing the door, she remembered to lock it and turn the deadbolt. As she dried her hair, her mind was swirling with thoughts. She did not question her decision this time. Now that she had a face to go with the imagined body, he didn't seem so threatening, not really. And she had determined that she would not allow any more than surface-level conversation between them. She had already brought Michael through the darkness and out the other side, but she would not do the same for his brother. She would listen to what he had to say about the possibility of helping her, but that was all. He was no more family to her than he had been to his own brother after all these years. She would never see him again after this, and with this final decision made, she felt lighter and self-assured.

As she exited the elevator, she heard Artemidoros's voice. He seemed to be in an animated conversation with someone, probably a new arrival to his establishment. His laughter filled the room at one point. Coming around the corner, she looked for him only to find Stephen and him in conversation. Not surprising, she thought. But a bit unsettling to her. She slowed her pace as she approached the men. Stephen saw her first.

"Ah. There you are." He had turned from Artemidoros and was giving her his full attention.

"Hello, again. Am I interrupting?" She looked at Artemidoros when she asked the question.

"Oh no, not at all, Mrs. Bingham." She noted his formal address to her and couldn't help but smile at him. "We were, Mr. Bingham and I, just chatting about travel. He has some good stories to tell." He looked back at Stephen and grinned a boyish grin, as if the two of them were complicit in their dealings with one another. "Please excuse me. I have things to attend to." He nodded to the two of them. And to Stephen, "I enjoyed our chat, very much. Mrs. Bingham?"

Stephen nodded in return. Then turning to Alison, he said, "Shall we?" He gestured toward the restaurant's seating. Still early enough before the middle meal of the day and well after the breakfast diners, the place was almost their own. An elderly couple sat in the back corner lingering over warm cups, oblivious to anyone around them.

"May I order for you? Perhaps some tea, coffee? Something to eat?"

"No, thank you. Well, perhaps coffee. I just finished breakfast." She caught herself as she remembered that she had told him that she had overslept. "I had an apple in the room, enough to get me started." She saw nothing on his face that would indicate he had even questioned her. *Relax,* she told herself.

Having ordered, Stephen readjusted himself in the seat. It was uncomfortable, he didn't mind letting anyone know who would think to ask. All for the sake of state-of-the-art furnishing. Its wrought-iron back and seat felt as though they were digging into every part of his body that came in contact with them.

"Not the most comfortable, are they?" She surprised him with her question.

"Funny. I was thinking the same thing. At my age, lots of cushioning is required, as I do not carry it naturally anymore." He smiled at his humor and saw that she was doing the same. "Mrs. Bingham, I…"

"Please, call me Alison. I am comfortable calling you Stephen, if that is all right with you?"

"Yes. Of course. Thank you. And I want to thank you again for agreeing to meet with me. I have been wondering how I can be of any help to you. The shock of losing Michael, well, I cannot imagine what you are going through. But the least I can do is offer my help, if you need it." She was focused on him, and he saw no indication that she was unwilling to listen further. "I thought that I could help you with the arrangements for Michael's return to the States. I am somewhat familiar with the French way of doing things. I don't know if you are aware that I have made my home in France?" He paused, waiting for her to respond.

"I do know that, Stephen."

He continued. "If you would allow me, I will work with you to have this accomplished quickly. Am I correct in assuming that you will want him home for the burial? Forgive me, but I don't know his circumstances, his past, you know. Where he might have plans for burial. I hope that I am not becoming too personal here."

"We never discussed it. To be honest with you, it never entered our minds that our marriage would end this way and this soon. I am completely unprepared." Her openness took her by surprise. "I'm unsure of the next step. I just know that I want him to come home with me as soon as possible."

"I understand. Where is home?" His efforts to be consistent in the tone of his voice, the compassionate one, were paying off.

"Los Angeles. Well, that is home now for the two of us."

"LA. Busy place. I don't think that I could live there. At this stage of the game. Too fast a pace and geared toward the younger ones, I think."

"Had you lived there before?" She felt the skin on her arms prickle at the thought that he might have been within driving distance of Michael all of this time.

"No, never. Never had the desire to. I spent a good deal of time on the East Coast in my productive years and I don't believe anything can compare to New York City. A bit biased, I suppose. I was raised in California, though, as you may or may not know. Funny the way life works. I met my wife in Boston and it turned out that we were both from the same region in California." He stopped. What was he doing? Babbling on like a schoolgirl. Her gaze had not changed its direction as she continued to focus on his face. Perhaps he had done nothing wrong in revealing some details. She seemed to be interested.

"Your wife?" Her curiosity was getting the better of her.

"She passed years ago. But we had a steady run until then. After she died, I found myself at loose ends, so decided to travel. I found myself in a small village just outside of Paris, Tigeaux. Do you know it?"

"No, sorry. Pretty much have been a stay-at-home, at least until I met Michael." She looked away from him as her eyes filled with tears. Fighting to keep them from falling, she gave in and, with the back of her hand wiped her eyes dry. "Sorry."

"Please, there is no need to apologize. Are you okay?"

"Yes, thanks. Please continue."

She was looking at him again. "It is the perfect place. I

fell in love with it almost immediately, decided to leave the States only temporarily, but the years continue to come and go, and I stay."

"I see. So, you have no connection with the States now?" A far-reaching question, she thought, but she wanted to know.

"Actually, I do." He would avoid the issue of his human connection. Which was to say, none. He knew that in doing so, no red flags would be raised. "I've kept one of my properties, having given up my homes on the East Coast."

"Homes?" Did she suddenly resent him? Had he done that well in life while his only brother had held on for dear life? And in all that time, he had never reached out to Michael in any way? She tried to calm the rising tide of negativity that filled her thinking.

"That was a while ago. Yes, I managed to procure a few homes during my younger years. I was fortunate, I suppose, to be in the right place at the right time. But that was then, and this is now. A far cry from those days."

"So, you do have a home in the States? Where?" She fought the urge to yell at him.

"Believe it or not, in California, where I started. Full circle, I guess." The ease with which the conversation was flowing continued to take him by surprise. She was easy to talk to and obviously interested in what he had to say. But he would need to get back on track. He didn't mind spending his valuable time bringing her around to his thinking, but he had not expected the conversation to be so deep. *Be careful*, he admonished himself. "As a matter of fact, ...well, this might sound quite inappropriate, but please know beforehand that nothing is meant by it other than my sincere offer to you, ...I have a place in Central California, in the mountains. A cabin, but much nicer. It has been added on to over the years by various owners, so to describe it as a cabin is a misnomer. However, that is how it began. It's quiet and in a beautiful setting. Not far from civilization, just up the coast highway. If you would consider staying there for however long you like before getting on with your life in LA, I would be honored. You would have it all to yourself. Time to get your bearings, to recover?" He had gone well over the line now. He'd planned to get to this point, but not this quickly. He was sure that any progress made had been ruined by his carelessness.

The thought of being alone in the mountains in a strange place without anyone around her was unsettling. As appealing as the quiet sounded, she could not quell what she could only identify as fear. Of what, she was not sure.

"There is so much to do. I need to concentrate on bringing Michael home, settling our affairs, before I take time for myself. I appreciate your kindness, but I hope you understand. Perhaps a rain check, if I need it?"

Not what he wanted to hear but not surprising, he thought. "Of course. I understand completely, and you are quite right. As I think about it, you might consider saying yes to my offer after you have completed what you are about to tackle. I am sure you will appreciate it better being free from worry. It is yours for the asking, anytime."

The anger has disappeared. Perhaps she had misjudged him. She could not blame him for where his life had taken him any more than she could blame Michael for becoming a junkie. Who was she to judge his actions? He was an old man now. What was done was done. He wasn't to blame for any of it. Not the distance created between the brothers, not really. Certainly not anything that happened to either one of them when they were so young. And she could find no reason to blame him for Michael's death. Even though, had it not been for Stephen, Michael would never have gone to Paris. Perhaps, on second thought, if she tried hard enough, she could cast a morsel of blame his way. But she knew better. Fate. Simply that and nothing else. Just as it had been fate that Michael wandered, drunk and out of his mind on drugs, into traffic and then into her life.

"I could use your help with making the arrangements for Michael's body to return home. After that, I'll be fine. You said that you are familiar enough with the process?"

"Yes. Let me accompany you to Paris, and from there we will take care of Michael."

"Fine. That would be most helpful. I appreciate this, Stephen. I really do. Thank you."

He was standing behind her, pulling her chair out for her. "So, I will purchase our tickets for later today, perhaps early evening, whatever is available out of Athens?"

"I can be ready to go anytime. I do have my return ticket to LA for the day after tomorrow. Do you think that we can take care of everything by then? Perhaps I should cancel it and start over?"

"It might be wise to do so. I am familiar with the process, but I can't guarantee time issues. Why don't you cancel, and we can make flight arrangements when we are ready to?"

"Of course. That makes sense. I'll do it as soon as I get up to my room. Will you call me when you have our flight time to Paris?"

"You will be the second to know." He laughed, and she heard her own tempered laughter join his.

Chapter 25

He found Adrastos in his office. Unable to wait any longer, he had left the hotel as soon as he saw Alison and Stephen leave the restaurant and enter the elevator. He knew why he had come, but he wasn't so sure that he could articulate it sensibly to his brother. All he knew was that none of this had been right: Alison, Michael's horrible death, and now this newly arrived brother-in-law. He could not leave it alone. Perhaps that was why he stood in front of his brother's desk now, needing to talk with him, the only one who could help him understand.

"I expected you, but sooner." Adrastos glanced up at his brother to acknowledge his presence and then continued to rifle through a small pile of papers on his desk.

"What are you doing?" He wondered how his brother could focus in the dimly lit room, certainly brighter than the shop but not enough to suit Artemidoros.

"Do you know what I have here?" He rested both of his hands on the papers, some still stacked while others had been strewn on the desktop. He did not look up.

"I have no idea." For a moment, he put aside his own concerns and was intrigued by his brother's ambiguousness. "Please don't make me guess. I've got too much on my mind right now."

"You are about to have more, little brother." He picked up one of the sheets, turned it so that it faced Artemidoros, and brought it closer in his view. "Do you recognize the script?"

It was as if his father had just entered the room and joined them. His father's script was easily identifiable, an elegant record of a time long gone. "Yes, of course. What do you have there?" He pulled a chair around the desk and placed it next to Adrastos'. In his quick estimation, there must have been over a hundred sheets of parchment paper, each filled from top to bottom with his father's handwriting. "My God! Did he write all of this?" He turned to his brother, a paper in one hand and an incredulous expression on his face.

"It appears so. I was going through some boxes under the counter in the back of the store. You know, the corner where he waited?" Artemidoros smiled as he recalled the image of his father hidden in the darkened corner. He had always thought that he was playing a game with the visitors to the shop and as a child had wanted to play as well, but his father would send him away when the customers came in.

"I remember."

"It never occurred to me to do it before now. But after Mr. Bingham's visit, I kept coming back to that corner and I had no reason to do so. None that I could understand. And then my eye caught their shape's outline in the recess of the shelf and I suppose my curiosity took over. At the bottom of the second box, I found these…," he waved his hand over the sheets, "bound in two bundles with ribbon. It was as if he had hidden them. They were under old pieces of fabric and odds and ends that perhaps he couldn't sell but did not want to throw away." He pointed to the box that held only clutter as far as Artemidoros could tell. "The other box was the same, but I found no papers."

"Have you read them?" He felt a growing excitement at the prospect of his father communicating with them again, but with that feeling he could not ignore another, less identifiable but nevertheless as strong and growing stronger. Perhaps that was why he was now feeling torn as to knowing the boxes' content.

"When I found them last night, it was quite late. I was not so sure that I wanted to discover him again, to be privy to his thoughts but not be able to talk with him about them. Perhaps a foolish way to be, but I was sure that my unanswered question to him would consume my thinking and, I must tell you, Artemidoros, it frightened me. I had only gotten through the first bundle when you came in." Turning to his brother without breaking eye contact with him and about to speak again, he heard the bell attached to the shop's front door alert him to someone entering. "Oh, excuse me. I need to attend to this." He pushed his seat back, stood, and then rested his hand on his brother's shoulder. "Go ahead. Read. Then we can talk."

Artemidoros could hear his brother's friendly greeting to his customers somewhere within the shop. He went to the office door and quietly closed it. Returning to the desk, he sat in his brother's chair, pulled the desk lamp closer, and began to hear his father's voice. At one point, he felt an intruder as his father's innermost feelings about his wife became detailed and, to his own thinking, private, certainly not meant for his sons' eyes. Was this a kind of diary, then?

As he read on, his suspicions were confirmed as, page after page, the minute details of each day had been recorded with great thoroughness. Thankfully, for both him and Adrastos, their father had included the entry date each time he had put pen to paper. Artemidoros flipped through the pages, noting the earliest entry date to be January 1, 1944. Achaïkos had been twenty years old and just married. Each page revealed day-to-day events within the village, in his personal life, and what he knew of the horrors of the outside world. It read like a book, each character carefully revealed as his father had gone along. Their mother had borne five children. Artemidoros reread this sentence. Five? Who was the fifth? He read farther only to discover that the fifth child, a girl, had died within hours of her birth. He could find no explanation as to why. Of the four brothers, only he and Adrastos had made Oia their home. The other two had left the island years ago, one settling in South Africa, the other in Argentina. In numerous entries, their father had lamented the fact that these sons were not closer to him physically and emotionally. It seemed that their communications to their father became less and less after their mother died. Artemidoros, upon reading this, was reminded that his correspondence with them both had been infrequent. Sitting at the desk, he wondered when he had last heard from them and couldn't remember. Had they even come to their father's funeral? Had anyone told them about it? He knew he hadn't, but perhaps Adrastos had? He just could not remember.

The second bundle, which Adrastos had just begun reading, began with the entry date January 1, 1984. He wondered what the last entry date was and so thumbed through the pages to find the final entry written on July 14, 2005, the year that their father died. As he quickly calculated dates, he realized that his father had died three months later, exactly to the day of this entry. He wondered why the entries had stopped three months before his death. Perhaps he was not as well as he appeared to be during that time? When he turned eighty, he had been admired by so many for looking and acting younger than his chronological years. Artemidoros only hoped that he would do as well as his father had.

"Sorry. You know how it can be. One comes in, they all come in." Adrastos moved to his seat and waited for Artemidoros to vacate it.

"Did you read all of the first bundle?" He asked the question as he stood up and sat back down next to Adrastos.

"Yes. Interesting. I had no idea that we had a sister, did you?"

"None. I did start the next bundle. Much of the same, day-to-day recordings. I cheated and went to the last entry date, July 14, 2005." He flipped the pages to the entry. "Look. Three months to the day of his death. I find that interesting."

"Ah. I hadn't seen that yet." Adrastos added, "October 14? Was that the date?"

"Yes. Why do you think he didn't keep the entries going? I mean, after all, he had been faithful to this for, what is it?" Again, quick calculations. "For sixty-one years!" As he spoke these words, he shook his head slowly in disbelief.

"We will never know. And what does it matter? We were close enough to him in his last days. I don't think that we have missed anything." Both men did not say anything more for several minutes as if they had fallen into deep contemplation, individually, but as one in the love they shared for their father.

"I am curious." Artemidoros's question broke the silence. "What does the last entry say?"

Adrastos, as if shaken from a deep sleep, swallowed the wrong way and coughed uncontrollably. In between spasms, he managed to say, "Water," and Artemidoros brought him a glass of the cold liquid. Gulping it down, he wiped the tears and his nose, the result of the unwelcome convulsion, cleared his throat, and stood up. "I'm sorry. Where were we?" He needed to stand, to readjust his body.

"I want to read the last entry. Here, sit down and we can read it together. Do you want me to read it aloud?"

Settling back into his chair, Adrastos said, "If you wish." He shoved the last few pages over to Artemidoros, who had pulled the desk lamp even closer. With the last entry in front of him, he lifted the first page, adjusting it under the dusky glow of the old bulb and, before beginning, commented to his brother that shedding more light in here would be a good idea.

Chapter 26

Stephen had done the necessary legwork. Two one-way flights to Paris were booked for a six-thirty departure today. That would give Alison and him tomorrow to arrange for Michael's return to the States. Although it was just before noon, he felt a growing fatigue from having done nothing at all. Frustrated by his body's limited stamina, he sat down and called Alison's room. When he confirmed with her the time of departure and assured her that he had already taken care of the hotel room for her short stay in Paris, she was more than grateful to him. They decided on a meeting time to leave for the airport. A short boat ride to the mainland and then they would be on their way. Satisfied and recognizing his persistent fatigue, he decided to give in and, leaning forward, unlaced his shoes, took them off and placed them neatly side by side at the edge of the bed, loosened his pants and the top buttons of his shirt, and collapsed on the freshly made bed, too tired to pull down the quilt.

**

She had approximately four hours before she needed to meet Stephen. Feeling a bit more settled, she considered venturing out and taking in the beauty of this village and its surrounding waters one more time. She knew that she would never return here, not after all that had happened. Surprised that she was not hungry, she decided to get everything together so that when she returned, she would not be late for Stephen. It was only when she saw Michael's suitcase, still open, most of his clothes still packed other than the ones he had taken with him to Paris, that she broke down again. Taking many deep breaths to regain control, she gently refolded the clothes that had been disturbed by his hurried efforts to grab something to take with him and before placing them back into the case, she held them, one at a time, to her nose, breathing Michael back into her broken heart.

**

It was harder than he thought it would be, reading aloud what his father had written. He found his throat constricting numerous times as the words produced Achaïkos, who seemed to be standing in front of them both. Adrastos heard the catch in his brother's throat each time and fought back his own emotions as Artemidoros's voice filled the room. Much of the beginning of the entry was similar to so many others. Their father's daily ritual, noting the beauty of the day soon to be changed by the oncoming storm clouds and the unusual chill in the air for July. He had recorded in great detail those whom he had greeted that morning, the majority being the locals who were beginning their day as well. In each entry, he had made a point of ending the day by going to a high place, always alone it seemed, and painting a picture with his words, as if each one was a different hue in the spectrum of colors, of the sunsets that blessed this place every day. However, this entry did not include a sunset, nor was there mention of the day ending.

What he had filled the pages with was an encounter, and as Artemidoros read the words to his brother, he could go no farther. Dropping the pages on the desk, he turned to Adrastos who was looking straight ahead, almost lifeless in his movements and expression. Artemidoros's eyes searched the shadows, looking for his father somewhere now in the room. He was sure that his brother was doing the same.

**

Entering the lobby, she made a point of looking for Artemidoros. She wanted to thank him for all that he had done for her in the past days before heading out for one last sightseeing adventure. Not seeing him immediately, she went to the front desk. She was told that he had left for the afternoon on business and was not sure of his time of return. Because the young woman had used the word *business,* Alison did not ask where he might be. It was none of her business, and she was sure that the information would not be given to her anyway. "May I leave a message for him, then? Give me a moment and I'll be right back." She did not wait to hear the woman's response. Heading back to her room, she remembered that the hotel stationery still sat untouched on the table. She would be able to compose a decent and thoughtful note in the quiet of her room. It was the least she could do.

**

Fitful stirrings did not allow his mind to sleep. Yet, he could not wake up. The dark palette of his subconscious entertained fragments of images, all familiar but colorless, void of defined shapes but whose voices he knew. Rushing air through tall growth lifted him above the surface of something; he could not determine what. Children's laughter collided with pulsating thuds whose increasing noise drummed out any lingering lightness. A woman's gentle voice broke through the din but could not complete a thought. Bits of her words lingered, however: "…is okay," "…over." Breathing. No, not breathing. Unable to hear his own breathing. A man's voice, violent, familiar, unforgiving, malevolent. A brother's voice hushing him. Any words? He couldn't remember. Screaming, cries from somewhere. His cries. A louder voice than his blocking those cries from being heard. *Cry harder, harder, harder!* Deathly stillness—no sound, nothing. Then small whimpers that evaporated into the dank dark. His name. Was he hearing his name? Whose voice? Calling his name over and over again until it, too, evaporated. Silence.

He turned to his other side, still enclosed in the wrappings of fatigue. He was aware that he had done so as he adjusted his aching hip against the firmness of the bed. With a deep sigh, he felt himself once again dragged down under from any light of day.

**

"If you would be sure that Mr. Metaxas gets this?" She handed the desk clerk the envelope with her message for Artemidoros sealed inside.

"Of course. As soon as he returns."

"Thank you." She turned to go but thought better of it. She would ask directions. "Sorry, one more thing. I have a few hours before I leave and thought that I would take the stairs down to the fishing village…," she paused and checked her map, "Ormos Armeni? Don't know if I am pronouncing that right. Sorry."

"You did very well." The clerk reminded Alison of a French teacher she'd had in junior high. No smiles for a job well done, just a textbook confirmation that she had done what she was expected to do. "The staircase is very near. See, here we are and there it is. Just go out the door to the left. You will see signs along the way. And if you become lost…"

Alison interrupted her. "I know. There are plenty of people to ask along the way. Thank you." She took the map back and stuffed it in her purse. "Oh, can I make it there and back in the next three hours?"

"If you are a good walker and don't mind climbing stairs, you have plenty of time to…" The clerk abruptly stopped speaking. Then she said, "Oh, Mrs. Bingham. Please forgive me.

Your husband—I mean his loss is so new. May I ask if you will be all right? Would you like someone to accompany you there and back? I am sorry. I should have thought of this sooner."

Alison could sense that she was sincere and felt grateful to her for caring. "It is fine. Please. Thank you for the offer, but I will be just fine. It will do me good to get some fresh air. I'll be just fine." She left the desk and opening the door of the hotel, she wondered if she would ever be fine again.

∗∗

From the top of the cliff, he could see no ground below it. Nothing but a darkness that was deeper in its shade than the hills that surrounded it. He heard the waves breaking against the rocks, receding from the shore as they churned between the stones that jostled for position as the force of the water swept all around them. He sensed that his arms were heavy, strained, tense. He couldn't release the burden from them that they were obediently carrying. He was trying to drop them forward, pushing them into the darkness only to return to him with their cargo. Stepping closer to the edge. Trying one more time. A thrust of his whole body working in tandem with his aching upper limbs to release, to let go. Again, they returned burdened. As he moved farther into the darkness, he looked down to see that his toes were no longer on the cliff's edge but jutting forward, resting on nothing. They seemed unnaturally long, and he thought to reach down and feel if they really were there at all. But the burden would not let him. *Drop it, drop it!* he cried to himself. The pain was becoming unbearable. From somewhere behind him, he heard a noise. Footsteps? An animal? He tried to turn to see what was close to him, but his body would not move in any direction but forward. He fought the rising fear that now accompanied the intolerable weight resting heavily in his arms. He tried to open his mouth to ask, "Who's there?" but his teeth were clenched, and his lips sealed shut as if the two had become one. And it was upon him. A sharp pain shot through his back and into his body. Another, and then another until, still with his burden, he felt himself in midair and rapidly descending into the blackness below him.

**

"Keep going. Finish what we have started, Artemidoros. You know that we must." Adrastos spoke softly and with reverence as though the Holy Book were in front of them. "It is his wish that we do so. Go on."

Artemidoros found comfort in his older brother's words. He was right, he knew. Perhaps within his father's recordings his own suspicions would be confirmed for good. He searched for the last sentence he had read to his brother. Placing his finger on the place, he took a deep breath and began.

"I was under the impression that the couple was happy. But the man is not. He does not hide it. Perhaps unhappy with me that I have taken an interest in his wife? No, not that way. God bless my wife's soul. I still love you. No, Mrs. Bingham, Eliza, has taken an interest in me. She lingers with me, wanting to know about our village, its history, its geology. It is as if she thirsts for conversation, for the finest of details that I can offer to her. As I speak she does not write down my words, but I know that she keeps each one safely within, and she asks me for proper spellings. I speak with her about our volcano, our home here on the caldera, and of the history of Greece. As much as I can remember. If we could have years to do so, our conversation still would not be completed. So much like a daughter to me. I can feel

this so strongly. May God forgive me, but could she be our little one? Rest in peace. God forgive me. Our child has been spared the possibility of sharing her life with someone like Mr. Bingham. He is impolite, to be sure, but more than that. He is not loving to his wife. I can tell these things. I have feelings that come to me and will not leave me alone. And I see the sadness in her eyes. She hides it well in front of me, but it is there. I am unsure whether to mention this to her. My instincts tell me not to, as do you, my darling wife. But I fear for her. I fear that she will never be happy while she is married to him. But it is not my place. She is, after all, a stranger to me who has come to my shop and who will leave in a day or two. I will never see her again. But I have thought of a way for her to always remember me, remember our talks, remember my motherland. Upon my death, she will receive the gifts of my father to me and his father to him and so on and so on. She will receive them as a daughter might receive the love of her father. It is that love that Eliza shall inherit.

As for her husband, I can only pray that he will love her as he should. And if not, the gods will know best what will become of him.

Artemidoros continued holding the page as he turned to his brother. "Tell me what you feel about Mr. Bingham." A simple question from which, he hoped, a similar opinion would appear.

"He does not strike me as a man of good intention. My dealings with him have been nothing but uncomfortable and all business. I don't find him sincerely interested in our father's wishes. Not even in showing any respect for him. I suppose that I am asking too much, but even so..." His words drifted off slowly.

"I feel the same way, my brother. There is something not right. I am not afraid to say that I am uncomfortable with Alison, Mrs. Bingham, in his company. She is in no condition to make decisions, especially with someone who has just entered her life whose connection with her is nothing other than by name in law. And even that is not right. I don't know what to do."

"What I do know is that there is a reason for these boxes to be opened, for us to have found our father's words so sharply speaking to us now after so many years. There is a reason and because of that, we cannot ignore him. More importantly, we cannot ignore that the gods of old are present and standing in this room with us." He looked around the room as if ready to greet them, but stood up, turned off the desk light, and motioned to Artemidoros to go with him.

"I cannot tell you what to do, Artemidoros. I wish that I could. But I do not hold the answer. Perhaps, if you listen carefully to the words that are all around us, you will be given an answer. And perhaps," he turned back to face his brother so that their eyes met in the fading light of the shop, as he said the last words he would ever utter about this, "our father has already answered for us."

**

He never reached the bottom. Waking, suddenly free from his subconscious drama, it took him a moment to understand where he was and that what had been so very real a moment ago was nothing but a bad dream. His breathing now under control, he lay there a bit longer until the last vestiges of remembrance had vanished. Checking his watch, the blurred face was a mystery until he reached for his glasses and put them on to find that it was already five thirty. He had slept the afternoon away! Upset with himself for wasting so much time, he pushed his body up and into a sitting position. Bracing for balance, his arms served as supports as he pushed his weight onto them while slowly swinging his legs over the edge of the bed. How could such a simple maneuver exhaust him so, he wondered? He would need to move. Very little to pack, and a shower would revive him and put him in a better mood for the journey ahead. He had time before he needed to be in the lobby.

**

Standing at the top of the stairs that led down to Ormos Armeni, she stopped, taking in a view that took her breath away. Below her, the small fishing village seemed dwarfed by the mountains that towered over it. She turned back to Oia, trying to make out the remnants of the volcano in its entirety, but found it difficult to do. She kept the images in her mind that she had seen in the travel books, though, so that she still had a sense of where she was standing on its caldera. If things had been different, if Michael were still with her, they would have toured the landscape and learned more about the place. He would be standing right next to her now, encouraging her to take the next step, not to be afraid of the descent, much less the ascent. She could feel his energy. It was surrounding her as she reached out to the railing for support. But she could not take the first step. She did not want to as she gave in to her loss, her whole body from head to toe beginning to quiver and then shake as though what was moments ago solid footing beneath her now gave way as she sank onto the caldera's surface and succumbed to her grief once more.

**

When Artemidoros arrived, the desk clerk did not see him come in. A large party from Australia was overwhelming not only the lobby but the clerk. Had he paid attention, he would have seen her frantically appeasing the newly arrived tourists, who were eager to get their vacation underway. He might have appreciated her even more. But his mind was not on anything but Alison. Entering the elevator, he tried to calm himself before speaking with her. He had no idea how to begin, and it frightened him that he might make things worse. He might, in his endeavors to alert her to what both he and his brother suspected, push her away, especially in light of what she was going through. As the doors opened, he hesitated. None of this was his business. Who did he think he was? As the doors began to close, he stepped forward, thrusting his arm between them so that they retracted, allowing him one more chance to complete what he was compelled to do.

There was no answer to his knock. He waited, but it was obvious that she was not there, although it crossed his mind that she could be sleeping. He started to walk away but stopped and pulled out his cell. Dialing the hotel's number, he was surprised to be greeted by his own voice thanking him for calling and saying that "we are unable to answer the phone right now." Then the menu of possibilities so that valued customers were not turned away but intentionally made to feel as though they were important and would be connected momentarily. "Ridiculous," he mumbled and ended the call.

Back in the lobby, he now saw the reason for his frustration. He was pleased to know that it would be a full house tonight. Though his mind was still focused on Alison, he managed to disguise his concern for her and plaster upon his face the genuinely welcoming smile of the hotel's manager who was at each guest's service. He greeted the guests who were still clogging the lobby, some having registered while others waited in line. Seeing how overwhelmed the clerk was, he excused himself from a woman whose animated conversation with him continued even as he walked away and back around the counter. "Keep up the good work," he said to the clerk as he took his place next to her. "Yes, next please?" In the rush of appeasing these strangers who were his livelihood, Alison slipped from his mind.

**

Spent from convulsions of grief, she remained where she had fallen. A fatigue had snuck up on her so that even the cooling breezes that rose from the sea below were not enough to fully revive her. But she couldn't stay where she was and was a bit surprised that no one had come this way and seen her. Perhaps this little adventure down the staircase was not as popular as she had thought, and although she would like to see the village below, her body was telling her otherwise. And she had a plane to catch, now only two hours away. With a heavy sigh, she stood up, brushed the caldera's skin from her own, and started back the way she had come.

She would miss this place, she thought as she leisurely wandered through the streets leading to the hotel. She made a point of taking a bit of time to soak everything in so that she would remember the beauty of the place in light of the tragedy it also held. Michael would have wanted her to, she thought. Lost in thought, she found herself on the street leading to the hotel's entrance, and she suddenly felt disappointment. She was in sight of the end of this journey. And she had reconciled herself to accepting that she was leaving a part of Michael behind.

Crossing the street, she quickened her pace and entered the lobby. Checking the time, she was grateful that she'd had the wherewithal to have everything ready since her return trip had taken her longer than she'd thought. Still enough time, though. Turning the corner to reach the elevator, she remembered.

The desk clerk did not seem as gracious in her greeting as earlier and her face communicated weariness. A long day for her? A long week? Alison could relate to a full week's worth of work and what it could do to you. "Yes, hello. I wondered if Mr. Metaxas was given my note? The one I left with you earlier?" The young woman's face revealed that she hadn't, and Alison thought that she might break into tears, so distraught had she become.

"Oh, I am so sorry. So sorry. He was here, and I forgot.

We were so busy with guests arriving, and I was so relieved to have his help, that your note slipped my mind. It is entirely my fault, Mrs. Bingham. I will be sure that he receives it as soon as he returns."

"You mean he isn't here? But he was here?" This was becoming almost comical.

"He was here about thirty minutes ago but left again. He asked me if I knew where you were, and I told him that you wanted to see the village. He didn't say where he was going but assured me that he would return shortly. I thought that he might have found you. I feel terrible about this."

"It's not your fault. Don't worry. It's just that I would have liked to have said goodbye and to have thanked him in person. I thought that he would be here. But I guess it's not meant to be." Glancing at her watch, she excused herself. "I need to get my things. If you could just be sure to give him the envelope, I would really be grateful."

"Of course, of course."

Once in her room, she replayed the young woman's words: "…asked me if I knew where you were." How strange. It made some sense, she supposed, as he probably wanted to be sure to see her before she left. Courtesy demanded it on his part, she assumed. It would be a shame not to say goodbye but not the end of the world. Her note would be an acceptable substitute.

Stephen was waiting for her in the lobby, as planned. He had already gotten a taxi for them, which she could see through the lobby doors.

"Sorry to have kept you waiting," she said as she approached him, even though she knew that she was on time; in fact, she was a few minutes early. He turned to her and smiled.

"Here, let me take them for you." He reached for both her and Michael's bags.

"No need to take both. I can handle one of them at least." She took Michael's back.

He was relieved as he felt the weight of them. He had grown used to his overnight bag.

The bellhop appeared. "Would you like me to take your

bags, sir? Madam?" He waited patiently but eagerly, expecting to end his day with a tidy pocket of tip money.

"Yes, that would be fine," Stephen said. "Just to that cab." He pointed with his free hand. "Are you ready, then?" Lightly placing the palm of his hand on her back, he led her through the doors. She glanced behind her, thinking that she had heard her name, but saw no one other than the young woman behind the counter, who briefly looked up from her computer and then back down as if Mrs. Bingham no longer existed.

As he turned the same corner that Alison had turned a short time ago, Artemidoros saw a taxi pull away from the hotel entrance.

Chapter 27

With arrangements made to transport Michael's body back to LA on a separate plane, Alison began to feel some relief as she sat comfortably in First Class, at Stephen's insistence, on her way to LA. She had had her doubts about Stephen, to be sure, and still harbored caution in her dealings with him. But, even so, she was grateful for his support now. He had a way of perceiving when she wanted to be quiet, not keep a senseless conversation going just for the sake of companionship. She appreciated him giving her some much-needed space. She wondered if he was doing it for her or for him or for them both. It didn't matter. She was just grateful for it no matter what the intention was.

He had not mentioned the cabin since he first brought it up. She had not been in any state of mind to think anything through clearly then, but the fog in which she had barely functioned for the last two days had lifted. She had business to tend to in LA before she could entertain the idea of a cabin somewhere in the woods. She needed to focus on burial arrangements for Michael first. His list of contacts was limited, she realized. She would need to contact the bookstore, of course. Certainly, let the facility know, if anyone there remembered him, that is. It never occurred to her that the people in her own life would want to know. And then their place. The one thing that she dreaded, the more she thought about it, was opening the door to their home. How would she be able to live there without him? Everywhere her mind's eye took her within its walls, she saw something that was Michael's or was there because of Michael. She had heard others talk about how difficult it was to start over, and all sorts of variations on the theme. It was an individual call as to how one came through it, she decided. As she glanced out of the plane's window to see below her the tops of clouds, she could not begin to know where she would be in the months to come. One step at a time, she reminded herself.

In the taxi on the way to Alison and Michael's apartment, Stephen had assured her that he would arrange for a hotel close by once he knew where she was located in LA. They both managed a half-hearted laugh about it. That he had come all this way with her but had no idea where he was going. At his age, he had told her, he needed plans in place, but this time, he had been too caught up in just getting them both here and Michael.

As the next week came to an end, Stephen looked forward to leaving LA behind. With Michael's small funeral completed, his burial in some cemetery whose name he hadn't bothered with remembering, and the forced patience of meeting the few people who bothered to show up for Michael and Alison, he was exhausted. The last hurdle was convincing Alison that she needed to accept his offer and take the time to adjust in the peace and quiet of the forest. Had he mentioned to her that the coastline was an easy walk away? He would need to remember to do so.

"Have you thought any more about my offer of the cabin?" They were sharing a meal together somewhere in LA in one of those overrated sidewalk cafés that Stephen disliked but the Alison had been drawn to.

"Well, not really. It crossed my mind at one point, but nothing more. Tell me again about it, Stephen?" She was sipping on lukewarm iced tea, a sprig of mint entwined artfully through the lemon's fibers to appear across the thin layer of yellow skin that was skewered to the tinted glass rim. He had never seen anything quite like it.

"I have only suggested it because I thought that you might like the time alone. You've been through so much and, quite frankly, I can't imagine how one could ever hear one's self think, much less enjoy substantial rest, in this city." He had gotten off track. And he saw her look up from her tea, a quizzical expression on her face. "Sorry. I only speak for myself. Too many years of quiet and ease. I probably needed this trip just to remind me of what I have left behind and to appreciate what I now have."

"No, I get it, really. There are times when everything here

becomes just too much. Sitting in traffic, the lines for anything, the heat and smog. Doesn't sound that appealing, I guess. But it's home."

"Yes. I guess it must be. However, a break is important for anyone under even normal circumstances. Yours have been far from normal. So, as you may remember me saying, the cabin is up the coast from here in the Ventana Wilderness area, around Big Sur. Have you heard of it?"

"Sure." She continued to nurse her tea.

"I bought it some years ago now but haven't been back since Eliza died. She loved being there and it is hard for me to imagine myself there without her. I am sure that you understand." He stopped and looked down, avoiding eye contact. He hoped that she would interpret this as his own internal conflict to come to grasp with his loss, as long ago as it was.

"Of course."

Barely heard above the din of the street noise and the conversations around them, he silently congratulated himself on his dramatic skills. "I just thought that I could accompany you there, help you settle in, and then leave you to your own devices. You can stay as little or as long as you need. When you are ready to return home, just let me know. I will make the arrangements on both ends for travel."

"You really are kind, Stephen, to offer. I've got to say that it is very tempting. Would I have some form of transportation if I chose to do some adventuring?"

He hadn't even considered the possibility. She would have no time to venture anyway. But he thought better of hesitating and said, "Yes, I can arrange that." At one point in his planning, he had considered renting a car and driving up the coast with her but decided against it, as it would only take more time, and he was beginning to feel anxious about closure. It was within clear range now, if she agreed.

"You know, I'm probably not paying attention to my better judgment, but I will take you up on the offer, Stephen. It could be just what I need, and to know that you are willing to let me decide when to come home—I mean, you staying in the States away from your home—well, that's beyond generous of you. Are you sure? Where will you stay?"

"I wouldn't be offering if I wasn't. I have friends in the city, San Francisco, whom I haven't seen in some time. They will take care of me. Not to worry. I'm glad that you have said yes. I know that you will look back on your time there as a blessing in disguise." He fought the urge to celebrate his success as he controlled his voice and the muscles in his face.

She was not sure that she had made the right decision, not really. Alone in the apartment, she repacked her bag, let her neighbor know that she would be out of town for a short time, probably a week or two, and said if she could keep an eye on the apartment, she would appreciate it. The task that still lay before her was not going away and would be waiting for her when she returned. She had not touched any items that were Michael's, had not put away the few toiletries that he had left out on the sink's counter in their haste to make their flight to Athens. Tempted to put the used towels that hung precariously from his towel rack into the wash, she decided against it. She wasn't ready. Besides, she wasn't going anywhere that prevented her from returning home, and the towels and the memories of Michael would be waiting for her just as she'd left them.

Chapter 28

Stephen had arranged for them to fly into Monterey. The drive down the coast would be less than an hour to Ventana, he had assured her. To come into San Francisco, as she'd hoped they would, would have added another two hours to the journey.

He'd had the sense to hire a real estate firm that managed the cabin's upkeep in his absence. The drive into the property had been paved. Stephen had made sure to have this done. It bore no resemblance to his vague memories of it. The cabin's exterior and the grounds around it had been kept up over the years so that anyone coming upon it would assume that it was occupied. Never imagining that he would return here but keeping it as an investment whose value would come in handy if he ever found himself financially strapped, he found it hard to believe that he was heading down the driveway. He found it even harder to comprehend that he was sharing this place with another woman, someone who, for a short time at least, would be allowed here. But there would never be any permanency in this place.

Alison had not made much conversation with him on the drive from Monterey. She was happy watching the coastline pass by, its beauty a match for the island's that she had recently left behind. But this coastline was rugged in most places and certainly uninviting to the casual beachgoer. Where she could see access to the beach, she also saw long, winding paths through the cliff's brush that dropped from sight, not revealing the final approach to the waiting sands. Coming around hairpin corners, she gasped aloud a number of times at the view. And looking back, she realized how high they must be as the cliffs and their long-ago separated selves sat like small haystacks floating in rough seas. It wasn't long, however, before all of this changed, and the redwood groves lined the highway on both sides, casting their shade in all directions. Leaning forward, she tried to see the tops of the trees, but they towered over them well beyond her line of vision.

"Beautiful, don't you think? We're almost there." Stephen continued to look straight ahead as he said this.

The cabin was directly in front of her, waiting at the end of the long driveway leading from the highway. It was, at first glance, as Stephen had described it. Deep within the forest, it was surrounded by more redwood groves that grew far enough apart to let the sunlight find its way through to the cabin's windows. Someone had kept the area around the cabin neatly tamed. Even the raised boxes on the far side of the drive, although empty, had been recently rebuilt, the wood not yet aged by the seasons. It did not dawn on her right away that a small car was parked by the side of the cabin just at the end of the drive. She wondered who would be meeting them.

"Are we expecting someone else to be here, Stephen?" She suddenly felt a bit betrayed.

"Oh, no. Not at all. That car is for you. Remember? I made arrangements for a rental to be delivered here for your use. I hope that is all right?" He knew that it was.

"I can't believe it. That's great. Thanks, Stephen." She was now even more comfortable with her decision to come here.

The interior surprised her. He had told her that no one had been in it since he left years ago, but it was almost pristine in its appearance, as if the housekeeper had just finished for the day. The furnishings were of an older style, but they added to the quaintness of the rooms, she thought. And the kitchen cupboards. Each one held dishes, utensils, and cookware, while the refrigerator was stocked with food and drink. She wanted to explore the upstairs, but Stephen interrupted her exploration.

"What do you think?" He stood in the middle of the living room. She came around the corner from the kitchen.

"I thought you said that no one had been here since you left? How can that be? It's as if someone cleaned house just for us."

"Well, I will admit that I made some calls to the people who manage the property before we left Paris and told them to take care of business for me. It appears that they have done so."

He looked around the room and was impressed. His preparations were paying off.

"It really is lovely, Stephen. I am feeling a bit guilty about staying here and you having to get back on the road."

"Don't worry. I have already made plans with my friends in the city. They are looking forward to seeing me. It's been many years for us. However, a cup of tea would hit the spot before I head out. Would you mind?" He started for the kitchen, suddenly feeling very much at home.

"Of course not. As a matter of fact, why don't I become familiar with the kitchen and prepare dinner for us? It's not too early, is it?" She was trying to remember when they had eaten last. By the number of grumbles coming from her stomach, it was long enough ago.

He looked at his watch, not noting the time for it didn't matter. He knew that he was not going anywhere. "Well, I suppose I have time. Just don't want to drive back in the dark. Eyes don't work as well as they used to once the sun goes down. Let me help you."

"I am putting my foot down about that, but politely. No thank you. You have done more than enough for me. Have your cup of tea, take a nap, and before you know it, I'll have something ready."

Her efforts were not up to her standards, but the meal was passable. Not comfortable in someone else's kitchen, she wasted time hunting for ingredients, not finding the ones she needed so substituting this for that and then giving up, only to start over with a completely different meal in mind. He didn't seem to mind one way or the other as he sat down, observing her efforts. His only comment had something to do with her quick work and the lateness of the day. Placing the spaghetti-and-meatball dish on the table, she had to admit that the aroma of the sauce was enticing. She'd finished by warming a small baguette and defrosting some peas. Well, if nothing else, it filled the hole.

They ate in relative silence. She had questions about the place as her curiosity overwhelmed her thinking. But she held back, trying to understand her reluctance to strike up a conversation with him. He looked up infrequently as he ate and when he did it was as if he had heard something, expecting someone to walk in the door. He reminded her of a meerkat, the way it stands straight up on its hind legs, alert and observant, and in a blink of an eye disappears into their ground holes again.

He knew that keeping his silence was bothering her. He didn't care. He had too much on his mind to be distracted by vacant female noise. He reminded himself to compliment her on the meal, as mundane and tasteless as it was. As he formulated the next hours of his and her lives, he was torn between two sets of emotional pathways, both of which would accomplish the task that had not changed. The closure that he had looked forward to since his meeting with Michael and learning of Alison was imminent. He just had to be sure not to take a misstep. She was not a fool, he had come to realize.

She heard him place his knife and fork down on his dish. "That was very good. Thank you." She looked up to see that he had not left a morsel on the plate.

"I'm glad you liked it." She finished the last two bites on her plate. "Afraid that dessert does not exist tonight."

"No need. I am satisfied. You?" His eyes were on hers.

"Oh, yes. But would you like another cup of tea, or some coffee before your drive?" She looked at her watch and saw that it was already four thirty. She was sure that he would excuse himself, not wanting to linger any longer.

"Well, now that you mention it, a cup of coffee sounds wonderful. But I will need to be on my way soon and you must want to settle in a bit before it gets too late." A fatherly concern found its way into his voice, intentionally.

Perhaps over coffee, she thought as she prepared two cups and brought them into the living room, she could start up a conversation with him about the place. And they hadn't really talked about Michael, not the way she longed to. There were gaps in his life that she wanted filled. Anything that Stephen could add from his four-year-old memories would help her say goodbye to Michael as she knew she must to go on. As for Stephen, she reminded herself that his existence did not concern her beyond his experience with his brother. He had chosen to lead his life as though he had no brother at all. It angered her, when she thought about it. But she knew that the anger she felt was about water under the bridge and she had to let it go.

She caressed the hot mug in her hands, letting it send a vibration of warmth through her. Noticing a chill in the air, she looked around the living room for any open windows. She saw only shut windows and doors. *The draft is terrible in here,* she thought.

He noticed her drawing her legs up under her and a kind of hunkering down into the cushions of the couch as she held the cup close to her chest. He had forgotten how early darkness and the chill from the dampened air seeped in and around the house.

"Don't hesitate to turn on the heat or build a fire. You are very close to the ocean and when the fog comes in, you will feel its effect right through the walls. You get used to it, I suppose, as it never really bothered me after a while. As a matter of fact, I looked forward to its arrival."

"Certainly not LA weather, is it?" She appreciated his noticing her discomfort.

"I don't know how long you will want to stay, but you should not cut your time here short because of this." He pointed to the window across from them that now revealed little in the way of the details of the world outside, as the gray shroud had almost completed its coverage.

"Hmmm. We'll see." She took a sip and then another of the hot liquid. Feeling warmer physically, she snuggled her body even deeper into the cushions while pulling what appeared to be a brand-new throw that had been folded neatly over the back of the couch onto her legs. She was relaxing, she realized, something that she had not done since before Michael's and her arrival in Athens.

"So, did you live here long with your wife?" She wanted to reach out and quickly gather the words back into her mouth as the expression on Stephen's face changed from passivity to sudden confusion. "I'm sorry. I didn't mean to upset you."

He hadn't expected this. He had planned to guide the conversation, if there was to be one, and he knew that there would be. Hiding his surprise as best as he could, he continued. "Yes, for a number of years. She was very happy here." He would go no farther.

"I am sorry, Stephen. May I ask how she died? She must have been fairly young?" Her plans were not on track, as she had really wanted to have him talk about Michael. She would need to bring the conversation back to him and soon. Glancing outside again, she saw that although it was not dark yet, the fog had submerged them in a light darkness, if there was such a thing.

"She was. Or I believe so." He stopped. He must choose his words carefully if he was to go any farther.

"What do you mean, you 'believe so'?" She readjusted her body so that she sat up a bit.

"It's been a very long time and I try not to think about it, you see." He would ply her with his words, sympathy being the result he hoped for. "She disappeared one day. I came home to find her gone. I thought for the longest time that she was still alive somewhere, but I gave up thinking that, not after all of these years." *Careful,* he cautioned himself.

"No trace of her at all? Was there an investigation, a missing person's report?" Now she sounded like she was on the job and that was not called for, she knew. "I mean, that is terrible, not to know." She had pushed herself up now so that her legs swung over the cushion's edge and her feet rested on the floor. She turned to him. "Sorry. I don't mean to pry."

This was his cue to change the subject. "All that was necessary was done long ago. I have come to peace with it."

Neither one of them spoke for what seemed minutes. She recognized his desire to end the topic. It left a strange taste in her mouth, though. Something about his revelation stayed with her, trying to penetrate her brain, insisting on being noticed.

"You know, I must be heading out. I've done just what I did not want to do and now I also have the fog to contend with. Stupid of me." He had risen from the couch, slowly and painfully. A reminder to him of the damage the dampness could wreak on a body.

Against her better judgment but too late to retract them, she heard her words. "Why don't you stay and leave in the morning?"

How well this is going, he thought. "I would, but they are expecting me tonight. I shouldn't disappoint them, not after all these years."

Too late now, you idiot, she thought as she continued. "I'm sure they would understand, Stephen. What is another few hours after all these years? Besides, by the time you arrive, your evening will be over anyway. Give them a call."

With a heavy dramatic sigh, he looked at her. "I did not want to impose on your privacy, you understand. But perhaps you are right. Better to be safe than sorry, I suppose." He took the cell from his pocket. Remembering that the reception was "iffy" in this place, he had found the perfect excuse not to have to make the call in front of her, the call to no one. "That's right. I had forgotten. I'll need to drive up to the highway for some clear reception. It will only take a few minutes."

"You mean I can't use my cell here?" This did not settle well with her. She looked forward to some solitude, but in case of an emergency?

"Yes, you can, but I neglected to tell you about this." He held up his cell. "We had a landline as well, but I canceled that when I left. I thought that if I sold the place, the new owners could reconnect, so to say, if they chose to do so. I had no use for it. Sorry not to have given you a heads-up on this sooner. But it's a nice little walk up to the coast road from here, no more than a few minutes' walk." So much energy expended on a slip-up that he should have thought of earlier!

She had agreed to stay in a log cabin, after all, she reminded herself. Not wilderness, really, but close enough, as she'd realized on the drive from the highway. If she had been in a better state of mind, she might have asked him all the pertinent questions beforehand. "Well, let's just hope I don't do anything foolish like trip over a rock or something in my adventures around the place. I'm not the most sure-footed person in the world." She added a bit of laughter to this last statement in order to ease the hint of intensity that had appeared between their words.

He felt the heat rise to the surface of his face and then subside just as quickly. The outside. He had not given any thought to the outside of the cabin. None. He had imagined in his planning only the interior of the place. He had not considered that she would, naturally, want to spend time outside. All the more reason why, as he had planned, time was of the essence. The sooner the better.

"So, go ahead. Make your call. I'll clean up in here." She was standing now and reaching for the coffee mug that he had gripped overly tightly in his hand.

He released the mug to her. "Thank you. I'll be right back." Feeling for the keys in his jacket pocket, he gave her an old man's nod and left the cabin.

She watched the car move slowly up the drive as it disappeared into the fog.

Sitting in his car just off to the side of the drive and well out of sight of the cabin, he had time to think. Quite frankly, he was growing upset and weary at the direction the evening was taking. He had had no intention of making it so easy for her to be comfortable but, at the same time, he had to be sure she wouldn't insist on leaving the place after having seen it. A fine line that he thought he had balanced upon quite well.

But it was beginning to feel more like she was in control and he couldn't let that continue. He had allowed her to make dinner, not in her kitchen but in a borrowed one, and she had managed to accomplish it without complaint. She had made him coffee and was doing the dishes at this moment. So familiar did she seem to what was not hers. He imagined that she would explore the upstairs in his absence, hurriedly to be sure, as she would not want to appear nosey. He wouldn't be surprised if, upon his return, she would play the innocent and ask him to show her the upper level.

And what would she see up there? A bedroom still

containing the furniture and bed that he and Eliza had shared but nothing else in the room. He had emptied all the drawers and the closet of everything long ago. And she would come upon the room that once held hundreds of books where now only empty shelves clung to the sides of three walls. The desk was still there. Her desk. And the red couch that he had wanted to get rid of at the time but had not. Not having seen it in so many years, he could only imagine its unwelcoming appearance. No. Even if she snooped around, there was nothing that could tell a story—not its beginning, middle, or end.

As he had predicted, she was sitting in the living room waiting for him. He glanced around and found the kitchen to be almost immaculate, and the table gave no indication that anyone had just shared a meal on it.

"Were you able to get through?"

"Yes. They understood my delay. I'll leave early tomorrow morning." He was fighting a growing resentment of her. It was none of her business, really. And did the appearance of the kitchen fuel it even more?

"Good to know. Makes feel me better about getting ahold of someone if I need to." She watched him as he removed his jacket and hung it carefully on one of the hooks by the front door.

"Well, I think that I will call it a night. You can use the bedroom upstairs." He pointed to the staircase just off the living room. "I haven't checked it, but it is supposed to be made up. Clean sheets, towels, you know. The bathroom is attached to the room. I will not be using it. All yours." He wanted to say, "You know. The one you already snuck into," but held his tongue. He felt strangely uncomfortable for a moment. Almost embarrassed. Foolish, he thought.

"Thank you. Where will you be staying?"

"Down here." He nodded toward a closed door on the far side of the living room wall. "It's a guest bedroom with its own facility, so I will not be bothering you nor you me."

"Will I see you in the morning before you leave?"

Surprised that she hadn't taken the opportunity to ask to

see the rest of the cabin, he managed to respond with the fiction that he had been weaving together. "Yes, I won't be heading out at an ungodly hour. Probably about nine or so. I'll be in the city in time for lunch." Then he thought again. "However, if you want to sleep in, which I hope that you do, I will be quiet. No need to get up to say goodbye."

She rose from the couch and came over to where he was standing. "Stephen, do you think that you could manage another hour before going to bed?" She had hoped that the evening would not end so soon. And now there would be no time in the morning.

What did she have up her sleeve, he wondered? He did not want to spend another hour chitchatting, which he was sure was her aim. He needed to retire so he could focus on what needed to be done. Listening to her go on and on about, well, he wasn't quite sure what, though it didn't take a genius to suspect that it would have to do with Michael and him, was to be avoided at all cost.

"I don't think that I can manage it, really. I can't understand why you aren't exhausted. My age won't let me consider anything else." He turned to leave the room.

"No, Stephen. I am not exhausted. As a matter of fact, I feel like I have a second wind and it is strong." She was smiling now. "I just thought that we could spend some time together. I guess, maybe finding some closure?" She knew that she was imploring him to turn back but subtly, so as not to scare him off. "I really think that I need it, Stephen. And, I have a suspicion that you might as well. Who knows when or if we'll ever be in contact again?" Perhaps, she thought, adding this last bit—that she was not expecting to ever see him or bother him again— would encourage him to get it over with.

Keeping his back to her, he allowed an unnaturally long silence to rest between them. As if he had given it due thought, he turned to her. "Perhaps a few minutes more." He moved toward the chair by the front window that faced the couch.

"Good. Thanks. Let me make you something. A night toddy? Tea? Anything?" She threw the words over her shoulder as she began to rummage through the kitchen cabinets. "I'm going to make myself some tea."

"No, nothing. Thanks." He wanted to get on with it.

Waiting patiently for her to join him, he could feel his fatigue growing. How he hated getting so old! To bed well before the rest of the world, only to wake up as if it were the middle of the day and then to find that the clock read one or two in the morning and sometimes as early as midnight. And in the pitch black of night, wandering around the house as if it were high noon with a few more chores to see to. Fighting the urge to let his eyelids drop, he shifted in the chair, uncrossing and then crossing his legs.

"Sorry to keep you waiting, Stephen. Are you sure you want nothing?"

"Very sure."

She sat and cupped the hot mug in both of her hands. "I'm not sure where to begin. There are gaps in Michael's life that I need to fill." She stopped, kicking herself for beginning so abruptly. "I'm sorry. I don't mean to sound so demanding."

"I am not so sure that I can help you with that." He had memories, most certainly, but even with Michael's admission to him that he had shared their family's darkness with her, he wasn't really sure what she knew and what she didn't. He had no intention of meeting darkness tonight. At least not that one. "You do know that I was very young when I saw him last. I think somewhere around ten or eleven. And even during that time, we had been separated for so long that I have no distinct memories of any of our time together." That was a lie. He didn't care.

"Do you remember anything at all about before that time? When you were very young?" She took a sip of tea, surprised by its heat against her lips.

"Do you mean before we were separated the first time?"

"I think so. Something Michael told me about your father and how he was so cruel to you both?" *Careful. He is not your patient and you have probably just crossed a line that you cannot withdraw from,* she told herself.

He wanted to uncross his legs but that would indicate to

her that he was further engaged in the conversation, an impression that he could not afford to create.

"He spoke to you about our father? Well, I suppose you being his therapist, he would. I am sure that he told you everything that we both remembered. I don't think that there is anything that I can add."

"Michael was traumatized, Stephen, when I met him. I mean traumatized by what had happened so long ago. Yes, he did speak with me about your father and what he had done to you both. But he couldn't speak for you. He couldn't express what he didn't know, and that haunted him during our marriage and well before I ever met him. It killed him that he didn't know about you, couldn't ask you how you were. Everything that came out of his mouth was fiction when it came to you. Because he never got the chance to be with you long enough to help heal your wounds, to let you know that he had not abandoned you, that you were left on your own through no fault of your own." She had said so much more than she'd intended. The words just fell to the floor in front of her as if piling higher and higher, forming a barrier between them.

He leaned forward, uncomfortable now, feeling a tingling in his calf and moving toward his foot. Slowly, he unwound his legs and let them drop to the floor, feet now side by side and firmly supporting his upper body. "And if he had been able to, what good would it have done either one of us? You have no idea, none. You sit there talking to me about a brother who, when convenient for him, calls me out of the blue, right in the middle of a life that I had made for myself. *I* made for myself. No one else. Me. He calls me as though I would drop everything and run into his arms, my poor lost brother. That was never going to happen. Never." He was suddenly breathing hard and his voice was louder than he had experienced in years. Holding back further words, his mind raced, trying to sort out the emotions that were beginning to take control of him. Fear? Anger? Bitterness? Sadness? He had to regain some self-control and now, he thought.

"I can understand, Stephen, why you refused to connect,

to reconnect. I get it. But…"

"You don't 'get it'!" He added air quotes for emphasis. His voice level had not diminished, nor had he been able to regain control. "My father died by my brother's hand. Did he tell you that? Did he?" He was now leaning farther forward, still at arm's distance from her.

"Yes, he did. He was protecting you and your mother." She was afraid now. She had stepped into territory that, even though familiar to her, was only so because of Michael's revelations to her. Stephen she just did not know, and she was beginning to think that she no longer wanted to know anything about him. About his interpretation of the past. About his trauma, his memories, his wounds. She only wanted to have completion with Michael. She regretted that she had begun the conversation.

"Did he tell you about the darkness?"

She was not sure, at first, what Stephen was referring to. "The darkness?"

"He didn't tell you about leaving me in there? Hearing his voice calling my name but never getting me out? Do you know who got me out? *She* did. She pulled me up and I remember screaming; the pain was unbearable. But she reached in and grabbed me and lifted me over the wall." He stopped and sat back. She saw him gently rocking back and forth. "She protected me. She held onto me. Not him. Not Michael. I would have died in there and he knew it. But my mother, wounded and crying from her own pain as she brought me back up—she was the one who saved me." He closed his eyes, still rocking.

"Why do you blame Michael? You can't blame him, Stephen. He did all that he physically could. He stood between the two of you and your father. Did you know that? He stood up to your father and he was only eight! My God, Stephen. He was only eight!" She shook her head slowly, as if suddenly acknowledging the truth of that statement.

"I was four!" He slowly stood up but did not move toward her. "What was I to think?" He felt the urge to walk out the door, get in his car, and leave her here. Never mind his plans.

None of that mattered now. He wouldn't let her drag him any deeper than she already had. But he could not move.

"Yes, you were both so young, Stephen." She could feel the intensity diminishing between them and found herself breathing more slowly. "Stephen, I am sorry that any of this happened to either one of you, and to your mother. And I am sorry about what just occurred between us. I should never have pushed as I did." She meant what she said to him, but she also recognized that she was not satisfied. That there was more that he could share with her. Hesitant to say more until he acknowledged her, she fell silent.

Relieved that she was the first to give in, he sat back down in the chair. "There is so much, and it is too late to drag anything up from that time. With Michael gone, there is no point. I wish that you would let it rest now. What is done is done."

"Yes. I suppose you are right. May I ask only one more question, Stephen? No more after that, I promise." *Where is this coming from?* she thought.

"I don't think that that is wise on either of our parts. One question always leads to another and another. You know that." He was tired and drained.

"Please, Stephen?" She tried to be respectful of the man across from her.

Exaggerated or not, his sigh filled the room. An indication to her that she had won. Not waiting for his permission, she began. "What do you know about how your mother died?" One question delivered.

"I have already told you. By my father's hand." He resented having to repeat himself.

"Did you see him kill your mother?"

"That is the second question, you realize that, don't you? Do you always break your promises?" There was a hint of anger in his voice and he knew it. *Let it simmer before seeing where she's going with this,* he thought.

"You're right. I mean one question leading to another. Sorry. And yes, I keep my promises. We're dealing with a different kind of promise." How much more defensive could she appear?

"I am not obligated to answer it, but I will. No, I did not see him kill her. And before you ask the third question, let me be very clear with you. I did not see him end her life, but my mind has been tortured with the image of her lying in front of me, rivulets of blood clogging the hairs of her head while streaking down her swollen, wounded face. The image sleeps within me until it chooses to invade my sleep, my mind, with its reminder of what I need to forget. I must forget."

She hesitated, knowing full well that what had seemed the climactic point only moments ago had not occurred. What they had just been through together was a warmup, she feared, for a climax that might devastate them both if she continued. She knew better. She could sense every intuitive bone in her body screaming out to her to stop. Instantaneous debates battled within her brain, confusing her even more. He wanted to forget, not to acknowledge any of it. She suddenly disliked him immensely because of it. He needed to remember just as Michael had and to acknowledge to her—no, to himself—that he was a victim just as his brother had been. If she could remove him from the façade of his successful life so that he could see where he began and why he had become who he was now as he sat across from her, she might be able to sleep tonight. She even went so far in her thinking as to entertain the possibility that this might not be the last time they see each other, that she might be able to call him her brother-in-law and mean it.

"Michael shared with me something that you should know. For him, it was one of the two hardest things for him to acknowledge and then to tell me. The first I have already shared with you. If he could be sitting here with us right now, Stephen, he would ask your forgiveness for leaving you behind. He had never intended to do so, not the way it turned out." She searched his face for some softening, some sign of understanding. She found none but refused to end the evening without having said what he needed to know. He needed to know the truth. As if a force beyond her control was pushing her forward, step by step, so close that she could smell his breath, almost hear his heart beating, she continued. "I need you to…"

"You need to stop talking." He had put up with her long enough, had allowed her to have the upper hand, had succumbed to his own mental weakness and physical decline so that she had taken advantage of him.

"But, Stephen, you don't understand. I am trying…"

"You must stop talking." Regaining his adversarial nature and confidence, the intonation of his voice could not be mistaken. This was not a request but a command. A warning to her.

He had suddenly changed, she knew. The intangible line that divided sanity and insanity was recognizable to her, too familiar. Not unlike the numerous interactions with some of her patients in which she was put off guard, but only momentarily, knowing full well that just on the other side of the door was help. All she had to do was push the button or yell loudly. Then she would no longer be alone with an unknown. The reality now was that she was alone, very alone. Fighting a growing fear of him, she kept quiet, unsure of any next step on her part.

"I am going to bed, something I should have done over an hour ago." He made a point of looking at his watch as he said this. "If I don't see you in the morning, I wish you a good life, Alison."

He crossed the room and opened the door to the bedroom. He did not turn back, as he suspected she thought he would, but closed the door behind him and turned the lock. He purposely did not turn on the light. He leaned closer to its wooden surface and strained to hear movement on the other side. The kitchen faucet was running. She was probably washing up the recently used mug. He could not hear her footsteps but did hear the staircase creak under her weight as she climbed it to the upstairs bedroom. He stepped away from the door and looked for any light seeping under it from the space on the other side. None. He had forgotten how pitch- black nighttime was here. Satisfied that she had finally retired, he turned on the light switch, which softly illuminated one corner by the bed. Enough for his purposes, he thought. Sitting on the edge of the bed, he began to undress, eager to rest and to think clearly. As he was unbuttoning his shirt, he remembered that his bag was still in the living room. Frustrated with himself, he quietly unlocked and opened the bedroom door, allowing enough light to seep into the black space before him so that he could make out the outlines of furniture. He moved cautiously into the room and saw his bag next to the couch. Trying not to make a sound, he gingerly lifted it and started toward the bedroom.

"Stephen."

Her voice came from somewhere in the darkness. It was strained, he thought. Or was that his own poor hearing's reception? He stopped and peered into the blackness and saw no one. Now unsure if his mind was playing tricks on him, he responded.

"Alison?"

The silence in the room was deafening to him as he tried to hear any movement. Any response. "Alison? Are you in here?" He whispered for no other reason than the darkness seemed to dictate that he do so.

"Stephen."

He put down the bag and reached for the lamp's switch. The light was shocking to his system and blinded him instantly. Wiping his eyes, upset that he had left his glasses in the bedroom, he searched the spaces around him only to find that he alone was in the room. Moving to the staircase, he looked up, sure to see Alison standing at the top, having remembered one more thing she wanted to discuss, but he saw no one. *Now I am hearing things,* he chided to himself. *Foolish old man.* Turning off the light, he lifted the bag and headed for the dimly lit bedroom. Once in the room with the door closed and locked behind him, he continued readying himself for bed.

She had been unable to respond to him, so surprised was she by his announcement. As if nothing had just taken place, he had bid her good night and goodbye. Just like that. And she had let him. As she lay in bed, comfortable and warm under the down cover, but unable to fall asleep as it was only nine thirty, much too early to go to bed, she replayed the last hour with the man. She was angry with herself that she had pushed so hard. Having come so close to what she wanted to say but unable to say it, she knew that she could not leave it alone. He was about to walk out of her life forever, leaving her with the weight of Michael's soul upon her. And now that same weight was to be shared between the brothers. Her own doing, she conceded. Leaving her with no closure. She could not allow that to happen. He had no right to ignore her or his brother. He had no right to deny the havoc that was his life, that had dominated his brother's and that had bound Michael and her together. But he was going to, she was sure of it. He would get up in the morning, slip out of this place, and be gone. And she knew that he would make sure that she would not find him again. Sleep could evade her tonight, she thought. She would have to find a way for this man to allow her to face the next day knowing that she would be all right. Knowing that it was possible. Sleep would come once she had the answer.

This time, he knew he had heard something on the other side of the door. It woke him from his sleep, fitful as it was. He lay straining to hear further sounds. And then he noticed the thin line of light under the door. She was up and making no secret of it, he thought. He reached for his glasses, put them on, and checked his watch. Two in the morning! How long had he been sleeping? Almost five hours. Maybe less. He quickly calculated the recent passage of time. Once his head had hit the pillow, he had slept soundly, so much so that upon being awakened and lying there he felt strangely revived, wide awake. He would wait her out. She probably came down for water. Maybe she'd had a hard time falling asleep. He wouldn't doubt it, as she had been so revved up before going to bed and he had made a point of exiting at her peak, it seemed. More noises. Opening and closing of cupboards, more running water. The building steam in the kettle about to shrilly whistle its presence if she didn't pick it up soon. The scraping of chairs on the hardwood floor of the kitchen—not just one; he heard her dragging each chair out from under the table and then methodically, one by one, pushing them back under the table's surface, never once lifting its legs to assure silence. As he continued to lie there, he began to feel agitated but curious. He also fought the feeling that was slowing angering him: there was a stranger in his home who somehow made him feel that he was the stranger now. All he needed to do was get out of bed, approach her, and tell her to be quiet. He needed his sleep. Not to be so rude. Who did she think she was?

The bedroom was a shade darker now. He pushed himself up on one elbow and saw no light coming from under the door. After all of that, he thought, she had managed to quietly leave the room and climb the stairs to her room. Letting himself fall back onto the bed, he pulled the covers around him so that he felt the warmth of their fabric enclose his body. He closed his eyes, grateful that another encounter had been avoided. Determined to deal with her in the morning, he now focused on nothing but his own breathing and the desire to fall back asleep.

She decided that she would be waiting for him in the morning. Perhaps have coffee ready for him; she would see. But she was determined that he would not leave the cabin without speaking with her. No—without letting her have the final word. She did not care how he received it, at this point. She only cared that he heard her. What he chose to do with the information was his business. She set the alarm on her cell for 4 a.m., noting that only forty minutes had passed since he had dismissed himself for the evening, and she had snuggled under the covers and begun her ponderings. Closing her eyes, the fatigue that had kept its distance as she struggled to come to a decision descended upon her, embraced her, and dragged her quickly into a numbing slumber.

Chapter 29

She was awake before the alarm rang and found it hard to believe that she felt no fatigue. Her body was nagging her to get up. Wondering if she had been overly conscientious about being up before him, she strained to hear any noises downstairs. She shoved her slippers on and wrangled with her robe as she went to the bedroom door. Carefully opening it, trying to avoid any noise, she leaned her head out into the hall. Still no sounds. Good. Closing the door, she quietly got dressed, washed her face, and headed downstairs.

His bedroom door was shut. That didn't prove anything, so she went into the living room and looked outside to see two cars still in the drive. He was here, not up yet. Breathing a sigh of relief that she had not missed seeing him before he left, she crept into the kitchen and made a cup of tea. She would use the next hour or however long she had before he arose to organize her thoughts. She contemplated even writing them down in a short outline format, something she could inconspicuously refer to if need be. Feeling very unsure of how he would react seeing her waiting for him, she would need to be very clear and definitive with him. And she knew herself well enough to know that it wouldn't take much in the way of some attack on her emotional fragility to throw her completely off guard and off track.

The fact that Michael had been responsible for their mother's death would be difficult for him to accept. But she was determined that he know and that he might try to feel some pity for his brother, who had had to carry this with him all his life. If she could make Stephen understand the truth and accept it— that Michael had been the cause of her death but that it had been an accident and that he had been trying to protect Stephen—she would know that she had done her part in finishing what Michael may or may not have started. She had never gotten that far in speaking with Stephen, nor had he brought it up. However, somewhere deep down, she was sure that Michael had not revealed this to his brother.

And then there was the book. They had told no one that he had been writing one, mainly because he did not write with the intention of authoring a book. Very early in the first year of their marriage she had known that he was writing, for she'd surprised him one afternoon having had come home early from work to find him at the laptop, his notebook open, and he had seemed to be copying from its pages. His fingers had been flying over the keyboard, almost frenetic in their work. He had not looked up when she opened the front door nor had he when she shut it, dropped her keys on the side table, and walked toward him. He had been startled by her standing behind him and his body physically reacted with an almost imperceptible jump, but one that she felt as she rested her hand on his shoulder. Not wanting to pry, she had remained silent aside from a greeting and a kiss on the top of his head. He told her that he'd been transcribing the notebook pages. Something that he wanted to do just to have a clear history of where he had once been in his life. Taken by his desire to revisit his past but this time without fear, she had encouraged him to keep going, to perhaps add more of what he had now confronted. And he had taken her encouragement as another sign of her love for him.

As the months passed, then into the second year, he had announced to her that he wanted to write a book about his family. She was touched when he offered it as a possible means for readers who might recognize their own life reflected in his to seek help, to know that they were not alone and that there was a way out. She had never asked to read his manuscript and had waited patiently for him to offer. He never had, and she had accepted his decision. She had not pushed him toward publication and knew that if he had wanted her input and help, he would have asked.

Her patience paid off when he had finally announced its completion. Having worked at the bookstore, he had done research and had spoken to visiting authors about the process of book publishing. Not that he had written anything, he'd continued to assure them, but he was curious as to how they had become recognized. Some were inclined to give him lip service as their sole agenda was to sell their books, autograph each one sold, and bear with the banal chatter of an adoring fan, while a rare few gave him invaluable information, including a favorite editor's name.

With his acquired knowledge, Michael had contacted publishing houses, sending his manuscript with the hope that someone would be ready to contact him with an offer. His relationship with the words on a screen had become a reality. The offer had come. Their trip to Greece had been, in part, a celebration of the manuscript's acceptance by a top publishing house. Michael would have had the first book of the edition in his hands by Christmas. He had told Alison that he'd planned to write a second book, a continuation of his story. Something about reconnecting with the Greek family who had left such an impression upon him when he first met the patriarch. It had been only an idea rummaging about in his brain, and he'd been the first to admit that there might not be any fodder to work with once he revisited the family. But then again, he had told her that there was a reason for him to return to them. He'd had no idea why and had been intrigued by the prospect of something more. And if he had come away from the trip with nothing more than a pleasant vacation with his beautiful wife, he had reassured her, it would have been well worth it.

She reread her notes several times before she put the pencil down. Feeling stronger now and much more prepared than she had been two hours ago, she stood up and walked over to the front window. She was taken by the beauty of the place even from this angle. The driveway leading up the slight incline, the trees that surrounded them in any direction she looked, and the light. The fog was lifting, and the rising sun's rays began to penetrate their warmth through the thick umbrella boughs to the earth below. She wanted to take in clean air and revive herself a bit. It was only six o'clock and with no movement behind the bedroom door yet, she opened the front door and stood out on the porch, leaving the door ajar behind her. Holding onto the porch railing, she focused on her deep breathing while imagining that the healthy sea air filled her lungs to capacity as she blew out the stagnant nighttime air that had kept her alive during her sleep. With each breath, she felt an intensifying clarity that seemed to lift her spirits and her energy. Closing her eyes, she concentrated on the forest's earthy aromas. Michael would have loved it here, she thought. And as his body stood next to hers on this porch in the wilderness, she tilted her head so that it rested on his shoulder, only to dissolve as quickly as he had appeared when she heard footsteps approaching.

She turned to see Stephen standing in the doorway, fully dressed as though he had been up for quite some time. How long had she been out here, she wondered.

"Good morning." She did not move.

"Good morning," he mumbled and turned back into the living room. She heard him open cupboards in the kitchen.

"I hope that I didn't wake you. I woke up early and couldn't get back to sleep. So I got up. I was just enjoying the early morning out there." She had moved into the room and was closing the front door behind her.

"No, I didn't hear you, but I did last night." He turned to her as he said this. She did not mistake the perturbed tone in his voice but was at a loss as to why.

"I'm sorry. What do you mean, 'last night'? Did I disturb you getting ready for bed? I really tried to be quiet." She was not going to move any closer.

"All I can assume is that you must be quite tired. Could you not sleep?"

Now completely confused, she was not afraid to show it. "I really don't know what you are talking about, Stephen. I fell asleep quite quickly and slept right through."

Now he was confused and regretted having even brought it up this morning. He had told himself while shaving that he wouldn't, that there was absolutely no point, and that the less time he engaged with her before leaving, the better.

"What did you hear? I mean, I'm just curious. More likely than not, you were dreaming it."

"I...I...Well, perhaps so." If it had been a dream, he thought, it had been too real, and he assured himself that he had not dreamed. He knew what he had heard and seen. Ill at ease, he would concede to her suggestion, again, avoiding unnecessary banter.

"So, what time are you leaving?" She came to the table and sat down.

"As soon as I have something to eat." He was fumbling with the plastic tie on the bread bag, his fingers rebelling against him as they pretended not to know how to function. Dropping the bag on the floor, he swore loudly, surprising her as she debated whether to offer him some help. She thought better of it.

"I made coffee, if you want some."

He did not look at her as he stood up, bag dangling from his hand, but nodded that he had heard her.

"Stephen, before you go, I need to tell you something. Well, two things. Two important pieces of information that you are entitled to know." She watched him, his back to her, as she spoke and saw his shoulders rise as if taking a very deep breath before responding. "I know that you don't want to talk to me, that you want to be gone from here. But I can't let you. Not until I have had my say." Even she was taken aback by her offensive stance as she saw him turn toward her with an incredulous look on his face.

"I beg your pardon? I will leave when I choose to leave. As a matter of fact, to hell with breakfast and to hell with you!" He slammed the bread bag down onto the counter and brushed by her toward the bedroom.

Without thinking, she followed him and stood in the doorway as she watched him gather his belongings and throw them into his bag. She would not wait any longer.

"Stephen, Michael killed your mother!" If nothing else, she hoped that this statement would freeze him in his tracks.

Stephen did stop what he was doing but did not turn to face her. Instead, he shoved the bag from the edge of the bed and dropped his body into its place. Still not giving her any eye contact, he sat as if he had been punched in the stomach.

"Stephen. I am sorry. I had no intention of blurting it out like that, not in that way, but you gave me no choice. You had to know before you left, if for no other reason than for the sake of Michael. He didn't tell you, did he?" She knew the answer as she watched the man in front of her slip away from her and the reality of the moment. "Stephen, please speak to me."

He remained silent and distant.

"All right then. If you won't speak to me then I will to you. Michael's greatest guilt was that he was the cause of your mother's death. It was not intentional. He had stepped in between your parents to stop your father from hurting her and, in doing so, he pushed her out of his way. But she lost her balance, Stephen, and fell against stones that were strewn on the ground. Her head hit a stone that caused her death. Stephen, Michael had borne the weight of this tragedy along with your loss, not to mention killing your father, all his life. He had wanted to tell you himself, but that did not happen."

Her tears were forming as the tragedy that was the brothers' history overwhelmed her with a greater sadness than she had ever experienced. She gulped for breath, fighting the brimming moisture that was aching for release. But she needed to finish, and she needed him to respond to her.

Stephen had heard every word. He fought off the anger that was rising from within. He fought the despair that was consuming him as the knowledge about his mother's death sank in. And he secretly, through all the turmoil that his body was busy producing, congratulated himself on taking care of Michael when he did. He knew that he had been justified all along. He just didn't know why. Slowly, he gathered his senses so that he to respond to this woman who thought that she had the upper hand. He had let her have her way and now it was his turn.

He stood up, turned halfway, and with one hand straightened the quilt whose wrinkles indicated he had been there. Pulling down on the hem of his jacket and then adjusting the sleeves so that the shirt's cuffs were just peeping out, something that he had done every morning of his working life and something that he had not given any thought to since he had stopped working until this very moment, he marveled at his behavior. Almost as though nothing had just transpired between the two of them. But her voice broke through his thoughts.

"There is one more thing. Will you at least tell me that you are hearing me?" Her sadness had dissipated, so now frustration with him was setting in quickly.

"I do hear you." Nothing more from him was required, he thought.

"Michael has written a book, Stephen. A book about what happened, about your lives with your mother and father." Alarmed by his facial expression, which had, only moments ago, been unnaturally passive but whose flesh now suddenly grew taut, as though something or someone was pulling it across his skeletal structure in opposite directions at the same time, she stopped, sensing that to go on was dangerous. She took a step back, unaware that she was doing so.

"A book?" That was all he could produce for the moment.

What that word meant to him, she could only guess. A revelation about him that was now no longer only his well-hidden secret but for the world to know? An admittance of the horror that had been no one's business but his own? A literary demolition of his life? Of who he thought he was? Was it a betrayal by his brother? No. Michael had tried to include Stephen. Had done everything that he could to bring them closer to one another, only to be met with resistance. Even the tragic meeting in Paris would have to have made some progress for the two of them. She would never know, at least not from the perspective of the only man she had ever trusted. The man standing in front of her frightened her, was a stranger to her, and was unpredictable. The sudden urge to flee sent her pulse into overtime as she dismissed the need to tell him anymore, but only to figure out how to be away from him.

His thoughts were exploding, one by one, as if tiny detonations of anger kindled a growing fire within. He would not, did not, want to smother them either. With each thought of his mother, his father, Michael, his rage built. All the while he was aware of the woman standing in front of him, this messenger from hell who was determined to destroy him in any way that she could. He would not let her do that, just as he had not let Eliza and Michael. And this final blow from her? He recognized it as his destruction, as there was no turning back. But perhaps there was.

"This book." He forced himself to hold back the anger that pushed his words forward but was now out of his control. "Is it published?" His eyes were locked on hers.

Feeling as though any possibility of escape was futile, she answered, fully expecting his wrath to come down upon her. "Yes. Yes, it is in the process. It will be coming out in December." She was surprised at the calmness in her voice. Perhaps it was because she was back on solid footing, dealing with only facts and not the tightrope of emotions that was suspended between them and upon which neither of them had any semblance of balance.

"Dear God in heaven! How can this be happening? Dear God in heaven!" He was yelling now, not at her but at the ceiling. Suddenly he turned on her. "You...you are to blame for all of this. You and your fucking therapy mumbo-jumbo. You think you saved him? You think that just because he married you, you healed him? Made him into a needy runt of a puppy that keeps you company? Oh, no, wait. *Kept* you company. My mistake. How do you know if he loved you? How do you know that he wasn't playing a game just to keep his head above water? What if I told you that he never loved you? Never. Just saw you as his way out. What do you think about that? You have no idea and now you never will. You know what you've done, don't you? You have destroyed him and now me!"

"What is wrong with you? How can you be so cruel?" She was reeling from his verbal blows, but she was not going to let him scream lies at her. "You are the one who has no clue! You're the one who wouldn't let him in, wouldn't open your life to him! You're the one to blame if you want to blame someone. Not me. How dare you! How dare you! He never would have had to write a book if you had just one time said yes to him. Maybe you'll get it when you read your own brother's words. Better late than never!"

She was spent but was afraid to let him see it. Her words had come so easily and with such vehemence. Who was she in front of this man? She didn't recognize herself.

He moved away from her and picked up his bag, not bothering to zip it shut. As he pushed his way by her, she barely managed to move her body before he could slam into it. Was he just going to walk out the door with no response to her?

"What are you doing? You can't just leave like this. Stephen!" She followed him through the living room and came upon him as his hand reached for the doorknob. "No, you can't walk out of here forever after what you have just said to me. I can't be left here replaying what I said to you."

"I will not play any games with you, not like my brother did. You are to blame, Alison. You will always be blamed. Lucky for you, however, that there isn't anyone left to blame you except me. Well, maybe not so lucky." He was smiling now, with no trace of anger on his face. She stood, frozen in place, trying to comprehend what was taking place.

"What do you mean by that? Are you threatening me? Because if you are, you have no idea what you're doing. Has it occurred to you that I know probably more about your past and that of Michael than anyone else? You're right about one thing. There was no one else except you. But now there is me. And I will not let Michael's life and everything that he went through until the day he died be forgotten. Do you understand me, Stephen? You cannot go back to your little village in France, lock the door, and ignore who you are anymore. Both Michael and I will not let you!"

She felt his hands grab her by the shoulders before she could register that he was attacking her. Surprised by the strength of his grip, she realized that she was falling backwards, losing her footing as his hands pushed her downward. Even in his elder years, he was stronger than he looked. An odd thought that shot across the bow of her thinking as if slow motion had taken over, giving her time to linger on odd thoughts as she sensed the floor coming up to meet her. His weight now fully on her body, she tried to wriggle out from under him, but he had pinned her so that her middle could go nowhere. And then his hands were on her throat, groping for a solid, crushing grip. It was at that moment that she knew she had to act. With every ounce of her strength, she propelled her middle up against his so that his surprised body gave way, leaving just enough room for her to draw her knee up and into his groin. It took only one time for him to react but for good measure, she did it once more, this time with more force as he unintentionally left room for her attack, his body collapsing in pain to the side of her.

Without a moment's hesitation, she was standing and then running to the kitchen counter. Grabbing her purse and the keys for the rental, she opened the door and ran to the car. She took her first breath since starting the engine as the coast highway appeared before her. She turned south and did not look back.

Writhing in pain, a pain that he had not felt in years but that reminded him that he still had his manhood to protect, he stayed on the floor, fighting off the rising nausea that he knew would overtake him. How long he suffered, he wasn't sure, and it was only after he managed to crawl to the bedroom and lift himself onto the bed that he began to remember all that had transpired. Where was she? He listened, straining to hear her somewhere in the cabin. He wouldn't be surprised if she was packing with every intention of leaving. He could not let her go. That had never been his intention. He had a plan, well thought through, and when completed it would relieve him of any worry. His life would be his own again.

But as he lay there, the sickening realization that none of that had occurred brought him to a painful sitting position. He had almost ended her life. He had been that close. There was no way that she could still be here. She might have moxie, but not enough to jeopardize her life.

Slowing turning his body so that his legs now hung over the side of the bed, he gingerly stood, placing one foot down and then the other. What he had tried to do to her and what she had done to him had depleted him of any confidence that his body was going to perform for him. Placing his hand on the mattress for support, he pushed himself up and slowly, one foot in front of the other, managed to make his way to the bedroom door.

He knew it before he confirmed it. She was gone. The car was gone. *You fool!* he admonished himself. His first thought was to go after her. Not to reason with her but to silence her. And then he remembered the book. What good would it do to silence her? Not now that the whole world would know. And all he had done was attack her, not hurt her. Just frightened her. She knew nothing that would damage him other than whatever Michael had put in his precious book. And none of that really mattered, because Michael did not know about his little brother's past. No. He knew nothing about Eliza other than what he had chosen to tell him. The longer he thought about Alison, the less inclined he became to do anything at all.

Chapter 30

She played back the last hours of her life over and over again, barely aware that she was behind the wheel of a ton or so of steel and plastic. She had not taken any notice of her surroundings, so engrossed was she in thinking. He had tried to kill her. Not able to fathom this, she kept going over the moment when his hands found her throat. Unaware that her own hand kept reaching toward it, she forcefully rubbed its skin each time as if wiping away his flesh upon her body. She was not hurt. Nothing ached, nothing broken. She couldn't identify what she was feeling other than having been trespassed upon.

Once, maybe more, she couldn't remember, shortly after turning onto the highway she'd looked in the rearview mirror. Cars came up behind her but none she recognized. She must have been traveling below the speed limit, she realized, as car after car passed her and then sped off ahead of her. She hadn't been giving her full attention to her driving, she knew, and she said a tiny prayer of thanks that she hadn't run off the edge of the road and into the Pacific Ocean. When she came to a pull-off, she stopped the car and got out. The full blast of cool ocean air hit her squarely in the face, forcing her to take a gulp to catch her breath. Walking to the edge of the cliff, she kept a safe distance as she took in the air, coming to second by second.

What was her plan now? She told herself that she needed to pull it together and think beyond the next turn in the road. Heading back to LA was her goal, of course. To be home in familiar surroundings, as hard as it would be without her husband beside her. She knew that as soon as she stepped in the door, everything that had been Michael would overwhelm her with sorrow. The familiarity that she longed for would cause unbearable pain. She wasn't sure that she was ready to say goodbye as she knew she must eventually. Probably the sooner she did, the sooner a better frame of mind would take over. And she needed to bring herself back to a semblance of normalcy.

Work still waited for her, people who depended upon her for all kinds of reasons. As she thought more about the workload, she was surprised by a sudden burst of energy and positivity that cleared away all thoughts of the horrors that the early-morning hours had sprung upon her.

Revived by the fresh air as well as a shift in her thinking, she returned to the car and just before pulling out onto the highway, remembered her suitcase. She had left it in the bedroom. It never occurred to her in her haste to escape. What did she have in her bag? Anything that she had really wanted to save? As she took a mental inventory of its contents, she breathed a sigh of relief. Just a few changes of clothes, easily replaceable; two pairs of shoes, one of which she had really liked but also replaceable; and a book that she had started just before their departure to Greece. Everything of real importance she had kept in her purse, which she reached for just to be sure that it was really there. No, she had left nothing of herself behind that mattered. And even if she had, she would never go back to retrieve it.

Oh my God! His notebook! She had packed it in her suitcase at the last minute with the intention of reading it through one last time before she stored it along with some of his other belongings that she knew she could never part with. Of the few of his belongings that she had unpacked when she first returned to the LA apartment, the notebook was one of the first to find its way back into her hands. She had set it aside, not willing to decide its fate. But the thought of peace and solitude gifted to her by Stephen had been the deciding factor in bringing it with her to the cabin. There, without any pressure, she could let Michael speak to her one last time in all his anguish as well as his joy, the little of it allowed him. She'd wondered if he'd taken it with him when he met with Stephen? He had wanted to start the second book upon their return and had been excited about what the near future would hold for him and for the contents of the new manuscript. She couldn't have lost his notebook. Not in the way she feared she had.

The car behind her had been patiently waiting for her to

pull onto the highway, she realized, as the harsh sound of a horn broke through, startling her. Looking in the rearview mirror, she saw the driver holding both hands above the steering wheel as if to say, "What gives? Move it, lady!" She waved an apology to him as she entered the highway once again, still heading south.

As she drove on, it suddenly dawned on her that his book would substitute for the notebook. It had to now. The only unknown for her was what he might have added to it while in Greece. But all of this was moot. There would be no second book. There was no notebook from which to compose it and no Michael to do so. Did it really matter if Stephen found it and read it? In a humanly kind mental gesture toward him, she entertained the thought that it might be good for him to see Michael's words as he originally recorded them. Perhaps, in some unknown way, he might come to appreciate who his brother had been. A reconciliation that would take place between the living and the dead? It was possible, she thought.

She reached LA just as the evening sun was at its lowest point in the sky before dropping below the horizon. She was prepared for the traffic, a rude awakening back to the world she had left behind days ago and that, if anything, now seemed even more frenetic than before.

Closing the apartment door behind her, an exhaustion the likes she had never felt before overwhelmed her and the simple effort of placing one foot in front of the other seemed an impossibility. She was tempted to crumple in a heap right where she was. *Come on. You've made it this far. Just a few more steps,* she told herself. She purposely did not stop once started but headed for the bedroom. Now undressed, she stumbled into the shower stall, turned on the hot water, tempering it with the cold tap only when she could bear the heat no longer, and let the stream wash over her. Subconsciously, her hands moved along her neck in a sideways movement as if massaging the stress-related kinks that were preventing her from moving it to the left or right with any kind of ease. She reached for the bar of soap and lathered herself in its sweet-smelling foam, paying extra attention to her neck as she soaped and rinsed it not once, but over and over again until a chill ran through her as the hot water ran out of its healing warmth and the cold reminded her, unsympathetically, where she was.

She had decided that she would go in to work the next day. Perhaps a half day. They might even insist on a shortened day or tell her to take more time to grieve. But she would assure them that she wanted to work, to be among the living. It would do her a world of good and would help her heal, she would reassure them.

As she suspected, she had been at her desk no more than fifteen minutes before the first of many co-workers found their way to her cubicle, offered their condolences and to help in any way, and then went on with their lives. Ready for all of the kindness to be done, she debated whether to leave and take work home with her or hang in there. Frankly, she figured that everyone had had the chance to have their say and that should be the end of it. Even her boss had made a personal appearance and was generous in his suggestion that she take the rest of the week off. As it was only Tuesday, she could probably use it, he had added. It sounded appealing for a moment, but she had thanked him and told him that she wanted to stay.

As she plowed through the back paperwork that someone had thoughtfully left on her desk that morning before she arrived, it felt good to be doing what she knew she was meant to do. With each review of her current patients' standings, she felt less and less alone. She realized that even with all of the kind condolences shared with her earlier, none of them made her feel as though she really existed in anyone's life. But as she ran her fingers over the first, last, and middle names of her clients, one after the other, she could not deny the connection that she felt with each one of them. Even the new one, someone who had only come under her watch since she'd been gone, called to her. A confirmation that she was home, safe and secure in these surroundings. And then she chuckled aloud at that last thought. Well, maybe not all that safe, but far more than she had been just a day ago. As quickly as the aged crazed face appeared before her did she dismiss it, wipe it clean from her mind's eye, and refocus on the day's workload before her.

She was proud of herself that she was running ahead of schedule and promised to be sure to maintain her promptness from here on out. Fully caught up on the paperwork, she felt as though she had not skipped a beat, had not been away at all, much less had gone through what she could not bear to think about right now. Passing his old room on her way to the meeting room, she purposely willed herself not to register that once, on the other side of that door, Michael had survived one day at a time. Quickly stepping aside to the right of the hallway in order to avoid the door opening and her slamming into it, she turned to see who had shoved the door so forcefully and carelessly into the hallway. She stopped in her tracks as Jared, still holding the door open to its full extent, did upon seeing her.

"Whoa! Sorry about that," he said as he let the door close after him.

She struggled to say something, anything at all, but was dumbfounded to see him. She couldn't recall how long ago she'd last spoken with him.

"Alison? Man, it's been a while. You okay? I didn't get you, did I?" He looked back at the door and then to her.

Her words emerged as she heard her meager attempt to respond. "No. I'm fine." She turned and began walking down the hallway, knowing that he was only a few feet behind her.

"Hey, wait up." He caught up with her and now walked by her side. "Just wanted to say I'm sorry about your husband."

As he spoke these words, she tried to remember how long ago it had been since they had last spoken. At least three years. How could that be? In the same building, doing the same work, she was aware of his rise in stature and her stagnant career. Had they managed to avoid each other until this moment?

"I never met him. Michael, right?" He thought he detected a slight nod but was not sure. She did not turn to acknowledge him, nor did she slow her pace. "I guess it's been too long. No worries. Just wanted you to know that I was thinking about you. Really sorry for your loss." He pivoted so that in one movement he was facing the opposite direction and walking away from her.

In the days that followed, she let the work consume her and found herself falling back into the same habit of staying well after hours, reflecting on the work of the day, all the while attempting to keep up with the endless reams of paper that screamed for her attention. She knew that she was avoiding the inevitable and the longer she stayed at the office, the less time she would have in the apartment—only enough time to shower and sleep. Catching something to eat before going home was convenient and added to the avoidance, not to mention a ding to her budget. She would take care of it all, but not just yet. Even though Michael was gone, his stuff was not and, strangely, she found some comfort in that.

For the first few nights, and for that matter, at unannounced moments during the day, she wondered about Stephen. Where was he now? Was he going to come after her when she least expected it? Should she have reported him to the police just to be on the safe side? Was she being too cavalier about the possible danger he could be to her? Those moments paralyzed her. She fought against replaying anything having to do with him by submerging herself deeper into her work. She occasionally left her desk and walked through the corridors, distracting herself with professional human contact. Only twice had his presence invaded her thoughts while with a client. It had been embarrassing. Because she registered nothing during that time, her clients fell deeper into their own confusion, with no help from her until her mental battle with Stephen fought him off and freed her to return to the moment at hand. It worried her that her behavior would be reported and that she might need to be the one behind a door just off the hallway. But as time wore on, he began to fade from her consciousness. She had moments when she realized that she hadn't thought about him for days, even weeks, and soon all thought of him left her.

It was then that she knew what her task must be and that avoiding it any longer was out of the question. Without the memories of Stephen, she felt lighter, unrestrained, and ready to move forward. As she emptied Michael's side of the closet and cleared out the chest of drawers that held his belongings, the tears came. She knew that they would, but this time she was in a better place to greet them and to understand that the process of grieving was never over; it was just handled differently as time went on.

She began to understand now how her grandmother could relate to her stories of her grandfather, his escapades as a young man and his loving gestures toward her, without her ever shedding a tear. In fact, she sprinkled smiles and laughter among her voiced memories and because of that, Alison recalled so clearly those precious moments with her grandmother. Even when she was dying and everyone in the family who could come surrounded her deathbed, there were no tears in her eyes but only gentle, barely whispered assurances of her love for each one as they reached for her hand, one last touch, one last connection made. And when it was Alison's turn to come to her side, she had touched her grandmother's hand, avoiding the tubes that sank into her almost tissue-thin skin, only to hear what others had not.

"I am not afraid."

Chapter 31

He was in no hurry to leave. He had no place to be. He had made sure of that. As he sat at the table sipping his coffee, he contemplated what he should do now. With her gone, a deep and deafening silence had filled the room so that the only sound he could detect was the slurping of his own lips against the hot liquid that entered his mouth. He smiled remembering the movie *2001: A Space Odyssey*, the scene in which Dave had become ancient in appearance and was sitting alone at a dining table, the only sound breaking through the silence the clanking of his silverware against the china plate. A disturbing and invasive sound, it had seemed to him at the time, just as his slurping was to him now. He put the cup down and stood up, still feeling the remnants of her attack.

Not speaking aloud but allowing a stream of curse words to drive her out of his mind, he decided to get some air before making flight arrangements. The thought of returning to his own home, to the quiet village that would not welcome him with open arms, a situation he knew was of his own making, but would be waiting for him just as he left it, lifted his spirits. He decided to make a clear path for himself now and live out his days, as limited as they were, in Tigeaux. And in going home, he would bring nothing back with him of his time here, as there was nothing left. Even though she was alive, probably heading back to LA right now, she was not a threat. In fact, she was meaningless to him now, just as his life had been to this point, he realized, even with its successes as well as its failures.

He had no intention of going far, just off the porch to wander a bit around the perimeter of the cabin. One last look, as he intended never to come back. He had already added to his mental list to call the real estate management and tell them to put the property up for sale. Get back home and sell the place. He had a plan. Satisfied with his decisions, he noted that the pains he suffered earlier had diminished to the point where he had to think about his groin to acknowledge its recent trauma. Feeling much better, he picked up the pace a bit, still wary of hidden dangers just below the surface that might trip him up. "Don't be too sure of yourself, you old fool," he reminded himself aloud.

As he came to the back of the cabin, he saw what appeared to be a mound of earth in which rocks of different sizes, barely visible, were partially buried. Remnants of what were once green, thriving tendrils still clung to the rocks' surfaces but were now dried and emaciated, their brown, withered capsules that once held life having become part of the rocks, fastening themselves to their hard surfaces even in death. He stood in front of the mound trying to recall its beauty, but all he saw was neglect. Perhaps the management company thought the same, which would explain why the area had not been attended to.

Not wasting any more time, he turned to go back to the cabin. He noticed how overgrown the underbrush had become, especially farther back into the groves. Obviously, only the very immediate cleanup had been done for their arrival. Never mind. It was not going to be his problem anymore.

Coming around the corner of the cabin and onto the drive, he thought he heard something and turned backed. Standing still, he strained to hear any sound. His hearing, he knew, was not getting better but only worse as time went on. He couldn't trust it to communicate to his brain with any accuracy. But he had heard something, and he knew it had not been the wind in the trees or the tapping of a red-headed woodpecker somewhere high above him or the crush of fallen brittle branches trod upon by a rabbit or deer. He knew those sounds. But whatever it was that he had heard did not repeat itself as he stood a bit longer, silent and alert. *Imagining it. That's what you're doing,* he thought. *Get a move on!*

He turned and walked back to the porch. And then he heard it again. This time he could almost identify it but still was not sure. A whooshing sound? No. More of a clatter? Not continuous or in any rhythm he could identify but sudden, and then silent. Without questioning himself, he moved toward what he thought was the direction from which it was coming.

Stopping at intervals, he waited quietly. Nothing. Until he took a step forward. It was louder this time but still indistinguishable. He stumbled and spread his arms out to his side to regain balance. Once he'd established both feet securely on the ground, he looked down to see what had tripped him up.

Stones. Scattered all about him, surrounding him as if they had seen him coming and were just waiting to move in place, encasing his feet within their circular growing wall. He watched in horror as the stones silently climbed over one another, making their way higher and higher as they worked together to support one another. He tried to scream, to slam them down to the ground as they continued to surround him, blocking any way out, so much so that he couldn't even turn his body, so encased was he becoming. And then the only light that appeared was just above him, barely illuminating the stones that stood triumphantly encircling the small opening. When he looked forward, there was nothing but thick black velvet darkness, but he could feel the chill of the stones filling what little air there was around him. Again, he tried to scream, but even though he knew his mouth was open, no sound came. He looked up once more, blinking rapidly, trying to adjust his eyes from the darkness to see the little light that waited for him above. And then he saw him. Only his face, whose mouth was also open, trying to make sound. Their eyes locked even as the distance between them seemed to be growing so that within an instant, his face was only a spot against the diminished circle of light. And then Michael was gone.

In front of him as he looked straight ahead, the blackness held two images, impossible to make out. He struggled to focus, to see more clearly what he knew was within his reach if only he could move his arms to do so, but the cold stones kept him in place. He closed his eyes, hoping that upon opening them, they would be gone, that all of this would be gone. Sensing that nothing had changed, he reluctantly opened them. His fear only grew as he made out two pairs of eyes, wide open and staring at him. They were not facing him as he was them, but one pair, the older eyes, lay beneath the younger pair, a vertical display of such intensity and despair that even as he tried to close his own eyes to avoid seeing what he was forced to see, the darkness slowly revealed the restraint that had been invisible a moment ago and that held the eyes, balancing one on top of the other, in place: a stone.

What brought him to he couldn't say, but as he lay sprawled on the ground, he gradually understood that he had fallen. His head hurt on one side, and he reached up and felt a bump on his forehead. Slowly rolling onto his back, he lay there and watched the morning sky, a clear robin's-egg blue, change as haphazard swishes of fog swept across the canvas as if someone was finger painting. He marveled at its beauty. Then a sharp pain seared from one temple to the other as the bump on his forehead made itself even more known. Taking a slow accounting of the rest of his body, he determined that, aside from a sore knee and elbow, nothing was out of order.

He carefully rolled onto his side and pushed himself to a sitting position. The ground was not even. He could see that now. Grabbing onto the protruding rounded surface of two stones, he used them to push his way up to a standing position. As if each one of them had just given him an electric shock, he moved his hands from their surfaces quickly and rubbed his palms against his pant legs. Strange, he thought. "Better attend to this head," he mumbled, reaching up once again to feel that the swelling had grown. So had the headache that had come on as he regained full consciousness.

After swallowing a couple of aspirin with the cold coffee that he had left behind and rubbing ointment on his grazed knee and elbow, he collected himself. Not feeling completely well but enough to get on with business, he made his reservation for a red-eye flight from San Francisco to Paris arriving early in the morning. He looked forward to the sleep that he knew would come once on the plane and after a couple of bourbons. The second item on his list would take more than one phone call, but he would start the process by letting them know he wanted to sell. The rest he would need to do at a distance.

A sudden yearning to be home consumed him as he hung

up the phone. He wasted no time packing the little he had with him and then took one last walk through the cabin. Nothing left behind, he thought, as there was nothing there to begin with. He debated about checking the upstairs. He knew what was there. Nothing. However, he needed to be sure.

As he entered the bedroom, he saw it sitting, open, on the bed. Her suitcase. *Damn.* He wanted nothing to do with it but couldn't just leave it there for someone to find. He would need to get rid of it. Zipping it closed, he decided that he would take it with him, and somewhere along the way, dispose of it.

He closed the house behind him. Taking one final glance at the property from the porch before getting in the car, he felt nothing other than the searing pain on his forehead and the need to return home. He threw his bag and her suitcase onto the backseat.

He never saw her. Never sensed Eliza's presence as she came toward him from the stones and followed him up the drive, only to evaporate with the morning fog as the coast highway came into view.

Chapter 32

He had not forgotten how the morning light intensified the beauty of the countryside but was still taken by surprise as he watched it pass by from the inside of the taxi. Thankful that the driver was not one to chat for the sake of chatting, Stephen enjoyed the quiet atmosphere and the opportunity to adjust to the rest of his life in this village. As the taxi pulled up in front of his home, Stephen felt in an especially generous mood, paying the fare and then adding a tip that almost doubled the journey's expense. The driver was grateful and jumped out of the taxi, opening the passenger door and helping his fare out as he struggled with his bag.

"*Non, non.* Let me." He reached in and carrying the small bag in one hand, he offered his other arm to Stephen, who gratefully leaned on it as he made his way up to the front door.

"*Merci beaucoup, monsieur,*" he said to the driver, who handed him his bag. "*Au revoir.*"

"*Au revoir, monsieur, et merci, merci.*"

Stephen fumbled with the keys for just a moment before he heard the familiar click as the key made contact with the lock. Pushing the door open, he was confronted with the stale smell of firewood smoke. The house seemed to suck in the fresh air as Stephen stood in the front room holding the door open. Dropping his bag to prop it open, he moved through the house, opening windows. Even though it was stale and stuffy, he sighed deeply and was glad to be back.

He had only glanced at the yard when he came up the walk with the driver. Now, remembering Jean-Pierre's promise to him, he went back outside to see what the boy had accomplished during his absence. He had done a good job, Stephen thought, as he moved closer to inspect the plantings. The plants were still young but healthy and promising, and he was curious as to what to expect once in they were in full bloom. Jean-Pierre would regale him, he knew, with all of the details.

Turning to go back in, he remembered his command to the boy. *No rocks!* Turning once again, he moved back to the plot. Nothing but freshly turned earth harboring its new charges. *Good,* he thought. He would have to remember to give Jean-Pierre a little extra when he paid him.

He was hungry and hoped that something decent awaited him in the kitchen. He couldn't remember what he had left behind. He was in luck, finding that not only had the carrots not spoiled, but he had one potato and a frozen chicken breast. Enough to tide him over until tomorrow. Setting the chicken on the counter to defrost, he felt a draft around his legs. The door. He had forgotten that it remained propped open. Lifting the bag, he closed the door. He needed a shower and a shave. He flung his bag onto his bed and, in doing so, felt a sharp pain somewhere in his chest. It disappeared as quickly as it came on. Paying no attention to it as his head had begun throbbing again, he undressed. A shower would feel so wonderful, he thought, as he closed the bathroom door behind him.

Now refreshed but with his head still throbbing, he ingested two more aspirin. He knew that he should take it easy for the rest of the day. There was not much else to do than read, which he was tempted to try if only the headache would cease. If improvement didn't come soon, he would give in and see the doctor.

The bag waited for him. He had forgotten it was there. For just a moment, he wondered if his memory lapse was not just the laughable forgetfulness that everyone assumes a person over the age of fifty comes by naturally, and no one really takes that seriously, or if he truly was suffering from the onset of dementia. He wouldn't be surprised. It seemed that he was constantly forgetting something. Pushing this depressing thought aside, he focused on the practical. Unpack, maybe do some laundry depending on whether he could get away with a few more days' wear of the clothes in the bag, have a light lunch to tide him over until dinner, and then see where the rest of the day would take him.

As he unzipped his bag, his mind wandered to Alison's

suitcase. He had rudely gathered its contents against his upper body as he approached the dumpster. Self-conscious, he struggled to free himself of a woman's intimate as well as everyday clothing. It occurred to him, a fleeting thought, that he had planned no explanation for his actions. So as not to draw attention to himself, he moved as quickly as he could. The last of it now covering someone else's trash, he closed the heavy lid, free of this burden. As he pulled out of the parking lot of the local market, leaving Big Sur behind for the last time, it suddenly dawned on him that he still possessed the suitcase. Why he had separated the contents from the suitcase, he had no idea. It was stupid, and now he had one more problem with which to contend. And he had. Pulling off the highway, he removed the suitcase from the backseat and tossed it over the side of a cliff. It dropped quickly and unceremoniously to the churning waters hundreds of feet below him, its only remaining contents, Michael's notebook, which was securely lodged inside a zippered pocket that Stephen, in his haste and determination to free himself of this last burden, had overlooked.

The two small boxes lay under the clothes and had found their way to one corner of the overnight bag, having landed there after so many jostles. At first, he was puzzled by them, not recognizing them at all. As he lifted each one from the bag, flashes of a darkened room came quickly while bits of conversation trickled in and out of his thinking. And then he remembered. The inheritance. Eliza. He had been carrying these with him all this time. So much had transpired since he had been given the gifts that they had completely been lost in his memory. *So, after all that,* he thought, *I am not completely free.*

He sat on the bed, the boxes balanced in his lap. The easiest thing to do would be to throw them away without opening them. Why put himself through any more of this? But he wasn't thinking clearly, he knew, as he put one of them on the bed next to him. The other, he opened.

The velvet material was a deep crimson, and its soft folds

and shallow crevices disguised the shape of the object within its embrace. For a moment, he entertained the thought that a thing of great value lay just within his reach. Perhaps his efforts were about to pay off. He could put up with this last intrusion considering the possibilities it might hold. Without going any farther, he reached for the box next to him and opened it, only to find the same enticing packaging. He stood up and carried them both to the kitchen and set them on the table.

Gently, as if a careless move could destroy the fragility of the contents, he unwrapped the velvet of the first box. Resting on top of the object was a neatly folded sheet of paper. The familiarity of this moment sent a chill through his body, but he couldn't identify its source. Lifting the paper from the box, he saw a rock. Not very large at all, no bigger than the palm of his hand as he lifted it out and examined it. Its surface was a dull white. Smooth and cold. Quite ordinary and disappointing, he thought. He realized that he was strangely and unexpectedly calm as he put the rock down next to him and opened the second gift. The same greeted him, another rock, very similar to the first.

Unfolding the first paper, the familiar script appeared in front of him. The writing seemed blurred for a moment as he forced his eyes to focus. The pounding in his head had diminished slightly, but he wondered if he had done some real damage as the lettering remained difficult to read. He took the paper over to the reading lamp and held it under its brighter light. Rubbing his eyes, he tried again to make out the words. The paper under the light revealed its age, the parchment's color faded, almost matching the variations of whiteness of the rock upon which it had rested. But the black ink that formed the letters appeared as if it had penetrated the paper only yesterday. Odd, he thought, as he began to read.

My Dear Eliza,

You honor our friendship and my family by accepting these gifts. I am sorry that I am not with you to explain my intentions, but

I am sure that you will understand their meaning once you read on. They come to you not only from me but also from my father and his father and all the fathers before us. Keep them safe.

The note continued:

This rock appears plain, with no striking characteristics. If not for its color, it would be lost among all the other rocks. But it is the color that draws your attention. I have seen this rock in my father's possession even as the youngest of children. It sat on a shelf in his shop in the same place that it sat for all the fathers of our family. The second rock did the same. As if brothers, never to be separated, but meant always to be together. That is why you have both in your possession now. It was never meant that they should be apart.

The first rock was taken long ago, during ancient times, from its original site, the Acropolis in Athens. It is said in our family that this was done by one of our fathers. It is limestone and comes from the earth upon which the Acropolis was built. You may understand better if I explain that the word Acropolis, in Greek, means "The Sacred Rock, the high city." The Acropolis rock has been a part of the earth since the late Cretaceous period. This acropolis had its own underground water supply in the form of a deep well, dug at the north end of the rock, which could be used by the defenders during a siege.

The second rock is from Cyprus, which is home to some of the oldest water wells in the world. This stone comes from one of the many excavations of the area of the well-preserved Neolithic village of Khirokitia, whose wells date to around the 10th millennium B.C.

I believe that these rocks traveled through time within our family for a reason. They have been waiting for you, Eliza. I do not know the reason, but I do know that they can no longer stay with us. I do not question which of the gods' hand is at work here or why. Neither should you. Hold them near as the gods intended.

With my warmest regards,

Achaïkos Metaxas

Had he been feeling better, he would have taken the time to reread the text for after reading it the first time, certain words lingered with him. Somewhere, deep within the recesses of his memory, he thought that they made sense, but he had difficulty determining what that sense precisely was. And the man's superstitious references to the gods were just an old man's folly, he told himself. Besides, none of it mattered now. Passing by the fireplace, he moved back to the table where the rocks waited. The pounding in his temples had gained intensity, and he held his palms against them to ease the pain. Why weren't the aspirin kicking in? Bearing the pain a bit longer, he put each stone back in the box that had contained it, wrapping each one in the rich red velvet blanket that waited patiently for its return. The note, like the others, now lay crumpled among the ashes and charred wood, the remnants of the most recent fire in his home.

He knew he shouldn't sleep, but he could bear it no longer. Instead of lying on his bed, he decided to remain sitting up, in hopes that getting off his feet and closing his eyes for just a short nap would allow the medicine to do its work. Straining his eyes to read probably hadn't done his head much good. Leaving the boxes on the table, he moved to the chair in the living room, his favorite, and sank into its welcoming cushions.

Leaning his head back, he shut his eyes, trying to block out the thumping sounds in his head. *Deep breaths, relax. Relax.*

The pounding subsided into a more defined percussion. Trying to identify it, he awoke from his sleep and looked toward the front door. The knocking was on the other side of the wooden entry, not in his head, and for that he was grateful. Taking a moment to orient himself to his surroundings, he managed to call out, "A moment, please."

The knocking stopped but when he stood up, he was reminded of the swelling on his forehead as he took a step forward. Reaching to touch it, he was amazed at its size. It felt as though it covered the whole area above his eyes and as he explored it, he flinched from the soreness of the wound. He would need to remember to look at it in the mirror afterward.

On other side of the entrance, Jean-Pierre stood, hands clutching his cap as he held it in front of him. His smile quickly changed upon seeing the old man standing in front of him. "Oh, *mon Dieu! Monsieur,* what is wrong?" He lifted his cap toward Stephen's face.

"Oh, nothing. I took a little fall yesterday. It looks worse than it is," he lied. "You have come for your payment, I am sure. Give me a moment." He did not give the boy time to respond but turned back into the house leaving Jean-Pierre waiting, his expression unchanged.

As he passed the kitchen table on his way back, it dawned on him that he was going to give the boy an extra amount for his good work. However, he was very low on cash until he made a trip into the village. He had only just enough with some spare change left over to pay the boy. And then he remembered. The rocks. He was sure the boy would consider the gifts of the rocks something very special. And they were already boxed for presentation. Yes, that was the answer. He would get rid of the rocks and, at the same time, express to the boy his appreciation for his efforts.

"You have done a good job there." He pointed to the new plantings. "Will you tell me what you have planted?"

"But of course, *monsieur.* Do you see the two bushes in

the back, the ones with the silvery green leaves?"

Stephen stepped out onto the front walk, following the boy, and nodded.

"Well, that is lavender, and it will grow very big, and you will have flowers of lavender for many months. Do you like the scent of lavender?" he asked as he stepped carefully through the plants and picked a stem. Crushing it between his fingers, he lifted it to his nose and then came back to Stephen. "Please, smell. It is the scent of the flowers. The whole plant holds the scent, not just the flowers. Do you like?" He dropped the crushed plant into Stephen's hand.

Holding it to his nose, Stephen was surprised by the powerful aroma that seemed to rush through his nostrils and into his lungs. "My, that is powerful."

"You can use lavender for medicine as well. My mama uses it in her cooking. It is a good plant to have in your garden. It will take care of you." He glanced at Stephen's angry forehead and then looked away.

"And the others? Are they as medicinal?"

The boy's quizzical look alerted Stephen that communication can be tricky when English is your second language. "I mean, are they medicine too?"

"Ah, yes. Some. I have planted a few herbs for you to use. You need to buy a book on their many uses. I can explain them to you then. But these," he pointed to the plants in the foreground of his botanical canvas, "these are meant to bring you happiness, for when they bloom, you can bring them into your house so that you can enjoy them in both places. Shall I write down all of their names for you? That way you can read and learn about them. I have left small labels next to each one to identify them."

"You could do that, yes. It is a little too far down for me to read each one." He couldn't even imagine how he would untie his shoelaces this evening as the pounding continued to grow inside his head.

"I will, and I will bring you the paper tomorrow. I will write down all of the names for you."

"Good, thank you. Now, here is what I owe you, I believe." He handed Jean-Pierre a small stack of euros. "And, because I am very pleased with your work, I want you to have these. They are very special." He handed the boy the two boxes.

"*Monsieur,* I cannot take these gifts. You are too kind, but I cannot." He started to hand them back to Stephen.

"Yes, yes you can. I would not give them to you if I did not mean for you to have them. Open them. Go ahead."

Jean-Pierre put one box on the ground while he opened the other. Stephen watched him delicately remove the velvet from the rock and thought that he heard a quick intake of breath, not his own.

"Oh, this is beautiful!" He lifted it from the box and held it up away from the shadows of the house so that the sun's light played on its surface. "Do you know what kind of rock this is?" he asked without looking back at Stephen as he turned the rock in different directions.

"Yes, it is limestone, and it is special because it comes all the way from the Acropolis in Athens, Greece. You must have learned about the Acropolis in your school studies?"

"I know something about it. One day, I will go there. Thank you, *merci.* You are too kind." He put it back in the box and set it down as he lifted the second one. "Is this a rock too?"

"Open it to find out, young man."

"Ah, yes. Another rock." He lifted this one with the same care as the first and examined it in the same way. "And this one?"

"Yes, this one is from Cyprus and is very old. You have heard of Cyprus?"

"Yes, I think so, but I do not know anything about it. Perhaps another place that I will visit when I get older."

"Well, I am glad that you like them. Now, if you will excuse me, I am not feeling all that well." He stepped back into the house and reached for the door.

"*Monsieur,* shall I call the doctor for you? He will come to your house. Your head is very bad." Jean-Pierre's look of concern was not lost on Stephen and he did feel rotten.

"I think that would be a good idea, Jean-Pierre. I do. Thank you." He started to close the door again.

"I can call from your house. I can stay with you until he comes." He stepped forward and looking into the room.

"No, that isn't necessary. But if you could call him as soon as you arrive home—that would be good." He couldn't begin to fathom having another person in his home, not in the condition in which he was finding himself and certainly not a conversationalist like Jean-Pierre.

"I will go fast." And picking up his boxes, he ran down the walkway and continued to do so until he was out of sight.

Thankful for the boy's help but glad that he was now alone, Stephen imagined that, if the doctor appeared at all, it would not be right away. He could not expect that he would be dragged away from a patient in much worse circumstances than his own. However, the sooner he had some relief from not just the continuous throbbing but now the soreness that he detected as the stretching skin tried to make room for the swelling below it, the better. He should have applied ice to it long ago. What was he thinking? Probably too late now to do any good, but he needed to do something.

The ice tray held frozen cubes that had been there for a very long time. He couldn't remember the last time that he consumed an ice cube, much less filled the tray. But at their sight, Stephen was grateful for them. Dropping them into a small plastic bag, he grabbed a dish towel and sat back down in the chair in the front room. This way, he would hear the doctor's arrival and be ready for him.

The coolness hurt his skin at first, and he was tentative as he tried to rest the wrapped plastic bag against his forehead without causing more pain. He was frustrated. He recognized this, and the more he thought about how stupid he had been to begin with—to take the time and for what purpose, to have one last look? He swore that he would never think about that place again. For that matter, any place that he had been. This was his home now. This was the life he wanted and that he had created. Everything would be all right, he knew. He just wanted the wounds that plagued his body to heal. That was all he asked for. Just peace.

He felt the bag drop from his hand, and he vaguely saw it slide in front of his face to the floor, landing somewhere. He could not tell where. The pain in his chest that had risen from within was so intense that it dulled the throbbing in his head. He reached his hands to his heart and covered his chest with both palms wide open as if to rub the pain away. But it did no good as he felt the constricting stabs moving rapidly across his front, across his back, and into his shoulder and then back again, clutching his heart in their ferocity and with no pity.

Struggling now to breathe, he tried to keep his eyes open, to stay focused on the door in front of him, but it moved upward from his sight as his body gave way and slumped to the floor. His eyes, filling with tears, allowed him nothing but increasingly blurred vision so that nothing they rested upon was recognizable. Nothing. He needed to see clearly just one more time, needed to know that he was going to be all right, that he was, once again, staying out of harm's way, needed to cling to something, anything.

The tears seeped from his eyes and he could feel, even in his pain, their damp rivulets forming across his cheeks, some finding their way into his ears, some touching the edge of his lips, finding the slightest opening between them so that the salty liquid found its way into his mouth. He tried to swallow, so thirsty had he become. But the liquid was no longer salty and moist but thick and acrid, clinging to the inside of his mouth and refusing to follow the gravitational path into his throat. It glued his lips together and he could not speak, could not cry out. He forced one hand from his chest and wiped his mouth to clear it of the goo. Feeling the liquid on his hand, he drew it to his eyes, trying to identify the blur in front of him. The pain in his chest, in his head, in his body demanded to be heard but was drowned out by some internally ancient and bestial cry heard only by Stephen as his eyes momentarily cleared enough for him to see the thick, sticky crimson liquid dripping from his hand. Closing his eyes to hide from it, a palpable darkness took its place.

Chapter 33

He had left no instructions for final arrangements. Nothing that the authorities could find in his belongings. No next of kin listed, no acquaintances. It appeared that he was truly alone in the world.

He was laid to rest in the village's cemetery; the small church's budget was tapped to cover the expense of a simple casket, a hole dug, and nothing else. There was no service, no headstone. The unmarked grave hugged the border of the cemetery, away from those who truly deserved to spend eternity in its hallowed ground.

But overnight, it seemed, a grave marker did appear. A simple wooden cross whose two lengths had been neatly lashed together with a dried grass. Etched into the cross bar and difficult to read, as the carver was certainly an amateur, were two words: *Monsieur Bingham.* On the freshly turned-over soil that had only recently covered the remains lay a small bouquet of lavender, kept together with the same grass tie. And next to the fragrant stems, neatly placed, one above the other in a perfect vertical line, lay two white stones.

Chapter 34

As the months passed and with Christmas just around the corner, she had thrown herself into her work. And with each passing day, affirmation that she was moving on and in the right direction came to her in different ways: the smile of a client who was searching for some peace while on a confused and fragile journey; all the little breakthroughs that each one of her clients made, even if she was the only one to recognize them at the time for what they were; the paperwork that continued to overwhelm her but that she knew she could conquer; the brief moments when she could actually get outside, for lunch or maybe just a walk, but conscious decisions on her part to take better care of herself; and her relationship with her aging mother, who seemed to mellow as time passed so that both daughter and mother looked forward to their brief times together. All of this and more was good, she reflected, as she walked toward her cubicle to begin another day.

Not noticing it at first, she sat down, opened the bottom drawer of her desk, and dropped her purse into its empty space. She had left her desk as she always had so that the surface immediately in front of her was orderly. To her left, her in-box sat containing the day's work and, below that, the out-box sat empty. She smiled, satisfied that all was as it should be. She was looking forward to her meetings today. One of her clients, whom she had struggled with both from her end and from his, might just be turning a corner if she was careful in her handling of him. But something told her that she would have success today, and she clung to that thought.

Reaching into the in-box, something caught her eye just behind it. A loose paper whose corner had protruded from its containment, she thought. Leaning forward, she reached for the errant sheet only to discover something more substantial than a piece of paper. The box came from behind the in-box easily. She recognized it as soon as she pulled it away from the darkened corner. As it sat on the desk in front of her, her mind swam with distant moments in time, with memories that were not complete but enough to be recognizable, with feelings that were not so easy to identify.

Slowly opening the lid, nestled as it had been the first time, the granite rock stared up at her. She sat back for a moment and then pulled herself forward again, trying to focus on its presence and what it was supposed to mean. As she suspected, a note was taped to the bottom of the box, and she carefully pulled it off and opened it.

"I guess we don't have to talk to one another to know that we both exist. So, I want you to keep this as my invitation to you to climb the mountain when you are ready. I can be there, if you want. If not, I'll be there in spirit. Jared"

Chapter 35

She floated home as if in the Good Witch of the North's transparent bubble. His note had meant more than she could comprehend at the time. Nestled in her purse, the box traveled safely with her. Somehow, she could feel its strength as she, too, felt stronger. She had not said anything to him, had not even emailed him that she had received it. She didn't know what to say to him and thought better of spewing meaningless and thoughtless words his way. She wanted to think things through. She wanted to figure out if he had a place in her life.

Arriving home, she found a note stuck on her door. Her neighbor had a package for her that the mailman had tried to deliver. Not wanting it lying around only to be stolen, he had knocked on her door. Thankfully, she had been at home and had no problem keeping it for Alison.

Her apartment did not hold the heat well and she felt the chill in the air as soon as she walked in. True, she lived in LA, but that didn't mean it didn't get cold. She put the package on the couch, took off her coat, and dropped her purse by the door. Turning up the heat, she kicked off her shoes and replaced them with her fluffy slippers, a gift from her mom last Christmas as she worried about her daughter's feet freezing.

Digging in the freezer for anything that she could microwave quickly, she found some concoction of so-called healthy foods all put together in one easy-to-prepare microwavable dish. *It fills the hole,* she thought. Pouring a glass of wine, she set the timer for three minutes and started the process. Then she remembered. Jared's rock.

She placed it on her bookshelf and left the box next to it. Both held significance to her now. And she could see it from anywhere she sat in the living room. She stood in front of it, admiring it in a way that she hadn't before. What had he said about granite? Something about its strength? Wasn't the mountain made of it? She couldn't remember exactly. A ding.

Dinner was ready. She decided to eat in the living room, something she rarely did since most nights she didn't eat at home. But something drew her here tonight, to the comfort and security of her home, as much as it was. One day she would have a house, maybe.

The package lay on the couch where it had landed. With her hot dish in one hand and the glass of wine in the other, she put them on the end table, shoved the package over to make room for herself, pulled the throw from the back of the couch, and nestled into the corner, bundled under the warmth of the woolen weave. Taking another sip of wine, she reached for the package. It hit her squarely between the eyes as soon as she saw the return address. The book! Michael's book was in her hands! She placed the glass on the end table and ripped open the wrapping. All she saw was his name drawn by an artist whose job it was to create an appealing cover. Everything else was a blur. She didn't register the title, not at first. Opening to the first few pages of Chapter 1, one by one, she ran her hand over each surface as if to feel Michael's presence. She closed the book and held it to her heart. Then, almost as an afterthought, she opened the book again and stared at the title page, the copyright page, and the page before the first chapter, a dedication. "To Alison, my rock. I clung on and I lived."

Her tears did not fall. Instead, she could not stop smiling as she looked across the room, eyes lingering on the piece of granite whose permanency she had now secured, and then back down as she turned the page, her full attention now on Michael's book that lay open to page 1, Chapter 1 of *Crossing the Line*.

Appendix

1. **Achaïkos**: The name Achaicus is a biblical baby name. The meaning of the name is "a native of Achaia, sorrowing, sad." People with this name tend to be idealistic, highly imaginative, intuitive, and spiritual. They seek after spiritual truth and often find it. They tend to be visionary and may inspire others. If they fail to develop their potential, they may become dreamers or misuse their power.

2. **Acropolis**: In Greek: "The Sacred Rock of the high city". The Acropolis of Athens is best known. There are many acropolises in Greece. The Acropolis's rock has been part of the earth since the late Cretaceous period. It is part of the late Cretaceous limestone ridge that cuts through the Attica plateau in the northeast to the southwest axis and includes the Likavitos Hill, the Philopappas (museum) hill, the hill of the Nymphs, and the Pnyx. The Acropolis of Athens had its own underground water supply in the form of a deep well, dug at the north end of the rock, which could be used by defenders during a siege.

3. **Adrastos**: Gender masculine. Greek mythology: Means "not inclined to run away" in Greek. This is the name of a king of Argos in Greek legend.

4. **Artemidoros**: Greek name composed of the name of the goddess Artemis and the word "doron" meaning gift; hence "gift of Artemis".

5. **Metaxas**: Greek. Derived from Greek metaxi "silk" and most likely referred to a silk merchant or another occupation that dealt with silk.

6. **Ventana**: In Spanish: Window, window pane.

Bibliography

Ancient-Greece.org, History of the Acropolis, Geography, 2002-2018 Ancient-Greece.org, pp.1-2, ancient-greece.org/history/acropolis.html, Accessed 15 April 2018.

Ancient-Greece.org, The Parthenon, 2002-2018 Ancient-Greece.org, p.1, ancient-greece.org/architecture/parthenon 2.html. Accessed 15 April 2018.

Behind the Name: Greek Surnames, pp. 1-2, surnames.behindthe name.com/names/usage/Greek. Accessed 15 April 2018.

The Big Book of Mother Goose. Kenosha, Wisconsin, John Martin's House, Inc., 1946.

Male Greek Names, pp. 1, 5, www.2000names.com/male greek names.htm. Accessed 15 April 2018.

Oia, Greece-Wikipedia, edition 17 January 2018, pp. 1-3, en.wikipedia.org/wiki/Oia_Greece. Accessed 15 April 2018

Prehistoric Cyprus-Wikipedia, edition 30 March 2018, p. 2, eb.wikipedia.org/wiki/Prehistoric_Cyprus, Accessed 15 April 2018.

"Orthodox Prayer for Healing", The Saint Gregory Palamas, Prayers from the Tradition of the Holy Orthodox Church Outreach, p. 1, www.saintgregoryoutreach.org/2014/04/orthodox-prayer-for-healing.html, Accessed 15 April 2018.

Acknowledgements

This book thrived because of the support of my family and friends. Without their thoughtful comments, their ongoing encouragement, and the often-asked question, "How's your book coming?" I would not be expressing my many thanks.

Thank you to my husband who read and reread the initial attempts. His eagle editing eye caught the obvious errors and the more obtuse. I never heard a sigh, a groan, or saw a grimace when I asked him to read it one more time.

Thank you to Lisa Wolff who edited the book. Her notations, queries, and suggestions propelled me forward and gave credence to my work. Her professional background as an accomplished editor will always be appreciated by me, a fledgling author.

Thank you to Geoffrey and Amanda whose creative talents, attention to detail and professionalism produced a book cover that I could only imagine.

Thank you to my sons, Geoffrey and Jason, who continue to encourage me to "Go for it!"

Thank you to Susan, a good neighbor, who kept me on track with my character, Allie. Susan's professional experience and guidance brought validity to this fictional character.

Thank you to Heidi and Molly who allowed me to read an early passage to them and for their encouragement to keep writing.

Thank you to Anna, my niece, who took the time to talk with me as one writer to another and whose insights were taken to heart.

Thank you to my "Book Club" friends who wanted to read the book and threatened to withhold wine and hors d'oeuvres if my efforts were not published and soon. Find the bottle opener, dear friends!

About the Author

Stephen has haunted Linda Mutty for forty-five years. She met him in 1972 when he appeared in a story she was composing for a graduate course in short story writing. Three and a half pages was all he, the main character, demanded at the time. Forty-five years later, Linda and he have been reacquainted; he frozen in time and she a recently retired middle school English teacher. He knew, all along, what the result would be of her newly found free time, and stubbornly refusing to be confined to those few yellowed pages any longer, he emerges as the antagonist in this, her second novel. No specter now but still in control, or so he thinks. Ironically, the original short story was entitled, *Home Again.*

Linda lives in Carmel, California with her wise and loving husband.

www.ingramcontent.com/pod-product-compliance
Lightning Source LLC
Chambersburg PA
CBHW021832010726
47493CB00005B/1365